The Fourteen Day

Soul Detox

THE COMPLETE SERIAL

RITA STRADLING

This is a work of fiction. Names, characters, incidents and places are the product of the author's imagination or are used fictitiously. Any resemblance to actual events, locations, or real persons, living or dead, is coincidental.

Copyright © 2016 by Rita Stradling.

All rights reserved, including the right to reproduce, distribute, or transmit this book in any form or by any means. For subsidiary rights please contact the author.
Email: ritastradling@yahoo.com

Edited by: Monique Fischer
Cover and Interior:
Title Font by WC Fonts
Author Font on Cover by Tup Wanders

This book is for my sisters and girl friends, because if I
did not have such true friends in my life, I would
never be able to write them.
You inspire me.

Contents

The Fourteen Day

Soul Detox

The Day Before

The Birthday Luncheon Intervention

Day Zero: Seven O'clock

I woke with a massive headache. And when I say massive, I mean my first thought when I opened my eyes was, 'oh, fuck this day.' Yet, I did open my eyes as my phone alarm insisted on beeping repeatedly. Grabbing my phone off my nightstand, I slid my finger across the screen and laid back into my pillows.

Sarah sat up next to me, her hair sticking out of her head at odd angles. She blinked around the lightening room like a little fish.

"Hi, angel," I said to her, smoothing her hair down. "I didn't realize you climbed in here with me. Remember, go potty, that's the first thing we do."

She turned around, her eyes closed halfway as she laid back on my shoulder, curling into a ball.

Kissing her forehead, I whispered, "Time to wake up baby, you need to get ready for the bus."

"No bus. I'm going to keep sleeping," she said, before yawning. Her little voice sent a new stab of pain into my head.

"No baby," I whispered. Extricating my shoulder from under her head, I peeled myself out of bed. Massaging my temples, I stepped onto the late-seventies shag carpet. I staggered through my room, stepping over a doll that lay face down on the carpet. Poor Mary Ann the Gymnast doll must have come in with Sarah but been discarded halfway to my bed. I made it all the way to my door, and turned on the light, but nothing happened.

"Ugh," I groaned. "The effing power better not be out, I know I paid it."

Well, I paid the past due, but they'd never shut the power off on me for being a month behind yet.

"What's the matter?" A man's voice from the living room called out.

"Oh, sorry, Cameron," I said, grimacing. "I didn't mean to wake you." I walked to the hallway light-switch and turned it on. Yellowish light illuminated the little hallway that connected all four rooms of my apartment—the conjoined living room and kitchen, two bedrooms and a bathroom.

I turned to see Cameron's body fill the doorless entry to my living room. He stretched up his arms, grabbing onto the doorway above his head, also yawning. I couldn't help but appreciate the view of his muscles straining as he stretched forward. A night on my couch had done a thorough job of mussing up his dark hair. He met my gaze, eyes hooded. "Everything okay?" he asked.

"Yes, I'm sorry for waking you. The stupid bulb in my room is out," I said with an annoyed glare back at my room.

He grinned lazily at me. "Where do you keep spare light bulbs?"

"I'm probably just going to take one from the bathroom fixture and switch them," I said.

He raised a brow at me and shook his head. He leaned in, his eyes glinting with amusement. "Hey beautiful, happy birthday."

"Uh, huh," I said back, "Sure it is." My body brushed against his as I slipped under his raised arms and into the living room.

His fingertips brushed down my side as I passed, but didn't linger.

From behind me, I heard his low chuckle.

"What's so funny?" I asked as I moved to the coffee maker. Thankfully, the coffee made itself on a timer this morning.

"You're still in your clothes from last night… again," Cameron said in his low voice.

"You try working until two-thirty in the morning then driving home," I said.

"No thank you," he said, his voice muffled as he must have been a couple rooms away.

Grabbing a bottle of aspirin out of my spice cupboard, I looked between the bottle and my coffee machine. It was a hard choice.

If I took the aspirin, I could go back to sleep after Sarah went on the bus, but I'd have to be awake without coffee for the hour until then. If I drank the coffee, I'd both get rid of my headache and my lethargy, but I wouldn't be able to nap. My gaze went back and forth between them.

"Good morning, Sarah," I heard Cameron say in the other room.

After a long pause, I called, "Sarah, can you say, 'good morning' to Cameron?'"

"Who won the Gold Medal in the 2012 London Olympics?" Sarah said, her voice getting louder. I turned to see her in Cameron's arms as he carried her out of the bedroom and set her on the couch.

Crossing to the cupboard, I grabbed two coffee mugs. I filled both with coffee, and went into the fridge to find the half and half.

"Hmm, in all around gymnastics?" Cameron asked Sarah.

"Gabrielle Douglas, USA," Sarah said.

"Baby, if you ask someone a question, you need to give them a chance to answer," I told her.

Cameron took his cup of coffee from my outstretched hand, gave me a wink and said, "I don't mind."

Sarah ran over into the kitchen. "Who won the silver in London in all around?" she asked.

Cameron turned to Sarah with a smile. "Wouldn't that be Shawn Johnson, from the USA also?"

"She won in Beijing." I whispered, "It's Viktoria Komova from Russia."

"Beijing!" Sarah yelled. Then she smacked Cameron on his arm.

"Sarah!" I said.

Sarah spun and ran into her room. "Go to time out!" she yelled before slamming the door to her room.

Squeezing my eyes shut, I groaned. "She keeps hitting you, I'm so sorry Cameron."

He took the coffee cup out of my hand. His arm wrapped around my waist while his lips moved down to my ear. "It's fine, Jamie."

He pulled my body into his and I couldn't help but melt a little against him.

"You are such a saint for babysitting her all the time," I said back.

"It's not like it hurts when she hits me," he said.

"Not really the point," I whispered. "And now she's doing it at school, too."

"She's just eight," he said.

"Which is way too old to be hitting other kids or adults," I said.

"Too old for other kids, maybe, but not for her. And she'll move past this, it's a phase," he said.

I moved out of his arms, whispering, "Yeah." Opening the aspirin bottle, I shook out a couple pills and washed them down with coffee. "Sarah, you can come out of time out," I called in a loud voice.

I heard the toilet flushing, then the water going for a long time.

I stared at the hallway. "She doesn't want me to check on her while she brushes her teeth anymore. I'm not sure how good of a job she's doing at it lately..." I tapped my foot, "but I just want her to have a good morning."

"They're all going to fall out anyway. Isn't it a good thing she's becoming more independent?" he said.

"I guess," I said, still staring toward the hallway.

After a minute, Sarah came out. She wore her favorite purple 'Junior Gymnast' shirt and purple stretch pants. Staring down at her purple rhinestone covered shoes, she trudged forward. I waited for a minute for her to apologize on her own, but gave up and said, "What do you say to Cameron?"

"I'm sorry. No problem, Sport," she said, still staring down at her shoes.

Cameron mussed up her hair, grinning. "Hey, that's my line."

"Do you want a bagel, angel?" I asked her as she took a seat at our tiny, light wood, two-chair breakfast table in the small nook at the side of our kitchen.

"Yogurt, bananas, juice," she said.

"Okay, but you have to eat it this time," I said, grabbing out a peach yogurt from the fridge. When she was eating small spoonfuls of her yogurt, I sprayed detangler in her hair and tried to comb through her tangled, thick, blonde hair. Sarah glared up at me a few times, making annoyed sounds, but I reminded her, "Do you want me to cut your hair short?" And she would turn her glare back to her food.

Grabbing an oversized hoodie, I pulled it over my head. That, and pulling my hair in a pony-tail, was all I was going to do to get dressed.

"You're going to need to wear a jacket, baby," I said, when Sarah was done eating and I was zipping up her purple-rhinestone covered backpack.

"No," she said, glaring at the level of my hoodie.

I breathed in through my nose. "You have two choices. Do you want to wear a jacket, or a sweater?" I held up the jacket.

Sarah shrugged it on, letting me zip her into it. Opening the door, we walked out into the morning. Dew settled on my face and hands. All around us little lines of dew fell, drops too dainty to be rain.

"It's raining baby, put on your boots," Sarah said to me.

"No Sarah, you don't need your boots. It's just dew, it'll burn off soon. Look, no puddles." Grabbing her hand, we walked down the street to stand in front of my neighbor's banged up sedan, where we waited for the bus every day.

"I love you so much," Sarah said.

I swallowed. "I love you so much, baby. Are you going to do a good job at school today?"

"Yes," she said.

"No more hitting, right?" I asked.

"No hitting," Sarah said.

"Are you going to listen to your teacher?"

"Yes," she said.

The long yellow bus pulled around the corner. After the bus stopped in front of us, an overwhelming volume of shouting voices released out of the opened door.

"Morning, Jamie," the thin, fifty-something-year-old bus driver called out over the cacophony inside. He adjusted his tie-dye T-shirt while giving me a half-smile, half-grimace.

"Hey, Henry," I said.

"It's pretty loud on here today, you think Sarah can handle it?" he asked, kindly.

"No bus!" Sarah shouted before taking off and running down the street.

I lunged after her, but saw she was running up to our duplex door. Sighing, I said, "I guess not. Thanks anyway, Henry."

Back in the house, I found Sarah sitting at our breakfast table, eating another banana.

"No bus?" Cameron said, coming to stand close to me, smelling like toothpaste and soap.

I shook my head.

"Want me to take her in?" he asked, his hands rubbing my shoulders.

"No, it's fine. I took the morning off for that stupid lunch thing anyway. You're going, right?" I asked.

"No, I guess it's a females-only birthday thing, or that's what Amy said," he pulled me even closer to him as he talked.

"Weird," I said. "There's only going to be like three people there then, since both Jessica and Beza need to work."

"I'll be here when you get back from dropping off Sarah, though," he whispered in a low voice into my ear. "I have a present I want to give you."

I pulled back to look up into his heated gaze. Stepping back from Cameron, I turned away to grab my now lukewarm coffee and guzzle it down. Pinching my thighs together, I forced my mind to unsexy things, like the Coffee Stop's taxes and whether or not I could afford to hire someone after all the taxes were finished.

"Okay, sounds good," I whispered, refilling my coffee mug. I was on my fifth cup by the time I pulled into Coral Beach Elementary. Pressing the dial to turn Sarah's CD off, I turned around in my seat. My phone lit up with a text message from my coworker-friend Nancy.

Nancy: For some reason your sister just uninvited me to your lunch thing. Just didn't want you to think I ditched. See you at the bar tomorrow night.

Me: Wtf?

Nancy: No idea why, sorry.

Sighing, I turned to the back seat. "Baby, why don't you have your seatbelt on?" I said, suppressing the need to yell and trying to keep my voice calm.
"I undid it," she said, smiling.
I took a deep breath and exhaled. "Not safe, baby. You need to keep it on until I stop the car."
"No," she said.
"Yes, or no more kids' CD in the car," I said.
"Yes, kids' CD!" she cried, her body bowed stiffly in her seat.
"Wait," I said, climbing to sit backwards in my seat and reaching back to her. "Ready, we need to take gymnast breaths, okay?"
She started screaming and kicking the chair.
Exiting the car, I climbed into the backseat beside her. Reaching out, I put an arm over her so she wouldn't fall out of the car seat while she kicked.
When her kicking slowed down, I leaned in close and said in a calm voice, "Do you want a squeeze?"
Big tears coursed down her face as she said, "Yes, squeeze."

Grabbing her under her legs and behind her back, I lifted her into my lap. She curled up and I squeezed her tightly against me. "It's so important for gymnasts to take deep breaths," I told her. "Can you take some deep breaths with me?"

She didn't respond.

"Sarah," I said in a quiet voice into her ear. "Are you a gymnast or not a gymnast?"

"Gymnast," she whispered.

"Okay, you ready to take ten gymnast breaths with me?"

"Yes," she whispered.

We both breathed in deeply and then exhaled. "One," I said. We did it again and I counted, "Two." At ten, I opened the car door and we both climbed out into the parking lot. Giving Sarah my hand, we walked into the school campus. By the time we got there, the bus had already arrived and Henry gave me a wave as we walked by.

"Good morning, Sarah," a school attendant whose name I couldn't remember said as we passed by.

When Sarah didn't respond, I stopped. "Sarah, she said good morning," I said, smiling at Sarah and gesturing to the attendant.

"It's okay," the older lady said with a smile, "Don't worry about it."

"Hi!" Sarah said. We walked up the hallway to Sarah's classroom, passing several kids carrying trays of breakfast food. Murals stretched along every wall at Coral Beach School, most were done by kids but some were elaborate and professional, like the one we were walking next to of international students holding hands.

"Hi Sarah!" A boy called, but he rushed off when Sarah didn't respond.

"Remember to say hi to people, angel," I said when we got to her classroom. As we stepped inside, three teachers and my friend Beza glanced up and smiled as we entered.

"Hi, Sarah, hi Jamie," Ms. Ivy said as we entered the classroom.

"Hi," I said, sliding my sunglasses to the top of my head.

Sarah took off into the classroom, bee-lining to the small trampoline they had in the corner.

Ms. Ivy stood up, following Sarah, "Remember Sarah, just jumping. It's not safe to do gymnastics in the classroom."

Sarah pulled the trampoline down from where it was propped against the wall and started jumping.

"Hey lady, happy birthday," Beza said, stepping up next to me. Beza was one of the most beautiful women I'd ever seen up close. She was half-Sudanese, half-Native American and born in America. She had been an international supermodel before she had Aiden.

"Thanks," I said, giving her a hug.

"You look hung-over," she whispered, chuckling.

"I wish," I said, "Then at least I would have had fun last night."

"I bet you had fun this morning though," she nudged me.

"Not yet, but I plan to," I whispered.

"You're bad," she said, winking at me. "How old are you turning today anyway, twenty-five?"

"Yep, twenty-five, you got it in one," I said.

"Yeah, sure. Me too." She rolled her eyes with a smile and placed her hand on my arm. "So, I think I should tell you, Susan was hurt when Amy uninvited her to your birthday lunch."

"What? Susan was uninvited?" My jaw slackened. What the hell was going on with my sister?

"Yes, this morning," Beza sighed. "She just felt she was making some headway with your sister, but felt pretty persecuted that she'd be uninvited."

"Oh, no, it wasn't just Susan, I guess Amy uninvited everyone without telling me. I mean I know Amy has her weirdness, but I don't think she was singling Susan out." I looked over to where Sarah was still jumping on the trampoline, but now with Aiden. "It's just so weird, I mean, I'm cool with just having lunch us two, Amy never has time for that. But why have me invite all my friends, just to rescind the invitation?"

"That is strange," Beza said. "Well, are we still on for our birthday sleepover tonight?"

"Yes, as long as you and Susan are still cool with us sleeping over."

"Are you kidding me? We'd never miss a birthday sleepover. You know what's crazy, Susan pointed out this morning that you two have done this every year since you were Aiden and Sarah's age."

"Yeah, that is trippy… and those two have been doing it since birth," I gestured to the pair, who were now taking turns on the trampoline.

The first bell rang and Beza whispered, "We should go." Raising her voice, she called, "Aiden."

"Aiden, honey, it's time to go to your classroom," Sarah called back, making all of us smile and Aiden laugh. Aiden ran over to us, and into me giving me a big hug.

I patted his braided hair. "Hey cutie. You are so sweet to visit Sarah every morning before class," I told him.

"I like it," Aiden said with a whistling voice, smiling up at me with his front teeth missing. "Happy birthday!"

When we exited the classroom, Beza said, "I wish you still dropped Sarah off every morning, I miss this."

"Yeah, me too," I said, "Though I'm so touched that you guys kept up this tradition even though she takes the bus now." I shifted down my sunglasses so I could hide just how touched I was.

"Aiden gets as much out of it as Sarah does," Beza said, giving me one final hug. She whispered, "Don't look now, but Hunky Dad was right behind us and he was looking over here."

"Looking at you, I'm sure," I said, glancing down at my dirty jeans and sweatshirt ensemble. Beza on the other hand, was dressed in a tailored suit and she was, you know, a former supermodel.

Glancing over my shoulder she whispered, "Nope, definitely at you. Wait here for a minute, maybe he'll finally talk to you."

"Um, that's okay. First, I'm kind of excited to get home, and second, I'm not even sure whether or not I brushed my teeth this morning. I don't want this to be the picture he has of me."

"As opposed to what? Sweatpants and a festival T-shirt?"

"You..." I said pointing at her, "... you B-word I can't say in front of children."

"Mom, I'm going to be late to class," Aiden said.

Beza smiled at me. "I have to go. See you at five-thirty. Bring your sleeping bag."

A second later, Hunky Dad passed me. He wore a suit, but then again, he always wore a suit. This one was charcoal grey. His blond hair was neat, combed back with a side part. As he passed, he sent a grin over my direction. "Hi," he said, with a friendly smile.

My stomach did a little flip. Even though Beza had told me that Hunky Dad had been looking over at me, I had to resist the urge to check behind me to see if he was greeting some other parent.

"Hi," I said.

"You're Sarah's mother, right?" he asked.

"Yep," I said, seemingly only able to come up with one syllable words. I honestly didn't blame myself. He was so gorgeous—like movie star gorgeous.

"My daughter Kay is in her class. She talks about her all the time. I think they're friends."

I bit my lip, looking back to room three where I'd just dropped Sarah off. I knew most of the parents from Sarah's special day class and I definitely would have noticed Hunky Dad if he had been in there before. I was almost certain that his daughter Kay would have to be in Sarah's typically-developing class she went to after lunch. To be sure, I asked, "In room seven?"

"Yeah, with Ms. Keller," he said. "Would you ever be interested in setting up a play date with the girls?"

"Oh, um, maybe," I said, glancing over at him to find him still smiling. I wasn't confident on how to proceed without being rude. "I... I've only ever really set up play dates with parents of room three kids or with my friends. I think we do things a little differently than the other parents do."

"No worries," he said, "We can do it your way. I'm Patrick by the way." He reached a hand out for me to shake.

"Jamie," I said, shaking his hand.

"I used to see you around here every morning," he said.

"Yeah, I work in the mornings usually, so Sarah takes the bus now."

"At the bar?" he asked, holding the main door open for me.

"Not in the mornings." I cocked my head. "Wait, you know where I work?"

He shrugged, looking adorably sheepish. "I take clients there once in a while."

I stepped back out into the day, which had cleared up in the short time I'd spent dropping Sarah off. I turned back to Patrick. "Weird, I feel like I would have noticed you there. Am I that oblivious?" I mumbled the last part to myself.

"We don't usually sit at the bar," he said.

"Well, next time say 'hi' and I'll buy you a drink," I said.

He stepped closer to me and grinned. "I'd rather buy you one."

Did Hell just freeze over, or was Hunky Dad, himself, flirting with me?

"Yeah," I said in a teasing tone turning back to him, "But if you bought me a drink and I drank it, I'd get fired." I winked. It was a barefaced lie; I could burn the bar to the ground and not get fired. I stopped when I reached my used sedan at the curb.

He grinned. "Well, maybe—"

"Patrick!" A woman's voice yelled.

He turned away and I looked over my shoulder to the source of the noise, feeling a little annoyed. I really wanted him to finish his sentence.

I didn't feel any less annoyed when I saw who it was. Whitney Cooper rushed toward us in her high heels; she wore a dress and full makeup. The woman must wake before the sunrise to look that picture perfect. I was pretty sure she didn't have a job either. And, I mean no disrespect to stay-at-home moms, more power to her, but if I didn't work I would never get dressed up in the morning again.

"Patrick, I was hoping to run into you," she said, marching toward us. Her gaze passed on to me, and the smile on her face faltered. She replaced it with a little too wide grin. "Oh, hello Jamie, how are you doing today?"

"Good, Whitney, you?" I said, though I really didn't care.

"I am great, and happy I ran into you two. I presume you're both going to the *Principals and Principles* fundraiser next weekend?"

"Next Saturday?" Patrick said, rubbing the back of his neck.

"Yes, that's the day," Whitney said, smiling.

"Oh, yeah, sure, Kay and I will be there," he said.

"Sorry, no," I said.

"Oh, that's too bad," Whitney said with a small grimace at me. "This would be a great opportunity for you to help raise some money for all those services you are demanding for your child."

I gritted my teeth at her. I was pretty sure if I drop kicked her here in the parking lot in front of the school, no one would believe it was an accident. "What services are you exactly referring to here, Whitney?" My calm delivery of the question was Oscar-worthy.

"Oh, the ones you and your husband are so vocal about in the school board meetings," she said, flashing another plastic smile my way.

"Do you mean when I said that the school board shouldn't lay off one of the two SDC teachers and combine the classes? Are you referring to when I said that having thirty-three SDC children aging between four and eleven in one classroom was not acceptable to their parents? That their vast age differences, overwhelming numbers and varying levels of disabilities will not be conducive to providing these children with a safe and intellectually supportive atmosphere? Are those the *services* you're talking about?"

She shook her head. "Obviously, this is a very sensitive subject and you look like you had a long night." She looked up to my messy ponytail as if it was pitiable. "It's unfortunate that there's just not enough money in the budget for—"

"But there's enough for a dance instructor to come in to teach the children daily?"

"Dance is very important," she said, looking affronted. "It is arguably essential for children's development. And not every family has the money to send their children to private dance classes."

"Says one of the richest parents in the school to one of the poorest," I grumbled.

She sighed, shaking her head. She was cool as the morning frost and I was ready to spill over with hot tears. Patrick the Hunky Dad had been following the conversation back and forth with his gaze, but shifted a little to stand beside me so that we both looked over at Whitney.

Whitney rolled her eyes as if the whole conversation was ridiculous. "Please don't make this personal, Jamie. And, as I said, the fundraiser next week is essential so the school can have both dance class and services for those with special needs. I would think that you would be jumping up to help."

"Unfortunately, I work Saturday nights," I said.

"Oh, yes, at that bar. I forgot." She gave me another icy smile. "Well perhaps your husband could come in instead. He's always so passionate at the meetings, I'm sure he'd be happy to help. He's a mechanic, isn't he? They don't work long hours."

Rolling back my shoulder, I told her, "Cameron isn't my husband, he's just a friend."

She blinked at me, and then looked down at my wedding ring. "Oh," she said.

I touched the wedding band, twisting the ring around my finger. Patrick also looked down at my hand.

It was so awkward that this guy, of all guys, had to witness this school-side drama.

From Whitney's small smile, I could tell she didn't believe for a minute that Cameron was simply a friend. Honestly, if any other woman told me that Cameron was their 'friend', I'd doubt it too. He was just too sexy, plain and simple. And even though I didn't care what Whitney thought of me, my daughter was going to go to this school for a while, and Whitney was the head of its PTA.

My mother always said that the best time to kill gossip was before it ever began, and being a teacher, my mother would know. I hated talking about what happened with Logan, but I could practically feel Whitney heating her iron to brand me with a big 'A' for adultery.

I looked between both their faces, and then exhaled. "My husband died about a year ago. I still wear the ring at work; I must have forgotten to take it off. Cameron was my husband's best friend and he helps us out a lot."

"Oh wow, I'm sorry," Whitney said, giving me a 'your life sucks' look.

Patrick, however, didn't look at all surprised. He gave me a sympathetic straight lipped smile.

I nodded. "Thanks. Anyway, I can't make it to your fundraiser and I have to go now. So, good luck with it all." Waving, I crossed up to my car door and crawled inside.

Day Zero: Nine O'clock

Before I even started my car, I texted Beza:

Me: You are in so much trouble.

Beza: Who me?

As I pulled out of my parking spot, Patrick looked over at me. He stood a few cars down, still talking to Whitney. He raised a hand, and gave me a slight smile.

I returned the smile and the wave, but the moment I was out of the parking lot, I called Beza. When she didn't answer her cell, I called her work number. Normally, I would never stoop this low, but I was feeling pretty low right now.

"Karen Blanche Wedding Services," a female receptionist answered.

Gasping and making my voice sound as if I was crying, I said, "Hello, I'm a bride, I mean I'm a client of Beza's, can I speak to her?"

"Can I get your name?"

I made a crying sound into the phone, and the receptionist must have connected me because suddenly I heard Beza's voice, "You've reached Beza."

I stopped pretending to cry. "Hello my supposed friend. You set me up," I said in a serious voice. "I know that you are at work and I don't want to get you in trouble. I'm going to ask you a series of yes or no questions and you better tell me the truth. Got it?"

"Yes, Miss Summers, I have a minute," she said in a professional voice.

"Did you talk to Patrick the Hunky Dad about me?" I asked.

"Yes," she said.

"You buttface, I knew it. Did you tell him I was single?"

"Yes, I did," she said.

"Did you tell him that I think he's cute?" I asked.

I could hear the smile in her voice when she said, "Well..."

"No, you didn't! You did not tell him I call him the Hunky Dad!"

"I did," she said.

I paused. "Is he single?"

"Yes," she said.

"Okay, last question: if I murdered you, do you think I could get away with it?"

"No," she said, not sounding the least bit worried.

"You are officially the worst friend ever," I said.

"I know. You're welcome," she said before hanging up on me.

Pulling up to my duplex, I jumped out of my car. Upon exiting the parking lot, I looked to my neighbor's yard. Finding it empty, I rushed up to my door.

I turned the knob quietly and slowly, finding the door unlocked. "Hey Cameron, sorry I took so long," I called out as I opened the door. "Whoa," I said, stopping right inside.

Cameron, just on the other side of the door, stood only an inch from me. He reached behind me, shutting the door but left his arm on the door, boxing me in.

Backing up, my back hit the door behind me. "Hi," I whispered.

His other hand reached to the door on my other side, surrounding me. "Hi," he said. Then his lips moved into mine. At first he kissed me slowly, but then he kissed me furiously, as if he was unleashing a kiss that had been pent-up for hours. The length of his body pressed into mine.

I wrapped my arms around his shoulders and my legs around his waist, climbing him. A little gasp escaped me as he ground against me.

He pulled his lips away from mine for one second to say, "I need to be inside of you." Then his lips pressed back into mine.

We broke our kiss only for a moment so that he could pull off my sweatshirt and shirt.

His hands went to my breasts and I felt him groan against my lips. "I love that you're not wearing a bra," he whispered.

I laid my head back against the door, closing my eyes as he ground into me.

Uncurling my legs from around him, I set them down to stand on shaky legs. His hands immediately went to my button and zipper, and mine reached for his. As soon as my pants were undone, I wiggled out of them.

Cameron's hands wrapped around my ass and he lifted me until he was poised to enter me. He paused and I pressed my knees into his hips, breathing heavily.

Leisurely, he pushed into me. When we'd both reached our release, he let his body collapse into mine against the door.

"Oh, baby," he whispered into my ear, chuckling, "Baby, baby, baby." He then whispered something so low I couldn't hear him.

"Huh?" I asked, blinking up at him.

He pulled out of me, setting me down on the floor, and tucking himself back into his pants. His face came down, lips just brushing over mine. As his fingers combed into the hair at the back of my head, he intensified the kiss. After a minute, he pulled away. "I really want to do that again, and take my time this time."

"But...?"

"But I am supposed to open up the shop at ten-thirty, and I'll already be a little late for that."

"Of course," I breathed.

"And you have that birthday lunch," he said.

"Oh, yay," I said without enthusiasm.

He chuckled. "Want to shower together?"

"Um, you go ahead, I haven't eaten anything and I'm starting to feel a little lightheaded," I said.

"Let me make you something," he said, leaning back and looking at me, concerned.

"No, no, I'm just going to microwave some oatmeal. You go shower," I said.

He kissed me. "You sure?"

"Yeah, I'm good," I said, nodding.

He walked backwards away from me, looking sexy with his pants open and boxer briefs riding low. He gave me a huge grin. "You keep standing there all naked and ravaged like that, and I'm going to fuck you again."

"Is that a threat or a promise?" I asked.

"Oh, sexy, you're going to get me in trouble. I'm forcing myself to turn around now," He turned, saying, "I have a new customer, wants some custom work done on all of his cars and a bike, top dollar."

"That's great," I grabbed the sweatshirt off the ground and shrugged it on. It hung to just below my butt and I kept the hood on.

"I thought so. And he has friends who need work done as well. Things go right, I might be able to hire another guy or two and free up some time during the day."

"Oh yeah?" I asked.

He turned around at the bathroom doorway, and said, "You know, to spend more time with you and Sarah. Dinners and stuff like that."

"Yeah?" I said, steadying my voice, "That'd be great, fingers crossed."

"Fingers crossed," he said, turning around and moving out of sight into the bathroom. After a second, I heard the water turn on.

My body slid down the door and I curled into a ball. Tears coursed down my face.

"What am I doing with my life?" I whispered. Sobs ripped from my chest as I rolled forward onto the ground. My face brushed against the shag carpet.

It was disgusting and I wanted to get up, but as the tears and sobs continued, I couldn't make myself.

Day Zero: Ten O'clock

I dug my fingers into the coarse carpet as the ragged sobs continued.

Hands grabbed me, and suddenly Cameron lifted me into his arms and carried me across the apartment into my room. He set me on my bed, curling up around me and holding me to his chest.

"This is so embarrassing," I whispered, my words broken with sobs.

"Please, no, don't be embarrassed. I don't want you to hide it from me." He kissed me on the back of my neck. "Can I be here for you, or do you need me to go?"

"Um…I… I think I'll go take that shower with you," I said as I scrubbed at my face.

"You sure?"

"I'm sure. That carpet made me all itchy," I half-cried, half-laughed.

"Yeah, I hate your carpet. The people who own this complex are serious cheapskates; it should have been re-carpeted years ago. Come on, I'll wash you," he said.

When I climbed off the bed, I realized that Cameron was already naked and I had not noticed. I had obviously lost my sanity for a minute there, because when Cameron was naked, I was pretty sure all the angels in Heaven started singing.

I ran my hands down the muscles of his back as we crossed the hall into the bathroom, just because I could. He smiled over his shoulder at me, a glint of white teeth.

"You feeling a little better, baby?" he asked.

"Yeah," I said.

"Okay, I just need to do one quick thing." He turned, grabbing his phone which had been sitting on top of a pile of his folded clothes on the bathroom counter. He texted a message, then set the phone back. "Oh, and don't let me forget to give you your birthday present."

I looked down. "I thought you already did."

"Funny girl," he said. Grabbing the bottom of my sweatshirt, he pulled it up over my head, so that we were now both naked.

Switching the faucet to the shower-mode, he turned on the hot water, then the cold. Keeping his hand under the flow, he turned his attention back to me. "What I did to you in the living room was a present I gave to myself. I have an actual real material present I *bought* for you."

"Oh, okay," I said, smiling—or trying to smile. "I love presents."

"I know you do. Here, come on in," he said, gesturing to the shower.

Climbing in, I pushed my face into the hot spray. The water pelted me, beating against my eyelids and cheeks.

"Here, get your hair wet," Cameron said.

Bending my neck forward, I let the water saturate my hair.

Hands on my hips pulled me back a step. There was a squirting sound, and then Cameron's hands were in my hair. He massaged soap into my scalp, rubbing his fingers from the top of my head, behind my ears all the way to the base of my neck.

A small groan escaped my mouth.

His hands guided me around and he pushed me back a step, into the spray. I closed my eyes as he continued to massage the soap out of my hair. His hands again went to my hips and he led me a step forward.

Opening my eyes, I looked over to where Cameron was browsing through the bottles at the side of my bathtub.

"I do know how to wash myself, you know," I said with a smile.

"Yeah, but why would you when I'm so happy to do it?" He grinned up at me. "Close your eyes."

I rolled my eyes before I closed them. "Okay," I said.

There was another squirting sound, I smelled my lilac bath soap, and then Cameron's hands were slowly massaging my shoulders. He rubbed the soap up my neck, then down my arms. His hands worked down my chest, taking a very long time rubbing soap into my breasts.

"My boobs must be very dirty," I said with a laugh.

"Very, very dirty," he said in a low voice close to my ear. His hands moved down, washing my stomach, over around to my back and butt, then down my legs.

When he pushed me back into the spray, I whispered, "I think you missed something."

Cameron went to his knees. "That part I clean with my mouth." He looked up, raising an eyebrow at me. "Hold onto something."

I grabbed the faucet above me as Cameron's hands spread my legs apart. My back pressed into the cool tile, while the warm water sprayed across my middle.

He lifted one of my legs, placing it over his shoulder, then did the same with the other.

Exhaling heavily, I looked down at him. The corner of his mouth turned up as his eyebrows lifted. He lowered his mouth.

Mere minutes later, the aftershocks of pleasure pulsed through me. My throat was so dry, I let the spray from the shower run into my mouth.

I realized the water hitting me was ice cold, and I couldn't help but breathe a laugh.

Cameron looked up at me. "I thought I could brighten your mood," he said with a self-satisfied smirk.

I moved my shaky legs off his shoulders. "Uh, yeah, you could call it that. But what about you?" I said, pointedly looking down to where he was *very* ready for round two.

"I... am going to stay in the shower and cool off," he said.

"Are you sure?" I asked, smiling.

"No, definitely not." He got up off his knees and rubbed my arms with his hands. "But, if I don't get going, I'll probably lose this customer."

"Yeah, we should probably be responsible adults," I said, kissing him. "I'm getting out though, it's freezing in here."

He smacked me lightly on the butt as I climbed out. Wrapping my hair in one towel and my body in another, I looked for some spare towels but couldn't find any. It had been over a week since I'd done any laundry. Yet another thing I had to do.

As the towel around my body was only damp, and the one around my hair was already soaked, I left the damp towel on the rack for Cameron.

I dried the rest of me with the soaked towel and threw it on the wet floor on the bathroom.

As much as I wanted to wear sweatpants, I knew that I would have to go into work for a little while after lunch, and I didn't want to have to change later.

Unfortunately, the only clean jeans I had were from about a year ago and a full two sizes too big. When I threw on my too-big Coffee Spot T-shirt, it looked like I was dressing up in someone else's clothes. I put on a belt to make sure the pants didn't do a diving act, and slipped on some tennis shoes.

The water turned off and I heard Cameron singing something to himself in the bathroom.

Peeking in on him, I found him drying himself off and singing in a low country voice.

A chuckle escaped from my mouth.

Wrapping the towel around his waist, he turned away from me swaying his hips back and forth.

"Woohoo," I called.

He flexed his muscles, then flashed me a smile over his shoulder and dropped the towel.

I laughed. "I feel like I should go get some dollar bills."

"Dollar bills? That hurts." He chuckled.

"I'd give you twenties if I had them," I said, grabbing the only remaining semi-clean towel off the floor and hanging it back up. I kissed his shoulder before leaving the bathroom.

Even though I would be heading out to meet my sister for lunch in less than an hour, I headed into the kitchen and made myself some oatmeal. Dumping the peaches and cream packet into the bowl, I filled it with water and put it into the microwave.

"I'm kind of disappointed I won't be able to drop by your shop at lunchtime today," Cameron said when he emerged a minute later fully dressed.

"You can still stop by to grab coffee when I'm not there," I said as I took the oatmeal out of the microwave.

He stopped right in front of me. "Yeah, maybe I will," he said, then kissed me over my oatmeal bowl. "You working at the bar tomorrow night?"

"Yeah," I said, spooning some oatmeal into my mouth.

"Okay, I can get here at around five-fifteen with dinner, that okay?" he said.

"Cameron, you don't need to babysit every time. I mean, Susan and Beza would do it, or Amy, it doesn't always have to be you," I said.

He gave me another kiss. "Fuck that," he said.

"I just feel bad," I said.

"Well don't." He paused for a second. "Is it okay if I give you your present when I see you tomorrow?"

"Yeah, sure," I said.

"I just want to be there when you open it, and I'm already late."

"Of course," I said.

After crossing the room, he turned back. He stood at the door for a second, hand on the knob, looking at me intently.

"I'll see you tomorrow," I said, giving him a little wave and a straight-lipped smile.

"Yeah, baby, see you then." He opened the door, and left.

Staring at the front door, I slowly ate the peaches and cream oatmeal. Setting the bowl in the sink, I ran water into it. I glanced into the otherwise empty sink, then at the clean kitchen table. "Oh my god, Cameron, stop doing my dishes," I whispered, rolling my eyes.

I took a seat at the kitchen table, laying my head down on my arms. Looking up to the shelf above my refrigerator, my gaze found the black brass urn sitting there. A large circle brass moon silhouetted a black howling wolf on the otherwise black urn.

When I picked it out, I remember my dad saying, 'That looks like something you'd pick up in one of those new-agey wannabe Indian gift shops.' My stepmother Sharon had smacked his arm saying to me, 'Don't listen to your father, honey, it's beautiful.'

Still, I don't know what had possessed me to buy that one. It did look like a Native American wannabe picture. Like those patterns you found on 'color your own felt' posters at a superstore. Yet the urn had called to me in a weird way, a way I couldn't refuse.

The tears didn't rip out of me this time, just slid out, dripping onto my arm. My phone buzzed in my pocket, and I pulled it out.

I wiped my face with my hands, looking down at where a text from my sister lit up the screen.

Amy: You should leave in five minutes to make it to the restaurant on time.

I glared at my phone.

After a minute, I texted back: Are you going to even be there? Or is this a birthday lunch party of one?

Amy: Of course I'm going to be there.

Me: It's just that you uninvited everyone else.

Amy: I'll explain when you get there. You should probably leave now.

Me: You could have handled it better, Susan thought you uninvited her because she's gay.

Amy: My goodness, I am not homophobic. Why does everyone always think that? Don't answer that. You should have already left by now. We'll talk when you get to the restaurant.

Me: Okay, will do.

Amy: Stop texting and get in your car.

I smiled at my phone.
Then I texted: I might have to go to the
bathroom first.

Amy: Then go.

Me: It might be a while.

Amy: I might kill you.

Me: Happy Birthday to me. Alright, I'll see you
in ten.

Amy: I really hope so.

Day Zero: Eleven-thirty

Knowing that lunch with Amy would be horrible if I took much longer, I got ready in a rush and left the house. Even though I didn't speed, I arrived at the restaurant five minutes early.

Rolling my eyes at the time, I parked in the little lot next to *Mickey's*—my dad and stepmom's favorite harbor side restaurant. I laughed and shook my head as I saw my father's big Buick parked right in front of the staircase leading up to the restaurant.

Salty, fishy air greeted me as I climbed out of my car. After making my way through the parking lot, I patted the side of the black Buick. "Dad, you are officially the worst surpriser ever," I mumbled to myself.

I started up the steps to the pier the restaurant stood upon. A mother and her daughter passed me going the opposite direction, and I paused to watch them. Her extended belly screamed pregnant, and her attention was fixed on her phone as she walked down the staircase. Her young daughter's pigtails flopped up and down as she rushed to keep up with her mother. She was maybe three years old or so, and was shouting, "Mom, can I go play with Cynthia? Mommy! Can I go play at Cynthia's house?"

"Maybe later, sweetheart," the mother said while she stowed her phone in her purse.

"But why, mommy?" the girl said, holding her hands up in question.

"Because Cynthia is at preschool," her mother said. "We need to go to get—" She looked over at me, squinting and furrowing her brow.

I startled. "Sorry, excuse me," I told her. "Um, congratulations." I turned back to the steps and continued my ascent.

Seagulls plucked up what seemed to be pieces of bread on the dock's planks just outside the restaurant. A happy and familiar crab greeted me on the restaurant door as I pulled it open.

Walking through the group of people gathering around the host stand, I said to no one in particular, "I'm meeting people." Not waiting for a response, I entered the main dining area of the restaurant. Walking between tables, I scanned the dining room for my sister and froze.

"What the...?" I whispered under my breath. Halfway down the long wall of windows, my half-sister Amy sat beside my mother.

I spun on my heel, ready to head back to the entrance of the restaurant, when a strong arm wrapped around me.

"Hey kiddo, happy birthday!" my dad said in his booming voice. His arm wrapped firmly around my shoulder. His sandalwood soap smell enveloped me.

"Hey Dad, thanks," I said, looking over at him.

I couldn't help noticing a few people staring at my father, which wasn't anything new. He stood about six-four on a short day, and had a white mustache that took up a good third of his face.

"Your mother, stepmother and sister are waiting to see you," he said, leading me toward the table with his arm.

"Wow, yeah. The thing is, I think I left my oven on," I said, trying to dig in my heels.

"Shoot babe, well, how about you give me your keys and I'll run over to your house to check? I wouldn't want you to miss your birthday lunch," he said, still leading me to the table.

I looked back toward the door. "Um, I'll just be a—"

"Nope," my dad said, leading me straight to the table. "Look who I found!" he said to the group.

My stepmother, Sharon, and my sister, Amy, looked up at me. There was very little of my father in Amy except for her height, otherwise she was pretty much Sharon minus twenty years.

Sharon gave me a guilty looking smile. "Happy birthday, sweetheart," she said, her Cuban accent thicker than usual.

Amy gave me a smile I could only label as tense.

"Aren't you going to say happy birthday?" I asked.

"Happy birthday, big sis," she said, before pinching her lips together.

"Uh, huh," I said. I looked over to my mother; her dark blonde hair was still the exact shade as mine. She looked older, wrinkles gathering at the corners of her eyes and one creasing her forehead. "Hey Mom," I whispered.

My mother did not look up, instead she squeezed her eyes shut, her face somewhat turned down. "Hey sweetheart," she said.

My father pressed down on my shoulders and I dropped into a chair at the head of the table. We all stayed silent as my father took the seat beside Sharon.

"You think it's too early for a beer?" he said, elbowing me and throwing me a conspiratorial grin.

"You better be kidding, Mike," Sharon whispered.

"A beer sounds pretty good right now, Dad," I said.

"So—" Amy said, drawing out the word, "How does it feel to be thirty?"

"Pretty much the same as twenty-nine," I said, trying to unfold my napkin from my silverware in jerky motions. The silverware was wrapped so tight, I gave up.

"Hello, I see you're all here now," a cheery, blond, college-aged looking guy said as he stopped by our table. He beamed at me. "Can I get you something to drink?"

"Iced-tea please, and some water," I said.

"Water for the table," Amy said.

"You all look nice," I said, glancing around. I was definitely underdressed for my present company. Sharon and Amy were each in three-piece suits and my mother wore a trendy-looking bohemian-style top and slacks. Well, I was underdressed for the company, except for my dad. He wore jeans and a T-shirt just like I did, though his was collared and quite a bit better quality than my work shirt.

"Thank you sweetheart, you look very nice too," Sharon said.

My mother finally opened her eyes, her gaze moving over me. A tear dropped from her eye, and she turned away. "You've lost so much weight," she commented.

I rocked back in my chair. "Seriously, Mom?" I said under my breath.

"Like twenty pounds," she said.

"Not twenty pounds. And, seriously, we haven't talked in nine months and that's the first thing you say to me?"

Her mouth opened, jaw falling slack before her brow furrowed. "And whose fault is that, Jay Jay?"

"So you decide to ambush me?"

She leaned toward me from across the table. "You won't answer my phone calls."

"Because I need some space right now," I whispered.

"Your birthday is a special day for me too, Jay Jay. You and Sarah are all the family I have left," she said.

"You can see Sarah anytime at the school. I know you do," I grumbled.

"It's not the same, and I don't see her all that much, just in the hallways between classes. I am all alone," she whispered.

"No you're not, Mom. I know you spend every Sunday with Susan."

"I love Susie, she's like a daughter to me, but she's not my daughter." She reached across the table, touching my hand. "You shut me out."

"I can't do this," I said, pulling my hand away from hers and starting to stand.

"Jamie," my dad said, looking up sharply, "Sit."

"Really, Dad? I didn't expect this of you," I said.

"Just because your mother and my marriage didn't work out, doesn't mean that we stopped being a team when it comes to you. All three of us are a team," he said, throwing an arm around Sharon. "And we all think it's about time you stopped punishing your mother for doing the right thing."

"Yeah, okay, sure," I said, grabbing my purse and turning around. I almost smacked into the waiter as I turned around.

"I'm so sorry ma'am, but we're out of iced tea," he said.

"Oh, good, because I'm actually leaving," I told him, before stepping around him. "Thanks anyway."

"Jamie," I heard my father say in a warning tone.

"Ground me, fire me, I don't care, Dad. But, I'm not staying here," I said, and walked away from the table, shaking my head. I rushed through the lunch crowd, squeezing between bodies.

When I exited the restaurant, the fishy smell seemed stronger, as if it had intensified while I was in the restaurant.

Rushing down the dock steps, I jogged through the parking lot and unlocked my car. Once inside, my urgency drained and I slumped forward in my seat. My head rested on the steering wheel, as I took deep breaths in and out.

I wasn't that surprised when the door to my car opened and shut again.

"What the hell is wrong with you, Amy?" I said, not looking up but knowing from her floral perfume that it was her.

"Your mom called me a week ago; she wanted to see you on your birthday. What was I supposed to say to her?"

"Um, 'no' would have worked," I said, head still on the steering wheel.

"Actually, no, it wouldn't have. If I ever treat my mom as bad as you treat yours, I hope someone shoots me in the head," she said.

"Do you want to shoot me in the head, Amy? Because let me tell you, that'd be a better birthday present than the one you got me," I said. "You couldn't have warned me?"

"Would you have come?"

"No."

"Uh huh. You know what, Jamie? I'm tired of it. I'm tired of feeling sorry for you. I'm tired of everyone tiptoeing around you and not bringing up how screwed up you are. I'm especially tired of everyone not mentioning this." She grabbed my left hand.

Surprised, I lifted my head away from the steering wheel, only to have Amy shove my wedding finger into my own face.

"And don't you dare tell me that you wore it for work, because I know for a fact that you never take that thing off," she said.

"What, do you have cameras in my shower?" I said, pulling my hand back to cover my wedding finger with my other hand.

"Why do you still wear that thing? Is it just to ensure that you can never move past losing Logan?"

"It's been a year, Amy. A *year*," I said.

"If he was still alive, you wouldn't even be together after what he did to you," she said, rolling her eyes in apparent frustration.

"And that's supposed to make this easier?" I said.

"To move on, yes. Have you even talked to a guy who wasn't ordering a drink from you since Logan died?"

"Yes," I said.

She pointed a finger at me. "I'm not talking about you sleeping with Vanessa's ex-husband. You know how screwed up I think that is," she said, glaring at me.

I stared at her, dumbfounded. "Are you and Vanessa talking again?"

"No, of course not," she said, smacking her forehead before throwing up her hands. "But that doesn't change the fact that I think you sleeping with Cam is all kinds of screwed up. Like either of you need any more baggage."

"Thanks, Amy. Please, don't hold anything back. What else am I doing wrong with my life?"

She closed her eyes, breathing through her nose. "I wasn't trying to—I didn't mean to dump all of this on you on your birthday, okay? It's just hard. I want you to be happy and you obviously don't want to be."

"Unfortunately for you, you can't control other people's lives. I know you know everything and you have this perfect life with your perfect husband and all, but I was dealt a different set of cards." I crossed my arms over my chest.

She placed her manicured fingers to her temples. "See, it's when you talk like that that really bothers me, and not because you're trying to insult me and Peter. You're thirty, not ninety, stop being so self-defeating. And for God's sake, eat something; you always look so sickly lately. Can't you at least eat at that money-hole of a coffee shop?"

I glared at her.

She sighed, dropping her hands. "I'm sorry," she said, but she didn't sound sorry. "Will you come back into the restaurant?"

"No, I'm not hungry," I said, raising my eyebrows at her. "And I need to go throw some more money into a hole."

"Fine," she said, looking to the car's ceiling. "Well, are we still going to that kids' movie this Sunday? What was it called?"

"*Lucky Stars*," I said. "Sarah and I are going; you can come if you want to."

"Well, I do, and Peter does too," she said.

"Great, see you at the theater," I said.

"I guess I'll bring you everyone's presents then." She heaved a sigh. "Happy birthday."

"Thanks," I grumbled as she exited the car. "Hey Amy!" I called out to her.

She ducked her head back into the car.

"Thank you for sparing me the humiliation of doing that scene in front of everyone."

"Yeah," she said, before closing my car door.

Day Zero: Twelve-Thirty

I texted Susan while still sitting in my car in the restaurant parking lot.

Me: Why can't you be my real sister?

Susan: Amy crawl up your ass again?

Me: With a pitchfork. I seriously don't know where she gets it. Both my dad and Sharon are such nice, well-adjusted people.

Susan: Maybe from all those teeny-bopper sitcoms she used to torture us with.

Me: Omg I forgot about those! Those were horrible.

Susan: Fucking awful.

Me: Btw I'm killing your wife tonight.

Susan: Yeah she told me, something about her introducing you to the guy of your dreams.

Me: She would spin it like that.

Susan: Gotta go. Boss coming. See you soon. And, you're not killing Beza.

Backing out of my spot, I drove the half mile downtown where The Coffee Spot sat sandwiched between a Cajun restaurant and the public library building.

The familiar mural on the library wall of Jack climbing a beanstalk to a paradise made entirely of books greeted me as I exited my car. Jack had a happy-go-lucky look on his face, having no idea that a fearsome literary giant was waiting for him in a castle made of the classics. Like everything else in this town, the library architecture was done in a mission style, all red tile roofs and thick white walls.

The Coffee Stop stood out from the library's cutesy exterior. Six years ago, when Logan and I bought The Coffee Spot's building, we remodeled the whole thing to look like a Parisian shop. We designed the exterior and interior, and even had one of Logan's friends do the installations so we could be there through every step of the process.

Huge windows spanned the outer wall, all of which was sheltered by a long, red awning. 'The Coffee Stop' was written in wide letters across the windows. The sun was going full blast above, though the wind blasting through the street was fighting it for dominance. The blossoming cherry tree planted in front of the coffee shop swayed as if it was waving. Petals blew past like a whirlwind of pink snowflakes, catching on my shirt and hair.

Flicking the petals off me, I hurried up to the shop's entrance and threw open the door. As soon as I was safely inside, I shut the door on the wind. The warm coffee smell comforted me with its familiarity as much as the soft classical music did.

Turning, I watched the petals swirl past the windows in the wind. Some petals took a straight path, flying onward like they wanted to reach somewhere other than the drainage holes on the sides of the street. Other pink petals were in no hurry, they swirled around, forming small columns of color.

"Look! It's the birthday girl!" A familiar voice shouted from behind me.

Spinning on my heel, I turned to see Chris beaming at me from across the cash register. The line of customers in front of him glanced over at me. One older woman gave me a smile and a nod, though I didn't recognize her.

Smiling back, I made my way to the opening behind the coffee counter.

"Hey Chris," I said, patting him on the shoulder as I passed. Chris looked too big behind the coffee counter, and like any great baker, he only got bigger the longer I knew him.

I slid past him to the back where I kept the spare aprons. After making sure to grab one of the smaller aprons—Chris's spares could wrap around me twice—I washed my hands and stepped up behind Chris. "You want to take off?" I asked him.

He turned a wide smile on me, his white teeth contrasting with his dark brown skin and short black bristle beard. "I'm good," he said. "I'll help you close."

"Are you sure? Haven't you been here since four-thirty?"

"Yeah, it's all good," he said.

"Okay, if you're sure," I said, shrugging. "Well, what do you want to take, register or espresso machine?"

"Register," he said.

Jumping on the espresso machine, I adjusted the grind. Chris tamped down the ground espresso beans harder than I could, and if I pulled shots from his grinds, they'd be weak and watery.

It took a few wasted shots, but soon I was pulling great shots. Taking the small pitcher of milk, I let the steam wand rest just under the milk's surface and turned the knob to start the steam going.

When the temperature of the milk was right and the foam at the top was just perfect, I turned off the steam. Lining up the cups, I made the dry cappuccino first, using the majority of my foam.

I called out the order, placing the cappuccino on the bar. Turning my attention to the next drink, I stirred the flavor in with the shot, and then poured the hot foamed milk in while holding the foam back with a spoon. When the cup was almost full, I let the foam pour in. Shaking my hand back and forth, I then did a quick motion up, making a white fern leaf in the foam. I repeated the process with the next drink, but made a heart instead.

As new orders came in, I hurried between the espresso machine and the blenders and ice for the cold drinks.

Chris kept the cups coming, chatting up both the new and regular customers alike. He was almost constantly laughing, and if I didn't know the customer, I could never tell whether they were unknown, or someone Chris was friends with at college. When the lunch rush dwindled, I blew out the steam wands and wiped down my station.

Chris always managed to keep it pristine when he worked the espresso machine, while I worked in a general mess of chocolate and coffee grind spills until the lulls in customers.

"Happy birthday to you, happy birthday to you," Chris sang, holding a banana nut muffin out to me.

I closed my eyes and blew out an imaginary candle. "I wish for a million dollars," I said.

"No, you're not supposed to tell," he whispered. Then he stuffed the muffin into my mouth.

"Ah," I garbled with the muffin hanging out of my mouth, before taking a big bite. After swallowing, I raised my finger at him. "I'd be pissed if that didn't taste so freaking amazing. Is that a different recipe?"

He grinned. "I'll never tell."

I took another big bite. "Crack, you put crack into it, didn't you?"

His smile grew wider. "So how is your hot sister?" he asked.

"Still married," I said before stuffing the rest of the muffin into my mouth.

"That's fine with me; I just meant she's nice to look at." He shrugged his wide shoulders. "You know, even though she knew I was covering for you here, she called to un-invite me just in case I might change my mind." He furrowed his brow and a grimace turned down the corner of his lips. "I've always been so nice to her. Is she racist or something?"

"Um, I've never heard her say anything racist that I can remember." I shook my head. "If it makes you feel any better, she uninvited everyone I invited. I'm pretty sure she was rude to everyone else too."

"Good, because I was thinking of starting a petition to stop you having her plan your parties," he said.

"My signature will be the first one on there, trust me," I said, raising my eyebrows at him. "Hence me coming in an hour earlier than expected."

He glanced over at the clock. "Whoa, I thought it was later! That bad?"

"Worse," I said as I grabbed a clean towel and ran it under warm water. "Remember when that rock busted through our door window a couple years ago and a piece of glass stuck in my arm?"

"Yeah, I remember, that sucker was this big." He held his thumb and index finger up about two inches apart.

"Ten stitches," I said. "I'd take five pieces of glass to avoid another birthday luncheon planned by my sister." I held up my hand, extending out my fingers for emphasis.

Chris whistled.

Wringing out the towel, I nodded. "Anyway, I'm going to get a head start on closing."

"You doing that birthday sleepover thing with those hot lesbians?"

I smacked him with the damp towel. "Shut up you," I said.

He threw up his hands with a grin. "Just asking. Touchy, touchy."

With quick efficient movements, I wiped down the tables and chairs around the shop.

The only remaining customer, a regular who usually came in during the morning, called to me from across the shop, "I'm just going to pack up here in a minute, Jamie."

"No worries, Margret, we're still open for another hour. Just getting a head start," I said. "You want me to grab you any water or anything?"

"Oh, no, I'm great, thanks Jamie," she said, turning back to her laptop.

Leaning over, I cleared the kid's books from the coffee table before wiping it down.

The door jingled behind me, but I figured that Chris would handle the customers.

A cookie had exploded across the couch cushions and I was furiously wiping it away when I heard a low familiar chuckle from right behind me.

I jumped up and spun around.

Cameron stood a few paces away, his eyes still on my backside with a half-amused, half-heated look on his face.

"Enjoying the show?" I asked, attempting to glare at him, but I had a hard time fighting a grin.

He stepped closer and said in a low voice, "Loved the show."

"How long were you standing there?"

He just bobbed his eyebrows. Then he narrowed his eyes. "I thought you weren't going to be here."

I shrugged. "Yeah, the whole thing got canceled. I'm really not that disappointed."

Behind the counter, Chris widened his eyes at me then shook his head.

I focused back to Cameron. "You want your usual?"

He paused before saying, "Yeah, that'd be great."

I walked around the counter, and set up a double shot on the espresso machine.

"Hey Chris, how's it going?" Cameron said as he walked up to the counter.

"Good, Cam. You?"

"I am doing perfectly, got a great new client today and he's got friends who need a lot of custom work," he said with a grin.

"Oh good, that went well?" I asked.

"Better than I even thought it would." He gave me a grin and a wink. "Things are looking up, fingers crossed."

I nodded. "Fingers crossed."

Chris's gaze went back and forth between us, and then he smiled at Cameron. "Well, I'm happy for you, bro. You deserve good things coming your way."

"Thanks, buddy, I really appreciate you saying that. So," he drew out the word, "what's the favorite for today."

"Lunch or pastry?" Chris asked

"Banana muffins," I said as a fake-cough.

"I'll take a banana muffin," Cameron said with a grin and a quick glance over at me.

"Here's your drink," I said, leaning over the register. As I handed him his dark roast coffee with a double espresso shot in it, his fingers brushed over mine. His thumb brushed across my hand once before I pulled it away.

After insisting on paying, as he always did, he held up his pastry bag and said, "Later."

"Yeah," I said, biting my lip as he turned away.

The moment the door clanged closed behind Cameron, Chris turned on me. "So when are you guys getting married?"

"Um, never. What are you talking about?" I turned back to the espresso machine. Grabbing a towel, I started scrubbing under the machine. "Speaking of marriage, how's Melissa? Isn't it about time you put a ring on her finger?"

When I looked up at Chris, he was just shaking his head at me. "Smooth," he said.

"What?" I said. "Cameron and I are just friends. We'd never get married... in a million years."

"Does he know that?" Chris asked.

"Yes, he knows that." I slammed the double filter holder down over the trash to empty the wet grinds.

"If you say so." Chris raised his hands in surrender. "And, Melissa's good. She wants to wait to get married until we both graduate. She's actually been bugging me about bringing you and Sarah over for dinner."

"I'd love that. But, we'd probably have to meet at a neutral location, or at my house. Melissa just has way too much nice stuff for Sarah to knock over."

"Oh, she's not worried about that," he said, waving a hand in the air.

"Just you wait until Sarah tries to do a handspring on your coffee table. Trust me, it'll be better at my place," I said.

"Whatever works." He shrugged.

"Well, if you're determined to stay until we close, mind covering the front while I check through the papers in the office? I'm hoping to find a couple more exemptions before I take the shop's papers to my tax advisor. I was thinking that if we got enough of a refund, I could hire someone else on, maybe keep the shop open on evenings and weekends like the old days. What do you think?"

"Like I told you last week, Jamie, I think… you should take that offer and sell the shop," he said.

I blew out my breath, shaking my head. "You're so eager to be out of a job, are you?"

"We both know I wouldn't be out of a job for long. I've been working here since the day it opened, and I'll be here until the day it closes. Businesses love that stuff. And you'd give me one hell of a reference," he said, giving me a smile.

"You think so, do you?" I said, throwing my towel at his face.

He caught it out of the air.

"I don't get it, Chris. You're the only one who loves this place more than I do."

"I'd miss this place like crazy, but you should sell it," he said. "Aren't you tired of paying off a property you've already paid off after years of working your ass off? And it's a mean lien the court put on this place. At our current earnings you'll be paying it off for another ten years. And, I know you're paying yourself minimum wage."

"That's why I think we should hire someone. We miss out on a lot of the business on the evenings and weekends," I said. "We could do open mics and stuff like that."

Chris shook his head. "The time is right now, Jamie. You might not get an offer like this again. That offer was for more than what you owe. You and Sarah would even have a little to start over. Put a down payment on a house or something."

I touched Chris's arm. "You're a good guy, Chris," I said before turning toward the back office.

"I was here in the beginning, Jamie. I remember, it was his big dream, not yours," he said.

"It was both our dreams," I said, not turning around.

"Wait, no, I can prove it," Chris called.

Rolling my eyes, I turned around. "You can?"

Chris grinned widely, held up a hand and walked backward to where we always stored our personal stuff. He pulled a small square present out of his old, worn satchel.

"What's that?" I asked.

"Your birthday present," he said, his grin growing even wider. He handed it over.

"Why am I scared?" I asked him, smiling.

The moment I pulled the blue wrapping paper away from the CD, I started laughing. "No way! Where did you get this?" I asked.

"eBay. I had to get a bunch of other early 2000's pop CDs with it, but it was worth it."

"I think that this might be the best present anyone has ever given me," I said, meaning it. "I lost this, you know, with everything else." I held it up.

"You were pretty hot back then," he said, looking at the picture on the cover of the CD.

I smacked his arm. "Back then?"

"Jesus, you don't need to get violent. Okay, fine, you were hot back then, but now you're gorgeous," he said.

"Better," I said.

"And wowza, look at Susan and…" he paused, looking up at me with a grimace.

I swallowed. "It's okay, you can say it, Vanessa was super hot back then too." I looked down at our picture. Our blonde hair was up in pin-up girl style while we stood in super short cut-offs and red and white striped crop tops, giving the camera attitude. "We were all such babies back then, and look at us, we're practically naked."

"Yeah, sure, I'll look," he said.

"Yeah, yeah," I said, pulling the CD back to me. "My fifteen minutes of fame, immortalized in a compact disk."

"Let's put it on," Chris said.

I looked over to Margret who was still working away on her computer. "I'm pretty sure we'll drive away Margret for good." She was a professional looking young woman; this was probably her office away from her office.

"Hey Margie," Chris called.

"Yeah?" Margret called, not looking up from her laptop.

"Did you know that Jamie here was in an early 2000's pop group?" he called back.

"Are you serious?" she said, looking up with interest. She walked up to the counter. "Early 2000's were my years. Were you famous?"

"No," I said.

"They were a one-hit wonder. 'Cherry Pie', you ever heard of them?"

Margret gave me an apologetic smile. "I can't say that I have."

Chris sang, *"Don't you want to love me, baby? When the sun goes down. Don't you want to touch me, baby, when I'm not around?"*

I buried my face in my hands. "Now I'll definitely not be able to listen to it, I'm already too embarrassed."

"Oh, can we? It sounds familiar, but I'm not sure," Margret said.

"Oh, fine," I said, face still in my hands.

A second later I heard the oh-so-familiar opening notes from the first song of our CD before Chris skipped forward to our famous song.

The intro notes played and Margret burst out laughing. "Oh my god, I remember this song. This was like senior prom for me. That was you?" she asked.

I nodded.

When the chorus came on, both Chris and Margret sang along, *"Don't you want to love me, baby? When the sun goes down. Don't you want to touch me, baby, when I'm not around? It's been so long, baby, and to you it might sound sappy. But it's been so long, so long, baby, since I was happy."*

"Come on, Jamie, you know the words," Chris said, nudging me.

"Fine," I said with a smile, and I joined them for the next chorus.

When the chorus ended, I stopped singing too, though I remembered the words.

When the song was over, Margret smiled at me. "Well, I'm going to have to go buy a copy of your CD and have you autograph it for me."

"Good luck," Chris said, "Took me forever to find it. You can buy the track off iTunes though, and have Jamie sign a napkin. Cheaper that way too."

"No, I'm determined." she smiled. "Have you ever been on one of those 'where are they now' things?"

"Nope, but my friend Susan was." I pointed to her on the cover. "But, only because she married an international supermodel and they 'retired' together. Susan's partner was the main article."

"Well, that's very cool," Margret said, "I'm going to go pack up and get out of your hair, guys. I'll see you Monday."

"Thanks for coming in Margie," Chris said.

When the next song started playing, I pressed eject on the CD player and replaced the CD in its case. I slipped the CD case in a pastry bag, taping the ends down.

"What was that?" Chris asked, raising a brow at me.

I gave him a sheepish smile. "I don't want the case to get scratched. Thank you so much Chris, this really was the best present ever."

"What else did you get?" he asked.

"Nothing yet," I said, shrugging.

"Well, the point I was trying to make earlier, was that when I first met you six years ago, you told me you wanted to go back to your singing career. You told me that you were just putting things on hold until Logan's coffee shop and bakery was on its feet."

Shaking my head, I stowed the CD in my purse, making sure I zipped up the purse so it wouldn't fall out. "Dreams change, Chris. Even then I knew it would be hard to be a professional singer and a full time mom. No matter what, I'd need a day job."

"Not for a little while if you took that offer," he said.

"Even if I didn't need a day job financially, I'd *need* a day job for my sanity. Just having the morning off today proved that to me."

"Work for Cam, he'd hire you in a heartbeat," Chris said.

"At a custom body shop? Um, no. What would I do?"

He gestured to me. "Be a receptionist? I don't know, help him manage it?"

"I am not working for Cameron," I said, snorting and suppressing a grin.

"Fine, well, I'll hire you when I start up my cupcake shop. It'll probably be a year or two, but I can hire you in the meantime to help with all the start-up paperwork and stuff that I have no idea how to do. I'll pay you more than minimum too," he said, pointing at me.

Two sudden tears splashed down my face. "You would hire me?"

"In a heartbeat, Jamie," he said. "Hey, stop crying." He pulled me into a hug.

I loved Chris's hugs; they were all-consuming and substantial. He smelled like coffee grinds and flour.

"I'll help you with your paperwork, Chris. You don't need to pay me."

"Ah, shut up, Jamie. Of course I'd pay you," he said, stepping back from me.

Wiping my face off, I smiled at him. "That means a lot, Chris, so much."

"You going to sell the shop?" he asked.

"No... I don't know Chris. It just doesn't feel right selling Logan's shop." I closed my eyes. "But, I'll think about what you said, and no matter what, I want to help you with your future cupcake empire."

"Well, it's up to you." He shrugged.

The door clanged and a family walked in.

"Hey, I'll take the customers. You go do what you have to do," he said.

Day Zero: One-forty

Instead of heading to the office, I smashed down the recycling, flattening milk cartons and ice-cream boxes. As I passed the office door on the way to the back exit where we kept the trash and recycling bins, I forced myself to look away. Out behind the store, the smell of the trash mingled with the briny smell of the not-so-distant ocean.

Reaching into my pocket, I pulled out the key to the dumpsters. Turning, I jumped a foot in the air when I saw a man looking at me. All the recycling I was holding fell to the ground.

"Oh, I'm sorry Jamie!" he said, getting to his feet.

I grabbed at my heart. "Mitch, you scared the crap out of me. You know you're not supposed to be back here," I said.

He wiped at his nose, leaving a smear of dirt across his face. "I'm sorry, Jamie," he said again, his loose jaw moved too much with his words.

I doubted Mitch was much older than I was, but he was already missing a couple teeth and had several deep wrinkles. "It's just so cold with the wind, and they call the cops behind the ice cream place. The shelter doesn't open for a while, you know. Can I just stay? Just for a little while. I won't touch anything."

I looked around the alley; the only thing he could possibly touch was our locked dumpsters.

"Go on ahead around and into the shop. Tell Chris I said to hook you up with a coffee and something to eat."

He slumped forward, staring at the ground.
"Nah, Jamie, that's okay. I'm not looking for a
handout, just a warm place to sit."

"Well, unfortunately Mitch, I can't have you
back here. Tell you what, if you help me out with
picking up all this recycling for me and throwing it in
the bin, I'll repay you with a coffee, something to eat
and you can sit in the shop while we close."

"Like, as a payment?" he asked.

"Yeah, like that," I said.

He grinned. "Yeah, um, that'd be great. So I've
been meaning to ask, do you have any liquor in there?
Like do you add it to the coffee, ever?"

"Nope, sorry," I said.

"That's cool, no, that's fine. I love your coffee,
thanks." He stood up, scrambling to gather the boxes I
had just dropped.

I unlocked the dumpster and held it open for
him to throw the boxes into. He moved like I was
timing him, practically jumping back and forth from
the ground to the bin. When he'd grabbed the last box,
I let it drop, and locked it. I walked with him around
to the front entrance, holding the door open for him.

"Anything in particular you'd like to eat?" I
asked him as we made our way through the shop.

"Um, can I have a cookie?" he asked, eyes
bright.

"Of course you can. Chocolate chip or peanut
butter?"

"Chocolate chip." He grinned like he thought it
was funny.

"Do you want a bagel too?" I asked.

"Oh, that's too much for what I did. Just a cookie and a coffee would be great," he said.

"Alright, if you're sure, but we have a bunch of them left over and they just get stale if we don't eat them," I said, heading back behind the counter.

"Hey Mitch, how's it going?" Chris asked, looking up from wiping down the counter with a big smile on his face.

"Real good, Chris, great. Love this place, love this city. I couldn't be happier," he said.

I handed Mitch a plate with a cookie, then asked, "Where are you going to sit, on the couch?"

"No, I wouldn't want to..." he trailed off mumbling. "Right here is good." He gestured to a table away from the windows.

"Alright, I'll fix your coffee and bring it to you," I said.

After fixing Mitch his coffee, I checked the store and bathroom for any other customers. When I found it empty, I switched the sign on the window from 'open' to 'closed' and locked the front door.

After wiping down all the tables except Mitch's, I flipped the chairs up and mopped under them. When I returned behind the counter, Chris had already cleaned up and closed down the espresso machine, put away the pastries and was working on the till.

"I'll do those," I said, grabbing the credit card receipts from Chris. I printed the closing receipt and a long line of receipt tape came out. "You must have had a crazy rush this morning."

"Yeah, it was going pretty good in here for a while."

"If we keep having days like these, we'll definitely be able to hire on more help," I said.

Chris didn't respond, so I turned my attention to counting the number of transactions and making sure we had the same number of signed receipts.

I glanced at Mitch, wondering if he was watching us count out the money, but his attention was fixed on the tree outside our window. He seemed completely content, almost dreaming.

"We are twenty-five cents off," Chris said with a frown.

"Here you go," I said, leaning down and grabbing a quarter from where it must have dropped to the floor. I set it next to the change rolls. "Wow, exact. That never happens when I'm on the register."

Chris chuckled. "Yeah, I know."

"Ha, ha," I said, holding the deposit bag out for him.

He set the money in the bag, and I zipped it up.

"Alright, I'm going to take out the trash and ask Mitch to join me so you can take care of this stuff. I'll lock up the back if you get the front," I said.

"Sounds good. And happy birthday, Jamie, I love you," he said.

"Love you too, Chris," I said, giving him a hug.

Taking off my apron, I grabbed my purse and hung it over my shoulder. I grabbed up a trash bag in each hand. "Hey Mitch," I called. "We're all done in here and have to go. Mind helping me with the back door?" I asked.

"No, of course not!" Mitch said. "Do you want me to clean my table and my plate? I can do it, it's no problem."

"No worries, Mitch, I'll get it," Chris called.

"Okay, because it's no problem. But, I'll... I'll help you with the door. Want me to get those?" he reached for the trash bags in my hands.

"No, I got them. But the door would really help," I said.

Mitch rushed forward, pushing open the back door and doing a wide sweep of his hand to gesture me out.

I grabbed up my keys, locking the back door and then unlocking the dumpster.

"Would you mind holding it up for me?" I asked Mitch.

He rushed over to the dumpster, holding it up way more than I needed him to.

After dumping the trash and locking up, I turned to him. "Do you want a couple bucks, Mitch?"

"Oh, no, that wasn't worth a couple bucks. I'll take a dollar, if you have it."

After I gave him a dollar, he asked me, "Can I stay back here? Just for a little while. I won't do anything, just sit, I swear."

I rolled back my shoulders. "Thing is, I'm part of the business association and we're not supposed to let people loiter back here." I hummed to myself. "How about... I'll just walk away and not notice that you're back here, yeah? I have no idea that you're here." I winked at him.

"This was a very nice day," Mitch said, grinning at me and settling onto the ground near the dumpster.

"It was nice to see you," I told him, before walking around the building to the front. I ran my hand along the jack and the beanstalk mural as the wind buffeted against my back.

When I climbed back into my car, I sat in the warmth for a second before starting it. Petals clung to my windshield and hood; I even found a few in my hair.

When I drove past the shop, I caught Chris just as he was locking up and my hand hovered over the horn but I thought better of honking at him.

Most of downtown was empty of pedestrians, though the wind sent ripples of movement in every direction. Trash skipped down the sidewalk under swinging signs clattering back and forth. Several other blossom trees sprayed out their petals, though some of them dotted the ground with a deeper red.

The only human traffic I saw was clustered around a burger shop on the way out of downtown. Crossing into the residential neighborhood, the houses passed by my car, growing bigger and bigger.

Turning, I made my way to the end of the drive where Coral Beach Elementary abutted a beach park. It was one of the prettiest public schools I had ever seen. Unlike most of the town, it shied away from the mission architecture; instead it shone out with hundreds of windows throughout its modern exterior.

I usually waited for Sarah's aide to walk her out to the parking lot, but I was a little early so I walked through the main entrance.

The school secretary peeked up at me as I passed, but turned her attention back to a kid who stood in front of her desk. The indoor hallways were thankfully warm as I walked over toward Mrs. Keller's classroom. When I was within ten feet, I saw a familiar head of blond hair waiting in front of the closed doors with a couple other parents.

Right, this is room seven, where his daughter Kay goes to class. I stepped backward, considering sneaking back out to wait in my car when Patrick the Hunky Dad spotted me.

"Jamie," he said, walking through the group to come stand by me.

"How's it going?" I said with a wave, rocking back on my feet.

"Pretty good, you?" he asked.

"Good." I swung my arms back and forth. "So," I drew out the word, "my friend, Beza, confessed to talking to you about me. And, I just want to apologize, my friends and family are either trying to fix me or smother me lately."

His brow furrowed.

"Sorry, I'm awkward and confusing. I'm just a bit embarrassed, I guess, that my friend went up to you to talk about me. Please, don't feel obligated to... whatever, because of my situation." I stepped back, looking over my shoulder toward the red 'exit' sign.

"I asked your friend about you," he said, with a smile. "You know, because our daughters are friends."

"Yeah, uh-huh," I said, scratching my nose. "Um, never mind everything I just said."

"Why did you think she approached me?"

Pinching my lips together, I shook my head. "No reason," I said.

"Anyhow, would you like to go to dinner sometime?" he asked.

My jaw slackened as he grinned a wide, amused grin.

I narrowed my eyes at him. "Are you serious or are you messing with me because I just made that super awkward 'my friend was trying to set us up' speech?"

"Can I say both?" he asked, eyes twinkling with amusement.

The bell rang, and a tide of children came rushing out of the doors all along each wall.

As a long line of children filed past us, Patrick asked, "So, about that dinner, yes, no, maybe so?"

I looked over. "Can I say *maybe so*? Is that a real option?"

"I was stupid enough to add it, so I guess, yes. Unless, you'll let me amend my choices to 'yes, yes, and definitely yes?'"

"Let's stick with maybe so," I said.

"Dad!" a little girl ran up throwing her arms around Patrick. Her hair was darker than his, almost brown. She jumped up and down, talking a million miles per hour about an art project.

Patrick's attention was solely on her now, his smile warm as he nodded along with her story. He slipped her backpack off, throwing it over his suit shoulder.

"Are you Sarah's mom?" A little boy asked me as he passed. Red hair poked out of his head in all directions and freckles dotted his face.

"Yep," I said.

"I knew it!" he shouted, before hurrying off.

"Okay," I whispered to myself, smiling.

Sarah and her aide came out of the door together. The moment Sarah saw me, she grabbed the straps of her backpack and ran. "Mom!" she shouted, "Mom!" She plowed into me, and I threw my arms around her as she buried her head into my stomach.

I looked up to Ms. Brown, trying to gauge her expression. She was a few inches shorter than me, and probably a couple years younger than I was too. She smiled at me and the tension in my shoulders relaxed.

"Was it a good day?" I asked, giving her a hopeful smile.

Ms. Brown nodded, making her bobbed black hair flip up and down. "For the most part, yeah. The class just watched movies, went to art and stuff and we had a Friday fun day raffle, so it was a pretty easy day. She had a little trouble transitioning from speech, kicked over a trash can, but yeah, all in all everything went pretty well." She pushed her glasses up her nose.

"No hitting?" I asked.

"Nope, no hitting today," Ms. Brown said, nodding.

"Oh thank god," I said. I looked down at Sarah, who was grabbing onto me like I might leave her behind if she loosened her hold. Patting her head, I said, "Nice work at school, angel."

"I'm ready to go home and have the weekend," she told me.

"I bet," I said.

"Oh, the principal did want me to ask you to talk to Sarah about not doing her gymnastics while she's at school." She turned to Sarah, saying, "It's very important Sarah, no gymnastics at school, okay?"

When Sarah just looked away from her, I told Ms. Brown, "I'll talk to her about it. How are you doing?"

She beamed at me. "Oh, I'm good! John and I set the date, so this time next year I'll be Mrs. Harriet."

"Awesome, wow. Congratulations!"

"Thanks," she said. "I have to go head to a meeting, but you guys have a great weekend!"

"Yeah, you too," I said. "Hey Sarah, angel, you need to give me a little space so we can walk to the car." When she didn't step back, I said, "If we can't walk to the car, we can't go to the sleepover tonight at Aiden's."

"Mom," Sarah said, looking up at me. "I want to watch the artistic women's beam final from the North Greenwich arena at the London Olympics."

"Um, we might have time before we have to head to Aiden's, but we have to go now."

She stepped away.

"Excuse me, Sarah's mom," said a young girl's voice from behind me.

I turned to see Patrick's daughter, Kay, standing right behind me, looking up.

"Her name's Jamie," Patrick said, smiling over at me.

"Um, my name is Kay. I love gymnastics too. Where does Sarah go to do her gymnastics? I go to the Y. Sarah is really good, she's better than me. But she's not supposed to do gymnastics on the playground. She does it anyway though."

"Hi Kay," I said.

"Sarah told me she does gymnastics at the Olympics, but I don't think that's true," she said. "I mean, she's only eight like me."

"It's kind of true," I said, "Or it will be soon. She wants to join something called the Special Olympics; do you know what that is?"

"No, but it sounds cool. Can I join it too?"

I glanced up at Patrick with an apologetic smile on my face. "Sorry, Kay, it's only for people with special needs like Sarah. The Special Olympics is open to people a little younger, but one day Sarah plans to join the main Olympic Games. Isn't that right, angel?"

"USA, artistic gymnastics," Sarah said.

"That one you can join, but I think you have to be sixteen," I said. "Sarah goes to a coach who volunteers with the Special Olympics at her studio."

"Oh, wow, can I go?"

"Yes," Sarah said.

"No, sweetheart," Patrick said, looking down at his daughter.

"No, dad, just to watch, I mean. Can I go to watch?" She turned big, brown pleading eyes to me.

I scratched behind my ear. "I'm not sure, I could check with the coach," I said, looking over at Patrick.

He gave me a half smile and shrugged. "You walking this way?" He gestured toward the parking lot.

"I was hoping to," I said, putting an arm around Sarah, and leading her toward the exit.

The wind blasted us as we exited out of the main doors. Both Kay and Sarah had to grab at their hair as it blew into their faces. Grabbing two hair bands out of my purse, I offered one to Patrick.

"Want this?" I asked.

He took the little pink hair band, and gave me a big grin.

I gathered up Sarah's hair and tied it back. "Want me to do Kay's too?" I asked as I could see he was struggling.

"Thanks, I'm still not that good at all this girl stuff."

"No problem." I collected her hair up in a high bun. When I was done, she grinned up at me, touching her hair like it was delicate and might break.

"Well, see you Monday, probably?" I said.

He grinned, "Or maybe sooner."

"Maybe *so*," I said, with a flirtatious grin, "It's a small town."

"Alright then," he said, his eyes glowing and grin growing even bigger, "Maybe so."

Day Zero: Three O'clock

When we turned off the street Sarah's school sat on and onto another residential street, I pressed the button for the CD player to start working.

"Oh, Buffalo Gals will ye come out tonight, come out tonight, come out tonight. Buffalo Gals, won't you come out tonight, and dance by de light of de moon?" Sarah and I sang at the top of our lungs along with the kids' CD. We kept singing, and I saw the seat next to me bump forward every couple notes as Sarah kicked it.

"I danced with a gal with a hole in her stockin', And her heel kept a-knockin', and her toes kept a-rockin'," Sarah sang in a low, masculine sounding voice which was an amazing impression of the singer from the CD.

"Wow, that's really good," I said, looking back into the rear view mirror at her. I squinted into the mirror. "Sarah, are you wearing your seatbelt?"

"I'm wearing it!" she shouted. I glanced over my shoulder, just to be sure, but she was wearing it.

"Sorry, I just needed to be sure," I said turning back to the road.

"Shit!" I screamed.

A woman was in the road. Time slowed down as she turned to me while I drove straight at her.

My foot slammed down onto my brake pedal.

Her brown ponytail flew back and her eyes widened in shock.

The car skidded toward her. A loud screech and a pungent smell of burnt tire overwhelmed my senses.

My back locked up as the car jerked to a stop, my body slammed forward into the steering wheel.

The woman had her hands out toward my car, as if she would have been able to stop it. Her fingers were only a couple inches from my hood. Her tight running suit expanded with her labored breaths. Her jaw hung open, giving her pretty young face an even younger expression.

Shifting into park, I heaved out a breath.

"*A frog he would a wooing go, m-m, m-m. Whether his mother would let him or no, m-m, m-m,*" the song played on my speaker until I used shaky fingers to turn it off.

The woman straightened up, hand going to her mouth.

I rolled down my window. "I am so sorry! Are you okay?" I called out to her.

"Oh my god," she said under her breath. "I thought I was going to die."

"I'm so sorry," I repeated. "I should have been paying better attention. Are you okay?"

She nodded, though I saw that her arms were trembling. With quick steps, she jogged to the other side of the road. She turned back to me, staring for a minute. "Thank you… for stopping in time. Be more careful next time, okay?"

"I… I will. I'm so sorry," I said.

She nodded, walking at first but then jogging away down the sidewalk.

A loud honk made me jump and woke me from staring after the girl.

I looked back at Sarah. "Baby, are you okay? Are you hurt?"

"I want a glass of milk," she said.

The car behind me honked again. Taking a deep steadying breath, I shifted the car back into drive. I drove five miles under the speed limit all the way home, never once letting my concentration waver from the road.

My hand shook as I shifted into park after pulling into my assigned parking spot. I heard Sarah's seatbelt click off and a moment later she climbed over the central divider.

"Mom, I want some milk. Can we watch the artistic women's beam final from the North Greenwich arena at the London Olympics?" she asked.

"Yeah, angel," I said in a whisper.

Opening the car door, I let her out behind me. We walked down the path that led to our little duplex. My neighbor Clarke stepped out of his apartment as we approached. A big hairy head appeared over the small fence that ran around the front of his apartment.

"Buster!" Sarah said, moving toward the sheep dog.

Glancing over at Clarke, I pulled her away and in front of me. "Not right now, angel," I whispered.

Clarke put an elbow on the fence, leaning over. His sport's jersey was so white it reflected the sunlight. "Hey Jamie, hey Sarah," he called out.

"Hey Clarke," I said waving while I pushed Sarah toward our door.

"Hey Jamie, were you putting up pictures earlier or something?" The grin Clarke gave me made me cringe a little. He ran his hand over the short stubble over his strong jaw, his eyes glinting with amusement.

"Um, no," I said, turning away but narrowing my eyes in thought.

"By the front door," he said.

I felt my face go hot and heard Clarke start laughing.

"Now that's a noise I won't complain about," he said.

"Come on Sarah," I said in a low voice, again pushing her toward the house.

"Oh come on, Jamie, don't be like that. I was just joking," he said, still chuckling. He raised a beer and took a long drink. He pulled down the beer, pointing it at me. "I love that my neighbors are so... happy. You ever need help putting up pictures, just knock on my door. I'd be happy to be... neighborly."

"No thanks," I said as I managed to unlock my front door and push it open.

Locking both my bottom and my top lock, I turned away from the door and squeezed my eyes shut tight.

"Mom, can we watch the artistic women's beam final from the North Greenwich arena at the London Olympics?"

"Yeah, sweetheart," I said. Grabbing my laptop from the living room, I set it on the table and pulled up my YouTube Olympics playlist. Scrolling down, I selected the 2012 artistic bar final.

After pouring Sarah a glass of milk, I grabbed my phone and walked out of the room.

I sat on my bed and dialed Susan.

"Hey bitch," she answered on the second ring.

"Hey," I said, before swallowing.

"What's the matter?" she asked.

"I almost hit a kid with my car. I mean, she wasn't really a kid, but young. I don't think I should be driving. I don't know what's wrong with me," My voice was thick with the tears that started pouring down my face.

"I bet I can guess if you let me," she said.

"Please do," I said while wiping the tears from my face. "Unless you're going to tell me I'm losing my mind, because then I don't want to know."

"When's the last time you ate anything?" she asked.

Putting my head in my hands, I started sniffling. "Oh, crap," I said.

"Love, your brain needs calories to function, go make yourself a fucking sandwich then call me back."

"Okay," I said, hanging up.

Walking back into the kitchen, I looked into the fridge, scanning the contents. It was full of veggies and fruit, and ingredients to all our favorite dishes, but in the end, I grabbed a frozen meal out of the freezer.

"Want a snack, angel?" I asked Sarah.

"Apples and peanut butter," she said.

"I'm waiting for another word, a polite word," I told her as I poked holes in the plastic cover on the frozen enchilada plate.

"Apples and peanut butter... please!" she said the last word with enthusiasm.

I laughed to myself as I dialed the front office on my phone. Holding the phone to my ear with one hand, I grabbed out an apple and held it under cold faucet water it with the other hand.

The dial tone rang three times before I heard a woman pick up. "Sunset Estates, this is Denise," she said.

"Hi Denise, is Richard there?" I asked. Using my shoulder to hold my phone to my ear, I grabbed out a cutting board and knife.

"Sorry, he's gone for the weekend. Can I take a message?" she asked.

"Um, I guess. This is Jamie Scott in apartment thirty-six B. Richard said he was looking into finding another apartment in the complex for my daughter and me to switch over to."

"Sorry, that really is something you'll have to speak to Richard about," she said. "I'll definitely leave a message for him if you want, though."

"Yes, please do. Will you say it's pretty urgent? I already told him why," I said.

"I will, and that's Jamie Scott in...?"

"Thirty-six B," I said.

"Got it, Jamie. You have a good weekend," she said.

"Thanks, you too," I said, setting the phone back down.

I cut up the apple, putting a small dollop of peanut butter on the plate. When I set the plate in front of Sarah, she said, "More peanut butter."

"Nope," I said, grabbing an apple slice and dipping it in the peanut butter.

"Hey, Mommy, that's not yours," she said.

"But it's so delicious, I just can't help myself," I said, tickling her side and making her giggle.

Taking the tray out of the microwave, I pulled away the plastic and ducked back from the cloud of hot steam that poured up.

I sat down beside Sarah just as the Romanian competitor fell off the bar. I draped my arm around Sarah's back as I ate.

"She'll have to tighten up her whole routine," Sarah said, right before the announcer said the same words.

"I think she was very brave to keep going," I said to Sarah. "It's important to just keep going, keep fighting."

"And I'll tell you that is not an easy skill," Sarah said, exactly in sync with the announcer.

"It's funny, the ones that look easy are always the hardest," I said between bites.

When Sarah's favorite American competitor took the beam, I reached to my laptop to skip forward.

"No!" Sarah yelled.

"You hate it when Gaby slips," I told her.

"I like to be sad," Sarah said.

"What?" I said, sitting back in my chair.

"I like to be sad," she repeated.

I paused, then said, "Um, okay." Letting the recording go, I stared at Sarah as she watched her favorite gymnast take the beam and slip in one of her landings.

Sarah screamed at the laptop.

Immediately, there was a banging from the wall that connected our apartment to Clarke's.

I paused the video on the computer. "Angel, quiet, okay? Or I'm turning the laptop off. Let's watch another competition, not the finals for a little while." I skipped to another video.

Wandering into my living room, I took a seat on my overstuffed couch. When I closed my eyes, vivid images ran through my mind. First, I saw the mist parting around Sarah as she ran away from me and the bus. Then Aiden's braids bounced in every direction as he held Sarah's hand and jumped on the trampoline. Whitney's long black lashes came together and separated as she glared down at my wedding ring. Cameron smiled over his shoulder at me as he shook his hips. My sister's red fingernails made small circles at her temples. The pink blossoms blew in all directions around my body. Chris's eyes squinted with a smile as he and Margret belted out my pop song. Mitch looked out of the shop's window as if he was perfectly content. The girl in the road's hands reached to stop my car. Sarah, smiling with her little dimples showing when she said, 'I like to be sad.'

A knock sounded at my door and I got up to answer. When I opened the door, Susan, Beza and Aiden stood outside, smiling at me. "Happy birthday," they said in unison.

"I need to change my whole life," I said.

Day Zero: Four-thirty

Beza and Susan shared a look.

"Well, let's get inside then," Beza said.

I stepped back but Aiden ran up to hug me. "Hey, Aunt Jamie. Where's Sarah?" he said.

"Hey cutie, she's in the kitchen," I said, moving aside so he could run past me.

As we stepped back into my living room, Beza asked, "Have you packed up Sarah yet?"

"I'm sorry," I said.

Susan stepped in front of me, so close her pregnant belly almost touched me. "Okay, this is how this is going to go." She paused to grab up her long blonde hair, tying it into a knot on the top of her head. "Bee is going to take the kids to have a sleep over at our place. I am going to stay here with you, and we're going to figure out your life."

"No, we don't have to tonight," I said.

"Yes we do," Susan said.

I turned to Beza. "I feel bad, our plans—"

"Are not as important as this, Jamie," Beza said. "Anyway, it will be nice to have some special time with Sarah."

"Wow, you guys are so intense about this," I said.

"We've just been waiting for you to wake up for a while, and we're ready," Susan put an arm on my shoulder. Then she lifted one of her legs backward and grabbed her ankle with her hand.

"Susan, I thought you were going to hug me, but you're just using me as a stretching pole?" I rolled my eyes.

"I am f-u-c-k-i-n-g uncomfortable," she said.

"That spelling words out thing isn't going to work for much longer," Beza said, pointing at Susan and pursing her lips. "I'm going to go pack a bag for Sarah." She turned, heading to Sarah's room.

"Stay right there," Susan said as she walked over to my other side, stretching her opposite leg.

"You know I do have walls and furniture you could do that on."

"You're just the right height. Don't you dare move," she said. "So, it sounds like your day fucking sucked."

"I heard that!" Beza yelled from Sarah's room.

"Crap," Susan mumbled under her breath.

"I'm not sure, in a way it was horrible, but not really. Sometimes, I think that life is only a series of moments. And today, moments were just shooting at me left and right. It was like I didn't have a single thing really happen for a year, then just today, a million things happened. Except for almost hitting that girl, they weren't even that big either, just there."

"Maybe you were walking around asleep for the past year, and some... power determined that you were ready to wake up," she said.

"If life is a series of moments, and you have a year without any real moments, I guess you wouldn't have really lived that year. And then maybe you could live a whole lifetime in a day filled with moments like the ones I had today."

"Maybe you're just paying attention again, and seeing what you forgot how to see," she said.

"How am I going to fix my life, Susan?"

"With a pen and paper," she said.

"You make it sound so easy," I mumbled.

She sighed, letting go of my shoulder. "I'm going to go lie down on your couch. I always thought you and Beza were just being big whiney babies, but oh my god, this pregnancy thing is exhausting."

"That is why you got to do it this time around," Beza said as she reentered the room with Sarah's small suitcase.

When I walked over to the kitchen, all I heard was giggling. Aiden spoke along with the announcer of the gymnastic event, though he obviously didn't know the words. He said in a low voice, "That lady just did a flip-de-loo, and now she's going to do a wa-de-ka. Don't fall lady, the snakes!"

Sarah's shoulders shook with her laughter.

"He has a pretty good announcer voice," I said to Beza. "Maybe he has a future career in being a goofball." I tickled Aiden as I said it.

He giggled, trying to grab my hands. "Mom, Aunt Jamie just said balls!"

Susan started laughing from the other room.

"I did not," I said, still tickling him.

"Aiden," Beza said in a warning tone, though I heard suppressed laughter in her voice. "That's what it's been all this week." Beza shook her head. She turned to Sarah. "Hey cutie, you ready to go? You're going to have a sleep over with just me and Aiden tonight."

"I'm ready to go," Sarah said, jumping off her chair. She jumped up and down. "Bye mom!"

"Wow, I'm glad you're so excited," I said, breathing out a laugh. "Come give me a hug." When she did, I told her, "Now behave for your aunt Beza, okay?"

"Yes," she said. After walking the group to the door, I stole another hug from each of them.

"Unlock your car so I can grab your booster seat," Beza said.

"Oh, shoot, you want me to switch it?"

"No, I got it, Jamie," she said, giving me a kiss on the cheek.

I unlocked the car remotely and watched the group walk away.

When I reentered the living room, Susan laboriously moved her feet down and sat up. "Come over here and help me get my pregnant ass up," she said, holding a handout to me.

"Who knew you were going to be the biggest baby of all of us," I said as I helped her stand.

"Shut the fuck up," she said.

"What, are you trying to get your swearing out while Beza is not around?"

"Yes, she's on my case," she said.

"I'm surprised she's put up with you for as long as she has," I said.

"Me too, me too," she said, plopping her butt down on my kitchen chair.

"Will you make me something to eat? I'm starving," she said.

I rolled my eyes. "Yes, but I'm microwaving it."
I opened my freezer, "Enchiladas or lasagna?"

"Ooh, lasagna," she said. "And grab me a pen and a piece of paper, too. Oh, and a glass of milk."

"Holy shit, Susan, I thought you were here to help me," I said.

"I am, hence the paper. Move, woman, I'm not getting any less pregnant here," she said.

With a sigh, I warmed up the lasagna and brought her everything she wanted.

She clicked the back of the pen. "Okay so, you want to change your life," she said.

I sighed. "I guess."

Her bright blue eyes drilled into mine. "You do or you don't?" she snapped.

"I'm pretty sure I need to change things," I said, looking away.

"Oh, you need to change things. That's a definite. I'm just asking if you're willing to change things, if you've given yourself permission to change things yet. I don't want to spend all this time figuring out how to make you better, just to have you go back to punishing yourself."

"Why would I punish myself?" I asked, rocking back in my chair. "I didn't do anything wrong."

"I'm not saying you have a good reason, I'm just saying that you're doing it." She rubbed her hand over her belly and looked away from me. "When my mom died, it felt like the worst thing that could ever happen in my life, but it wasn't. It was Logan's death that truly destroyed me. I wake up thinking about him. I still cry myself to sleep. Sometimes I even still call him and leave a message on his answering machine, hoping like hell that you don't still check those messages."

"I don't," I whispered.

She wiped a tear from her cheek. "Losing Logan felt like more than I could bear." She turned her gaze on me. "But you know what? I can still have a healthy relationship with my wife. And you don't see me slowly destroying my body. And I definitely don't make monthly payments into some huge inflated lien on Logan's coffee shop. Because you know what, even when you pay that off, he'll still be gone. You're not immortalizing him; you're immortalizing the shit situation he left you in."

"There's nothing left," I said to her, tears again coursing down my face. "We don't have the house. I don't have a single thing of ours."

"You have Sarah," she said, eyebrows raised.

"You don't get it," I said.

"Oh, I get it," she said. "Do you need his permission to move on? Because, you know what? Logan and I shared a womb. Most people said we shared a personality too, and I can tell you, it's okay to move on. If I got myself killed in some screwed up way that left Beza and Aiden in a ton of debt, I would want her to sell my fucking bones if she had to, to get out of that debt."

I shook my head.

"I know he screwed up, I know he went off the deep end and you guys probably would have split no matter what, but even so, I know he loved you and

Sarah more than anything. All he would want now is for you two to be happy. He'd want you to move on."

Pressing my palms into my eyes, I whispered, "I have to sell the shop, don't I?"

I felt Susan's hand on my back, rubbing up and down. "Yes," she said. "And a lot more, I think you need a whole life detox."

"How do I do that?" I said, half laughing, half sobbing.

"We'll start small," she said. "First, we'll just write down the things to fix your health. Then we'll figure out the rest."

"I have to quit Cameron, don't I?" I whispered.

"Or be with him for real," Susan said.

"I can't do that," I said.

"You're in love with him. He's in love with you and your daughter; I can't fathom why you two can't be together." When I didn't respond, she made a huffing sound. "No... really, Jamie? You have to get over that."

I looked up from my hands. "I can't. Don't you think I've tried? Don't you think that I've thought these exact same thoughts a hundred times? I'm never going to get over it."

"Then yeah, you have to let him go," Jamie said, shaking her head and looking away.

"That's going to be hard," I said, swallowing.

"So, if say, you were with a guy and you were in love with him and loved his kid, and you spent all of your free time trying to be with both of them. Then you went and played mommy three times a week, watching his kid. But all this time, the guy knows there's no future for your relationship, but he refuses to pull the plug because it would be too hard to let you go."

"Sounds like an asshole," I said, blowing out a breath.

"Honey, you're an asshole."

I let my face fall into my hands. "You're right."

Susan put her pen to the paper. "My fourteen day soul detox," she said, while writing.

"You're giving me a deadline?"

She met my gaze and pursed her lips. "Yes. Alright, let's start with your body. You need to gain fifteen pounds."

"Fifteen pounds in fourteen days? That's impossible," I said.

"Women going back to the creation of the holiday season would beg to differ. You just need to... cut back on coffee. That will be up here at number one," she said while writing.

"Nope, vetoed," I said.

"You only get one veto, you really want to use it on coffee?" she asked.

"Do you know me at all?"

"Better than even you do, soul sister," she said. "Okay fine, I'll put a 'to be decided' by it. When's the last time you exercised?"

I smirked at her. "This morning."

"That," she pointed at me, "does not count. I'm talking like a run, or a Zumba class or something."

"I hate those dance classes, I can never learn the routines and I'm just stumbling into everyone."

"Yoga," she said as she wrote it. "You can come with me to my class."

"You don't go to yoga. How come I've never heard of this yoga class?" I said.

"Okay, so I've never actually gone there, but I was given the brochure a couple months ago, and I kept it because I thought sometime soon, I might actually go. We can try it together."

Susan and I spent the rest of the evening working on my detox list.

The Fourteen Day Soul Detox

In the next fourteen days, I plan to:

Body

1) Cut back on my coffee intake.
2) Gain some of my weight back.
3) Start getting some exercise again. Yoga?
Maybe.
4) Sleep.

Mind

5) Take on my daughter's school board.
6) Sell my coffee shop.
7) Go on a date.

Soul

8) Stop wearing my wedding ring.
9) Spread my husband's ashes.
10) Forgive the woman who killed him.
11) Stop sleeping with her ex-husband.

12) Remember what love feels like.

13) Be happy.

~~14)~~ (Vetoed and erased from the list.)

Day One

Dying a Slow Coffee-Deprived Death

Day One: Eight O'clock

I woke up staring at the USA 2012 Artistic Gymnastic Olympic team. The young women grinned from ear to ear, all holding medals—three of them held two. I blinked my heavy eyelids as I scanned the room. It was difficult untangling myself from the purple bed sheet, but when I finally managed, I sat up and pushed my feet into the shag carpet.

Trudging out of Sarah's room, I walked to the cupboard and grabbed a mug. The coffee maker beckoned me forward with its delicious promise of wakefulness, and I smiled. Grabbing up the carafe I poured it over my mug.

Nothing came out.

I glanced at the glowing buttons beneath on the coffee maker control panel, where the timer button was not lit up.

"Don't tell me you don't remember," Susan's voice said from behind me.

I looked over my shoulder to find her big pregnant belly sticking out of her tank top. She folded her arms over her chest.

"Oh, no," I said, my hand going to my forehead. "I changed my mind."

"Nope, I don't think so," she said. "Go get dressed; we're going to the health food store."

"I'm better, my soul is detoxed. Give me my coffee," I said.

"Nope," she said.

"You're just doing this to me because you're pregnant and can't have coffee; so you want me to suffer with you," I said. I collapsed forward onto the counter, laying my head on my arms.

"Yep, that's exactly why I'm doing this," she said. "I love watching you suffer. Now go get ready."

"Can't we start with a different thing? Like, I could go eat an entire cake or go on a run or take a nap."

"Nope, you have to at least start on one task per day, going down the list in order. You can do things early, but you can't skip anything. Otherwise, you'll give up when the hard part comes. You only get one day off, and you'll need it later," she said.

"This whole thing is ridiculous," I said. I filled my cup with water, and then crossed to my cupboard to retrieve my aspirin bottle.

"If you are good, you can have one cup of coffee before work tonight," she said.

After swallowing the pills, I asked, "Why the hell did I ask for your help?"

"Because you finally actually wanted help, and not a pat on the back," she said.

Laughing, I said, "You are so mean."

"Get dressed, I'll drive," she said.

"I can drive," I said.

"Um, no, I'm probably going to insist on pushing the grocery cart around, too," she said.

"Ugh," I said at her as I passed on my way to my bedroom. "You made my bed?" I asked as I entered my room.

"You're welcome," she said.

"I'd be thankful if I liked you," I grumbled.

Opening up my dresser, an empty drawer stared back at me. When I opened another drawer, I realized I was out of sweatpants too. "Crap, I'm out of clothes!" I made a 'ugh' sound and laid back down on my bed.

"You're not out of clothes," Susan said, crossing over to my closet, "This thing is stuffed."

"Have you talked to Beza yet?" I asked.

"Yeah, the kids are fine. After breakfast, she's going to take them to Reynolds's Beach Park, we can meet them there. Here, you can wear this."

Some material smacked me and I rolled over to find a white, eyelet maxi dress.

"Oh, I love that dress," I whispered.

"Wear it," she said.

"It's too big," I said.

"Wear a belt. Seriously Jamie, if you don't stop bitching and whining, I'm going to smack you."

"Ugh, go away," I said, but I grabbed the dress.

After slipping on the dress, I fished my leather cowboy boots from the very back of my closet. Crossing to my bathroom, I finished getting ready and walked out to the living room.

Susan grinned wide as I walked into the kitchen. "Wowee! Hot mama!" she called. "Is that makeup I see on your face? I wonder."

"You're one to talk, can you say midriff?"

"Your shirts don't fit me the way they used to," she said, pulling her tank top over her belly.

"That's my shirt? I didn't even recognize it," I said, turning my head to the side.

"My old shirt was nasty. Pregnancy makes me sweat. I'm sweating right now," she said.

"The shirt is yours, keep it," I said.

She smiled. "I think I'll try on some more shirts then. I always wanted a Warped Tour shirt... or maybe an Aerosmith on Tour—"

"I don't care if you're pregnant, touch it and die," I said, pointing at her.

She heaved a sigh. "Okay then, let's go get you some healthy shit."

"You're going to freeze." I pointed to her belly.

"Ha ha," Susan said as she pulled a big, knit sweater over her head. "The moment I put this sweater on I start sweating. I'm so over this. Can I be done?"

"You have two months to go, my friend," I said. As I was slipping my phone into my purse, it lit up with a text.

Cameron: I woke up wishing I was at your house with you. Think I'm going to cancel my afternoon so I can come earlier... if you're available.

I chewed on my lower lip, staring at the message.

"Cameron?" Susan asked.

I looked up at Susan. "I should cancel on him, shouldn't I? I mean, if I'm going to break it off with him, I shouldn't have him babysit."

She raised her hands. "Don't ask me, I'm on team Cameron. That is up to you."

"*Team Cameron?* What, are you twelve?" I said, staring back at my phone.

Me: I have to do a bunch of boring stuff, like laundry.

Cameron: I love boring stuff.

Me: Okay, when do you want to come over?

Cameron: How about one?

Me: Sounds good.

I looked up at Susan. "I suck at this."
"You have a couple days for that one, girl. We either need to leave your house or I need to take this sweater off," she said.
I opened my front door to the sight of my neighbor Clarke's tan, shirtless back as he stood in his front yard. Averting my gaze, I stepped out into the cool misty morning.
"Whoa, looks like you lost your shirt, friend," Susan said as she exited my house.
Gritting my teeth, I turned my attention to locking up my door.
"Oh, sorry," I heard Clarke say from behind me in a good-natured voice. "I just woke up and came out here to feed my dog."
"You're the new neighbor?" Susan said.
"Yeah, I've been here for about a month and a half. I'm Clarke."

I turned to see Clarke offer a hand over his fence.

Susan gave Clarke a close-lipped smile, "Susan. Sorry, I have a little cold so I'm not shaking hands today."

"No problem," Clarke said, pulling back his hand as Buster jumped up on the fence.

"Cute dog," Susan said.

"Thanks. Morning, Jamie," Clarke said as his gaze found me. He smiled as his gaze moved down my body.

"Good morning," I said, giving him a small wave and starting to walk toward the parking lot.

"You look really nice in a dress," Clarke called after me.

"Thanks," I said, waving at him again, though I didn't look over. "Later."

Susan caught up to me. "So, new neighbor, huh?" she said.

I glanced over my shoulder, but now only Buster sniffed around the ground in Clarke's small yard. "Uh, huh," I said as I clicked my keys to unlock my car remotely.

"Is it just me, or is that guy kind of weird?" she asked, also glancing back. After a few seconds when I didn't respond, she said, "I'm sorry; I shouldn't say stuff like that. You have to live next to him and I'm sure he's perfectly normal. He's good-looking... for a guy—" she nudged me. "Now, move over, I'm driving."

I walked to the passenger side of my car. "It isn't just you," I said, under my breath.

In the midst of opening her car door, Susan froze. "Did he do something?" she asked in a serious voice.

"No, Susan, chill out," I said, climbing into the passenger seat.

She sat down next to me, glaring. "What's going on?"

"Nothing! Don't fly off the handle. I'm just not a big fan of him, that's all," I said.

"I don't 'fly off the handle'," she said, scoffing and shaking her head.

"Oh no? How about when you and Logan beat the crap out of that guy for groping me?"

"I was like nineteen back then, and drunk," she said, rolling her eyes.

"You were charged with assault," I said.

"The charges were dropped," she shrugged, but when she looked back at me, her expression was serious. "You'd tell me if something was going on, right?"

I rolled my eyes. "Yes, of course I would. I just... I don't like him. He bangs on the wall every time Sarah makes a noise. Well, every time she makes a loud noise. But he doesn't smoke pot right next to Sarah's open window, so I guess he's an improvement from the last lady."

"You want me to talk to him?" she asked.

"No, let me handle this. I've got it, okay?"

"Fine," she said, starting up the car.

Pulling out my phone, I texted Beza.

Me: Everything okay?

A minute later, I got her reply:

Everything is wonderful. We are heading to the beach now.

"Is that Bee?" Susan asked.

"Yeah," I said.

"Ask her if she wants me to pick anything up for her at the health food store."

After relaying the message, I read the message I received back, "Carrots."

"Cool," Susan said, pulling into the parking lot.

Susan weaved around pedestrians, circling the parking lot four times before someone started pulling out of a space.

A red truck pulled up in the oncoming lane and turned on their blinker for our spot.

"No fucking way," Susan said as she rolled down the window. "Are you really going to steal the spot of a pregnant lady?" she yelled out her window.

"What?" A woman said, poking her head out of the truck.

"I'm pregnant! You are going straight to hell if you steal my parking spot," she yelled.

"That's a little intense," I said as the red truck drove off.

"It's the truth," Susan said, taking the vacated spot. After exiting the car, we had to wait for six cars to pass before crossing the parking lot and entering into the crowd gathering inside the health food store.

"So many healthy people," I said.

"Oh, yes, I forgot this is sample day," she said excitedly, looking at a woman offering what looked like potato pancakes. She joined the line waiting to get the sample.

"Oh, no," I said, pulling her out of line. "You're getting me that caffeine replacement thing you promised, and then we're going to go to the beach. I'm not spending my entire Saturday in line for free samples."

She turned a grumpy look on me. "Fine," she said, "Okay, we're heading to the smoothie line."

We went to stand behind five women in the line. Papier-mâché fruit hung above us on all sides like giant healthy Christmas ornaments.

"So, now that we are in public, I have a confession to make," Susan said.

I turned a glare on her.

"And remember, I'm pregnant. So if you attack me in here, everyone here will take my side."

"How many times are you going to play your pregnancy card?" I asked.

"Oh, sweetie, I'm going to be playing it until the moment I pop this little guy out," she said.

"What did you do? Out with it," I said.

"So... a couple of days ago Beza kind of set up a play date with Aiden and that kid of that dad you think is sexy."

"Why would I care about that?" I asked, shrugging.

"Because she set it up for today. I mean, for this morning. He's there at the beach with her. Beza had this big plan of introducing you to him this morning."

Susan shrugged. "Obviously, this was before it just happened naturally—"

"What?" I yelled at her.

Day One: Nine-fifteen

All the women in the line turned. Seeing who I was yelling at, the elderly women next in line to us glared at me.

Susan gestured to the glaring lady with a small nod of her head and chuckled.

"I'm going to kill her, for real this time," I said under my breath. "And you too."

She raised her hands in protest. "Don't kill the messenger," she said with a huge smile.

"I thought you were…" I did air quotes with my fingers, "Team Cameron."

"I am. But Beza isn't." She shrugged, with a 'what can I do?' gesture.

"Honestly, I'm just trying to figure out my life, do you really think I need all this… effing interference?"

"No, but like I said, Bee arranged this days ago. If it makes you feel any better, that guy doesn't know either," Susan said. "Well, he probably knows now as Sarah is there with them, but he didn't know when she arranged it."

"You are a pair of devious… witches," I said, glaring.

"Ooh, I like that. And, if it makes you feel any better, I promise we won't do it again," she said.

"You speak for your betrayer of a wife?" I said.

"No, but if I find out about any nefarious plot, I'll tell you this time," she said.

"Swear on your life," I said, crossing my arms over my chest.

She traced a big, 'X' with her finger on her chest.

"Hello?" A woman's voice called out, "Excuse me ladies, you're up."

We both turned to see a lady jumping up and down behind the smoothie counter. Her blonde, frizzy bob circled her smiling face like dandelion fluff.

"We'll take a Nutty Berry smoothie with protein powder, a wheat grass shot, and I want a Merry Berry smoothie with yogurt and honey," Susan said.

"Awesome." The woman gave us a receipt, and said, "You take this up to the counter to pay."

After grabbing some muffins and carrots, we paid for our drinks and groceries. Returning to the counter, I found a little shot glass of green next to our drinks.

Susan grabbed it and lifted it up to my face. "That's for you," she said, smiling.

"You serious? Is it gross?" I asked.

"No, it tastes good," she said, grinning wider and giving me an exaggerated wink.

"Meaning it tastes horrible, right?" I asked.

"Yep, tastes like ass. Drink it. Your date awaits," she said.

Rolling my eyes, I tipped the contents of the shot glass into my mouth. The taste that exploded into my mouth was as if I'd lain down on a freshly mowed lawn and scooped a big pile of lawn trimmings into my mouth.

I coughed. "Seriously Susan, if I'm going to taste something that bad, I at least want to get drunk from it."

She laughed, handing me my smoothie.

"Please don't tell me this one tastes like tanbark," I said, taking it from her.

"I'd say more like asphalt."

I paused with my mouth over the smoothie.

"Joking! That one is good," she said.

Opening up the lid, I sniffed it, inhaling a nutty raspberry combination scent. Running my fingers over the plastic lid, I took a small sip. "Almonds and raspberries?" I asked.

"Like I know. I just chose yours at random," she said as we avoided shopping carts on our way to the sliding glass doors. "Feel up to driving yet?" she asked.

"I feel like a slug, but I can drive," I said.

"I still think I should get points for telling you that this guy is going to be there at the beach," Susan said before taking a big sip of her drink.

"You've got to be kidding me," I mumbled as I opened the car.

"I'm going to get in trouble for it," she said while settling into the seat and using the lever to push it back.

"If you want points, go sneak Sarah out," I said.

She laughed, "No way, you chicken shit."

"Exactly, no points," I said while looking over my shoulder to check for pedestrians before backing up out of the parking space.

"Want a muffin?" Susan said with her mouth full.

Above us, large stretches of blue interrupted the dissipating fog layer. Birds flew between lamp poles, swooping in happy flight. The car keeping pace with us on the main road had surfboards on top and men without shirts inside.

"Looks like it's going to be a beautiful one," Susan said while taking off her sweater. "By the way, I'm eating another muffin."

"Traffic is not horrible, but it looks like people are going to be heading our way." I pointed to a bunch of college-aged kids in bathing suits, loading a cooler into their car. "I hope we can get parking."

"Oh my goodness gracious," she covered her mouth, "You are so excited to see this guy."

"Shut up." I smacked her leg. "Will you text Beza and make sure everything is okay?"

"Everything is okay," she groaned. "She would have called if there was a problem, mama hawk."

"Just do it," I said.

After a minute she said, "Sarah is fine, everyone is fine. Eat a muffin."

After she stuffed a muffin in my hand, I took a small bite. It tasted decent but it wasn't in the same universe as the muffin I ate yesterday.

In the parking lot, we slowly moved along as people imitated cars and walked in the middle of the road.

"There!" Susan shouted, pointing to a car backing up. "Yes, it's right in front!"

After shifting into park, I ran my hands over my face. "I am so nervous. I hate you for doing this to me," I said into my hands.

"Oh, get over it. If you humiliate yourself and he hates you, you'll only have to see him every day until Sarah graduates from high school."

"I fire you, you are officially fired," I said.

"Bitch, you can't fire me, I'm a self-employed best friend," she said while hobbling out of the car. Yet again, the bottom half of her belly fell out of her tank top.

"Sweetheart," I said crossing over to her. "Just roll your shirt up so it looks like you're wearing a bathing suit." I grabbed up the material, folding it up.

"My stomach will get burned. My belly hasn't seen the sun in months," she said, even though she raised her hands so I could help her.

"I have sunscreen in my purse," I said, pulling the blue glue-stick shaped container out.

"Of course you do, sometimes I swear you and Beza have twin souls," she said.

"I'd take that as a compliment any other day," I grumbled.

"Oh get over it. This is how Beza says she loves you," she said, rubbing sunscreen over her belly.

"I would have preferred a card," I said.

Kids ran all around the grassy park that led up to the rocky cove. A little girl in a yellow polka-dot dress tried to get a red and blue superhero kite into the air. She ran around, throwing it up repeatedly, while her mother and father sat on a blanket, cheering her on.

"Does that type of scene make you sad?" Susan asked, pulling my attention away from the family.

"What type of scene?" I asked as we walked down the sidewalk toward the beach.

"The happy family. You were staring," she said, nodding back to the family on the blanket.

"Logan and I weren't ever really like that family," I said, shrugging. "It would have been you, me and Beza watching our kids from the blanket anyway."

"I guess that's true," she said, her jaw clenching after she said it.

"He was a good dad," I said, looping my arm through hers.

The beach was painted in colorful blankets, with people moving in a chaos of movement. The cove was almost completely surrounded in man-made tubular rocks, the heavier waves passing the placid cove by. Babies bobbed on floaters next to their parents in the water, while the children ran in every direction.

Immediately, I spotted Sarah's iridescent purple one-piece. She was cart wheeling about while the beach-goers on nearby blankets turned to watch her. Beza sat a few feet from her, snacking on some grapes and cheering every time Sarah landed.

"There's Aiden playing with a girl and her dad," Susan said, pointing to the water. "Is that the guy?"

Looking to where she was pointing, I saw Patrick, kneeling down in only board shorts, building a sand castle with Kay and Aiden.

"Oh my goodness, you're blushing. It has to be him," she said. "And wow, the boy is ripped. What do you think, gym or hard labor?"

"Gym, he comes to the school every day in a suit," I said.

"That's... different. Okay so, suit or board shorts, what do you like better?" she nudged me.

"I can't decide," I said.

"He builds a mean castle too," Susan said before taking a sip of her smoothie.

"Does he? I wasn't looking at the castle," I said.

Right then, probably catching sight of two women staring at him, Patrick looked straight at us. His hand went over his brow to block the sun from his eyes, and then he waved with a huge grin growing across his face.

"Oh, look, he's so happy to see you," Susan said.

"Shut—"

A small body hurled into mine, making me take a step back.

"Mommy!" Sarah said while she got a death grip around my waist.

"Angel." I squeezed her to me. "I missed you, my love. Did you have fun with your aunt Beza?"

"Oh my goodness, she runs so fast!" Beza panted. "Hey baby," she said, giving Susan a kiss.

"How did you manage to get her to let you do braids in her hair?" I asked, touching the two French braids in her hair.

"Aiden told me that she wanted braids like his, but we settled for these. Does this mean you're not mad at me?" she asked as her head settled on Susan's shoulder.

"Oh, I'm plotting my revenge, you just wait," I said.

"I really like him." Her eyes glowed as she talked. "He's only thirty-four, divorced for three years, very smart, funny, and healthy. Aiden loves him. He has a steady source of income—"

"Beza! I don't need you to write him a dating profile for me, okay?" I whispered at her. Patrick was walking up the beach toward us with the kids jumping around him, vying for his attention. "What did you do? Give him a questionnaire?"

She pinched her lips together in an amused smirk. "You give me no credit."

"Oh, I'm giving you credit for a lot of things," I grumbled, before taking a long sip of my smoothie.

Sarah grabbed my cup from me and took a big sip. With a loud, "Pah!" she spit the smoothie out onto the sand.

Susan laughed really loudly, and then held out her smoothie. "Drink this one, baby."

"I thought you had a cold," I said.

"No, I just said that because I didn't want to touch your weird neighbor," Susan said.

Taking Susan's smoothie, Sarah took a big sip and kept drinking.

"Can I have some?" Aiden lisped out as he caught up to Sarah. "Hey, can I have some of that?" Then he turned to Susan. "Mom, Sarah's not sharing!"

"Tough," Susan said.

"No, we need to share, Sarah, you can have it for ten more seconds and then it's Aiden's turn. Then you can have it after Aiden," Beza said. After ten seconds, she held her hand out to Sarah.

"Sarah," I said in a warning tone when she didn't hand the smoothie over. "You listen to your aunt or you're not going to get anymore smoothie," I said.

Sarah finally gave it up as Patrick and Kay joined us.

"I'm Susan, Beza's wife," Susan said, holding her hand out to Patrick.

"Patrick. Nice to meet you," he said with a big, genuine smile on his face as he shook her hand. "And this is Kay." He put a hand on his daughter's back."

"Nice to meet you, Kay," Susan said.

"I don't have class with Aiden, but I play with him on the playground sometimes. I like boys; I don't think they're gross. We're friends."

Susan chuckled. "That's good to hear, Kay."

"Hey," Patrick said to me. His blue eyes practically twinkled in his tan face.

"Hi," I said, giving him a half grin.

"Hey kids, I have snacks on the blanket," Beza said smiling and herding the kids away from us.

"You look really nice," Patrick said when the group had walked away down the beach. A small smile played on his lips.

"Thanks. If I return the compliment, are you going to think I'm a perv?" I asked, glancing down at his perfect chest and smiling back.

His grin got wider. "Probably, but I don't mind."

I blew out a laugh, then looked away and bit my lip. "So, I'm sorry my friends are stalking you. I swear I had no idea Beza was going to do this."

He laughed, running his hands over his blond head. "I'd mind more if she wasn't trying to set me up with a gorgeous former pop star."

"Oh no!" I covered my face with my hands. "She did not tell you that!" I peeked out of my hands to find him grinning widely at me.

"So, you're famous?"

"No, not at all. It's really not what you'd think," I said.

"I'm very curious," he said.

"Okay fine, I'll tell you while we walk."

He chuckled.

"See, you're already laughing at me."

"Nah," he said, looking over.

Turning toward where our group sat on a big blanket, I exhaled an almost-laugh and started walking. "So, Susan and I grew up with this girl named Vanessa. The three of us were inseparable since we were in, like, first grade. Vanessa lived with her mom in Coral Beach, but her dad was a big time music producer in LA. Every summer, she went to stay with him and met all these pop stars and went to these fancy parties. So obviously, Vanessa was obsessed with the music industry and was always writing songs and making us perform them with her."

I glanced over at him, and shrugged. "So, for Vanessa's eighteenth birthday present, her dad offered her full use of the studio and their staff so she could record a single. And she said she wanted to share it with us."

I looked away, remembering. A hot feeling rimmed the underside of my eyes and I shook my head to rid myself of it. "Anyway, we did fantastic, the studio loved us. We'd been performing Vanessa's songs since we were ten, so we were just natural together. We recorded an album, did a short tour opening for another group, one of our songs got popular, and then we quit."

"Why did you quit?" he asked.

I laughed. "Beza actually."

He furrowed his brow. "How'd that work?"

"Well, on our tour, we opened for this boy band called 'Dream Big'."

"I've heard of them," he said.

"Listened to them, did you now?" I asked.

He shook his head. "Nah, of course not," he said with a big 'I might be lying' grin on his face. "Okay, so Kay likes them."

"Well, yeah, they were famous even back then and we had one hit song. We basically played that song over and over and over again."

"And Beza?"

"Was the girlfriend of the lead singer in Dream Big, she was an international supermodel then, pretty famous."

"Oh, I see where this is going," he said.

"Yeah, Beza and her boyfriend was this media darling couple, and when she fell head over heels in love with Susan, the press went crazy. Actually, Beza's boyfriend was a pretty great guy. I think they were more friends than really romantic; he basically just told her that he was glad she was happy. But the newspapers and tabloids made Susan out to be this lesbian home-wrecker. And at that time, homophobia was a lot more mainstream, you know? Susan was getting a lot of grief—random people calling her names and spitting on her. Some people sent the studio hate mail for her. One of the letters was so messed up the studio had to call the cops. Vanessa, Beza and I sat down one day and decided it wasn't worth it. So, we all came home to Coral Beach and Beza broke her contract and quit modeling completely."

"Do you regret it?" he asked, bumping me with his arm.

"Quitting? No." I shook my head. "I do regret that we stopped singing though."

"You know, now that I think about it, I faintly remember that scandal," he said.

"I'm not surprised. The tabloids kept it going for a long time. They only really left Beza and Susan alone when they threatened to sue three different magazines for libel and defamation of character."

When we reached the blankets, I looked over to where Beza sat with Susan leaning against her.

"Don't think that hiding under that pregnant woman is going to keep you safe, Beza!" I yelled at her.

"*Don't you want to love me, baby? When the sun goes down,*" she sang at me then ducked behind Susan when I threw a handful of sand at her.

"Hey," Susan said as she got smacked with the sand. She pointed at Aiden, who was now holding a ball of sand in his hand too. "Don't you dare follow your aunt's bad example."

He chucked the ball of sand at her, and then giggled furiously as he ran to the other side of the blanket while Susan tried to get to her feet. She lumbered after him as he ran in a circle around the blanket.

Susan ran straight over our little picnic at Aiden, which seemed to surprise him. He squealed with laughter and it took him a second to run away. She managed to get in front of him and stopped him by tickling him, sending Aiden into a fresh bout of giggles.

Sarah popped another grape in her mouth, stood up and walked up the beach to the large vacated area behind our blanket.

"Where's she going?" Kay asked.

"I think she's going to do a routine," I said. To Sarah, I yelled, "Angel, is there food in your mouth?"

"No," she said, striking a pose with her hands held up to one side. She moved through the choreography in graceful, exact movements. She did several tumbles before ending with a front tuck, her purple iridescent bathing suit painting a line of color across the beach. Turning around, Sarah lifted her arms and moved them through the choreographed poses.

"Wow," Patrick said, looking at me with wide eyes.

"Yeah, she's really good," I said, not taking my eyes off her.

"Is she just making that all up as she goes?" he asked.

"Uh, no, I'm pretty sure that one was a floor exercise from the qualifying rounds at the last Olympics. She just exchanges the really hard moves for ones she can do," I said as Sarah did three aerials in a row and another flip.

She did two more passes before ending her routine with a pose.

Aiden ran forward. "And the score from our judges is, sixteen-million! Sarah Scott wins the gold medal!"

Sarah's smile couldn't have been bigger as Aiden grabbed up her hand and held it up like she just won a boxing match.

I turned back to say something to Patrick, but he was gone. Glancing around, I found him walking toward a guy who was standing, facing us, but looking at his phone.

"Hey, that's not cool," I heard Patrick say to the guy.

"Huh, what?" the guy said looking up, he was shirtless and looked probably college-aged.

"Either delete that, or hand it over so I can delete it." Patrick held out a hand toward the guy.

"Sorry, man, I'll delete it," the guy said, fiddling with his phone.

"You better. I'm a lawyer, and you don't film kids and put them on the internet without their parent's permission," he said.

"I just thought it was cool. It's deleted, okay?" he said, turning away.

"What a dick," Susan said, glaring at the phone guy who was now walking down the beach.

"Susan!" Beza said.

"Oh, sorry," she said, still glowering at the guy. "Thanks for doing that, Patrick. I didn't even notice that guy."

"Yeah, thank you," I said as Patrick plopped down beside me. When his gaze met mine, I gave him a grateful smile.

He sighed, wiping his hand over his face. "No problem. I hate to see that type of thing."

Susan shook her head. "It..." she glanced at Beza, "*Freaking* pisses me off. Filming a kid when their family isn't looking, what the hell is wrong with people?"

Sarah came over to me, practically falling into my lap.

"You're amazing," I whispered to her, before kissing her forehead.

"I'm going to go swim in the ocean," she said, smiling up at me.

"We're going to go soon, angel. But maybe we can go swimming at our pool while I do laundry."

"Yes! Pool!" Sarah yelled.

"You can come swim in our pool," Kay said as she took a seat directly beside me. She looked up with a huge smile on her face.

"Oh, thank you, sweetheart," I said. "Sarah and I will probably go to our pool though, because it's right next to the building where we do our laundry and we need to wash our clothes.”

“You can do your laundry at our house,” Kay said, scooting even closer.

I laughed. “Not this time, sweetheart.” Looking back down to Kay, I touched her hair. “You kept your ponytail up,” I said, noticing her hair was the same as when I pulled it up yesterday after school, though now strands stuck out in every direction.

Kay touched it gently.

“She wouldn’t let me take it out.” Patrick grimaced.

“Oh.” I bit my lip, looking closer and noticing that her hair was tangled around Sarah’s hair band. “Kay, do you want me to fix your hair? Or maybe do a braid?”

Her big blue eyes widened at me. “Would you? Can you do a braid? Because I don’t know how to. I’ve tried on my dolls but I’m not any good at it.”

“Well, Beza is the best, but I know how to do it,” I said.

She nodded emphatically. “I really, really want one.”

“Well, I’d be happy to do one for you. Can you turn around to face your dad?” To Sarah I whispered, “Off my lap for a second, honey.”

After Sarah climbed off and went to sit with the rest of the group, I turned to Kay.

Her little body shook, shoulders bobbing up and down. “I’m so excited! I’ve always wanted a braid!”

Patrick exhaled heavily, before giving me a nod. "Do you mind if I watch? I should probably learn how to do this."

"Of course not, I'll try to explain how to do it too," I said as I slowly, gently, worked the hair band out from where it was caught in Kay's hair.

"Do you want a comb?" Beza asked as she pulled a wide-toothed comb from her bag.

"Thanks," I said grabbing the comb from her hands.

"Do you need a comb?" Patrick asked as he knelt beside me with all his concentration on his daughter's hair.

"No, but it makes it easier." I combed out her long, dirty-blonde hair, working out the knots. I leaned forward, asking Kay, "One braid, or two?"

"One, please," she said.

In a low voice, I said to Patrick, "So, first you divide the top part of her hair into three sections, like this, near her forehead. Then you start weaving the sections in and out of each other, like this. Using the comb, or you can just use your fingers, pull more sections in, adding them to the original three, and keep weaving them. When you run out of hair, just put in the hair band, and done" I said. When I'd finished the braid, I turned to Patrick.

His eyes were glued to his daughter's hair, like if he just concentrated hard enough, all the secrets of life would be revealed.

He nodded. "Yeah, I think I got it," he said. He turned his blue eyes on me. "Thank you for teaching me."

"Anytime," I said. "So, you're a lawyer?"

He gave me an almost sheepish grin. "Tax law. It just doesn't intimidate people all that much when I say it."

"Ha!" Susan said. "Sorry, I was eavesdropping, but that was just too funny."

Day One: Eleven O'clock

Patrick grinned. "I like your friends," he said in a low mock-whisper to me.

"That's because you don't know them that well," I said, grinning to myself and digging my feet into the warm sand. "They're really pretty awful."

"Stop talking trash," Susan said. "That... b-word would die for us. She loves us so much it's sickening. Don't listen to a word she says."

I rolled my eyes. "If you say so." Then to Patrick I mouthed, "Nah."

He chuckled.

"Well," I said, clapping my hands on my legs. "It's probably time for Sarah and me to head home."

"Can I go with Aunt Jamie?" Aiden asked as he looked between his mothers. "Please!"

"It's fine with me, if it's okay with you," I said.

"Are you sure?" Beza asked.

"Yeah, of course. Have some time just for the two of you. I can drop him off on my way to work at about five-thirty. I think I have some clothes of his too from a little while back, so he can wear that after the pool."

"Thanks, babe. That sounds really nice," Susan said.

Beza pointed at Aiden. "You better behave for your Aunt Jamie."

"I will!" he said excitedly, jumping up and down on his knees.

Sarah started jumping too, making loud excited sounds.

"Can I go, dad?" Kay asked.

"Oh, I'm sorry," I said, giving Patrick an apologetic look. "You're welcome to come too."

Susan gave me a wide-eyed look like, 'are you serious?'

I held my breath, gritting my teeth together, waiting for Patrick to answer.

"Thanks, but it doesn't work for us today. We have to go meet my brother," Patrick said.

Turning away, I let out the breath I was holding.

To his daughter, Patrick added, "We have to meet him and Aunt Carrie very soon," while running a hand over her hair.

"Dad, no, don't mess up my braid!" she said, pushing his hand away.

"Oh, sorry, sorry, Kay-bay. We probably should be off too." Patrick grabbed what looked like a cloth grocery bag and pulled out a shirt. Unfortunately, he then put the shirt on before he started gathering sand toys. He looked over at me. "Can we walk you to the car?"

"Sure," I said as I stood, brushing sand off my lap.

After saying our goodbyes to Susan and Beza, the kids ran ahead while Patrick and I followed them up the beach. The sun was in full-blown roasting mode now. All down the beach, families ducked under sun tents or gathered around barbeques while college-aged kids carried coolers down.

"I wonder where all these college students came from," I mused.

"Probably down from the UC, that's what we used to do," he said.

"That's where you went?"

"For undergrad," he said.

"We used to come to Coral Beach looking for a less crowded spot." Patrick said, looking around.

"Well, those kids didn't find one, this place is getting crazy."

"Where did you go?" he asked.

"To college?"

"Yeah," he said.

"I didn't." I shrugged.

He looked over at me, his brow furrowing, then he quickly looked away. "Oh," he said.

I glanced over at him when he said nothing more. After another couple seconds of silence, I looked back at the kids, who were now waiting for us on the grass near the parking lot. Aiden and Kay talked animatedly about something, heads close together, while Sarah cart wheeled around on the grass.

"Not even a junior college?" Patrick asked, though when I glanced over, he was still not looking at me.

"Nope, nada," I said.

"Oh." After another couple seconds of silence, he asked, "Why didn't you go to college?"

In a completely serious voice, I told him, "My career as a prostitute during the day and a stripper at night just didn't leave me the time."

Patrick glanced sharply at me and I burst into laughter. "I'm sorry," I said, and ran ahead to where the kids were standing now all giggling. Putting one arm around Aiden and the other around Sarah, I told Kay, "It was great to see you again, sweetheart."

"Will you do my hair in a braid, again, next time I see you? Next time can I have two like Sarah's?" she asked.

"Maybe sweetheart, but definitely give your dad a chance to try to braid your hair, yeah? He watched me do it, so he'll probably do as good a braid as I did. It might take a couple practices though, so be patient with him," I said.

"I will!" she said, grinning up at me.

I turned to Patrick, giving him what I hoped looked like a friendly smile. "It was nice seeing you. You guys have a great rest of your weekend."

He took a step toward me. "Yeah, it was really nice to see you too. And—" he paused, running a hand over his head, "I—I hope we see you again... soon."

"Thanks," I said, smiling and stepping back with the kids. "Yeah, I'm sure we will. Later." Taking both Aiden and Sarah's hands, I walked toward my car.

"Jamie!"

Turning around, I found Beza running up after us. Patrick too, was just standing where we left him, staring after us. When I made eye contact with him, he waved. Putting an arm around Kay, he walked with her toward the parking lot.

"The kid's boosters are still in my car!" Beza called when she got close. She jogged up, not out of breath at all when she reached us. "I'm parked over here," she said, gesturing a little further into the lot.

After we transferred the booster seats and got the kids buckled inside, Beza gave me an amused twist of her lips. "So what do you think?" she asked.

"He's nice," I said, giving her a quick smile.

Her expression fell into a frown. "Oh, you don't like him. I thought it was going so well."

"It was, but it took a sudden turn for the worse on the walk to the car. I think he was just a very nice fantasy guy, you know?"

"And I ruined it for you, I'm sorry." She exhaled heavily, her shoulders dropping. "I shouldn't have pushed you into this."

I laughed and shook my head. "Yeah, you shouldn't have. But, I'll forgive you... if you promise to never, ever do it again."

"Fine," she said, giving me a lemon-scented hug. "Alright, I'll see you at five-thirty at the house?"

"We'll be there," I said as I stepped away.

When I sat back in the car, I rubbed my face and shook my head.

"What are you doing?" Aiden said from the back seat.

"Your Aunt *needs* coffee, bad," I told him.

"Then go get some," he said.

"That is a fantastic idea, buddy," I said. Driving five blocks out of the way, I pulled into the parking lot of the drive-thru coffee shop. Pulling up to the speaker, I rolled down my window.

"Welcome to Harrington's, can I take your order?"

"Do you kids want anything?" I asked into the back seat.

"Chocolate milkshakes!" Aiden said.

"Two juice boxes," I said to the speaker. To the back seat I said, "Anything to eat?"

"Doughnuts!" Sarah yelled, and then the pair giggled.

"Goodness, I have a pair of comedians in the backseat." I shook my head, making them giggle more. Back to the speaker, I said, "Okay, what type of sandwiches do you have?"

He listed off a list of pre-made lunch foods, of which I ordered three turkey sandwiches. I inhaled deeply, and then blew out the breath. "And a coffee," I said in a rush.

"Just regular coffee?"

"No! No coffee! Sorry," I said, my head falling into my hands. "Do you have tea?"

"We have bagged tea or tea lattes," he responded.

"Give me whichever one has the most caffeine, please. Chai latte, probably. And that's all," I told him.

"You got it. Your total comes out to twelve-eighteen at the window. Please pull forward," he said.

After paying for our food and drinks, I handed sandwiches and juice boxes back to the kids and drove forward. At the first stop light, I lifted the Chai out of its cup holder.

"Are you making me a cheater?" I whispered to the Chai.

It said nothing back.

"If you're going to be like that, I'm just going to drink you," I told it.

The light turned green and I set the Chai back in its holder while I drove. It stared at me all the way home.

Finally as I pulled into my parking spot, I couldn't stand it anymore. I took out my phone and sent Susan a text.

Me: Is Chai cheating?

Susan: Just this once, no.

Me: Oh, you're so magnanimous.

Susan: You know it.

I practically inhaled the Chai, finishing the whole thing in almost one big gulp. "Did you finish your sandwiches?" I asked when I was done drinking as I looked into the rearview mirror.

"Yes," Aiden said.

"Okay, make sure to grab your trash," I said.

"Let's go to the pool!" Aiden yelled as he opened his car door.

"You need to let your stomach settle. Also, I have to change into my bathing suit and grab the laundry first, sweetheart," I told him as we all walked toward the duplex. As we approached my front door, I quickly scanned Clarke's yard. Buster was the sole occupant, sleeping in his open crate.

"Shh," I whispered to the kids. "Buster is sleeping." We tiptoed up to the house, though the kids giggled under their breath. Putting the key in the lock, I opened the door slowly and quietly.

I gestured to the kids to come inside, and closed the door behind them, making sure to lock it.

"Here, I'm going to put a movie on for you two," I said.

"Gymnastic floor exercises!" Sarah shouted.

"No, something Aiden wants to watch too this time," I said.

"I don't mind," Aiden said, shrugging.

"Sweetheart, you don't always need to go along with what Sarah wants. What about cartoons or something?"

"No really, Aunt Jamie, I don't mind," he said, grinning his gapped-tooth smile at me.

"You're such a sweet kid," I told him, as I walked over to my computer and set up the video for them.

They squeezed into one chair, barely fitting, and sat watching floor exercises from the last Nationals.

"Don't you want your own chairs?" I asked them.

"No," Aiden said.

"Alright," I said, taking the other chair and unwrapping my turkey sandwich. I took a bite and my mouth filled with a heavy mustard taste. There was a good amount of cheese and turkey, as well as some lettuce and tomato, but the mustard drowned out the other flavors.

"You guys liked this?" I asked the kids as I held up the sandwich.

Aiden glanced up from the computer screen. "Yes."

"Wow, this is a pretty sophisticated taste," I told him.

"Well, we're somistifacated," he said as his focus returned to the computer.

"You sure are," I said with a grin before taking another bite.

Day One: Twelve-thirty

My phone buzzed in my purse and I pulled it out.

Cameron: I'm about to leave my house, do you guys need me to pick anything up on the way?

Me: No, but bring your swim suit, I promised Sarah and Aiden I'd take them swimming. I'm watching Aiden.

Cameron: Will do. See you in thirty.

"Hey Sarah, you want to do the quarters?" I asked after my last bite of sandwich.

"Yes," she whispered, her gaze still glued to the screen.

"She says yes!" Aiden called to me. "I'll help too, I remember how."

"Okay, cuties," I said as I went to get my spare-change jar from the closet. Setting the jar in front of them, I let them have at pulling the quarters from the mass of change.

Aiden plunged his hands in and called out, "Money! Can I have some?"

"Aiden sweetie, if there's any quarters left over after we do the wash, you can have them. Remember to wash your hands when you're done, you guys," I said.

My laundry pile had been threatening to overflow its basket for a while now, but as I entered my bedroom, I realized that it must have succeeded this morning without my knowledge. I usually sorted the lights from darks, but today I just opened my laundry sacks and started shoveling the contents of my laundry in.

Less than ten minutes later, I had two huge sacks of laundry and an empty basket. Thankfully, my bathing suit and throw-over were clean, so I quickly dressed in that before dragging my laundry out of my room.

"How's the money counting going?" I asked my team.

"Look," Aiden said, pointing to a big pile of quarters.

"Wow, you guys are fast!" I emptied the money into a sandwich bag then put that bag with my laundry soap.

"Can I have some money? Like you said?" Aiden asked.

"Only if there's some left over," I reminded him.

"Is Sarah getting half of the money or is it all for me?" he asked.

"Why don't you ask her if she cares," I said.

"Sarah, can I have all the money?" Aiden asked.

When Sarah didn't answer Aiden, I closed the laptop, which made her look up at me.

"Aiden asked you if you want to share the quarters with him," I said to her.

"I want to watch the floor exercises," Sarah said as she grabbed my hand and tried to pull it away from the computer.

I sighed. "I think it's fine, Aiden." Picking up the computer, I told Sarah, "Baby, we're about to go to the pool. Make sure you go potty first." After Sarah ran off to the bathroom, I turned to Aiden. "Make sure you do too after Sarah, buddy. Also, rub on some sunscreen. Please give it to Sarah when you're done." I handed him the bottle.

Looking into the closet, I realized I still didn't have any towels. We would have to swim until the towels went through their wash and dry cycle. Grabbing the other pool toys, I folded up the single towel in the bathroom just as I heard a knock on the door.

As I reentered the living room, I saw Sarah answering the door. Cameron stood in the doorway behind her with a big smile on his face. "Hello, sport," he said.

"Sarah! Always wait for mom to answer the door! That's dangerous!" I yelled.

Sarah threw herself at Cameron, giving him a big, wide-armed hug.

"Your mom is right, Sarah, you never open the door. I could have been anyone." He patted her head.

I walked over, crouching down in front of Sarah. I pulled her away from Cameron so she had to face me. "Sarah, never, ever answer the door. That's dangerous," I said again.

Sarah let out a bout of nervous laughter and hit me smack dab on my nose.

"Ouch!" I said, grabbing my face.

Sarah ran away from me. "Go in time out!" she screamed as she ran into her room and slammed the door after her.

"You okay?" Cameron asked as he helped me up.

"I'm fine. That's a nice scene to walk in to. I'm sorry," I grumbled.

He examined my face. "Let's get you some ice."

"Are you okay, Aunt Jamie?" Aiden asked.

"I'm fine, cutie," I said, patting his head as I walked by toward the kitchen.

Cameron pulled my blue ice pack out of the fridge, and opened the right drawer to find the clean kitchen towels. He gently pressed the covered ice-pack to my nose. Even with the towel, it was shockingly cold.

"You know your way around my kitchen," I said.

He gave me a warm grin, his free hand going to the back of my neck. "I haven't seen you in a dress in over a year," he said.

"Laundry day," I said.

"If only every day could be laundry day," he whispered before grinning at me.

"You bring your trunks?"

"I'm wearing them," he said. "I brought some towels too."

"Oh good." Pulling my face away, I looked down to find he was indeed only wearing his board shorts and a T-shirt. "We should probably get the kids out there. Do you mind taking them into the pool while I start my laundry?"

"Yeah, of course, but let me carry the bags to the laundry room," he said.

"Sarah, you can come out of time out!" I called.

The door opened and Sarah walked out slowly. After about thirty seconds of her just standing there, looking at her toes, I asked, "What do you say?"

"I'm sorry," she whispered.

"Okay, angel, let's go to the pool," I said, giving her a hug.

Cameron helped me carry all my bags to the laundry room and waited while I unlocked the door. I handed him my keys, showing him which one was the pool key, then he and the kids headed off to the complex's pool.

As I propped the door open with a rock, I took a deep inhale of the dry laundry scent, smiling a little to myself. Flipping up the light switch, the florescent lights flickered on. I dragged my bags inside and glanced down the line of washers.

"Crap," I mumbled, seeing that all of them had a zero on their time monitoring screen. When I checked down the line, I found all four washers full. "Ugh," I called in exasperation and walked toward the exit.

When I was about three feet away, Clarke stepped into the doorway. His light brown hair fell loose over his chiseled, angular face. He was looking down at his phone as he walked, but his face came up and his dark deep-set eyes immediately found mine. A big grin spread across his mouth as his gaze slowly moved down my nearly-transparent bathing suit cover.

"Excuse me," I said, as I pulled a bag up in front of my chest and tried to step around him.

He stepped into my path. When I tried to go the other way, he stepped into my path again.

"Clarke, let me pass," I said in an annoyed voice.

"Hey, I'm about to move my stuff, you can have the washers," he said, standing so close that the bag I held up between us brushed his chest.

I forced myself to shrug. "Oh, that's okay, I'm in no rush. I'll just come back later."

"It's just going to take a minute. If you're in no rush, why can't you wait one minute? If it's too cramped in here, just wait outside. Here, do you want some help with that? It looks heavy." He tried to take my laundry bag, but I pulled it back.

"I've got it," I said, pulling it to my chest. "No problem, I'll just wait outside."

When he stepped out of my way, I walked past him, hugging the wall as much as possible. Outside of the laundry room, I moved the rock that I had used to keep the door open, and I used my hand to close the door slowly. Right before it was completely closed, I called out, "I'm going to do my laundry tomorrow. See you later."

Grabbing up my laundry bags, I walked around the building to where the large black gate surrounded the pool.

I stuck my face through the gate, looking to where Aiden and Sarah were both pretty-much attacking Cameron in the pool.

"Hey Cameron!" I yelled.

He looked up and seeing me, he waved.

"Can I get my keys? I need to go to the other laundry room, that one was full," I called.

He walked out of the pool with the kids still attached to him like barnacles.

"Hey, Aunt Jamie," Aiden said, when the three headed monster walked up to the bars.

I smiled as Cameron winked, handed me the keys and headed back to the pool, kids still clinging to him.

My laundry grew very heavy as I carried it to the next laundry room over, which was behind the building's main office. I quickly divided the clothes into three loads and started them going. Setting my phone timer for the right amount of minutes, I stowed it in my bag. As I exited the laundry room, I held my hand up against the glare of the sun. When my vision cleared, I saw Clarke standing feet away and looking straight at me.

I inhaled sharply, rocking back on my heel.

Clarke looked to the building behind me, then again into my eyes, raising an eyebrow at me.

Giving a half hearted wave and a forced smile; I turned and walked toward the pool. When I looked back over my shoulder, Clarke's broad-muscled back seemed to strain against his shirt as he walked in the opposite direction toward where our apartments were.

Immediately, I picked up my pace, jogging until I reached the gate leading to the pool area. I let myself in with the keys, and then leaned back against the gate. My hand pressed into my chest, feeling the rapid beat of my heart.

When my breathing and heartbeat settled into a more steady rhythm, I walked into the pool area. Both Sarah and Aiden splashed at Cameron as if their lives depended on it, and Cameron gave as good as he got. They were all smiling and laughing loudly. They were all so concentrated on each other; none of them noticed my approach.

Dropping my stuff off at a chair and pulling off my swimsuit cover, I walked to the deep end of the pool. Diving shallowly, I submerged in the cool pool water and stayed under. I swam under the water, opening my eyes and aiming for the group across the pool. The chlorine stung my eyes so I closed them until I thought I was likely close to the group. I popped out of the water right beside Cameron. They all stopped splashing for a moment, looking at me in surprise. Then I did a wide sweeping splash at both of the kids.

"War!" Aiden yelled, before splashing full force at me and Cameron.

Cameron grabbed me, pulling my body in front of his like a human shield.

"This is how you treat your reinforcement?" I yelled at him as I was splashed nonstop.

"All is fair in love and war, baby," he called back, his head hiding behind my back.

"Ha—" I gurgled as a large amount of water went into my mouth. "Okay!" I shouted after probably ten more minutes of the nonstop splashing. "We surrender!"

"No, I already tried that, it's worse," Cameron said into my ear, chuckling.

That's when Aiden and Sarah swum up and started tickling me mercilessly.

"Escape!" I said, diving under the water. A strong hand grabbed my ankle and reeled me back in.

"Oh, no you don't," Cameron said as he wrapped me in his arms. "You're not going to escape that easily."

"Whose side are you on?" I said, trying to squirm out of his arms.

"He's on our side!" Aiden yelled.

Sarah made a loud excited sound and jumped on us, laughing.

A loud beeping sound came from the side of the pool.

"What's that?" Cameron asked.

"My alarm! I set an alarm for when the washer would be done!" I laughed and finally squirmed away from the group. I swam over to the side and pulled myself out of the pool. Pulling out one of the towels Cameron brought, I dried off my hands and turned off the alarm. Looking over at the gate, I chewed on my lip.

A hollow feeling grew in my stomach. Turning toward the group in the pool, I called, "Hey Cameron."

He smiled over while swimming breaststroke to the side of the pool. "Yeah, babe?" he asked, when he was right in front of me.

I crouched down and said in a low voice, "Would you mind going to transfer the laundry for me?"

"Of course not, everything okay?"

I exhaled heavily. "Sort of. One of my neighbors was in there when I went to put my wash in and they kind of creep me out."

"Is someone bothering you?" he asked, and even though his expression remained calm, there was an edge of anger in his tone.

"It's probably all in my head. I'm just not a fan of... that person," I said.

Cameron did a push up out of the pool, water cascading off his body as he climbed out. Grabbing a towel, he dried his hair and body before looking up at me. He gave me a seemingly casual smile. "So, who is it?"

I rolled my eyes. "I'm not telling you."

He stepped in closer to me. "Why not?"

"Because you'll try to handle it for me, and then I'll either have to live near a neighbor who has a huge vendetta against me, or I'll be kicked out of my apartment."

"Would that really be so bad?" he asked.

I glared at him. "You have to be kidding me."

"I have a three bedroom house and a beautiful five acre piece of property," he said.

Turning away from him, I said, "Yes you do, it's beautiful. Alright, I'm going to go swim with the kids. Thank you for transferring my laundry. Please don't intimidate any of my neighbors."

He said nothing as I walked away. An invisible fist clenched its fingers around my stomach and lungs, replacing the hollow feeling and making it hard to breathe.

Day One: Two O'clock

I sat on the edge of the pool, my feet splashing in the water.

"Aunt Jamie, we're going to race and you judge," Aiden said as he and Sarah lined up on the other side of the pool.

I cupped my hands like a megaphone. "Ready! Set! Go!"

They swam toward me. Aiden was a tornado of movement and splashing, water flying from him in all directions. Sarah, instead, pushed off the wall, and then crossed the pool in a fast and precise breaststroke."

Sarah touched the side of the pool. "I won!" she yelled.

A second later, Aiden caught up and grabbed onto the side of the pool. "Aww." He hung his head. "She always wins."

"I won!" Sarah yelled again, smiling.

"Oh," Aiden said, frowning and folding his arms on the edge of the pool.

"Aiden, we should race again," Sarah said.

"I don't want to," Aiden grumbled.

I ran my fingers over Aiden's braided hair. "Sweetheart, Sarah practices gymnastics constantly and we go swimming here at least once a week. You just don't have as much experience. If you keep practicing, you'll be as good as her one day."

"No, I won't," he grumbled.

"I'm thinking it's time for a snack break," I said to the pair.

Sarah swam to the stairs and climbed out. She went straight to my bag, sopping wet.

"Angel, towel off first, my phone is in there," I called. After seeing that she did, I turned back to Aiden. "Come on out, sweetheart. Get a snack."

"I'm not hungry," he said, his fingers tracing the lines in the cement.

"Well, you still need to get out. I want you two to get out of the sun and put on a little more sunscreen. You can just watch us eat if you're still not hungry."

"Fine," he said with a heavy, almost adult-sounding, sigh.

Cameron walked back in the gate just as the two kids sat down with snacks all wrapped up in Cameron's towels.

"Are we getting out?" Cameron asked.

"We're taking a break," I said, smiling at him.

Cameron stepped up close to me. "So this guy that's been bothering you, does he live in your building?"

"I never said it was a guy," I said.

"It's a woman?" he asked.

"It's an I'm-not-going-to-tell-you," I said.

He leaned in and whispered into my ear, "I have ways of making you talk."

Giving him a small smile, I said, "I'll never tell."

"We'll see," he said, before walking backwards with a smug grin, then turning to take a seat with the kids.

I set an alarm for when the dryer should be done, then ate a banana and some chips with the kids.

After loading up on calories and rehydrating, we all reapplied sunscreen and waited a few minutes before jumping back in the pool.

Cameron and I took a seat at the edge of the pool while Aiden and Sarah again took to splashing each other between attacks of giggles.

"I'm actually considering moving out of here. Though I was thinking more along the lines of buying a house," I said.

"You have the money for that?" he asked, his brow furrowing.

I closed my eyes, blowing out of my nose. "I'm going to sell the coffee shop." A hot tear leaked out of my eye as I said it.

Cameron's arm wrapped around me and he pulled me into his body. He said nothing, just held me securely.

"I talked to both Chris and Susan about it, at length, and they convinced me it was time. I think I need to find a property lawyer because even though I already have an offer, the shop has a judgment lien on it and I'm pretty sure that complicates things."

"I know a guy, a customer and friend. He could help you out," Cameron said.

"Thanks, I'd rather go with someone you trust. I don't want to get screwed," I said.

He whispered in my ear, "Don't you?"

"Ha!" I leaned back and shoved him into the pool.

With a surprised look on his face, Cameron toppled right into the pool. He came out, shaking the water out of his hair. His gaze met mine. "Oh, you're in trouble now," he said, amused.

I jumped to my feet and dodged away just as Cameron grabbed for me. I ran away from the pool, laughing hysterically.

"Hey, don't run by the pool, mom!" Sarah yelled.

"Sorry! Sorry," I said and walked very fast away from where Cameron was climbing out of the pool, still grinning.

"Hey Sarah, is jogging okay?" Cameron called.

"Yes!" Sarah and Aiden called.

Cameron jogged toward me.

When I started jogging away, Aiden yelled, "Aunt Jamie is running!"

I pointed at Aiden as I jogged away. "I am not, I'm jogging—" I screamed as I was scooped into Cameron's arms.

"Hey baby," he whispered, before throwing me into the pool.

"No!" I screamed all the way down until I hit the water. I surfaced glaring up at Cameron who was casually standing there, grinning down at me. Pointing my finger up at him, I said, "Just you wait."

"Do your worst, baby," he said not sounding the least bit afraid. When my phone alarm went off he said, "Looks like your time for revenge just ran out. I'll carry the stuff over to your apartment."

"Thank you, Cameron. We'll meet you there in a couple minutes?"

"Sounds good to me," he said, giving me one more grin before walking over and putting on his shirt.

It took me another twenty minutes to herd the kids out of the pool and gather up our stuff. I wrapped them up like caterpillars but still heard little teeth chattering as we walked to my apartment. I paused when we got close; looking over into Clarke's yard, but it was completely empty this time.

The kids remained quiet as we walked up to the house, as if the water had washed the energy from them. When the doorknob turned without resistance, I opened it quietly and closed it quickly behind us, again locking both the locks.

"Hey!" I called out.

"Hey," Cameron called from the back rooms. "I hope it's okay, I already took the first shower."

"Of course... that's good. Aiden you go next but don't take a long one okay?"

He nodded and hurried to the bathroom.

Sarah looked at me. "I want to shower, Mom."

"Aiden is the guest, Sarah, angel. You can go next."

Going into the back room, I pulled out the clothes of Aiden's I had set aside. As Aiden had yet to close the bathroom, I set the clothes on the counter. "You have some clean clothes here, sweetheart," I said as I closed the door.

I grabbed a throw from the couch, wrapping it around Sarah, who was still clinging to her towel. I led her to the kitchen table, where she followed without protest. "Here you go, angel," I said as I opened my laptop and pressed play on the gymnastic Nationals.

Walking into my back bedroom, I found Cameron folding my clothes. He turned, grinning and putting an arm around me.

"What are you doing?" I asked, touching his back.

"Not much, I just thought that this was just one more thing you have to do."

"You don't need to do all this, Cameron," I whispered. "My dishes, laundry, babysitting, I feel like you're always giving and I'm always taking."

He shook his head. "It's just the laundry, baby. It's not a big deal."

"Okay, but don't feel like you have to do these things."

He kissed me gently. "You don't get it; I'd fight tigers for you."

Squeezing my eyes closed, I whispered, "Cameron..."

He put his hands on my arms and whispered, "I know I shouldn't talk like that. And I'm sorry about the house comment I made at the pool, too. You just acted like it was nothing, but I shouldn't have said it. Just know there are no expectations from me, I'm not trying to change things or push things forward."

Opening my eyes, I met his gaze. A tear slipped from the corner of my eye, slipping down my cheek.

"Aunt Jamie," Aiden said from the door.

Startling, I turned. "Yes, sweetheart?"

"I'm really thirsty, can I have some juice?"

"Of course, you don't have to ask. Do you know where the juice boxes are?"

"They're not where they usually are," he said. He was fully dressed in the clothes I laid out for him, jeans and a T-shirt.

"Oh, I'm sorry, I forgot. I'll go get them," I said, stepping away from Cameron.

Steam and the scent of kid-shampoo wafted from the bathroom as I entered the hall. Hearing the shower going, I closed the door to the bathroom.

I grabbed a package from the extra stores of juice boxes and grabbed one out.

"Here you go, cutie. The rest are going to be in the fridge, okay?"

"What are we watching?" Cameron said as he joined us in the living room.

"Sarah's stuff," Aiden said, shrugging. "You can watch it with me if you want to."

"I'm going to go grab Sarah some clothes," I said. Walking back into my bedroom, I examined the bed covered in neat piles of clothing. Cameron had folded everything, even my underwear. I crossed over to the pile, smiling to myself at the sight of lacey little thongs being folded so gingerly.

My brow furrowed. I lifted the pile, and then searched around the bed itself. "What the...?" I whispered.

Walking into the living room, I asked, "Hey Cameron, could anything have been left in the washer or dryer?"

"I don't think so, I double-checked," he said.

"Some things are missing," I said.

"What's missing?" he asked.

"Um, come over here," I said, motioning him to follow me.

When we stepped back into my room, I told him, "My underwear is missing."

His eyes gleamed with amusement. "No, it's right here," he pointed to the pile of lacey thongs.

"No, my normal underwear is missing, like, my boy short underwear and… just the regular ones. Did you see any ones like that? Here, I'll show you an example…" I went into my underwear drawer then made an annoyed sound. "I completely forgot that I only had my sexy nonfunctional underwear left."

He pointed to the bed. "These are all the underwear I found. I can go check," he said.

"Or I can, if you don't mind keeping an eye on the kids," I said.

"No, Sarah's just about to get out of the shower and she might need your help. Also you have some creepy neighbor, right?"

I nodded. "Thank you so much, Cameron. Make sure to take the keys. And… would you mind locking the front door on your way out?"

The shower turned off a second later.

"Oh, crap," I mumbled. Then I yelled, "Sorry, angel, I'm going to bring you some clothes in one second." I grabbed a purple outfit from the newly laundered pile.

When I knocked on the bathroom door, I got no response.

"Angel, I have your clothes," I said toward the crack in the door.

Sarah opened the door a little and smiled through the crack. When I held up the clothes, she took it, and then closed the door.

Going back into my bedroom, I checked through all the piles of clothing, finding nothing else missing.

I heard the metallic sound of the key turning in our front door and walked back into the hall to see Cameron walk in the house empty-handed.

"No luck?" I called out to him.

He crossed the living room to me. "Nothing, I even checked the trashcans and nearby washers." His hand came up to rub my shoulder.

I leaned into the soft feeling of his fingers. "This sucks, somebody stole my underwear. I mean, who does that?"

"At least you know it was probably a woman," Cameron said.

I furrowed my brow. "Why's that?"

"Because if it was a guy, wouldn't he have taken those?" He pointed through my open door, to the bed where my lacy thongs were still piled.

I sighed. "You're probably right. I should go shower and get ready for work. Would you mind entertaining the kids while I do?"

"I would love to entertain the kids," he said.

"Thank you for everything, Cameron," I said before wrapping my arms around him. When his arms wrapped around me, I squeezed him tighter, inhaling his soapy smell. "Did you use my body wash?" I asked, laughing.

"Yes, do I smell like a chick?"

"You so do," I said.

"That's embarrassing," he said, but he didn't sound embarrassed.

The door to the bathroom opened and Cameron and I broke apart. Sarah came out, smiling, dressed from head to toe in purple.

"Oh shoot, I forgot to take out her braids," I said.

Her hair was still weaved into loose braids, though strands of her blonde hair escaped in all directions.

"No!" Sarah said, putting her hands on her head to protect her hair from my interference.

"You go get ready. I'll see what I can do," Cameron said.

"Are you sure?" I said.

"Yeah, go get ready it's already past four," he said.

"Are you serious? I need to leave at five because I have to drop off Aiden," I said.

He grinned at me. "Then go, baby."

"Ah, I'm going," I said, walking into my room. Quickly, I put away all my clothes that hadn't been stolen, leaving out my clothes for work. When I came to my underwear, I stared at the pile of little thongs. I almost never wore sexy underwear to work for two reasons: first, it was uncomfortable after a few hours of running around behind the bar. Second, when I bent down to get anything, which I had to do constantly, the back of my thongs always tried to come out to say hello to my customers.

Now, I realized, until I bought new underwear, I had a choice between wearing a black lacey thong, or wearing no underwear at all.

A queasy feeling punched my gut. My hands covered my face as I sat back onto my bed. Heavy breaths whistled between my hands.

Day One: Four-thirty

My pre-programmed phone alarm went off, 'Get ready for work', flashed across the screen.

"Shit!" I said, jumping. Twisting around, I turned the phone alarm off. Even on days where I didn't have to go out of my way to drop off Aiden, I was supposed to be getting ready right now. I grabbed the pile of clothes I had set aside for work and the thong on the top of the pile.

After a quick shower, I dressed in the bathroom. I was too nervous to really concentrate on anything and I rushed through getting ready. Squeezing clear gel into my hand, I scrunched it up into my hair. The underwear I wore under my jeans felt foreign and wrong every time I moved. The lacey curls on the sides of the thong felt abrasive to my legs.

I unbuttoned my jeans, considering just wearing nothing, but the idea sent another wave of queasiness into my stomach. Buttoning back up, I exited the bathroom and rushed over to my phone.

Scrolling down my list of contacts, I stopped on 'Safe Ride—Gina' and I pressed on her number. Crossing to my bedroom door, I closed it then went to sit on my bed. The phone rang three times before a gruff, older woman's voice said, "You need my services already, Jamie?"

"Not exactly, Gina," I whispered.

"Well, what can I do for you?" she asked.

"You used to be a cop, right?" I asked.

"A million years ago, I might have been," she said.

"I have a... problem; can I burden you with it?"

"You definitely can."

"The only thing is, my dad can't really know about it. Can I trust you not to tell him?" I asked.

She paused for almost a minute. "Are you in some kind of trouble, Jamie?"

"I didn't do anything illegal, if that's what you're asking," I whispered.

"Alright. Now, are you in some sort of danger?" she asked.

I didn't respond.

"Well, you see, your dad and I have been friends for over forty years. I won't feel right knowing you're in danger and not telling him about it," she said.

"Okay, Gina. I understand," I said.

"Hold up," she said in a loud voice. "There's no way that I'm okay with you being in danger with no one to help you. So, if you'll only let me help you if I keep it from your dad, that's what I'll do."

"Really?" I asked.

"But I'm going to tell you to tell your dad. I'm telling you that now," she said.

"I know, it's just complicated. I thought that I could handle it, but things seem to be escalating," I said.

"Well, tell me about it," she said.

"I can't really now, I'm already running late for work. Can I call you tomorrow morning?" I asked.

"Is your dad going to be at the bar tonight?" she asked.

"No, he started taking weekends off," I said.

"How about this, what time do you take your break tonight?"

"Eight-thirty."

"I'll be there at eight-fifteen, find me at my usual table," she said.

A tear leaked from my eye and I wiped it away saying, "Thank you."

"Anytime, darling girl. I'll see you tonight," she said.

Slipping into my work shoes and pulling myself together, I walked out of my bedroom. "Hey, Aiden cutie, I need to get you back to your parents."

Cameron stood from where he was sitting with both kids, playing a board game.

"Yum, yum, yum, I ate your arm," Sarah said as she held her game piece to Aiden's.

"Sarah doesn't play the way you're supposed to play, but I don't mind," Aiden told me as he got up from the table.

Sarah stood up, and ran over to Aiden, wrapping him in a hug. Aiden hugged her back, his eyes squeezing closed.

"I love you so much," Sarah said.

"I love you too, Sarah," he said.

Another bout of tears fell from my eyes, and I didn't break up their hug, even though we would definitely be late now.

When they broke apart, I wiped off my face and smiled at Aiden. "You ready to go?"

"Yeah," he said, though he ran over to give Cameron a quick hug too.

Cameron gave me a small grin and said, "I'll wait up for you."

"Thank you for doing this. I'll see you later tonight." Unable to muster a grin, I crossed to the freezer, grabbing out a frozen dinner. Over my shoulder, I said, "If you get tired though, don't worry about waiting up."

"Alright. You have a good day at work," he said.

"Thanks, Cameron."

As Aiden walked with me toward the door, I whispered to him. "Want to have a contest?"

"Yes," he said.

"How about we see who can be quiet all the way to the car?"

"Aunt Jamie, I know that one." He rolled his eyes. "My parents try to have quiet contests all the time."

"Well, this one is a really short one," I said.

"Fine," he said with a heavy, put-upon sigh.

Holding my fingers to my lips, I slowly opened my front door. After Aiden followed me outside, I quietly closed the door behind us and locked it with my key. Putting my hand around Aiden, we began walking away.

Behind me, I heard a door swing open. I didn't look back, just kept walking when I heard a dog bark.

"Hey Jamie," Clarke's voice said from behind me.

Not turning around, I gave a wave. "Hi, Clarke," I said, while still walking away.

I heard his laughter behind me, but it was so low, almost inaudible.

"Aunt Jamie, can I come over tomorrow and go swimming again?" Aiden asked in the parking lot.

"Oh, sweetie, Sarah has gymnastics tomorrow. But we'll go swimming again soon," I told him when we got to my car.

When we were both locked in my car, I group texted Beza and Susan.

Me: We're running late. Be there in twenty minutes.

Susan: We'll wait outside, so you're not late for work.

On the drive to his house, Aiden told me about his teacher, the kids he liked, and the kids who were mean to him. Then he told me every detail of his second grade presentation, where he showed a collage of pictures about everything that was important to him. "You and Sarah were on there," he told me.

"That means so much to me, Aiden," I said.

"Another girl in my class has two moms, and a boy in my class has two dads and a mom, but they're divorced," he said.

"Wow," I said.

"I'm friends with the boy but the girl isn't my friend, she says she hates me and I stink."

"Well, you don't stink. Girls can be mean sometimes," I said.

"Was Uncle Logan mean to you when you were in first grade together?" Aiden asked.

"No, we were good friends. He actually had a really hard time in first grade because your grandpa and grandma—"

"The one that died?"

"Yeah, sweetie. Well, in kindergarten they let your mom and Uncle Logan be in the same class together, but they didn't make any friends because they only wanted to play with each other. So in first grade, they kept them apart. And your mom and Uncle Logan had never been apart in their whole lives. So, in first grade, Logan was always sad. Now, back then, I was really goofy like you are."

"You're still pretty goofy, Aunt Jamie," he said.

"Thanks, cutie. Anyway, I had decided that it was my mission in life to make Logan laugh. I had just learned to write, so I drew him a picture of a poop with a face on it, wearing a cape."

"What? Are you serious?" Aiden yelled, laughing.

"I did," I said, smiling into the rearview mirror at him. "Under it I wrote, 'This is Doo Doo the Super Poo!' Then under that, I wrote, 'Will you be my friend? Check yes or no.' He passed the note back, and he had checked yes."

"That's how you met Uncle Logan?" Aiden asked.

"Kind of. It's how we became friends." I turned from the main road and into a residential street. The high-roofed houses were in neutral colors, all the windows had cute decorative shutters coming out to their sides. A line of trees grew up and over the street, creating an arch above the car.

"When did you become friends with my mom?" Aiden asked.

"That day at lunch," I said.

"Wow. Did Cameron go to first grade with you too?" Aiden asked.

"No, I met Cameron in high school. He was friends with Logan first."

"But then he married Vanessa?" Aiden said.

"A long time later, cutie," I said.

"But they're divorced?" he said.

"Yes," I said.

"Is he married to you now?" Aiden asked.

"No. If I ever get married again, you'll be part of the wedding," I said.

"Was I part of your wedding to Uncle Logan?" he asked.

"Nope, you weren't even alive yet."

"I was part of my moms' wedding," he said.

"I know, I was there," I said, smiling back at him.

"It was illegal for them to get married for a long time. They would have gone to jail," he said with complete surety.

"I don't know about jail. The courts just wouldn't give them wedding licenses back then; it's the piece of paper that says you're married. But they're married now," I said.

"I know, I was there," he said repeating my words.

Beza and Susan waited on the street, under the shade of the tall tree that partially blocked the view of their house.

I rolled down my window as we approached.

"Don't get out, Jamie. We have this," Beza called.

Beza and Susan opened Aiden's door. One grabbed Aiden, the other his booster seat. Susan shut the door and leaned in to yell, "We love you. Go! Go!"

I rushed off for their benefit, but slowed down a little ways down the block.

Pressing the button for the radio, I turned up the volume, switching from a slow, melodic love song to dance music, and then to classical. After a second, I switched the music off. I shook out my hand at my side, surprised when I accidentally hit the cold box of my microwave dinner.

Downtown looked completely different than it had yesterday. The streets were packed with people walking from place to place. Restaurants overflowed with people. As I passed, a strange mesh of different music poured through my open window.

Turning down a side street, I pulled into an alley and parked in a spot that had a large white sign that read 'Mike's Saloon Employee Only Parking'.

Glancing at my clock, the time read five fifty-five. "Yes," I said, grabbing the frozen food box and jumping out of my car. I jogged across the alley, unlocking and opening up the back door of the bar. After stuffing my meal into the staff room's mini-fridge's freezer, I rushed into the bar through the adjoining door.

Glancing around the light, wood bar, and old style Saloon tables, I saw a few customers, but only at the tables. There were also a few people tucked up into the raised booths. Musicians were setting up on the small, wooden stage. The décor showed touches of my father's wood artistry—inlays on the tables, decorative pieces at all the edges.

Behind the bar, Nancy, our only server and bar-back during the slow times, lifted trays of clean cups out of the dish sanitizer. Bartenders Carl and Jose cleaned their stations, not looking up at my arrival.

Looking at the clock, I said, "Yes! Just under the wire. I'm not late."

Carl looked up from wiping the bar, glanced over at the clock, and continued wiping the bar, shaking his head. "Congratulations, we're all so impressed," he mumbled

"Good job," Nancy said, bumping her hip into Carl as she walked by. Nancy was barely more than head and shoulders taller than the bar, but her black hair was blow dried big today, giving her a little more height. Her dark red lips stood in stark contrast to her otherwise makeup-free beautiful, pale face.

I rolled back my shoulders. "I rushed here thinking I could avoid getting evil mutterings from friendly over there, but next time I'll just be late."

Nancy set the tray of clean cups on the under bar. "Just ignore Carl," she said, waving a hand. Her painted nails made black lines through the air.

"Uh huh," I said as I crouched down, quickly checking that all the bottled beers were stocked. Finding them all full, I moved on to checking the alcohol bottles, which were also all full.

"Hey Jamie," José said from behind Carl. "Nice to see you today. Have you been enjoying this fine weather?" He elbowed Carl as he said it. José had a big smile across his baby-face.

Appearance wise, Carl and José were as different as a fish and a bird. Where José's features just screamed 'wholesome', Carl struck me as the ultimate bad boy. His pale muscular arms had two full sleeves of tattoos. His dark hair made his light blue eyes stick out in a way I swore could only be contacts.

"I have enjoyed the weather, José, thank you for asking. I went to the beach and to the pool, it was very nice. How was your day?"

"We worked," Carl said, giving me an insincere smile.

"Well, you don't need to work anymore, Carl, your shift is over. I'll finish cleaning," I said as kindly as I possibly could.

"Yes, boss," he said under his breath.

"Hey, if anyone can be the boss here, I'll give it a stab. Carl, take a hike, your station is clean," Jose said, clapping Carl on the back.

Carl shook his head, chuckling, but gave me a glare as he passed toward the communal tip jar.

Taking his place at the bar, I went to check my sugar and salt containers, but they were fresh. My fruit tray was also practically overflowing.

Gritting my teeth, I turned. "Thanks for setting up my station, Carl."

"That's what a good bartender does," he said, not looking over.

"I don't do that. It's supposed to be the bartender's job to set up for themselves at the beginning of shift," José said, shrugging.

"It's also a little hard to set up for the morning crew the night before, though I restock the bottles if it's not too busy," I said as I washed my hands under the bar.

"That's what's great about day shift, it's never busy. You should try it," Carl muttered under his breath.

"She has a kid," Nancy said, hitting Carl with a towel.

"You here until closing?" I asked Jose.

"Yes siree. Hopefully things pick up, it's been pretty dead since I got here an hour ago," he said.

"Dead all day," Carl added from behind us.

"I saw a lot of people on the street, my guess is we'll get an after-dinner rush," I said.

"Good for you," Carl mumbled again.

"Shut up, Carl," Nancy said.

"Alright, I will. Later guys," he said.

"See you tomorrow, buddy," Jose said, waving.

"See you later, alligator," I called over my shoulder.

When the door to the staff room closed behind Carl, I said, "That guy hates me so much."

"Don't take it personally," Nancy said.

"I don't, but it's unpleasant to deal with," I said.

"At least you don't have to ever work shifts with him. And he set up your whole station just to prove something to you. I mean, he can say *eff* you to me anytime by doing my work," José said.

I shrugged. "True. As you are both busy, and I have nothing to do, I guess I'll check if anyone needs a refill."

"Thanks babe," Nancy said.

I walked around the bar, going table to table getting drink orders. After pouring two shots of whisky over ice and a pint of beer, I brought the drinks to their tables. As I was crossing back to the bar, a crowd of people came in all at once.

When several people sat in my section, I quickly filled their orders. I poured myself a tall glass of caffeinated soda, sipping it between orders. The musician on the stage strummed his banjo a few times, and then a fiddler did the same. I looked up just as the group started playing a lively blue grass song.

"Should I keep your tab open?" I asked a well-dressed, middle-aged woman who handed me her card.

"Yes," she said, smiling and turning back to her companion. Walking to the little plastic filing bins we kept next to the register, I flipped through the cardboard pieces until I found the first letter of her last name. I filed her card and turned back to the bar, but I stopped suddenly.

Smiling, I walked over to Patrick, who sat at the end of the bar in my section. "Hey, here for that free drink I promised you?"

He grinned back tentatively, looked down to the bar, then looked up and offered a stronger smile. "Sure," he said.

"What can I get you?" I asked.

"Scotch, on the rocks," he said.

"Alright, you have a preference or do you want me to pick?"

"You pick," he said.

After pouring the drink, I handed it over. "Not much of a Scotch drinker myself, but this one is my father's favorite and everyone else seems to agree."

He tasted it. "Great," he said as he pulled out his wallet.

"No, this one's on me. Unfortunately, if you need to order drinks for clients, I can't comp you those."

"I'm not here with clients," he said.

"Oh, okay. Well, do you need any other drinks?"

"Another one of these?"

"Just a heads up, it's sixteen dollars a drink, that cool?"

"Sure," he said.

I poured the other drink, handed it to him, and then took his card. "Do you want this open or closed?"

"Open?" he said like a question.

"Okie dokie," I said. I filed his card under his last name—Kelly. When I was done, I wrote down his drink on the comp list, writing my name and the drink next to the cash value. I turned to go to the next customer, when Patrick said my name.

Turning to face him, I saw that instead of grabbing his drinks, Patrick set them down and leaned over the bar toward me.

"What's up?" I asked.

"Can I say something to you? It will only take a minute," he said.

"If you don't mind waiting for me to help all these customers first," I said with an apologetic smile. "I can come find you; it might be a little while."

"Thank you. I'll come back," he said, drumming his fingers against the bar.

Day One: Seven O'clock

Turning to the next customers, a group of young looking girls, I said, "IDs please."

Two of them rolled their eyes, while the other one smiled and handed her ID over as if she had it ready. After they'd each showed me their IDs, and I'd checked them thoroughly, I poured a couple mixed drinks, and then moved down the bar. After about forty-five minutes of serving drinks nonstop, I grabbed a towel and walked toward where Patrick had sat down a couple minutes ago.

"I'll just be one more minute," I said as I passed.

Starting at the end of the bar, I gathered all the empty glasses, setting them in the dirty dish tray. I also grabbed up any tips left behind, sticking them in our communal tip jar. Last, I used my towel to quickly wipe up all the spills.

After I had finished, I stopped in front of Patrick. "I'm here, but I apologize in advance because I might have to run if a new customer comes."

"I'm sorry for bothering you at work. I just couldn't get what I said to you out of my head. I was driving my brother and sister-in-law nuts being so preoccupied all day. She insisted I come apologize and my brother drove me. So, I just want to apologize for what I said."

"What you said?" I frowned.

"Or how I acted when you said you didn't go to college... Obviously it wasn't as upsetting to you as it was to me."

"Oh. I'm sorry Patrick; it's been a really long day." I looked him in the eyes. "Like, a year long. And no worries about the college reaction, I wasn't as offended as you probably thought I was."

"I was being a pretty big dick," he said.

"Can I be honest with you?"

"Always," he said.

I pointed at him, smiling. "You might regret that answer some day." Shaking my head, I continued, "It just seemed like you had some sort of list in your head you were comparing me to, and I was falling short."

"I have no list, and you definitely don't fall short of anything," he said quickly.

"Okay, let me put it this way: I've had a crazy, beautiful, adventurous life, and I have not regretted a single decision I made. And I really don't feel like letting someone I barely know regret the choices I've made."

He leaned back in his barstool, twisting his lips into a contemplative expression. "You might be right. I may have a list in my head. And now that I think about it, it wasn't a list that worked out in the past."

I shrugged. "I probably do too. But, I really appreciate you coming out here to apologize."

"I'm getting a feeling that the 'maybe so' answer you gave me earlier is much closer to a 'no' now."

Biting my lip, I played with the towel in front of me. "Can we try friends, and then get back to that question down the road?" I looked up at him. "I need to be fair with you; there is another guy in the picture.

We're not really together, not officially anyway. And, I've decided to end it. But, there are feelings there and out of respect for him, I need to end things before I even consider moving on."

"Oh." He drummed his fingers on the bar again. "I guess I'll be straight with you too. Being a single, full-time dad, and having a full-time job, I haven't gone on a date in two years, I haven't wanted to. And, I like you. I know I don't know you that well, but I noticed you long before your friend Beza tried to set us up. Getting to know you in the past day and a half just makes me want to get to know you more. So yeah, I'd be honored to be your friend. But, down the line I am definitely going to ask you out again." He exhaled heavily. "Wow that was a long speech... And a little embarrassing."

I grinned at him. "Accepted. Do you want another drink?"

"I think I need one," he said grinning.

"How about for your brother?"

"Yeah, two of the same, please," he said.

"You got it, and then I have to head over to refresh drinks, okay?"

"Yeah, of course," he said.

After pouring two more shots of the scotch, I told him I'd talk to him later, and headed down the bar.

Nancy came up to the bar. "Who's the sexy older guy?"

"He's not older, he's my age," I said.

"Oops, sorry, I forgot you were old," she said with a teasing smile.

"No, you're just a baby. Don't worry, you'll get your growth spurt someday," I said.

"Oh, I'm going to get you for that one. Well, anyway, I have a drink order for you if you're done talking to the hottie."

"Go for it," I said.

She rattled off a list of drinks, and I got to work. Setting a tray on the bar, I set the drinks down one by one.

"So did he ask you out yet?" I whispered over to her, shooting a glance toward José.

Her shoulders sank. "No." She looked up at me, biting her lip. "Um, so, I guess Carl did though." Her face tensed.

My brows rose. "What did you say?"

"I said yes. Don't hate me," she said in a rush.

My head rocked back. "Really?"

"He's nice to me, Jamie. And during morning shifts we flirt, like, constantly."

"Well, it's how he treats you that matters. I just hope you don't start hating me for his benefit someday," I said.

Her jaw dropped open. "I never would!"

"And what about... you know?" I gestured over to Jose.

"I don't think I'm his type," she said.

"Trust me, you are, it's completely obvious," I said.

She shrugged. "If you say so." With expert balance, Nancy grabbed up the tray of drinks and carried it across the floor, dropping off drinks at tables.

As I went down the line, refilling drinks or filling new orders, I peeked over at Jose every so often. He kept moving, filling drinks and chatting up customers, but every now and then, his gaze would find Nancy.

The bar steadily picked up pace with more people coming in. Soon I had a line of customers standing behind the barstools. I poured myself a second half-cup of soda, though I barely had time to drink it. Lining up drink after drink, I eyeballed shots and poured mixers with quick, precise movements.

A hand on my back made me turn around. "You're on double duty for the next thirty minutes, and then it's your turn for break," José yelled over the sound of the crowd and the odd notes of bluegrass we could hear over the crowd.

"Sounds good," I yelled back. I went down the bar, working as quickly as I could covering his orders, mine and Nancy's when she brought hers to me.

What felt like a few minutes later, José tapped my shoulder again. "Your turn, Jamie," he said.

"Thanks, José," I said as I finished shaking a Kamikaze shot and pouring it into a tumbler. Handing it over the bar, I told the pretty young brunette woman who ordered it, "Six dollars."

She handed me eight, giving me a crooked smile and said, "The change is for you."

"Appreciated," I told her, knocking the bar once. After ringing up the order and putting the tips in our tip jar, I headed for the staff room.

Taking my frozen meal out of the small freezer section of the mini-fridge, I pulled it from its box and pulled up a corner of its plastic wrap. I stuck the tray in the microwave for seven minutes, and then pressed start.

Reentering the bar, I made eye contact with none of the customers as I walked to the side of the bar.

"Excuse me," I said to the crowd of expectant drink patrons blocking the exit to the bar.

"Sorry, beautiful," A large hairy guy said as he moved out of my way.

I gave him a smile as I passed. The crowd wasn't as thick steps from the bar. People either sat in tables or gathered around the stage where the bluegrass band was finishing their set. I immediately saw Gina sitting at her one person table with the 'reserved' sign still on its top. She had headphones in her ears and a book in her hands. She lifted the straw of her diet soda to her lips, never taking her eyes off her paperback.

She wore her graying hair up in a twist, that, and her beautiful, elegant features made her look odd in the oversized T-shirt she was wearing. I knew that the shirt was one she had printed herself at a local printing shop; it read 'Designated Driver Volunteer,' in big thick, black letters.

As there were no other chairs at her table, I stood on the other side, waving.

Gina looked up and when she saw who it was, smiled. She plucked her headphones from each ear, and said, "Hey, babe, pull up a chair."

"Would it be okay if we talked in the staff room? It's private in there and I have some food in the microwave."

"Well, of course, let me just gather up my stuff," she said, while she slipped a bookmark into her book and stored it in her tote bag along with her phone and headphones.

We remade our way through the crowd, asking them to move aside again at the edge of the bar. When we were in the staff room, I opened the microwave and pulled out my lasagna tray. Peeling back the plastic, I held the tray out as the cloud of hot steam rose.

"Are you hungry? I could split this in half," I said.

"Not at all, eat your food," Gina said. She took a seat on the big green worn-in couch that I've been hounding my father to replace. Though Gina was not a large woman, she never lost her muscles from her years of public service.

"I like the flowers," Gina said.

Looking around, I noticed a large bouquet of colorful daisies in the corner. Their large blooms exploded out of an overtaxed glass mason jar.

"Wow, I didn't even see those. I bet José brought them in from his garden."

"How many times have you been in here today?"

"Twice," I said, blowing on my food.

"You need to pay better attention to your surroundings, especially if you're in some kind of trouble." She pierced me with blue eyes—eyes that had probably seen through a thousand deceptions by paying attention to small details.

"You're probably right. I feel like I'm constantly on autopilot," I said, taking a seat next to her.

"With your life, I'm surprised you're even awake to talk to me," she said.

"Yeah, me too." I took a bite of lasagna, chewing slowly and looking away.

"You have fifteen minutes left to tell me, babe. I'm assuming this is a hard thing to tell me about since you're obviously not rushing to talk," she said, her gaze never leaving my face.

I sighed. "It's my neighbor, he's been harassing me."

"Sexually or otherwise?" she asked.

"Sexually, I guess, but it's tricky to explain. I actually tried to tell the complex's manager about it. I asked to be moved to another apartment. It's just he never says the wrong thing, he never says anything inappropriate, it's how he says it."

"Give me an example," she said.

"Yesterday, he overheard me and…" I cleared my throat looking away.

"Do not be afraid to tell me." She touched my arm. "Your shame is his weapon against you."

Taking a deep breath, I met her gaze. "He overheard me and Cameron together; we had sex by the door of my apartment. Later that day, Clarke, my neighbor, asked me if I had been putting up pictures by my door. When I blushed, he laughed and told me if I ever needed to hang pictures again, he'd be happy to help."

"I see," she said.

"He's been making comments like that since I first met him. At first I thought maybe I was just imagining things, but I know that I'm not. And when I tried to tell the manager, I really, really sounded like I was imagining things. I told him that Clarke told me he got a new big screen TV he wanted to show me, or that he had the steam cleaner for an extra day and offered to clean my carpet. He's said nothing overtly wrong; it sounded like I was just paranoid."

"What did the manager say?"

"That he'd already moved two of my neighbors due to noise complaints about Sarah. That he understood about our particular situation. That he'd keep an eye on the situation and move us as soon as there was a suitable apartment."

"Basically, he gave you a fat load of bullshit," she said.

"It would have helped if I could have given him a specific example of Clarke clearly sexually harassing me. And he never does it if anyone else is nearby to hear, except for Sarah."

"Have you told anyone else?"

"No," I said, my head falling into my hands.

"Sweetheart," she patted my back. "Most women do not report sexual harassment, probably for all the reasons that you haven't."

"It's just if I told any one of my friends or family, they'd tell Susan or Cameron. Either one of them would automatically threaten, or more likely, attack Clarke. When the cops came, Clarke would only look like a victim. I have absolutely no proof that he's doing anything wrong. Both Susan and Cameron have a history of violence, and they're so hot-headed."

"So you've just been living with it alone?" she asked.

I nodded.

"For how long?"

"A month and a half," I said.

"But something happened today that scared you enough to risk speaking out," she said.

I nodded again.

"What happened today?" she asked.

"He cornered me in the laundry room, insisting that I wait until he moved his stuff, he blocked my path out. I agreed to wait for him to move his stuff, but when I was past him, I told him that I was going to wait another day to do my laundry. Instead, I went to another laundry room and started my stuff there. He was waiting for me when I exited. He didn't say anything, just gave me a look. Then later, when I got my laundry, all of my normal, not sexy underwear was missing."

I paused to wipe tears from my face. "At first I thought it must be Clarke who took the underwear, but then Cameron told me that a guy would have probably grabbed the lacey thongs instead of taking the more normal pairs. I agreed with him until I realized I had only two choices now, sexy underwear or nothing."

"He's controlling you," she said simply. "Was he waiting for you when you left the house?"

"He came out as I left, called my name," I told her.

"It makes sense," she said.

"Yeah, I know. But I imagined telling this to the complex manager or a cop that doesn't know me. They'll think what Cameron thought."

"They might. I'm assuming you're seeking my help because you want my advice from a cop's point of view, am I right?"

"I just want your advice, period," I said.

"Alright, first, eat your food while I talk, you only have five minutes of break left."

"Alright," I said and took a bite of lasagna. The tomato and parmesan flavors were even stronger with this bite.

"As a cop, I'd tell you to first find a way to avoid all contact with Clarke. Then, go in and make a police report. Tell your friends and family about what is going on. If you do see Clarke, find some way to record what he says to you."

"But he's my neighbor, how do I avoid all contact with him?"

"Go stay with friends, or with your dad. Not as a cop, but as someone who was waiting outside your delivery room, I'm telling you to move. It's very hard to prove harassment, especially because he is so careful. Getting a restraining order against him would be difficult. You'll have to present evidence of harassment at a hearing and he'll still be allowed to be in his house and yard."

"I might have the money to move soon," I said.

"I'd suggest you move now, at least to a temporary place," she said.

"I'll think about it… I'll try," I said, sagging forward.

The door to the bar opened. "Hey Jamie! I need you out here!" José called out.

"Sorry, one second," I called. I looked at the clock. "Shoot, I'm five minutes over." Standing, I threw away my lasagna tray and plastic fork. "Thank you so much for all the advice," I told Gina.

"You call me, day or night, Jamie. You have one person who believes you, and I have a nine millimeter pistol and a concealed carry permit."

I wiped another tear away. "Thank you, Gina."

"Now get back to work. I'll follow you out," she said.

I walked into the bar, finally feeling as if I had taken a little control of my situation back.

Day Two

Eating My Feelings

Day Two: Two-forty AM

After exiting my car and crossing the parking lot at the side of my duplex, I peeked around the building. Soft white light outlined my front door and porch. Almost no light escaped into Clarke's neighboring yard, and I had to squint to bring the yard into focus.

Unless he was ducking behind our adjoining fence, he wasn't in his yard. I took a deep breath.

Behind me, a loud swooshing sound broke the silence.

I jumped, spinning to see a neighbor stepping out of the light and away from their open window.

Exhaling heavily, I turned back to my duplex.

Clarke still wasn't there, no one was there.

"You're being such a chicken shit," I whispered to myself. Taking my phone out of my purse, I pulled up Cameron's name.

Me: You awake?

Cameron: Yes.

Me: Will you open the front door for me?

A second later, Cameron opened the door. He stepped out, looking around. The light silhouetted his dark hair, giving him a crown of light.

I hurried up to him, not quite running, but close. "Hey," I said in a low voice.

"Everything okay?" Cameron asked when I stopped a step away from him. Though shadows entirely masked his features, I could feel his gaze intently on mine.

I nodded. "Yeah, fine."

"Okay, good," he said, stepping back inside.

After following him in, I turned, making sure to lock both locks before looking back to Cameron.

He smiled down at me. "Hey, baby, how was work?"

"Busy, busy. But I made almost three hundred in tips."

"Nice," he said, leaning down and giving me a soft kiss on my lips. "I still haven't given you your birthday present," he said, stepping back but taking my hand.

"Oh, yeah," I said, grinning. I tossed my purse onto the table we walked past.

"Yep, it's all wrapped up in your room," he said with a smoldering grin.

I laughed. "That type of present, is it?"

"You'll have to see," he said, bobbing his eyebrows at me.

"Ha, okay. I'll just check on Sarah, and then meet you in there," I said, lifting his hand up and giving it a quick kiss before releasing it.

Sarah was fast asleep in her bed, her leg thrown over the covers. She snored softly, her wavy hair streaks of blonde in a sea of purple.

I tucked her foot back under her covers and smoothed the blanket over her. Giving her a soft kiss on her forehead, I whispered, "I love you, angel."

Quickly, I checked that the window in her room was securely locked, and then I left her room, closing the door behind me.

I walked into my room to find Cameron lying across my bed.

I stopped, just taking in the sight of him lying across my bed. His head was propped up with his hand. The grin twisting his lips invited me closer.

"I never see you on my bed," I said, then I corrected, "When I'm not in it."

"Do you want me to sleep in your bed?" he asked, and though his expression stayed casual, his gaze seemed intense.

"Well... Sarah still crawls in bed with me most nights," I said, shrugging.

"If you warned her first, I think she can handle it. I've been staying over for close to a year now and she sees how we act together."

I swallowed. "Maybe... Could we talk about it later? I'm just a little too tired to talk about anything serious."

"Yeah." He nodded, and then looked down. Looking back into my eyes, he took a deep breath. "Alright, well, come over here I want to give you your present."

He held up a medium-size rectangular package, wrapped in tissue paper.

I crawled onto the bed toward him.

Cameron dropped the box, and grabbed me, leading me to straddle his lap.

"Is it a book?" I asked, looking down at him.

"You'll see," he said with a grin.

Picking the package up from where it landed on the bed, I ran my finger under the tape. The tissue paper tore in a long fissure up the length of the present. Pulling the paper away, I stared down at a photo-montage frame.

"Is this..."

"The Ultimate Sunshine Tour," he said, with a grin.

There were three pictures, one with both of us screaming, the other was just of me, looking over my shoulder at him, almost lost in the immense crowd. In the third picture, I was kissing his cheek, Cameron's eyes squeezed closed, and a smile stretched wide across his face.

"I thought you lost that disposable camera?" I said excitedly. I pointed to the fourth frame. "Wow, Cameron! And those are the tickets. You kept the tickets."

"Of course I did," he said.

"How old were we here? Seventeen?"

"Sixteen," he said.

"We look so young..." I laughed. "Remember how everyone was so mad at us for ditching that end of summer bonfire thing."

"Yeah," he said.

"That was... to this day, probably the best concert I ever went to. We had so much fun. I don't know if you remember this, but you kissed me while we were dancing."

"I remember," he said.

I smiled at him. "Me too. I had such a crush on you that summer. But, you know, you were brand new to town, and I knew you kissed a lot of girls, so I didn't think too much of it."

"Who told you that I kissed a lot of girls?" he asked.

"I don't know... probably Logan," I said, laughing. "He was so jealous after we went to that show, so angry and brooding. He wouldn't even talk to me for days and then, bam, he asked me out. We were always in this 'maybe' place, and then suddenly he asked me out after all those years. I always wondered if the idea that I had a crush on you was what prompted him to ask me out."

"Probably. Logan knew that I was really into you, I'm sure that helped encourage him to act too," he said.

"You were?" I asked, surprised. I looked up from the picture to smile at him. "I always thought you just thought of me as a friend back then. Aside from, you know, how much chemistry we had—but you were so popular with the ladies, you seemed to have chemistry with everyone."

His hand came up to run through my hair. "I was crazy about you."

"How funny," I breathed out a laugh. "Imagine how things would have been different if you'd just asked me out first," I mused, meeting his gaze.

He didn't say, 'I have imagined that,' but the serious expression he regarded me with said it loud and clear. Finally, he said, "I'm glad things happened the way they did, even though some of it was rough, because we have Sarah in our life."

I swallowed heavily. "She's the center of my life."

"I know," he said, he looked deeply into my eyes as if he was saying something silently that I could almost hear.

"Well, I love the present," I said, leaning over to place it on my nightstand. "Thank you so much."

Cameron's hands came up to my hips as I moved, then pulled me back to him. His hand grazed up the side of my body, as I looked down at him.

"Hey beautiful," he whispered.

Leaning down, I kissed him.

His hands immediately threaded through my hair, pulling me closer into him. He kissed me deeply, our breaths soon coming heavily between us. I felt him lifting at the hem of my shirt and I broke away to let him lift my shirt off me. With a quick flick of his fingers, my bra followed. With one arm around my back and the other cupping my head, Cameron rolled us over so that he was now on top of me.

Letting out a little gasp, I smiled up at him.

He gave me a mischievous grin before his lips started making their way down my chest as his fingers unbuttoned my jeans, and slowly let down the zipper. His hand caressed over my lacy underwear, then slipped under.

Minutes later, we were both naked and my body was liquid with waves of pleasure washing over me. Cameron poised to enter me.

His eyes locked on mine, and I stared up at him, completely captivated. Again, it was as if he was speaking to me only with his gaze. His lips came down hard on mine as he entered me gently.

A long time later, Cameron collapsed over me, his breath heavy. "Hmm, this is my happy place," he whispered, chuckling before pulling out of me.

My hand slipped over his back, feeling over the ridges of muscle. "I like this feeling. You're so heavy, but it feels really nice." I closed my eyes, but blinked them open. "We need to shower, and I think I might need to change my bed sheets too. We're so sweaty."

Cameron slipped down my body, so that his head rested on my stomach. "If you just stay here for one more minute, I'll do the bed sheets and let you take a shower alone."

"Okay, but you have to wake me if I fall asleep," I said, closing my eyes.

"I will," he said, kissing my stomach. Then a second later, "Baby?"

"Huh?" I said, blinking furiously. My heavy eyelids glued themselves together.

"You fell asleep," Cameron whispered. When I fought my eyes open, I whispered, "Whoa, you moved."

"You fell asleep," he repeated, kissing me lightly on my lips. "Do you want my help in the shower?"

"Um..." I sat up with some effort, but immediately sagged forward while I scanned the room. "No, I have it," I said. Scooting forward off the bed, I trudged to the bathroom across the hall.

Turning on the faucet to the right temperature, I stepped into the spray. The tears came then, hot and immediate, as if the faucet had turned them on too. Stuffing my hand in my mouth, I muffled the sounds of my sobs. I turned from the spray and moved my hand away to take a couple deep breaths.

"I can't keep doing this," I whispered, pressing my head into the cool tile of the shower wall.

Turning off the faucet, I wrapped a towel around me. I took a deep breath before walking into my bedroom.

Cameron looked up from where he was laying a new top sheet over my bed. He smiled over at me.

"You don't need to do that, Cameron," I said.

"That was our deal, remember?" he said. "Now come lie down and I'll tuck you in."

"I can't just yet, I have to put on some pajamas," I said, not quite able to meet his eyes.

"Alright, I'll wait," he said.

"Cameron, I..." I looked up into his gaze, into his beautiful, smiling face. "Are you okay with things just staying as they are between us?"

"Yeah," he said, automatically.

"Forever? Or, until someone else comes along for you?" I said.

His eyelids narrowed and brow furrowed. "Jamie, it might take a while, but one day you're going to be ready to move on completely. I can wait for that day."

I sat down on the bed, tears running down my face. "I don't want you to be waiting for me to move on, Cameron. It's not fair to you," I said.

He kneeled down in front of me. "I don't want to be anywhere else."

"No, it's not fair to you... because we're never going to end up together. Not in any real way."

He rocked back. "Why would you say that?"

"Because, we're each other's history, we're never going to be able to move on if we cling to the past through each other."

"That's what you're doing? You're clinging to the past through me?" His shoulders came up, as if he was pulling into himself.

"What Logan and Vanessa did to us, and then we started sleeping together only a few months later... how are we supposed to ever make something real out of that?"

"What are you saying, exactly? What has this relationship between us been to you? Some elaborate revenge against Vanessa?" He glared at me as he spoke, his nostrils flaring.

"Of course not!"

"Shit, Jamie. I thought—" His head fell back, his hands covering his face. His hands fell away and his eyes came back to glare into mine. "I thought you loved me. But I'm just some long, elaborate grudge-fuck for you?"

Tears came faster now. "No. You know that I love you, Cameron. But that's not—"

"Not, what?"

"You knew!" I shouted at him. "You knew for weeks and you never told me. You even covered for them," I said. "I've tried so hard to move past it, because I'm in love with you. But I can't move past it, I can't. Every time we have sex, the words beat into my fucking head. He knew. He knew. He knew!"

Tears coursed down his face now, too. "I'm not fucking perfect, Jamie."

"I know, and I know I'm far from perfect. I'm a big fucking mess. But, I really want to move forward in my life, and you and I are just carrying around our past everywhere."

"You just had sex with me, right here, just a few minutes ago, and now you lay all this on me?" he said, before shaking his head.

"I'm so sorry. You just keep saying and doing these amazingly sweet things, and I'm so filled with guilt. You deserve better," I said.

"Yeah, I do." His hand came up to my cheek and his thumb brushed my tears away. "I do deserve better from you. Like a little fucking understanding about what I was going through at that time. I'm going to the living room to sleep. We can talk about all this stuff later. I'm not in the right mindset right now."

"Okay," I said, tears still coursing down my face.

He stood, but didn't walk away for a second. His eyes squeezed together. "I really wish that this wasn't the way you told me that you loved me for the first time."

"I'm sorry," I said.

He opened his eyes, and stared directly into mine. "Yeah, me too. Goodnight, Jamie."

Day Two: Ten-thirty

When I opened my eyes, light filled my room. I had thrown off my blankets sometime in the night, but the leg that was still covered felt like it was baking. Looking beside me, I found an empty bed.

"Sarah?" I called out.

"She's out here," Cameron called from the kitchen.

Glancing over at the clock, I read the time: ten-thirty. "Whoa," I said, under my breath. After crawling off my bed, I trudged out of my room.

"Wow, I slept in. I'm sorry, Cameron," I said with a yawn.

Sarah and Cameron sat at the kitchen table, a puzzle on the table before them. They'd put together the edges, as well as a gymnast, midair between the uneven bars.

"No worries," Cameron said as he connected another puzzle piece. "I promised Sarah I'd do this puzzle with her in the morning."

Sarah smiled up at me, her hair big and crimped.

"Morning, angel." I kissed her forehead. "Are you hungry? Oh, you already ate," I said, noticing the plate left out for me, a pot lid covering it.

"Yeah, sorry we didn't wait for you," Cameron said, standing up. "Can I talk to you a minute?"

"Yeah, sure." I attempted to keep my voice even.

He tilted his head to the living room and I followed him when he headed that way.

When Cameron turned around to face me, he gave me a straight-lipped smile. His hand came up and brushed up and down my arm. "Hey," he said.

I swallowed. Looking everywhere but at him, I said, "Thanks for everything this morning, letting me sleep in, and the breakfast and everything."

"Of course," he said. "I—"

"It was really wonderful of you, staying overnight too."

He nodded. "No problem. I want—"

"And the present you gave me was so special."

"Jamie, please."

My hand came up to my face. "Okay." I finally looked into his eyes.

"I need a couple days. I have to figure out my head, think some stuff over, you know."

"Of course." I nodded, then bit my lip before saying, "I can get someone else to watch Sarah on Thursday, it's no problem."

"It's up to you, but that's not what I want. Thursday is a long way away," he said.

"It is. Just... don't feel obligated to do anything. I want you to do the right thing for you. What I mean is, I can get a babysitter, so only come Thursday if you want to." Heaving a deep breath, I met his eyes. "It's up to you. Just let me know."

He rubbed down the sides of my arms again, looking into my eyes. "I never feel obligated to do anything, Jamie. This isn't about that, okay? Even though I'm going to take a few days for myself, I still want you to call me if you need me."

I nodded, breaking eye contact. "Alright. Well... thank you for coming over."

"Of course," he said. He sighed and wrapped his arms around me, clutching me to him.

My arms moved of their own accord, and suddenly my hands were clutching at his back.

He kissed my forehead lightly. "See you in a couple days, Jamie," he said. His hands dropped away from me.

"Okay," I whispered, squeezing my eyes shut. I felt Cameron moving away, but I couldn't seem to force my arms to release him.

Instead of breaking my hold, Cameron's arms encircled me again, squeezing me to him. "I'm not going to be too far away," he whispered. "No matter what."

"Okay," I said, hoarsely. "Okay." I forced my arms to drop from around him.

Immediately, Cameron turned away from me. He crossed to the kitchen and gave Sarah a quick kiss on the top of her head. Without another word or a glance back, Cameron walked out of the door, making sure to lock the bottom lock on his way out.

Watching the closed door for a minute, I was not quite able to make myself move. I walked to the door and unlocked the bottom lock. The knob felt cool as I turned and held it.

"Jamie, no way, no how are you going to run after him," I whispered. I released the knob, taking a step back. With a deep inhale, I unlocked the top and bottom locks.

I found Sarah still at the table, fitting another piece into the puzzle. She smiled over at me as I sat beside her with my breakfast plate.

"Hey beautiful girl, did you have a good morning?"

"What are we going to do today, Mom?" she asked, enunciating every word.

I took the lid off my plate, finding toast, eggs and sausage. "Did you eat this, angel? Or did you eat a yogurt?"

Sarah made a loud, annoyed sound. "What are we going to do today, Mom?" she repeated.

"Oh, sorry. Gymnastics. We're going to gymnastics today. I'll tell you the rest in a second," I said, standing up. When I checked the fridge, I found one of Sarah's yogurts gone. When I looked into the trashcan, I found an empty yogurt container and a banana peel near the top.

Taking the seat beside Sarah again, I said, "So today is Sunday..."

"So there's no school today. Yep, that's right, angel," Sarah said, giving me a wide grin.

"Yep, that's right, angel. In an hour we're going to go to gymnastics. I think Heidi said you're going to practice on the beam today."

Sarah squealed, waving her hands up and down.

"And then, we're going to go to that Lucky Stars movie with Aunt Amy and Uncle Peter."

"Is it a movie about gymnastics?" Sarah asked.

"No baby, it's about a horse. Remember, we watched the preview."

"And then?" Sarah asked.

"Then we'll either go to dinner or go home," I said. A hot feeling surged up my face, and my eyes started to tear up. I took a deep breath to push the feeling back. Stuffing a big bite of eggs in my mouth, I began to chew. The eggs were a little cold, but I just shoveled another bite into my mouth.

"And then we'll go to ice cream," Sarah said.

"Maybe," I said, but then decided, "Yeah, okay, we'll go to ice cream." Finishing my meal, I stood and walked over to the fridge. "You should probably eat lunch before we go to gymnastics."

"I will go get ready," Sarah announced, jumping up from the table.

My purse vibrated from where it was still sitting on the table. Pulling out my phone, I saw that Susan had already texted me three times.

Susan: Morning. Welcome to day two, eat up.

Susan: I hope you're eating a good hearty breakfast my friend.

Susan: We were just invited to a barbeque at Patrick the Hot Dad's house. You're invited too.

I sent her a message back.

Me: I'm about to have a second breakfast, and it's Patrick the Hunky Dad FYI.

Her response came immediately.

Susan: Well... I'm thinking you're the main invitee, but Patrick doesn't have your number, so he called Bee. We're totally going to the barbeque after we hang out with your mom anyway, though. Free food and beer, and he has a pool.

Me: You can't have beer, you're pregnant.

Susan: It's the idea. And anyhow Beza can, not that she will. You could too, I'll drive you.

Me: I probably can't, can you tell him sorry for me?

Susan: No, you call him, you big chicken.

Me: I don't have his number.

She sent me his number.

Me: I hate you.

I saved his number into my phone as Patrick Kelly, feeling like I'd stolen his last name since he'd never mentioned it to me. I pressed the button that opened the screen to text message him, but closed it. Opening my phone app, I took a deep breath and called him.

The phone rang twice before Patrick answered with, "You've reached Patrick."

"Um, hey Patrick, it's Jamie," I said.

"Hey." His voice, which had sounded casual and professional, now sparked with interest.

"So…" I drew out the word, "Susan passed on your number and an invite to your barbeque."

"Good. I was hoping your friends would," he said.

"Is it a dinner time thing?" I asked.

"Yeah, around five-thirty. And, it's definitely going to be a friend barbeque, not at all like a date," he said. I could hear the smile in his voice.

I breathed out a laugh. "Okay, well as long as it's not a date. I was very worried," I said, grinning. "But, unfortunately, I have plans with my sister and her husband for dinner."

"Oh," he said, his voice losing all of its enthusiasm.

"Unless… until what time will your barbeque be? We might be able to drop by after dinner."

"Sure, or if you want, you can just bring your sister and her husband," he said.

I paused, looking down at the puzzle spread over my kitchen table. "Maybe, I'll ask them."

"Great, I can't wait to see you… as a friend, nothing more," he said, making me laugh again. He added, "I'll text you my address, just come whenever you can."

"Alright," I said.

"And I hope it's okay, I'm planning to save your number. Just a warning, I might put your name down as 'Sexy Mom'."

"Ha, I forgot I have to kill Beza for telling you what I called you," I said, feeling my face get hot.

"Just so you know, you're now Patrick the friendly dad."

"That's unacceptable. I am absolutely going to have to change your mind on that," he said.

"You can try," I said through a smile. "I'll see you later."

"I'm counting down the hours... in a friendly way," he said.

"As long as it's in a friendly way. Bye, Patrick," I said before I hung up.

A smile had taken over my face but it fell away as I set my phone down next to the scattered pieces of the puzzle. Standing, I crossed to the cupboard and opened it to stare at my coffee beans.

"I miss you," I told them. They missed me too, I could tell from the way they slumped forward in their bag. "No one would know," I whispered.

Then I sighed and turned to my fridge. I opened it and peered in at the contents. There was an overwhelming assortment of choices that would all expire if I continued to overlook them. I settled on sandwich fixings, and made Sarah and me grilled ham and cheese sandwiches.

As I served the sandwiches on plates, Sarah returned to the kitchen dressed in her gymnastics leotard.

"Sweetheart, you can wear that now but when we're outside you'll have to put on clothes over it."

"No," she said as she took a seat at the breakfast table.

I blew a breath out my nose and looked to the ceiling for patience. The ceiling gave me nothing.

Grabbing half of my sandwich, I ate it on my way to my room. After getting dressed, I grabbed Sarah some shorts and a light sweater.

"Hey baby," I called as I reentered the living room. "Do you want to see Mommy drink grass?"

Sarah looked up from her sandwich with wide eyes.

"What do you say? Do you want to see me drink grass or not drink grass?" I raised my eyebrows in question.

A big smile spread across her face and she nodded. "Yes, eat grass!" she shouted.

"Well, I'll probably drink it, but it tastes really gross."

She giggled furiously.

"But you have to put on your clothes, otherwise we won't have time to go get the grass before gymnastics," I said, holding out outfit.

Sarah jumped up and put the clothes on. When I held out her jacket, she immediately shrugged it on also. "Mom, are you going to drink grass?"

"Yes," I teased as I grabbed my purse.

She giggled again, grabbing her stomach.

I grabbed the other half of my sandwich and placed our empty plates in the sink. When I turned again, I caught a flash of black in my vision and looked up to Logan's urn. It seemed to be looking down at us. I reached up and ran a finger over the wolf as I passed, and then took a big bite of my sandwich.

I opened the front door as quietly as possible and whispered to Sarah, "Let's be really quiet, can you do that?"

I looked up as I pushed the door open and saw Clarke in his yard. I straightened, putting an arm around Sarah and holding her to me as I locked my front door.

When I turned, I glanced over into Clarke's yard. He leaned down over Buster, the hook of his leash in one hand. He looked up, meeting my gaze.

"Hey, how's it going?" he asked, giving a little wave.

"Hey," I said, grabbing Sarah's hand and turning away with her.

"Well, have a good day," he called.

I glanced back at him, but found him petting Buster.

"Yeah, you too," I mumbled as I turned back toward the path and led Sarah to the parking lot. When we'd reached the car, I glanced over my shoulder once more, but no one was behind us.

The parking lot for the Health Nut was thankfully much less crowded than it had been yesterday. Sarah and I snagged a parking space near the front of the parking lot and had little trouble walking in.

As we stepped into the short smoothie line, I leaned down toward Sarah. "That's the grass," I said, pointing toward a glass case of wheat grass on the smoothie counter.

Sarah smiled at the counter, eyes lighting up with excitement.

The same lady with hair that looked so much like dandelion fluff, waited behind the smoothie counter with a big smile on her face. "What can I get you ladies today?" she asked us when we stepped up to the counter.

"A wheat grass shot," I said.

Sarah squealed again and jumped in place.

The lady behind the counter smiled down at Sarah. "You sound excited. Is the wheat grass for you?" The lady gave me a wink as she said it.

"No!" Sarah shouted.

I laughed before saying, "Sorry, she's just excited to see me drink it."

The woman grinned over at me. "Well, would you ladies want anything else?"

"Strawberry smoothie!" Sarah ordered.

"Do you have a kids' size?" I asked.

"We do," she said, pulling out a twelve-ounce cup.

Sarah continued squealing and jumping around until I relented. "Alright," I said.

"Okay, take this up to the front," the lady said. There was no line to pay, and when we returned to the smoothie counter, our drinks weren't finished yet. The smoothie lady called out another man's order, and he walked past Sarah to get his drink.

"Hey, who's your favorite gymnast?" Sarah yelled at the man.

The short, older man turned, gave me a questioning glance and then looked down at Sarah.

"Hey, who's your favorite gymnast?" Sarah called at him again.

"Angel, not everyone has a favorite gymnast," I told her, giving her a squeeze and smiling at the man.

He smiled down at Sarah. "Well, I do," he told Sarah with a wink. "Do you know who Sawao Kato is?"

Sarah shook her head, eyes wide and focused on the man.

"He is from Japan, like me. One of the best gymnasts who ever lived. You should look him up."

Sarah nodded at the man and looked down at her feet.

"Thank you," I said to him.

He gave me a small smile and a nod, and then walked past us, sipping his smoothie.

"Wheatgrass shot, Strawberry Sunshine," the smoothie lady called out to us.

"You ready for this?" I asked Sarah as I brought the wheatgrass shot to my mouth. I lowered it. "You want to taste it first?"

"No!" she shouted as she jumped up and down excitedly, waving her hands in the air.

"How about smell it? You want to smell it?"

"No!" she shouted again, and then gave another squeal.

"Okay." I brought it to my lips. "I'm going to drink it." The smell hit my nose before I downed the shot. Maybe it was because I was so prepared to be disgusted this time, but the astringent grass taste did not overwhelm me. It was less bitter than I remembered.

For Sarah's benefit though, I stuck out my tongue and said, "Oh, yuck."

She giggled, jumping up and down in a circle.

"Okay, angel, here's your smoothie. Let's head to gymnastics, yeah?"

She beamed all the way to the car.

"I'm going to drink that if you don't," I told her as I fastened her into her booster, pretending to lean down and take a sip.

"Hey Mom! That's not yours," she shouted as she pulled her drink away and stuck the straw in her mouth.

"Okay, okay, you keep it." I smiled and closed her door.

Day Two: One O'clock

The gymnastics studio was on the other side of town, up through the industrial buildings and tucked back in an office complex. I parked in the small empty lot that hugged the side of the warehouse building. Sarah's seatbelt clicked the moment I parked the car. She tried to pull open her door, but groaned when it didn't open.

"Wait," I told her, exiting the car and opening her door. "Wait for me to cross the—" I grabbed Sarah's arm as she made to run for the building. "Stop! Sarah, this is a parking lot, it's dangerous."

Sarah tugged against my grasp as I shut both our doors.

"Sarah, do we need to practice getting out of the car again? Or can we be safe?" I said through gritted teeth. I held my breath as a car passed, speeding through the parking lot.

Sarah danced in place, eyes focused on her gym. "Be safe!" she yelled, and even though she was shouting, she stopped tugging on my arm.

"Okay, angel, look now that there are no cars we can cross and be safe."

As we walked up to the glass doors on the warehouse, the doors opened.

"Hey ladies, nice to see you," Sarah's coach Heidi called with her thick Texan accent, as she stuck her head out of the door. She propped the door open by kicking down the door's stand.

Sarah ran up to Heidi, throwing her arms around her.

Heidi leaned over, barely a foot taller than Sarah. "Hey, monkey, you driving your mama bananas, or what?" She leaned back. "Saw you by your car. You scared me running toward the parking lot like that. Remember to wait for an adult every time you cross the street."

Sarah nodded furiously, her eyes wide and expression intent.

"Okay there, sweetie, go on in and start stretching while I talk to your mama," Heidi said, stepping back and gesturing for Sarah to go in.

Heidi patted my arm, "How's everything going?"

"Fine. She had a pretty good week, nothing too major happened. But the principal did mention she's been doing gymnastics on the playground."

Heidi grabbed up her mass of curly, gray-streaked red hair while she listened to me, grabbing it all together in a messy bun the size of her head. "Oh, I'll definitely to talk to her about that," she said, nodding.

"Thanks. Lately every time I tell her to do anything, Sarah just tells me 'no'. But she'll listen if you tell her," I said.

"Well, that won't do. But I do think that it's rather typical, especially at her age. We'll have a little talk about needing to listen for safety, if you don't mind," she said.

"Please, have at it," I said with a grateful smile.

"Alright, well, go ahead and take a load off for a while. I brewed a whole pot of coffee for you as well, so help yourself."

"Oh, thanks," I said, biting my lower lip as I turned away and headed toward the benches near Heidi's office. I glanced at the long line of gymnastics team photos spaced along the wall. Gleaming gold and silver trophies jutted out from every flat surface, ribbons hanging from their bows. Sitting down, my eyes found the words emblazoned in white, 'Every Champion was Once a Beginner' contrasting out from its black background.

Taking a seat on the bench closest to the office, I leaned back against the wall. Across the room, Heidi stretched along with Sarah, moving through their usual routine.

The room buzzed with a sound that was nearly silence, but not quite—an echoing quiet. Closing my eyes, I let the wall behind me take all my weight. My fingered threaded through the holes in the bench, and I grabbed onto the metal.

Opening my eyes, I grabbed my purse from where I had dropped it on the floor and pulled out my cell phone. I scrolled to Susan's number and texted her.

Me: I think I did number eleven early. Last night actually.

I held my phone on my lap as I watched Sarah move into some of her exercises. She stood on her head upside down, practicing quick kicks back, then slower, then quick again. They ran across the floor, practicing different moves each time. My phone buzzed, pulling my attention away.

Susan: Shit. I'm sorry. What happened?

Me: I acted stupid, went about it in the worst possible way. We got in a fight. This morning he said he needed some time away to figure out his head.

Susan: How you holding up?

Me: Pretty well on the outside. On the inside, I think I'm shattering.

Susan: Want me to come take over?

Me: No. I need to hold it together. I have to go to a movie and then that barbeque. As for me and Cameron, it's probably the right thing anyway.

Susan: 'Probably' doesn't sound too sure.

Me: 'Probably' doesn't feel too sure either. 'Probably' feels like shit.

Susan: If you need to duck out of the barbeque just text and I'll cover for you.

Me: I think I need the barbeque.

Susan: If you say so. I'll see you there then.

"Hey."

Surprised at the voice, I glanced up to find my sister Amy standing over me. A hesitant expression played on her lips as she regarded me. She pointed to the space beside me. "Is this seat taken?"

I scooted down a little. "It's all yours," I said.

She sat, her gaze drifting to Sarah and Heidi practicing on the beam. "This place brings back memories," she said.

"Yeah. You know your picture is still on the wall over there." I pointed to one of the team photos down the wall. "You have that super early-nineties hairdo."

Her lips twitched, but her gaze didn't wander. "I'm so glad Sarah got in with Heidi."

"Yeah, me too. You really made it all happen for her," I said, watching the pair.

We were silent for a long time before Amy said, "So, I'm assuming you're still mad at me."

I looked over at her. Her thick, dark brown hair draped around her face so perfectly, she could have been at a photo shoot. She stuck her stiletto boot out in front of her, as if she was examining it, but I could tell her attention was fixed on me.

"I'm not sure mad is the right word," I said with a sigh. "Maybe more like mistrusting."

She sucked in her lips, closing her eyes and breathing in heavily through her nose.

"That sounded worse than I meant," I told her, shaking my head. "It just felt like everyone decided that I'm too incompetent and weak, and decided to take over my life."

"I don't think you're either," Amy said, finally looking over.

I laid my head back against the wall. "Yeah, thanks. I can't help but feel like both a lot of the time."

"If you think you're weak, you should probably reexamine your idea of strength. You've always been this warrior woman, this warrior mom. You're just... I don't think that you're not managing, Jamie. I couldn't manage everything you do, not even close."

"I'm just...?" I said, raising an eyebrow.

"Just stuck," she said.

"Maybe you're right. I... I'm going to change a couple things."

After a pause where she continued to look at me expectantly, she said, "Like?"

"I made a list."

Her eyes widened and a smile spread across her face.

"Oh my goodness, all I need to do is say the word 'list' and you pee your pants."

"Don't pick on me, I love lists. What kind of list did you make?"

"A fourteen-day soul detox. I'm on day two, and it's scary as a hell. I'm supposed to do one thing a day every day."

"What's today's?"

"Gain some weight," I said.

"You made this all up?" She sounded skeptical.

"Susan," I said.

"That makes more sense. So you have fourteen things to do?"

"Thirteen, I vetoed one." I looked away.

"Is it what I'm guessing?" she asked in a quiet voice.

"Probably. I'm just not ready yet," I said in an equally quiet voice. "I'm not ready for a lot of the things I'm supposed to do, either."

"Like what?"

I leaned down and pulled out my wallet from my purse, extracting the note from where I stored it in the bill fold. "Here," I said, handing it to her.

Her eyebrows slowly hiked up her forehead as she read the list. "Wow," she said when she was finished.

"Yeah, I know, ambitious," I said.

She folded the list and handed it back to me. "I feel like no matter how I respond to that, I'm probably going to get in trouble, so all I'll say is that if you need any help, Peter and I would be happy to help you."

"Thanks, Amy. Where is Peter anyway?"

"Working. He's meeting us at the theater. I took a car over here; I wanted to talk first, just us."

"Yeah. How's everything going with you two, anyhow?"

She smiled. "Fine, we're great. Yeah, everything is great."

"Everything?" I asked, meeting her gaze.

"Yeah," she said, looking away, but she looked back at me. "Well, not everything, I guess. You know how we've been trying for almost a year now?"

"Yeah," I said.

She swallowed. "Well, Peter is wondering if maybe we should get some tests done. He thinks I might be infertile." Her voice was controlled, but I could hear the suppressed tears.

"Are both of you getting tests done?"

"Mostly me," she said.

"Well, that's bull."

She shook her head. "Not really. I'm twenty-seven, and I've never even had a pregnancy scare."

"Yeah, but weren't you on birth control until last year? And you're religious about shit like that. I had pregnancy scares because I was constantly messing up my birth control."

"I just always pictured myself as being a mother. I was going to get my MBA, work for two years, and then have two children. I cleared it with my work. We renovated the second office into a nursery."

"Now who's being self-defeating? In the words of the wise Amy, 'you're twenty-seven not eighty-seven,' go have lots of babies. And if it doesn't work for you biologically, there's always adoption. You always said you wanted to, and you and Peter are, like, the ideal candidates."

She closed her eyes. "Peter and I talked about it, but we decided not to."

I raised my eyebrows at her. "You both decided not to?"

"Just let it drop," Amy said.

"Alright, if you want me to," I said.

"She's so good, I was never that good," Amy said, staring off toward where Sarah was rehearsing her beam routine. She flipped on the beam, doing a slight balance check.

"That was a great landing. She needs to work on her dismounts. I think that's what they're working up to today," I said.

"Aren't you afraid she's going to get hurt?"

"Every moment of my life. But if I try to stop her, she'll just be more determined to do it. And, I don't want to teach her that she's not enough. The world is already so determined to do that to her," I said softly.

Amy took my hand, giving it a squeeze. "You're a good mom."

"Thanks. I hope so."

We watched the rest of Sarah's lesson in silence. Heidi had Sarah practicing her dismount for the rest of the session, though they only actually did the dismount three times.

After they finished practicing, they stayed on the mat. Heidi spoke to Sarah for a long time and claimed Sarah's undivided attention. Sarah nodded once, and then they both stood and walked toward me. After putting on her clothes, Sarah made a beeline for us, climbing directly into Amy's lap.

"Hey, adorable," Amy said.

"I thought I saw you coming in, Amy," Heidi called over, a wide smile on her face.

"Hey there, Ms. Heidi, how are you?"

"I am doing just fine, just fine, thank you for asking. You look very nice. How is your job in advertising?"

"Marketing," Amy corrected. "Fantastic."

"And how is that handsome husband of yours?"

"Wonderful, he couldn't be better to me. We're very happy," Amy said, a smile fixed securely on her face.

"Well, that is good to hear. Unfortunately, ladies, as much as I'd love to visit with you, I have a class coming in at three I have to set up for. I'll see you two next Wednesday," she said, pointing at me and Sarah.

"Thank you so much, Heidi," I said.

"It's my pleasure," she replied with a wave as she turned around and headed back for the mats.

As we walked out of the gym, all three of us connected by our held hands, I turned to Amy. "Oh, I forgot to mention, I was invited to this barbeque thing this evening. You and Peter were included in the invite too, but I understand if you'd rather do dinner just us."

"Probably, but I'll text him," she said as she pulled her phone from her purse with her free hand. "Whose barbeque is it?"

"A guy named Patrick, his daughter Kay is in Sarah's—"

"Not Patrick Kelly?"

"You know him?"

Amy laughed. "Yes, what a coincidence. He's Peter's friend, they play tennis and golf at the club."

"Crazy. We're kind of becoming friends," I said, shrugging.

"Which kind of friends?" she asked, her lips twitching with what I guessed was a suppressed smile.

"The kind that go to barbeques. Don't make too much of it," I told her, as I clicked the beeper for my car.

"So he asked you out?" she said.

I gave her a warning glare as I helped Sarah into her seat and buckled her in. "Nap if you need to, angel." She curled up, eyelids heavy.

When I straightened, I saw Amy's shoulders bobbing up and down as she laughed under her breath.

"It's just so funny," she said.

"Why's that funny, Amy?" I asked, rolling my eyes.

Amy got into the passenger seat, still looking all too amused. "It's just that he's something of a celebrity at the club. He's from an *extremely* wealthy family and I guess he practically grew up there. He's the best tennis and golf player there, by far, and he's friends with everyone. His wife was pretty much shunned when she left him for her boss."

"I don't get why any of that is funny," I said, starting the car.

"Because the women there throw themselves at him left and right—even the married ones—right in front of his daughter. It's so bad; it's something of a joke between me and Peter. Especially since Patrick doesn't give any of those women the time of day. He's always nice but dismissive. Then he goes and asks out my sister, a coffee-shop owning bartender who hates rich people."

"I don't hate rich people. Half the people I love are rich. Everyone in this city is freaking rich," I said.

"I'm not talking about our kind of rich," she said.

"What other kind of rich is there?"

"Trust me, there is a whole other world of rich. So, I'm taking an educated guess here and going to say you turned Patrick down, didn't you?" she said.

I didn't answer her, which just made her snicker some more. Finally, I said, "I like him; we're going to try out being friends. It's funny that you described him like that, though. He just seemed so… lonely to me. But I guess he's surrounded by friends."

"You can be surrounded by friends and still be lonely," Amy said. She then turned a too-bright smile on me. "So is he the 'Hunky Dad' you're going on a date with from your list?"

"I might have to amend that one. I think I changed my mind."

"Please, no," she begged. "Give him a chance. He's sweet, not stuck up or pretentious. He's one of the good ones."

"Uh huh. You know, you're one to talk about me hating rich people; I thought you despised that country club. I thought all those women referred to you as 'Peter's Mexican wife' even though you told them you were Cuban-American?"

She waved a hand dismissively through the air. "Not everyone there is like that. And, networking with those people is really important for both my and Peter's careers."

"I get how it's good for Peter, but how is it important for *your* career?"

"In a lot of ways. And Peter's career is very important to me, too. He'll be the main provider when we eventually have kids."

"Alright, but I hope you don't let those people walk all over you."

"I don't," she snapped before fixing her attention on her phone in her lap, her fingers flying across her screen as she typed out a text message. A minute later, she said, "Peter would love to go to Patrick's barbeque." She looked away.

"Awesome, then we'll go. I do like Patrick, and Kay is adorable."

"Yes, she sure is," she said, though her mind seemed to be elsewhere.

Day Two: Three Twenty-Five

"Park here," Amy said, pointing to a spot in the parking lot in front of the movie theater.

"I think I can get a closer one," I said, scanning the lot.

"If you spend any more time circling the lot, we're going to be late," she said, tapping my dashboard clock.

"Amy, we have ten minutes—"

"Which will be barely enough time to get snacks."

"—and there are always fifteen minutes of previews on these kids' movies," I continued.

"If you're going to miss this spot, drop me off in front so I can go get the tickets," she said.

"It's not going to sell out," I grumbled as I took the spot she indicated.

"How can you be so sure? It's a Sunday afternoon—prime kids' movie time," she said, opening her car door.

"I want popcorn," Sarah's voice bubbled from the back seat.

"You're awake," I said, smiling into the rearview mirror. "Last time I looked back you were fast asleep."

"I want popcorn *and* candy," Sarah said as she unbuckled her seat belt.

"You do, do you?" I said.

"I'm going to run ahead and get us tickets," Amy said, having already exited the car.

"Do what you have to, Amy," I grumbled.

"Unless you're getting out now because then I'll wait," she said.

Grabbing my purse, I exited my car and walked around to open Sarah's door. Sarah bounced out of the car, beaming.

"You woke up happy, angel," I said as I closed the door behind her. When I turned, I found that Amy and Sarah were already three cars away, hurrying hand in hand toward the movie theater.

I followed them at a normal pace. By the time I reached the ticket counter, Sarah and Amy were next in line.

"This one is on me." Amy pulled out her wallet to purchase the tickets.

When she walked out of the line, tickets in hand, I asked her, "Shouldn't we wait out here for Peter?"

"He's already inside, saving us seats."

"Cool."

There was almost no line for the concessions, and Sarah bounced on the balls of her feet as we stepped up to the counter.

"Can I help you?" The pretty blonde teenage girl behind the counter asked with an air of impatience. Music buzzed out of the earbud in one of her ears. When she turned, the earbud that wasn't in her ear swung around her cash register.

"I really hope that you're going to tuck away those headphones before you serve us," Amy said.

The cashier gave us a cold smile, and pulled the headphones from her ears, shoving them into her back pocket. "What can I get for you?" she asked with a small roll of her eyes.

"A large popcorn with no butter, please, and…" I looked down to Sarah who was holding four bags of candy. "Only one, Sarah."

"Two," she said.

"One. Pick now or no candy," I said, turning back to the girl as she placed the large popcorn in front of me. The popcorn glistened up at me as it settled.

I looked back at the girl who was watching me expectantly. "Sorry, I ordered no butter."

"No butter. No butter. No butter," whispered Sarah under her breath.

"You said butter," the girl said, practically glaring at me.

"She said no butter, you just didn't hear her because you had headphones in," Amy said exasperated.

"Actually, no, I didn't. I put my headphones in my pocket before you even ordered," the girl said.

"It's fine." I put my hand out toward Amy. "My daughter can't have butter."

"It's not actually butter, it's like vegan," she said.

I took a deep breath to steady myself. "It's the texture on her hands, it freaks her out. She can't do the butter; I ordered no butter, please."

"No butter. No butter," Sarah said.

"I'm going to go get my manager," the girl said.

"This chick is going to make us miss our entire movie," Amy grumbled, pulling her phone out to text something into it. "It hasn't started yet," she said after a minute.

Another tall, middle-aged woman walked up, her salt-and-pepper hair in a high bun. A big smile spread across her face as she stopped in front of us. "Samantha tells me you have some questions about our butter?" she said in greeting.

"No, I ordered a popcorn with no butter and got one with butter and—"

"No butter!" Sarah screamed, she grabbed for the popcorn but I intercepted her. I picked her up, holding her to me as she made loud distressed sounds and kicked out in my arms.

"My niece has special needs. We ordered popcorn with no butter for her. Please go get it," Amy said to the woman.

I grabbed out my wallet and threw it on the counter. "I'm going to take Sarah over there," I said as I walked out of the crowd.

"It's okay, angel, aunt Amy is getting it," I whispered over and over again, as she continued to thrash and whimper in arms. People cleared from our path, gawking as they passed.

I sat Sarah on my lap, giving her squeezes until she calmed down. "Do you want to do gymnast breaths?"

"One," she said, breathing in shallowly.

"Two," I said, breathing in deeply and gesturing with a hand for her to do the same.

As we finished breathing to ten, Amy walked up with two big tubs of popcorn and stopped a few feet away. "You still want to go see this?" she asked as we stood.

"I think so," I said, leaning down to Sarah. "Do you still want to go to the movie angel?"

"Yes movie," she said.

"Okay, let's do this then," Amy said, tilting her head toward where the theaters were. She lifted the two big tubs of popcorn. "They gave us one for free."

"Wow, how generous," I said, dryly.

"It's all yours, Jamie. Peter already got us one. You said you're trying to gain weight," she said, lifting the basket up sporting a small, amused grin.

As we walked in the theater, a golden retriever flew across the long black movie screen, his cape billowing behind him. 'Space Pup Returns, Coming May 4th' lit up in big letters.

"See, still previews," I said as we scanned the dark theater.

"There he is," Amy said, pointing. Walking halfway down the aisle, Amy stopped in front of her husband.

Peter looked up from his phone on his lap. "Oh, hey honey, I was just texting you," he said as he stood.

"Hey Peter," I said, reaching over to give him a hug.

"Hey Jamie, Sarah," he said, giving me a pat on the back and waving at Sarah. He motioned past him. "Here, go on in."

"Thanks," I said. I made my way down the aisle first so Sarah would be sandwiched between me and Amy. We pushed down our velvet seats and sat down.

Sarah smiled at me, shoving a handful of popcorn into her mouth. I picked up a piece of the non-butter soaked popcorn and examined it for a minute before popping it in my mouth. Whatever the girl had poured all over the popcorn, it sure tasted like butter. It tasted like butter and salt exploding in my mouth.

I cringed a little, but after a minute, I scooped up a handful of popcorn and shoveled it into my mouth.

The movie started with a loud trumpeting sound. Sarah bounced up and down in her seat, popcorn flying out of the bucket in her lap and going in all directions.

I grabbed the bucket and placed it at her feet.

"Candy," she demanded.

"Shoot." Leaning over to look at Amy, I whispered, "Did we get candy?"

Amy nodded and kept her eyes on the screen as she pulled a bag of candy out of her purse. She opened it, handing Sarah a couple, but keeping the bag.

Sarah gobbled up all the candies in record time. "More," she said to Amy.

"You know the deal, Sarah," Amy said.

Sarah kicked out her legs and refocused on the movie.

The movie started with a racing scene: a small man was on top of a horse, gripping the reins, then the camera panned to the horse's feet thundering down the track.

Sarah's eyelids were wide, the lenses of her eyes reflecting the movie. I focused on the plot and felt myself being drawn into the plot as the racehorse tripped mere feet after crossing the finish line. I shoveled handfuls of popcorn into my mouth, my gaze never once wavering from the screen.

The protagonist, a preteen boy, turned to the jockey and yelled, "Dad! They're going to kill Lucky!"

"Oh, son." The boy's father pulled him into a hug. "Sometimes an animal's injury is just too great and the vet needs to put them down."

"Not the doctor, Dad! He said Lucky could heal but never race again. Mr. Jones and Mr. Hamilton are going to kill Lucky so they can get twenty million dollars from their insurance! Please, Dad, you have help him!"

"I'll help him, son," the jockey said.

A tear crawled down my cheek. As the jockey went to guard Lucky Stars until the doctor and police got there, more tears spilled from my eyes. For the rest of the movie, my face was wet with fresh tears.

And at the end, when Lucky Stars raced again, winning the Kentucky Derby, I was positively sobbing. I stuffed yet another handful of popcorn in my mouth, and when I went for another, my fingers scraped the bottom of the bucket.

A hand touched my elbow.

Wiping my face on the shoulder of my shirt, I turned.

My sister was leaning over Sarah, who was still completely captivated by the movie.

"Hey, you okay?" Amy whispered.

"Yes," I whispered back.

"You sure? You're a little bit... loud. Go to the bathroom, I'll keep an eye on Sarah."

"I'm sorry." I laughed, wiping the tears away with my hand. "Yeah, maybe I should go to the bathroom." Standing, I stepped over each of their legs in turn, and then walked up the aisle. At the trash can, I threw away my now-empty, large, popcorn container.

In the bathroom, my reflection stared back at me. I looked like an absolute mess. Red splotches covered my pale face and gathered at the tip of my nose. I washed my face over the sink, scrubbing at my cheeks.

"Did you watch a sad movie?" the elderly woman at the next sink over said.

I tried to grin at her. "Yeah." I grabbed a handful of paper towels and dabbed my face with it.

"Which movie was it?" she asked as she pushed down the lever for the paper towels.

"Um, it was called Lucky Stars," I said.

"The kids' movie?" she asked. "I saw that with my granddaughter. It had a happy ending."

"Yeah, I'm a sucker for a happy ending. Have a nice day," I said and rushed out of the bathroom as fast as I could without running.

I waited outside the theater as the doors opened and people started pouring out.

A couple walked by me with a pair of young kids. The man leaned in close and whispered to his wife, "That's the woman who was bawling."

I quickly looked away from the couple, fixing my gaze on a 'Space Pup Returns' poster. The golden retriever had a tongue lolling out of his mouth as he flew superman-style through the air.

"Hey Jamie," a voice said from beside me.

I turned to see Peter step up beside me, he smiled but his gaze quickly turned to the Space Pup poster. "Amy took Sarah to the restroom; she says she'll meet us here. So... how's everything going with you?"

"Fine, just suffering some minor humiliation for bawling my eyes out at a kids' movie," I said, trying on a smile for him.

He shrugged. "I doubt anyone noticed."

I raised an eyebrow. "I appreciate the kind lie, thanks. How's everything going for you? How's life at the firm?"

"Very busy. I'm sure Amy told you that I've made junior partner, so, definitely been great," he said.

"Yeah, congratulations. That's huge, right?"

"I suppose," he shrugged, though there was a hint of a smile on his face. "So, Sarah has class with Patrick's daughter? That's quite a coincidence."

"I know," I said.

"And Amy says Patrick asked you out?" he asked, his lips fighting what I knew was a smile.

I shot a glare toward the women's restroom.

"Kind of. Not really. We're sort of becoming friends," I said.

"That'd be interesting, if you dated Patrick. I'd love to see how people reacted to that. It would be like the two opposing sides of Amy's life coming together.

She'd probably love you to come to the club sometime," he said.

"Uh-huh. But Patrick and I are not dating. And no offense, but I don't think the country club is really my scene," I said.

Peter was definitely smiling now. "No, I don't suppose it is."

"Excuse me, Peter. I think I'm going to go check on Amy and Sarah, they've been gone for a long time." I patted his arm as I passed on my way back to the bathroom.

Just as I reached the restroom, Amy and Sarah came out. "Hey, I was going to meet you back at the theater. Didn't Peter tell you?" Amy asked.

"Yeah, you were taking so long I decided to check on you."

"Oh, yeah sorry, there was a long line," Amy said as we turned and continued walking toward Peter and the exits.

"Did you like the movie, angel?" I asked as I leaned down to kiss Sarah on the head.

"Yes. You cried," she said.

"Yes, a lot," I said, taking her hand.

Amy cleared her throat. "So what time is this barbeque? I think Peter wants to pick up a host present on the way."

"Shoot, I didn't even think of something like that. What are you thinking of getting?"

"I'm going to leave that up to Peter. Patrick's his friend. Do you know what time the barbeque is?"

"Um, I think Patrick said the barbeque would be at five-thirty," I said.

"Five-thirty? You mean five minutes ago?" Amy checked her phone, nostrils flaring.

"Calm down. It's casual. You know, I think I'll call Patrick and ask if he wants me to bring anything. Oh, and I should probably tell him that you're coming," I said.

"Hmm, maybe that's a good idea," Amy snapped.

"That's me, always full of great ideas," I said as I pulled out my phone. "Need a great idea? I'll give you seven, one for every day of the—"

"Oh my god Jamie, just call him," Amy said.

Day Two: Five Thirty-five

I grinned as I peered down at my phone, and thumbed through my contacts to 'Patrick Kelly'. I offered my other hand to Sarah, who took my hand only to use it to twirl herself around, again and again.

"Hey there," Patrick answered in a low voice. I could almost hear his smile when he said, "I knew it was you because 'Sexy mom' popped up on my screen.

"Ha," I said, turning away from where Amy hastened ahead to Peter.

"So, I've been meaning to ask you... do you and Sarah like steak?"

"We love steak," I said.

"Good, because we already have a couple steaks on the grill. You ladies heading our way?" Patrick asked.

"Yeah, we are. So... weird coincidence, I think you know my sister and her husband."

"Really?"

"Yeah, Amy and Peter Smithson? They're members, or whatever, at the same country club as you."

"Oh." The cheerful tone had disappeared. After a short stretch of silence, he said, "Bring them along. It'll be great to see them, too. We've got plenty of food."

I paused, confused by his hesitation. "Are you sure? Because we can totally sit this one out." Sarah finally got dizzy twirling around my hand and I grabbed her with one arm, holding her weight.

"No, really, that's the opposite of what I want. I'm sorry. The grill distracted me. Please, come. And bring them too, it'll be great."

"If you're sure. Is there anything we can bring?"

"Just yourselves," Patrick said.

Sarah broke away from me and I spun round to see her running over to where Amy and Peter were deep in conversation. When they both turned to her, I turned back and said, "Okay, but if you think of anything, just text—oh, shoot! Are the kids in the pool? I completely forgot to bring Sarah's swimsuit. I might have to take a quick trip home and be there a little later," I said.

"No problem, Sarah can wear one of Kay's," Patrick said.

"Are you sure?"

"Yeah," he said.

"Okay, that works, thanks. Are you going swimming?"

"I will if you do," Patrick said, the smile returning to his voice.

I breathed out a laugh. "Probably not tonight," I said.

"Alright then, I'll see you real soon," he said.

"Yeah, soon," I said before hanging up.

When I walked up to my group, Peter immediately turned to me. "What did he say?" he asked, his gaze intent on mine.

"He said you guys are welcome to come. He's got plenty of food and we just have to bring ourselves," I shrugged.

Amy stepped toward me, lips pursed and said in a low voice, "Peter wants to run by a liquor store to pick up a host present, but I was thinking I could go with you and watch Sarah while you get ready."

"I'm ready," I said, then following her gaze, I glanced down at my ripped jeans and 'The Rolling Stones US Tour T-shirt'. "This is what I'm wearing. Did you guys want to grab your suits?"

Amy frowned. "No, definitely not. How about you follow us to the liquor store, then we'll follow you to Patrick Kelly's house."

"You probably know the way better than I do," I said.

Amy shrugged. "Either way. Would you mind texting me his address?" she asked.

"Sure." I scrolled up to the text and forwarding it to her.

"Well, let's not waste any more time," Peter said, glancing at his watch.

Sarah did a cartwheel as we walked through the lobby toward the exit.

"Sarah, don't do that," Amy said in a low voice with a hand to her chest. "There are a lot of people around."

"Not here, angel," I said, rushing forward and grabbing her hand. "Did you know we're going to Kay's house to go swimming?"

Sarah jumped up and down and squealed. Then she asked, "Do you want to go swimming in the pool, Mom?"

"Probably not tonight. How about you, do you want to go swimming?"

"Yes!" she shouted.

"Well, you definitely can. Let's get to the car," I said. When I looked up, Amy and Peter had already left the lobby and were waiting outside, locked in what looked like a tense conversation. I tried not to disturb them as I exited the theater, but they immediately looked over.

"Hey guys, I feel really bad. I totally changed plans on you and it seems like it's stressing you out. We could still cancel if—"

"No, really, let's get going there. We're already late," Amy said.

"Are you sure?" I asked.

"Definitely," Peter said as he pulled out his keys. They turned to the parking lot, Amy's arm threaded through Peter's.

"Peter is parked over here, we'll pull around to you," Amy said over her shoulder.

"Okay," I said, heading the other way.

By the time I got Sarah in her car seat and gave her my phone to play with, Peter and Susan had already pulled up in his sleek gray sports car. When I pulled behind them, Peter sped ahead. He weaved through the traffic, and by the time we exited the movie theater parking lot, having followed him by cutting off three people, I stopped trying to keep up. A few blocks up, Peter stopped dead, waiting for me.

Sarah's game blared out, playing the same chord of music over and over. "Angel, if you don't turn your game down, I'm going to take the phone away."

"No take the phone away!" she shouted as her game music decreased.

"Thank you," I whispered as I caught up to Peter's car.

He slowed his pace and after a few minutes pulled into a strip mall I'd never been to before. The strip mall was lined with upscale boutiques and salons. We parked in front of a small store. The windows were frosted and bare, except for a decorative silver logo that read 'The Scotch Cabinet'. Peter got out of his car and entered the store, only to exit a minute later with a wooden box.

He rushed back to his sports car, pulling out of the spot and barely waiting for me to pull out of mine. We drove deeper into the southern coastal neighborhoods I had never visited before. As we weaved through neighborhoods, the houses bulked up so large only two of them could fit comfortably on a block.

Peter turned down a road lined with heavy, reaching oaks. We came out along the beach, where the few houses were separated from each other with stretches of sand dunes.

"Look how pretty it is out here," I said to Sarah. When she didn't respond I said, "Isn't this neat? Kay lives on the beach."

Peter parked in front of a sprawling one story house, behind what I recognized as Susan's car. I parked between two cars a little way down the road.

"This is beautiful!" I said to Amy as I exited my car.

The roof slanted out at all angles, interspersed with dormers, in a long low cottage-style house.

Windows stretched the length of the house, giving the illusion that the house was made of glass.

Peter and Amy waited by the walkway as I helped Sarah exit her door. Sarah rushed up to join them and the group turned and headed up to the large wooden door.

The door opened and a woman's head popped out, her brown curls bouncing as she smiled at us.

"Oh, wonderful!" she exclaimed. "Come in, come in." She pulled the door open wide, and I got a good look at her. A huge smile spread across her gorgeous heart-shaped face. She wore a long silky maxi dress that cinched at her waist, and was barefoot.

"I'm Carrie, Patrick's sister-in-law. Are you Jamie and Sarah?" she asked.

"Yeah—"

She crossed the distance and hugged me. "You are exactly how I pictured you. I've been talking to your friends, and I absolutely love them. They are so sweet." She pulled away and looked at Sarah, "And you are adorable. How old are you?"

"Ten," Sarah said.

"She's eight; she just likes the number ten, right angel?" I corrected.

"I do too," Carrie said to Sarah, "But my favorite number is seven."

"My favorite number is ten," Sarah mumbled as she pressed her face into my stomach.

"This is my sister Amy and her husband, Peter," I said, gesturing to Peter and Amy who stood with smiles fastened on their faces.

"Actually, we've met at the club," Peter's voice sounded too bright.

Carrie turned to Peter, her smile wavering for a second. "Oh, of course, it's so nice to see you both."

"How is your flower business?" Peter asked, taking a small step forward.

"Oh, it's wonderful, especially this time of year. Everything is blooming. But, honestly, I thought it would be more work owning a flower shop," she laughed. "I do almost nothing at all, except arrange a bouquet once in a while. Who knew owning your own business could be so easy?"

Amy and Peter laughed, their eyes fixed on Carrie.

Sarah took a step back and started to walk off, but I took her hand and said, "Wait for us, cutie."

"I am so rude! I'm hogging you all to myself. Let me take you down to the party," Carrie said, linking her arm through mine and leading us through the house. Up close, I could smell a light perfume and a stronger tang of alcohol.

"This place is awesome," I said as we walked through an open sitting area and glass doors that led to a wide stone patio. A few steps down, a long white deck stretched into the sand dunes. A pool sat to one side. Beside it, a small grotto area surrounded a Jacuzzi.

My gaze caught Susan sitting, kicking her feet into the pool, as she watched Aiden and Kay splash each other. On the other side, a large stone wall with a grill set into it was surrounded by Patrick, a guy who looked just like him, and Beza. Each had a drink in their hands and a smile on their face.

"Beza, are you drinking beer?" I asked in disbelief as I approached the group.

"It's a root beer," she said, shooting a smile my way.

"Oh, good, I was about to die of shock," I said, wiping pretend-sweat off my brow.

"One of these days. But not today. I need to be supportive of my wife. Susan's sad she can't have one." Beza said the word 'wife' with clear enunciation, her gaze flitting to Amy and Peter and away. She hugged me and Sarah, then gave Amy and Peter a quick wave before excusing herself to go join Susan.

I turned to the guys. "Hey, how's it going?"

"This is Jamie," Carrie said, beaming at the man I assumed was her husband. "And that's Sarah," she said, gesturing at Sarah. "And this is Jamie's sister and brother-in-law..."

"Amy and Peter. It's great to see you. Thanks for coming." Patrick leaned over the wall to shake Peter's hand.

"Thanks for having us," Peter said. He lifted the wooden box in his hand. "This is your favorite, right?"

Peter took the box, and his brother looked down at it and whistled. "Eighteen-year-old. Good taste," he said.

"Wow, man, you have a great memory. Thank you," he said, opening out the doors to the box and pulling out a bottle scotch.

"You ever try this one?" Patrick asked grinning, his gaze meeting mine.

"We don't carry that one at Mike's Saloon, and I told you scotch isn't really my thing," I grinned.

"You're missing out."

"I'm going in the pool," Sarah said, tugging on my hand.

"I have that swimsuit for Sarah, if you want," Patrick said, coming around the wall to meet us.

"Definitely. Is it okay if she eats first?" I asked, pulling Sarah in for a hug.

"Sure. Would she prefer hot dogs or steak?"

"What do you say, angel, hot dogs or—"

"I'm going to the pool!" Sarah cried.

"Angel," I crouched down in front of her. "You need to eat if you want to go in the pool. You had gymnastics today, and now you want to swim. It's important to eat nutritious food when you get so much exercise. After you have some dinner, you can get your suit on and join the other kids."

Carrie patted my shoulder. "May I help her get some food? I love kids. Besides I want you to enjoy yourself."

"Sure, if you're up to it. Thank you," I said, standing.

"Hey, Sarah, cuteness, I'm really hungry too. Would you mind coming and eating with me? You can choose what I eat, if you want."

Sarah looked at Carrie with wide eyes. I poised to catch her, in case she ran in the other direction, but when Carrie offered her hand, Sarah accepted.

They walked to the barbeque and Patrick's brother walked around the small wall to stand next to

Patrick. He cleared his throat, giving Patrick a pointed look.

"Oh, sorry." Patrick smiled and gave an exaggerated exhale. "Jamie, Amy, Peter, I apologize in advance for doing this to you, but allow me to introduce my brother Derek."

"Nice to meet you people." Derek's grin was all for me as he reached out a hand to shake mine. "You go to that concert?" he asked, nodding to my T-shirt.

I turned around and pointed at my back. "This one is from 1978, but the shirt is actually from the concert though. I won it from our dad."

"Wow, tough break for your dad. How'd you win it?"

"An epic beer pong competition in Belize. Amy and I were tied with our parents, three to three. My stepmom and our dad are good, but Amy is the best." I patted Amy on the back as I spoke.

Amy breathed in through her nose and glared at me. She shook her head slightly, but I was sure only I picked up on it.

I shook my head right back at her and rolling my eyes, I continued, "So we decided to make it more interesting, if we won, they made Amy's next car payment and I got this shirt. If they won, Amy and I cleaned their house once a week for the rest of the summer. We won."

Derek turned to Amy, and said, "We should play. Oh, shit, we haven't offered them beers yet, have we?"

"No, we didn't," Patrick said, leaning down to a cooler.

"I'll take one," Peter said, accepting a beer from Patrick. He swung an arm around Amy, squeezing her to him. He shook his head at the beer Patrick was holding out to Amy. "Amy doesn't drink beer anymore. The story Jamie told was from when Amy was in college."

"We have wine, or I could go make you a drink. Unless you want to make an exception," Patrick said, still holding out the beer.

"Yeah, make an exception. I used to be something of a beer pong champion myself. I'd love to match skills," Derek said, eyebrows raised.

Amy's gaze fixed on the beer, but then she blinked and shook her head. "Wine would be wonderful," she said.

"I'll take it," I said, reaching for the beer before Patrick lowered his hand.

"So, I guess your sister is out, but are you up for an epic game of beer pong." Derek gave me an exaggerated wink.

"Oh, no, I would fail miserably. Amy definitely carried me, I suck at beer pong." I took a sip of beer, then added, "And I'm driving."

"You don't have to drive. My brother has plenty of bedrooms here." Derek slapped Patrick on the back and Patrick's cheeks reddened slightly.

"Thanks," I said with a small laugh, "but Sarah has school in the morning and I have work."

"Doesn't Sarah go to Kay's school? Patrick could take both of them and you could drive to work?"

Patrick cleared his throat. "Derek, seriously? They just arrived and you're strong arming them into staying the night?" He turned to us. "Any of you hungry yet? The tri-tip isn't quite done, but a couple of the steaks look good to go."

"We all ate at the theater. We can wait for the tri-tip," Peter said.

"Yeah," Amy smiled.

"I've been meaning to challenge you to a tennis rematch, my pride's been smarting since the last time we played," Peter said, taking a step forward and just slightly in front of Amy and me.

"I'd like that Peter, we definitely should." Patrick stepped back and looked over at me. "How about you Jamie, are you hungry?" he asked.

"You know, due to unforeseen circumstances, I ate an entire large buttered popcorn by myself, so I'm not that hungry yet." I pause, looking away. "Actually I take that back I am weirdly hungry. I'd love a steak."

Patrick laughed and I couldn't help joining in.

"I'm kind of on the opposite of a diet right now. So, bring on the barbeque and whatever else I guess," I said.

"Great. I'll make you a plate," Patrick said.

"Oh, thanks, but I could do that," I said.

"It's no problem; I was going to make one for myself anyway." Patrick rounded the barbeque, forking two large steaks onto plates. "Want any salad?" he asked.

"Sure," I said.

"Grilled zucchini?"

"Yeah, why not."

"Pasta salad?"

"I'll just have a little bit of everything, if that's okay."

"Finally! A woman with an appetite. Maybe we could still have some sort of competition," Derek said, clapping me on the back.

"Well, you said you had hot dogs, right? I can eat them pretty fast," I said.

"Seriously?" Derek said, eyes bright.

"No, that's disgusting," I laughed.

Day Two: Six Forty-five

Patrick came around with two heavy laden plates of food. "You want to go eat over by the pool or at the table with Sarah and Carrie?" he asked.

"Um, by Sarah, if you don't mind," I said.

"No, that'll be great." He led me further down the patio and down a step to where Sarah and Carrie were eating at a sturdy table.

"I don't really know any gymnasts, who should I like?" Carrie was saying as Patrick set down our plates. She took a big bite of salad and gave us an awkward, chipmunk smile as we sat. She held up a finger as she chewed, then said, "Your daughter is telling me all about the American—is it?" She looked at Sarah for confirmation, "...The Women's Artistic Gymnastics National Team?"

"The Women's Artistic Gymnastics National Team. Aly Raisman is your favorite. Say, my favorite is Aly Raisman," Sarah said, pointing at Carrie.

"Aly Raisman is *my* favorite, but Carrie might not know who that is," I told Sarah as I took the first bite of steak.

"I don't, but I'll definitely look her up," Carrie said.

I pulled Sarah in for a hug and kissed on her forehead. "Wow, you ate so much, good job."

"I like all of them, all of the Women's Artistic Gymnastics National Team, but my favorite is Gabby Douglass," Sarah said to Carrie.

"Sarah is an amazing gymnast herself," Patrick said.

"Are you?" Carrie said.

"I'm going to go swimming now," Sarah said, getting up.

"Wait a couple more minutes for your food to settle, okay?"

She groaned as she stood.

"Okay, I'll make a deal with you. Go sit with your aunts for five minutes. You can put your feet in the Jacuzzi, then I'll go get you and you can go swimming. Deal?"

"No," Sarah said.

"Okay, you can sit here with us, or go put your feet in the Jacuzzi. Pick one," I emphasized.

"Jacuzzi," she bellowed as she walked away. I watched her as she walked toward Susan and Beza, but turned around when she sat beside them.

"Your daughter is too cute for words," Carrie said.

"She's a handful," I said.

"One day I want to have a little girl just like her. One like her and one just like Kay, and they'll be best friends," Carrie said.

"You can borrow Kay whenever you want," Patrick smirked.

"Speaking of Kay, you have to teach me how to do those braids. I'm afraid I'm rather useless on all those mommy things, but you just made her so happy," Carrie said.

"Sure, I'll teach you. It's actually really easy. It just takes practice," I said.

"I never had any sisters—or girls really—in my life at all until Kay," Carrie said.

"There's Emily," Patrick said, then to me he added, "My sister's daughter."

"Yeah, but Emily always has short hair. Besides, she's awful and she hates me," Carrie said, shaking her head.

"Sorry to change the subject, but I just have to tell you that this is *the* most beautiful spot for a house I've ever seen. I didn't even know that this part of Coral Beach existed. How long have you lived here?" I asked Patrick.

"See, isn't it beautiful? It's the best house in town. But Patrick hates it," Carrie said, tsk-tsk-ing under her breath.

"I don't hate it, Carrie. I actually love it here..." He shook his head and exhaled heavily. "You're always stirring the pot."

"On that note, I'm going to get another drink," she grinned and winked at me.

Patrick gave me a small smile. "It's complicated... because of my father."

"You don't need to talk about it if you don't want to." I took another bite of steak, filling my mouth with the juicy, spicy meat.

"I don't really mind. I mean... it's fine. My father is just very patriarchal, and I spent, well, pretty much my entire adult life trying to rebel against that. Which sounds way cooler than what I did. Basically, I just refused to work for him, or anyone he was friends with. When Shelly and I split, the firm I was working for started complaining about the amount of hours I needed to take off. They weren't happy that I could no longer work late nights or weekends—even if there was a big international client coming in. They asked me to take a look at my priorities, and I did. So I quit.”

“Good job,” I said.

“Thanks,” he grinned. “In the three months of furious job searching that followed, I received only one job offer that would both provide for us and be flexible with my hours.” He gave me a meaningful look.

“Your dad,” I said.

“You probably think I’m a joke now, huh?”

“No, I work for my dad. Mike’s Saloon… my dad is Mike. My dad gave me a similar job offer after Logan died. We weren’t making it, and I wasn’t about to take on loans I couldn’t possibly pay back, so I made the same choice you made,” I said.

“You and your dad get along?”

“Yeah,” I said.

“There’s the difference. My father is a cold front, and I’m the warm front and whenever we come together, it’s like there’s a tornado,” he said.

“I didn’t know tornados formed like that,” I teased.

“Well, I think there also has to be a thunderstorm. The rest of my family is the thunderstorm,” he said.

“Alright, I get it. But, if you don’t mind me asking, how does any of this make you hate where you live?”

“Sorry, I got a sidetracked with analogies. After I decided to work for him, my father threw me a surprise ‘I finally own you’ party at this house.”

"Did he put 'you are my slave' on the cake?" I asked.

He chuckled. "I think it was, 'Welcome to the Company,' but the meaning was the same. At first I thought this house was just an event rental, but at the end of the party, he gathered the hundred or so people around and announced that this house was a gift for me and Kay. Then he took Kay and the rest of the party to her new bedroom, which is basically a princess castle room. It had everything she could ever want in there."

"Oh, I get it. That does suck," I said before taking another bite.

"Yeah. The house we used to live in was much smaller. It didn't have a pool or the beach, but I bought it, and paid it off entirely on my own. Most of the furniture had been bought in pieces from online stores, but Kay and I had put them together and she'd added bits of art to all of them."

"What happened to the house and stuff?" I asked.

"I've been renting it out furnished," he said.

"Well, at least you can always go back," I said.

"Maybe," he said. "But, to be honest, this place is growing on me. We've been here for a while now, and it's feeling more like our place than my father's gift. He still has a key and feels no need to knock, but he's too busy to just show up, so it works out."

"Well, there are definitely worse places to be forced into," I said with a smile.

"Very true," he said.

I set my fork down on my now empty plate. "By the way, this food could not have been better; I can't believe I ate all of that."

He grinned. "I'm glad you liked it. I love to cook, but I rarely do."

I glanced over my shoulder. "I want to talk more, but I have a feeling if I don't get Sarah into that bathing suit, she'll just go in in her clothes."

Patrick stood, grabbing our plates. "Yeah, of course. Here, follow me."

"Thank you. Do you want some help washing the dishes?" I asked.

"No," he chuckled. "I'd much rather you just have fun."

I cupped my hands around my mouth. "Hey Sarah!" I called over.

When she looked up, I gestured her over.

She bounded over to me, and we followed Patrick.

Patrick grabbed a swimsuit and towel from where it was stacked on a pillar. "The bathroom is just in the house, want me to show you?"

"Do you mind if I show them? I was just in there." Amy said from my side, startling me.

"Oh, of course, go ahead," Patrick said with a smile. He set the towel and bathing suit in Amy's outstretched arms.

"Thanks Amy," I said, taking Sarah's hand.

"You're welcome."

Upon reentering the house, Amy gestured for us to turn left down a hallway, and then pointed to a door on the right. "It's through there, baby," she said, handing Sarah the bathing suit.

When Sarah had disappeared inside the restroom, Amy turned a glare on me, her arms crossing over her chest.

"What did I do now?"

"Will you stop saying embarrassing stuff?" she hissed.

"What did I say that was embarrassing?" I asked.

She hushed me and glanced around. "The beer pong story, the hot dog eating contest... stuff like that."

I rolled my eyes. "Why is that embarrassing? Derek thought it was funny."

"Do you even realize who these people are? They're not laughing with you; they're laughing at you."

"No, they're not. And even if they are, why would I care? I have enough to worry about without caring what random people I don't even know think about me."

"That's easy for you to say. You don't have to see them all the time. You don't have to be known as the beer pong champion. I have spent a lot of time and energy on my image. I do not want to be known as the trashy daughter of a guy who owns a bar downtown. And with one comment, you undid all of that to the people who own this town."

"You might have been a beer pong champion, Amy, but you were never trashy. You competed with grace and decorum, and you never once slurped your beer. Not once," I told her.

"You don't even feel bad at all," she huffed and walked away.

"What did you think, Amy?" I called after her. She paused and looked over her shoulder at me. "Did you think you were going to come here tonight and I was going to be someone other than me?"

She closed her eyes and exhaled through her nose. Her hands came up to her forehead, and she rubbed her temples. "I'm sorry, Jamie. You're right; I shouldn't expect you to not be yourself. I'm just used to these two parts of my life being separate."

"Honestly, Amy, I think these people would prefer the beer pong champion," I said.

She dropped her hands from her face. "Maybe they would, but they wouldn't respect the beer pong champion. It's complicated, okay? Be yourself, fine, just leave me out of it."

"Alright, fair enough," I said. "I love you, I wasn't trying to embarrass you."

"Yeah, I know," she sighed, "I love you too, Jamie," she said before turning away.

A moment later, Sarah came out of the bathroom in a bright pink bathing suit. "Bye Mom, I'm going to the pool," she told me.

Laughing, I said, "Wait for me. I'm coming too, goofball." Walking into the bathroom, I grabbed her gymnastics leotard and clothing, before following Sarah.

Sarah walked up to the pool and jumped in right beside where Susan was sitting.

"Hey!" Susan laughed. "You splashed me, you little stinker."

Sarah broke into a fit of giggles as she treaded water. Susan kicked a little water toward Sarah, which made her giggle even more.

I grabbed a couple sodas from the cooler, then stepped up next to Susan.

"Watch out, I think this is the blast zone," Susan said.

I glanced back to the Jacuzzi where it looked like Beza was napping. "You think Beza is okay in there? Should I check on her?"

"Yeah, she's fine; I checked on her a few minutes ago. She's not sleeping, just taking a break," she said.

"I get that." I kicked off my shoes and rolled up my jeans before taking a seat beside her. "Got you a decaffeinated soda. Did you get anything to eat?"

"Are you kidding me? I'm pretty sure I ate an entire cow," she said, accepting the soda. "How about you? You having fun over there with your caffeinated soda?"

I shrugged. "Sure," I said.

"Uh, huh. I saw Amy follow you into the house, and now you look unhappy. Two and two equals your sister's lame."

"She just cares a lot about what people think about her."

"Peter completely ruined her," Susan said.

"Don't say that," I said, splashing my feet into the water and watching as all the kids flipped into underwater handstands.

"Fine, I'll think it and you'll think it, but we won't say it," she said. "I just remember when she was like this glowing vibrant human and now it's as if she's fused into his shadow."

"Seriously, Susan, let's talk about something else," I said.

"Okay, okay. I wanted to tell you something... oh, yeah, the yoga class. It's at three o'clock tomorrow," she said.

"Oh no, I can't go," I said.

"Unless Beza picks up both the kids from school and you leave straight from work in workout clothes—and Beza says that's totally fine with her," she said.

"Well, Beza is on the list of people allowed to pick Sarah up. I just feel bad for depending on her so much."

"That's what family is for, we're both going to help you through all of this," Susan said, gesturing widely with her hands.

"Well, I'll have to go over the plan with Sarah so she's not—Shit!"

"What?"

"Oh, I screwed up." I put my head in my hands.

"What's wrong?"

I looked up. "I totally forgot I was going to ask if Sarah and I could spend a couple nights over at your house. I completely forgot until right now."

"Of course you can," she said.

"Thanks, but I don't have any of Sarah's clothes or her backpack, and it's already almost her bedtime...

and I would need to tell her in advance or she'll be
super dysregulated at school."

"What's going on? Why do you have to be out
of your apartment?" Susan asked, leaning in, her gaze
serious.

"They're, uh, spraying… for bugs," I said.

"Bugs? What kind of bugs?"

"Um… cockroaches."

"Cockroaches?" She made a face. "You
seriously need to move out of that place. It has
cockroaches?"

"Not my apartment, but they spray the whole
building tomorrow. You know what, they're not
spraying until tomorrow… so we'll be fine there
tonight. But, can we stay with you tomorrow night and
for a couple nights after?"

"Of course. But is that really what's going on?"
Susan's eyes narrowed.

"Yeah… why would I lie?" I scoffed.

"I don't know, but you're making that
expression you do when you're lying,'" she said.

"I don't have a lying expression. You're crazy," I
told her.

"Fine, whatever. And yes, you can stay
whenever and for however long you need, you know
that," she said.

My gaze drifted over the sand dunes to where
the blue of the sky had ripened to a deep purple. A few
tenacious stars broke through the lingering remains of
the daylight. The last sliver of sunlight slipped over
the horizon, leaving lingering rays of its light.
Recessed lights in the pool and lanterns all around the

patio all lit up at once, as if the lights knew to perform along with the sunset.

Susan whistled. "I need to get me one of these beach houses."

"I know, right?" I chuckled.

Day Two: Seven-forty

"Mind if I join you?"

I looked up to see Carrie smiling down at us.

"Please do," Susan said, while I nodded.

"So can I ask you ladies a question?" Carrie asked, sitting down beside us and kicking her feet into the pool.

Susan stiffened, but she said, "Sure, go ahead."

"Jamie called you and Beza Sarah's aunts, are you two sisters?"

Both Susan and I relaxed.

"Oh, no, we're not sisters. Susan is Sarah's aunt from Logan's side," I said.

"Oh, wow, that's so beautiful that you stayed so close after the divorce," Carrie said, patting me on the arm. "After Shelly and Patrick split, we just never saw her again. It was as if suddenly she didn't exist. I even ran into her at a restaurant once and she hid her face from me, didn't even say 'hi.' I was so sad too, because we used to be pretty close."

"I'm not divorced. I'm a widow. My husband died in a car accident." The warm expression fell off Carrie's face and a hot blush spread up her cheeks. "Oh, I'm...so sorry... I..."

"Please don't be embarrassed, people always think it was divorce," I said.

"I'm am so sorry," she said again, before biting her lip.

"Don't be, she's fine," Susan said. "Yeah, Logan was my twin brother. But Jamie and I are kind of like sisters anyhow, we've been best friends since we were eight."

"Wow, I have to say I'm a little jealous. I grew up with only older brothers, I've never had anything resembling a sister," she said.

"They can be a pain, even the honorary ones," I said, knocking my body into Susan's.

"And you and Annie are half-sisters?" Carrie asked.

"Amy. Yeah, but my mom and dad split up when I was a baby. My dad married Amy's mom, Sharon, before I could even remember, so Sharon is like my mom too."

"You and Amy are very different from each other," Carrie said. "It's a lot easier to believe that you two are sisters." She nodded to Susan.

"People always say that because of their coloring, but if you really look at their faces you can completely see the similarities," Susan said.

"I meant more... personality wise," Carrie said, meeting my gaze with one of her brows slightly raised.

"Yeah, we're pretty different, but we're also *very close*. She's one of the people I care about most in this world." I gave Carrie a straight-lipped smile and held her gaze for an extra second before looking back to the kids in the pool. "Anyway... you said you own a flower shop. Do you ever work with Karen Blanche Wedding Services?"

Carrie looked at me with pursed lips before giving me a bright smile. "I most definitely do. Karen is actually a friend of mine."

"Small world. Beza's one of the wedding planners. Maybe you guys will work together in the future," I said.

Carrie turned her head. "You know, I thought your wife looked familiar, Susan, but I just assumed it was because she used to be a model."

We all turned to where Beza definitely looked like she was sleeping.

Susan made to stand up, but I touched her arm. "I'll go check on her," I said.

"Thanks… I feel like a walrus," she said.

"Well, you don't look like one. I hope I'm as gorgeous as you when I'm pregnant," Carrie said.

I crossed over to the Jacuzzi and crouched down beside Beza. "Hey, babes, I think you fell asleep," I said as I patted her shoulder.

"Huh," she said, raising her head and looking around blearily. "Jamie?"

"You were sleeping," I told her.

"Oh, thank you," she said.

"Hey baby, you really tired? Maybe we should go." Susan called over.

Beza wiped water down her face. "Yeah, I think maybe we should. I'm definitely feeling a little tired."

"Yeah, it's fine with me. And I'll drive. Jamie come help me up," she said, holding her hands out. Before I reached her, she turned and called, "Aiden! Time to get out!"

"You better not tip me into the pool," I said as I grabbed Susan's hands.

"I wasn't thinking about doing that before," she said.

"I'll take you with me," I promised.

"Fine," she said, using me to leverage herself up.

"Sarah, we're going in a second too. It's time to get out," I called over.

"But then I'll be all alone," Kay said.

"I'm sorry, Kay, but by the time we get home, it'll be pretty late," I said.

"You should probably be getting out pretty soon too," Carrie said.

Kay swam to the side of the pool, following where Aiden and Sarah were climbing the steps. "I'll get out now. It's boring to be in the pool all by myself. Um, Sarah's mom, can Sarah sleep over?"

"Not tonight, sweetheart," I said to Kay as I wrapped Sarah up in a towel.

"Wait a second, baby, I have a towel for you," Patrick called from somewhere behind me. He rushed up with a towel, wrapping it tightly around Kay and giving her a quick kiss on the forehead.

"Hey, I'll take the kids up to change if you want to say your goodbyes," Susan said.

"You sure?" I asked.

"Yeah, Beza already headed up there and I want to check in with her."

I grabbed up the Sarah's clothes and handed it over to Susan.

"And I'll help Kay get ready for bed," Carrie said, putting an arm around Kay and practically scooping her away from Patrick.

A moment later, Patrick and I stood alone next to the pool.

He looked at me, then at the group disappearing into the house. "I have a feeling that was intentional," he said, a smirk poised on his lips.

"I think you might be right." I huffed out a laugh. "Thank you so much for inviting us tonight Patrick, and for extending the invitation to my sister and her husband."

"Can I tell you a secret?"

"Always," I said.

"You might regret that answer someday," he said, taking a step closer.

"Ha," I said. "I probably won't. There's nothing I love more than secrets. Tell them to me."

"This barbeque was pretty much for you," he said.

"That was very friendly of you, Patrick," I said, grinning. "Can I tell you a secret?"

"Sure."

"I kind of guessed. Your family was pretty obviously sizing me up," I said.

"I'm so sorry, that wasn't my intention."

"It's cool. They know we're not actually dating, right?" I asked, taking a step closer to him.

"We're still not dating?" He took one more step in.

"Nope, definitely just friends," I said.

"Okay, I'll try to remember that," he said.

I glanced down at his lips, then back up to his eyes. My words came out a little breathily, "Good, it could get very awkward if you don't."

"Do friends ever go out to dinner together?"

"Yeah, but they have to go to crowded, unromantic places, like Kids' Pizza Arcade or Spanky's."

He burst out laughing. "Those are two very different places."

"They were just the first two places that popped into my head," I said.

"Well, I've actually never been to either, so as a friend, I think it is your duty to broaden my horizons," he said.

"Um, maybe Kids' Pizza Arcade. I'm not all that into sports. I get enough of it Thursday nights at the bar," I said.

"How's Tuesday sound?"

"For a non-date to a pizza arcade with our kids?" I asked.

"Exactly," he said.

"Yeah, that sounds... that sounds like fun," I said.

"Am I allowed to kiss you at the end of a non-date?" he asked.

I bit my lip to stop myself from smiling. "Only in the friend kissing-zones zones," I said.

"Where are those?"

"Cheeks and forehead," I said.

"Oh, good to know, thanks," he said.

"Mom!" Sarah plowed into me and I had to take a step back.

"Whoa, angel," I said, smiling down at her wet head. "It's just about bed time, ready to go home?"

"No," she said.

Shaking my head, I said, "Well, we have to, no matter what. Let's go say our goodbyes to everyone." We hugged everyone, including Amy and Peter, who had gratefully accepted Patrick's invitation to stay longer.

Even though Susan, Beza and Aiden walked out with us, Patrick, Carrie and Kay insisted walking us to our cars.

"Let's do this again," Carrie said as I rolled down my car window to say one last goodbye.

"Definitely," I said.

As I started to drive away, I read the word, "Definitely," on Patrick's lips as he watched us pull away.

"When we get home, you have to take a quick shower then straight to bed," I told Sarah. When I got no response, I asked again, "Did you hear about bed time?"

Glancing in the rearview mirror, I found Sarah fast asleep.

As we turned east, back toward town and home, the gibbous moon rose over the Transverse Mountain Ranges. Only one of her eyes was visible tonight, as if perhaps the moon was looking elsewhere.

My hands shook as I drove the final stretch to our apartment. I circled through the whole parking lot, examining every guest parking. I exited the parking lot, and drove up and down the street. Finally, I turned back into the parking lot and circled the parking lot again. I ended at Clarke's assigned spot. It was empty. Sighing, I drove up and parked in my assigned spot.

I quickly climbed out of my car, and opened Sarah's door. Unbuckling her from her seatbelt, I picked her up as gently as I could.

Sarah mumbled, but settled her head on my shoulder.

I locked my car with the remote, but threaded my keys through the fingers of my free hand, making a fist around them. I peeked around the wall. The street light failed in its reach, leaving the entire area leading up to my apartment dark.

I looked back toward my car, taking a step in that direction. I held my breath as headlights approached and a car parked in the spot next to mine.

I exhaled in relief as my neighbor Sammy and her boyfriend got out of her car.

They climbed out, carrying wetsuits in their arms, and were turning to walk in the opposite direction when I said, "Sammy?"

"Hey Jamie, everything okay?" she asked as she turned around. They both blinked over at me with bloodshot eyes.

"Kind of. Would you guys mind walking me to my door? I forgot to leave my porch light on and it's pitch black." I said, lowering my voice when Sarah groaned on my shoulder.

"Yeah, no problem," Sammy's boyfriend said.

"Yeah, of course, Jamie," Sammy echoed. They changed their direction, walking with me toward the back of the parking lot.

"You two just come back from surfing?" I whispered.

"Yeah," Sammy said in a hushed vice.

"How was it?" I asked.

"Beautiful weather but not many waves to catch. It was nice to be on the beach all day though," Sammy said.

"Really nice," her boyfriend echoed.

They waited for me to unlock my door, and I turned the porch light on for them once I was inside.

"Thank you guys so much," I whispered out the door.

"Anytime, Jamie, nice to see you," Sammy whispered back.

Once inside, I double locked the door before going to lay Sarah down in her bed. I tucked her in and kissed her forehead. Before leaving her room, I checked all her windows to see if they were locked.

I checked every window and place large enough to hide in the house.

When I'd checked the house thoroughly, I whispered to myself, "Oh, my god, Jamie, you are acting like a crazy person." But still, I checked the house one final time before going to sleep.

Day Three

Downward Facing Dog

Day Three: Seven O'clock

I woke with Sarah's cheek smashing into mine. "Space, I need space," I said in a muffled voice.

"Good morning, angel!" Sarah shouted as she bounced off me, and stood up to jump on the bed.

"No," I whispered, "stop doing that. Oh my god, you have so much energy," I grumbled. I made my way to the kitchen in a blurry haze.

I stared at the empty carafe of coffee. "I hate you, Susan," I whispered as I wandered back into my room to where Sarah and my pillows were still bouncing on my bed. "Come take a quick shower baby. You didn't have one last night," I said. I walked across the hall into the bathroom and turned the water on. "Time to shower, Sarah," I called when she didn't come over.

After a few more seconds, the springs on my bed ceased their screeching, and a loud thump sounded. A moment later Sarah appeared in the bathroom.

"I will take a shower now, Mom," Sarah said.

"Thank you baby, I'll set clothes out for you on your bed. Do you want me to make you something for breakfast or just yogurt and fruit?" I asked.

"Yogurt, bananas, juice," she said.

"Sounds good. Don't take too long because you have to go on the bus today," I told her before leaving the bathroom.

Trudging back into my room, I dressed for work, cringing when I opened my underwear drawer only to find the stupid lacey thongs.

"Shit, I forgot to go stupid underwear shopping," I grumbled as I grabbed a red lacey g-string. I finished dressing in my work clothes, then went to Sarah's room to make her bed and lay out her outfit for the day. I packed two additional bags. One overnight bag for me and Sarah, and one bag with my yoga clothes.

Going into the kitchen, I grabbed two yogurts from the fridge and two bananas from their basket. While eating the banana, I checked Sarah's backpack to make sure it had everything she needed in it and set it by the door.

"Time to get out of the shower, angel," I said at the door and waited until I heard the water turn off.

My phone beeped with a new text and I crossed back into my bedroom to grab it.

Cameron: Good morning beautiful.

I bit my lip. A million hummingbirds took flight in my stomach, but a strange bout of tears welled up in my eyes.

Me: Hey yourself.

Cameron: I had a dream about you.

Me: A good dream?

Cameron: A sad dream, I just needed to check in.

Me: Oh, well, I'm fine, Sarah's fine, just about to head to school. You okay?

Cameron: Yeah. Are you going to have a moment to talk today? I have some stuff I want to talk to you about.

Taking a deep breath, I closed my eyes on the exhale. A single tear dropped from my lashes and slowly made its way down my cheek. I wiped it away.

Me: I was thinking of closing the shop early today anyway; want to just come by at your usual time?

Cameron: Sounds good, I'll see you then.

I reread the entire text conversation before stowing my phone in my purse.

Sarah's bedroom door opened and she walked out of her room.

"Did you brush your teeth?" I asked her as she walked through the living room toward the breakfast nook.

"Yes," she said, opening her mouth in a big, exaggerated way.

"Ha, ha, okay, go eat your breakfast," I told her. I brushed out her tangles as she ate, ignoring her glares and grumbles.

"Alright, bus time," I told her after she finished her yogurt.

I walked over to the door and hoisted the duffle bag and sports bag.

After unlocking the door, I cracked it open, and peered around it. Clarke's yard appeared to be empty. Without making a sound, I led Sarah out into the mist, making sure to lock my door after we exited.

The thick mist rested on the ground, leaving only what was a couple feet in front of us clear. We walked up the path to stand in front of one of my neighbor's cars. A glance over my shoulder told me Clarke's car was now in its assigned space.

"Aunt Beza is going to pick you up from class today, baby. We're going to spend the night at aunt Beza and Aunt Susan. You and me are both going to spend the night there."

"I love you so much, Mom," Sarah told me.

"I love you so much too, angel." I gave her a quick kiss on the top of the head as the growl of the school bus's engine approached.

The bus pulled up in front of us, and when the doors swung open, the loud voices of a bunch of children speaking sounded out from the doors.

"Hey Henry," I said, as the bus driver looked down at us.

"Morning Jamie. Another loud morning," he said.

Sarah walked up the steps to the bus, turning and walking away from us down the aisle.

"I think it'll be okay. She had a really good morning," I told him.

"Alright then," he said, looking back over his shoulder and into the bus. He turned to me. "You have a great day."

"You too," I said as the doors closed.

The rows of kids passed by as the school bus returned into the fog.

Turning away from my apartment, I started the much longer path around the entire section of duplexes. The eucalyptus trees lining the sidewalk dropped leaves, fluttering down around me. I plucked one from the air and inhaled its strong scent. My gaze darted around the empty street. The street lights were still lit, the fog clearly outlining their path.

I examined each parking spot and the spaces between them as I made my way to my car. When I reached my car, I jumped in, locked the doors and drove out of the parking lot.

Turning the radio on to a classic rock station, I sang along at the top of my lungs until I parked alongside the mural of Jack climbing the beanstalk. Walking up the sidewalk, I stopped before the tree that stretched out its branches in front of my shop. Nestled among its big, green, heart-shaped leaves were three stubborn blossoms. The street showed no trace of the buds that had so recently splattered the sidewalks.

I turned to the store and unlocked the door.

"Morning sunshine!" Chris called out from behind the counter the moment I stepped inside.

"Morning moonshine," I called back.

"I wish! Everything's ready if you want to open her up," Chris called.

I flipped over our sign from open to closed and said, "Ta, da." Walking behind the counter, I put on a clean apron and washed my hands.

"So, I have big news," I said while my gaze was still glued to the hot, soapy water on my hands.

Chris stepped up next to the sink, and I had to look up at him. "You're pregnant," he said.

"Shut up! Don't even say those things out loud!" I told him, splashing him with soapy water when he started laughing.

"I'm sorry, I actually thought you were going to say that." He wiped his face off with a rag and threw it in the bin designated for dirty rags.

"No, I'm not pregnant. I'm taking your advice," I said. "And I'm going to…" I choked up.

"Oh, sweetheart," Chris said, wrapping me in a hug. "I already knew, Susan called me."

I hugged him back. "That busybody. I can never make my own freaking announcements."

"Well, for what it's worth, I'm proud of you," he said, stepping back and giving me a grin.

"It's worth a lot. But I haven't actually done anything yet. I'm going to close the shop early today, as soon as the breakfast rush is over. I need to get all my paperwork together."

The bell over the door dinged and I turned to see our first customer walk in the door.

"Mind if I start on the register today? I'm trying to resist temptation," I said.

Chris beamed, holding a hand out toward the register. "Be my guest."

I stepped up as a middle-aged woman stopped before the register.

"Good morning. What can I get you?" I asked.

Her gaze was fixed on the completely full pastry display case. Scones, muffins, Danishes and croissants lined up in perfect rows from the glass in the front to the mirrors in the back.

"Are any of these gluten free?" she asked, her gaze still intent on the pastries.

"Um, Chris, do we have any gluten-free pastries today?"

"Yeah, the savory and sweet scones on the far right. They should be labeled," he said.

"Hey Chris, I didn't see you back there," the middle-aged woman said as she beamed over at Chris.

"Good morning," he sang, "Can I get a drink started for you?"

"Double shot skinny latte," she said.

"For here or to go?" he asked.

"Oh, to go, please," she said.

"Great," he said, marking it on a cup.

"Anything to eat? We also have gluten-free bagels," I told her.

"I'll take the savory scone," she ordered with a wide smile.

By the time I rang her up, a line had formed behind her, the bell ringing every few minutes. I moved between the cash register and the bagel station in the back as The Coffee Spot filled with customers. When there was a break in the line, I bussed tables and wiped them down quickly so new customers could sit.

"This is killing me," I said as I stood over a large carafe refilling with coffee. I inhaled the fresh coffee scent as I watched the stream pour down.

"You're not drinking coffee?"

"Susan says that I'm disgustingly addicted and I'll never be healthy until I cut down."

"Cruel woman. But you can still drink some coffee?"

"I'm allowed small doses once I've proven I'm not addicted," I said.

"Why are you letting her control you?"

"That's a seriously good question. I hate authority." I heaved a sigh. "I've just never been very good at...structure. So, I guess I'm borrowing her ability to get stuff done."

"Whatever works." He held up his hands.

The bell rang again and I spun to see a woman already waiting at the counter, and another couple lining up behind her.

"I'm sorry, what can I get for you?" I asked the tall blonde woman wearing a three-piece suit.

"I want a mocha with half and half, no whip cream," she with quick, clipped enunciation.

"Alright, for here or to go?" I asked.

"To go," she said, drumming her manicured fingers on the counter.

I marked up a cup and handed it over to Chris.

"Is that going to be all?" I asked, forcing myself to give her a warm grin.

"Yeah, just the drink," she said, holding her card out to me.

"Alright, that's going to be five dollars," I said.

"Actually, it's four," she huffed, pointing at the large wooden sign over my head.

I lowered my voice. "I'm sorry, the half and half is extra when it's in a mocha. It says it right there at the end of the menu." I pointed. "We could do it with whole milk instead."

"No, the half and half. But you're definitely not getting a tip," she said.

When I handed her the receipt and a pen, she picked it up, and started to walk away.

"Sorry, I need you to sign that one, this one is for you," I said.

She spun and glared at me. When she returned to the counter she wrote, "No tip!" in the space provided for a tip, and signed with a slash across the bottom of the paper.

"Okay, thanks," I said as I took the receipt from her and added it to the receipt pile in the cash register.

The next group, an elderly couple who were regulars, needed another minute, so I waited at the counter for them to decide.

"Mocha with half and half, no whip," Chris called, putting the drink up on the coffee counter. The woman walked up in her tall heels, grabbed her drink from the counter and strode out of the shop.

"What a psycho," the elderly man, Avery, who was next in line said.

His wife Charlie chuckled. "I think you handled her well, Jamie. I would have smacked her."

"We definitely get all types here," I said under my breath.

Chris came up behind me and pressed the button to open the register. He grabbed the women's receipt and started laughing.

"Let me see that," Avery said. When Chris passed him the receipt, he cracked up so hard he had to grab his side.

Charlie grabbed the receipt. "Ha. Like her spare change was going to put your kid through college." She handed me the receipt back.

I shook my head and put the receipt away.

"Should I make you your regular?" Chris asked.

"Yes, without a doubt," Avery said.

"Don't you speak for me, Avery," Charlie said, but she winked at me and Chris. "Yes, I'll have my regular."

"Ha, okay, anything to eat?" I asked.

"We can't decide, so we'll have one of each."

"Good choice," I said, winking back.

When I had gathered one of every pastry onto four plates, I rang them up.

Charlie paid the tab with her credit card and pulled a twenty out of her wallet, stuffing it in our tip jar. "That is for you two lovely people," she said.

"Thank you so much you guys, you didn't have to do that," I said.

They waved it away.

"If there's anything left over, bring it up and I'll wrap it in plastic, okay?" I said.

"Don't worry, there won't be," Avery said, patting his wife on the back.

The bell chimed again and again as several more customers entered, one after the other. I ate my third muffin as a seeded onion bagel toasted. When the bagel popped up, I washed my hands before preparing a lox special.

I placed the plate on the counter and called out, "Lox special!" Turning back to the register, I stopped dead.

Clarke stood at the head of the line, a placid grin on his face. He held up a hand in greeting.

I exhaled slowly, my gaze fixed on his face. Forcing a smile onto my face, I walked to the cash register. "Hey Clarke, how's it going?" I asked as casually as possible.

"Great, Jamie. So you work here?" he asked me, glancing around.

"Yep. Can I get you something?"

"Yeah, what's good here?" He ducked down over the display case, examining the few lingering pastries.

"What do you like?" I asked.

"The berry scone looks good. I'll have that." He stood, coming back up to the counter.

"Uh, huh," I said, inputting it into the cash register with shaky fingers. "That'll be two fifty."

"I want a drink too," he said, gaze on mine.

"Sure, what would you like?" I asked.

"What do you recommend?" he asked.

"Coffee, black coffee," I said, meeting his gaze.

"Okay, I'll take that, medium-sized," he said, grinning.

"Alright, that'll be four even," I said.

He gave me the four cash and then dropped another large wad of cash into the tip jar. "See you later," he said.

Day Three: Ten-thirty

I poured Clarke's coffee as fast as possible, grabbed the berry scone, and put both into to-go containers. "Black coffee, berry scone," I called out as I placed both on the coffee counter, pointedly not looking at him as I did.

Without glancing his way, I focused on the line of customers waiting for drinks. When everyone was helped, I grabbed a dish towel. As I walked through the shop, wiping up spills and clearing plates, I looked from face to face. Carrying a stack of plates to the bussing station, I heaved a sigh, closing my eyes.

"Everything okay?" Chris asked, stopping next to me.

I gave him a smile. "Yeah, I'm just feeling the coffee deprivation."

"Did you know the caffeine in tea is different than the caffeine in coffee?" he asked.

"I didn't," I said.

"It's a little known fact, but true. Have you ever had a green tea latte?" he asked, cocking an eyebrow.

"I can't say that I have," I said.

"Well, hold tight, you're in for a treat," he said.

While Chris made my drink, I tidied up the bagel station and wiped the spills from the counter.

"This is a green tea latte," Chris said, holding a drink out with one hand and flourishing his other hand out.

I looked into the cup. "It's definitely green."

"Just drink it," he said.

I took the handle of the mug, lifting the cup to my lips. The aroma that rose from the drink was a little like green tea, but not as strong, and sweeter.

"Drink it," Chris growled.

"Fine," I said, smiling as I took a small sip. "Mmmm... tastes so good."

"I told you. That's your new favorite drink," he said, smacking me lightly with a rag.

"It just might be," I said. Glancing down, I examined the large wad of cash still sitting at the top of our tips in the tip jar. I raised my gaze to Chris's. "Hey, Chris?"

"Yeah?" he said.

"Did you see that guy who came in here earlier?" I asked.

"You're going to have to be a little more specific than 'that guy'," Chris said as he returned to the espresso station.

"Never mind," I said, taking another sip of my tea latte. "So, I was thinking about calling this lady who made the offer this afternoon, what do you think? I mean—Cameron said he knew a property lawyer, so maybe I should wait until I talk to that guy but... I don't know, I'm kind of terrified. I kind of want to get it over with, and at the same time I don't really want to do it."

"Wait and talk to the lawyer," Chris said.

"You're right," I said, nodding before I took another sip.

"It'll be fine," Chris said then he looked up. "You have a big group incoming." The bell over the door chimed as a group of about thirty cyclists walked into the shop.

Chris and I worked through the orders, running out of pastries entirely too soon after the bicyclist group.

A regular came up in the line right after the last pastry was taken from the display case.

"Hey Pat, I saved you a muffin if you want it," I said in greeting.

"Thanks Jamie, I'd love it." His striking blue eyes sparkled, contrasting strongly with his trim white beard. He gave me a dimpled grin that would have made me melt if I was a few decades older. "You ran out early," he said looking at the empty display case.

"This morning was hopping. That's the first time in a long time that we ran out of pastries entirely before noon."

"Double cappuccino dry," Chris said, holding the drink over the register to Pat.

"I didn't even get a chance to order," Pat said with another grin.

"I saw you coming up in the line," Chris said as he returned to his station.

I grabbed the muffin bag I had set aside for him and handed it over to him.

"Oh, I meant to tell you happy belated birthday. Chris told me that was why you were out last Friday," he said.

"That's so nice, thank you," I said as I rang him up.

After helping the last few customers in line, I glanced up at the clock. "Oops, Chris, it's eleven thirty-five."

"Oh, good, I am feeling it this morning," Chris said, folding down his apron. He crossed over to the tip bucket. "Look at this thing," he whispered, lifting it up. "And I know Charlie put a twenty in here too."

I looked down at money, seeing that same wad of cash just visible under a layer of loose tips. "You keep it all today," I said to Chris.

"You serious? Nah, you have to be kidding me," his voice went a little high when he said it. "There has to be like two hundred or more in here."

"You always work half your shift with no one here and no tips, and I work my whole shift every time with tips. That doesn't even come close to evening things out," I said.

"Ah, Jamie, you're so sweet." He gave me a one-armed hug. "I'm not going to say no. Melissa's birthday is next week so I'm in definite need of money."

"Oh, shoot, I forgot... What day is her birthday?"

"Next Thursday. She wanted me to invite you out with us, but I know you can't because of work," he said.

"Oh, that's sweet. Are you guys going out downtown?"

"Probably," he said.

I threw out my hands. "Come by the bar, first round is on me."

Chris grinned. "I'll run it by her."

"I want to get her something, what does she want?"

"I'll get back to you on that one. I kind of need to get out of here, Jamie, I'm wiped," he said.

"Yeah, just take all the tips and don't worry about doing anything else, okay?" I patted him on his arm.

"Text me if anything happens today with selling the shop?"

"Of course," I said. Grabbing a piece of paper, I wrote, 'Shop closes at noon today, sorry for the inconvenience.' Taking a few pieces of tape from the back, I taped the sign under the 'Open' sign.

I cleared the recently vacated tables, wiping each down in turn. The moment the clock struck twelve, I walked back to the front and turned over the 'Open' sign to closed.

"You're closing?" one of the only lingering customers asked.

"Yeah, we're closing early today. If you want anything on the espresso machine, I can get something before I shut it down.

"Oh, no, I'm fine. I'll just pack up here."

"No rush," I said, waving a hand through the air.

Going back behind the counter, I cleaned out the display case and the bagel stations completely. Next I shut down the espresso machine. Chris had already cleaned it. I started on the dishes and only glanced up when I heard the bell ringing over the door. Each time I saw someone exiting rather than entering, so I returned my attention to the dishes.

After each dish was on the drying rack, I returned to cleaning the main part of the shop. When I saw no one was inside the shop, I locked the front door.

I was turning the chairs over onto the tables when someone knocked on my front door.

Turning, I looked through the window and up into Cameron's beautiful face.

A grin fought its way across my face and I had to force my feet to move slowly across the floor to let him in.

"Hey," I said when I managed to get the door open.

"Hey, baby," he said, grinning down at me.

I stepped back to let him in and locked the door behind him.

He stepped past me, his fingers grazing my hip as he passed. He peered around the shop. "Anything I can do to help?" he asked.

"No, I'm almost done. Actually... That property lawyer you're friends with, do you think it would be possible for me to talk to him?"

"I talked to him. That's why I'm here," he said.

"Oh—okay..."

"That's not the only reason I'm here." He brought his hand up to my face. His thumb brushed back and forth over my cheek. "I also want to talk about us," he said.

"There's still an us?" I asked, my voice quiet.

"There's always an us," he said.

"Okay," I said. "So let's do that part first, otherwise the stress will kill me."

He huffed out a laugh. "Well—I thought a lot about what you said last night. I don't agree with a lot of it, but one thing you definitely got right."

"What's that?"

"We're still dragging our past around with us. And not just our past, we're dragging around Vanessa and Logan too. If we keep going on this way, they'll always be part of us and that's not what I want. I want us to start over, from scratch. I want it to be as if I had asked you out after I kissed you at the Ultimate Sunshine Tour concert, like I wanted to."

"How do we do that, from scratch?" I asked.

"I'm not sure yet, but I was thinking maybe we could take a step back. Instead of acting like we're pretty much already married, we could try dating."

"No sex?" I asked, a small smile on my lips.

"People still have sex when their just dating," he said.

I tapped my chin. "I don't think they do."

He leaned in and gave me the lightest kiss on my lips. "They definitely do," he growled.

"I need to—someone asked me on a date," I said, meeting his gaze and biting my lower lip.

"What did you say?" he asked.

"I told him that I was sort of with someone, though not officially. And I said that until we'd figured out what we were doing, I couldn't start something new."

"But you didn't say no?" he said.

I shook my head.

"Did you want to say no?"

I looked at him for a few seconds, then shook my head again.

"Are you going to go out with him?" he asked.

"Maybe, I don't know—I was curious, I can't even remember what a date is like. And, he's a really nice guy."

"Are you going to sleep with him after your date?" he asked, his gaze intent on mine.

"Probably not," I said.

"Would you tell me if you do?"

"Do you want me to tell you?" I asked, cocking my head.

"Yes, I'd want you to tell me before you planned to do it," he said.

"Why?" I asked.

His hand came up to rest on my shoulders. "I heard what you said two nights ago… but where I'm coming from is different. I don't just want to be with you, Jamie, I want to end up with you. I want to move in together, get married, maybe even make Sarah a brother or sister together. If that means we need to take a step back and date other people to figure out if we want to be with each other, I can handle that. But I don't think I could get over you sleeping with someone else. If you want to do that, it'll be over between us. And, if I find out after, it will hurt me a hell of a lot more."

I reached up to touch his hand covering my shoulder, running my thumb over his knuckles. "Thank you for being so honest with me."

"I think that's what we need—a fuckload of honesty between us," he said.

"A fuckload? How much is that in shit-tons?" I grinned.

"They're the same thing," he said, pulling me into him for a kiss. "Hey, Jamie," he said against my lips.

"Yeah?" I murmured.

"I dare you to go on a date with me this friday." He leaned back a little to grin down.

"Look at that grin! You're so sure I'm going to accept?" I asked, grabbing his biceps.

"I know you. You never turn down a dare," he said.

"You fight dirty," I said.

"Hmm, dirty." He gave me a heated look and moved his hands down my sides, gripping my hips.

He glanced over my shoulder. "Here, come over here," he said, nodding toward the back of the shop.

I glanced back over my shoulder to see a couple pass by the shop. "It's fine, it's really hard to see in when the sun is reflecting against the windows like that," I said, but when Cameron grabbed my hand, I followed him back to my office.

Once inside, he shut the door behind us.

My breaths came faster when his hands came back to my hips. "I know what you're thinking and we—probably should..." I trailed off.

Cameron grinned down at me. "Probably should or probably shouldn't?" he asked.

I ran my hand up under his shirt over the muscles of his stomach. "What if it's like a health code violation?"

"It's not a health code violation. It's not like I'm bending you over your bagel bar," he said.

"Bagel station," I breathed.

He chuckled as his lips came down onto mine. His kiss was a slow caress, a wet glide over my lips. His tongue just barely moved against mine before he pulled his mouth away. "But I'm not going to fuck you right now," he said.

"You're not?" I asked as I blinked up into his gaze.

He kissed me lightly once. "Nope, I'm taking a step back, remember?"

"How far a step?" I asked.

"Far enough so that we can actually see each other again, and not just in the relationship we've thrown ourselves into," he said.

"So, if I go on a date with you, I get sex?" I asked.

"What do you take me for, a sure thing?" he asked, pressing his hips into mine and telling me in the most carnal way possible how much he wanted me.

"Um, no. But I just might be," I said.

"And I love that about you," he said, grinning down.

"Yeah, I bet." I rolled my eyes. "So, this means you're not going to sleep with anyone else too, unless you tell me?"

"That's exactly what this means," he said.

"But you might date other people?" I asked.

"Would you have a problem with it if I did?" he asked.

"That's a complicated question." I shook my head, and looked away. "Of course I wouldn't be jumping for joy, but I want things to be fair and…" I sighed. "We probably both need a little perspective, you know?" I met his gaze. "But I don't want to know about it—actually I do…" I shook my head again. "Nope, I don't."

He laughed, pulling me to him and wrapping his arms tightly around me.

"I'll check and see if Sarah can spend the night with my dad and Sharon this Friday. Maybe we can spend the night at your place?"

"You're making a lot of assumptions," he said.

"I shouldn't get a babysitter?" I asked.

"No, definitely get a babysitter. Do you mind if I plan our first date?"

"Not at all," I whispered.

"Thank you, baby," he said. Then he stepped back to pull his phone from his pocket. "And the other thing. The property lawyer said you can call him at twelve thirty-five, and that's in about five minutes."

"Oh awesome," I said, taking his phone. "I'm just going to grab that offer…" I looked through my desk, first finding the offer I had turned down a couple months ago, then pulling out the second, much more recent offer from the same company.

I pulled them both out, glancing over the numbers once more.

"How much was the judgment lien on this place?" Cameron asked, looking over my shoulder at the numbers.

"Two million, fixed," I said.

"How much do you still owe?" he asked.

"One million eight hundred thousand and change," I said.

"You made that kind of profit in one year even after you cut your hours in half?" Cameron asked.

"Yeah, Chris and I got it up to twenty-five percent. Loyal customers, Chris's amazing food, low labor cost and very little waste," I said.

"No wonder this lady wants to buy it so much. Is this offer over market?" he asked.

"Yeah, two million is still the estimated value. Okay, I'm dialing him now," I said as I pressed the phone button on Cameron's screen.

"Mark Hamm's office," a man's voice answered.

"Hello, my name Jamie Scott—"

"I'll patch you through, he only has a minute," the man said before there was a ring on the other line.

"You've reached Mark Hamm," a more masculine voice said.

"Hello, my name is Jamie Scott, I—"

"Cameron's friend, I've been expecting to hear from you. Look Jamie, a client needed to come in during my lunch break, so I only have a second, but if you can set up a meeting with the buyer's broker tomorrow morning before nine-thirty, I'll be able to go with you."

"Um, I can definitely try. Do I need to sign a contract or something with you?" I asked.

"No, I'm going to be doing this as a favor to Cam."

"Oh, you don't have to—"

"I won't hear it, Jamie." His tone was all business. "But it's important that I note that I'm not your attorney, I'll just be going in an advisory capacity, is that okay with you?"

"Yeah sure, I—"

"I'm pretty sure that's all you'll be needing, but if you need to hire me on as an attorney, we'll talk about that if it comes to it. Do you have a fax machine handy?"

"Yep," I said.

"Okay, write down this fax number," he said, before reading out a fax number to me. "Okay, I want you to send me every scrap of paper you have related to the offer, the judgment lien and the shop's worth as soon as you possibly can."

"Okay," I said.

"Great. My client just arrived, so I'm going to have to let you go. Leave me a message with my assistant as soon as you get a meeting time with the buyer."

"I will. Thank you so much, Mr. Hamm."

"You're welcome, talk to you soon." He hung up.

"Wow," I said as I handed back Cameron's phone.

"Yeah, he's definitely got a take-charge personality," Cameron said, chuckling. "Great guy, though. And he has 2014 Benz black series." He looked off at nothing with a small grin on his face. "I love that machine."

"Well, thank you for setting this up," I said, giving him a quick kiss on the cheek.

He wrapped one hand around the back of my neck and pulled me in closer to him. Our lips met, as if they were the opposite poles of two magnets, meant to join. He opened my mouth with his, deepening the kiss as his fingers threaded through my hair.

The length of his body pressed into mine and I couldn't stop the small moan that came from my lips. He echoed my moan.

I pulled back to whisper, "Are you still not going to fuck me?"

"Oh, I'm going to fuck you. I'm just not going to fuck you right now," he said, grinding his body further into mine.

"Tease," I whispered.

He laughed. "Aren't you supposed to be faxing papers?"

"I would be if you weren't here distracting me," I replied, grabbing his waist.

"Well, I need to leave anyway, lunch is over," he said.

"Oh, no, you didn't get anything to eat! I shouldn't have closed the shop... Let me go make you a bagel or something."

"You really think I'd rather have a bagel than this?" he asked, leaning down for a kiss again. "I'll just stop by the burger place on the way out of here."

"Are you sure?" I asked.

"Definitely," he said, giving me on last quick kiss before his hand squeezed my butt cheek.

"You," I said smacking his butt once as he left my office chuckling. After a second, I rushed out of my office after him. "Ha, sorry, I forgot, I have to let you out." Unlocking the door, I gave Cameron one more quick kiss before he left.

Right after I locked the door, Mitch walked up, giving me a big smile and pulling on the door handle.

"Sorry," I mouthed to him through the window while I pointed to the sign.

The smiling expression on his face fell.

"Wait," I said, holding up one finger. Rushing back to the coffee counter, I lifted the carafes and found them all hot and full. I filled up a to-go cup and brought it back to the door.

After unlocking the door, I held out the cup to Mitch.

"Oh, hey Jamie, so, um, is that for me? Because I was just sort of wanting to come inside for a minute, but I don't really have the money for a cup of coffee right now."

"No Mitch, this was extra. I was just about to throw it out," I told him. "I'm so sorry but I have to close early today."

"Well, if you're just going to throw it out," he said, taking the coffee. He gave me a wide grin, showing all his missing teeth. "I'm all cleaned up, you see?" he asked.

My gaze passed over his clean shaven face, recently washed sweatshirt and weather worn jeans. "You look great, Mitch. Are those new clothes?" I asked.

"Yeah. I have a job interview today. Someone set it up for me," he said, beaming. "It's at the full service gas station right over there." He pointed down the street. "If I get a job there, will you and Chris come say hi when I'm at work?"

"I definitely will, and I'll tell Chris. I'm sure he'll want to too," I said.

"It's through an outreach program so I really think they might actually hire me. They're supposed to do that, right? Hire people in outreach programs?" he asked.

"Um, I really don't know about that, sorry," I said.

"Oh, that's okay Jamie, that's okay."

"I have to do a couple things, so I really need to get back inside, Mitch. Good luck with your interview, I bet you'll do great."

"You think so?" he asked.

"Yeah, I really do," I said.

"Okay, well, you have a great day, Jamie. Next time I see you, I'll be able to buy anything in your store."

"Sounds awesome, Mitch. Good luck." I closed the door and locked it, giving Mitch one more wave before returning to my office.

While the two offers I received fed through my fax machine, I pulled out the judgment lien folder. I leafed through the court documents and the fifteen year pay back deal I'd made with the owner of the lien.

I read under my breath, "This agreement is made between Timepiece Corporate, hereafter referred to as the creditor, and Jamie Scott, hereafter referred to as the debtor." Sighing, I added the form to the pile feeding into the fax machine.

Next I pulled out some tax and asset forms, detailing the worth of the shop's equipment. When all the forms had gone through, I sat down on my office chair and pulled out my phone. With shaking fingers, I dialed the number on the offer, pressing the speaker button on my phone after the first ring.

"You've reached Nicole Murphy's office," a woman's voice said.

"Hello, is this Harrington's corporate office?"

"Yes, but this is not the main line, would you like me to transfer you?"

"I'm not sure. My name is Jamie Scott, someone from your company sent me an offer on my coffee shop a week ago. Actually, they sent in two offers, but it's really hard to read the signature," I said.

"If it was an offer, it was probably from the company's broker, but just give me a moment and I'll check with Ms. Murphy since you were given her direct line."

"Thanks," I said.

Crackly classical musical played over the line, sounding suspiciously like Beethoven. A smooth sounding voice came over the line, "Harrington's Coffee Shops, they're more than just coffee shops, they're your home away from home." Then the crackly Beethoven continued. After another couple seconds of butchered classical music, the sound silenced.

"Hello," the same woman's voice said.

"Hi," I said.

"I'm connecting you through to Nicole. One moment please," she said.

"You've reached Nicole," a low, feminine voice said.

"Hello, my name is Jamie Scott, I—"

"I know, Clara told me. You're calling about the offer I sent to you a week ago. This is for the shop downtown, right? The Coral Beach shop?"

"Yeah," I said.

"And you're willing to sell?"

Sighing, I said, "I think so. I definitely want to set up a meeting if that's possible."

"It is. What time works for you?" she said.

"The best time would be tomorrow at eight, if that's at all possible?" I said.

"At the shop?" she asked.

"We could, but it's pretty loud and busy here in the morning," I said.

"Could you make it to Harrington Corporate offices? We're about fifteen minutes North?"

"I could make it at eight-fifteen," I said.

"Could you give me one second, Jamie?" she asked.

"Of course," I said, and was rewarded with more distorted classical music, this time Mozart.

After about five minutes, the line went silent and Nicole said, "Jamie?"

"Yeah?" I asked.

"Eight-fifteen works just fine for us, we'll see you here. Do you know our address?" she asked.

"Is it eight four three Sea Breeze Way?" I read off the offer form.

"That's it exactly. Take the elevator to the third floor then come straight back and my receptionist will help you."

"Okay, I'll see you then. I'll have a property lawyer with me, if that's okay? I'm not sure if you're aware, but there's a judgment lien on the property—"

"We're aware," she said.

"Alright, well, he's going to help me figure out how to transfer. If I do transfer—that is."

"That should be fine," she said.

"Oh, good, thank you," I said.

"See you then," she said before the line went dead.

Day Three: One-thirty

After calling back Mr. Hamm and telling his assistant about the meeting's time and place. I walked back into the shop and behind the counter. I pressed the button for the final receipt and as the long tape printed out, I texted Chris.

Me: I might have to come in an hour late tomorrow for a meeting with the company that made the offer. Is that going to be okay?

Almost instantly, my phone rang, Chris's number flashing on the screen. "I'm so sorry Jamie," he said in a low, raspy voice that didn't sound much like him.

"Oh, no, are you okay?"

"I think I'm sick, it just suddenly came on," he said.

"Oh no, Chris! I'm so sorry," I said.

"I don't think I'm going to be able to make it tomorrow," he said.

"Oh, of course not. Is there anything I can get you?"

"Melissa is at the store now, she left work early," he said. "I really hope I didn't get you or any of the customers sick."

"I feel fine, I'm sure everyone is fine. Just take it easy and call me if you don't feel better on Wednesday. I'll figure it out."

"I feel so guilty," he said.

"Shut up. I don't even remember the last sick day you took. You are more than due. Just rest and feel better."

"Okay," he said.

"Call me if you need anything," I said.

"Okay, I will," he said before hanging up the phone.

After counting the money and totaling up the receipts, I added up the daily till, finding the register to be a dollar and fifteen cents short. After putting the money and receipts into the bank deposit bag, I walked into the back office and slipped the bag into the safe.

On a piece of paper in thickly printed letters I wrote: 'Store Will Be Closed on April 19th. Sorry for the inconvenience.' Walking up to the front, I replaced my hastily made sign that was already on the door with the new one.

I finished sweeping and mopping the floors before emptying the coffee carafes and filling them with water so they could soak. When everything was clean, I took two trips to the dumpsters in the back, first with the recycling, then with the trash bags. After locking up the back, I returned behind the counter to grab the gym bag I'd stashed there.

Going into the shop's bathroom, I changed into yoga pants, a sports bra and a tank top. When I leaned forward to examine my outfit, my hair fell into my face and I inhaled a strong coffee smell.

"Oh my god, I want coffee," I whispered as I pulled a chunk of hair to my nose. Reluctantly, I pulled my hair back into a ponytail.

My phone buzzed and I picked it up from where I had set it on the counter.

Susan: You coming to yoga?

Me: Yes, just leaving work now. Text me the directions?

When she did, I typed them into the Maps app on my phone. After gathering all my stuff, I turned off all the lights and locked up the shop on my way out. On the way to the car, I updated The Coffee Stop's social media pages, announcing that the shop would be closed tomorrow. Even before I had climbed into my car, my alerts dinged with and comments from regulars saying that they'd miss us in the morning, or asking if something was the matter.

"Oh, that's so sweet," I mumbled to myself as I took a seat in my car, but left the keys in my lap. I responded to the comments, saying everything was fine and that we would miss them too.

I drove down the main street to the opposite side of downtown, reading the signs above the storefronts until I saw 'Namaste Yoga Studio' in big decorative blue letters. I pulled in front of the studio into a metered spot.

Using my credit card, I paid for an hour and a half at the pay kiosk, not really knowing how long a yoga class went for.

The doorbells jingled as I opened the door and was met with a strong lavender scent.

I stepped up behind a woman who was filling out some sort of paperwork.

"Hey."

I turned to see Susan in neon green stretch pants trying to fight her way off a couch along the wall.

"Beep, beep, beep," I said, offering her hands.

"You're not funny. That'd only be funny if I was backing up. So, is this the first time you've worn those yoga pants actually to yoga?" she asked as she grabbed my hands.

"Yep," I grunted under her weight. "Though I think I might be getting enough exercise just helping you stand all the time."

I turned to head back to the desk the other woman had been standing behind before, but Susan said. "I already did all that for you, just come back with me." We stepped into a hallway and up a long staircase to the second level.

"I'm glad I'm with you. Can we stand in the back where no one will notice us?" I asked as we walked into a large room.

Long gleaming lines of wood stretched across the studio's floor, seeming to stretch on forever into the walls of mirrors on three sides of the room. The third side was a long line of windows that looked down on the downtown street.

Before the windows, a young woman with frizzy brown hair sat almost cross-legged, with one foot in front of the other, on a mat. She greeted us with a wide serene smile. "Good afternoon, ladies. Please, go ahead and grab a mat and some blocks and find a nice open place to lay it out." She gestured across the room to where a pile of rolled up pink mats and purple foam blocks sat side by side.

I glanced at the other women in the room as we passed, my gaze passing over three women before I halted mid-step. I looked from woman to woman.

Quickening my pace, I caught up to Susan just as she pulled a mat from the pile.

I leaned down to her and whispered in a really low voice, "Susan, this is pregnant lady yoga."

"Yeah?" she said back, not whispering at all.

"I'm not pregnant," I whispered, glaring at her.

"Yoga is yoga," she said in a low voice with a shrug. "Anyway, I'm not supposed to go to regular yoga classes." She grabbed her belly. "You know, because I'm pregnant."

"I didn't need you to go; I could have gone by myself."

"But I wanted to go, I've been wanting to do this for months," she said.

"You have to be kidding me. What if they kick me out?" I asked.

"It's not a problem," she said, handing me a yoga mat. "I wrote on your intake form that you're two months pregnant, if anyone asks, you're just not showing yet."

"This was completely premeditated. I'm going to kill you," I whispered.

"You've been saying that for twenty years, yet I survive," she said "Now, could you grab me some blocks too?"

I glared at her as I grabbed four blocks. We walked to the back of the group, laying out our mats and placing the blocks at the end.

"Welcome friends, my name is Jennifer. Thank you so much for joining this class and being here and present with me." She grinned around at us. "I'm going to ask you all to sit as I am in siddhasana, or if it's too hard, go ahead and sit cross-legged. First, I just want us all to get very grounded in our bodies, and our breath. I'm going have you place one hand at your heart, while your other arm crosses over your belly, really embracing your baby."

Following the rest of the class, I took one arm and wrapped it over my stomach.

"Now close your eyes and really concentrate on the sweet little presence that is growing inside your womb. Some of us know a lot about our babies, whether they're a boy or girl, what they're name is going to be, while others of us are just beginning to be introduced."

I shot a glare at Susan, who was sitting eyes closed with a happy serene smile on her face.

I closed my eyes again as the instructor continued.

"So throughout this yoga session, I want us to let our minds really center on the little one inside us and let our breath extend out."

We took several guided breaths while the instructor detailed 'our' babies' development in the womb.

"Alright ladies, go ahead and open your eyes." She blinked around at each one of us. "Hello."

The ladies around the room chuckled.

I looked over at Susan. When she met my gaze, I pursed my lips and raised my eyebrows.

Her shoulders bobbed and she grinned at me before looking back to the front of the studio.

"We're going to be moving into our poses now, but it's really important to remember to go at your own pace. Some here are on their thirty-eighth week, while others are on their eighth." She raised a hand and pointed straight at me.

Several heads turned around to glance back at me.

Susan made a noise that distinctly sounded like laughter.

I made myself wave and grin at the women before they returned their gaze to the front.

"Okay, so let's pull out our legs a bit and move into our bound angle pose, really feel that stretch. Feel free to bounce gently in your legs. This is a pose that will really help us open up our hips and relieve our lower back pain, in turn, getting ready for when we go into labor."

Pulling my feet together, I moved into the pose with my knees out to either side of me. We continued to move through poses fluidly, first through different sitting poses, to all fours, and then to standing poses.

After an hour of stretching out muscles I didn't know I had, and staying in a squat for longer than I would have thought possible, we stood. The entire class raised out arms in a big circle until our hands met in the middle, we then lowered our hands into a praying position and bowed to each other.

"It was lovely spending this time with you ladies. Make sure to drink lots of water."

"That wasn't so bad, was it?" Susan asked, grinning over.

"No, I guess it was pretty nice. And... I'm now the soil cocooning a growing acorn, that's pretty neat," I said while rolling up my yoga mat.

"Healthy dirt, you are healthy and dirty," she said.

I smacked lightly her on the head with my yoga mat. "Go drink water."

We walked toward the group of big bellied ladies gathering around the yoga mat pile.

"Excuse us!" Susan pretty much yelled, making most of the women glance back and a couple of them shift out of our path.

After we put our equipment away, I turned around and just avoided colliding with a big pregnant belly.

"Oh, sorry," I said, contorting my body so that I wouldn't rub bellies with her.

She smiled. "Oh, that's fine, just trying to put my mat away too," she said with a thick southern accent.

Seeing a break in the ladies, I stepped out of her path.

Her short, straight red hair flopped around her sharp features as she turned back to me. "So you're only eight weeks?"

"Um—yeah," I said, trying to back out of the crowd of women without bumping into any of them.

"How are you feeling? Do you have morning sickness?" she asked.

"Yeah, she has it bad. Vomiting all the time," Susan said, patting me on the arm. "Sometimes in the afternoons too, poor thing."

When I turned a look on her, Susan just kept her placid expression.

"Oh, don't be embarrassed. We all had it." The woman offered her hand. "I'm Savannah."

"Jamie and Susan," I said.

"And how many weeks are you, Susan?" Savannah asked. They started talking and Savannah accompanied us all the way to my car. I tuned them out as they discussed their labor plans.

"I ideally want a water birth, though I know sometimes they won't allow it depending on the circumstances," Savannah was saying.

"My wife had a water birth with our son," Susan said.

Immediately, Savannah's cheeks turned a bright shade of red. "Wow, that's beautiful," she said, her voice a little choked.

"It was beautiful," Susan said.

"Yeah, it really was," I agreed, turning to them.

"Well, will you ladies be coming back, do you think?" Savannah asked, her voice cheery and smile verging on manic.

"Probably," Susan said.

"Well, it was nice to meet you and congratulations on your babies and your—marriage."

"Oh, that's not my wife, that's my sister-in-law," Susan said, her cheeks fighting a grin.

Savannah's shoulder's visibly relaxed. "Oh, well, again, it was nice to meet you. See you later." She walked away from us up the street.

"She was nice," Susan said, chuckling.

"Are you really going to come back?" I asked skeptically.

"If you do," she said.

"Unless I really start putting on the pounds, the ruse wouldn't last long," I told her.

"Or you could just go get pregnant," Susan said.

"Shut the fuck up. That's the second time someone said that today—third if you count Cameron saying he'd like to make a sibling for Sarah one day."

"Holy shit, he said that to you?" Susan said.

"Kind of. Where's your car?" I asked.

"Beza and I carpooled today; she dropped me off on the way to pick up the kids. So you can give me a ride home and give me all the juicy details."

"Alright," I said, unlocking my car remotely.

When we were both inside, Susan turned to me. "He came to your work?"

"Yeah, I closed early so I could call the company that made an offer on the shop." As we drove to her house, I gave her all the details of the phone call with Mr. Hamm, the one with Nicole Murphy, and what Cameron and I had decided about our relationship.

"I have always thought that boy had a beautiful soul," Susan said.

"He's pretty special," I said as I turned onto her street.

"Are you going to lose your shit if he starts dating someone else?"

"I'd like to think that I'm the kind of person who could be okay with him doing what I'm asking for of him. If that makes any sense," I said.

"Yeah, it does. Well, Beza and I will definitely watch Sarah for your date this Friday," she said.

"Honestly Susan, I really feel like I'm asking too much of you two. You guys don't need to do everything for me. Sharon is always begging for time with Sarah and my dad doesn't work on Fridays anymore. So together, I think they could manage things without it being too stressful."

"Well, it's up to you, but watching Sarah is never too much for us. Actually sometimes it's less work since she and Aiden entertain each other for hours."

"Okay, well, I'll ask my dad and if he says he can't, could she stay with you?" I asked. "I also feel kind of bad passing her off to other people so much."

"Stop with the mommy guilt," Susan said.

"Fine," I said as I parked on the street before her house.

Day Three: Four-thirty

After grabbing the overnight bag from the backseat, I followed Susan up to her house. As we stepped inside, I dropped my bag and purse onto the bright green entrance table. The colorful interior of the familiar house immediately made me smile. The multicolored furnishings and walls managed to both clash and complement each other. Large multi-colored tapestries covered every wall.

I paused by one, touching its edges. "I loved Peru, I wish we could go back there someday."

"We should, we'll do it when the kids are teenagers or something," Susan said, running a finger along the tapestry's edge.

We walked into the dining room, following the excited voices. Sarah and Aiden sat at the table, excitedly spooning macaroni and cheese into their mouths and talking to each other with their mouths full.

Beza was laughing so hard, tears were running down her face.

"You guys look like you're having fun," Susan said, giving Beza a kiss before taking a seat next to Aiden.

"How was yoga?" Beza asked.

"She tricked me, it was prenatal yoga," I said, pointing at Susan. "I always fall for these things." I shook my head as I sat down, swinging an arm around Sarah's chair.

"And you always will," Susan said. "It's because you're so trusting. You and Beza are the exact same, always believing everything everyone tells you."

"And we should know better too, with that one," Beza said, pointing at Susan.

"With both of you, you've been pretty devious lately too. I think Susan is a bad influence on you," I told Beza.

"Oh, I definitely am," Susan said.

"I'm a good influence on Sarah," Aiden informed us. "When I'm at the playground, people don't pick on her."

"That means you're a good influence on the other kids, baby." Susan said, her fingers running through Aiden's braids. "Do other kids pick on you, Sarah?"

"No," Sarah said.

"Are the other kids nice to you?" Beza asked.

"Yes," Sarah said, taking another big bite of pasta.

Aiden said, "Only sometimes they're mean. There are some girls in second grade that say mean things if Sarah's not listening to the teacher and they tattle on her to get her into trouble. They're mean."

"Sometimes kids your age really care about the rules. And if they see a kid breaking the rules, it gets them really upset," I told him.

"I don't care about the rules. I just want people to be happy," Aiden said.

Beza and I shared an amused look.

"Well, I hope you at least follow the rules," Beza said.

"I do, Mom," he said, rolling his eyes and giving an exasperated huff. He threw up his hands. "I just don't care if other kids break the rules and I never ever tattle."

"That's my boy." Susan gave him a kiss on the head.

"Sarah knows she's not supposed to do gymnastics at school," I said, looking over at Sarah.

She groaned with her mouth still full of food.

I held up my hands in surrender. "It's important."

She made groaned again and glared at me.

"Okay, okay," I said, half-laughing.

"You ladies hungry? I'll start on some dinner," Susan said, making to stand.

"Want me to help?" I asked her.

"How about, I cook, you clean," Susan said.

"Jamie doesn't need to clean," Beza said, "You cook, I'll clean."

"No Beza, let me do it this once, please?" I said.

She grinned. "Okay, if you really, really want to."

When the kids finished their macaroni, they jumped up and ran outside. I watched through the open door as Sarah climbed up into the giant trampoline and Aiden followed her.

"Did they go on the trampoline?" Beza asked, craning her neck.

"Yeah," I said.

"Okay," Beza said, sighing and getting up from the table to follow them out. "You need to take turns flipping okay? I don't want any more collisions.

Whoever's turn it is, the other one stands on the side," Beza called out.

"We know Mom!" Aiden yelled at her.

"Don't yell at me, Aiden, or it's going to be a time out," she said.

Aiden huffed and muttered something under his breath, but followed Beza's directions.

"He's always angry at me lately, and it's only me, he never even talks back to Susan," Beza frowned as we sat together at the outside table.

"I feel you, Sarah's always mad at me lately, too. It's like I'm constantly annoying her.

"Aside from that, how you feeling? We haven't really talked in a while."

"Oh, I'm good. Things are going pretty well at work lately. I haven't been working much with Karen Blanche lately, and that's always really nice," she gave me an amused smile.

"Ha. You know that woman from the barbeque last weekend? She's friends with your boss."

Beza laughed. "Yeah, Carrie Kelly, I actually know her. She didn't even recognize me though, and I didn't correct her. I've worked with her company for eleven weddings, they're ridiculously overpriced and so snobby—but Karen Blanche insists on using them. I'm not a fan of Carrie."

"Really? She seemed so nice," I said.

"Well, I don't really know her that well, just in a work relationship. She's probably very different socially."

"That's so weird, I didn't know you knew how to dislike people," I said.

She rolled her eyes. "Well, I usually don't. Except of course for Karen, but there are some people I'd rather not spend my time around."

"Yeah, I hear you."

My phone beeped with a text and I checked the screen. "Speak of the devil," I said, grinning.

"Carrie?" Beza asked.

"No, sorry, Patrick, I guess we weren't actually talking about him."

"But you were thinking about him?"

"Maybe, maybe not," I said as I read the message.

Patrick: Are we still on for dinner tomorrow night?

Me: I'm not sure if the food they serve there really qualifies as 'dinner', but I'm definitely up for whooping your ass at arcade games.

Patrick: That will never happen, I am an arcade master.

Me: I have a second degree black belt in arcade games, so we shall see.

Patrick: Want to meet there at six-thirty?

Me: We'll be there.

I stowed my phone and looked up into Beza's grinning face.

"So... How's everything going with you?" she asked.

"Fine. I don't know—I might be selling my coffee shop tomorrow."

"That's really big," she said.

"It feels really big. I'd be selling it to another coffee shop chain and they want to buy everything, the machines, the displays, furniture, even the signs and stuff so the shop will kind of still be there. I'm sure they'll change the appearance somewhat, since they're a chain and they all look pretty alike, but I'll be able to go back and visit."

"I remember the opening day. Chris was so young then, how old was he?"

"Sixteen. You know, we weren't even planning on hiring anyone. Logan and I were planning on working the whole store alone. And then, before we opened, Chris walked by with a group of friends after school and struck up a conversation with us while we were painting the outside. We showed them the store, because they were curious and Chris got so excited when we showed him the full baking setup in the back. He'd asked us for a job and we told him we didn't even have the money to pay ourselves at that point. Then Chris said that if he came back before we left for the night with the best thing we'd ever tasted, we had to give him a job. He came back an hour later with éclairs, and we gave him the job. We actually took out an additional loan just to do it, best business decision we ever made."

"Did he work mornings in high school?"

"Yeah, we were so worried about it too. He worked from five am to seven am every morning and early shifts on Saturday mornings too. He still earned a really high grade point average and it was what he wanted to do. No one could talk him out of it. He never quit either," I said.

"Would he lose his job if you accept the offer?" she asked.

"Basically, yeah. The offer says that they want to retain the equipment, staff and general goodwill of the customer base, so I'm assuming they'll offer him a job. But I looked into it and the company only pay their baristas minimum and they have an affiliated company that provides their pastries. I seriously doubt Chris could live off minimum wage. I know his parents paid for his college but I'm pretty sure he's on the hook if he wants to go for his MBA, which I know he does."

"He would get another job in a heartbeat," Beza said.

"Yeah, I know that and he does too." A tear dropped down my cheek. "It's just the end of an era, I guess. Chris and I have been through a lot together, and it's going to be hard not seeing him every day. I'm going to miss him the most, but, I'll miss the shop too. It has so many memories."

Beza's hand rubbed my back.

"Thanks," I told her.

"Dinner ladies," Susan said, stepping outside. "What did I miss?" She looked between Beza and me.

"Just feeling a bit sad about selling the shop," I said.

"Yeah, I'm feeling a little sad about it too," Susan said. "Remember when Logan hosted that brownie eating extravaganza for charity with all those bands?"

"Yeah, we got in trouble for that one, the fire department was called and we had to kick everyone out."

"I have never eaten so many brownies in my life. I couldn't eat another one for a year," she said.

"Umm, brownie," Susan said.

We walked into the house, eating Susan's food and telling stories about the Coffee Spot.

Day Four

Good in Bed

Day Four: Six O'clock

I was sitting in my living room of my old house, staring out the window at the streetlights on our old street. I touched my bright green couch, which should have been a darker shade in the low light.

"This is a dream, I'm dreaming," I said to the empty room.

A knock came at my door, and I stood slowly. When the knock came again, I rushed to open the door. Glancing through the peephole, I inhaled my breath sharply. My hands shook as I opened the door.

Standing framed in my doorway was a middle aged woman police officer.

"My daughter is sleeping," I whispered to the cop.

"Are you Mrs. Scott?" the officer asked me in a low voice.

"This isn't how this happened," I told her. "Cameron comes first. Cameron comes to the house first, then you come." But when I looked back to the door, the police officer was gone and it was Cameron there.

He said nothing, just stood there in the doorway, my porch light casting deep shadows on his face.

"Hey Cameron, what are you doing here? Is everything okay?" I whispered.

He said nothing in return, his face ashen and eyes fixed at my feet.

"Do you want to come in?"

After another minute of silence, I said, louder, "Talk to me. You're scaring me. What happened?"

"Vanessa just called me from the hospital, but I didn't go to the hospital—I came here." His voice was so quiet and hard to hear because he talked to my feet, not me.

"Is she okay?" I asked.

"She's fine."

I startled awake from the dream, tears coursing down my face. "Shit," I whispered, wiping my nose on my sleeve.

There was a small groan beside me and I saw that Sarah must have left Aiden's pullout bed and crawled in with me. She lay curled up into a fetal position on top of the covers.

I wrapped the blankets back around her, careful not to jostle her too much before crawling out of bed.

Checking my phone, I saw that I still had another hour until I was supposed to wake up. Finding my purse on the side of my bed, I extricated the folded up list from my wallet and read today's task: Sleep.

"Of course it is," I whispered, rubbing my hands over my face. Climbing out of bed, I walked to the adjoining bathroom. I pulled the garment bag off where it was hanging on the door and took it with me. When the bathroom door was closed, I turned the light on and hung the hanger on the shower curtain pole.

After unzipping the bag, I examined the three-piece suit.

"It's a skirt suit," I said, examining the bottom half. I zipped up the bag again, hanging it back on the door. I searched the drawers of the bathroom one by one until I finally found a razor. Sitting on the side of the tub, I shaved my legs using the bath faucet to wash off the soap and razor. When I was finished, I tried on the suit. I buttoned the navy blazer, examined myself thoroughly, then unbuttoned it.

"Jamie?" I heard Susan say. There was a knock on the door, and a moment later Sarah's loud crying.

I opened the bathroom door to find Susan standing, droopy eyed, holding onto a bawling Sarah.

"Oh, no," I said, leaning down to scoop Sarah up.

"She came into our room and started crying. I think she couldn't find you or something," Susan said.

"Oh, I'm so sorry baby, I was just in the bathroom," I said, moving her side to side while she cried out loud, ragged sobs. "I'm sorry, Susan," I said.

"It's fine, it's about time for us to get up anyway," she said.

I walked over to the bed and set Sarah down. Gently I moved the wet strands of hair out of her face. "I'm so sorry, angel, were you scared?"

Sarah made a loud sound and made to hit me, but I caught her hand. "No, baby, no hitting. Do you want a squeeze?"

"No!" she shouted, crying harder and now kicking and screaming.

"Is she having a meltdown?" I heard Aiden say from behind me.

I spun to see Aiden standing in the doorway.

"Yeah, sweetheart, she just needs a moment to reset," I told him as I walked over to give him a kiss on the top of his head.

"Can I help? Sometimes Sarah listens to me but not to anyone else," he said.

"Not this time sweetheart. Could you give us just a minute?"

"Sure, aunt Jamie."

I went and lay down beside Sarah, not touching her but making soothing sounds. "It's okay, it's going to be okay," I said. "I screwed up, I super screwed up. I shouldn't have closed the door to the bathroom. Let's just calm down, and take gymnast breaths."

Sarah's sobs and kicking subsided quickly and she crawled into my lap.

"You want a squeeze?" I asked her.

"Squeeze harder," she said and she grabbed one of my wrists and pulled it toward her.

I wrapped my arms around her, squeezing her to me as tightly as possible. "Are you ready for gymnast breaths?" I asked. We took ten breaths together, and then started on another set of ten when I heard a light knock on the door.

"Come in," I said.

"Hey guys," Beza said, stepping inside. She held up another garment bag. "I was thinking you might need another suit, Jamie."

I looked down to see the one I was wearing was wrinkled and had a substance that looked suspiciously like snot on it. "I am so sorry!" I told her.

She made a 'pisha' sound. "I never wear that one anyway and the drycleaners will clean it."

"I'll pay for the dry cleaning," I said.

"I get a better deal when I do them in bulk; it's not a problem at all. I'm going to hang this one on the door."

After starting a shower for Sarah and encouraging her into it, I unzipped the new garment bag. Seeing that this one was a pantsuit, I sighed and shook my head. Carefully, I took the snot-covered suit off and hung it back up before putting the clean charcoal gray pantsuit on. After a few minutes, Sarah started singing in the shower.

I examined the high-heeled stilettos that were sitting next to where the garment bag had been. Then I looked over my shoulder to where my flats sat next to the guest bed.

"Definitely flats," I said to myself, and walked over to slip them on.

When I heard the shower turn off, I called over my shoulder, "Sarah, there's a towel hanging beside you and pile of clothes on the toilet for you to put on."

After a minute of silence, I said, "Your toothbrush and toothpaste are by the sink." I sat on the bed.

Susan stuck her head in the room. "Hey Jamie, what do you two want for breakfast?"

"I'm going to wait for Sarah to get out so she doesn't get upset again," I told her.

"No problem. I'll just cook you up some food while you're waiting."

"Thanks, Susan. I can really eat anything. Sarah usually wants something light, like yogurt and fruit, but she can eat other stuff too if you don't have that."

"We have yogurt, I'll just set some up for both of you, that work?" she asked.

"That's perfect, thank you so much," I said.

Sarah came out of the bathroom a few minutes later, fully dressed and smiling.

"Are you feeling better, angel?"

"Yes!" she said, jumping around the room and making loud noises.

"Okay, great. Let's go eat some yogurt, and then aunt Beza is going to drive you to school," I said.

"No bus?" Sarah asked.

"No bus today."

She made a loud, excited sound.

"First, drive with Aunt Beza, and then?" she asked.

"And then school," I said.

"No school," she said.

"It's Tuesday, you have school on Tuesday," I said.

"No school!" she shouted, then she ran out of the room, down the hall and when she got into the dining room where everyone was sitting, she pulled over a chair so that it fell backward.

"Sarah! Stop!" I said, as I ran up behind her, grabbing her arm.

Everyone at the table looked over.

Sarah screeched loudly and tried to kick over another chair.

"Sarah, stop doing that!" I yelled. "Stop it!"

I righted the chair while holding her with one arm.

"Sit down!" I yelled at her.

Sarah smacked me right in the nose.

A white hot surge of pain shot up my nose. I closed my eyes, concentrating on my breathing.

"Hey, I got this. Sarah, come over here and eat please," Susan said sternly. "Sarah, now."

I let go of Sarah and let Susan lead her to a seat with a bowl of yogurt with chopped fruit in it.

"I'm sorry about the chairs," I said.

"Jamie, it's fine, come eat," Susan said, pointing to the chair next to Sarah.

"I think I need to take a walk around the block or something," I said.

"No problem, take your food, it will make you feel better," Susan said.

"Yeah, okay," I said, grabbing my food from the table. Exiting into the morning air, I ate as I walked down the sidewalk under the archway of branches. The fog sat just above the trees, giving the world a low, gray ceiling.

I dug my spoon into the yogurt, scooping up a couple slices of strawberry. The sweet, milky, fruity taste burst in my mouth as I chewed, contrasting starkly with the dark, gray morning.

A middle-aged man walked out of one of the houses to stow his briefcase into the backseat of a luxury sedan.

"Morning," he said, waving.

"Hello," I said, trying to disguise the fact my mouth was full, and raising my spoon in a wave.

Crossing the street, I walked back the way I came. A block and a half away from Susan's house, I passed a realtor's 'For Sale' sign. I peered over my shoulder up the driveway to the small, cottage style house. What looked like brown shingles covered the entire exterior all the way up to its slope roof. A tall shuttered window looked out on the street.

I committed the house number and realty company to memory, then crossed the street. When I approached the house, Susan, Beza and the kids were just stepping out the front door.

"We're going to keep this open for you. Mind locking up with your key when you leave?" Susan asked as she held the front door open.

"Yeah, I definitely will but I'm thinking that maybe I should cancel my meeting and keep Sarah with me," I said.

"Of course, if you like. And, the house is yours. But, you know, Sarah did fine over breakfast," Beza said.

"Yeah, she calmed right down and ate every bite," Susan added.

"Oh." I sighed. "Maybe she was just feeling my stress. If that's the case, it actually might be better if she doesn't spend the day with me."

"There's a pretty easy solution to your stress," Susan said while unlocking her car.

"Yeah?"

"Eliminate your stressors. Go sell your shop," she said.

"Maybe. I'll go grab Sarah's booster," I said.

"No need. Beza bought one for Sarah," Susan said.

"I realized I didn't have one for her when I went to pick her up from School yesterday," she said.

"Wow, thank you. I'll pay you back for it," I said.

"You don't need to pay me back... or maybe pay me back by getting one for Aiden in your car? We've been silly just switching back and forth for all these years," she said.

"Alright, I will definitely do that," I said.

Beza and Susan loaded up the kids in the car and I walked over to Sarah's side.

"Have a good day at school, angel," I said, kissing her at the top of her head.

"I love you so much, Mom," she said, patting my cheek softly.

"I love you too," I said, sniffing back a sudden wave of emotion. "So, so much."

Walking back into the house, I washed my plate and grabbed my purse. My phone read five minutes to eight o'clock when I extracted it from my purse.

"Crap," I said, stowing my phone and heading for the front door. After locking the house and climbing in my car, I used my Maps app to speak out directions at me.

"Head West on North State Street," the vaguely female mechanical voice said.

"Alright, which way is west?" I asked her as I started driving.

"At the next intersection, do a u-turn to head West on State street," the voice said.

"Okay, that way is west," I said, glancing into my rearview mirror.

After doing a three-point turn, I followed the directions the disembodied voice gave me. The voice led me to the freeway and told me to go North.

The sun had already burnt through large patches of the fog layer by the time the freeway pulled up along the ocean.

"Take the next exit onto Sea Breeze Way," the voice told me.

"Okay," I said as I merged into the right lane. I exited the freeway, turning left and going through the underpass. The road drove along a large freshly mowed park. Ducks settled on large ponds, avoiding the many fountains in their midst. Framing and webbing through the park were paved footpaths, interspersed with unoccupied benches.

Several large matching buildings approached on my left, their walls made of glass, each curving in an out in an 's' shape. As I drove past the building and the reflected light followed me, the buildings looked almost as if they were rolling waves.

"In three hundred feet, your destination will be on you left," the voice told me.

I turned into the parking lot, driving around until I saw a man standing next to a Mercedes Benz with a brief case.

I parked several spaces down and rushed to get out of my car.

"I'm sorry, am I late?" I asked him.

He looked down at his wrist watch. "No, you're just on time." He walked over, stretching out his hand to me. "Nice to meet you. I'm Mark Hamm."

"Jamie Scott," I said.

"Let's walk and talk, Jamie," he said, gesturing an arm out toward the large wavy glass building ahead of us. He wore nice suit that fit well on his trim body and complimented his handsome square-jawed face.

"I thought your car was going to be black," I said with a smile as we passed his Benz. "You know, because it's a black series."

"They had black, but I prefer the gun metal shade," he said with no trace of a smile on his face. "I've looked over your files and though I believe you will be able to sell and satisfy your judgment lien with little trouble, I don't think you should verbally agree to sell or sign anything until you've spoken to the Timepiece Company."

"Do you think there's a possibility they'll refuse to settle early?" I asked.

"I just don't want you to get in a legal bind. They have the right to not let you sell the property before you settle," he said. "My paralegal called Timepiece to see if their accounting team had any availability this morning, they said they could accommodate us. I, of course didn't give them any personal information about you. If it's before nine-thirty I can accompany you there. Would you like to go talk to them?"

"If that's okay with you. It would be amazing," I said.

"Ideally we could get an update offer that addressed the lien and bring it to them," I said.

"Thank you so much for doing this Mr. Hamm, this is such a kind thing you are doing for me and I sincerely appreciate it," I said.

He nodded brusquely, then opened the glass entrance to the office building for me.

We entered into an entrance hall lit with natural light from a windows roof five stories above. Walkways crisscrossed the open gallery, each at an angle and echoing the wave design of the building.

A small café opened out to one side. On the other side of the building, elevators lined up in a perfectly spaced row.

"Good morning," a petite woman security guard said from behind a wave shaped reception desk. "Are you visitors?"

"We have a meeting with Nicole Murphy," I said.

She typed something into her computer. "Jamie Scott at eight-fifteen?"

"Yes, and this is Mark Hamm, a property lawyer," I said.

"Alright, please step in front of this camera," she said, pointing to a camera mounted on her desk. We took turns getting our photo taken, then waited for her to print our name tags.

I looked down to the black and white photo of me grinning next to my printed name. Leaning in just a little, I looked at Mark's name tag before he stepped away. He wasn't smiling in his picture.

"You can go on up to the third floor," the security woman said, turning back to her computer.

We walked to the side of the building and pressed the button for the elevator. "So did Cameron work on your car?" I asked.

"He customized the stereo system," he said.

"Neat. I didn't even realize that Cameron did that," I said as we entered the elevator.

"He's good," he said.

"How long have you been a property lawyer?" I asked.

"Twelve years," he said.

"Wow, you must have started young," I said.

"When I was twenty-five," he said.

"So, are you really into cars?" I asked after a moment of silence.

"Moderately," he said.

The doors dinged open onto another open reception area. Large freestanding banners hung down in front of the wall on each side, each depicting coffee related images. A woman sat at the reception desk, grinning at us as we made our approach. Frosted glass doors stood behind her on both sides, each with the Harrington's logo.

A blonde woman opened one of the glass door and held it open for us. "I have this, Miranda," she said to the receptionist. "Are you Jamie Scott?"

"I am," I said.

She grinned at me, and crow's feet lined both sides of her beautiful face. "I'm Nicole, come on in."

"This is Mark Hamm, the property lawyer I mentioned on the phone," I told Nicole.

Nicole gave Mark a wide grin. "It's very nice to meet you, Mr. Hamm."

We walked down a line of office buildings, many with assistants in desks before them or in small offices leading to bigger offices.

I peeked through open doorways as we passed, mostly seeing people on phones or computers.

"So this is the offices for Harrington's?" I asked.

Nicole glanced around. "Some of them, this whole building is the Harrington's headquarters."

"Oh, wow," I said.

"Well, we do have eighty locations across the state and four coffee roasting warehouses," she said, grinning back.

"You look incredibly familiar, have you been into The Coffee Stop before?" I asked.

"I've checked it out." She opened the doors to a wide, open meeting room. "Right through here," she said, gesturing us to a long black table. "Let's just all gather to one side here."

"Thank you," I said, taking a seat at the end.

Nicole took a seat behind a big stack of paper. "Would you like something to drink? We have tea, coffee and water," she said looking between us.

"I'm fine," I said.

"A water, please," Mark said.

"Oh definitely," Nicole said with a grin on her face, she stood walking across the room to a small mini-fridge. "Bottled water okay?"

"That's great," Mark said.

"You sure I can't get you one, Jamie?" she asked.

"Since you're up, sure," I said.

Nicole returned with our waters and a smile. "So, do you want us to go over this offer from beginning to end or would you rather just ask me questions?" Nicole said.

"Best you go over it," Mark said.

"Well, the offer is two point one million dollars. Included in the purchase price would be all the personal property at eight four two Main street, all property at the site and/or associated with the business, including but not limited to furniture, tools and fixtures, all permits and special licenses. In addition to this we require goodwill, all customer lists, accounts payable, and stock and trade. For real property, the building and lot at eight four two Main street, the recorded casements of public utilities would be included in the price. As for special conditions, we would require an employment contract with you, Jamie Scott, and to retain the current employment contract with your employee Christopher Johnson. We—"

"Sorry to interrupt," I said.

She looked up, a small grin on her face. "No, go ahead."

"When you say an employment period, are you asking us to work for a transitional period?"

"Well, both your and Christopher's employment contract renegotiation would go a little differently. In your case, we will be requiring you to sign a three-year contract."

"Excuse me?"

"That is an unusual length of time," Mark said, leaning over the table.

Nicole put her elbows on the table, threading her fingers together. "Let me be frank with you here, Jamie. We're interested in your business and its location enough to make an offer on it. But we're making this specific offer because of your shop's twenty-five percent profit margin. With only thirty-five open hours open a week, you have outperformed every one of our shops in the county, all of which have twice as many open hours. You also surpassed three of our shops in gross profit. We would like you to join our team."

I played with the sleeve of my suit. "Honestly Nicole, I'm flattered, but it really wasn't due to my efforts. It's pretty much all because of Chris. He's an incredibly talented person and I can't speak for him."

"I'm going to have to disagree with you there, Jamie," she said. She pulled out a stack of papers. "Christopher—Chris is an incredibly talented young man. I'm not fighting you on that point. We have every intention of utilizing his skills to the fullest scope of their potential if he chooses to remain with us. However, Chris has been working for your company for six years, and until this year you made a steady eighteen percent profit margin for all five years, except for dipping down to seventeen percent last year. After you took full management of the shop, it almost immediately increased its profitability."

"I—I have very specific hours I can work, and— I... Nicole, truly, even with the sale of the business and the money I'm going to be making from the sale, I can't continue to work for minimum wage for three years," I said.

She grinned wider at me. "We're not asking you to work minimum wage." She pulled out a small stack of papers clipped together from her pile. "We're asking you to be the general manager for all the Harrington's in the county—seven store locations. It's a salary job with benefits. As for the hours, you can continue the thirty-five hours you have now."

"Jamie, I'm going to recommend that you talk to an employment lawyer about this," Mark said, leaning in. "This isn't my area of expertise—"

"No, it isn't," a voice I recognized said from behind me. I turned to see Pat, the regular from the shop, standing with his shoulder leaning into the wall just inside the open door to the meeting room.

"Hey Pat," I said, raising my eyebrows at him. "Do you... work here?"

"This is actually my company—one of them," he said, walking across the room and taking a seat next to Nicole.

"Oh," I said.

He grinned at me, flashing his dimples. Tapping the paperwork in front of me, he said, "If you want to get a lawyer, by all means do it. But there's no hidden agendas in here, no misleading language that says 'promise', but isn't binding. I'd like you to work for me; I'd like both you and Chris to work for me."

"Okay—thank you for the offer, Pat, I'll take this with me and go talk to Chris. I have a lot to consider," I said, starting to stand.

"Such as?" Pat said.

"I appreciate it, I do, but I still need to really think about if it's right for me and the shop," I said, hovering half-standing.

"Why wouldn't it be? I've seen your tax records; you don't get paid much right now. This would dissolve your debt and put you ahead, it would offer job security for three years." His bright gaze bored into mine.

I sat back down, forcing myself to hold his gaze. "Thank you, but I actually don't have anything to sell right now. There's a judgment lien on my business, and until I talk to the lien holders, I can't make any decisions."

"I am the lien holder," Pat said.

"What... what did you say?" I whispered.

"I own the lien on your business. Timepiece is also my company."

I jumped out of my chair and it tumbled to the floor. I stared down at him, unable to tear my gaze away from his. "What the hell is wrong with you?" I asked, fighting to keep my voice down.

Silence engulfed the room. Mark and Nicole stared at me with a mixture of confusion and shock. Pat's expression bordered between concern and annoyance.

"Jamie—"

"Don't say my name like you have a right to say it to me—like a friend would. You came into my shop every day, talked to me every day... what is wrong with you? What? Were you spying on me?"

He pushed the employment contract toward me. "Put past grievances aside here..." he touched his chest, "I have, and—"

"I would rather die than work for you," I said.

"That's a little dramatic."

"You want to know what's dramatic?" I asked, putting a hand on the table and leaning forward. "What's dramatic is having your husband die and being sued for three million dollars three days later."

"I actually sued for eight million dollars but the estate was only worth three," he said, leaning back in his chair. "The three million didn't even compensate Timepiece for half of the damage your husband did."

"But you didn't sue my husband. My husband is dead. You sued me!" I exclaimed.

"I sued the estate during probate, it was well within the law," he said.

"And you exercised every loophole of the law to ensure you got everything. You didn't just take Logan's half, you took every single penny me and my daughter had. Every penny I had earned from years of working my ass off," I said.

"You kept the business," he said, his brows lifting.

"In name only, and only if I paid off two million dollars in fifteen years," I said.

"Which at your current profit rate, you could do in ten and a half years. If anything, I'd say you thrived in this adversity."

"Thrived?" I spat. Shaking my head, I leaned down and righted the chair. I looked back to Nicole and said, "Is the offer still available if I don't join the company?"

She glanced over toward Pat, then back at me. "I'm sorry, no."

"Alright, I'm going to have to turn down your offer. Thank you for your time," I said.

"You're making a mistake, Jamie," Pat warned.

"I hope you enjoy the furniture my father made my daughter for her birthday," I spat. I walked out of the room, wiping hot tears from my face.

Day Four: Nine-Fifteen

"Jamie."

I turned to find Mark jogging toward me.

"I am so sorry, Mark. I just ran out of there not even thinking of you," I said.

"Perfectly understandable," he said, catching up. "I'll walk you out of the building." He pulled a handkerchief out of his pocket.

"Thank you, but I'm fine." I held up my sleeve, and the wet spot on it.

He walked me past the reception desk to the bank of elevators. We were silent as we rode down the elevators and crossed through the bright reception atrium, and as we walked all the way through the parking lot to our parked cars.

Mark stopped in front of his car. He pulled a business card out of his pocket.

"He gave me this to give to you, I can dispose of it if you'd like," he said, handing it over.

"Thank you, but I'll take it for my voodoo doll," I said, reaching for it.

His face remained impassive as he said, "I am assuming you no longer wish to discuss your lien with Timepiece. I had thought it odd that they were located in the same business park."

"The fuck?" I said, looking down at the card. "Pat gave this to you?"

"He did," Mark confirmed.

"He is sick. There is something seriously wrong with that guy!"

"I'm not going to argue with you there," Mark said.

"Ugh, this makes me so mad!" I looked up at Mark. "You've been so generous with your time, but can I ask you one more favor?"

"You can," he said.

"Timepiece is a finance company?"

"Accounting and finance placement," he said.

"I'm going in there," I said.

"Why?" he said.

I turned the card around. "Pat's full name is Patrick Kelly Sr. Just so happens that another Patrick Kelly—a young, blond, good-looking dad of one of my daughter's friends has been asking me out lately. I actually spent the weekend hanging out with him."

"I'd recommend you don't go in there. This company has already sued you once; they could file charges against you if you act in any way aggressive or threatening toward Patrick Kelly Jr. in his place of employment."

"I'm not going to do either, all I'm going to do is go in there and say hi. I just want him to know I know and I'm not doing it over the phone," I said.

"I'm sorry, Jamie. You'll have to this on your own, though I strongly recommend against it," he said.

"I understand. Thank you for all your help," I said.

"Just between you and me, I think what that man did to you and your family was very wrong under the circumstances. However, I think that what he's doing now, with this offer—which he has not rescinded—could have motivations your anger is blinding you to." He turned to unlock his car. "And with that, I will leave you."

"Thank you, Mark," I said, stepping back so he would have room to back out.

I got into my car and pulled out my phone, searching for Timepiece's location. I clicked on the address, and pressed the button to have my phone direct me.

"Turn left onto Sea Breeze Way," the mechanical voice said.

I followed the directions past five more identical buildings, to yet another identical building. I parked in the back of the lot and again stared at the business card.

"Fuck him," I said, grabbing the stack of papers I'd placed on the passenger seat and climbing out of my car.

After crossing the lot, I entered an almost identical atrium, though in this building, the interior walls were covered in a green, grassy substance. A plaque on a nearby wall declared it to be 'Green Art'. The area smelled fresh, rather than dirty or mossy.

I walked up to the security personnel lady sitting behind a similar desk as the building I had just left.

"Hello," I said to her. "Patrick Kelly Sr. asked me to go over some paperwork with a tax attorney of the same name... I think it was in this building." I held out the business card so she could see Patrick Kelly's name and the cell phone number he had handwritten under it.

"Yes, you're in the right building. And you've already been given a guest pass and been entered into our system?" She leaned forward to squint at my name tag through thick glasses, giving me a clear view of her neat gray bun.

"Yes, the other guard registered me," I said.

"Alright, go ahead in. Top floor..." she typed into her computer, then said, "Suite five fifteen."

"Thank you," I said, heading to an elevator at the side of the atrium. A man in gym clothes got on the elevator with me, getting off at the third floor. I rode to the fifth floor alone, finding an entrance room very similar to the one in the Harrington's building, though there were large photographs of seemingly important people rather than free-standing wall hangings.

I gave the twenty-something male receptionist the same story, showing him the card. "He's actually expecting me, his father called him," I said.

"Your name?" the receptionist asked, his focus on the screen.

"Jamie Scott," I said.

He typed into his computer. "You are in our system as a guest of Harrington Company," he said.

"Yeah, I had a meeting with Nicole Murphy and Patrick Kelly Sr. They made an offer on my business. But Timepiece has a lien on my business, so I—"

"Oh, was it your attorney that called this morning?" he asked.

"Yeah," I said.

"I've already cleared the meeting with another team member in accounting, but you say that Mr.

Kelly asked you to speak to Patrick Kelly Jr directly?"
he asked.

"Yes, he told Patrick that I'd be here in a couple
of minutes," I said.

"Okay, go ahead back to suite five fifteen," he
said.

"Thanks," I said, walking through the frosted
glass door, this one with the Timepiece logo on it. I
read the plaques beside each door until I saw, 'Suite
515: Patrick Kelly, JD, Senior Tax Manager'.

I stepped through the open door to a small
fore-office with a single desk and a young woman
sitting in front of it. She didn't look up as I
approached, her focus pointedly on her cell phone in
her lap.

I glanced at Patrick's office door, then back the
way I came. Closing my eyes, I shook my head. On an
exhale, I turned back the way I had come walking
toward the office door.

"Can I help you?"

I turned to see the receptionist looking up, her
short, multi-colored hair sticking out from her face in
all directions as if she's just stuck her finger in a light
socket.

"Are you looking for someone?" she asked.

"I was, but I think I changed my mind. Sorry to
bother you," I said.

I turned back to exit the small office when I
heard the door behind me open and Patrick say,
"Jamie?"

I spun slowly until I faced Patrick.

His brow was furrowed into a look of confusion until the expression fell away. His shoulders dropped slightly. "Oh," he said.

I licked my lips, and looked the other way. "Could I talk to you for a second?" I asked.

"Yeah, um…" he stepped back into his office, "Come on in."

I stepped into his space, taking in the floor-to-ceiling view of a park ending abruptly to overlook the ocean. I took a seat at his desk, glancing between his photos of Kay: Kay as a baby, laughing in a posed photo with him, Kay on a swing set, Kay spinning in a tutu.

He didn't sit in his desk chair; instead he stood with his profile to me, facing the wall.

"So this was some sort of corporate espionage thing? And just for the record, that sounds way cooler than what you did."

"What did my father say to you?" he asked.

"He wants me to work for him under a three-year contract; he offered to buy my shop, offered more than it's worth by a hundred thousand…"

"You should do it," he said.

"Why? So I can get my very own 'Welcome to the Company' cake?"

He turned with a grimace on his face. "I really don't think he's trying to make you his slave. What I said to you—that was about my relationship with him. Not about the way he treats his employees."

I huffed out a laugh. "Just some advice; the barbeque was completely overkill. I was planning on selling the shop to Harrington's before I realized who was behind the offer. You could have saved yourself a small fortune in beef. Free advice for next time," I said, getting up out of the chair.

"The barbeque wasn't about my father's offer," he said.

"Yeah, whatever. I thought coming up here and rubbing your face in the fact that I know who you really are and what you were really doing would feel satisfying, but it doesn't. This just feels sad... and disgusting. I'm going to go. I guess I'll see you around Coral Elementary. Yay," I said, dryly.

"I'd like a chance to explain," he said.

"I don't really need an explanation. I barely even know you. I just don't appreciate the falseness of what you were doing. It's funny, because my sister warned me about you and your family and I totally dismissed it."

"We weren't being false," he said.

"You didn't know who I was when you asked me out? You didn't know that your company took everything from me?" I asked.

"I knew," he said.

"That's what I thought. Oh, and since you started working here three months after you got divorced two years ago, you were working here while your company sued me. See, I might not have gone to college, but I can do the math. You were probably even part of the legal team, weren't you?"

He sucked his lower lip into his mouth and let is slowly roll out from behind his teeth. "Only in an advisory capacity," he said.

"You knew who I was when they sued me?" I asked.

"No. I found out a month later at that school board meeting. I'd seen you dropping off Sarah in the mornings before that, but I never knew your name." He paused to run a hand through his blond hair. "I found out and I... used it against my father. I was very angry with him at the time. I'll be honest, I told him to hurt him, not to help you. I threw it in his face that after all his speeches about making the world a better place he had just beggared a new widow who had a child with autism."

"You used my child's diagnosis as your weapon against your father?" I asked, blinking at him and shaking my head.

"I'm not proud of it, but yes, I did. I found out that he was barely familiar with the case, he'd just been briefed about the accident, then on the financial aspects and the repayment plan acceptance."

I didn't respond, just stayed standing and staring at Patrick.

"All year he kept asking me about you—asking about Sarah, so I told him what I knew. I asked your friend Beza about you... not to tell my father the information, but because I was interested in knowing more. I also... I asked you out on a date for me, not to trick you into any kind of deal with my father. And, my brother and his wife don't know any of this."

After standing for a full minute, staring at him, I said, "Okay. Thank you for telling me what I hope is the truth. I don't want to date you..." I shook my head, "Or be your friend. But I'm not going to confront you again or freak out on you, so don't worry about that. I'll be as friendly as I can be under the circumstances, but please don't seek me out, especially at my work."

"Jamie, I—"

"And no Pizza Arcade this evening, though I'm sure you could have guessed that one. I don't even really like that place anyways." I turned away from him, heading for his office door.

"If it makes any difference, this is the closest I have ever seen to my father admitting that he was wrong," he said.

I grabbed the handle to his office door. "I'm really not interested in signing away three years of my life to ease his conscience."

Day Four: Ten-twenty

No one stopped me or even looked twice at me as I left Patrick's office and retraced my path out of the building. Across the parking lot, I climbed into my car and sat, staring out the window. The edges of my vision blurred as my eyelids grew heavy. My stomach growled at the same time a headache pounded in my skull. I blinked away the light, and found it difficult to reopen my eyes.

I closed my eyes and leaned forward.

The sound of people talking somewhere nearby had me shaking my head and opening my eyes. I felt sweat gathering in my armpits and behind my neck.

I blinked at the clock. It read twelve-ten.

"What the—?" I rubbed my face with my hands. "Oh, crap."

Glancing around my car, I saw hordes of people dressed in business attire walking in groups to their vehicles. After a quick scan of the parking lot, I didn't see Patrick.

Starting my car, I rolled down the windows, sticking my face out to take a few gulps of fresh air. Backing out of my space, I joined the traffic feeding onto Sea Breeze Way, and continued to stop and go all the way to the freeway entrance.

When I reached my apartment building, I circled the parking lot. A sigh of relief left me when I saw that all that was sitting in Clarke's space was a puddle of oil. Circling around, I parked in my space.

Trudging from parking lot, I unlocked my house, relocked it on the other side, set my phone alarm for an hour later and passed out on my couch.

What felt like minutes later, I woke to an incessant beeping. "Get up, Jamie, go shower," I whispered. But instead, I reset my alarm for thirty minutes later and passed out again.

On the second time waking up to my alarm, I forced myself up. Going into my room, I changed out of Beza's pantsuit and into jeans and a 'Flaming Lips' T-shirt. My hair felt sweaty as I gathered it up the best I could into a ponytail.

Leaning forward, I washed my face. The cold water, followed by the coarse feeling of the towel, finally rid my eyes of the heavy feeling.

When I reentered the living room, my phone lit up with a text message.

Cameron: Did everything go okay today?

Me: Today was horrible.

Immediately the phone rang with Cameron's smiling face lighting up the screen.

"Hey," I answered.

"Hey, baby, what happened?"

"Turns out the potential buyer also owns Timepiece and is the lien holder on the Coffee Stop."

"They were trying to screw you over?" he asked.

I sighed. "Not exactly, they were more trying to acquire me and Chris with the shop, but I have no interest in working for them."

"I get that after what they did. Did they want you to keep running the shop?" he asked.

"They've been keeping careful track of our profits and I guess we're outperforming them by a decent margin. They wanted me to be their general manager for the county, but I'd have to sign a three-year contract."

There was a pause on the other end of the phone, then Cameron said, "No matter what you choose, I'll be behind you, okay?"

"Thank you Cameron... but there's no possible way I'll work for them. They didn't just kick us when we were down, they shot us with a bazooka, then smashed our itty bitty remains under their boots. I've spent the worst year of my life crawling my way out of the hole they blew us into. And it might look like they're offering me a ladder, but I have a feeling it's a lot closer to a greased up slide into a much bigger hole."

"You're probably right. I just hate to see you stuck for fourteen more years with this debt," he said.

"Maybe someone else will make an offer. Except—shit, they probably won't let me sell to anyone before I settle the debt if they're trying to force me into their deal."

"What about filing for bankruptcy?" he asked.

"My dad looked into it right after this all happened. The debt is non-dischargeable because it was a DUI and that security guard broke his leg. I should have just given The Coffee Stop up in the first place—now I'm even more trapped than ever."

"No, we'll find a way through," he said.

"Okay, if you say so. You doing okay?" I asked.

"Yep. I got a couple sweet kisses from a beautiful woman yesterday, and they're keeping me going through another long day at the shop."

"You working late? Maybe we could drop by."

"Actually, I'm taking off at two-thirty today for a late lunch thing," he said.

"With that amazing client?"

"Nope, a different one."

"Alright, I need to go get Sarah from school," I said.

"I'll talk to you soon," he said, before hanging up.

When I peeked out my front door, I found Clarke's yard still empty. After stepping out of my house, I turned to lock my front door when my phone rang.

"Shit," I whispered, fumbling it from my bag and turning it to silent. The screen flashed with the words 'Sunset Estates Office'.

"Hello," I answered in a quiet voice.

"Hello Jamie, this is Richard, the property manager of Sunset Estates," a man's voice came from the other end of the line.

Behind me, a door swung open, making a screeching sound.

I glanced over my shoulder to see Buster run out into Clarke's yard.

"Hello? Ms. Scott?" Richard said.

"I'm here, sorry just one second," I said in a low voice, walking quickly down the sidewalk.

When I reached my car, I realized my keys were still held out in my hands, my house key pinched between two fingers. I unlocked my car, and once I was inside said, "Thank you so much for getting back to me."

"No problem. Is there any way I could have you come down to the office to discuss your housing situation?" he asked.

"Right now?"

"That would definitely work for me," he said.

"Sorry, but I'm on my way to pick up my daughter," I said.

"Well, we can definitely make an appointment for later in the week," he said.

"I can come in thirty minutes, I just need to pick up my daughter and then I could be right back there," I said.

"I have a meeting with some prospective renters in half an hour," he said.

"I thought all the units were full," I said.

"We might have some openings next month," he said.

"Oh good. But honestly Richard, could we meet later today, maybe after your appointment? I can't keep living like this," I said.

"I am sorry, Ms. Scott. I do have some time open tomorrow during the day," he said.

"I have to work and then my daughter has gymnastics, but could we make some time over the phone maybe?"

"Yes, that'll work for me," he said.

I started up my car. "Would three-thirty work?"

"That'll work," he said.

"Thank you so much. I really need this," I said before backing up my car.

When I arrived at Coral Elementary School, the children had already exited the school's doors and dispersed like colorful fish in a coral reef. Ms. Brown stood with one hand looped in Sarah's back pack, her gaze roving back and forth over the parking lot.

I pulled the car in front of the pair. Climbing out of the car, I rushed around the front. "I am so sorry. I'm running late," I said.

Sarah's head shot up to look at me. "Mom!" she screamed, plowing into me. She made a loud sound, smacking her head into my stomach again.

"Baby," I said, running a hand over her hair. I looked up into Ms. Brown's face.

She pushed up her glasses, her face set in a grimace.

"How was today?" I asked.

"Well—it was pretty rough. Yeah, I'd call it a rough day." She gestured out to Sarah. "Nothing really bad happened, she just didn't want to listen and we had a really hard time calming her down. She's been really emotional."

I squeezed Sarah tighter to me. "Oh, sweetie." I looked back to Ms. Brown. "But no—hitting or anything?"

"Yeah—yeah she was hitting me a lot, but not hard." She held her hands out in a reassuring gesture. "And not the other kids."

"Oh, I—I am so sorry," I said.

"It's okay. Did anything happen... like at home, that could have set her off?" she asked.

"Yeah, um, we stayed at her aunts' house last night because our complex was spraying chemicals. Everything was fine, but then she had a pretty intense morning."

I leaned over to open Sarah's car door. "Time to get in, angel."

When she refused to release her hold on me, Ms. Brown asked in a quiet voice, "Did they spray chemicals today?"

"No, I think we can go back to our usual schedule," I said in an equally quiet voice.

"Alright, I need to head into a meeting. Goodbye Sarah, see you tomorrow."

Sarah made no response, just continued to hold onto me.

"Thank you so much," I said to Ms. Brown as she backed away from us with a concerned look still heavy on her face.

"Sarah, if you don't let go of me, we can't drive home," I said.

Sarah leaned back. "Mom, are we going to Pizza Arcade today?"

"Um, not today baby, but we can do something else fun if you want. Pick a place, like the beach or the playground or a restaurant, and we'll go there."

"I want to go home," she said.

"Okay, climb on into your seat," I told her.

Day Four: Two-fifty

The moment I sat in my car, my phone dinged with a text.

Chris: I think it was just a twenty-four-hour bug. I'll definitely be at work tomorrow.

Me: I am so sorry Chris, I meant to check up on you. I'm glad you're feeling better. Unfortunately, the offer was a bust. I have a lot to tell you.

Chris: Too bad. See you bright and early.

After buckling Sarah in, I slowly drove through the lot and back onto the road.

"Mom, can we listen to the kids' CD?" Sarah asked.

When I pressed the button for the CD, the song we had last been listening to blared out, *"He rode right to Miss Mousie's den, mm mm, mm mm..."* I skipped past the song. A new song played with a group of kids singing, *"Itiskit, Itasket, green and yellow basket, I wrote a letter to my love, And on the way I dropped it..."*

I sang along under my breath all the way back to our apartment.

When I circled the lot, Clarke's spot was once again vacant.

Parking in my own spot, I reached back and unbuckled Sarah's seatbelt.

Sarah screamed at me and tried to fasten the latch back into the seatbelt receptacle.

"I'm sorry! I forgot! Sarah—wait, I'll help you," I said.

She furiously pushed my hands away.

"Sarah, let me buckle you back in and then you can unbuckle yourself—there," I said, putting my hands up in surrender.

Sarah took another minute to calm down but finally unbuckled her own seatbelt.

"Okay, let's just go home," I said.

We climbed out of my car. The leaves on the bushes around my duplex rustled softly, swaying back and forth. The building cast a severe shadow across the entire walkway. Goosebumps ran up my arms.

I pulled out my keys to unlock my house, sticking the key in my lock but the door simply pushed open.

"Huh?" I whispered, hand still hovering with my keys in the lock.

Sarah barged forward through the door.

I grabbed her around her torso and held her to me. "Wait baby."

I turned on the hallway light, glancing around what I could see of the living room and kitchen. I examined every inch of the kitchen, then moved into the living room, keeping Sarah's hand in mine. I continued looking through the bathroom, checking behind the shower curtain, and then into the bedrooms.

When the entire house was searched, I locked the front door.

"I want to watch the artistic women's beam final from the North Greenwich arena at the London Olympics."

"Right now the choices are to read books or do art, baby. You didn't have the best day at school today and we have to earn videos," I said.

I pulled some art material down from the shelf, and went to Sarah's room to grab a couple books from her shelf.

"I'll do art in books," Sarah said, grinning with a crayon in her hand.

"Ha. Not in those books." I grabbed them back off the table. "I'll go get your coloring books."

I walked back to the room, grabbing Sarah's coloring books and leafing through their pages on my way back to her. "This one has a lot of free pages," I said, handing it to her. "Alright, I'm going to be right back."

Turning, a low buzzing started ringing in my ears. Concentrating on my breathing, I walked slowly back into my bedroom. From the doorway I could see where my underwear drawer had been left just the slightest bit open. I glanced around the room again, but just as when I'd checked five minutes ago, I didn't see anything else out of place.

Closing the distance, I slid the drawer open. At first glance, I only saw the same lacey thongs that had been lying haphazardly in my drawer since this morning, but then I saw it. I dug my hand through my other underwear and pulled out a gray boy-short pair.

"Oh my god," I whispered.

The underwear slipped from my fingers and back into the drawer.

I pulled my phone from my pocket, thumbing through my contacts and calling Gina.

"This is Gina," she answered.

"Gina, this is Jamie, I think he came into my house when I wasn't here," I said.

"Whoa, slow down there Jamie. You neighbor came into your house?" she asked.

"I, um, yeah, I think so."

"What happened? Did you leave your house unlocked or did he break in?"

"He must have broken in. I locked...wait I—I was going to lock it but then the property manager called and... I didn't lock it," I said.

"How do you know there was an intruder?" she asked.

"He left a pair of my underwear, one of the ones that went missing from the laundry," I said.

"Now Jamie, I'm only going to ask you this because this is the first question many people will ask you, but I want you to know that I believe you that this man is harassing you; is there any way that you just accidentally didn't include this underwear in your laundry and they're lying around the house?"

"They were in the laundry, I know for a fact they were there," I said.

"I believe you. Are you still in the house?"

"Yeah," I said.

"You need to leave," she said.

"I can't Gina, it's too hard on Sarah. She gets so thrown off when her routine is messed up, especially on the weekdays. It's not fair to her to be moving her around like this," I said.

"We are talking about the safety of you and your child," she said.

"I just—I just can't do it to her right now," I said.

"Is there anyone who can stay with you?" she asked. "I have designated driver duties, but I can cancel if you need me."

"I'll call someone," I said.

"Promise me you'll call someone, and I'm hoping that someone is your dad," she said.

"It won't be my dad, but I will call someone and ask them to come here. I'll probably call Cameron," I said.

"As long as I have that guarantee from you, and that you'll call me if he can't come," she said.

After I hung up with Gina, I scrolled down my contacts, until I found Cameron's number. Taking a deep inhale through my nose, I pressed the call button next to his name.

After three rings, a woman's voice answered with, "Cameron's phone." Her voice was accompanied with the loud sound of people chattering along with a periodic tinkling.

I didn't say anything for a few seconds, and then I said, "Oh, I'm so sorry, is he busy?"

"Darn it. I can't hear you... I am so sorry, I'm in a really loud restaurant. Cameron has one of these blasted old fashioned flip phones and I have no idea how to turn up the volume. Is this the client he's waiting for a call from?"

Her deep melodic voice, the way she said his name... I realized who it was. Blinking around my room in surprise, I walked over to my bed and took a seat. "Vanessa? It's Jamie," I said.

"I am so sorry... I can't hear a word you are saying. I know he's waiting for your call, but he stepped out to go get something from his car. Can he call you back in just a minute?"

"Sure," I said.

"Shoot, I still can't hear you... I'm just going to assume you said yes and I'll tell Cameron that you called," she said.

"Thanks," I said, hanging up.

Grabbing a pillow from the head of my bed, I pushed my face into it and screamed. I screamed until I needed to come up for air, and then I took a deep inhale, pressed my head back into the pillow and kept screaming.

After what felt like forever, I dropped the pillow onto my lap. Squeezing my eyes shut, my fingers rubbed my eyelids. I looked back to my phone, scrolling down my contact list. Finding the name of the one person in the world I wanted over at my house right now, I texted her.

Me: Will you spend the night at my house?

After a couple minutes with no response, I stood up and walked into the kitchen to check on Sarah.

"Hey, angel, are you hungry?" I asked.

"I am hungry for milk. What are you hungry for, Mom?" she asked.

"I am *thirsty* for water," I said.

My phone beeped and I scrambled to pull it out of my pocket.

Amy: Tonight?

Me: Yeah.

Amy: Yeah, sure. Everything okay? Do you still have a wireless connection?

Me: Yes to the wireless. I am having a horrendous day, I have a seriously creepy neighbor, Cameron is on a lunch date with Vanessa and you were right about Patrick and his family, they're super villains from an evil empire.

Amy: I definitely didn't say that. I can be over in about three hours. I might have to do some work over there, though.

Me: That's fine.

Amy: How creepy is your neighbor?

Me: Like I need to move creepy. Don't tell dad.

Amy: I won't, but you have to tell me about what's going on. I also want to hear about this

Vanessa thing. I'm going to finish what I have to do here so I can head home and pack a bag to come over.

Me: Thank you so much.

After pouring a glass of milk for Sarah, I sat beside her.

"Can I have that one?" I asked, pointing to a picture

She glanced over, "Yes."

Taking a blue crayon from the box, I started working the color between the lines. After I had finished coloring in half the picture, I paused to look over at Sarah.

"Everything is going to be okay. It's all really tricky right now, but I am going to make all of these things right, I promise you. I'm going to make it work."

Sarah looked up at me, smiled, then turned back to her drawing.

Day Five

Stick it to the Woman

Day Five: Five-fifteen AM

My eyes opened to a rattling sound on my roof. Standing, I climbed off the bed and away from where Sarah was sleeping as carefully as possible. When I lifted up a blind on my window, faint morning light fed through a stream of rain water.

I cringed as the rattling grew in volume, looking back to where Sarah was fast asleep.

Her leg was hooked over her blanket, pulling it down. I slid the blanket around her and covered her again.

Stepping out into the hall, I found Sarah's bedroom light on. The scent of freshly brewed coffee wafted through the air.

I popped my head into Sarah's room to find Amy sitting on Sarah's bed, her fingers clicking quickly over the keyboard of her laptop.

"You're killing me, Amy," I groaned.

"I'm sorry, Jamie, did I wake you?" she asked, looking up with glasses poised on her nose.

"It's the smell. I'm going to start floating toward the coffee pot like an old cartoon."

"I was planning on finishing the pot before you woke up," she said.

I walked into the room and took a seat across from her. Sarah's toys were organized orderly on their shelves in a way they definitely had not been last night when we went to bed.

"Are you always up this early?" I asked her.

"My alarm is set for four-fifteen, but I usually wake up earlier," she said, looking back to her screen.

"So that house near Susan's is a little over three hundred thousand, and that's only because there's numerous problems with it. Thankfully, they're mostly cosmetic, and since you're good at that stuff, the house would be livable and you could get other things fixed over time. The downside is most of the loans you might qualify for require a pretty high down-payment."

"You spent all morning doing this?" I asked.

She looked over her screen. "I'm not going to leave you in this situation Jamie, no matter what you say."

I pointed at her. "You swore on Peter's life you wouldn't tell anyone."

"Am I telling anyone? No. But I'm not leaving you in a house where some psycho is breaking in to play with your underwear," she said.

"I'm probably going to have to get another apartment. I'm just getting the distinct feeling that they're not going to help me at the main office."

"And you're absolutely positive about the job?" she asked.

"I knew you'd be rooting for me to take that stupid job," I whispered.

She raised her eyebrow at me in response.

"Yes, I'm sure I don't want to take a contract job at evil headquarters."

"Actually, after I heard that story, I thought even more highly of Patrick and his family. It sounds like they want to do right by you."

"And I think you're biased by your rich people blinders," I said.

"I have no idea what that means," she said.

"You think that they're like a higher breed of human or something," I said.

"I don't think that at all. If you asked me, you would know what I think. But you don't ask me, you just judge me," she said.

Sighing, I climbed off the bed. "I'm sorry. I love you and I really appreciate everything you're doing."

"Of course, you're my sister, I'd do anything for you," she said, returning her focus to the computer. "So, what's on your detox list for today?"

"Taking on the school board," I said.

"Because they laid off her teacher? I thought the school board voted to keep her on part time?" she said.

"They did at first, but then they held another meeting where a couple of the parents from the PTA fought really hard for the dance teacher to have her job extended to full time. They did a revote two days before the cutoff last month and decided that without knowing the future enrollment next year, they should 'temporarily' lay off the second special needs class position."

"That's ridiculous, isn't the number of kids going into special education rising?" she asked.

"At least at Coral Elementary, yeah. Several of the moms of incoming kids even came to the meetings. But I know why the school board did it." I shook my head. "Some of these PTA ladies have a lot of financial sway on the school. It's technically a public school, but a huge amount of their funding for equipment and day-to-day stuff comes from private donation," I said, leaning against the door frame. "When these parents have ideas about how the school should allocate the funds, the school board always votes in their favor."

Amy cocked her head to the side. "What are you planning to do?"

"I was thinking about writing some letters to the district and the state board," I said.

She shook her head slowly.

"What?" I asked.

She closed her laptop, turning fully to me. "You need to force their hand."

"How could I possibly do that?"

"You start a social media storm," she said, her eyes bright.

"I have absolutely no idea how to do that. I'm still confused on how to update profile pictures."

"I could help you," she said.

"You know how to do it?" I asked.

"I know how people do it; there's no guarantee that it will take, but if you do it exactly right, there's a good chance."

"Could they sue me or something for revealing info about the school?"

"You have to be very careful about what you reveal and to only state the exact truth. And you have to be sure that you are willing to face the social consequences, Jamie. You're going to be forcing the school board to take action, and these rich PTA parents will not thank you for it. They might retaliate against you personally."

"Half of them already hate me because I'm the only one who points out their bullshit at the meetings. What would I have to do?" I asked.

"You would need some powerful branding, a viral post or video. The video would be better since it could draw national media attention. You'd probably need to use your celebrity status and any celebrity contacts you have."

"I don't have any," I said.

"What about Beza?"

I nodded. "She definitely has a lot of them, but I don't want to force her to commit parent-social suicide with me. She's on the PTA and friends with a lot of these parents."

"She could do it anonymously, like I'm going to. I probably know a lot of these parents, too." Amy shrugged. "But, there's a lot of behind the scenes things she can do to help without anyone ever finding out."

"I'll ask. How would we create a viral video?"

"It needs to be short, poignant, inspiring, and if at all possible, entertaining. What if you sang?"

"Seriously?"

"You're a semi-famous singer, that's the best weapon in your arsenal," she said.

"I'm not even close to semi-famous," I said.

"You can call back whatever little fame you had, especially if you have help from other celebrities."

I looked down. "But this might not work?"

"I'd say you have about a forty-percent chance of it going viral if you had more than ten celebrities with a decent-sized fan base endorsing your video."

A nervous fluttering formed in my stomach. "I would have no idea what to sing. I mean, I've never written a song before..."

"I'll do it. I can do the research too," she said with a small grin on her face.

"That sounds like a whole lot of work to do today, along with your more than full time job," I said.

"Jamie, this will be invaluable experience for me. Also, if there's something I can do, I want to help."

"Oh, this is terrifying, I haven't sung in like... in years. Not like that. When do you want to do this?"

"Aren't you supposed to do this step today?" she asked, her grin growing.

"Oh, I don't think that's so important," I said, my voice pitching.

"Well, I do. I can get everything together today. Also, we're both pretty busy for the rest of the week."

"Oh, my god Amy, I don't think I can do it," I said, laughing.

"You are so going to do it. I'll meet you during Sarah's gymnastics. The sun will be just a little west-facing, and the warehouse walls will make for a perfect backdrop. We need to avoid recognizable buildings."

"Except that it's raining." I shrugged. "Too bad. We'll just have to do it another day," I said.

"It stopped raining, Jamie," she said.

Peeking out of Sarah's window, I realized she was right. The sun was almost entirely broken through the clouds.

"Shit," I said.

Amy laughed behind me. "I am pretty excited."

"I am most definitely not," I said.

Amy laughed so hard she snorted. Her hands flew up to cover her face.

I spun to smile at her. "Oh wow, Amy, I haven't heard you snort in years!"

"Oh, that's so embarrassing," she said.

"Not in front of me. It reminds me of when you were little," I said.

She rolled her eyes. "Well, I'm going to start setting all this up so you have to do it."

"Oh no," I said as I walked out of the room. Before I had even completely stepped out, I walked back in the room, closed my eyes and said, "Fine, I'll do it. You're right; they'll just ignore me if I try to do it the conventional way. They've been ignoring me all year."

Day Five: Six-twenty

After listening to some absolutely terrifying ideas that Amy was mulling over about the intended-viral video, I walked into the kitchen to stand by the coffee pot. I picked up the carafe and swished the coffee contents around. The hot steaminess almost exuded from the metal exterior.

Sighing, I crossed over to my refrigerator and opened it. Grabbing up a super food drink I had run out for the night before, I held it up near my face and whispered, "I know what you're trying to do but you will never replace coffee, not ever."

It tried to look innocent, but I wasn't fooled.

"Whatever." The cap snapped and crackled as I broke the seal. I took a deep drink of the thick smoothie, tasting the tangy, carroty taste.

Grabbing up my phone, I returned to sit beside Sarah and read through old text messages from Cameron. What I was looking for wasn't there. After a moment, I realized I couldn't find what I wanted because we had our last conversation over the phone instead of text.

Closing my eyes, I tried to remember exactly what he had said. Had he said that he was having dinner with a client, or had I? And if he had said it, was she just getting some work done and they took the opportunity to catch up? Or, was it like it sounded like, and they were actually on a date?

Could I ask him point blank?

Was there any possible way that I could ask it that wouldn't at the very least sound judgmental?

I leaned back against the headboard. I'd always loved to play with Vanessa's long-thick blonde hair. We had never reached the level where the studio provided us with a hairdresser for every show. So, in a sort-of round table, we'd each done each other's hair in the style the hairdresser had modeled for us.

Even years later, on the last day I'd been close with her before the accident, she'd wanted us to do each other's hair the moment she'd put her lips to a glass of wine.

We sat in my old bedroom, both of us sitting on the multicolor bedspread on my and Logan's bed. Unlike usual, Vanessa hadn't cracked a smile through the entire dinner party.

My hands were combing through her thick strands as I began to say, "You want your usual do—Vanessa?"

Reflected in the mirror we were both facing, she wiped away a tear, smudging a streak of mascara. Red splotches rose on her nose and cheeks.

"Sweetheart, are you okay?" I leaned forward so I could peer into her face.

"Fine... I'm fine, Jamie." Her smile fell short as another tear dropped onto her cheek.

I grimaced. "Obviously not all that fine. Are you sure you don't want to talk about it?"

Tears painted two thick black streaks down her face. "I screwed up, Jamie..."

I hugged her from behind.

She put her hand on my arm and squeezed it tight, as if she wanted her fingers to sink into my skin.

I pulled my arm away, but returned to hugging her. "What's going on?"

"I—I..." She dissolved into sobs and didn't continue.

I kissed the top of her head. "Oh, Nessa, it's okay. Is this about Cameron?"

"Yes," she said through her sobs. She made eye contact with me in the mirror. "It's also about—" She squeezed her eyes closed and didn't continue.

"Nessa, you can tell me. I care about Cameron, but you are my best friend. No matter what you did, I'll always be on your side, okay?"

She didn't respond but she sagged more as if she crumpled into herself. "I love you... Jamie, I'm a horrible person..."

"No you're not. You're crazy and emotional, and sometimes you make crazy, emotional, not-so-well thought out decisions, especially when you're drunk..."

Another sob burst from her.

I ran a hand over her hair. "But you are a wonderful person. I should know, I was your maid of honor... and your conjoined twin that one Halloween."

I thought she would laugh at the memory, but instead, more silent tears coursed down her face.

"You don't need to talk about it now, Nessa."

"Cameron told me that I'm... supposed to... I— have to tell you." Her eyes met mine. "But somehow telling you is so much harder than telling Cameron."

"Then don't tell me, Cameron is your husband not your boss. Just let me love you and tell me when

you're ready, okay?" I squeezed her to me. The warm wine feeling in my stomach mixed with the warm love feeling in me.

Vanessa's hand covered mine, and she said nothing more as she sobbed.

I opened my eyes as Sarah's head fell onto my shoulder and woke me from my memory.

She blinked open her eyes.

"Good morning, sweet angel," I whispered as I craned my neck to see her.

Her eyes shut, but after a second, she peeked one open at me.

"Hi. Are you going to wake up?"

"No, I'm going to keep sleeping."

"Okay..." I glanced at my phone, "You can sleep for another four minutes."

Her head settled on my shoulder as I squeezed my eyes shut and tried to dislodge the gloom that had settled in my chest ever since I'd heard Vanessa's all-too-familiar voice last night.

After a very short time, the alarm on my phone started beeping.

"Good morning, angel!" Sarah popped up, a big smile on her face.

"Good morning, angel," I repeated.

"I'm going to see Aunt Amy!" She scooted off the bed and ran out of the room.

I heard an 'oomph!', then Amy said, "Good morning, love bug." There was a kiss sound. "You should probably go to the bathroom, right?"

There was silence, and then the bathroom door closed.

"Jamie!" Amy called from the other room.

I made my way over to Sarah's room, where I found that Amy had not moved from the last time I was in there.

She looked up from her computer again. "How about I get Sarah ready and take her to the bus so you can go ahead over to the coffee shop?" She said it as a question but in that way of hers that almost sounded like an order.

I ran my teeth over my bottom lip. "Um, I want her to be on her usual routine..."

By the look on Amy's face, I could tell she thought I was being ridiculous. "I know her routine, Jamie, and I'm fantastic at routine, okay? But, don't you think it's Chris' right to have an opinion about this offer?"

I looked away. "Amy..."

"And if you show up during open hours, he won't be able to discuss it with you."

I rolled my eyes. "You're only saying this because you want me to take the offer. If you didn't you'd be saying it was my decision to make."

"No, I wouldn't." She turned back to her computer. "I think you should talk about it with him." She turned her computer around to face me. On the screen was a beautiful shot of the cottage house. "If you took the offer and put twenty percent down, you could pay a lot less monthly for this than you do in your apartment now."

"Subtle, Amy."

"The numbers add up, Jamie. Just go talk to Chris, okay? That's all I ask. If nothing else, do it for my peace of mind because you're not letting me do anything about your neighbor, like go to the police... which is what I truly want to do."

"Okay!" I held up my hand in surrender. "Okay, I'll go to talk to Chris. But seriously Amy, don't expect anything to change."

"Thank you. You know, you can always negotiate in a job offer before it's accepted." She raised her brows at me.

"I'm not accepting it; don't get your hopes up. And don't clean my house while I'm gone, okay?"

She rolled her eyes. "All I'm going to do is get Sarah ready. This afternoon, I'm planning to meet you at the studio at around three-fifteen with the script and possibly costumes?"

"Yeah, but I'll have to step out for that phone call with my rental company." A nervous embarrassment surged up from my stomach to the back of my eyes. "Oh, God, I don't want to be in this video."

"Call Beza, see if she can set up the endorsements? It'll take me a couple days to edit the video, but the sooner we coordinate with the celebrities, the better. I already pretty much have an idea forming of what I want you to do, but I'm not ready to explain it."

"Okay." My voice came out way more high-pitched than usual.

Amy smiled at me. "It'll be great, Jamie. Now go get ready."

I covered my face with my hands. "I'm going to die of embarrassment."

"No you won't."

"Oh, fine." I turned to go get ready in my room. Even though all I wanted in the world was to wear comfortable underwear, I couldn't make myself put on the pair that Clarke had left for me. I picked it up between two fingers and dropped it into the trash. I wiped my hand on my pants. My fingers felt tainted.

After getting dressed for work, I walked into the living room to find Sarah and Amy sitting at the table. Sarah was somehow already dressed and eating, her hair brushed back into a ponytail.

I kissed the top of her head. "Hey baby, you okay with Aunt Amy taking you to the bus?"

She smiled at me, her mouth full of banana. "Mm-hmm."

"Okay. Amy, are you—"

"Go, Jamie." She glanced up from her oatmeal. "We're fine."

I sighed. "Okay, I'm going, fine. Thank you, even if you're a complete dictator while you help me."

"I'm not a dictator." She rolled her eyes and shook her head. "But you really should go."

"Ha, okay, I'm going." I grabbed my purse and crossed to the door.

Fifteen minutes later, I parked in my usual spot next to the Jack and the Beanstalk mural. I stepped out into the cool, low-hanging mist and pressed the button to lock my car before hurrying down the sidewalk.

A warm glow wreathed The Coffee Stop's windows in the misty dawn morning. I stopped to glance through the window in the door, seeing Chris loading pastries into the display case. I could almost imagine Logan in there too, standing next to Chris, laughing in that way of his that seemed to wrinkle every part of his face.

I sighed, sticking my key into the lock and opening the door to break the imagined scene.

"Whoa!" Chris said, jumping up. "You just scared the hell out of me, Jamie. I thought you were someone breaking in to rob me for a second."

"I am. Give me your muffins!" I laughed. "Wow, that sound way dirtier than I meant it, sorry."

Chris shook his head but his face broke into a grin. "Reporting you to the boss."

"How are you feeling?"

"One-hundred percent better."

"Oh, good." I turned to lock the door. "So… Amy spent the night last night and she pushed me out the door this morning so that I could talk to you about the offer."

"I thought it was a bust?"

I turned back. "It was… kind of."

He turned and continued placing pastries in the display case.

After depositing my stuff and putting on an apron, I walked over to the nearest table and pulled the chairs down, flipping them and tucking them under the table. I looked back to Chris and opened my mouth to speak, but closed it again and moved to the next table.

After I had flipped the chairs on all the tables, I returned to the front to find Chris starting up the credit card machine. He looked up. "So, are you going to tell me?"

"Yeah. The offer was by the same guy who owns the lien."

Chris' jaw sagged. "Are you serious?"

My knuckles thumped the counter. "That's not all of it. It's from Pat."

"Pat? Dry double cappuccino Pat?"

"Yeah." I nodded.

His mouth made an 'oh' shape before he shook his head again. "You're messing with me?"

"Nope."

"That's messed up." He looked away, but his gaze returned to me. "Take the offer. Let them pay you off or whatever for what they did."

"Yeah, except there's a catch. They want us to work for them. At least for me, they want me under a three year contract. I'm not sure about you... I stormed off pretty soon after I realized who they really were."

"Three years doing what?"

"For me, being a general manager. I suck because I didn't ask about your job. Sorry."

"So understandable, Jamie."

"Well, they did say that 'they would use your talents' or something, I don't know."

He nodded.

I punched the counter again, looking down. "I kind of freaked out on them... and ran off."

"Yeah, only what they deserve. So, what do you think now?"

I met his gaze. "I don't know Chris... I still hate what they did, but a lot of heat has gone out of my anger. I half think they're still trying to screw me—us—over, and half think that maybe this is some sort of guilt deal. The way it was explained to me—by Pat's son, who I am sure is really biased—is that Pat offered me this deal to take care of me and Sarah after he decimated our lives. At the same time, this past year just made me way too cynical for that."

Chris didn't say anything.

"I could find out about what they're offering for you for a job if you—"

"Nah," he said, shaking his head. He opened the cash register and started opening the coin rolls.

"Are you sure? if they're offering me a job as a general manager they could be offering you—"

"Nope." He spilled the quarters into the drawer, making a loud clattering. "I stand behind you, Jamie, always."

I swallowed. "And I stand behind you too, Chris, whenever, whatever, I hope you know that."

"Duh." He shook his head. "So since you're here, are you going to help me open the shop or what?"

"Whatever you say, boss." I grinned at him.

He pointed at me. "Get to work, young lady."

Day Five: Seven-forty

Walking around the coffee bar, I jumped on the espresso machine, turning it on. The machine's light blinked its hello at me a couple times before the light turned into a solid red. Turning the knobs, I blew out the steam wands into clean cloths and tried out a few shots on the machine. The shots pulled way too long so I adjusted the grind and started again.

While the shots poured in a slow stream, I pulled one of the large carafes from the coffee brewer, filled another hopper with our organic roast, and started brewing into a new carafe. The air filled with the smell of fresh, newly roasted coffee as I placed the full carafe next to the others on our counter. Inhaling the aroma, I grinned and closed my eyes.

"Still jonesing I see," Chris laughed.

"You have no idea. I'm going to force you to teach me how to make that green tea thingy."

"How about I steal those shots you just pulled to make myself something and then I'll make a green tea latte for you?"

"Then you will be my very favorite person on this whole wide world."

"As if I wasn't already. Trade me places, lady." He stood against the wall so I could squeeze past him.

As Chris heated pitchers of milk, I did a final wipe of the counters, tables and chairs. A classical rendition of a popular pop song by Dream Big was playing over the speaker system and though it was entirely instrumental, I sang the words to the song under my breath as I worked. Everything had been stocked throughout the shop, so I just went to stand beside Chris.

"Ta-da!" He handed me a cup with a green heart in the foam.

"Yes!" I held the cup up, inhaling its sweet aroma. "Thank you, I worship the ground you walk on."

"Naturally. So you want to be on register again today? I don't mind if you do."

"Maybe. Yeah, it might be best, I'm just really hoping that a certain regular doesn't come in."

"If Pat comes in, I could write 'go to hell' on his cup." He bobbed his eyebrows at me.

"I'd say yes, but he's still the lien holder on the shop and I'm pretty sure I already did enough damage."

"I was joking, Jamie, I'd never do that."

"Oh." I grinned, tucking up my shoulders. "Sorry, I guess I would do that." I blew on my drink and took a sip. "*This* is amazing, Chris."

"No problemo. Oh, and today the best thing in there is the savory scones." He walked back behind the coffee machine with his own drink.

"I'll get right on that." A minute later, I realized that he was very right. The scone was some sort of buttery, cheesy Cajun spiced miracle that simultaneously melted and crunched in my mouth. After collecting every last crumb from the plate, I washed my hands and called over, "You ready for me to open her up?"

"One hundred percent."

When I headed for the door, I saw that a couple people were already waiting outside. I waved before I turned over the sign to open and unlocked the front door.

"Morning Steve, morning Carol," I said as I ushered the couple past me.

"Morning, Jamie," Steve said in his gruff baritone voice as he passed. "Hey Chris, what's good today?"

"Like you don't know, Steve," Chris called as he pumped coffee into a cup. In unison, he, Steve and Carol all said, "Everything."

"You guys are just too much. Every single morning," I said, shaking my head and grinning.

By the time I stepped back behind the counter Chris had already set out both Carol and Steve's coffees.

"Except yesterday morning, we sure missed our pastries."

I rang up their order. "Well today... The savory scone was like... I don't even have words to describe how amazing it was."

"I'll take one of those," Carol said. In contrast to her husband, her voice was shrill. They were both thin but Carol was also almost a head taller than Steve.

"One for me as well," Steve said.

They didn't tip, they never did, but they gave us each warm grins and thanks before taking their scones and coffees to a table.

The bell dinged over the door and a couple more regulars came through the door. As the customers kept rolling in all morning, many of them mentioned how we'd been closed the day before or how they'd missed us, even a couple customers that I didn't recognize. A couple customers mentioned leaving us messages on our social media sites. I'd told them all thanks for the concern and support and that we'd just needed a staff day.

When the morning rush finally slowed, I'd taken a moment to check our social media sites to find there were about fifty messages. "Wow," I said under my breath.

"What?" Chris said from behind me.

I spun. "Hey Chris?" I chewed on my lip and looked to the ceiling.

"Yeah?" Chris said after a second.

"Is there a... difference, since I've taken over the management of the shop, I mean, since I'm the sole manager?"

"Only a thousand differences. What do you mean?"

"I don't know. The profit margin is higher than it's ever been and we have less hours... stuff like that."

"Well, yeah. I mean, I loved Logan, but you're a better boss than he was. And let's be honest, Logan was pretty much the boss before he died."

"How so? I mean, they said they wanted me to be their general manager, but I have no idea what I could really do to improve stores that I've never even worked in."

"I'm not pretending that I know anything about it but... okay, I told Logan a thousand times that we should switch flours. The flour he insisted we buy was the same price for twice as much as the one I wanted, but I always ended up tossing half of it anyway. And Logan's flour didn't bond well, so I always had to use more eggs or other bonding agents to make the pastries. The first time I suggested it to you, you switched flours."

"Well, I don't know anything about flour."

"Let's be honest here, Jamie, neither did Logan. I mean, I know he loved baking, but there's a lot more to it than following a recipe. Even though I'm pretty sure he was aware that I was more knowledgeable about it, he never listened to me." He shook his head. "I feel bad talking about this stuff because he's dead, but it's true."

"Okay, so you're saying that I'm a better boss than Logan because I followed *your* orders?"

"Basically, yeah."

I laughed. "Okay, yeah, I'll change all the policies in all the stores across the county, thanks."

He shrugged. "I think you're a good boss because you didn't come in thinking that you knew everything and you listened to what I said, and what everyone else said too."

"Not everything."

"Yeah." He shrugged again. "But you listen. Even to what Mitch suggests. And when Colby came in that first time and said that it was hard to get around in his wheelchair, you had the whole shop moving tables. And you kept the tables that way, now Colby comes in twice a week. Also, you talk less to customers."

"Isn't that a bad thing?"

"Not really. You get drinks out faster and... I don't know, you still manage to make things personal but the shop moves fast."

The bell over the door rang twice in quick succession.

"Okay." I nodded. "Thanks Chris."

"See, you're doing it right now." He grinned.

"Doing what?"

"Listening to me."

I shook my head, feeling my cheeks heat as I turned to help the next customer. The smile that I had on my face fell away as I saw Pat walking up to the counter. He wore a dark brown suit, his light hair combed back. A black briefcase was held in one hand, which was new as I'd never once seen Pat work in the shop.

My stomach plummeted as I forced a placid expression on my face. "Hello, what can I get for you?"

He stared at me for a few seconds, then said, "Hello, Jamie, Chris, I was hoping to talk to you about the offer."

"Can I get something started for you?" Chris asked.

Pat cleared his throat. "Double cappuccino, dry."

"Awesome," Chris said as he wrote it on a cup.

I rang the order up then looked up. "Anything to eat?"

He looked over to the display case. "The spice muffin, please."

"That will be seven fifty, please."

As I ran his card, Pat said, "If you have a second, I'd like to discuss some modifications that I made to the offer that I believe will interest you."

"Thank you, but unfortunately it's not a good time right now. You're welcome to write a comment in the comment box with your phone number or email, and I will get back to you shortly." I grabbed a comment card from under the cash register. "It's just over there." I pointed to the comment box between the bathroom and our community bulletin.

"We check it every day," Chris added with a smile, and then he turned to the customer behind Pat. "Hey Clare. Just a mocha?"

Clare, who I hadn't even noticed behind Pat, grinned. "Hey, Chris! The mocha and a lot more."

"The whole salon?"

She giggled. "Practically."

Pat nodded then picked up the comment card from where I had set it on the counter. After Chris had called out Pat's order, he picked up his drink and for the first time ever took a seat at one of the tables.

While I helped Clare with her slew of coffee orders and then the people in line behind her, I glanced over to Pat periodically.

Pat sat with his back straight as he wrote on the comment card for at least five minutes. When he finished, he capped his pen and returned it to his briefcase. He pulled what looked like a packet of loose papers held together by a staple or paperclip and also a manila folder. After zipping up his briefcase, he crossed over to the comment box. One by one, he fed the comment card, the packet of papers and the manila folder through the slot.

As he turned, I returned my focus to the customer in front of me. "Sorry, did you say you wanted a muffin?"

The twenty-something-looking guy grinned. "Scone, this one." He pointed to the savory scone. "To go, please."

I grinned back. "Sorry. And, that's a great choice." As I went to grab him his scone, I glanced to where Pat was grabbing his briefcase.

He looked up and met my gaze, raising his eyebrows before turning to walk to the door.

Grabbing the scone, I put it on a plate and returned to the man at the counter.

He grinned again. "To go?"

I closed my eyes. "I am so sorry." I walked back and grabbed a pastry bag, using the tongs to transfer the scone into the bag.

When I returned to the guy, Chris set his finished drink in front of him. After ringing him up, I regained my focus through the remainder of the morning rush. When the crowd finally slowed down, Chris set a drink on the counter in front of me. This one had a green four leaf clover in the foam.

I looked up. "You have to teach me to do that one!"

"It's just a double heart."

"Too bad we already missed St. Patties, that would be an awesome special."

"Are you going to check?"

I took a sip of my drink and savored the delicious taste for a second. Shrugging, I looked up at him. "Check what?"

He raised an eyebrow.

"You check." I took another sip of my drink.

"Nah ah, I'll go get it for you, but whatever he left in there is for you."

I set down my drink and shook out my hands. "I'm not ready, Chris. Give me a couple more hours."

"If you don't tell me what he left before I get off my shift in..." he looked up at our shop clock, "forty five minutes, I will die from curiosity."

Squeezing my eyes shut, I said, "Fine. In forty minutes, I'll check."

He pointed at me. "I'm holding you to that."

I set about wiping up the counters and cleaning up the bagel bar, where I had somehow managed to create an onion, poppy seed and tomato war zone.

When everything was clean and there were no more customers to help, I walked around the shop, wiping down tables and bussing plates. Several people greeted me as I walked by with stacks of plates.

Even though the dish bin wasn't full, I got a head start on the dishes. When I was about halfway through I heard Chris call, "Yo, Jamie!"

I peeled off my gloves and set them by the sink.

Glancing back at the clock, I saw that it was, indeed, eleven twenty-five.

Day Five: Eleven twenty-five

Chris battled a grin.

I mock-glared at him. "Fine. You divide up the tips and I'll go check the comment box."

I crossed back through the Coffee Stop to the comment box. Using my keys, I unlocked the blue-painted lid. The lock was pretty silly as no one had ever tried to break into the comment box before, but a customer had recommended it, and ever since I put it on there we received twice as many comments.

When I opened the wooden box lid, the items Pat left peered up at me. I grabbed them up, closed the lid and relocked it. When I turned around, I saw that a small line had formed at the counter and Chris was juggling orders.

I crossed back through the shop and back behind the counter, depositing the packets and forms on a shelf above where we kept our stuff.

On my way to go wash my hands, Chris called over, "I got this Jamie, just go deal with the forms." He quickly rang up the customer in front of him, took their money, and moved on to the next customer.

"If you're sure," I said.

"I am positive."

Swallowing, I returned to the forms. I had set the comment card on top. Leaning over I read:

Dear Ms. Scott,
While I found your display today
immature, it did have the desired effect of

showing me that I was no longer a friend of the store. It is surprising how much this affected and saddened me, and that in turn, has me thinking of the reason that I wished to hire you in the first place. Your store and the way you have treated me as a customer, has created a sense of belonging for me, a feeling of enjoyment in the fulfillment of small daily traditions. Every morning, I see the same familiar faces and enjoy products with consistent quality and this in turn brings me a sense of happiness and fulfillment. While my stores have convenience and quality, they lack that feeling of belonging that you create with what seems like little contrivance to do so. For this specific reason, I wanted to hire you as the general manager for all local sites of Harrington's.

I hoped that after the shock of the situation had faded and you had a night to mull my offer over, your attitude would have changed. From my reception this morning, it is obvious that this is not the case. I will, however, extend an offer again with new terms, as well as detail the offer that I am extending to Chris.

I do still believe that to see a positive change with lasting effect, a number of years would be needed with you in our employ. Previously, I had acted under the assumption that three years of job security at a much higher salary than you are now receiving

I set the comment card aside and pulled the manila folder from the bottom of the pile. Sticking my finger in at the side, I pulled it across and ripped the package open. Inside sat a small pile of papers, the bottom ones thick and stiff as photo stock. When I tipped the folder over onto the shelf, a key fell out first, followed closely by the papers. The key's chain had a tag with 'Howard Storage' and an address printed on it.

"Huh?" I frowned as I lifted the papers in my hand. The thinner paper on top had a note in the same hand as Patrick's comment card. It read:

Below the note was dated this past Christmas Eve. I turned the page to find a photograph of an oak end-table, an inlaid wood artifact of my former life. The edges of my eyes heated and my lip quivered. The stack of photos protested as I slipped them back into their manila folder by catching halfway in.

I pocketed the key.

I set the manila folder beside my purse and left the stack of offers on the shelf. Walking away, I returned to the cash register where Chris stood, dividing up the tips.

"You're welcome to look Chris. There's a job offer in there for you, too. You can even take it with you, if you want."

He handed me my share of the tips. "I'd rather wait. I just wanted to make sure you looked while I was still here in case you needed me or something."

I pointed into his big, bristly face. "You are way too good of a person. I'm not even kidding, it's kind of disgusting."

"Yeah, sure." He shook his head. "I'm out of here, Jamie. See you tomorrow."

"All right, Chris. Take care."

I threw myself back into work after he left, finishing the dishes before returning to wiping down the store. A small rush came in during lunch time and I worked through the orders quicker than usual. When there were no more customers, I started doing pre-closing chores, just to do something. As much as I distracted myself, though, I couldn't stop my gaze from flitting to where the new revised offers sat.

When there was nothing left to do in the shop and no new customers coming in, I grabbed the window cleaner, squeegee and a towel and headed outside. I sprayed the cleaner across in giant splatters, then grabbed up the squeegee. Standing on my tiptoes, I stretched as high as I could reach.

"Hey beautiful," a male voice whispered directly into my ear.

I jumped forward. Pain exploded in my chin and chest as I rammed into the slick, wet window.

Hands grabbed me around my arms. "Shit, Jamie, are you okay?"

Cameron, it was Cameron's voice.

I half stepped, half fell back into him, while I grabbed my chin. "Owww."

"Is she okay?" I heard someone call out. When I looked over, I saw that it was one of my customers, holding the Coffee Stop's door open.

"Mfhhh... fine." I kept one hand covering my chin and waved at her with the other.

"What happened?" she asked, looking between me and where Cameron still held me up.

"I'm her friend, I just snuck up on her to say hello and I must have scared her so much she tried to jump through the window."

"Oops," the lady said, dryly.

"Yeah, oops," Cameron said.

When I glanced over, I saw that nearly all of my customers were standing or looking over concerned. I waved at them. "I'm fine," I called, my jaw throbbing as I spoke. Gasping, I lifted my other hand up to cover it.

"Let's go get you some ice." Cameron righted me, his hands rubbed down the sides of my arms.

I stepped out of his hands and walked into the shop without looking back. As I maneuvered through the crowd, more than one pair of eyes sought me out, making me think that my slamming into the shop window had to have been pretty dramatic.

Cameron's hand cupped my elbow. "Can I come behind the counter to help you?"

"Probably best not to, Cameron." I looked up at him for the first time.

His gaze met mine, brow furrowing. "All right, can I at least take a look at your chin and make sure nothing is broken?"

I turned away. "Nothing's broken; I'm fine, just need to get some ice."

"Yeah, okay." His hand dropped as I moved from him.

Behind the counter, I cleaned my hands then scooped a couple ice cubes into a clean towel. I hissed as I pressed the towel to my jaw. When I returned to the counter, Cameron stood in front of it, concern plain on his face.

His hand came toward mine, but fell short. "I am so sorry, Jamie."

Exhaling through my nose, I shook my head. "It's cool. You're probably doing me a favor, Amy wanted to film me singing today and I don't think that's possible now."

He grimaced. "And you're covered in window cleaner."

Glancing down, I saw that I was indeed wet and in some places frothy with cleaning solution. Thankfully, my hair was gathered into a ponytail, but from the strong astringent smell and tacky feeling on my chin, I didn't think that my face had been spared. I tried to laugh. "I guess I'm a little jumpy, lately."

"I saw that. I really am sorry, Jamie."

I shook my head. "It's really fine. I'll just get a new apron. Do you want your usual?"

He hesitated. "Sure."

Walking to where we kept our spares, I grabbed out another black apron, throwing my dirty one on top of my stuff so that I'd remember to take it home. Replacing my ice pack, I crossed over to the espresso machine and started pulling shots. "Want anything to eat?" I asked as I pumped the lever and filled a large cup with medium-roast coffee.

"Sure. What's good?"

"The scones. I ate one for breakfast and two for lunch."

"Okay. Jamie, is everything okay?"

I shrugged. "It's fine. Just a little shocked from colliding with the window, you know. How's," I paused, "everything going with you?"

"Pretty decent."

I stayed quiet while I poured his espresso shots into his coffee and grabbed his scone. Placing the coffee and pastry bag in front of him, I said,
"I tried calling you yesterday, but you must have been busy with your client."

"Why didn't you text?"

I shrugged. "It wasn't important."

He reached forward and ran a thumb over my knuckles. "Never, baby. Talking to you is my favorite part of the day."

Stepping away, I returned to pick up my ice pack from where I had set it down, and brought it back up to my chin. When I looked back at him, he was staring at me with a questioning expression on his face.

"Sorry, Cameron, my chin just really hurts."

He nodded. "Yeah. Okay, I have to get back to work anyway. Could you ring me up?"

"On the house."

He hesitated before nodding. "Thanks. I'll just see you tomorrow then."

I tried to smile at him, but the look turned into more of a grimace as my chin pinched with pain. "Only if you want."

"I do." He turned, and without saying anything more, walked out of the shop. When he stepped outside, I saw him lean over and set down his coffee and scone on the ground. He then grabbed up the squeegee and towel and cleaned my entire store window with quick, efficient strokes. When he finished, he set down the cleaning equipment, picked up his drink and food, and walked away.

"Hey, Jamie."

I turned to see one of my regular customers, an older woman that I blanked on the name of, by the counter.

"Hey, there. Can I get you another drink?"

"Nah, I'm just taking off, I wanted to make sure you're okay."

"Thank you, I'm fine. Was it really loud when I crashed into the window?" Every time I spoke, my chin ached.

"A little." She gave me a mirthless grin. "I think we were all just scared that someone was attacking you."

I laughed, but the pain cut it short. "Me too, I guess. But Cameron is a friend."

After the lady walked away, I walked over to my purse and grabbed out my phone. As soon as I pressed the button to get past the lock screen, text messages started scrolling across my screen. Eighty-five text messages. I had eighty five text messages?

"What the...?" I whispered. I checked my call log to make sure I didn't miss a call from Sarah's school or something, but only Amy, Beza and Susan had called me. When I looked back to the text messages, I found that most of the messages were group messages between those three and me.

I read through the last messages:

Beza: I'm so excited! Yeah, they're all going to be able to make it.

Susan: This is going to be amazing.

Amy: It looks like I can get us that equipment, but can anyone pick it up?

Susan: I can, probably. What time?

I put the phone down, forgetting what I had wanted to text and feeling a hot ball of nerves forming in my stomach. I knew I kept ibuprofen in my office, so as there were no more customers coming in, I walked back and popped a couple before returning to the stand behind the counter. As I was already ahead in closing, and there was little I could do until either more customers came in or left, I stood there, holding ice to my chin.

Images rose up in my mind.

The sunset had dyed the sky into a bright orange, setting over the beach-park near my old house.

Sarah's feet pumped as she soared back and forth on the swing. "Higher, Mom!" she said every time she swung back to me.

My hands pressed against the small of her back and I pushed her higher.

"Hey Jamie," came Cameron's low voice from behind me. I glanced back, seeing him walking alone across the playground. Though it was sunset, kids still hung from monkey bars and spun on the small merry-go-rounds.

"Higher, Mom!"

Sarah's back came to my hands and I pushed again.

"Hey, Cameron." I grinned at him. "Vanessa couldn't make it?"

He shook his head and came to stand next to me.

"Neither could Logan," I said, unnecessarily.

"Yeah, I know." He shoved his hands in his pockets, and looked off toward the sunset. "You and Vanessa talked last night when you went into your room?"

"A little. She was pretty upset. It's not really my business, but I got the feeling you guys were going through something." I gazed at his profile.

"Yeah, but obviously she didn't tell you what."

"Higher, Mom!"

I pushed her again.

The sun continued its descent, ripening the colors of the sky.

"How are things going with you and Logan?" Cameron asked in a low voice.

I glanced over at him, to meet his intent gaze. Sucking my lower lip into my mouth, I raised my shoulders in a half shrug. "I don't know, Cameron. He's going through some stuff right now. We both are. I think we just need to... get through it, and then things will be better."

Cameron's jaw clenched. "I haven't seen him sober in two months."

"Higher, Mom!"

"Cameron, not now, okay?" I tilted my head toward where Sarah flew away from me.

"He's a bastard."

"Cameron! Seriously?" I glared at him. "Don't do this here! What's your problem? He's your best friend. You have no idea what it's like to go through this stuff."

Cameron rubbed up his face and over his head. "I can't listen to you defend him—he's a bastard and she's a faithless coward." He turned to walk away.

I sighed. "Cameron, stay. You and Nessa are obviously having a hard time, let's not make it about me and Logan. Let's just chill, watch the sunset and think happy thoughts."

"Higher, Mom!"

"Okay, okay, goofball." I pushed her again.

Cameron grabbed the thick blue pole of the swing set and leaned against it.

The sun slipped down into a thin orange line over the ocean, its progress slowing. We watched in silence as the last sliver vanished into the ocean.

"That's lame. Susan was supposed to drop by with Aiden, they missed the whole thing," I said, as I pushed Sarah again.

Cameron continued to watch the darkening sky.

Grabbing the sides of Sarah's swing, I slowed her motion, moving with her until the swing stopped. "All right, cutie, it's time to go home now."

She kicked out her feet, rocking the swing. "No Mom, I'm going to keep swinging."

"Sweetheart, it's not daytime anymore."

She continued to kick out her legs, rocking the swing back and forth.

Cameron sighed. "I'll walk you two home."

My phone rang in my purse, and I grabbed it up from where I had set it and extracted out my phone. Susan's smiling face greeted me from the phone screen.

"You missed the sunset," I said in greeting.

"My stupid brother called me wasted off his ass and I'm here at the bar to pick him up and he's not anywhere. Has he called you?"

I swallowed. "No."

"Well, his car is gone, I'm freaked out he's driving around drunk again, especially this early in the day when there are kids out. I'm going to kill him."

"I really, really hope he would never do that." A hot wave of panic and anger surged through me. I pulled the phone away from my ear. "Cameron, have you heard from Logan? I guess he's drinking and Susan went to get him from the bar but he's gone."

Cameron stared at me, his gaze searing mine. "What?"

He blinked the expression away then turned back to the ocean. "Yeah, I know where he is."

"Where? Is he okay?"

He paused, again. "He's fine."

"Seriously, Cameron, where is he?"

Cameron closed his eyes, inhaling through his nose. "At Mike's, Mike went and picked him up."

"Oh." I put the phone back to my ear. "I guess he's at Mike's house."

"Well, the butthead could have called me to tell me he left."

"Yeah."

"I'm sorry, Jamie. You shouldn't have to be dealing with this shit either. I'm going to go, I have the neighbor watching Aiden and we have to go get Beza from the airport... I'm seriously going to kill Logan."

"I'm sorry, Susan. Call me later, yeah?"

"Yeah."

Day Five: One twenty-five

"Hey, Jamie?"

I looked up to the coffee counter to see Mitch standing there.

"Oh, wow, sorry, Mitch. I was just standing here daydreaming." I pulled the ice filled cloth away from my chin, which was now more just a cold, wet cloth. "Can I get you anything?"

Mitch grinned at me his gap-toothed grin. "Not right now, Jamie, not right now. But, really soon, I'll be buying stuff every day."

"You got the job?" I smile at him.

"Yeah... well, I... they said that they have more interviews they need to do. But, I think that they'll give it to me, because I'm in this outreach program, and they're supposed to give me a job."

I nodded. "That's promising! And no matter what, going to a job interview is good experience right? For the next, even better job that might come around."

"Well, I think I have this one. I'm pretty sure." He nodded furiously.

"That's awesome. Are you sure you don't want a coffee? On the house?"

"If—maybe could I owe you for it? I could pay you back, when I have the job."

"Um, how about this one is a 'congratulations on having a great interview' gift from me?"

Mitch looked around. I noticed then that he wore the same clothes from the interview, though they were now dirty and stained. "Okay, Jamie, this once, because of the interview."

"What about food, can I maybe get you a bagel too?"

"Nah, nah, Jamie, I ate in the park. Just the coffee, that will do fine for me."

"Okay then." Turning, I filled a cup with dark roast and returned to the counter. "Here you go, Mitch." Mitch told me all about his interview, and I tried to concentrate on what he said but my mind kept wandering. I nodded along, feeling a twinge of pain in my chin every time I did. When a customer came up behind him, I felt a little guilty for being so relieved. "Sorry, Mitch, I have a customer." I gestured to the man behind him.

"Oh, sorry!" He turned to the man. "Sorry!"

The young guy behind him waved. "No worries, bro."

"All right, Mitch, I'll see you later. Thanks for coming in!"

"Oh, thank you, Jamie. And yeah, I'll come in soon, real soon."

"Yeah, okay, Mitch, see you then."

I made eye contact with this new guy; he looked young, maybe late teens or early twenties. He had a surfer look, complete with bloodshot, half closed eyes and an orangey tan.

"Hello, what can I get for you?"

He grinned and pointed at me. "Are you Jamie?"

I nodded.

"Cool." He set his hand on the counter. "So this guy, I think he said he was your boyfriend, just gave me a twenty to come in here to say something like... shit."

I narrowed my eyes, but I couldn't help the small grin that crawled across my face. "Was his name Cameron?"

"Oh, I don't know... sorry. Oh yeah! Okay, he said, 'I'm not moving and neither are you'."

The smile dropped off my face as I stared, wide eyed at him.

"Whoa, lady, you okay? You just went like, sheet white."

"That wasn't from my boyfriend."

"Well, shit, he said he was... I think." The guy took a step back, then turned and started walking toward the door. "My bad, sorry."

I leaned forward over the counter. "Hey wait. Will you wait a second? Do you remember what he looked like? I'm going to call the police... will you wait for them to arrive?"

"Wait until you call the police?" He snorted. "Sorry, lady, no freaking way."

"Wait."

He waved as he got to the door. "Sorry."

I made my way around the counter, but there was little I could do short of tackling him on the street. I glanced around to see if there was anyone in the shop close enough to overhear, but there was only one customer close enough and they had ear-buds in their ears and their attention on a phone.

The bell rang and my gaze flew to the door, but it was only a group of college students walking in loaded down with text books. They stopped at a table to set down their books before coming over to the counter.

Forcing myself to grin, I helped them with their orders. After ringing them up, I said, "Hey ladies, just to let you know, we close in twenty minutes."

"We know, no problem," one of the girls said as she grabbed her latte from the counter.

I nodded, hoping that she actually meant what she said because I hated kicking people out. As no customers followed the girls in, I walked around the café, wiping down tables.

A loud crashing came from behind me and I spun around so fast, I banged my knee into a table. I grabbed my knee and hissed. "Twice in one freaking day."

When I looked around me, I saw the college girls both staring down at a book on the ground.

"Oh, no, is the spine damaged?" one girls said.

After all the tables were clean, I kept scrubbing around the people until the moment the clock struck two. Hurrying to the door, I turned over the closed sign. Walking behind the counter, I closed down the espresso machine and pulled out and wrapped up the few remaining pastries to sell as 'day-olds' tomorrow.

Each time the bell rang over the door, I glanced up, but only found customers leaving. The college girls, of course, left last. The moment they were out I rushed to the front of the store and locked it. Double checking that no one hid in the store, I returned to the counter and finished closing.

While counting the till, which was five and change over, sobs escaped my throat. Tears coursed from my eyes as I watched the receipt tape print, and I had to wipe them away to count the receipts.

"Screw him. Screw you, Clarke! You, you psycho asshole!" I kicked the coffee counter. Closing my eyes, I counted to ten. "I'm done. I'm not dealing with this anymore. I. Am. Done!"

After I deposited our money into the safe, I walked around the shop slamming the chairs onto the tables. I mopped the floor like I wanted to stab it to death. When I carried out the trash, I held my keys between my fingers, ready to claw Clarke if he waited back there. When I found the alley empty, I threw the trash in the bin, and then chucked the recycling in its bin with all my strength.

I was almost sorry when I had finished closing a little early, and I had nothing more to do but grab up my belongings. After exiting the shop's front door, I glared up and down the street, but saw no sign of Clarke. After locking up, I stomped up the street to my car and threw all my papers into the passenger seat.

The streets had few cars, as they often did this time on a weekday. As all the lights were green and four-way stops went to my right of way, I arrived at Sarah's school a full thirty minutes early. After parking in the lot I sighed and looked over at the pile of papers on my passenger seat.

"Universe, I think you are trying to tell me something." I picked up the new offer. After reading

through it, I found the offer on the store identical to
the first offer, so I turned the page, bending it back, to
look at the next paper.

On the top of the paper, there was a
handwritten note in an unfamiliar hand.

Ms. Scott,
This is a revised employment contract. The
previous contract offer is attached below.

"Okay." I read through the offer, and then
looked at the one behind it. Though the job
responsibilities in this revised offer were the same, it
was for a substantially lower salary yet still way above
what I earned at the shop now. Another major
difference was that this new offer only needed a
guarantee of a year, then a renegotiation of salary and
benefits.

I picked up my phone. Scrolling through my
contacts, I deliberated over each one. I bit my lip and
pressed the phone number under Cameron's name.

He answered on the third ring. "Jamie?"

"Hey." I closed my eyes and gritted my teeth.

"How's your chin?"

I reached up and touched it. "It's fine. It feels a
lot better."

There was an extended silence. "Jamie, are you
going to tell me what's going on or just leave me
guessing?"

"I can't go home. Like, ever again."

"What? Why?" When I didn't respond, he asked, "Jamie what aren't you telling me?" His voice was a growl.

I took a deep, steadying breath. "That neighbor has been harassing me, and it's getting really bad and scary."

"Jamie, why the Hell didn't you tell me?"

"I did, by the pool." In a whisper, I added, "kind of." I cleared my throat. "I feel horrible for doing this to you, because I gave you a bit of a cold shoulder earlier today. But you're the only one with a key to my apartment and I can't go home. I'd have someone else do it but I told Amy I'd meet her, and my dad works tonight and—"

"Jamie," his voice was quiet but it stopped my stream of words. "Please just tell me what you need me to do."

"Is there any way that you can go to my apartment and pack up a suitcase with my and Sarah's stuff?"

"Yes. Where are you staying?"

I paused. "Susan's probably. My dad's working until two-thirty tonight and Amy lives too far from the school, and—"

"You and Sarah are staying with me."

"Cameron, I can't ask that of you."

"You're not asking. If you and Sarah are in danger, I wouldn't feel right with you staying with anyone but me or your dad."

"Come on, Cameron, Susan is as tough as you are."

"Usually, yeah, but Susan's pregnant, and I don't think you want to put her, Beza and Aiden in danger either."

I swallowed.

"Jamie, it's easier for me to watch Sarah tomorrow if you two are staying at my house, anyway."

"I feel like I'm screwing this all up. Even after everything, I am thinking about taking this job and selling the coffee shop. I got a new offer from Harrington's and it's way less demanding. If I make the deal, I plan on buying a house. I already have a house in mind."

"Okay?"

"So, it probably won't be for that long, maybe a couple of weeks until I have a new place."

"Well, until then, please either live at my house or your dad's, Jamie. Can you agree to that? Because it's either that or I'm camping outside the window of wherever you're staying."

I snorted, picturing it.

"You think I'm joking, but I'm not. Will you please tell me everything about what's going on with this neighbor?"

The first bell rang at the school and the doors opened to let lines of kids stream toward the busses.

"Yeah, maybe. But not right now."

"Fine. Just come over when Sarah's gymnastics is finished. Do you want to come with me to get your stuff?"

"No. I really, really want to avoid going home right now."

"No problem, I'll get the stuff."

"Thank you so much, Cameron."

"Yeah. I'm just mad that you didn't tell me before. How long has this been going on? Just since last weekend or longer?"

Looking out my rearview mirror, I saw Sarah standing with her aide. She jumped up and down while Ms. Brown had a smile beaming from her face. "Sarah's out. I'll talk to you about it later?"

I could hear the sigh over the phone. "Yeah, I'll see you tonight."

Hanging up my phone, I climbed out of my car and crossed the parking lot to where Sarah still hopped up and down.

"Hi," I called over when I got close.

"Mom!" Sarah yelled. "Mom!"

"Hey, baby."

She jumped up and down in a circle. "Are you excited?"

"Sure. Are you excited, angel?" I asked.

"Yes!" Sarah hopped over to me.

"I can tell."

Ms. Brown grinned and pushed her glasses up her nose.

"I'm guessing it was a good day?" I hugged Sarah to me.

"A great day." Ms. Brown nodded. "Actually, even though a lot of the other kids were having trouble, Sarah did fantastic work all day." She leaned down to talk to Sarah. "I'm proud of you. Are we going to have another great day tomorrow?"

"Bye! I am going to gymnastics."

"Sarah, Ms. Brown asked you a question." I threaded my fingers through the strands of her hair that were loose from her ponytail and combed then back behind her ear.

Sarah waved. "Bye! See you at school! See you tomorrow! I am going to gymnastics!"

Ms. Brown's shoulders bobbed as she huffed out a laugh. "Okay, then, Sarah." She straightened to smile at me. "I have to be off now anyway; you guys have a great day!"

Nodding, I said, "Thank you so much!"

She waved as she turned. "My pleasure."

Turning with Sarah toward the car, I looked up and directly at Patrick Kelley Jr. The light hit his combed back blond hair as he grinned down at Kay. She seemed to be talking a hundred miles a minute while skipping along beside him. He walked away from me, so there was little chance that he would see me, but a squirming feeling still wormed its way through my stomach as my cheeks heated.

I blinked and turned my attention back to Sarah. "Okay, cuteness, let's get going to gymnastics."

She stepped away to smile up at me. "Do you love gymnastics, Mom?"

"I love that you love it so much. I love watching you do gymnastics." I offered her my hand and when she took it, we stood at the curb until a car stopped and let us pass.

When I buckled her into her booster, I gave her a grin and asked, "Hey Sarah, do you love gymnastics?"

"Yes!" She bounced in her seat and kicked the seat in front of her.

"Oh, I just had to make sure." I kissed her on the forehead.

The traffic was thick getting out of the school and it took a while to get to the gymnastics' studio as we had to go well around the high school to avoid grid-lock. The entire way, I told Sarah about how we were going to stay at Cameron's for a little while, what we were going to do there and how she was going to get to school.

Sarah happily kicked the passenger seat, but didn't say anything as I talked.

When I pulled into the studio's lot, I found it was full, which wasn't at all usual for Wednesday afternoons. I ended up having to pull back onto the road and park on the street down a block. By the time I parked, the clock on my car read three fifteen.

I turned back to Sarah. "Sweetheart, I'm going to have to get you in there and changed then run back to the car for a phone call, okay?"

Sarah giggled, her hands on her knees. "Are you happy?"

"Yes, goofball." As I walked her up to the studio, more cars pulled into the lot and we had to wait for a break to cross the street.

Unlike usual, Heidi wasn't waiting for us in the front of the studio. Also, when we stepped inside, the entire studio had been rearranged. The beams were lined up against one wall and all the other equipment crammed to the other side of the floor mat.

There were about twenty people in there, several guys and a man fiddling with what looked like a speaker system. On the mat, several older teen gymnasts practiced, doing what looked like a synchronized routine, dressed in costume and talking amongst themselves.

I caught a flash of Heidi's red hair as she came out of her office with an armful of ribbons. When I was about halfway to her, she looked up and grinned. "You're here! Great!"

"Um…" I looked to the practicing gymnasts, then back to Heidi. "It's okay if Sarah practices?"

Heidi blinked up at me. "She's not going to be in the video?"

I shook my head. "What?"

"Hey, Jamie, long time no see."

I spun to look up into a guy's face that I immediately recognized. "Holy shit." I covered my mouth a moment after the words came out. "Sorry—but, wow." Lowering my hand, I shook my head again. "Kevin? What are you—wow! What are you doing here?"

He laughed.

"Hey, give me a hug. How's it been going, Jamie?"

I gave him a hug, and though I felt a little embarrassed doing it, he hugged me tight and stepped back. "Um, good. This here is my daughter, Sarah; she's a big fan of you guys."

"Sarah, this is Kevin, he's in Dream Big, the group you like." I stepped back and looked down to Sarah, who glanced up at Kevin.

She waved. "Bye! I'm going to get ready for gymnastics now."

He grinned and waved back.

Heidi put an arm around Sarah. "Here, I'll take her to get ready."

"Oh, sorry. Heidi, did you meet Kevin?" I grinned a little manically at her.

"Yeah, we met." She nodded. "Sarah, you can change in my office. There are a bunch of people in the girl's room.

I turned back to Kevin. "This is too cool! How's life for you? How are the guys?"

"They're here." He leaned back and nodded to the group behind him.

Across the room, Nero and Markus waved over at me as a guy looked to be pinning a microphone to their shirts. "Hey, Jamie," they each said.

"Wow, hi guys." I smiled back at Kevin. "I never thought I'd see you guys again, besides on TV, of course. Congratulations so much on your success."

"Thanks, Jamie. Yeah, when Beza called we couldn't resist driving up here. You know, Nero's nephew has special needs too, and his sister has to deal with all kinds of hassles with the schools."

"Wait, what?" I blinked up at him. My eyes widened and lips puckered. "You're here for the video we're making?"

He laughed. "Bee didn't tell you?"

I shook my head. "Um…"

"So, she probably didn't tell you that the Rocketeers are coming too?"

My mouth hung open.

He laughed again. "Yeah, Nero told Clarice that we were coming out here to do a video for Bee's niece and they all just hopped in a van."

"They're still together?" I glanced over at Nero.

"Yeah, but only out of the spotlight. You know how it is."

"Yeah, I remember. This is just too crazy, but, wow. Thank you guys so much." My phone rang, vibrating my purse. "Shoot, I need to get that. I'll be right back, okay?" Rushing toward the door of the studio, I extracted my phone from my bag.

Several people walked in as I tried to leave, so I answered my phone. "Hello?"

"Hello, this is Richard, the property manager of Sunset Estates, is this a good time?"

"Yes, um, just give me a moment."

When the doorway was clear, I walked through to find Amy, Beza and Susan standing just outside talking.

"Aunt Jamie!" Aiden yelled as he jumped up and down, his braids flying in all directions.

The whole group turned to me.

"One second, sweetheart." I held up a finger. To the group, I said, "My landlord." I rushed down the side of the building where no one was.

"Hello?" Richard asked.

"Yeah, I'm here."

"Hello, Ms. Scott. So, I am pleased to tell you that we do have a three bedroom unit opening up at the beginning of May. The rent is twenty-two hundred a month, and it is one of our poolside apartments."

"Seriously, Richard, are you serious?"

"I am, this is what I have available at present."

"Did you tell Clarke I'm trying to move from my apartment?"

"It is our policy that when there is a conflict between tenants that we offer both tenants the opportunity to move units."

"He sent someone to threaten me at my work, Richard."

There was a prolonged silence on the other end.

"I don't feel safe in my unit; he's gone in there when I wasn't home. He's gone through my laundry when it was in your washers. I don't feel safe in your complex at all anymore. I'm not going back."

"Ms. Scott, if you are talking about breaking your lease, then there are certain procedures that we need you to take."

"How about this: my sister looked it up last night, and according to the Fair Housing Act, you refusing to help me after I reported sexual harassment from another tenant is considered discriminating against me based on my sex."

"We're helping you Ms. Scott, we're offering you another unit, and we offered your neighbor a chance to move."

"You offered me a unit I can't even possibly afford and all you did was tell the guy who's harassing me that I'm trying to get away from him. You put me in danger, you put my daughter in danger, and if you don't let me out of my lease agreement, I'm taking Sunset Estates to court."

"We have—"

I hung up on him.
"Good job."
I spun to see Amy standing a few feet away. She lifted her hands up and clapped a couple times.

Day Five: Three-forty

I gave a loud huff and sighed. "I'm so over this, Amy!"

"Sounds like it." She grinned at me, but the grin dropped. "What do you mean he threatened you at your work?"

I told her all about the stoned surfer guy and then about where I planned to stay.

She raised her eyebrows. "What are you thinking, Jamie? How are you going to break it off with him if you're living with him?"

I closed my eyes and leaned back against the warehouse wall. "I'm not even sure what I want."

"Did you talk to him about his date with Vanessa?"

I heaved a sigh. "No."

"Stay with me and Peter."

Shaking my head, I looked back at her. "You guys live on the opposite side of town from Sarah's school and both of you and Peter commute to work, and it would be insane."

"Mom can drive her, or—"

"I'm just going to do it this way, Amy, okay? I already told Sarah and Cameron's picking up my stuff from the duplex and everything."

"Jamie—"

"Amy, please."

"Fine, make your own stupid decisions."

"That's what I'm best at. I noticed that the little video we were planning to film turned into a circus."

She grinned and shrugged. "Obviously you didn't read any of our texts. Did you at least read the script I sent you in your email?"

I shook my head. "There's a script?"

She widened her eyes. "Um, yeah."

"Well, you know, unfortunately I injured my chin today so there's no way I can sing."

Amy leveled one of her infamous looks on me. "I don't see any injury."

I pointed to my chin. "It was right here."

She tilted her head. "Nope, nothing."

I glared at her. "It happened."

"You singing is essential to the plot of the video. I'm sorry, you're just going to have to suck it up."

"The video has a plot?"

"In a way." She grinned. "Thankfully for you, I brought copies of the script and they're inside. A lot of people showed up for this, Jamie, so you better be a good sport. I'm not even kidding."

She turned on her heel and walked toward the entrance of the studio.

I couldn't help giving out a little groan as I forced myself to follow her. "I can't believe I agreed to this."

"Stop whining." She didn't look back, just walked through the front doors.

The studio had more people in it than I had ever seen in there before, even during the couple competitions Sarah and I had watched.

The same girls continued to practice their gymnastics. On one side of the mat, Beza and Susan stood with four girls I recognized as the Rocketeers. I'd never met Clarice before, but I assumed she was the one with her arm swung over Beza's shoulders. They were all deep in conversation, looking between the packets of paper in their hands and each other.

A little way away, the three members of Dream Big were doing the same.

"Okay, here you go." Amy thrust a packet of paper into my hands. "You don't have much time; everyone else has had these for a couple of hours."

I read the first line and then looked up to glare at her. "'Jamie stands alone and starts singing?' Are you kidding me?"

She made a hushing sound. "Jamie, go memorize that thing."

Turning, Amy walked away and over to where Heidi stood.

I read through the script, which was actually just song lyrics and blocking. When I turned to look to the next page to the lyrics set with the accompanying sheet music, my brow furrowed. I leaned in to look closer.

"Yeah, it's hers," Susan said from just beside me. When I looked up at her in question, she gave me a half smile. "You didn't read the text messages, did you?"

"What? Amy called Vanessa?"

"No, I did."

I looked at her with my mouth hanging open and eyes narrowed. "Why would you do that?"

"Jamie, you know that me and Nessa still talk. I mean, I hate her for what she did, but we're still in touch."

"Yeah, but this is a video for Sarah."

"I know, but I thought maybe this could be a first step in you forgiving her. I mean, you're the one who said you wanted to, I didn't even suggest that. And even though Amy wrote decent lyrics, she did it to an old hokey song in the public domain. And she didn't know the first thing about having the lyrics match up to the song. Nessa put the lyrics to one of her originals and fixed them."

I nodded, looking back down at the lyrics.

"It wouldn't have worked otherwise unless we hired someone and that would have taken way too much time."

Sighing, I said, "And I'll be singing this in front of a bunch of famous singers, all alone for some reason even though I haven't sung in years?"

"Hey, look on the bright side, I haven't sung in years either and I'll be coming in at the first chorus all alone and preggo. You memorize it yet?"

"Nope."

"Let's go practice this outside."

Susan and I walked a short distance away from the entrance and into the sun, leaned against the wall and went through old warm ups I was surprised we even remembered. When we were finished, we practiced the first verse and chorus several times.

After about six times through, I was confident to sing it without looking, so Susan read the lyrics

while I sang. When I made it through, she said,
"Perfect," and came in at the chorus.

> *"I want to be your voice.*
> *I want to sing this loud.*
> *Please let me be your voice,*
> *To tell them all kids count."*

We moved on to the next verses, singing them
in unison as I took the melody and she the harmony.
After all these years, our voices still complemented
each other.

I pointed to the blocking on the script. "The
Rocketeers come in here, so we could just get quieter
if we wanted."

Susan laughed. "Or we could just lip sync at
that point."

"I like the way you think."

"Susan! Jamie!" A guy I didn't know stepped
around the corner. "Are you Susan and Jamie?"

Susan nodded. "You found us."

"Come on in, I need to set up your
microphones." He did a sweeping wave, indicating we
should follow him.

After following him in, he led us to the side of
the studio where the Rocketeers were practicing.
When they sang the chorus together, it sounded
amazing, like they'd been practicing the song for
years.

I looked down at the guy who was messing with
chords under me, then glanced at Susan. "Oh my God,
I'm so nervous."

"You and me both."

A clipboard was shoved into my face, and when I looked I noticed that Amy's arm was attached to it. "You guys both need to sign this." She tapped a pen on the paper, then offered it to me.

It was a release form with like a paragraph of legal jargon. Underneath the paragraph, there was a long line of signatures and printed names.

She pushed it forward at me. "Everyone has to sign."

I signed.

"Are you going to let Sarah perform with the other gymnasts? If you are, you're going to have to sign for her too."

I looked over. "What about all those teens?"

"They're all over eighteen and Heidi says she's talked with all of their parents."

"Wow, you are so thorough."

She grinned at me like I had just given her a really big compliment, which I guess to her, I did.

I looked to where Sarah and Aiden sat on the mat with the other gymnasts. "Should I let her perform?"

"I think so. She already knows the girls' routine and she really wants to be in it. Also, it goes along with the message."

I inhaled deeply and looked over at Susan. "What do you think?"

She lifted a hand toward Sarah. "Let the girl shine."

Returning my attention to Sarah, I rocked back and forth on my feet. "Yeah okay. If she wants to be in it."

The guy with the microphone equipment stood up. "Hold still for a minute here." Reaching forward, he pinned a small microphone to my shirt. "You don't need to sing into it, it should pick up everything."

"Okay, thanks."

When he'd finished pinning Susan's microphone, I pulled her away.

"So who is paying the microphone guy and that guy?" I nodded to a guy standing behind a huge camera on a tripod.

Susan shrugged. "Kevin hooked us up. Actually, these guys are friends of his and they're just doing it as a favor."

"This is just crazy." I shook my head.

"I know, it surprised the hell out of me, first when your sister texted us and then when everyone just said they were coming. Beza's kept in touch with these guys, but we've only actually met up with them a few times in the past couple years. One phone call and they're out here in force." She paused. "Maybe it doesn't surprise me all that much. It's just really cool."

Amy went to stand in the middle of the mat. I could see the tension in her shoulders, but her voice came out steady when she called out, "Has everyone who is going to be in the video signed the release?" Her gaze scanned the room. "Anyone?" When no one spoke up, she looked over at the microphone guy. "Greg, everyone ready?"

He gave a thumbs up.

"All right then, let's do a run through. After the run through, we'll start shooting. We're going for casual, unprofessional, so we're going to be doing this in one shot with no video editing. So, unfortunately, we're just going to have to restart if there are mess ups, so just be aware."

Susan and I made eye contact. Her nostrils flared and lips pursed as if the whole thing amused her.

I blew out a long breath and returned my focus to Amy to find her focus on me.

"Come on up, Jamie."

Holding my breath, I ignored the fact that everyone watched me as I weaved through the crowd.

"Barefoot, Jamie," Heidi called when I was about to step on the mat.

"Oh, sorry." I stepped on the backs of my running shoes and stepped out of them.

Amy gritted her teeth in an apologetic smile. "Oh that's the other thing; we all have to do this barefoot."

"Are you serious?" Clarice called from beside Beza.

The girls around her started laughing.

"Oh, this is going to be ridiculous." Clarice stepped out of her shoes, and lost four inches.

I turned my gaze away to avoid staring or smiling even though all of her friends were cracking up, including Beza.

"Stop laughing Bee, I'm doing this for you."

When I glanced back I saw Clarice pointing into Beza's still laughing face.

Amy came to stand before me and said in a quiet voice, "Come on, Jamie, I want to get through filming before the pizzas arrive at six."

"You bought pizzas for everyone?"

She nodded.

"Let me pay you back, that must have been a small fortune."

She widened her eyes at me. "You can pay me back by getting your butt up there; we only have an hour and a half."

I screwed up my face, but I walked to the center of the mat.

Amy went to stand by the camera man. "We're going to have to whisper through this, so just ignore us and keep going okay?"

I nodded.

Music started playing through the speakers. Though I'd read the notes, I'd never heard the song before.

Amy called. "Okay, start."

Swallowing, I fixed all of my attention on the glass lens of the camera.

"Mom!" Sarah yelled, running over to grab me.

Everyone started laughing as I staggered and missed my cue.

She buried her head in my stomach.

"Hey, angel, I was going to sing."

Heidi walked up to us and leaned down to Sarah's level. "It's hard to have our parents be the center of attention. But, Sarah, do you still want to perform with the other girls?"

Sarah looked over, her gaze going between Heidi and the other gymnasts.

"Do you want to perform? Yes or no?" Heidi smiled.

"Yes."

She offered her a hand. "All right then. We need to wait for our turn to go on."

After they walked off, Amy signaled to a guy and the song started again. "Okay, let's do that again."

I blew out a breath and at my cue, I began singing.

"I stood in front of the entire school board,
Said your needs can't go on ignored.
In a district where wealth's ranked at eighty,
Why won't they ensure your safety?
Looking away might still be their choice,
But maybe they just can't hear your voice?
Those outside the box we often ignore,
But you're the ones the world needs to change
for."

Amy caught my attention by doing a jerky gesture. "Susan, go."

"Wait, do I come on now or while she's singing?"

"As she finishes."

"Maybe she should go again so that I can practice my entrance right?" Susan gave me an exaggerated wink which I met with a glare.

"Jamie, just do the last line."

I sang the last line again and Susan walked on, singing 'world changes for' with me, then we moved on to the chorus.

As the chorus finished, Clarice and the Rocketeers rushed on stage. Instead of them all singing, Clarice started rapping.

"Listen, to our words and hear our voice.
We hear these words coming at us and not by choice.
In our culture, our media, our mainstream,
We're throwing derogatory words about people, not things.
We think it's funny to compare a person to a broken car,
Acting dumb or getting smashed down drunk in a bar.
We think that because we don't hear you shout: that won't fly,
That if we looked, we wouldn't see tears in your eyes?
We want to be your voice. We want to tell them no."

"Holy shit, that was awesome," Susan said.
I nodded while grinning. "Yeah, seriously."
One of the other Rocketeers said, "So I'm thinking we should all smile in greeting to each other, then watch and nod at Clarice until the last line. On the last line, we all sing while she raps."

"I like it," another one of the Rocketeers said, nodding.

"Okay, I'll back it up." Clarice rocked her head back and forth. "*We think that because we don't hear you shout: that won't fly, that if we looked we wouldn't see tears in your eyes?*"

All of us, but Clarice, sang, "*We want to be your voice, we want to tell them no.*"

"Sounds good, let's move into the next chorus," Amy called.

As we started on the chorus, this time singing *we want to be you voice*, Kevin, Nero and Markus walked on from different sides of the mat.

They came on to the middle and we all sort of huddled, as they threw their arms over our shoulders.

The moment the chorus finished, the gymnastics team came on around us, Sarah in the edge of them. As they performed their routine, we sang the final verse.

"In a culture that's taught us to dismiss,
We've stopped listening and your message we miss,
And yes we said we want to be your voice,
But actually no, that's just not true,
In the end, we really can't speak for you.
We want to lift your voice; we want to learn to listen,
We want to put the world's ear to those our culture's dismissin'."

In front of all of us, Sarah broke formation, doing several aerials and a flip until she was in front of all of us, before lifting her arms in the air.

"Whoa," Clarice said as we all paused to stare at Sarah.

Amy gestured with a lift of her hand. "Okay, one more chorus then you're done."

We all sang while the gymnasts finished their routine.

> *"We want to lift your voice.*
> *We want to lift it loud.*
> *Please let us lift your voice,*
> *To tell them all kids count."*

Day Five: Six-ten

The video took fifteen takes. Susan was by far guilty of the most mess ups. "Sorry, pregnancy brain!" she shouted at least five times. The moment we finished singing the last perfect take, Beza and Aiden started clapping and whooping from beside the camera man. A second later, everyone else in the room joined them cheering.

We stood there for a second, all huddled together and smiling before we broke apart.

We gave each other high fives and hugs.

Heidi stepped up beside Amy and raised her voice loud, "There's pizza for everyone. No eating on or near the mats please!"

As everyone else walked off the mat, Clarice grinned up at me. "If you can believe it, that was actually really fast for a three-minute video."

I exhaled a laugh. "Wow, it felt like forever. I'm going to be loading up on pizza."

She nodded. "Me too."

Instead of heading with the rest of the group to get pizza, I walked back to where I had set my purse. Pulling out my phone, I texted Cameron.

Me: Hey. We're running a little late here, so don't be worried.

Cameron: Thank you for telling me. I'm actually at your house right now. Anything specific you don't want me to forget?

I paused, and squeezed my eyes shut. Opening my eyes, I took a deep breath and wrote the message.

Me: Could you bring Logan's ashes? They're on the fridge?

Cameron: No problem, I see them.

Me: Thank you so much for doing all this, Cameron! I'll text you when we are on our way?

Cameron: Sounds good. I'll have some dinner waiting.

Me: No need, there's pizza here.

Cameron: All right, I'll see you tonight.

After stowing my phone, I looked across the expanse of blue mat to the laughing, smiling, pizza-eating group. In the middle of them all, Sarah wore a smile so big it threatened to burst off her face. Directly beside Sarah sat Aiden, and around them the gymnasts and musicians. All the gymnasts had pulled clothes on over their costumes. Sarah's t-shirt stuck out at weird places because of the ruffles underneath.

Aiden said something to the group that I was too far away to hear, but it had everyone laughing. Susan reached over and mussed her hand through his braids while Beza shook her head.

Heidi walked over from where she had been straightening mats. "Let me tell you, Jamie, it's days like these that restore my faith in humanity. I'm glad I'm here to see this."

"Me too, Heidi. And you know, I felt pretty down on humanity today." I sighed. "But I could never have even asked for this, I mean, all these people here to support Sarah."

"It touches my heart, too." She placed her hand on her chest. "Now, sweetheart, you better head over there and get some pizza before it's all gone."

After answering with a grin, I followed her instructions.

On a fold-out table an array of gourmet, I-would-never-pay-so-much-for-pizza-in-my-life pizzas sat. Taking a seat beside Nero and Clarice who were sharing a plate, I turned to Amy on my other side.

"Amy, I can't even—what you did was just too incredible. And I can't believe you pulled it off in a day."

Susan, who must have overheard, raised a cup of soda, "To Amy!"

Every one raised their cup, but as I only had pizza, I raised my slice.

Amy nodded at us in acceptance, her cheeks reddening.

While everyone else drank their soda, I took a bite of my pizza, letting the pine-nutty, pesto deliciousness overwhelm my senses.

I raised my pizza again. "To all of you guys, this was so amazing. You guys seriously restored my faith in humanity today."

"And to Sarah, the best eight-year-old gymnast I've ever seen!" Clarice raised her soda glass.

Sarah squealed, grinning ear to ear while bouncing up and down on her butt.

We all smiled and I took another bite as everyone else drank soda. When we finished eating, I helped Heidi put all her equipment back while everyone else chatted and packed up.

Sarah ran out of Heidi's office in her school clothes and pulled up onto a beam. "I am ready to practice gymnastics."

"Oh no, sweetheart." I walked over to her.

Heidi stepped up next to me. "Sarah, we already practiced today, we just did things a little differently. On Sunday, we're going to practice your beam dismounts again. Is that okay?"

Sarah looked between us for a few seconds, and then hopped down from the beam.

On the way out the door, we all exchanged one last hug and smile.

Beside me, Amy gave a few stiff, reluctant hugs. "I'm going to send out a few post write-ups to each of you, but you are welcome to change the posts or write your own."

"Sounds good." Kevin patted her on the shoulder. "Have you ever thought of going into the industry?"

Amy's voice came out a little reedy as she responded, "Oh, um, no, I don't sing."

She shook her head furiously, like he may force her to do it.

"No, in music video production." His hand remained on her shoulder as he grinned down.

Clarice turned from where she hugged both Beza and Susan, simultaneously. "Yeah girl, I like the way you just went with the flow when we changed things on you and all. Totally didn't expect that. We could give you the number of a couple guys that might be able to hook you up."

Amy shook her head again, her cheeks, chin and forehead now bright red. "I'm— Thank you, but I have a job. Though, I always appreciate making contacts in any industry, of course."

Both Kevin and Clarice nodded and turned their attention away.

After exchanging phone numbers and promises to keep in touch, we walked out in a group. Sarah's eyes had glassed over, so I made a hasty, final goodbye to everyone and walked with her down the road to my car.

The sun was fully in the west now, contemplating ducking behind the buildings at any moment. Even though the day was pretty much over, it was still warm.

The drive was almost silent until I realized that I'd pulled onto the street that led home. "Oops." I turned left, and then took another couple of turns toward where Cameron lived just out of town.

Sarah moaned from the back. "Mom, are we going home?"

When I looked through the rearview mirror she glanced around through the windows with a frown on her face.

"I'm sorry, baby, we're going to stay at Cameron's house, remember?"

She didn't respond but when I checked, the frown had disappeared.

Though his house was out of town, Cameron's was actually closer to the school than mine. The house was so familiar, though I hadn't seen it in over a year. To me, it had always been more his house than Vanessa's—even before the divorce. Though she had contributed the bulk of the money for the property, he had built the house from the ground up and it just felt more like him than her. It seemed Vanessa felt the same way. Cameron had told me that she'd all but insisted he take it.

The A-frame structure was interrupted only with a large, triangular dormer to one side that faced the driveway. Though they were impossible to see from the long driveway, the triangular walls on each side were walls of windows. The house was practically built into the hillside. With the way it was positioned and the fence that encircled the large lot of land, it was one of the only places I'd ever been in the central coast where you couldn't see your neighbors.

As I pulled up, Cameron opened his front door. He walked out, standing beside my car door when I opened it.

"Shoot, I forgot to text you."

"I figured it out. Looks like Sarah fell asleep."

I glanced back to find that she definitely had. "Oh, that sucks."

Cameron placed a hand on my car door. "Here, come here."

Climbing out, I stepped into his embrace. He squeezed me to him, his cheek on the top of my hair and arms wrapped all the way around me. Pulling back to look at my face, his hand came to my cheek. "We should get Sarah inside, huh?"

I covered his hand with my own. "Thank you for all of this Cameron. And you're okay with us staying another couple of weeks?"

He shook his head, but not in a 'no' more in a 'are you kidding?' way. "Jamie, I think you know how I feel about all of that. I asked you to move in here, remember?"

Walking around the car, we stopped outside Sarah's door.

Cameron turned to me. "Do you want me to carry her in?"

"I think I'm going to have to wake her up, otherwise she's going to be confused." Opening her door, I crouched down. "Angel, wake up, we're at Cameron's."

It took almost a full minute, but Sarah's eyes opened blearily and she looked to me, then at Cameron behind me. It took some coaxing, but Sarah followed us into the house and up the stairs to Cameron's spare bedroom. When we stepped inside, sudden tears filled my eyes.

Cameron had rearranged the room to the exact setup as Sarah's room in the duplex. Though his walls were at a bit of a slant, he'd pinned up her posters in almost the exact placement that they had been in at home. Her bedspread and most of her favorite toys were there too. The furniture was different, of course, but he'd rearranged it so that the room was almost identical.

Sarah walked in and bee lined to climb onto the bed and curl up into a ball on top of the covers.

"Angel, you need to at least go to the bathroom okay?"

"No, I'm going to keep sleeping." Her voice was muffled by the pillow.

I sat down beside her. "Just go pee, and then you can go straight to bed."

She made an annoyed groan, but lumbered off the bed and out of the room.

Following her, I showed her where the bathroom was, noticing that Cameron had set up our bathroom stuff too.

Stepping back outside, I closed the door and looked over to Cameron. "You did all this so that she'd be comfortable?"

He came to stand in front of me. "I didn't want her to get dysregulated with the new place."

I leaned in and kissed him gently on the lips. "Thank you so much."

The bathroom door opened and Sarah walked past us and into the room.

"Goodnight, angel." I flipped off her light and closed the door.

When I returned to look up at Cameron, he regarded me, his beautiful face so close to mine.

I leaned into him, stealing another soft kiss.

He leaned in even closer to me his hands going to the wall on either side of my head, and he whispered, "You're not off the hook yet, Jamie."

"What?" I whispered, leaning back into the wall.

He glared. "You've been in danger, you and Sarah have been in danger, and you've been hiding it from me."

I shook my head and forced myself to meet his eyes. "I told you, by the pool."

"You told me someone creeps you out, not that you were in so deep that you need to abandon your apartment."

I chewed on the inside of my cheeks and looked away.

"Jamie, what the hell?" he asked in a low voice.

I glared at him. "I'll talk to you about it, but not while you're boxing me in like this, okay? Give me some space."

He exhaled heavily and straightened up. "Fine, let's go sit somewhere or something." He offered me his hand.

After hesitating for a second, I took it. He led me down the staircase and into the main area of the house. The ground floor was one huge open room, stretching out into a kitchen and dining area on one side and a sunken living room area on the other.

We sat next to each other on the couch, but I folded up my legs and turned to him. When he met my gaze, I sighed and tilted my head. "Okay, yeah, I hid it from you on purpose."

He looked away, his jaw clenching. "Obviously."

"I was scared, okay? I knew what you'd do if I told you."

"Ask you to move in with me?"

"Actually, I was more afraid you'd go attack the guy."

"Hell yeah, I'd attack the guy."

I glared. "Exactly. Exactly like you attacked your old boss in college."

"What do you know about it, Jamie? You were off travelling the world with Logan." He said the last part with more than a little bit of resentment.

"I know you lost your scholarship, that you had to go to jail, that you missed finals and ended up having to drop out because of it."

"He deserved it."

I leaned in toward him, putting a hand on his chest.

"I know he did. Just like this guy deserves it. But he's just like your boss, he has the law on his side and if you went and attacked him, you would have probably have ended up in jail and he'd still be free to harass me. I didn't want that."

He leaned his head back, over the couch, stretching his neck out long. Closing his eyes, he said, "Fine. Just please tell me what's going on. I'm not going to attack him."

So I did.

I told Cameron everything, all the off color comments, the weird interaction in the laundry room that had set Clarke off to accelerate his harassment to a whole new level. When I told Cameron about discovering the underwear Clarke had left for me and my decision to have Amy spend the night, he looked over and interrupted me for the first time.

"You knew that he came into your place and you had your sister spend the night? What the hell, Jamie? What was she going to do, micro-manage him to death?"

"He never harasses me when other people are around."

Cameron gave me a level look. "He harassed you at your store."

I squirmed, because I hadn't even told him about the surfer guy yet. Blowing out a breath, I admitted, "I called you first, right after I found the underwear."

His eyelids narrowed. "You called... what? Once? If you really were trying to reach me, you would have."

Licking my lips, I met his gaze. "Vanessa answered when I called."

He looked at me for a second, and then took a long inhale through his nose. "Why didn't you say something?"

"Because if I brought it up it would be like I thought you owed me an explanation, and you really don't."

"Maybe I don't, but I would have rather given you one than have you give me the cold shoulder when I visited you at work. And I'd definitely rather you tell me what's going on than not reach me when you're in danger."

I looked away. "I'm sorry, Cameron. She's your ex-wife and she's also a person with whom I have a lot of feelings tangled up with. And when she answered your phone, it affected me. I was upset. But I also knew I didn't really have a right to be."

Cameron put his arms around me and gently led me to lean into him.

I let him. When his arms came around me, squeezing me into his chest, I grabbed onto his arms and laid my head to the side.

"Ness and I have been meeting up every couple of weeks for a while now. It started because we had some financial stuff to work out, but I was tired of hanging on to my anger at her. She hurt me and I was angry for a while, but I wasn't really feeling it anymore. The romantic feelings were gone. To be honest, they'd been gone before we split up. She was my best friend for years, and I missed her."

I nodded. "I miss her too."

Tears slipped out of my eyes. "And even though I think I want to forgive her for what she did, when I heard her voice again, it just all came up fresh and I—" Instead of finishing what I was saying, I pushed my face into Cameron's arm.

"No one's saying you have to forgive her, Jamie."

"I know."

"And, I'm not saying that I really forgive her either." He exhaled. "Jamie, I had feelings for you when I was with her. I always have."

"You did?" I asked, looking up.

He gave me a level look. "Come on, Jamie. You knew, she knew—Logan did too. And when Logan started drinking and everything he did, you and I started spending a lot of time together."

I stiffened. "She was *always* invited."

"She knew I was in love with you Jamie. She couldn't watch me help you through what Logan was putting you through. At the same time, she loved you and didn't want to stop me either. Yeah, she fucked up our marriage, but I did it first. I'm not going to pretend that I didn't."

Day Five: Eight-fifteen

We let the words sit between us, an admission of guilt that felt sort of like an accusation, too.

"Does she know about us?" I looked back into his face.

He nodded slightly.

"How'd she take it?"

"She cried when I first told her, but I'm pretty sure she's come to terms with it. She's seeing this guy now, younger guy, sounds pretty crazy about him."

"Are you jealous?"

He shook his head. "I thought I would be, but I just felt relieved when she told me. He sounds like a pretty all right guy, has his act together." He looked down to give me a half smile. "She asks me about you."

"What do you say?"

He shrugged. "Not much."

Nodding, I looked away.

"Can I move you?"

I sat up. "Oh sorry."

"Nah, I just want to get more comfortable." He scooted down to lay across the couch and pull me over him so that I was laying on top of him, my head on his chest.

"You're in love with me?" I whispered into his chest.

He kissed the top of my head. "I said I *was* in love with you."

"Oh."

"Do you want to watch a movie?"

I smacked his chest, which made him chuckle. He only laughed more when I pushed up to glare at him.

"Come here." He pulled me toward him, his lips finding mine. He kissed me with soft, gentle kisses which quickly deepened. Wrapping his arms around me, he rolled me over, pressing my body into the couch with his.

His hands came up to wrap around the side of my neck while he devoured my mouth. I broke away for air and gasped as his hand lifted up my shirt, thumb making a slow circle on my lacy bra over my nipple.

"Should we go upstairs?" Cameron whispered.

"No, we're less discoverable down here," I breathed.

"Good, because I want you right here and right now," he whispered into my ear. "And I want to have you for a very long time." He pinched my nipple, sending a shock wave of sensation through me that traveled right down to my center.

I gasped as he ground into me. "A very, very, very long time."

"Good," he said, again, then he lifted up to pull my shirt off. My bra quickly followed and his mouth replaced his thumb. My breath hitched as he unbuckled my pants swiftly pulled the pants and my underwear down my legs.

He raised his head, hunger and desire blazing from his eyes. His fingers dipped low. "You're already so ready for me."

"Yes," I breathed.

He kept his eyes on me as he arched up to pull off his shirt, then achingly slowly, unbuckled his pants and kicked them off. With his hands, he gently moved my legs apart, and then lifted my hands over my head. He settled between my thighs, his hands holding mine and stretching out my body. Though he was poised to enter me, he paused.

My breath came out in short bursts as I lay splayed out, begging him to enter me.

He leaned in and whispered into my ear, "Jamie, I have never loved anyone or anything in my life as much as I love you." And then he did what he promised, for a very, very, very long time.

When we were both sweaty and spent, in every sense of the word, I lay on top of Cameron on the couch.

"Are you still taking me on a date this Friday?" My fingers traced over his chest.

"I already have it all planned out."

I arched up to look at him. "You do?"

He grinned at me. "I'm not telling you."

"Did I ask?" I widened my eyes and shook my head. Laying my head back down, I whispered, "So, what are we doing?"

"Not a chance."

"Bowling?"

He shook his head.

"Not bowling?"

He squeezed me to him. "You'll find out on Friday."

I sighed and leaned into him. "Fine."

I looked over his chest and across the living room. "Whoa, Cameron!" I raised up my head. "We just did all that with the curtains open!"

He chuckled. "It's fine, there's no possible way anyone can see in here."

"Oh my God, I can't believe I didn't even notice!" I glared at him. "Do you swear on your life no one can see in here?"

He chuckled again. "Sure."

Laying my head back down on his chest, I whispered. "You better be telling the truth because otherwise I'm so going to kill you."

"That's fine." His thumb made a slow circle on my shoulder as we lay together. "What are we going to do about your job?"

"What do you mean?"

"If he's coming in there, you're not safe."

"Oh, yeah I forgot to tell you about what happened today." I filled him in on Pat's visit, the new offer and gift, and what I had decided to do about it.

"Hmm."

"Was that a yes, that's the smart thing to do hmm, or not so much?"

"It was an I wonder if you're rushing into this because you're feeling desperate hmm."

I splayed my fingers across his chest. "Maybe, or maybe the universe is sending me a very clear message, and if I don't listen, things are just going to keep getting worse."

"Maybe." His hand caressed over my hair, then continued down my back. "I just know that sometimes when a new thing comes along, it seems easier and simpler, but shit always gets real sooner or later. Sometimes, it's just better to work on the real thing that you already have going."

"So you think I shouldn't sell the shop?"

"That's up to you, baby. No matter what you do, I think we need to find out a way to keep you safe while you're at work."

"Yeah." I nodded, and then hesitated, biting my lip. "Actually, I didn't tell you the worst part."

"What?"

I closed my eyes. "I tried to get another apartment through my property manager. But even though I told him what was going on, he offered Clarke the apartment first."

Cameron jerked under me. "Are you kidding me?"

I shook my head. "I'm assuming that it's because Sarah and I haven't been the easiest to live next to."

"That dick."

"I know. So today, some guy came into my work and told me that someone paid him to say, 'I'm not moving and neither are you.' It really freaked me out. And, I think the guy was stoned because he kind of ran for the door when I suggested him talking to the police for me. I'm in way over my head Cameron, every sudden sound has me jumping... sometimes into the window. I'm scared to go out of my front door. I just want it all to stop."

He kissed the top of my head. "Yeah, baby, we'll make it stop." After another few minutes of

holding each other, we got up, turned on his home
alarm system and headed upstairs.

Day Six

Making a Deal with Evil
Headquarters

Day Six: Four O'clock

I woke as my bladder made it very obvious that it needed me to rouse. Bleary eyed, I climbed out of bed and walked through the room to the hallway. I blinked around at the space and to the lit bathroom across the hall.

I pointed at nothing in particular. "Cameron's house." Trudging into the bathroom, I almost tripped on Sarah's gymnast doll, who must have accompanied Sarah on a late night bathroom trip and been left behind. I relieved my bladder then returned to the guest room. In the low light coming from the hall, I had a clear view of the empty bed where I had hours ago fallen asleep next to Sarah.

"Sarah?" I turned on the lights, but she was neither in the bed nor had she fallen out of it. Crossing back into the hallway, I looked down the stairs, then into Cameron's room.

In the faint light I could see Cameron fast asleep on one side of the bed. Beside him, Sarah slept curled into a ball on top of the covers. She lay just beside him, the same way I often found her when she climbed in bed with me.

I watched for a second, leaning against the doorway. Walking back into the guest room, I grabbed Sarah's blankets from the bed and returned to Cameron's room.

Settling in beside Sarah, I covered us both with her purple blanket, and fell asleep.

I woke, hearing a faint distant beeping sound. "Huh?" I whispered, looking around.

Beside me, Sarah and Cameron continued to sleep. When the beeping continued, I walked over into the guest room to find my phone chiming out that it was seven in the morning. I walked back across the hall, lying down beside Sarah.

Combing my fingers through her hair, I whispered, "Hey, angel, it's time to wake up." When she didn't even stir, I whispered a little louder, "Baby, wake up."

Beside Sarah, Cameron stretched up his arms, turning over. His eyes opened. When he looked my way, he grinned, and blinked while yawning. "Hey, what are you doing here?" He looked down. "And Sarah, too?"

I shrugged. "She climbed in with you last night. Scared the hell out of me, I thought maybe she fell down the stairs or something. So I climbed in too."

His hand touched my cheek. "Good." He leaned back into the bed. "Is it seven already?"

"Yep."

He hissed out a breath. "Brutal."

"You don't need to get up Cameron."

He shook his head, sitting up. "I'm going to need to if I'm going to take Sarah. And I want to see you off."

"You don't need to take her."

He yawned, rubbing his hands down his face. "How else would you get to work on time?"

I shrugged. "I own the shop, I could just be late, Chris would understand."

Cameron stood up. "You can if you want, but I'm already up and I'm heading downstairs to make us

459

breakfast. We should have eaten something last night." He yawned again. "I'm starving."

After Cameron left, I turned back to Sarah, who blinked up and yawned.

"Hey baby, we're in Cameron's house, okay? We're not at our house."

She yawned again and curled into me. "I'm going to go back to sleep.

My phone beeped from where I had set it on the bed. When I check the screen, I saw the text from Amy.

Amy: The video is now live.

I covered my mouth. Another text came in with a website link. I lowered my finger and clicked on the link.

The website app on my phone opened to a video. Under the player the website said the video had five views. I clicked play.

Centered in the video, I stood far in the distance on the mat. As the music intro started, the video slowly zoomed in on me. When I began singing, the camera continued zooming in. My gaze was intent on the video screen, my blue eyes brighter than I had ever remembered them.

My voice sounded good, way better than I thought it would. I heard Susan's voice before she came into view. She took her place beside me. We had so much energy together, we glanced at each other then back to the camera as we harmonized.

Clarice and the other Rocketeers just seemed to pop on the stage as Clarice came in rapping. The camera panned out, centering on her with all of us surrounding her. She had such energy, such vivacity, as she addressed the camera.

The whole feel of the video changed the moment that Kevin, Nero and Markus came on. We were hugging, smiling at the camera, holding onto each other. When the gymnasts came on, flipping around us, the whole thing ended with a happy, uplifting feel, so changed from the sad feeling the video started with.

"Can we watch our video again, Mom?"

"Yeah, do you want to go show it to Cameron?"

She nodded, grinning.

"Okay, get ready for school, and then we can go down and show it to Cameron, yeah?"

Sarah climbed out of bed and crossed over to the guest room. I looked around for Sarah's suitcase, but Sarah crossed over to the dresser, opened the drawer, and started pulling out her clothes.

"Your clothes are in there?" I crossed over to the drawer to see that not only were Sarah's clothes in there, they were in the same drawers as her dresser at home. I pulled out the middle drawer and Sarah groaned at me.

"Sorry." I raised my hands in surrender. "You can get dressed by yourself. Remember to go to the bathroom and brush your teeth."

She groaned again.

"Fine, going, going. I'll be downstairs, that's where we're going to eat our breakfast."

While brushing my teeth and washing my face, I noticed that after a week, getting ready without coffee was considerably less painful. I walked back into Cameron's room and dragged my suitcase across the hardwood from where I propped it up last night, setting it on the bed. After throwing on some clothes at random, I shoved my feet in my sneakers and ran downstairs.

I jumped up behind Cameron who was frying something over the stove. "I have something I'm really excited to show you, but I have to wait until Sarah comes down."

"Do you?" He looked over his shoulder, smiling. "So, I grabbed your groceries and Sarah's yogurts are in the fridge."

I pointed at him. "Good thinking."

In the fridge, I found pretty much only my groceries. Leaning back, I smiled at him. "Is this when you tell me you're actually a vampire?"

He furrowed his brow, and gave me a half-grin. "What are you talking about?"

"You have no food. What do you eat? Everything in here but half a carton of half-in-half is from my house."

He shrugged. "I eat out."

"For every single meal?"

"Not when I'm at your house."

"How did I not know this about you?" I shook my head while I grabbed Sarah's yogurt.

When I turned, he was right there, grinning down at me. He leaned in and gave me a quick kiss, and when he pulled away, his smile had grown. "Come eat."

"Sure," I drew out the word. After placing Sarah's yogurt on the table, I started going through drawers.

"This one." Cameron pulled out a drawer filled with silverware. "Cups." He opened a cupboard. "And bananas." He opened a bare pantry; the sole occupants were my bunch of bananas on a shelf.

My shoulders shook as I forced down a laugh.

He raised his brows. "You think that's funny?" He stepped toward me.

"Cameron, bananas don't go in the cupboard, and where's all your food?"

He stepped into me, his arms going around my waist. "I don't have any; I'll just have to eat you." He nipped at my shoulder making me jump and laugh.

"I had no idea you were such a bachelor."

He kissed me lightly again. "Well, I'm planning on taking a vacation from being one."

"Watch this!" Sarah, who I hadn't even noticed come up, shoved my phone between me and Cameron.

Grabbing my phone before it fell, I broke away from Cameron. "Oh, hey, baby. You hungry?"

Sarah grabbed my phone from my hand and held it out to Cameron. "Watch this!" she squealed, jumping up and down.

"I promised her she could show it to you." I leaned into him, unlocking the screen and pulling up the video. I could literally feel my cheeks getting hot and tight as I pressed play on the video.

As the music began and I appeared on screen, he whispered, "What?" A grin grew wide across his face, and he looked between me and the screen. "When did you make this?"

"Yesterday."

When Clarice came on, he looked up, "Who are these people?"

"The Rocketeers, they're a music group... um, mega famous."

"Oh." He kept watching. "And those are the guys you used to tour with? The Dreamers?"

"I think this celebrity stuff is lost on you."

He grinned as we finished the song and Sarah came on with the other gymnasts. "I love it." He smiled over at Sarah.

"Do you love it? Say, I love it." She pointed into his face.

"I love it, Sarah. You did great."

She squealed, jumping around again. "Do you love it, Mom?"

"Yea." I nodded. "I love it, too."

Cameron started laughing.

I pointed at him. "You better not be laughing at me."

He shook his head, still laughing. "I just wish I could be there when that Whitney woman watches this video for the first time."

"Oh, God, me too."

We sat down together at the thick wood slab that Cameron had for a table. Cameron served me what he usually made on our Friday mornings: cheese and spinach omelets.

Halfway through my omelet, I paused to look at Sarah who was smiling while eating her yogurt. "Sarah, Cameron said he can drive you to school. Do you want to drive with me or drive with Cameron?"

"Cameron!" she shouted.

"Okay." I snorted out a laugh. "Nice to be wanted."

"Cameron! Can Cameron drive me, Mom?"

"Yes, baby."

"Mom, can Cameron drive me?"

"Yes, Cameron can drive you. Just, remember to make good choices, with him and at school, okay?"

She squealed her happiness.

Cameron stood. "I'll just run upstairs quick; I'll be down before you leave." His hand brushed across my back as he walked past to head upstairs.

"Shoot, I need to go grab Sarah's brush."

When I followed him, Cameron reached over and took my hand. He intertwined our fingers, not letting go of me all the way up the stairs. When I tried to release his hand at the bathroom, he turned and pulled me to him. When I was flush against him, his hands came down and gripped my hips.

I laughed. "Cameron, so not the time or situation."

"I just want one of these." He kissed me slowly, softly.

When he pulled away, I couldn't stop the smile that pulled up the corners of my lips.

"I like you here."

I grabbed his t-shirt and leaned in for another kiss. "I like being here."

"All right, I'm going to go get ready." He turned toward his room.

I smacked his butt.

Shooting me an amused look over his shoulder, Cameron walked into his room.

After grabbing Sarah's hairbrush, I walked back downstairs to find Sarah with my phone, replaying the video, again. As I brushed out her tangles, she repeatedly played the last thirty seconds of the video where she and the gymnasts came on. Every time the video ended she pulled rewind just a little.

"Hey baby, we're going to stay here tonight too. So after school, I'm going to pick you up and come home here, okay?"

"Mom, is this our house?" She looked up at me.

"Sort of, it's Cameron's house. We're going to be staying here for a little while."

"Do we live here?"

"For now."

Sarah looked back to my phone, replaying the thirty second interval again.

"Sorry, baby, I'm going to need that." I took my phone.

Cameron walked down the stairs, wearing his usual work-pants, boots and shirt with *Custom Designs* printed in yellow cursive over his breast pocket. He stopped in front of me.

"Are you going to go in early?"

"Yeah, there's always something to do." His eyes traveled from my eyes to my lips.

I glanced back at Sarah, who had returned her focus to her breakfast. Turning back to him, I closed the distance, giving him a light kiss. When I pulled away and headed toward his front door, I left with a grin. "All right guys, I guess I'm off."

"Bye, baby, see you after work."

When Sarah said nothing, I called, "Hey cutie, I'm leaving. Can you say bye?"

She grinned at me. "I love you so much, Mom."

Cameron stood. "Hey, do you need help with the code?"

"No, I got it." On the home security pad next to the door, I typed the four-digit code, and then pressed the button labeled 'disarm'. The red light next to 'armed' went out.

Stopping at the door, I glanced back. Neither of them looked over. From the corner of my eye, I saw a flash of something reflecting and I turned to peer into the living room. Above the free-standing fireplace, Logan's urn perched. It was turned in such a way that the wolf's head peeked out from the side.

Turning away, I pulled the front door open and walked out into the misty morning.

The drive to downtown was a little longer from Cameron's house. Though a gray haze lit the sky, I turned on my headlights as I made my way down from the foothills just outside of town. Turning on my radio, a pop song from the Rocketeers was just ending. Though I didn't really know the song, I hummed along. When the next song came on, a pop song from my era, I belted it out at the top of my lungs all the way down to the Coffee Stop.

As always, I parked next to Jack and his hopeful expression as he climbed on his way to his grand misadventure. As I climbed out of my car, I continued to sing the song, *"Live, love, laugh, dance. Dive head first into romance..."* I continued to sing all the way down the street and as I unlocked and walked into the shop.

When Chris looked up from the counter, I belted out, *"You only live once, so be sure to live free!"*

Chris laughed, but when I continued singing, he joined me, *"You're beautiful, magical, who you're supposed to be!"*

He shook his head. "You've been listening to Sarah's pop stations, again?"

"Not on purpose, it was on in my car and way too catchy. And Sarah is more into traditional kids' songs I'll have you know; she is a cultured eight-year-old."

"Well, of course." He pointed at me, grinning. "It's you I'm worried about. What, did you eat sunshine for breakfast or something?"

I walked behind the counter to drop my stuff off. "Maybe I did."

Grabbing the packet from the top of the pile of papers I brought in, I set it in front of him. "Here, you look this over and tell me what you think while I finish opening. I didn't look at it, so I want your honest opinion, okay?"

He looked up. "You're considering selling again?"

"Maybe. I'm teetering on the fence. But ignore all that, I want your honest opinion. Go take a seat or something, I'll handle all that." I gestured to the half-full pastry case.

"Bossy, bossy." He took the packet of paper. Instead of just taking a seat, he turned over all the chairs before sitting.

After washing my hands, I set to the task of filling and labeling the pastry case. When the case was full of buttery deliciousness, I moved on to starting up the espresso machine and setting out the coffee carafes.

"You haven't looked at this?" I heard Chris say from across the café.

I looked around the espresso machine and over to his stunned expression.

"Nope. I thought it would be a bit invasive for me to look over your job offer."

"Jamie, this isn't a job offer." He held it up. "This is the business proposal for my cupcake company that I uploaded to an angel investor website. It's an approval for a one hundred-thousand dollar loan in exchange for convertible debt."

I swallowed. "What is that?"

"Basically, a future share in the company... a big one." He turned back to the paper, just staring.

"Wow, Chris, that's amazing!"

"I—I just don't even know." He looked up, wide-eyed, but then his attention turned back to the paper. Chris didn't move the entire time I finished setting up for opening. When I finished, I walked around the counter and took the seat across from him.

He looked at me, his nostrils flaring. "I don't need it. I can get the funding some other way."

"What? You're not serious?" I looked down at the paper. "Is it not a good deal or something?"

"Jamie, don't sell your shop because of this. I can get funding."

"Oh, Chris." I reached across the table to squeeze his arm. "The offers are separate. The sale of the shop is only dependent on me taking my job offer."

Tears came down Chris's face, making two streaks of wetness around his nose.

"Oh, Chris."

His shoulders moved up and down in silent sobs.

I got up and came around the table to hug him.

His palms came up and wiped away his tears. "I just can't believe it."

"I can. I can completely believe it. No one deserves this as much as you."

He reached across and hugged my arm, silent sobs still shuddering through him.

A banging made me look up. Clare, who was probably here for her usual order of ten drinks, raised her fist and banged against the door again.

"It's Clare." I stood, and held up a finger to her.

She nodded her head at Chris, and raised her hands with a concerned expression on her face.

I waved at her in an 'everything's fine' way.

She pointed at the door and put her hands together in a pleading gesture.

"It's okay, you can let her in." Chris put his hands down on the table and pulled himself up.

"You sure, Chris? Because we can totally open late."

He chuckled. "No, it's—I'm good, Jamie. I might need to jump on the espresso machine first just so I can get my head on straight. I'll go get started on Clare's drink."

"Yeah, of course. I'll go let her in." The moment I unlocked the door, Clare practically bowled me over.

"Oh my God, Jamie, is Chris okay? What's going on?"

I took a step back and raised my hands in a conciliatory gesture. "Yes, Clare, he's fine."

"He's my friend, Jamie; I need to check on him!"

"Okay." I gestured for her to go ahead, and then held the door open for a few other customers who were heading in. By the time I returned to the counter, Chris already had a couple drinks out and Clare jumped up and down.

She threw up her hands. "That is just too cool!"

Chris grinned. "Yeah, I thought so too."

I joined them, smiling as I placed tabs on her hot drinks and maneuvered them into holders. "I'm just excited for the cupcakes."

"Oh, God, me too!" She hopped again, beaming.

"You have any food orders for me?" I asked her.

"Oh, yeah, sorry." She pulled out a list and read out six pastries and two bagel orders. I grabbed the pastries, putting them in individual bags, then inside a big paper bag.

Clare grimaced. "Don't hate me... I have to pay for a few of them separately, is that okay?"

"No problem, let's just do them one at a time." I charged three cards, and the rest with cash, printing out a receipt for each. By the time I had her rung up, Chris had all the drinks ready and started on the people behind her in line.

Giving her final change, I said, "All right, just give me a second for those bagels and I'll have you all set." When the next person stepped up to the counter, a tall, good-looking guy in a suit, I said, "Just give me one sec."

After washing my hands, I popped a couple bagels in our toaster oven and headed back to the register.

As Chris already had the man's drink ready, I rang it up and asked, "Good morning, can I get you anything to eat?"

"Nope, just this, I'm in a hurry." He glanced down at his wristwatch.

After charging his card and printing him his receipt I expected the guy to move on, but instead his phone rang and he answered it while still standing at the counter.

"Hello? Yeah, I'm at a coffee shop... about ten minutes away."

As he didn't seem to be moving, I took the opportunity to wash my hands again, popped back over to the bagel station, added the spread and wrapped them up. "Here you go, Clare." I set the bag on the coffee counter.

When I had returned to the counter, the guy still hadn't moved.

Chris already had the next two coffee orders ready and on the coffee counter, so I stepped to the side of phone guy and asked the woman behind him, "Can I grab you anything to eat?"

"Excuse me!" Phone guy glared at me. "I need my card back so I can go."

I startled, looking up at him. "I'm sorry, sir, I believe I already gave it to you."

"No you didn't, I've been standing here waiting for it." Then into his phone he said, "Let me call you back in a moment, I need to deal with this."

"I'm sorry; I know I always forget to put my card away, especially when I'm in a rush. Check your wallet. It's in there with your receipt." Noticing the guy—who had become decidedly less attractive—wasn't moving, I turned to the next customer. "I'm sorry, anything to eat?"

Phone guy finally pulled out his wallet, checked, then without saying anything more, walked out of the shop.

The woman glanced back at phone guy, shook her head, and then gave me a smile. "Sure I'll take something to eat, how about... a ham and cheese croissant. Is there any way I can get it heated?"

"Of course." I grabbed the tongs. "For here or to go?"

"Oh, definitely for here."

After setting the croissant into our toaster oven, I rang her up and moved on to the new customer. We moved through the line quickly, though the rush didn't have a break. An hour in, Chris set a latte with a green fern leaf on the counter next to him.

"Aw, thanks Chris," I said, before turning back to my customer. An hour after that, I was able to take a sip of my green tea latte.

"This is ridiculous for a Thursday," Chris said as the bell rang over the door. "And why are so many people looking at you weird?"

"What?" I looked over at him, furrowing my brow.

He nodded toward the shop.

When I looked, a couple customers who definitely weren't regulars looked away quickly. My stomach dropped. "Oh no, Chris."

"What?"

"I—I'll tell you in a second." I turned to the new group that had just approached the counter. "Hello ladies, what can I get you?"

The three girls that I swear couldn't have been out of high school giggled. "Um, can we get, like, maybe a soda?"

"I can do an Italian soda?" I picked up a cold cup.

"Um, yeah."

"Okay, what flavor and how many?"

"Can I have cherry?" the shortest one asked.

"Watermelon," the blonde one said.

"Lemon-lime," the first one said, her eyes alight and excited.

Chris grabbed up their cups. "Shouldn't you ladies be in school?" He grinned at them and shook his head, making a 'tsking' sound.

They all erupted in giggles.

"Stay in school." He shook his finger at them, but grinned before turning to make their sodas.

"Are you paying together?"

The first girl handed me a twenty.

After ringing them up, and handing them their change, the girls stayed at the counter for a second, nervous excitement radiating off them.

"Um—" one began to say, but they all started giggling and rushed off.

When they left, I helped a couple regulars and a long line of new customers. Even by eleven o'clock, the line still didn't seem to be slowing.

Chris came to stand beside me. "Hey, let's switch so you can eat and drink something. And, I'm going to stay until this lets up, Jamie."

"Are you sure?" I finished ringing in my customer's order and handed him the change.

Chris clapped me on the back. "For sure. I'm at least going to stay until you tell me what's going on."

I laughed as I walked back to wash my hands. "Yeah, okay."

Day Six: Eleven O'clock

Adjusting the grind on the espresso grinder, I timed a shot, dumped it, and adjusted the grind again. As the line still reached out the door, I had all four portafilters going at once. Lining up the drinks, I poured milk in each, holding back the foam with the mochas and making quick hearts in the foam for every latte.

"Mint mocha, double nonfat latte and vanilla steamer." I set the drinks on the bar and turned back to the next set of cups waiting for me.

"Excuse me?"

I turned to see a young guy with an eyebrow piercing looking over the espresso bar.

"Hello, what can I do for ya?" I grabbed a portafilter and hit it over the trash to dump out the grinds.

"Can I take a picture with you?"

I blinked at him. Gritting my teeth in apology, I said, "Sorry, I would but we're just too crazy busy right now."

"No, that's cool; I can take it from here." He turned, holding up his cell phone and took a selfie with me just sort of standing in the background. "Awesome! Thanks!"

I gave him a closed mouth grin. "No problem."

When I turned, I caught Chris smirking at me with an eyebrow raised. "Come on, Jamie. I am dying here. Did Cherry Pie come out with a new album or something?"

I shrugged. "Or something."

"Just tell me already."

Focusing on pulling more shots, I said offhandedly, "So, Susan and I did a video with some of our friends from back in the day and put it online. I'm thinking this crowd might have something to do with that."

"Yeah, you think? And, you owe me way more than that when I'm through this line." He turned back to his customer, who had been looking at the meager remains of the pastry case.

It took us close to another hour to have a lull, and by that time we were out of pastries. I sipped my now ice cold green tea latte. "You have to teach me how to make these."

"Then you wouldn't need me." Chris came to stand by the espresso machine. He grabbed my drink and threw it into the trash.

"Hey!"

"That's gross. I'm making you a fresh one. In exchange you can tell me about this video."

"How about, in exchange, I make us both bagels and then tell you about this video?"

"Deal."

I hurried over to the bagel bar. "I'm not even going to toast mine, I'm so hungry. Want me to toast yours?"

"Nope, just make me whatever you're having."

I threw together giant bagel sandwiches with everything on them and returned to Chris with his on a plate. We walked to stand outside my office so we could see the counter but people wouldn't have a direct view of us and stuffed our faces.

"If we keep having days like this we are going to need to hire someone," Chris said before taking another bite. "I'm not so young anymore."

"Yeah whatever, you baby." I elbowed his side. "Hey, are you and Melissa going to stop by tonight? Oh, shoot! I totally forgot to get her something."

"That's cool, Jamie. And, yeah, we're going to try to stop in. Melissa and I aren't all that into sports, but we'll stay for a drink or two."

"Oh, good. I want to buy you your drinks, at least something."

"It's all good, Jamie." He pulled out his phone from his back pocket. "So tell me how to find this video?" He unlocked his screen, and leaned his head forward. "Never mind! Whoa, like eight people texted me about it." He fiddled with his phone, and then the music from my video started playing. "Two million people have seen this?"

"What!" I turned to look at his phone, under the video '2M views' was printed. "No way, that has to be wrong. That thing's only been up for a couple of hours!"

I rushed over to my purse, grabbing out my phone. When I'd opened the lock screen, I stared at my phone for a minute. I had one hundred and fifty text messages and seventy-two missed calls. "Oh my goodness gracious." I thumbed through my call log to make sure Sarah's school hadn't called, then thumbed through the text messages, not reading any of them. It was like every person on my contact list, except the people I was close to, had called or texted me today. I didn't even glance at my social media sites.

A ding accompanied a new text message from Amy.

Amy: Thirty-eight and counting.

Having no idea what she was talking about, I scrolled up to her first new text message.

Six celebrities have now shared about the video. Here is a link to a post.

I clicked on the link. My web browser app opened to Dream Big's social media fan page.

We visited some good friends down in Coral Beach today. One of our friends who toured with us a couple years back, Jamie Scott from Cherry Pie, has a daughter with special needs. Recently, her daughter's Special Day Class teacher was laid off and the position eliminated, just days after the school hired a dance teacher on full time. Jamie's had a lot of trouble advocating for her daughter's rights and inspired by this, a family member of hers wrote her this song. Check it out; you might see a couple familiar faces.

I clicked back over to Amy's text. The next couple texts were counting how many celebrities had shared the post. Further down, I clicked on a link that opened my web browser app to an entertainment news site. The title above the article read

"Controversial Celebrity Video Goes Viral'. There was a video link and below the link a small block of text.

"A video Dream Big, the Rocketeers and the little known pop group Cherry Pie put out this morning, immediately went viral and not because it was a sweet song advocating for children's rights by some of the nations' favorite celebrities. To learn more, watch the video above."

My heartbeat coming fast, I clicked on the video.

Loud intro music came on as bands of color moved across the screen. A man with dark, greased back hair appeared on screen, sitting at a desk and grinning like he had a secret. "Good morning everyone. You're here with our entertainment news today. In breaking celebrity news, mega-celebrity groups Dream Big and the Rocketeers released a video today to help their former pop singer friend Jamie Scott advocate for her daughter."

He turned to another camera with a cheeky smile and continued, "Reportedly their friend, currently the owner of a local coffee shop in Coral beach, California, was having trouble advocating for her daughter's rights with the local elementary school. While the video was thought by fans to be sweet and inspiring, it was not what shocked the nation and had this video going viral within the first few hours of it being posted."

The screen filled with a still from our video, a shot from the end of the video where we were all huddled and hugging. On the screen, a red line circled around where Kevin had his arm around Susan.

The announcer's voice came over while the picture zoomed in on Kevin and Susan. "Yes, you're seeing correctly, people. Pop idol Kevin Dempsey is hugging Susan Scott, the woman who ran off with, and eventually married, his long-time girlfriend, former supermodel, Beza Yazzie, now named Beza Scott. In response to questions about Susan Scott on his social media page, Kevin Dempsey wrote, 'We're friends. We've been friends for years."

"While this might be the reason for the overwhelming media attention, the video's message has not gone unheard—"

"Hey Jamie!"

I turned to see Chris standing in front of a growing line of customers.

"Sorry!" I stowed my phone, washed my hands and returned to making drinks. Chris stayed with me all the way to two, when we had to kick out several customers so we could close.

"You don't have to stay Chris, I can close." I scrubbed tables, flipping chairs up onto them well before they dried.

He pressed the receipt machine to print out the closing receipt. "I don't mean this to sound rude, Jamie, but I just don't think you can do it in time to get Sarah. I mean, we didn't have time to think all day. And you're working tonight, so I'm going to help you whether you like it or not." The whole time he talked, he counted cash. "Shoot, we are way off."

"By how much?"

"Eighteen dollars under." He started recounting the bills.

"You know what, Chris? I'm surprised it's not more. You have to remember I was on all through that crazy morning rush. I probably just forgot to void something, I'll figure it out later."

After counting through the card receipts, he said, "Nope, I think I already figured it out. One of us must have rung in one of these card transactions as cash."

"Best guess, it was me."

"So now we're only two-fifty under. That's closer to usual Jamie till."

"Ha, thanks." I propped up the last of the chairs and walked over to grab our broom and mop. When the floor was clean, I set about washing the huge stack of dishes we hadn't managed to clean.

When I was finished, Chris called over, "I'll do the trash if you take out the recycling."

"Deal." I started breaking down boxes while Chris grabbed up trash bags.

I grabbed the stack of boxes in one hand and a bin full of milk containers in the other. "I feel bad; we didn't even talk about your cupcake business offer."

"I barely got to think about it." He shrugged as he passed me with a bag of trash in each hand. "I wouldn't need to be working regular hours in the cupcake shop for a while and I could balance both, at least for a while."

"Chris, I'm going to take their offer."

He turned to me just before we reached the door. "You are?"

I nodded.

After we were done with the trash, Chris and I only had time to lock up and rush out the door as I was already late to head to the school.

I speeded most of the way, but slowed a few blocks from Coral Elementary where children crossed the street away from the school. As I pulled into the school lot, Sarah and her aide came into view.

Seeing me, Ms. Brown waved furiously and pointed while nodding her head.

Pulling up in front of her, I jumped out of the car.

"I'm sorry I'm late!" I ran around the car.

"It's fine!" her voice came out high-pitched. She waved me toward her. "Here, Ms. Scott, you might want to get going fast now."

"Mom!" Sarah ran over to me, barreling into me. When I looked down, I realized I had forgotten to take off my apron.

Feeling my cheeks warm a little, I looked back up to Ms. Brown. "How was her day?"

Ms. Brown stepped up next to me. "It was great! But I think you really, really should get in your car now!"

"What? Why?" Looking around, my eyes widened. Among the kids, teachers and scattered groups of parents, were several parents I recognized. They were standing together a hundred yards away. Four of them were glaring at me, while the others were talking amongst themselves. Whitney stood to one side, she was definitely glaring.

"Oh, I see." I touched Sarah's shoulder. "Baby, it's time to get in the car now."

She looked up. "Mom, can I watch floor exercises?"

"Yeah, babe, um, let's get in the car." Leaning over, I opened her car door. When she let go of me, I ushered her in and buckled her into her booster.

Closing her door, I turned around to face a full crowd of angry PTA parents.

Day Six: Two fifty-five

"Heya Whitney." I waved.

"Hello, Jamie." She stepped up a little before the group. I stood off the curb, on the street. They were all glaring down at me.

I raised my hands in a 'what do you want me to do?' gesture. "Are you guys like the cheerleading squad coming to tell me I'm off the Social Committee?"

Whitney's voice was as calm and sophisticated as her way too fancy up-do. "Just because you have celebrity friends and power doesn't mean you get to throw your weight around here and bully people."

"Hmm, that sounds familiar. H-y-p-o-c-r-i-t-e... shoot, is that even how you spell hypocrite? I never went to college." I shrugged.

Mindy, another PTA mom stepped up next to Whitney. Though she had a pretty face, her mouth pinched and eyes practically bulged. "You think you're so cute, don't you? The school could sue you for defamation."

"Actually, Mindy, no it couldn't." The male voice came from behind me.

I looked over to see Patrick standing close by, holding Kay's hand.

"I'm pretty sure they could, Patrick."

He shook his head. "Well, I am sure that they can't, Mindy." He turned to me. "Can Kay go sit with Sarah?"

When I nodded, he leaned down and whispered something to Kay.

"Yay!" Kay opened my car passenger door and climbed in.

Mindy stood straight again. "Well, what she did was very uncool. We," she gestured, "You included Patrick, have done a lot of work creating goodwill toward the school and in just one day Jamie undid all of it. And it's just because she didn't get her way with the funding!"

"You've pushed the school board into making a decision that endangers my daughter and other children. I don't care about how many benefits or bake sales you've hosted; you're making decisions that you shouldn't have the power to make. All I did was bring attention to it. You're just mad because I called you guys out, and the world knows you're doing something awful."

Patrick stepped up next to me. "She's right; you guys shouldn't have the power to restructure the special education department, that should come from the district and the school board."

Whitney shook her head. "We didn't restructure the special education department. The school board made that decision."

I rolled my eyes. "Yeah, whatever Whitney. I'm done here, I've said my piece. You don't like what I have to say, I definitely don't like what you have to say. I'm just hoping that the school board rethinks their decision and reopens the position."

Lips pursed, Whitney shook her head. "They never said that the position was closed, Jamie. I think all of this could have been a big misunderstanding."

I pinned her with my glare. "I really hope it was, Whitney."

Mindy crossed her arms over her chest. "We expect an apology, a public apology."

I huffed out of my nose. "You can expect whatever you want, Mindy."

"Excuse me, I think she was brilliant!" Maria barged into the group, pulling her son Fernando behind her. Fernando grinned up at everyone, and even under the circumstances, I couldn't help but grin back, he was just so cute.

As if Maria was a bowling ball, most of the PTA parents scattered. Well, they drifted off, walking away.

Whitney stayed, Mindy close behind her. "See you tomorrow night, Patrick. Bye, Jamie."

I waved at her with an insincere grin on my face.

Maria stuck her phone in my face. "My son in high school designed this." On the phone was a picture of a t-shirt with #allkidscount emblazoned on it. "I'm just glad you did it, Jamie. I swear I'm growing so many gray hairs and I had no idea what to do." She pointed to her black hair, were I could see a couple gray hairs. She looked down to her son. "Fernando keeps running away because he can't handle the noise in the little classroom, and there are only sixteen kids in there. I just hope something happens. I am going to be selling these at the benefit tomorrow. I already had a booth planned, but my cousin's girlfriend works at a screen-printing shop and she said she can have them printed by tomorrow night. So I'll be selling these instead."

"Wow, Maria. That might not go well."

She shook her head. "I do not care what they think, Jamie. Also, a couple other moms offered to help me so I won't be doing it alone. I just hope we sell a couple and the people put them on directly."

Patrick nodded. "If I can buy one in advance, I'll wear it to the benefit."

I startled, having completely forgotten he was there.

"Give me your number; I'll try to get you one before the benefit." Maria pulled out her phone.

After Patrick gave her his number, I said, "How much is this all going to cost you?"

She waved it away. "Some of the other moms are helping me. Anyway, I'll probably make it back, and if I don't, it'll be worth it."

"I want to buy, like," I counted in my head, "Twenty-five of them."

"Sure, they're only going to be about five dollars apiece to make, so just pay me the cost price."

"Here, wait a second." I grabbed out my tip money, which was still in my apron pocket. "This is all the cash I have on me, it's—" I counted the money out, "—one hundred and eighty-two dollars. Here, take this and use what's left over toward making more shirts." When she took it, I added, "Sorry, there are so many ones."

"Oh, it's fine, Jamie." She put the large stack of bills in her purse. Glancing down at Fernando, who still smiled up at us, Maria sighed. "All right, we better go get started."

I gave her a hopeful smile. "Good luck! If there's anything I can do, text me."

"Thanks, Jamie. Nice to meet you, Patrick."

"Likewise." He waved.

I turned to him as Maria walked away. "Thanks, Patrick, very nice of you to defend me that way... after everything."

"No problem." He ran a hand over his head and pivoted to me. "They called me around lunchtime to invite me to join their mob; I thought maybe you could use some backup."

I exhaled a laugh. "They actually admitted what it was?"

"No, I think they said, 'will you come with us to ask Jamie to please take down her offensive video?' Not sure that is a direct quote, but pretty close."

"Yeah. Well, thanks anyhow."

He grinned. "I always enjoyed a little showdown by the school yard; I'm just disappointed it didn't end in fisticuffs."

"Who do you think would win, me or Whitney?" I bounced on my heels.

He regarded me with a look. "Do you really want me to answer that truthfully?"

"No way! You think she'd win?" My mouth hung open in indignation. "No way, I'm not listening to you, I'd totally win."

He chuckled. "If you say so."

"Ha, maybe I still am done talking with you." I turned to the car, then back to grin at him. "I'm just kidding."

"Good."

"Actually, do you have a minute?"

He looked down at his watch, and then scratched the back of his neck. "Unfortunately, no. We're running a little late for Kay's horseback riding."

"Oh. Okay, another time then."

He paused for a second as if he wanted to say something, but then he looked back to my car, going to open the passenger door. "Hey Kay bay, time to go, we're late for riding."

"Dad, can we go to ice cream with Sarah instead? Sarah's going to ice cream." Kay bounced up and down from where she knelt on the passenger seat.

"What?" I looked back at Sarah. "I never said anything about ice cream." I looked at Patrick and shook my head, grinning. "Little sneaker."

Patrick looked down at his watch again. "Unless we go right now, we're going to miss your entire riding session."

"Dad, can we go another day? I really, really, really want ice cream. Please!" She drew out the word, giving him the most pleading expression I'd ever seen.

"Wow, she's good at that."

"You have no idea." Patrick shook his head, and then looked up at me. "Are you guys going out for ice cream?"

"We could go out for ice cream. I'll even treat you guys to ice cream." I shrugged. "But I'm just warning you, I have a little bit of an ulterior motive."

He raised his eyebrows. "Do you?"

"Your dad gave me another job offer and I really want to get the opinion of someone who knows him and what he's about."

Patrick nodded.

"And, I sort of wanted to apologize for bursting in at your office. I can be a little... reactive at times."

"I'm getting that." He sighed. "Yeah, okay. Should I follow you or do you want to drive in one car?"

"You're welcome to drive with us, or we could even walk, the shop we go to is about five blocks down."

"Yeah, that sounds good." He turned to Kay. "Hey Kay, get out so Jamie can park, okay?"

"I could just sit in the front seat?" She grinned up at him.

"Nope."

"Please?"

"Nope, I'm already giving in to ice cream." He regarded her with a 'do you take me for a sucker?' look.

"Fine." She climbed out of my car and shut the door.

When I was in my seat, I finally took off my apron. I parked my car then grabbed all the papers that Pat left for me before climbing out. Sarah took my hand as we crossed the lot, but let go and yanked away as soon as we reached the curb. She ran to Kay and began bouncing.

"This way, just on the other side of the beach park." I pointed down the street. "Or we could even walk through the park."

"Yeah, let's do that."

"That way girls." I pointed to the path that curved through the freshly mowed grass. Palm trees lined on one side, their shadows crossing our path in even lines.

Kay and Sarah skipped into shadows, then light, over and over, as they held hands just a little way ahead of us.

"Don't get too far ahead!" I called through cupped hands.

Patrick and I strolled in silence for a few minutes.

"Is that the offer?" he asked, nodding down to the stack of papers in my hand.

"Yeah, uh..." I lifted my hand but dropped it, "I should probably wait to show you in the shop."

"What made you change your mind?"

"A lot of things."

He turned his concentration out ahead of us as he continued, "It's just a little surprising, after your reaction."

"I'm sure it seems that way. And yeah, it was a really big shock that the man who was about to buy my shop was the same guy who'd sued me a couple days after my husband died. I'm still not completely down with that. But then Sarah and I are pretty much homeless right now and I—"

"What?" He stopped to look down at me.

"That came out bad; we have a place to stay, but not a permanent one. And I want to buy a safe, decent house and work less and all that."

"Where are you staying?"

"With that guy I told you about. Cameron, who I'm kind of with."

"Oh." He nodded and continued walking. "So you guys are definitely together now?"

"Sort of. Yeah. Well, let's just say yes for now. But I'm hoping you and I could be friends?"

He shot me a smirk. "I thought you said you don't want to be my friend?"

"That was before you defended me against a pack of rabid socialites."

He huffed a laugh.

"And you have a pool; it's always good to make friends with people who have pools."

He really laughed at that one. "Fine, I'll let you use me for my pool."

"Your house too. I'd totally use you for that. Actually, Patrick, I kind of felt like an ass ever since I left your work. Not that I wasn't in the right, because I totally was."

"Of course." He glanced over, a smirk still on his lips.

"But showing up at your work was relatively inappropriate, and even though you should have told me what was going on with your dad and all, I probably wouldn't have if I was you."

He met this comment with silence as we caught up to the girls who were waiting for us at the base of a palm tree. The moment we caught up to them, the girls rushed ahead again.

"So what happened to your house? If you don't mind me asking. Or, have you always been living with this guy Cameron?"

"Oh, no." I looked over. "Just since last night. Um, my neighbor has been bothering us and threatening me."

He halted. "You're serious?"

I cringed. "Unfortunately."

He leaned in. "Are you okay?"

"Yeah. I mean, it was getting scary but we're going to be staying at Cameron's now and that makes me feel a lot safer."

"So you're now considering my father's offer because you're in a seriously bad situation?"

I started walking again. "That's part of it, but not all of it. Honestly, I just don't want to get screwed over here with this job contract. And I know you're his son, so you might be a little biased, but I wanted to ask your opinion."

He walked along side me. "I'll try to be as unbiased as possible."

"Thanks, Patrick. And, thank you for being so understanding about me freaking out at you and stuff."

"Well, you might be my coworker soon, so I figure I better mend fences with you now."

I glanced over at him. "Not really..."

"We handle most of the financial and accounting matters for all of my father's companies."

"Yeah, but both Timepiece and Harrington's are big companies, we would probably never see each other, right?"

He shrugged. "You never know."

We caught up to the girls again, who were standing at the curb where the park's path led out to the street. They took turns pressing the crosswalk button over and over again.

I grinned down at them. "It's like you girls are excited for ice cream or something."

They both giggled. After we all crossed the crosswalk together, we walked into the small parking lot in front of the ice cream and coffee shop.

Patrick looked around. "I didn't even realize this was here."

"They actually have pretty decent coffee."

"Are you going to get any?"

"No. I'm trying to cut down."

He opened the door to the shop, letting the girls go in first then waiting for me to go in. "That must be hard with what you do."

"You have no idea. But I'm thinking coffee ice cream isn't really cheating."

Day Six: Three-twenty

Inside the shop, on a hanging wood sign the words 'Coral Beach Ice Cream Shoppe Established 1920' were painted. The store was small, only holding two bright blue painted tables. Thick white lines of trim separated the powder blue walls, making the entire shop look a little like an ice cream cake. The elderly man behind the counter whose name tag read 'Tom', was dressed in powder blue with white stripes, making him look like an extension of the shop itself.

He grinned down at the girls. "What can I get you two ladies?"

Sarah jumped up and down. "Two scoops!"

"Dad, if Sarah's getting two scoops, can I get two scoops?"

I laughed a loud 'ha'. "Sarah is definitely not getting two scoops. She's getting a kids' scoop. What flavor do you want, sweetheart? They have strawberry, vanilla, chocolate—"

"Vanilla!"

Tom nodded. "Cup or cone?"

"Cup!"

Kay smiled up. "I want chocolate and I want a cone!"

"Also a kids' scoop," Patrick said.

Tom handed each kid their scoop, which they immediately took to a table and began devouring.

I glanced back at Patrick. "You want anything? It's my treat."

He narrowed his eyes on me. "My treat."

"Nope." I turned to Tom. "I'll take a scoop of that one in a cone." I pointed in at some sort of coffee, mocha, chocolate goodness.

"Good choice," Tom said as he pushed a heaping scoop onto a cone and set it in the cone-holder above the ice cream bar.

"What can I get for you, sir?"

Patrick looked between me and Tom. "I'll take the same as the lady, but in a cup please." He reached for his wallet.

"Don't you dare." I glared at him as I held out my card to Tom.

"Sorry, lady wins." Tom grabbed my card and rang us up. Just for that, I gave him a big tip on the credit card receipt.

As we went to sit down beside the girls, Kay looked up and said, "Dad, can we sit all by ourselves?"

Patrick looked at me and when I shrugged, he said, "Okay, Kay bay, but if anyone comes in we're going to have to share a table."

"Okay!" She turned back to Sarah and they started giggling.

Patrick and I took the other table and grinned at each other a little awkwardly.

"Do you want me to take a look at those?" He nodded over to the stack of papers I'd set on the table.

"If you would." I pushed them across.

He ignored his ice cream as he read the contract over. I had pretty much finished mine by the time he read the first page and had moved on the next.

His eyes moved quickly as he read. "This is the original contract proposal?"

"Yep."

"Mm-hmm. Well, it's pretty obvious that he's trying to get you to take the old one."

"Yeah?"

"Yeah, but this one isn't terrible, especially if you don't think you'll stay for more than a year."

"I'd like the option not to."

"Then this is the way to go. The wage is pretty standard at your managerial level, while the original wage was definitely on the higher side. The sign-on bonus is much lower, but that might be to your advantage—"

"There's a sign-on bonus?" I licked the ice cream off my lips.

He turned the paper around. "Yeah, that's what this line is."

"Oh."

He looked between the papers. "Twenty thousand with the three-year contract and five with this one."

"Oh, okay."

"If you quit before the term in either, you'd have to give the sign-on bonus back and there's a possibility, actually it's pretty likely, that you would be sued for damages because of the incomplete term of employment. This is standard, though."

"Okay." I bit into my cone.

He set down the papers. "It's not the best job offer I've ever seen. It's pretty clear he's trying to manipulate you into taking this one." He nodded toward the original offer. "But I don't see anything in there to *screw you over*." He took a bite of his now pretty melted ice cream.

"So you think I should take it?"

"Do you want to sell your shop?"

I took another bite of my cone and took time chewing. "I love my shop, but I already paid it off once. When Logan first died, it felt like the buoy I held onto in a storm, but now it feels more like an anchor, forcing me to keep treading water."

He nodded. We stayed silent as we finished our ice cream.

When I glanced back, I saw that Sarah and Kay were huddled together, no trace of their ice cream remaining. I turned back to Patrick. "Something's been bothering me since I found out you knew about Logan. Can I bring it up? I know we're mending fences and all, but I kind of need to know if we're going to be friends."

"Yeah, okay, Jamie."

"How much do you know about how Logan died?"

He rolled back his shoulders and set his spoon down in his ice cream container. "I'm sorry, Jamie. I know probably more than—I learned about it on paper, before I knew who you were."

"Yeah." I leaned back in my pastel-yellow chair. "That's kind of what I figured."

"Can I ask you about what happened, so that I know from you?" When I looked away, he said, "You don't need to tell me."

I exhaled, and shook my head. "Logan—we both were going through a really hard time right then, but Logan especially. He always drank, but things just got really bad, really fast. Like, he started drinking every day, during the day. He just stopped working so I was at the shop more than full time and depended on friends and family to help with Sarah." I looked out the window. "Logan wasn't coming home often, but I still had no idea that there were other women, actually to this day I wonder if Logan even knew that there had been. But, there were, I guess more than one, and my best friend Vanessa was one of them." I looked at him. "Vanessa was Cameron's wife then."

His eyebrows went up and eyes went wide.

"I know. We're so screwed up. Anyway, Cameron found out that Nessa had been with Logan and he told her that she had to come clean with me, I guess for a while, but she didn't—she chickened out. The night he died, Logan had called Susan to pick him up at his regular bar early, but when she'd arrived he was gone." I wiped away a tear with my palm. "I guess Vanessa had picked him up first and took him to a parking lot nearby the hotel she was staying in to try to convince him to come clean with me—probably so she wouldn't have to. I don't know what she was thinking. She was sober and he was blackout drunk, but for some reason she let him take her car and drive out of there without his seatbelt on. He didn't even make it out of the parking structure."

Patrick reached across the table, placing his hand on mine in silent sympathy.

"Thanks. You know, I don't ever remember telling that story out loud. Everyone just sort of already knew. Or, maybe I did tell people. I can't really remember all the details of those first few days." I looked back up at him. "What had you heard?"

"That he was there with a woman, that he'd had a blood alcohol level of point twenty-three percent."

I nodded. "Both were true."

"So Vanessa and Cameron got a divorce?"

"I guess they were already on their way to." I inhaled, deeply. "I should be heading back, I have to work at six tonight and I need to make sure Sarah eats something other than ice cream."

"Yeah, us too." Patrick stood, but paused looking at me. "Jamie, will you call me if you take the job?"

"Um, sure, okay."

"I'd just like to know."

"Okay, but next time I see you it'll be your turn to open all your old wounds and bare your heart, so you might not be so excited to be my coworker."

He shook his head. "I'll tell you right now if you want me too."

"I'm feeling a little too depressed for one afternoon. How about you tell me all the semi-inappropriate jokes you know but never say because you're too classy?"

He threw his ice cream container away, a small grin on his face. "I don't think I know any of those."

"Really? When you and the old men go off to drink scotch and smoke cigars you only talk about sports?" My look dripped skepticism.

"We sometimes talk about stocks."

"Sure." I turned to the girls. "Time to go, ladies."

They looked up from where they were huddled together, looking at the stickers on a binder that must have come out of Kay's now open backpack.

Kay stuffed her binder into her backpack and turned to look up at me. "Sarah's mom, can Sarah come over to my house?"

"Her name is Jamie."

"Not today, Kay. We need to go eat some dinner."

Sarah jumped out of her seat and came running over to me. "Mom, can we go watch videos?"

"Yeah, baby."

Before leaving, we shot a goodbye and one last thank you to Tom the ice cream guy, then filed out. The walk back seemed to be quite a bit shorter than the walk there.

"You parked right next to me," Patrick said, pointing to the only two cars remaining in the lot.

After we'd each strapped our kids into our respective cars, I turned to Patrick. "Thanks for everything. I'll see you later."

He grinned. "I'll be sure to learn a couple mildly-inappropriate jokes before then."

"Oh, come on, you already know them." I shook my head.

"See you later, Jamie."

"Yeah." I held up a hand as I opened my car door. When I checked my phone before driving, it coincidentally rang and lit up with a photo of Cameron's face. I rushed to answer it.

"Hey, Cameron."

"Hey, there. I've been trying to call you."

"Oh, sorry. I turned my phone on silent on the way to Sarah's school because people have been blowing me up nonstop all day. I'll tell you about it later."

"Are you at the house?"

"Nope, Sarah and I went to ice cream with one of her friends and her dad, but we're just about to head there."

"Okay, I'm just about to leave. I was worried because you don't have a key and I forgot to tell you where I keep the spare."

"Oh, it's all good; you don't have to leave work early."

"Nah, I want to. I've already closed up and I ordered us some Chinese food. I hope that's okay? I'm starving. I skipped lunch."

"I noticed. And Chinese sounds great, thank you so much. I'll pay you back."

"Of course not, baby. Anyway, the spare key is behind the house in the shed, I'll tell you how to find it."

"I'll just wait for you to get home."

"Okay, whatever you want to do. I'll see you soon. I love you."

I swallowed and said in a quiet voice, "You too." Quickly, I hung up the phone, biting my lip. Turning the car on, I backed out of my space and drove the short drive out of town and to Cameron's house.

After pulling up and parking, I turned to Sarah. "Hey, angel. I need to make a quick phone call. Do you want to wait in the car with the kids' CD?"

She unbuckled her seatbelt. "Kids' CD!"

I rolled down the window to the car and turned on the CD. Grabbing out Patrick Kelly Seniors' business card, I climbed out of the car and walked around to sit on the trunk.

For a full minute, I looked between my phone and the card. With shaking fingers, I typed in his number.

After several rings, the phone went to voicemail. "This is Patrick Kelly's voicemail. Please leave your name and a short message with your phone number." The phone beeped.

"Hello Pat, this is Jamie Scott. Um, I'd like to talk to you if you have a minute." I gave him my phone number, and then hung up.

As I hopped down from my car, my phone rang with Pat's phone number on the screen.

"Okay." I pressed the button to answer and put the phone to my ear. "Hello?"

"Ms. Scott?"

"Pat, you can call me Jamie."

"All right, Jamie, how are you doing?"

"Fine. How are you?"

"I'm doing well. I am calling you back; you said there was something you wanted to talk to me about."

I took a steadying breath. "Yes, I looked over the new employment contract and I'm interested."

"Interested in the new one?"

"Yes, and of course the sale of the shop with that."

"Good. Can you come in right now?"

"Come in?" I asked.

"To meet me and go over the details."

"Sorry, I can't, I have my daughter with me."

"You're welcome to bring her with you. I'd prefer to get this process started before I go out of town tomorrow morning."

"Sorry, Pat, I really can't today, I have to go into work at six and I need to get ready."

"You have a second job?" He didn't sound happy about it.

"Um, yeah, I work as a bartender two or three nights a week."

"Are you planning to continue this?" he said it like I'd just told him I robbed banks three nights a week.

"There was nothing in the employment contract about not having another job."

"Well, I proposed the contract with the assumption that you didn't have another job."

My jaw clenched. "I was sued, lost everything, barely made ends meet, was trying to save my business and feed my daughter, Pat. So, I work a lot, you know, so we can eat."

"Jamie, all of those matters will be settled if you come to work for me and sell the Coffee Spot. You also have had a good portion of your possessions returned to you; so much of what you said will be a non-issue. I just don't see how you'll be able to manage a high-demand position in my company and work in the evenings.”

As he spoke, Cameron pulled up and parked beside me.

I paused, and then said into the phone, “Are you going to change the terms on the employment contract or retract the offer?”

“No. But, I strongly suggest that you quit your other job if you come to work for me.”

“I’ll think on it.”

Cameron made eye contact with me as he exited his car then came around to grab out two full white plastic bags of food.

“Good,” Pat said. “Could you meet Nicole and me in the morning tomorrow?”

“At the shop or before we open?”

“We could come by the shop before I fly out, around nine?”

“Yeah, okay. But just to warn you, it might be really busy,” I cringed a little as I said it.

“That’s good, that’s what I want to hear. I’ll see you tomorrow morning.” He hung up.

“Who was that?” Cameron came to stand between my knees, setting a bag of Chinese food on either side of me.

“The lien holder, dun, dun, duh.” I put my head over the bag, inhaling the hot, delicious aroma. “Oh my God, that smells good.”

“So, you’re selling?”

“I’ll tell you inside. I need to get Sarah out of the car.” I hopped down in front of him so I was pretty much pressed against him.

I gave him a quick kiss and squirmed past him. "I'll carry in one of those bags. Leave it for me."

"Nah, I got it." He headed for the door, a bag in each hand.

I found Sarah in the driver's seat, turning the volume knob on the CD up and down, over and over again. Opening the door, I crouched down next to her and turned the car off auxiliary, grabbing the keys out. "Let's go in. Cameron brought Chinese food."

"Chinese food! I want to watch floor exercises, Mom!"

I grinned. "Yeah, of course."

We followed Cameron into the house, finding that he'd already set out the food and silverware, and was grabbing cups. "What do you want to drink?"

"Juice! Can I watch floor exercises?"

"After we eat." I turned to Cameron. "Just water. Can I help you with anything?"

"Plates. Just in there." He nodded to a cupboard.

After setting the plates out, I started opening containers.

Cameron came to stand beside me. "So this dad you went to ice cream with, is he the same guy who asked you out?" he said it so casually, like he was asking if I was going to want pot-stickers.

Day Six: Four-forty

I looked up at Cameron, who was concentrating very hard on dishing out Chinese food onto plates.

"It wasn't a date, Cameron. He's a friend; he just helped me by looking over the employment contract. And Sarah and Kay wanted ice cream."

"Oh yeah?" He continued to dish out Chow Mein. Handing the dish over the table, he set it in front of Sarah.

She immediately started eating, her concentration on my cell phone which she must have commandeered without me noticing.

"Cameron, look at me." I stepped in close to him.

His eyes came up to meet mine with a not-so happy expression in them.

I touched his arm. "I told him that we were together, that I was living here. He's a friend."

An almost smile twitched at the side of his mouth. He moved in closer to me, looking down, and asking in a low voice, "So are you still going to be going on dates with this guy?"

"No, but I might hang out with him because, as I said, he's a friend and pretty soon might be a coworker too."

"He works for Harrington's?"

"Kind of."

"Oh."

He set our plates in front of us and sat down, immediately digging into his food.

I sat beside him, eating in silence.

"What's his name?"

"Patrick." After a prolonged silence, I whispered, "Now who's giving who the cold shoulder?"

He glanced over. "Well, at least I'm asking you about it."

I rolled my eyes. "Oh, thank you so much."

"Can I meet him?"

I paused with my fork halfway to my mouth. "What?"

"Can I meet your friend Patrick?"

I shrugged, looking away. "Sure, you'll probably like him. He's nice."

"A nice guy, huh? No wonder you chose me."

I glared. "You're pretty nice, too, *usually*."

He smirked.

I concentrated on eating my Chow Mein, not really feeling like telling Cameron all the things I had been aching to before I saw him.

Sarah's game music played, loud in the otherwise silent space.

"Angel, no more phone at the table." I reached across the table and held out my hand. When she handed it over, we continued eating in silence.

After we had finished eating, I stood to clear the table.

Cameron also stood and stepped in close to me, taking the plates I had grabbed. "I'll do those; you can go ahead and get ready for work if you want."

"Thanks." I turned to Sarah. "Sweetie, do you have reading?"

"No!"

After checking her binder and confirming that she didn't have any homework, I grabbed my laptop off an end table, disconnecting it from the charger. I set up Sarah's videos from a playlist, and then gave her a kiss on the forehead. "I'm going to go take a shower upstairs."

As I started up the staircase, Cameron turned from the kitchen. He set down the plate he held and followed me. As I finished ascending, I heard him start up the stairs.

Instead of heading into the bathroom, I went into his room and turned to wait for him.

He followed me in, immediately striding to me. His hands came to my hips and he backed me into the wall.

I let him.

When his lips met mine, I returned the kiss, hungrily. He pressed me into the wall, kissing me deeply as his hands squeezed my hips.

He pulled away to look down at me. "I'm jealous."

"I can tell."

"I don't want to be." He gave me another quick kiss. "But I am."

I ran my hand over the back of his neck. "Even though we're not officially together, I told him that we were, Cameron. I told you that."

"Yeah, but in the back of my mind, I'm asking myself: do you want to be with me, or do you have to be because you're staying here?"

"Cameron, honestly... I'm not ready to officially be a couple. There's just too much going on right now in my life and in my head. I don't want to rush this. But..." I exhaled and sank into him, my head coming to his shoulder, "at the same time, I love you. And, I don't want to be with anyone else. Nothing ever happened with Patrick either; he asked me out, I said maybe and then changed it to no."

"If you still want to go on dates with other guys, I'm not going to stop you."

I leaned back to the wall to look at him. "Oh, come on, Cameron; don't say things you don't mean."

"When the time comes, I just don't want you to choose to be in a relationship with me because you feel like you have to."

I reached up and touched his cheek. "I swear to you, the only reason I will ever choose to be in a relationship with you will be because I love you."

"Good." His gaze burnt into mine. "I'm going to wait up for you tonight."

"You promise?"

"Without a doubt." He kissed me again, long and slow. When he pulled away, he regarded me with a mischievous grin. "I still want to meet him."

I shook my head. "Why?"

"I'd rather not just be a name to him, especially if you're going to work with him."

"Um..."

"And I know how big of a flirt you are, so I just want him to have a really good picture of who you come home to at night."

"*Who I come home to*?" My mouth hung open. "And I am not a *big flirt*."

He raised an eyebrow at me and kissed me on the tip of my nose. "Please, I promise I'll be nice."

I rolled my eyes. "Fine."

"Thank you. I'll see you downstairs."

After he left, I took a minute to choose a decent Sports Night at Mike's Saloon outfit out, that is, jeans and baseball hat and shirt. I grabbed a second outfit too, as there was about a sixty to eighty percent chance of a beer being spilled down my front, depending on the crowd.

I took a quick shower, dressed and then put my hair in a ponytail and fed it through my cap. After putting on minimal make up and doing other bathroom activities, I hurried downstairs to join Sarah and Cameron. They'd moved to the couch, Sarah sat under Cameron's arm as they watched my laptop sitting on the coffee table.

Taking the seat on Sarah's other side, I kissed her forehead. "I'm going to go to work, baby. You be good for Cameron."

She smiled at me. "I love you so much!"

"I love you so much, angel."

Cameron smiled at me. "I brought over Sarah's puzzles and some games. We're not going to watch this much longer, right sport?"

"I'm just going to watch floor exercises." She turned her attention to the screen.

Over her head, Cameron shook his head and mouthed 'nah.' He stood up, still smiling at me. "Come over here a minute."

After giving Sarah one last kiss on the top of her head, I followed Cameron over to the front door.

He grabbed the bill of my cap. "This is cute."

"Thanks." I grinned.

"I just wanted one of these before you go." He leaned in and gave me another kiss. His eyes met mine. "I love you, Jamie."

I reached up, running my hand over the little bit of dark stubble on his jaw line. "I love you. I love you so much."

"You do?"

"Yes. Don't you know that?"

"Yeah, I guess I do. But I'm never going to get tired of hearing it from your lips." After one last kiss, he said, "You be safe okay?"

"I will. I'll see you very late tonight."

He gave me a knowing grin. "Yeah you will."

I laughed. "Uh-huh, bye, Cameron."

Even though I was running a little bit on the late side as Cameron's house was further from the bar than mine, I didn't rush. When I parked in the spot designated 'Mike's Saloon Employee Only Parking' behind the bar, I was about five minutes late.

Before getting out of my car, I craned my neck to look both ways down the alley. Seeing no one in either direction, I climbed out and crossed the alley. My hands shook and I glanced once more in both directions as I unlocked the back door. Once inside, I remembered to click the remote to lock my car and closed the back door at the same time.

I exhaled heavily and hung my purse in the break room. Walking over to the door to the bar, I threw it open.

My dad's voice came booming out from behind the door. "Whoa there, cowgirl, you almost hit me."

"Oh, sorry, Dad!"

When the door swung closed, he stood there grinning at me. "Hey, kiddo." He gave me a one-armed hug.

"Hey Dad."

A cry of, "What the hell!" came from a guy down the bar. When I looked, he threw up his hand at the screen, which showed a golf game. All eyes were to the various screens around the bar, a few were showing golf, and others showed college baseball.

"Must be Thursday," my father said, giving me a squeeze.

"I never get why you don't switch your sports' night when football season is over."

He just gave me a look like, 'football season is never over.

"Yo," Nancy said as she set a tray down on the bar.

"Hey, lady, how're you doing? You look awesome."

She looked very like a cheerleader, in a blue mini skirt and white crop top. Her hair was blown big and lips painted bright pink. "Thank you! Your dad says it's too short." She frowned. "You look awesome, too."

"Thanks. And don't worry about it; my dad's an old man." I waved the idea away as I crouched down to check the fridge's stock of bottled beers.

"Fifty-four is not even close to old," my dad called from down the bar.

"Can I get a couple pitchers of the Blonde?"

"Yep." Standing, I filled up two pitchers, tilting them to minimize the foam. "How many cups?"

"Eight."

"So how are things going with you know who?" I grinned over my shoulder at her.

She grinned back. "We went on a date. Well, actually just out, but it felt like a date."

"Are you serious?" I lifted my shoulders, beaming at her.

She wrinkled her nose. "Yeah, I told you we were going to."

"Oh," I said, disappointed, "With Carl."

"Jamie, don't be like that." She rolled her eyes.

"Sorry, I didn't mean it like that. I just thought you were talking about another person." I set the pitchers and cups on her tray.

"Okay whatever." She rolled her eyes. "I'm going to take these out."

I checked the alcohol bottles, fruit, sugar and salt in my station and except for the limes, everything was full. Going to the store room, I grabbed up an empty beer box and filled it with the bottled beers I was low on, and then returned to stock the fridge. When everything was full, I went down the bar in my section, offering to get the guys and a couple girls' refills.

While my father chatted to customers, I casually wiped up spills and cleaned cups. The pace was slow and the crowd easy, nothing like it got during football. Unlike my morning crowd at the

coffee shop, no one seemed to recognize me that
didn't already know me.

Nancy came back to get more pitchers and
bring back empty ones from the booths and tables.
When I asked, she told me details about her date,
seeming to not hold a grudge about my original
misunderstanding.

"I like him, Jamie."

I placed a line of sugar rimmed shots on her
tray. "Oh, I'm so glad for you, Nancy. You deserve to
be happy."

"I think you would like him, too, if you got to
know him."

I shrugged, grabbing up a bottle of well vodka.
"I'm not the one with a problem."

"Yeah, I know," she sighed.

"Hey, Jamie, can I get a refill?" A regular whose
name I couldn't remember called from down the bar.

"I got it, Chuck, what are you having?" My dad
grabbed Chuck's old glass, setting it with the dirty
ones under the bar, and grabbed out another pint
glass.

I turned back to Nancy and poured the vodka
shots in a line. Next to the shots, I set a dish of lemon
slices.

Nancy grabbed the tray. "I'm working on him
okay?"

"Appreciated." I gave her a smile as she walked
away.

I turned to my father who watched a screen
focused on a batter, talking to a customer about him.

"Hey Dad, when you get a minute, I have some news I want to share with you."

He turned with a grin and then clapped me on the back. "I always have a minute to hear your news. What's going on?"

"I got a job offer. Actually, someone offered to buy the shop and the job offer came attached."

"Well, honey, that is fantastic! What type of job are they offering?"

"General Manager of all the Harrington locations in the county, plus, you know, the Coffee Stop."

"Ah, sweetheart." He wrapped me in a hug, and squeezed me tight. "I couldn't be happier for you. You are long overdue for a turn in your luck."

"Thanks, Dad. I actually brought the job contract in, thought maybe if you get an extra second you could take a look?"

"Yeah, bring it over now."

I shifted, bouncing on the pads of my feet. "The thing is, they'd want me to quit the bar. Would you be mad if I quit?"

He shook his head. "Not at all."

"Really, are you sure? Because I don't have to quit."

"Honey, I'd miss you, but it's easy enough to hire a new bartender. Maybe I'd finally get some peace of mind from stopping having to hear Carl's bitching all the time." He chuckled.

"I can still work for a couple weeks."

"Well, you don't have to. I can have Carl take your shifts and cover his Saturday days until I get someone new."

"I have another favor to ask."

"Shoot."

"Could you and Sharon watch Sarah tomorrow evening?"

"That's not a favor. What time?"

"Um, not sure when yet, maybe like five and could she spend the night?"

"Yeah sure. Now go get that contract while I refill a couple drinks."

Walking back in the break room, I grabbed the contract from where I had folded it in my purse and I delivered it to my father.

"Where's Gina?" I asked as I noticed her usual table was empty.

"Not feeling so good. All these guys are just going to have to man up and call taxis."

A guy at the bar barked out a laugh at that. While my father looked over the contract, I served my section and poured drinks for Nancy when she needed them.

"I don't see anything wrong with it." My father handed me back the contract. "But I don't pretend to be an expert. I never made any of my guys sign anything but their tax forms."

"Yeah, I know. Thanks for looking anyway." After returning the contract, I refilled a couple beers and poured one group of guys five tequila shots.

"Keep the change." The handsome older guy threw forty dollars on the bar.

"Thank you very much." I rang them up, putting the change in the communal tip jar Nancy and I would split at the end of the night.

When Nancy came back to the bar, she sent a wide smile my way. "Weirdest thing happened. Someone left this note on a booth that's been vacant. *And* they left this!" She held up a hundred-dollar bill.

"Wow, Nancy, woo-hoo for short skirts." I winked at her. "But, you totally should keep that; I'd feel too bad splitting it."

"No, it's for you, look." She held up her tray to show me a folded piece of paper that read: *To the hot blonde bartender.*

Day Six: Nine-fifteen

My eyes felt hot and my heart raced in my chest as I pulled the paper from her tray. The paper almost slipped in my fingers. It was thin, limp paper, like printer paper that had too much ink on it. When I opened the paper and saw the image inside, my hand went to my mouth.

A note was scrawled across the paper, '*worth every penny.*' Below the note was a photo printed directly on the paper.

In the photo, Cameron's living room lit with a yellowish glow. The outside of the curtains framing one side of the room revealed that the picture was taken from the other side of the windows. The camera had zoomed in so that Cameron's and my naked bodies took up most of the image. Cameron gripped me at the waist as I sat on top of him, riding him. My head was thrown back, lips open, mid orgasm.

The paper fell to the bar.

My breaths came short and fast as I covered my mouth. Tears slid onto my fingertips and dripped down my fingers.

The smile dropped off Nancy's face. "Oh my God, Jamie, what is it?" She grabbed the paper and opened the image. "What the hell!" She looked up at me. "This is you? Jamie what is this?"

My dad's voice came from right beside me. "Nancy, Jamie, everything okay?"

I jumped and reached over to grab the paper from Nancy's hands, crumpling it up in my fist.

"What's going on?" My dad looked between Nancy and my faces, hers was ashen and mine felt bloodless.

Several other people around us were looking on with concern.

"Nancy, Jamie, one of you better tell me what's going on."

"Someone left something really messed up for Jamie, but it's her business." Nancy looked to me, concern plain in her face.

"Jamie, let me see it."

I shook my head, my eyes hot and a few more tears leaking out that I couldn't stop. "No Dad." A wave of humiliation rushed through me, and I had to screw up my face to stop from bawling.

"Yes, Jamie, now!"

"Dad," I whispered, "It's a picture of me and Cameron... *together*. It's from last night."

The expression on my father's face was shock and horror and something else.

As tears started pouring out of my eyes, my father put an arm around my back.

"Nancy, you handle any orders for a few minutes, okay? You're the bartender." My father threw open the door to the break room.

"No problem," Nancy called from behind me.

When we were in the back room, my father turned to me. "Grab your purse, Jamie. I'm taking you to the police station."

"No, I'm okay."

"Like hell, Jamie. You're coming with me there or they're coming here. Those are your two choices."

He pulled out his phone and flipped it open. Pressing down the three button, he held the phone to his ear. "Carl, can you come in right now?" He paused. "I need you sooner than that." Another pause, then he yelled, "Because some sicko was here leaving his sick notes for my daughter and I'm taking her to the police station!" After a short break, he said, "Good," then hung up.

I wiped at my face. "As if the guy didn't hate me enough, already."

"Who cares, Jamie? You're quitting anyway."

I stared at him, my face wet and lip trembling. "Are you mad at me?"

"I'm so mad I could kill someone, but I'm mad at that sicko. Go get your stuff. I'm going to tell Nancy we're leaving."

I grabbed my purse from where I had hung it. The sound of my breath was loud in the quiet space. Across the room, the beautiful bouquet of flowers someone had left in the break room was wilting.

My father barged through the door. "Good, let's go. I'm driving you."

"Shouldn't we wait for Carl?"

"At this point I don't care if the bar burns down."

He put one arm around me and the other ushered me toward the door. Out in the lot, my father led me down to his big black SUV, opened the passenger door for me and closed it behind me.

After buckling myself in, I looked down at my hand, realizing the piece of paper was still clenched in it.

Outside the car, I heard my father on his cell phone. He opened his car door and climbed in. "Just talked to the chief, he's meeting us at the station."

"Dad, I want to talk to a woman."

He started his ignition. "We'll see what they can do when we get there."

My father said nothing during the ten block drive to the downtown police station. His eyes blazed at the road the entire time like he could melt it with his concentration. He pulled into the lot, taking one of the many open spaces.

We rushed through the lot and up the wide steps that led to the old mission-style police station building.

Only one middle-aged woman waited in the two rows of linked blue-cloth-covered metal chairs filling the waiting area space. The room was a long rectangle. On the far side a series of windows interrupted the wall. Through the windows, a larger area could be seen with a couple cops meandering or sitting at desks. Each window station sat vacant, except for one cop. The gray blue wall didn't quite reach the ceiling and voices from beyond it echoed quietly.

My father led me up the roped off space intended for a line to congregate. When we stopped at a sign that read, *'Please wait here',* a police officer looked up from the desk and waved us over, sliding a heavy window open.

The officer looked about my age despite the fact he was balding. His gaze darted between me and my father. "Hello, what can I help you with?"

My father leaned toward the desk. "Is Rudy here yet?"

"Not yet. Are you Mike?"

"Yeah."

"I'm going to buzz you in." He pointed off to the left to where a heavy looking door waited. "Go on in through there and I'll take you back to wait in his office with your daughter."

A loud buzzing blared out and my father paced over to the door and threw it open. He looked back grimly as he held it open for me.

The same officer met us on the other side of the door. "I'm Officer Kelper."

"Hi." My father shook his hand but didn't introduce us.

I shook his hand too. "I'm Jamie and this is my father, Mike."

The officer nodded. "Right this way."

I glanced at the series of desks, the majority of them open. The space was one large high-ceilinged room, doors led out on every wall.

The officer led us to our immediate right and straight to the first office on the wall. Opening the door, he held it for us and flicked on the light switch. The lights blinked on, illuminating a desk filling up a good third of the room. Two wood and leather chairs faced the desk.

The officer gestured. "Go ahead and take a seat, the chief will be here soon."

My father waited for me to sit then took the other chair. "Thank you, officer."

"Of course." He closed the door.

My father turned to me. "Do you want to call Cameron?"

I shook my head. "Not yet."

"He's with Sarah?"

"Yeah." I looked away.

"I didn't know that you two were a couple. Well, Sharon said she thought you were, but you never said anything to me."

"It's a bit awkward, Dad. I—please can we not do this now?"

He nodded. "He's a good guy. He was a great quarterback back in high school. Too bad he lost that scholarship—"

"Dad, please."

He nodded, again.

The door opened and we both jumped a little spinning around. A tall, broad man stood in the doorway. He wore a suit rather than a uniform.

"Mike, not only am I off duty, you interrupted a date with my wife. You better have brought some whisky with you."

"Rudy, some sicko is taking pictures of my daughter with her boyfriend during their intimate moments and leaving them for her at the bar, Cheryl will understand."

Rudy walked through the room, heading behind the desk to give us both a grim expression. He leaned over his desk offering me his hand. "I'm Chief Greer, but you can call me Rudy."

"Hi, Jamie Scott."

"All right, why don't you tell me what's been going on?"

Tears came to my eyes again. "It's really... embarrassing. Is it possible for me to talk to a female officer?"

He nodded. "It sure is, but you might have to wait a little while as I would have to pull one off patrol."

I looked at my dad.

He held his hand out and grasped mine. "I'll wait as long as you need me here."

I nodded. "Um, I—"

Rudy offered me a box of tissues and I took one, wiping my face.

"I guess I'll just tell you. I... I'm not sure where to start."

"How about if you have any idea who took the photo?"

I nodded. "Yeah, I'm pretty positive I know who. My neighbor Clarke. I don't know his last name."

Rudy's big, bushy eyebrows came down. "Do you think that the picture was taken from his residence?"

I shook my head. "The picture wasn't. We weren't at my apartment at the time. We were at Cameron's house. My daughter and I are staying there at the moment."

"I am sorry to ask you this, Jamie, but can I see the photo?"

My breath shuddered as I forced back the tears. I raised my hand that still clutched the ball I had crinkled the paper into.

Rudy sat up and reached out his hand for the paper. When I set it into his hand he sat back slowly.

My father's arm went around my back, and he squeezed me once.

Rudy unfolded the note, smoothing it out on his desk. His gaze moved over it, though his expression was impossible to read. After a few minutes of silence, Rudy asked, "Why did you decide to keep the curtains open?"

I closed my eyes. "We just forgot. Cameron lives on a three-acre property just out of town and there's no way any of his neighbors can see in. There's a fence and trees, and you'd have to be pretty far into his property to take this picture."

"Do you know what the message means?"

I swallowed. "He left a hundred-dollar bill with the note."

He silenced again, his concentration on the paper. After another thirty seconds, he exhaled heavily. "It's hard to tell with the wear and tear on the image, but it appears not to be professional, perhaps taken by a cell phone, and printed with a home printer. This is just my opinion from my observation."

I nodded.

"What makes you think it was this neighbor?"

"He's been bothering me for some time, that's why Sarah and I are staying at Cameron's."

"Sarah is your daughter?"

"Yes."

He turned the paper over and his eyes settled back on me. "How has this Clarke guy been bothering you?"

As Rudy took notes, I told him everything, though it came out in a disjointed mess. My mind felt fuzzy yet empty, the details taking way too long to fish up.

Rudy kept asking me questions like, "Those were his exact words?" and, "In what did he emphasize the words to make them sexual?" When I got to the part about the underwear, his brow furrowed and he said, "Don't you think it's more likely that if it was him, he'd steal the lingerie items?" After I explained the scene at my work with the guy who was paid to tell me not to move, Rudy said, "And he refused to give a statement?"

"This is why I didn't go to the police with this stuff." I shook my head. "If I wrote every word Clarke said to me on paper, there wouldn't be a sexual one in there. But not only is he doing all these things, he comes out to taunt me when he does them. He'll be waiting outside to give me heated looks. And, it's really embarrassing. If my dad didn't see me and my coworker react to the note, I would never have come here to report it."

Rudy inhaled through his nose, his chest expanding even larger in his suit. "Well, I definitely believe that your first move should be to file for a protective order, or a restraining order against your neighbor, Clarke. With this image and the police report that I will write up for you, you might have enough evidence for the judge to decide in your favor."

My father stiffened. "That's not enough."

"No, it's not. I want you to keep a log and document every interaction you have with this neighbor. Record everything he says, does, and the words he emphasizes along with the date and time of the encounter. If you can, record it with your phone or a recording device. Write down everything that has happened so far that you can remember and estimate the time and date as closely as possible.”

My father made a grunt of protest.

“I am going to give you the phone number of one of my officers; I want you to call her when anything happens, no matter how small.”

My father’s arm came from around me and he leaned forward. “Aren’t you going to arrest him?”

“That’s what I’m trying to do here, Mike. Right now, I have no proof of harassment and there’s nothing concrete linking her neighbor to the trespassing. I’ve seen arrests with eight times this much evidence be overturned by a magistrate in forty-eight hours or less. I’m going to send someone out there to take your neighbor’s statement, but I really can’t move forward with this until there’s something that will hold before a judge. A restraining order is a good way to start in this process, because if a protective order is in place and he continues to show at your places of employment, we can charge him with criminal contempt.”

Closing my eyes, I nodded.

“So she’s just supposed to sit there and continue to be harassed by some sicko, who obviously knows what he’s doing until he does something so bad to her that she can prove it?”

“Mike, you need to trust in the judicial process—”

"Bullshit! She's my daughter, Rudy. What would you say if it was Cody going through this, or Cheryl?"

Rudy leaned over the desk toward my dad. "If it was one of them, I'd tell them to get the hell out of town. I'd pack them up and take them out myself. But your daughter has a life and a family and she needs to make that decision for herself. The best decision Jamie—you," he turned to me, "can make right now, is file for a protective order, document everything, keep yourself out of situations in which you are vulnerable and do not, under any circumstance go to your apartment alone."

"Okay."

"And I am buying her a gun," my father said.

Rudy sat back in his chair and looked at the ceiling. "Mike, I'm going to pretend I didn't hear that."

Day Six: Ten thirty-five

After Rudy had an officer bring me a plastic freezer bag to put the note in, he gave me directions on how to find the forms to apply for a restraining order. Last, he gave me the phone number for the officer he was going to have be my contact.

My father brooded and glared the whole way back as we retraced the path to the parking lot. "Well, that was a fat load of bullshit." He threw the door open to the cooling night.

I didn't respond and he said nothing more until we were in his car.

"Hey, kiddo?" He looked over.

I buckled my seatbelt. "Yeah, dad?"

"Did you not tell me because you thought I wouldn't believe you?"

"No." I turned to him. "No, not at all. I didn't tell you because I knew you'd show up ten minutes later with a moving van and I was afraid that Sarah couldn't handle a move. Also, I had nowhere to live permanently, I have a year lease on my place and the apartments I'm in were being really fishy about giving me a new unit away from Clarke."

"You're damn right I would have shown up with a moving van." He started up the car. "Next time, you tell me."

"Yeah, I know." I watched out the window until I realized he wasn't heading to the bar.

"Where are you going?"

"I'm taking you to Cameron's."

"Dad, my car?"

"Will be fine behind the bar overnight. Please, just humor me in this."

"Okay. Do you even know where Cameron's house is?"

"I have a general idea. I think you better start directing me."

"All right, turn left on Mulberry avenue... Shoot, I should call and tell him we're heading there. Also, I haven't checked in or told him anything." I pulled my phone from my purse to see another slew of missed calls and text messages.

I dialed Cameron.

He answered after the first ring. "Jamie?"

"Yeah, hey Cameron."

"I've been trying to reach you."

"Is everything okay?"

"Everything is fine here. Chris came by your work with his girlfriend and your coworkers told him that some guy was bothering you and your father took you to the police station. I've been worried sick. Was it your neighbor?"

"Yeah, um, he left me something that freaked me out. I'll show you when I get to your house. My dad's driving me to you now. We're leaving the car behind the bar."

"Okay, good."

"I'm going to get off the phone so I can direct him, see you soon." I hung up. "Okay, Dad, take a left up there, and then you go straight for a while."

Opening my texting app, I wrote a message to Chris.

Me: I am so sorry that I wasn't at the bar when you guys came.

Chris: Are you okay?

Me: I'm being harassed by one of my neighbors. Going to file for a restraining order tomorrow.

Chris: Shit, Jamie! Is there anything I can do?

Me: No, but thank you! I'll tell you about it at work tomorrow.

Chris: Okay, I'll see you then.

Me: Tell Melissa I say happy birthday.

Chris: She says thank you and stay safe.

I stowed my phone, looking around us. "Sorry, Dad, I think we missed the turn."

He did a three-point turn. "Pay attention, Jamie, please."

"Okay, sorry." After we passed a few driveways, I pointed. "That one with the green mailbox."

My dad turned into Cameron's long driveway, the headlights reflecting off the highly sloped red roof and triangular dormer entrance. Pulling up to the house, he parked beside Cameron's car. We both climbed out and my father escorted me to the door.

Cameron opened it before we could knock. His gaze dashed to mine, quickly examining my face before he looked to my dad. "Hey, Mike."

"Hey, Cam, can I come in?"

"Yeah, of course." He stepped back, letting us walk past him.

Cameron wasn't a short guy by any means, but my dad still had a good three inches on him. He came to stand in the middle of the living room, and I couldn't help but notice that the curtains were still open.

Walking across the room, I pulled them closed.

Cameron watched me like he wanted to say something, but wasn't sure what he should or shouldn't say.

"So you know all about what this sicko has been doing to Jamie?"

Cameron's gaze met mine, and then went back to my father. "Yes, sir. Jamie told me yesterday."

"Jamie also told me that she's going to be living with you now and that you two are a couple."

Cameron glanced over then nodded again.

"I'm glad to hear it. Do you have a gun?"

"Yes, sir. In my safe."

"Good, if that psycho comes by here I want you to shoot him."

"Dad!" I glared at him. "No one is shooting anyone."

My dad regarded Cameron with a very serious expression. "You protect my girls."

"I plan to."

I dropped my head into my hands.

"Jamie, Cameron, I'm going to go. Cam, I like to see that you have an alarm on your house, that's good. What time do you want me to come get Sarah tomorrow, Jamie?"

I looked up. "No worries, I—or we'll drop her off at your house. I'll call you when I know when. Or, Cameron, if you know?"

"Would around four-thirty be okay?" Cameron asked.

"Why don't you head over right as Sarah gets out of school? Then you can go with Jamie to the courthouse to file those papers before whatever you're doing."

"No, dad, he works."

Cameron looked at me. "It's fine. I'd like to be there."

"Good. I'll see you two kids around three-thirty."

"All right, thanks Dad… for everything." I waved. "I love you."

"Love you too, honey." He waved on his way to the door. "Goodnight, Cam."

"Goodnight, Mike."

The moment my dad had left, Cameron came to sit beside me on the couch, his arm going around me. "Jamie, what happened? I need to know."

As I told him, his expression grew darker and darker. When I pulled out the picture and showed him, his whole body quivered.

I climbed off the couch. "I need to go check on Sarah for a little peace of mind."

Turning on the light in the guest room. Sarah clutched her gymnast doll, a foot thrown over the covers. I tucked her back under the covers before checking that her window was closed and locked.

As I descended the stairs, Cameron's back came into view as he paced to the window. He opened the curtain just a little and stood in the gap.

I stopped beside him. "Are you trying to figure out where he was?"

"Yeah." He turned to meet my gaze. "Will you help me in an experiment?"

"Yes."

"Okay, I want to open the window and turn on the lights like we did last night. I'll stay on the phone with you and you sit on the couch and tell me when you can't see me."

"No, Cameron, what if he's out there?"

"He better hope he's not out there." He glared out the window.

"This is dumb, it's pitch black out there and we already know that he came onto your property once."

"Jamie, he's invading my life too, and I don't want to just sit and wonder where he was and how he snuck up without me noticing. I want to figure it out so I can rig this place up with motion sensor lights and make sure nothing like this ever happens again."

"Okay. But this really freaks me out."

"Me too." He turned to me and for the first time of the night wrapped me up in his arms. "I just can't—you know me. I have to do something about it. And since I can't go over to his house and beat the shit out of the guy... I need to make sure we're safe here."

"Yeah, I get it." I pressed my face into his shoulder.

"Lock the door when I go out, okay?"

"No." I rolled my eyes.

"Jamie, just—please."

"Fine."

Cameron called my phone and I answered it, but kept it at my side as he walked to the door.

"Lock it," he reminded me with almost a smirk.

"Yeah, yeah." I locked the door the returned to the couch and sat, putting the phone to my ear. "Hey."

"Hey, I'm still walking around the house. You should see me in just a few seconds." He walked out into the small area outside the windows lit by the lights of the house.

"I see you." I waved.

He turned away from the window, holding up the photo in the freezer bag. He looked back over his shoulder and around the inside, then back to the photo. He took a few steps to the right. "I'm just trying to match these up," he said, unnecessarily. "Okay, tell me when you can't see me anymore." He stepped into the darkness.

After about ten steps, I said, "Now you're just a faint outline, I'm not sure I could see you if you were dressed in all black."

He took another couple of steps.

"Now I can't see you at all."

"I can see you, but I think he was closer." There was a pause. "Can you see me?"

I tried to look into the darkness. "Maybe a faint lightness, but not really."

"Okay, I'm going to mark the spot, hold on a second." There was a shuffling sound. "Okay, good. I'm coming back now."

"All right, I'll let you in."

"Wait until I'm at the door."

"Bossy, bossy," I said, waiting by the door.

"All right, I'm here."

I unlocked the door and opened it to look at Cameron's beautiful face. "Hi."

"Hey there." He walked inside, locking up the house and immediately turning on the alarm.

"I love your alarm. I love that you have one."

His hand rubbed up and down my arms. "Me too."

"Hey, can I ask you a huge favor?"

"Yeah?"

"We abandoned my car. Is there any way you could drop me off at the bar tomorrow morning?"

"Yeah, I'll do it on the way to take Sarah."

I hugged him. "You are way too good to me."

"Never." He kissed the side of my head. "I'm beat. Do you mind if we just go pass out?"

"No, not at all."

We closed all the curtains in the whole house before heading upstairs. After getting ready for bed in the bathroom, I stepped into Cameron's room to find him already lying on top of his covers in a t-shirt and boxers.

I smiled at him, looking so tired and tousled. "Goodnight, Cameron."

"Hey, come here."

I climbed onto the bed, lying down next to him. Reaching over, I threaded my fingers through his.

"Turn around and I'll spoon you for a little while."

"No, if I get too comfortable, I'll fall asleep."

His thumb ran over the back of my hand. "Or you could just stay."

"Sleep here?"

"Yeah. You ended up here last night, anyway."

I didn't respond.

"Here, just try it on for size for a minute?" He sat up and climbed off the bed, going to turn out the light. "Get under the covers and just turn around like that."

When I rolled over, he pressed his front to my back, clutching me to him.

"Now, I just hold you and we both feel happy."

"That's cute."

"I've always wanted to be cute," he whispered in my ear.

"Really?"

"No, not really."

I elbowed him.

"You're not supposed to be violent while spooning," he growled.

I laughed. "Then we're totally going to fail at this."

"You are getting very sleepy."

I huffed out a laugh, but closed my eyes. Minutes later, I fell asleep.

Day Seven

First Date and a Sure Thing

Day Seven: Seven AM

I woke to a loud beeping and found an arm wrapped around me. The arm was connected to a shoulder and the shoulder was connected to Cameron.

He opened an eye to look at me. "You going to get that?"

"Mm, but you need to let go of me first."

He squeezed me to him, my face pressing into his chest. "I like the sound of beeping."

"Mm-hm." I closed my eyes.

"Mom!" I heard from the other room.

"I'm in here, Sarah!" I called.

A few seconds later, a little body flew at us. "Get up, Mom! Wake up, Mom! Get up, Cameron!

"Ugh," I groaned as Sarah started jumping on the bed.

I tried to crawl away from Cameron and the bouncing bed, but he squeezed me tighter.

"Oh, make it stop."

He chuckled and finally let me go.

I climbed off the bed. "I'm up—Oh, holy cow, I'm up." Finding my cell phone from where I had left it last night, I swiped the screen to turn the alarm off.

When I looked back Cameron also climbed out of the bouncing bed.

"Hey Sarah, I want you to go get ready, we're going to have to leave extra early this morning."

She bounced to her butt and then climbed off the bed.

"Mom, do we live here?"

I swallowed. "For right now, cutie. Go ahead and get dressed."

Cameron gave me a sympathetic smile. "She asked me that a couple times last night, too."

"What did you say?"

"I didn't know what you wanted me to say, so I just said that you guys were staying here for a while." He opened a drawer and pulled a shirt out of it. Closing the door to his room and locking it, he grabbed the hem of his shirt and pulled it over his head.

I stared down at his beautifully muscled chest. "Are you going to change in front of me?"

He gave me a squinting, questioning look. "You see me naked all the time."

My gaze fell down to his boxers. "While we're doing it."

He barked out a laugh. "Well, now you get to see me when we're not *doing it*." He dropped his boxers.

I smiled as I stared, wide eyed.

"You're just going to watch?"

Glancing up at his smirk, I returned my gaze back down. "Um yeah." I sat down on the edge of the bed. "You're the one who dropped drawers; you can't blame a girl for staring."

He chuckled, again. "Fine, you can watch."

And I did, until all the exciting bits were put away, and then I stood.

Cameron came up behind me and kissed me on the shoulder, his hand going around my waist. "Aren't you going to change?"

"Yeah, in the bathroom."

"That's not fair."

"Life's not fair." I shrugged.

"Well, if I can't watch you get dressed, can I watch you get undressed tonight?"

I turned, biting my lip. "Maybe—okay, yeah."

"Really?" His eyes heated.

I nodded, still biting my lip.

He grinned. "With that promise, I'm going to go make breakfast."

He walked to the door and opened it, giving me one last glance back and a grin as he left. After I dressed for work, I crossed the hall to check on Sarah, but when I stuck my head in, the room was empty.

Downstairs, Sarah ate yogurt and hummed something at the large wood slab table. Cameron stood at the stove, making what looked and smelled like spinach and cheese omelets.

I came to stand next to him and grinned up. "Yum."

"It's quick and easy." He shrugged.

"Kind of like your mom." I poked him in the side. "Ooh! You so set me up for that one."

He leveled a look on me that clearly expressed he didn't think it was funny at all, but he fought a grin. "I'm going to tell her you said that."

"No, you're not! I want her to like me; Nessa always said she was the nicest woman in the world." I sucked my lips into my mouth, realizing how awkward that sounded.

"She's really nice. And, she'll love you; I don't think there's any possibility that she won't."

"Well, my dad seems to think the sun shines over your head, which has a lot to do with your high school football stardom, by the way."

"Does it?"

"I guess." I grabbed out some forks, knives and plates, setting them out on the table.

Cameron cut the massive omelet in half with the spatula and served us each half. "Whatever makes him like me, I'll take it."

I sat down next to Sarah, who concentrated very hard on her yogurt.

"Hey, baby, do you want to have a sleepover with Grandma Sharon and Grandpa Mike tonight?" I ran my hand over her head.

She grinned up at me. "Mom, can I go to Grandpa's house?"

"After school."

"First Grandpa's house, then school." She bounced up and down on her seat.

"First school, then Grandpa's house."

"Mom, will there be presents?"

I pursed my lips. "I don't know, baby." Though I was almost positive the answer was a resounding 'yes!'

"Mom, can I sleep in the tent?"

"I don't know, baby, that depends on Grandpa and Grandma and what they want to do."

"Mom, can I go to the gymnastics movie?"

"Baby, that one is out of the theaters, but I'm sure Grandma and Grandpa will do other fun things with you."

"Mom, can we go to Grandpa's house now?"

"Nope." I inhaled, forcing myself to be patient. "First we're going to drive to take me to my car, then Cameron is going to take you to school, then we're going to Cameron's house to get your stuff, and then, we're going to Grandma and Grandpa's."

"Mom, can we go right now?"

I stood. "Baby, I already told you. I'm not going to go through it again. Not...now, later." Taking my dirty dish to the sink, I rinsed it off and loaded it into the dishwasher.

Running upstairs, I grabbed Sarah's brush and returned to the table.

Sarah had grabbed my phone and was busy playing an app with one hand and holding a banana with the other.

Across the table, Cameron looked up from where he checked his text messages to shoot me a grin. "I have a few clients today, but I'm going to try to get back here by two-thirty, three at the latest."

"Are you sure?" I started brushing at the ends of Sarah's hair, though it wasn't that tangled this morning.

"Yeah, going in early helps, I should get everything done for the weekend. Worse comes to worst, I'll just go in for a couple hours on Sunday while you ladies are at gymnastics."

"Oh, yeah, okay." I looked back down. "Do you have any plans for the weekend?"

He grinned up at me. "I hoped to spend most of it with you ladies, and, obviously watching Sarah tomorrow night. Do you think the restraining order will go through before tomorrow?"

"I'm not sure; I think we might have to wait for a hearing or something. But I have a feeling that my dad is going to take me off the schedule anyway."

He looked at me, cautiously. "How do you feel about that?"

"Good, I hope he does. I'm pretty over this whole thing, you know. I don't want to be looking over my shoulder the whole time I'm at work, jumping every time I see a guy with brown hair."

Cameron nodded. "Yeah, honestly, I'd have a hard time knowing that he could come in any moment and I couldn't do anything about it. You want to do something tomorrow night, if you're free?"

I finished brushing Sarah's hair and gave her a kiss on the top of her head. "Actually there is something." I looked up to look at him a little bashfully. "There's this benefit for Coral Elementary, Principles and Principals or something. Some of the other mothers with kids in special day class are selling these t-shirts that say #allkidscount on them. I kind of love the idea and would love to go there wearing one, maybe work the booth for a little while."

Cameron grinned, his eyes full of laughter. "Always a rebel rouser."

I grinned, but then looked back down. "And you could meet Patrick, if you really, really want to."

I wasn't sure I liked the grin that spread across Cameron's face. "I definitely do."

"But you're going to be nice. I'm hoping we'll all be friends."

His eyelids narrowed. "I'm very nice."

I rolled my eyes. "When you want to be."

A small, knowing smile touched his lips. "I'll be nice, I promise."

"Maybe this is a bad idea."

"Too late." Cameron stood, going to put his plate in the sink. "We should get going if we want to get your car."

Day Seven: Seven-forty

After we'd all settled into the car, we made our way back onto the curving road that led to Cameron's house. Sarah sat in the backseat, the music of one of her games blaring out from my phone in her hands.

Looking over the back of my seat I started to say, "Angel—"

She didn't look up, but her finger moved to the volume controls on the side of the smartphone and the music quieted.

"So are you ready for this meeting with this Harrington's guy?" Cameron asked.

I turned to him and exhaled heavily. "No. I'm kicking myself that I didn't get an employment attorney like your lawyer friend suggested. Pat was just in such a hurry when I talked to him and—" I sighed again.

Cameron stayed silent for a moment. "Pat... like Patrick?"

I swallowed. "Um, Kind of. Not exactly."

He looked over before turning back to the road and shifting gear. "As in?"

"Pat, like Patrick's father."

"The plot thickens." Though he said it dryly, he had an amused expression on his face.

I sighed. "I'll tell you the whole saga later if you want to hear it."

"It's fine, Jamie. You don't need to tell me. But, if you want to, how about *after* our date, but before I meet the guy?" He shrugged before shifting gear. "As for a lawyer, why don't you send the employment contract to Amy's husband?"

"He's a defense attorney. It would probably only annoy him."

"Doesn't hurt to ask."

Blowing out a breath, I turned in my seat.

"Baby, I need my phone," I said to Sarah.

She didn't look up from the screen. "No."

"Yes." I held out my hand for it. When she still ignored me, I began counting down from five.

On five, Sarah put my phone in my hand. She smiled up at me. "Hi, Mom. Can I have your phone?"

"Not right now, cutie." Turning, I texted Amy.

Me: You think that Peter would be willing to give me some quick legal advice?

She responded immediately.

Amy: About your neighbor? Btw Dad called me, I was pretty surprised you didn't.

Me: Sorry. We literally passed out ten minutes after Dad left. But, it's not about the neighbor, it's about the job contract.

Amy: Yes!!!!!!!!!!!!

Me: I'm thinking you're a little biased here.

Amy: Biased for you. Email it now and I'll text it over, he's already at work.

Me: I'll have to email you photos of it.

Amy: Fine, whatever. Just do it ASAP.

Taking the papers out of where they were still folded in my purse, I smoothed them out on my lap. I tried to zoom in as close as I could on the text without cutting any of it out of the shot. After taking the photos, I emailed them from my phone. A moment later, my phone lit up with a text.

Amy: Got them and sent them. Leaving for work now, so Peter will call you.

Me: Thank you!

After closing the message, I thumbed through the ridiculous amounts of text message backup I had on my phone. "I think I'm going to buy a new phone just for my important contacts," I mumbled. When I looked up, I saw that we were pulling up in front of my father's bar.

Cameron looked over. "Where's your car?"

I grabbed for the handle to let me out. "Just around back. Thank you so much—" I cut off as Cameron started backing up the street to the alley we had just passed. "Or you can drive me to my car."

"Yep." Cameron shot me a grin as he stopped and turned into the alley.

We pulled up to where I'd parked my car behind the bar last night—probably for the last time ever.

Turning to Cameron, I forced a grin. "Thanks for the ride... and for driving Sarah."

"She still back there?"

We both glanced back to find Sarah grinning out the window.

Reaching back, I grabbed her purple sneaker cladded-foot. "You day-dreaming, cutie?"

"Mom, are there going to be presents at Grandpa's house?"

I laughed. "Sweetheart, you guys will have a great time and do fun things whether there's presents or not, okay?"

She grinned. "Will they be gymnastics presents?"

"It's official. Your grandparents have spoiled you." I leaned over the passenger seat to give her a kiss on the forehead and smooth down her blonde hair. "I love you. You be good, okay?"

"I love you so much!" She shouted the words back at me, inciting a laugh from me.

"Okay, monkey."

Sitting back into the seat, I grabbed my purse. "Thank you again, so much, Cameron." I glanced up at him.

Cameron's gaze fell to my mouth, then met my gaze in question.

I tilted my head slightly to the backseat, then shook my head.

His expression bordered on exasperated, but he gave me a grin. "No problem. See you at the house."

"Yeah, I'll head straight there after picking up Sarah."

We stared at each other for a second.

I opened the car door. "Bye, Cameron."

"Later."

I climbed into my car and sat for a moment, waiting for Cameron to pass.

He honked.

Glancing back, I waved for him to go.

Instead, he pointed to me then nodded to the road.

Rolling my eyes, I started up my car and drove out of the alley. We immediately parted ways as he turned toward Sarah's school.

Tears formed in my eyes before he had fully pulled away. My lip quivered and I bit it hard to stop myself from sobbing. A small sob escaped me anyway. I didn't even know why I was crying. Or more, I knew a thousand reasons why I could be crying, but I couldn't pin down any specific one.

After parking in my usual spot, I lay my head back against my headrest and closed my eyes, allowing the memories to wash over me.

Strangely enough, it had been Vanessa that watched Sarah while Logan and I had worked like mad to get the Coffee Stop ready for its opening. The whole shop had reeked of drying paint as we pounded the wood flooring in. Logan had been ecstatic all day, grinning at me and sneaking kisses every chance he got.

Blond bristles dotted his face and his blue eyes glowed as he looked up from nailing in the last board.

I grinned back. "Now we just have to sand it down and do a couple polyurethane coats on the whole thing."

He glanced down. "Are you serious? We're not done?"

I shook my head and laughed. "Duh."

He pushed down on a board which immediately squeaked. "I think it's good."

Grimacing down at the floor, I whispered, "I'm pretty sure it's not supposed to do that."

Logan reached to the second floorboard and pressed down. The board gave an immediate tweeting sound, like a bird.

I covered my face. "Oh no, we did it wrong or something."

Logan grinned wide. "Or maybe very, very right. Just think, we could call it the Musical Mug and charge extra. Five dollars just to walk across our floor." He leaned in and kissed me, his grin still wide across his face.

Back in the car, words slipped into my mind, and my lips whispered them almost inaudibly, "I'm not ready to move on from you."

I gripped my steering wheel.

The world had driven me to a cliff edge, a precipice my friends stood at, coaxing me to take the plunge. I thought that when I started up this path, I'd be ready when I got to the top, that I'd make myself ready, but instead, I was developing a sudden fear of heights.

I pulled the visor down and slid the mirror's little door open as I furiously scrubbed at my face with the other hand. The moment I saw my red, splotchy appearance, I stopped scrubbing.

"I can do this," I told my reflection.

The woman staring back at me didn't look convinced.

Sliding the door to the mirror shut, I pushed up the visor to see a large crowd of people standing outside the Coffee Stop.

Turning my ignition back on, I saw the clock read five past.

"Crap!"

Quickly climbing out of my car, I locked it and jogged down to the alley a block up from the coffee shop. Before turning the corner, I noticed that the crowd in front of my door was definitely larger than usual.

My gaze darted to and fro in the alley. The light was still low in the gray morning but I could see there was no one in there. The next alley behind the shop also stood empty.

My breath was loud in the quiet morning as I unlocked the back door to the shop and stepped inside.

"Jamie?" Chris's voice came from deeper in the shop, sounding a little off.

"Sorry I'm late, Chris!" I rounded the corner and found Chris loading the pastry case with shaking hands.

He looked up, eyes bleary. "I'm so sorry, Jamie."

My mouth hung open. "Oh, no, Chris. Please don't tell me you're hung over?"

His response was for his face to turn an even riper shade of green. "A little bit, but it's more that I didn't go to sleep last night."

Rushing over to the area where I kept our aprons, I grabbed one and threw down my stuff.

"Okay," I mumbled as I ran over to the espresso machine and turned it on. Grabbing the large coffee carafes from the industrial coffee machine, I set them on the counter. "Okay, Chris, we can do this. I just need you to pull through until ten, then you can go home to sleep. Yeah?"

"Yeah. Jamie, I'm so sorry," he repeated.

"It's fine, Chris. I should have thought about this, I mean obviously you would have gotten no sleep." I set a filter full of the organic roast in the industrial coffee machine and started it brewing.

Turning, I walked back over to Chris and patted him on the back. "You think you can make it until ten?"

He blinked at me. "I can make it."

"If you can't, tell me and I'll just close the shop early or something. I'm going to sell it today anyway, so there's no point in us killing ourselves."

He grimaced. "I think I should be on the espresso machine."

"Good call. I'm going to open up if you're ready."

He nodded. "Ready as I'll ever be."

Walking through the shop, I turned over chairs as I went. The shop wasn't dirty—we had done a decent job of cleaning it yesterday, but I usually gave it a wipe down. I definitely didn't have time for it this morning.

When I stopped at the front doors of the shop, I peeked at the line outside. It had only grown in the twenty minutes it had taken me to get inside.

After unlocking it, I yelled out, "Sorry everyone! We had a couple hold-ups this morning. Come on in."

"It's fine, Jamie," one of my regulars, Steve, said as his wife Carol stepped in beside him.

"Thanks guys." I propped the door open and quickly returned behind the counter. By the time I stood behind the cash register, a line had formed leading all the way out the door.

Beside me I heard the espresso machine running and saw Chris heating up the milk. His voice was hoarse as he called out, "Hey Steve, Carol, want your usual?"

"Hey Chris, what's good today?"

"Like you don't know, Steve. *Everything.*" Even though Chris delivered the line with almost no enthusiasm, the couple grinned and ordered what they ordered every morning.

When they stepped away, I found someone waiting in line who, unfortunately, seemed to have become a regular. Standing across the counter was none other than the rude phone guy from yesterday.

His arm lifted, making the sleeve of his gray suit ride up to expose his wristwatch. He angled the watch toward me, obviously conveying that I was taking my time.

Ignoring the gesture, I smiled. "Good morning, can I start a drink for you?"

Dropping his arm, he said, "I'd actually like to speak to your manager."

"I am the manager. But I'm sorry, sir, if you need to talk, it'll have to be after I get through this line. Would you like to order a drink in the meantime? I believe you like a double non-fat latte?"

"I've been waiting a half hour; I'm late for a meeting."

Taking a steadying breath, I said, "I really apologize, sir."

"As the manager, don't you think it's your responsibility to open your shop on time?"

I swallowed down the response I wanted to make. Diffusing this type of hissy fit usually came naturally, but today, I had nothing.

I took a deep breath and blew it out through my nose. *What the hell, I'll just tell the guy the truth. Maybe then he'd order his drink and move on.* I lowered my voice and said, "Sir, my late husband and I built this coffee shop, and I'm selling it today. I got an offer too good to pass up for my family. Twenty minutes ago I was bawling my eyes out in my car. I'm sorry I made you late for your day, if you want the latte, it's on me, but I just need to get through this line. And this day."

He stared, unmoved. "I can pay for my own drink."

"Latte?"

"Americano."

"What size?"

"Medium. What's your name?"

Giving him a tight smile before entering his order into the cash register, I mumbled, "Jamie."

Usually, at this point, I would ask him his name and try to turn his animosity into loyalty, but today I just couldn't do it. After ringing him up and running his card, I held it up in front of him. "Here's your card, sir, and here's me handing it back to you. Thank you and have a nice day."

"Thank you." He nodded, but hesitated at the counter. "I'm probably going to be seeing you around often soon, Jamie."

"That's... nice."

"At Harrington's corporate office. We'll be working together. I've been coming in to get a feel for your shop before the potential acquisition."

It seemed Harrington's was a pack of spies infiltrating my life. I called upon all the patience within me. "Awesome. I'll see you soon. Need to help other customers now."

Looking to the customer behind him, I called out, "Hey Clare, how many drinks you got for me?"

"I already ordered them with Chris and I'll pay it all with one card, Jamie." She sounded apologetic.

Leaning over the counter, she whispered. "That's the same jerk as yesterday, huh?"

I gave her a small nod, forcing a smile on my face. "Want anything to eat?"

She nodded. Reading from a list, she gave a long order of pastries, then read out the drinks she already ordered with Chris. By the time I'd finished ringing her up and had been able to bag all her pastries, Chris was done with her drinks and was placing them into carriers.

"How you feeling?" I asked as I passed him to set the pastries down on the coffee counter.

He gave me a half grin. "I'm fine as long as I'm just making the drinks. By the way, that Americano guy left his card for you, I tossed it."

I paused. "Not when he could see?"

Chris shook his head. "No, after he walked away."

I patted him on the back. "Thanks, Chris, but he's actually from Harrington's corporate, he wasn't leaving me his number."

"Oops."

I shrugged. "Doesn't matter. Pat's supposed to come by in fifteen minutes to buy the shop, but I just don't see how it's going to be possible. I'm going to call and cancel."

"No, I'll handle it, Jamie. Just let me get another cup of coffee into me... I'll be able to handle it."

"Okay." I said, though the uncertainty was clear in my voice.

When I returned to the line, I found two women who looked to be in their twenties waiting to be served. After they ordered, the shorter brunette grinned up at me, displaying her clear retainer. "Um, does Kevin Dempsey ever come here?"

I shook my head. "Sorry, he doesn't live around here."

"We know that," her blonde friend said, like she was telling me she knew the sky was blue.

"But you know him? You're his friend?" the brunette looked at me eagerly.

"Um, yeah, sorry ladies, I'm going to have to move on to the next customer here."

The brunette leaned over the counter. "Could you give him my phone number?"

"Um... I'm sorry. It might be months or years before I see him again."

"That's fine." She took a piece of paper out of her purse and held it out to me. Her friend beside her did the exact same thing.

Forcing a smile, I grabbed the papers and stuffed them under the counter.

Day Seven: Eight Fifty-five

The tables filled as we worked through the customers, but the line showed no sign on letting up. They were an incoming tide of talking heads. It was Logan's dream realized, in the weirdest, most inconvenient way.

Five minutes before nine, the bell over the door rang and Pat walked in with three other people. I recognized Nicole from the meeting, but not the other two people.

I rushed through orders, hoping I could get through the line. With a grin plastered on my face, I handed a pastry bag to a girl, rang her up, then moved onto the next couple. While I handed them back their card, the bell over the door rang and a crowd of ten people walked in.

Blowing out a breath, I looked over to Chris. He was keeping up with the drink orders, but I had heard a total of about twenty words from him all morning. That was so not like Chris, it was ridiculous. What I really wanted to do was tell him to go take a nap, especially since this might be our last day here.

I almost jumped as Pat stepped in front of the coffee counter. As if he read my mind, he said, "I have a solution for you, Jamie."

"Hi Pat. Uh, a solution for what?"

"A solution for your current staffing issue."

I glanced around at the ever-growing crowd, then to Chris, then back at Pat. Obviously I showed my mismanaging skills pretty blatantly here. "Okay, what is that?"

"I brought two managers from Harrington's, they can cover until we are finished with our meeting. I'm hoping we can start this meeting in a matter of seconds. I do have a plane to catch."

"I can't have non-employees working behind the counter; they won't be covered by my insurance."

He sighed and frowned at me. "We already ensured they'd be covered by my insurance in this location today. I really don't have time for this, Jamie."

"Chris, you up to do the fastest training ever?"

Chris nodded.

To Pat, I called, "Okay, fine. If you're sure they're covered."

His lips pursed. "I am absolutely sure. Let's move this along. I assume we are doing this in your office?"

"I thought we could do it in the shop—" Glancing out at the floor, I saw it would be impossible to do that. "But yeah, we can do it in my office; I'll just need to grab a couple chairs."

"Nicole will do that." He turned on his heel and a moment later, the two managers were walking behind the coffee counter. They were a matched set. Both brunette women were in their early twenties, tall, wearing high ponytails, glasses and identical grins plastered on their faces.

"I got this, Jamie. Go ahead to your meeting." Chris's voice was still a little scratchy, but I knew he wouldn't say he could handle anything that he couldn't. Turning to the pair, he asked, "Hey, how's it going? I'm Chris."

"We're actually both named Jessica," one of the Jessicas laughed. As they made their introductions and Chris gave them instructions, I helped the next three people in line.

"I'll take over," one Jessica said as she grinned at me.

"Awesome, thank you so much." Turning away from her, I rushed over to my purse. Feeling my way frantically through the contents of my bag, I fished out my phone. Just like yesterday, the phone had been overloaded with messages. Thumbing through my call log, I found nothing from Sarah's school.

I dodged Jessicas as I pulled up my text messages and scrolled through, looking for anything from Amy or Peter. Halfway down was a message from Amy.

Amy: Peter took a look at the contract. I've forwarded you the message from him.

Pausing in front of my office door, I pulled up the email. The message from Peter was short.

Hey honey,

Carlos took a look at these for your sister and wrote a short list of suggestions. They look good to me.

Below was a list of suggestions. Glancing over them and understanding nothing, I realized I would either have to sit down and study this stuff, or just take it all on faith that this guy Carlos knew what he was talking about. As I had no time, and I'd planned this whole thing out really badly, I was probably just going to have to bet on Carlos.

Walking into my office, I found Nicole and Pat already sitting on chairs. On the other side, filing cabinets threatened to brush their knees as they stood in rows. Framed concert posters glared out colors from every inch of available wall space in the small, windowless room.

Turning on the overhead fan, I closed the door and very carefully scooted by Pat and Nicole, so as to not knock their legs with mine on the way in.

I turned my rolling swivel chair toward them and sat. "Hi, sorry this is so cramped."

They each looked up at me from their devices, Patrick from a tablet and Nicole from the laptop perched on her lap. Nicole grinned, Pat did not. He was so tense it was as if my office was pressure cooking him.

Pat waved a hand dismissively. "It's fine, all of the Harrington's offices are about this size. All right, you've had sufficient time to review the paperwork. Let's get to signing the forms for this sale, contract and transfer. We have a great deal of paperwork to get through and I want to have it completed in the next hour."

I froze. "Pat, I get that you want this wrapped up and all, but this is my life that I'm overturning, and I don't want to rush through this and sign something I'll regret. Honestly, this is already too hurried for me.

If you have to go, can't I just finish the paperwork with Nicole?"

"I told you, Jamie, I've taken a special interest in this and I want to witness its resolution."

I looked straight into his deep blue eyes and, in that moment I was completely sure I was a problem for his conscience he wanted to be done with. "I get it, Pat, I do. And I'm honored that you're taking such an interest in my employment and my shop when you have thousands of employees—"

"Tens of thousands."

"Exactly. But, I've had a hell of a week and I just can't do it under this pressure. I'm willing to sell, I'm willing to sign an employment contract, but I need to do this right or not at all. And, I want to make some adjustments to the contract."

Pat sat up very straight then blew out a breath, settling just a little into his chair. "Fine, let's just get this started. Nicole, you pull up the contract file and we'll review these adjustments."

Pulling out my phone, I pressed in my pass code and looked back to the email I had left open.

Nicole looked up, still smiling. "I'm ready whenever you are, Jamie."

Tingles ran up my arms and I cleared my throat. "Okay... um, on line one, can we exchange the word 'year' for April eighteenth, twenty-seventeen?"

"Yes," Pat said.

Nicole looked down to her laptop, typing quickly then looking up.

"Okay, line seven, I'd like you to amend it from 'disabled' to 'determined disabled by a licensed physician'."

"Accepted," Pat said.

As we went down the list, and Pat accepted all the changes, I realized that Carlos—whoever he was—was a pretty thorough badass. When this was over, I was going to send the guy a fruit basket or something.

After we'd worked our way through my list, Nicole printed the new contract on my Bluetooth printer and handed it to me.

Her perfume wafted into my face as she leaned over me. "I'm just going to need you to sign here, and initial here, here, here, here and here." She pointed to the various places as she talked.

My hands shook as I took the papers and a pen from her. I swiveled my chair away from the pair to face my desk but also to give myself a moment. Closing my eyes, I made a fist around the pen.

As if I truly stood at a precipice, I felt a sudden spell of vertigo. The breeze from the overhead fan brushed against me, urging me forward.

Opening my eyes, I searched the paper, finding all my amendments one by one. Pressing the tip of the pen to the surface, I scratched my first initial. After I'd initialed every place Nicole had directed, I moved my pen to the bottom and signed my name.

Nicole was suddenly standing at my side. "I'll take that one, and I have a lot more for you here." She took my contract, exchanging it for a large stack of papers. "You'll likely be familiar with most of these, but if you have any questions I can help you with it.

The top few are tax and government forms, the USCIS Form I-9, and the New Hire Reporting form. After that we have benefits forms, which I will explain when you get to them." She pulled up the stack of papers to show me a form. Thumbing through it, she opened to a paper that was titled, 'At Will Agreement'. "When you get to the agreements, we'd like you to stop so that we can go over them together, all right?"

I swallowed. "Yeah, okay."

She smiled down at me. "You have any questions so far?"

Biting my lower lip, I shook my head. "No."

It took over an hour to get through the forms and agreements. Though the agreements were what I assumed was pretty standard, non-compete, non-disclosure, non-solicitation and arbitration agreements, my brain had a hard time processing any of it, and I had to ask Nicole to repeat information more than once.

I could practically feel Pat's impatience growing like a storm cloud trapped in the small office.

He pressed the button on his tablet, lighting up the lock screen with the time on it. "We need to get to the purchase of the shop now."

Nicole stood over me, seeming unruffled by Pat's impatience, she pointed down at the paper. "I just need your signature right here, initial here, then you're done.

Finishing up, I handed it to her. She handed me back another stack of papers and an apologetic smile. "On the top we have the business purchase agreement, next we have the shop purchase agreement. We needed to do them separately—for legal reasons. Let's get through those, and then we'll move on to the other agreements and what we'll need from you to finalize the sale.

My eyes could barely see the paper as I looked down at the sales agreement. They were blurry white-out messes, and the more I blinked, the blurrier they became.

Scanning down, I read the words in the bold font: '**This agreement and sale between Jamie Scott and Harrington's Coffee Company is effective on the date of...**' then it had today's date.

"The terms are the same that we gave you and you have had the time to review them for over a week now," Pat grumbled.

Closing my eyes, I muttered, "This is just a really big deal for me."

There was a quiet tapping sound behind me but Pat didn't interrupt again.

Opening my eyes again, I forced myself to focus. The purchase agreement really was identical in the details to the agreement I had read and reviewed so many times. At the bottom of the page, I signed away my business. At the bottom of the next page, I signed away the walls I had painted, the floors my husband and I had crawled all over to install, then crawled all over again after we rolled back and forth across our squeaky floor. I sold the fixtures we had debated over for thirty minutes at the hardware store, the counters we'd fallen in love with. I sold the laughter, the spilled drinks, the customers that had come to my husband's funeral, Chris's employment and my employment too.

By the end of the two purchase agreements, inescapable tears were rolling down my cheeks. Leaning over, I wiped my face on my shoulder. Without saying a word, Nicole took the purchase agreements from me, revealing the next paper—a tax form.

The squeak of a chair dragging back hit my ears and I looked back, startled.

Pat stood in the small space, his briefcase in hand. "I need to leave to catch my flight, I'm already on the late side."

He grinned at me, showing the first trace of his dimples. Reaching forward, he patted me on the shoulder. "Welcome to the company, Jamie."

Day Seven: Ten-twenty

"A lot of people cry when they sell their companies," Nicole said the moment Pat closed the door behind him.

"How long have you worked for Harrington's?"

"Ten years, but I've worked in HR for Pat's companies for longer than that. You're in good hands. I think you'll really enjoy working with us, Jamie."

Clearing my throat again, I said, "Thanks. So, does this mean that I should close up the shop, or hand you the keys?"

"Nope, continue as usual for today. After all the paperwork is filed and sent to our legal department, it will take a small time to process. Legal matters must be settled. We'll bring in a locksmith once everything has gone through, but you will get a copy of that key."

"And the money?"

"We'll go over all of that a little later in the paperwork, but basically because of the lien, once all the legal and tax matters are settled, we have to send the money to Timepiece, where they will settle the debt and cut you a check for the difference. Pat told me to assure you that he expedited the process, so it shouldn't take more than a week or so. As for the sign-on bonus, that should be coming to you almost immediately. We just need to set up your direct deposit."

"Okay," I whispered.

It took forever to get through the mound of paperwork for the sale of my business and property. Looking over my shoulder at the clock, I said, "Shoot!

Chris is supposed to be getting off now, and the Jessicas have already been working for over two hours."

Nicole smiled. "They expected to. You're welcome to send Chris home. I'm sure they can handle the shop until you're ready."

Glancing down, I looked over the papers. "I'm ready, I think." I looked up at her. "Unless you have another stack of papers."

She laughed. "No, I'm not that cruel. Well, if you'd like Jessica M and Jessica C to finish your shift with you, they are expecting to. They're some of our best at customer service and hardest working managers. They're both good candidates for taking over the running of this location if you assign them here."

"Okay." I nodded.

"If you don't mind, I'll camp out here and go over the papers just to make sure we didn't miss anything."

I gestured. "Make yourself at home."

It hit me then, as of that moment, it wasn't actually my office to make that offer anymore. Walking out into the main area of the coffee shop, I saw both Jessicas laughing at something Chris said. The line had quieted down for the moment and both girls had empty muffin sleeves in their hands. Chris's shoulders shook with laughter, and though I couldn't see his face, I could already tell he felt better.

As I walked, a dollar bill in its frame caught my eye.

We had our shop's grand opening planned for Sunday, but we'd been crazy busy preparing for it on the Saturday before.

A much slimmer teenage Chris busily baked in our kitchen, his mother beside him. Chris's mother, Shana, had come in often that first year to help us before she fell ill. Shana was holding two-year-old Sarah and arguing about the way Chris organized his supplies—teasing him really. More than once, I caught her fighting emotion as she focused her attention away from her teenage son with the excuse of playing with Sarah, who had glued herself to Shana's hip.

Unlike us, sixteen-year-old Chris wasn't the least bit nervous for opening day. He'd been all smiles all morning, filling the shop with the smell of baked cheese, fruits, and spices.

I turned to climb down from the ladder I balanced on as I wrote on the menu sign, when I startled so bad I almost fell off the ladder. "Oh!"

Logan, who had been stabilizing the ladder let go of it and grabbed me by the legs, pretty much lifting me off it.

The elderly woman, who I had originally been so startled to see standing at our counter shouted up, "Don't do that young man; you'll make her fall off the ladder."

The man beside her said, "Charlie, we scared the hell out of the poor girl."

Logan started laughing as he released his death grip on my legs. "I guess I don't have the best automatic reactions."

"Sorry!" I laughed as I climbed off the ladder.

"We're the ones who should be sorry, we thought you were open."

"Tomorrow." Logan held a hand over the counter, smile wide across his face. "How's it going?"

Charlie reached up to shake his hand. "We're great. I'm Charlie and this here is Avery."

"Jamie." I shook both their hands. "This is Logan and back there is our baker extraordinaire, Chris. Shana is also back there helping us out. Our daughter Sarah is the one trying to eat her hair."

"Baker extraordinaire you say? We're going to have to put that to the test." Avery grinned as he said it.

Logan grinned back, then shouted over his shoulder, "Hey Chris, we have some prospective customers questioning your 'baker extraordinaire' status."

"What!" Chris shouted from the back. "Give me three minutes."

Logan turned back to Charlie and Avery. "Do you have three minutes?" Amusement twinkled in his eyes.

They looked at each other.

"Well obviously this is very important," Avery mused.

Charlie barked out a laugh. "Are you kidding me? You couldn't force us out now."

Chris and Shana came out in less than three minutes, with four trays and Sarah balanced between them. As they set the trays across the counter, we all leant in just a little to stare at the pastry banquet they'd set out for us.

Avery grinned up at Chris. "Holy smokes, that's one beautiful sight."

Chris grinned back. "Try them."

"Which one?"

"All of them, any of them." Chris shrugged.

Avery had elected for the former, and his wife Charlie joined in. At the end of an hour long baked-goods bender, we were all laughing and wincing from the pain in our stomachs.

Sarah ran around our feet, jam smeared across her chubby little face.

"We'd like to pay you guys at least something," Charlie said, even though we'd already refused.

"Impossible," Logan said grinning. "But you're welcome to become our loyal customers." He winked.

"Well, that's a given, but we want to be the ones to give you your first dollar." Avery nudged his wife. "Charlie, you got a dollar?"

She rolled her eyes as she extracted one from her wallet. "I swear Avery..." She handed it to him.

Avery wrote for a minute on the dollar and handed it over.

When I took it, I read: 'For the sweetest people and the best damn baker extraordinaire we'd had the pleasure of meeting: your very first of many dollar bills.'

Six years later, the message was still visible across the dollar. Logan had had it framed that same day and hung it our opening day.

Turning back to Chris, I called over, "Hey Chris, I'm sorry it took so long."

Chris turned and waved it away. "No problem, Jamie. I got my second wind, or more like my first wind."

"You safe to drive home?"

He nodded. "So? Is this my last day?" He didn't sound happy about it.

I shook my head. "Um, no, they ask that you give two weeks' notice. I hope that's okay." I held up a hand toward him.

"I don't want to quit." He shrugged. "You think they'll make me stop baking?"

"Um, no, I'm the general manager, remember? And, I'm pretty sure this deal had everything to do with Pat's love of your muffins."

Chris turned and walked over to me. "Good, I'm not ready to leave this place yet." He wrapped me in a hug.

"Stop it, Chris. You're going to make me cry again." Contrary to my words, I hugged him tightly to me.

Chris pulled back. "Hey Jamie, is it okay if I come along this Sunday?"

"This Sunday? You mean for Logan's ashes?"

"Yeah, Susan told me what you were doing. I understand if you want to be alone but, if not, I'd really like to be there."

"I've been imagining just going off and doing it with Susan but, you know, I think I'd really like the company."

"Okay, because I was wondering... could my mom come too? It's totally fine if not, but she loved Logan and I think it'd really motivate her to get up and get going."

"You know I was just thinking about Shana. Of course she could come. I'd love to see her, and I know Sarah would too. And bring Melissa too if you'd like."

"Thanks, Jamie." He sighed. "I'm going to go ahead and turn in."

"Thank you so much for sticking it out this long, Chris."

"You're the best, Jamie. Anyone else would be mad I came in so wrecked."

"Oh oops. Shame on you." I pointed at his face.

He batted my hand away and grinned. "Shut up. When and where do you want to meet on Sunday?"

I bit my lip, thinking. "Susan really wants to do it in the same spot they scattered her mom's remains. It's pretty far out of town on the beach. Maybe we should have a meeting place nearby so we can all caravan?"

"Want to meet at the Harrington's on Main? That way we could grab a coffee and something to eat first?"

"Sounds good, Chris. How about nine-ish? Would that work for Shana?"

"Yeah, Jamie, that'd work great."

As Chris packed up, I pulled my phone out of my back pocket and did a quick check to make sure I had no missed calls from Sarah's school. After I'd eased my mind, I shot off a quick text to Susan.

Me: I just sold the shop.

After Chris left out the back door, I threw myself back into work. As Nicole had said, the Jessicas were excellent at what they did and had already learned our cash register and some of our regulars' names.

Jumping on the espresso machine, I focused on making drinks and introducing the Jessicas to my favorite regulars. Nicole surfaced from the office about twenty minutes later, having me initial one place I missed, before leaving.

All day it was as if an announcement had gone out and along with the new crowd of celebrity seekers, all our regulars had come in to show their support. Among them, Mitch had walked up the line and purchased himself a small coffee with change. Cameron had also stepped in, though he'd elected to just say 'hi' rather than hang around in the swarm.

By the time one-fifty rolled around, the crowd still looked to be incoming and no one looked interested in leaving.

Jessica M, who was starting the closing tasks when there weren't bagel orders, called over, "This is way more crowded than Harrington's. I'm surprised you've done this with just two people for so long."

"This is ridiculous. It's not usually this crowded." I started both my blenders going before turning to finish the mocha I had started.

"Because of your video?" Jessica C asked, turning from the register. "A lot of people have asked me about it."

My cheeks heated. "Um, yeah. The crowds will probably slow after a week or two."

"I doubt it," she responded, "You are a celebrity now. People love that stuff."

"Maybe a celebrity by the fact I know celebrities, but not by anything substantial." Pouring the cold drinks into cups, I covered them with whipped cream and set them on the coffee counter. I called out, "Two blended mochas for Miranda. Hey, everyone, we close in ten minutes!"

The bell over the door rang and a group of maybe fifteen high school kids walked in.

"They have to be cutting class," I grumbled as I put another couple hot drinks on the bar.

At exactly two, I turned to Jessica M. "How are you at kicking people out?"

She grinned up at me. "It's my specialty."

"Awesome. We need to clear this place and lock the doors before more people swarm in."

As I had a long line of drink orders, I focused solely on getting through them, sparing little attention for the scene around me. When I'd made my way through all the cups, I looked up to see a good number of the tables were now empty and wiped down, and several people were on their way out the door.

When Jessica M stepped behind the counter to grab a clean rag, I said, "Go you."

"Told you I was good at it." She beamed. "Now, I'll get everyone else out."

"Beautiful, thank you!"

Jessica C handed me a cup.

I looked over at the final customer in line, thankfully no one was behind her.

"Cool, last drink then I'm going to close the espresso machine."

"Okay," she said as she rang up the lady's order.

At ten past two, the shop was cleared and I discovered the beauty of having three people close, rather than one—or even two.

As I closed the till, which was nearly exact, the Jessicas cleaned the shop and took the trash and recycling out. As I zipped up our deposit bag, a loud knocking came on the window.

Looking up, I saw Susan standing at the shop's door.

"I'll go tell her we're closed," Jessica M said as she headed for the door.

"No, she's my friend; let her in."

"Okay, sure."

I turned to Jessica C. "Would you mind dropping this off in the safe for me? It's under the desk."

Her eyes widened. "Really? Um, yeah, okay, sure."

"Did I say something wrong?"

She laughed. "No, sorry, I'll go do that for you." She took the bag from me and headed off toward the office.

Feeling a little confused, I turned back to where Jessica M was letting Susan in.

"Hello," Jessica M said, stepping back and giving me a full view of Susan's tear-stained face.

Susan sniffed. "Hi, who are you?"

Rounding the counter, I rushed up to the pair. "Susan, is everything okay?" I called out.

Susan turned to me, tears still coursing down her face. Her lower lip came up as she nodded. "I just didn't expect it to hit me so hard."

"Oh, sweetheart." I wrapped Susan in my arms as she sobbed. "It's been hitting me really hard all day, too."

"I just couldn't stop thinking about the first time he told me he wanted to be a baker. We were so young, like five or six. And he just kept saying it. He wasn't even that good at it, but I remember how goddamned proud I was of him when you guys opened this place." She sobbed into my shoulder. "I'm sorry Jamie. You don't need this."

"It's fine. It's good. Now I'm not the only crazy one."

She laughed and cried. "Yeah, you can always count on me to lessen your insanity."

"What are best friends for?" I laughed.

She laughed again. "They kicked me out of work, I went too pregnant on them or something."

I pulled away. "You're not in trouble?"

"No." She wiped at her face. "Can I get a ride with you, though? I used that app thing to get a ride and Beza dropped me off this morning."

"Yeah, we're about done here, just let me—" I looked around, seeing that Jessica M had already turned over the chairs and was almost done mopping the floor. "Wow, you ladies are crazy efficient."

Day Seven: Two Twenty-five

After grabbing the stack of forms I printed out for the civil harassment restraining order, I needed to do little more than grab my purse and we were all out of there in record time. Actually, the Jessicas and I were out while Susan walked around the shop.

Outside, I turned to the Jessicas. "Thank you ladies so much! You both must be amazing at your jobs. You picked up on everything so fast and made this day bearable."

They smiled, glanced at each other, then smiled again.

"It was fun," Jessica M said. "We're actually both hoping to work at this shop in the future…" She left it open, a little like a question.

"Nicole did say that you'll be here next week, and the shop will need more staff permanently."

"Will the shop need a new manager?" Jessica M asked.

"Well, just so you know, if Chris stays I am going to promote him to manager of this shop. He probably knows the shop and the customers ten times better than I do."

Their smiles wavered a little, but they both nodded.

"Oh, okay," Jessica M said.

"But, if you're looking to become shift managers at this shop, I'll definitely consider either of you."

Jessica C took a small step forward. "I would, definitely. I'm a shift manager now."

"Okay, great. My head's not in a really great place to be making decisions or promises, especially since I don't actually start until next Monday, but I'm going to remember your awesome skills when I'm figuring stuff out next week. All right?"

She nodded and grinned, and they both shot a smile over their shoulder as they walked down toward a red sedan.

Turning back to the shop, I watched Susan's figure through the window as she wandered through the almost-dark shop. Her hand came up to touch an event poster Logan had had framed years ago, her fingers running along the frame.

I knocked on the window, making her look over.

'Sorry,' I mouthed. Pointing to my watch, I mouthed, 'Sarah.'

Susan nodded, heading for the door. When she stepped outside, she wiped away new tears that had sat on her cheeks. "Yeah, I'm ready to go."

Locking the door, I glanced over at her. "It's not going anywhere, you know. They may make me take some of the stuff down, but Chris already told me he plans to stay."

"Yeah, but it's not going to be the same." She shook her head and looked away. "I had no idea when I pushed you to move on, that some part of me wasn't ready either."

Swinging an arm around her, we walked together to the car. "Chris is bringing Shana this Sunday. We were talking about meeting at Harrington's—"

"Can we go over it later, Jamie?" She looked over. "I just can't right now."

I squeezed her shoulders. "Yeah, yeah, of course."

As Susan climbed in the front, I set the restraining order papers in the trunk.

We took the short drive in silence, though Susan squeezed my hand the entire way. At the school, no one waited for us. No horde of angry parents, no gorgeous son of my enemy who was also now my boss, no Sarah and no Ms. Brown. Pulling up to the curb, I stopped in the loading zone and stepped out.

Kids and their parents walked in all directions, crossing the lot and streaming around us.

"Oh, crap!" Susan said, climbing out beside me. She covered her mouth. "Oh, crud... I mean."

"What?" I smiled at her.

"Beza has a PTA planning meeting thing right now. I was supposed to take a car home and meet her and Aiden there. I'm sorry, Jamie."

"It's cool."

She groaned. "Kill me now, I don't want to go to that thing." She turned to me. "You want to come hang at my house for a little while?"

"Can't, it's date night remember?"

"Say what? With who?"

I shrugged. "Cameron."

Her mouth made an 'oh' shape. "Really?" she drew out the word. "Good, I'm glad that boy finally worked up the balls to ask you out on a date."

"Susan," I hissed.

"Oops, sorry. Worked up the testicles to ask you out."

I burst out laughing. "That is so much worse."

She shrugged. "It's the anatomical word for it."

I just shook my head.

"Well, I stand by what I said. The guy's been working up the courage for like thirteen years..."

"Thirteen years where I was with his best friend. That makes him sound like a real jerk."

"We both know that if any one of our lives was simplified into a paragraph, we'd all come out sounding pretty bad. No one is easy or simple, or good or bad, we all feel too much for that."

"You're getting way to deep for me with your hippie mumbo-jumbo."

She nudged me. "Shut up."

"Where's Sarah?" I scanned the area again, but she wasn't anywhere.

"Maybe they're just running late?"

Sudden fear swelled up in me. "Hey, wait by my car for a minute?"

"Sure," Susan drew out the word like it was a question.

I ran into the school, looking around frantically. When I reached room seven, I ran in through the open door. The room was lit, the desks empty. Sarah's photo caught my attention and I glanced over to see a poster with Sarah's photo on it that was titled, 'Student of the Week', something Sarah had not mentioned to me.

Dashing back through the door, I dodged kids as I ran down the hallways. At every passageway I paused to look around, but though I examined each child's face that I passed, none of them were Sarah.

While I ran my way up to Sarah's room three SDC class, the door opened. Ms. Brown stepped out, a large piece of paper in her hands. She stood against the door and Sarah passed her out of the classroom.

Halting in the middle of my run, I caught my breath.

Ms. Brown looked over as she stepped away from the door. "Oh, hi Jamie. Sorry we're late. I promised Sarah she could take her art home this weekend and she wouldn't let me forget it." She grinned at me.

"Oh, no problem," I exhaled.

"Mom!" Sarah yelled as she ran toward me, barreling into me.

I leaned down and squeezed her to me. When Sarah made a small squeaking sound, I released her. Laughing, I brushed her hair away from her eyes. "You have a good day, baby?"

"Mom, can we go to Grandpa's house now?"

"She's been talking about that all day." Ms. Brown grinned and held out the large picture paper.

Taking what I discovered was a glittery glue covered some-sort-of animal picture, I asked "How was today?"

"Great. A little defiance on the playground but it wasn't really that big of a deal. Besides that, I can't think of anything. Sarah followed the directions and made an animal in art today, instead of a gymnast, I thought that was pretty awesome."

"I see that." I grinned down at the paper.

"Mom, do dogs do gymnastics?" Sarah looked at me very intently.

"Um, not really, cutie. I love your picture."

Ms. Brown walked backward toward room three. "Well, you ladies have a wonderful weekend." She waved.

"Yeah, you too and thank you so much."

"My pleasure. Later, Sarah."

Sarah pointed at Ms. Brown. "Say bye, Sarah.'"

"Bye, Sarah." She smiled and waved once more before opening the door to room nine and disappearing inside.

When Sarah and I made it back, Susan was waiting for me, leaning against the side of my car. "Good. You found her. Everything okay?"

"Yeah, um, fine."

"It was like you were freaking out or something." She pushed off the car and walked toward Sarah. "Come give me a hug, you little monkey."

Sarah giggled, wrapping her arms around Susan's big belly.

Hoping that Susan would forget all about her line of questioning, I opened the trunk to set the glittery artwork inside and then helped Sarah into her booster. Leaning into Susan, I gave her a one armed hug. "See you later."

Susan pulled away. "So are you going to tell me or what?"

"About what?"

She gave me a look. "About why you freaked out."

"Oh, nothing, I'm just a little stressed."

"Okay." She shook her head. "Hey, Jamie, I've been meaning to ask you something extremely personal."

"Can I choose 'dare'?"

She pointed at me. "If you're that stupid. No, I just wondered if you've told Cam about the detox list."

"No," I scoffed. "And don't you tell him either. He doesn't need to know about it."

She raised her eyebrows, her expression clearly conveying that she had different thoughts about that, but she didn't argue. "It's up to you." She raised her hands. "I'm going to go see if these PTA things have food. Want to hang out tomorrow?"

"Maybe, probably. It depends on my plans with Cameron. Call me?"

"Sounds good. Have fun tonight."

"Have fun at the PTA meeting."

"Now that's just cruel. Love you and your offspring." She turned around, walking toward the front entrance of the school.

"Ditto," I called after her before climbing in my car. Handing my phone back to Sarah, aside from the music of her game, we took the short drive to Cameron's house in silence.

Outside of Cameron's house, I parked in the empty driveway and turned the car off. Locking the doors, I curled up in a ball and closed my eyes.

"Truth or dare?" I asked Logan.

Susan, he and I lay across his bed, our heads on the foot of his bed and our multicolored-socked feet on his pillows.

"Dare," he grinned at me with a mouth full of braces.

"Run across your roof naked."

"Gross!" Susan said, showing her own set of braces. "No one wants to see that."

"Shut up," Logan reached across me to push Susan, who grabbed onto me so she wouldn't fall off the bed. "But yeah, no one wants to see that Jay. Truth."

"If you had to marry someone from our school, who would it be?" Holding my breath, I waited for his answer.

"Mary Custard."

I turned to him, making a face. "Lame, why?"

He bobbed his eyebrows. "You know why."

"Pig!" Susan reached across me to push her brother, and he grabbed me so he wouldn't fall off.

"Ah, stop pushing each other. You guys are going to kill me!" I called out, making them laugh. "Evil bastards. Anyway, if you married Mary Custard, you'd have to be around her for the rest of your life, and then none of us would want to hang out with you because she'd be there."

"It'd be worth it."

"You suck," I said.

"Fine, I'll change my answer. I'll marry you." He leaned down and kissed me right on my mouth.

"Huh, no!" I pushed him hard and Logan went tumbling off the bed.

"Rejected!" Susan called out.

We both scooted over to look down off the bed to where Logan was grinning like a maniac.

"I totally just gave you your first kiss, Jay!"

"Doesn't count!" I yelled down.

Susan sighed resignedly. "Sorry, Jay, that totally counts."

Logan grinned widely at me. "Hey Jamie, truth or dare?"

"Truth."

"Who do you like?"

I rolled my eyes. "Dare."

"Kiss me again."

As Cameron's car drove up, I blinked out of my memories. It was strange, all these random memories surfacing when my mind had felt devoid of memories for an entire year.

"Mom, can we go to Grandpa's right now?" Sarah asked from the backseat.

"Really soon, baby."

Climbing out of the car, I smiled over at Cameron. He wasn't in the outfit I'd seen him in at lunch time, but rather new jeans and a button-down shirt.

"Hey, handsome."

He nodded over at me. "Hey." His voice held little enthusiasm.

"All right," I drew out the word. "Everything okay?"

He nodded again. "Fine. You want me to watch Sarah while you get ready?"

"I actually have to fill out a couple forms." I glanced toward the trunk then back to Cameron. "What do you think I should do first?"

"Maybe get ready then do the forms in the car? The clerk's office closes at four."

"Shoot! Seriously? Okay, you know what, if you just transfer Sarah over to your car, I'll get ready lightning quick, and grab her stuff for the sleepover."

He tossed me the keys and I caught them while running into the house. I left the keys in the door and the door open before sprinting up the stairs. I had already planned out my outfit in my mind, so I quickly shed my coffee-smelling clothing and bra, slipping on a much sexier black bra and dress. Rushing into Sarah's room, I quickly packed her an overnight bag, before grabbing her toiletries.

Since I had absolutely no time for makeup, I grabbed my makeup bag and brush and rushed back out the door. At the door, I spun on my heel and ran back to Cameron's kitchen to take out the bag with Clarke's note then rushed back to the door. It was tricky balancing everything in my arms, but I managed to set Cameron's alarm and close the door behind me, locking it.

Cameron and Sarah sat in Cameron's car, waiting for me. After dumping everything I held into the back seat beside Sarah, I called, "One more second."

I grabbed the paperwork from my trunk, climbed in beside Cameron and held it up, "My civil harassment restraining order paperwork is covered in glitter."

By covered in glitter, I meant drenched in glitter. Brushing it off on the way to Cameron's car had done very little other than coat me in the glitter too.

"That's not good," his voice was a little clipped, and he kept his eyes on the rearview mirror as he backed out of the driveway.

"You sure everything is okay?"

"Yeah, it's great. You look beautiful by the way." He wasn't looking at me while he said it, but behind him at the road.

"Thanks." Turning, I looked back at Sarah who was still playing with my phone. "Hey baby, we're heading to Grandpa and Grandma's house now, and you're going to spend the night there, remember?"

She squealed, bouncing up and down in her seat.

Glancing over at Cameron, I asked, "Do you need me to direct you?"

"No, I remember." *'From the funeral,'* he didn't say it, but the words were there. His attention stayed determinedly on the road, so I decided to focus on my sparkly paperwork.

After doing so much paperwork today, it felt second nature to me, even though the subject was so much more uncomfortable. I knew how to fill out almost everything, though there were a couple areas I was pretty sure I was supposed to leave blank. When I finally looked up, Cameron was pulling up to my father's house.

He shifted into park. "Is it cool if I just wait in the car?"

I looked over at him. "Of course." Going around the car, I helped Sarah out and grabbed her bag. "All right, we'll just be a minute."

Sarah ran ahead as I climbed the bottom steps to the newly refinished wooden porch. The porch showed hundreds of small details in the scrollwork from the eight full months it took for my father to fix it. Compared to the pristine porch, their blue Edwardian house looked rundown; it was one of the oldest standing houses in town. Both the historical tour and ghost tour made stops outside regularly, something Sharon loved and my father got a kick out of.

When Sarah reached the door, she stood up on tip toes and hit the door knocker over and over again.

"Sarah, just once," I called.

She hit it again twice when the door swung open.

"Could that be my favorite kid in the whole wide world knocking at my door?" My father boomed.

"Yes!" Sarah jumped up and down, giggling.

"Is that Sarah?" Sharon shouted from inside.

"Sure is, honey!"

"Tell her I have a present for her," Sharon called back.

I rolled my eyes, shook my head and laughed. "She knew it."

"Hey, kiddo." My father held out an arm to me, though he still held Sarah. "You feeling okay today?"

"I haven't really had a moment to freak out yet. So, yeah, I'm fine."

"Where's that guy of yours?"

"In the car."

My father leaned to look over at Cameron. "Well, tell him to get up here."

"Um, Dad, the clerk's office closes at four, and—"

Sarah pushed me. "Bye, Mom."

"Sarah," I warned.

"You say four?" My father let go of me to look at his watch. "Honey, that's in thirty minutes."

"Yeah."

He kissed me on the forehead. "Get going. We got Sarah, don't worry about a thing. We'll call you if anything comes up, so get what you have to do done and go have a nice time."

"Thanks, Dad." I gave Sarah a quick kiss on the forehead. "You be good for your grandparents, I love you."

"Bye, I'm going to Grandpa's now."

"Sure are." My dad turned toward the door with Sarah, but asked over his shoulder, "You brought a sweater, right?"

It was probably eighty degrees Fahrenheit out.

"Yep," I lied.

"Good. Love you, kiddo."

"Love you too, Dad."

Day Seven: Three-thirty

In the car, I waited for Cameron to say something as we passed the familiar houses and parks downtown, but I got nothing. As he pulled into the parking lot to our city's old courthouse, I finally turned to him.

"Are you sure everything's okay?"

He nodded.

"You're not mad at me about something?"

He shook his head, then glanced over. "Not at all." Cameron parked a couple rows back from the courthouse entrance.

"Okay." I drew out the word, grabbing for the door handle.

We walked into the building in silence, him beside me. Just inside the old, decorative building was a small area that resembled a miniature airport security station. As there was no line, Cameron and I stepped up to set our belongings into plastic bins and fed them through the bag-x-ray machine.

"Good afternoon," I called over to the security guy who was dressed in full uniform.

"Afternoon. If you would just proceed through the metal detectors." He waved us forward.

We stepped through one by one, walking toward another large security guard. As Cameron stepped through, a loud beeping went off.

The security guard behind the x-ray machine leaned forward to look. "Probably your belt. Please remove it."

Cameron stepped back through the machine, making it blare out again. He quickly took off his belt, setting it in a bin and feeding it through. I couldn't help noticing his jeans falling low on his hips as he walked through without a belt.

When Cameron didn't set off the alarm again, the big security guard smiled. "Go ahead." He waved.

"Thanks, um... where's the clerk's office?"

"Second floor. It closes in twenty minutes," called the security guard behind the machine.

"Thanks." Instead of putting on his belt, Cameron only grabbed his stuff and we headed toward the elevators. The building was an older, adobe and blocky space. The walls had those distinctive rounded edges so many of the older buildings in Coral Beach had. Large metal-framed display cases hung evenly spaced on every wall, many of them containing monitors with words scrolling across or upwards.

We stopped in front of the line of elevators, and after pressing the button, I turned to Cameron. Nudging him, I teased, "The clerk is going to be too distracted to help me if you don't put that belt back on."

Cameron looked down. "Oh, yeah." He fed his belt through, oblivious to my teasing, which wasn't like Cameron at all.

In the elevator, I glanced over at him several times. His profile was a set of perfect lines, though the line of his mouth was most definitely cast down. I thought of saying that perhaps tonight wasn't the best night for some extravagant date, under the circumstances. To be honest, going on a date was really the last thing I was in the mood for. I said nothing, though. I didn't want to alienate him further.

The clerk's office was clearly visible from the elevator doors as they opened. A small plaque beside the open doors read 'Clerk's Office'. It was the only office with glass doors on the entire floor. Though several people waited just inside, none of them seemed to be in line to talk to the clerk. She was the only clerk I saw in front of a long partition.

Glancing from face to worried face around the office and seeing no objection in their expressions, I stepped up to the long counter where the middle aged woman sat.

She looked up at me. "Please wait at the courtesy line until I call you up." She immediately looked back down to her papers.

"Oh, sorry." I stepped back to where Cameron waited, my cheeks feeling warm and tight.

Cameron's hand came up to my shoulder, rubbing it gently.

I leaned into his touch, the first real affection he'd shown me tonight.

The clerk looked up. "All right, go on and step forward now." She had an exhausted and not at all pleased look on her wrinkled face. Her no-nonsense short gray haircut added to the effect, making her look a little like a schoolmarm.

I set my papers down on her counter. "Hi. I need to file for a civil harassment restraining order."

"Do you have all your forms?" She held out a hand to me.

"Yeah, and I have the evidence." I held up the plastic bag.

She pointed at the bag. "Keep that, that's for the judge if there's a hearing."

"Oh, okay." I set the bag on the counter and handed her the stack of papers across the table.

She looked through my glittered-covered papers.

"Sorry about the glitter, I have an eight year old who—"

"It's fine. You don't have an emergency protective order?"

"No, but the sheriff is the one who sent me here."

She nodded. "You don't ask for a stay away order from your home. Is that intentional?"

"He's my neighbor—I'm going to move so I just figured that it'd be easier this way. I am asking for a stay away order from where my daughter and I are living right now, though."

"It's your decision. Do you want to talk to a deputy clerk about this filing process? They will not be able to assist you in any legal matters."

"Should I?"

She blinked at me. "Would you like to?"

I swallowed. "I just wonder about the timing of this process, I guess."

"Well, as it's..." she glanced at the clock, "After one-thirty, you can pick up the judge's decision after four p.m. on our next business day, which is Monday. He'll either issue a notice of hearing and a temporary restraining order, just give the notice of hearing or will dismiss the case all together.”

“How likely is that?” Cameron asked.

“That is a question I am not qualified to answer.” She looked back to me, giving me a tense smile. “Would you like to speak to a deputy clerk?”

“No, I don’t think so.”

She nodded. After giving me a lengthy explanation of my rights and about the judicial process, which all sounded very memorized, she dismissed us and we stood there for a few seconds before walking away.

“I thought that was going to be way more dramatic for some reason,” I said under my breath as we walked out of the glass doors and to the elevators.

“Yeah.” Cameron’s focus was on the elevators and not on me.

“So, where are we going now, dinner?”

Cameron closed his eyes and swallowed. He opened his eyes to peer over, giving me the smallest of smiles. “Yeah, then I have quite a few things planned for us.”

“Great,” I tried for enthusiasm, but fell short.

“Yeah.”

The elevators dinged open.

We stood a short distance apart and travelled all the way down to the car in silence.

As we crossed the parking lot, I whispered, “A lot of changes today. Good, I guess, but a lot.”

He glanced over. “You sold the shop?”

“Yeah. Thanks, by the way, for encouraging me to call Peter. He had some guy named Carlos look over the contract and change all this wording stuff that I would never have thought of.”

Cameron nodded. He opened my door for me.

“Well, thank you sir.” After stowing the horrible bag of evidence in the glove compartment, I waited for Cameron to climb in beside me. “It all felt rushed, but I’m pretty sure I knew what I was signing and it will work out.”

“That’s good.” Cameron looked over his shoulder as he backed up.

I wanted to ask him what his deal was one more time, but I knew I’d just sound like I was stuck on repeat.

A minute later in the drive, I smoothed down my dress on my legs and said, “So what restaurant are we going to?”

“I made reservations at—” Cameron cut off abruptly and veered off the road to pull onto the shoulder. Throwing open his car door, Cameron leaned out and started vomiting.

“Oh, no, Cameron! Are you sick?”

He coughed. “No, it was just something I ate… I’m fine we can still go out on our—” he cut off and started vomiting again.

Leaning toward him, I rubbed his back. “Oh, Cameron.” I suppressed a horribly inappropriate laugh. “Why didn’t you tell me you weren’t feeling well?”

“I’m fine,” his voice came out ragged as he leaned out of the car. When he sat back into his chair, his face was sweaty and pale.

“Cameron.”

He mock-glared over at me. "Why are you laughing?"

"Because you're such a dork. You totally were trying to hide the fact that you're sick from me so we could go on a silly date."

His lips pinched, but some amusement returned to his face. "I'm not sick, I just got some bad fish in my burrito at lunch. We can still go on our date."

"You're serious?"

"I bought tickets to—" he cut off once again to vomit out of his car.

I wrapped my arms around him and laid my head on his back. "You big dork. Let me drive, I'm going to go get you some sport drink thingy and then take you home."

Cameron wiped his hand across his mouth. "I bought tickets to the Death and Crumpets Tour for tonight."

"Really?" My eyes widened. Shaking my head, I laughed. "Okay, that was awesome of you, but we can go another time."

He sat up straight and closed his car door. "No, I can go."

I ran a hand through his hair and laughed again. "Come on, Cameron. We can't show up to the Death and Crumpets Tour with you barfing all over the place, we'd look like newbies that couldn't handle their liquor. Just think how embarrassing that would be."

He smirked, showing a little of his signature spark again.

Kissing the side of his head, I whispered, "Let me drive, please.

"Fine." He exhaled heavily. "But let me drive up just a little ways."

"Good plan." Kissing him on the cheek again, I whispered, "I'm glad you're not mad at me—not that I'm happy that you're sick, I just thought you were super pissed off at me for some reason."

He squeezed my arm. "Never."

"Ha, I'm holding you to that one."

Cameron rolled the car forward a bit then climbed out and as he walked around the car, I climbed over the center divider. After Cameron was in safely, I rolled down the window all the way and drove to the nearest grocery store.

Cameron turned to me as I parked. "I'll come in with you."

"Um, Cameron, you're looking a little green again." Sweat broke across his forehead. "Let me run in really quick and grab the stuff, yeah?" When he still reached for his door handle, I said, "Come on Cameron, please, I'll be fine in there. Let me take care of you for once."

He lay back against the seat, his eyes closing. "If you're not back in ten minutes, I'm coming to find you."

"Cool." I rushed out of the car and ran through the parking lot. My gaze scanned the lot as I jogged, but I didn't see Clarke or anything weird. The day was warm and the sky clear with a few happy clouds skipping through.

Unfortunately, unlike the colorful naturally-lit shop I usually shopped at, this store had a drab, crowded, halogen-light-dominated feel. I rushed through the aisles, unfamiliar with their organization. After purchasing Cameron's sick-supplies, I scanned the lot carefully before heading through to Cameron's car. It was still early and light outside, but after everything in the past few days, I couldn't shake that jumpy feeling.

I found Cameron's door open and him leaning into the car.

"Hey, you okay?"

He looked over at me. "Maybe we should head back to my house."

"Yeah, we really, really should."

We had to stop twice in the short drive up to Cameron's place so he could throw up.

As I shifted into park I turned to Cameron. "Maybe you should go to the doctor?"

He held a hand to his forehead, fingers pinching the bridge of his nose. "No, I'm good."

"If you say so."

"I'll get the groceries."

I laughed. "No, you get your sick ass inside and go lay down. I'll get the groceries."

He looked over, a small smile on his lips. "Bossy."

"Yep, now do what I say." I handed him the keys and gave him another kiss on the cheek.

Day Seven: Four-thirty

After grabbing the groceries from the car, I followed Cameron into his house. Locking the door behind me, I took the groceries to the kitchen and boiled some water for the rice.

"It really was the burrito; I didn't feel sick at all today before that, and it tasted a little undercooked." Cameron came to stand beside me. He must have dashed up to the bathroom because I smelled the fresh scent of toothpaste.

"Here, take this and drink this." I handed him the medicine and a sports drink.

He grinned and he snapped the seal open. "I like you bossy." Taking the pill I gave him, Cameron took a big sip of the blue liquid. He made a face. "Toothpaste and..." he read the label, "Blue ferocity do not go well together."

"You feeling any better?"

"Good enough to watch a movie with you if you want to."

"Okay, but only if it's in bed." I pointed at him. "I want you resting.

"I wish I had the energy to tease you right now." He leaned forward and gave me a quick kiss, his hand caressing my side. "I'll meet you up there."

After I had finished the quick rice and made toast, I filled a couple bowls with the food I had bought and balanced them all precariously in my arms. When I'd stealthily maneuvered up the stairs and into the bedroom, I found Cameron lying across the bed in only his boxers and undershirt, head down on a pillow.

"Well, hello, sir. I brought you your delicious dinner."

He glanced up and made a sort of grunting sound. "I think I feel worse."

"Oh, baby." I set the bowls on the side table next to his bed.

"Do I still get my strip tease?" he sounded incredibly depressed.

"Now?" I laughed.

"No, I couldn't do anything about it now. I just really wanted it."

I climbed in next to him. "Oh, little Cameron wanted his striptease."

He grabbed me, pulling me over to him, his body coming to rest most of the way on mine, his head on my stomach. "Don't mock me," he whispered into my stomach. "You've never done it for me before and I was really excited."

I laughed, my hands running through his hair. "Fine, I'll do it another day."

He looked up at me. "You promise?"

"Yeah, fine."

"Good, now I can die in peace." His head nestled back into my stomach.

"Are you always this big of a baby when you get sick?"

"I'm not sick. I was poisoned by a really nice lady named Jamilla who works at Tex-Mex To-go."

"Jealous ex-lover?"

He laughed. "She was probably older than my mother."

"Scandalous."

His hand reached under my dress, moving up my side.

I looked down at him. "What are you doing?"

"It's comforting to me." His hand moved up to my hip, fingers playing with the string of my g-string underwear. "You won't deny a man his dying wish?"

"We are not having barfy-sex."

He chuckled, his movement reverberating through my legs.

"I'm not sure I could manage it right now."

"That's a first. By the way, I brought you a feast: bananas, rice, applesauce and toast."

"Sounds amazing." He cringed.

"Don't even think about it, buddy. I am not a barf bag. So, do I need to cancel any reservations?"

"It's too late for that."

"Will you tell me what you planned? I'm really curious?"

He pulled me closer into him, saying nothing.

"Please?"

He spoke into my stomach, "Florentines for dinner."

"Wow, fancy."

"Then I was going to take you to the Death and Crumpets Tour, which would have gone to about midnight."

"Nice."

"Then I had a night booked at the Paradise Coral Beach."

I looked down at him. "Why there?" A sneaking suspicion crawled into my mind.

"Because that's where I decided that it was you for me."

"Seriously, Cameron?" I breathed out a laugh. "Senior prom?

"Yeah."

It didn't take much to bring up that night for me, as old memories had been fighting to come up for a few days now.

We all shared a table at prom, Cameron with his date whose name I couldn't even remember. She was beautiful with a blonde up-do, beaming around at our table. Logan's buddy Mike, and his girl Tammy sat beside Vanessa, whose date was pretty much trying to do her at the table all night.

Susan stood abruptly. "I'm over this, let's head up to Brody's suite." Her date was some punk guy with a mohawk none of us knew, who'd already took off. It'd actually been a pretty big scene, him leaving and saying, "Yeah, whatever," when Susan had asked if he'd hang out for a while. Susan folded her arms over her chest. "Prom sucks, let's go get drunk."

Half of the people at the table already were.

Logan leaned into my ear. "You ready, babe?"

I shook my head. "No, I want to stay here."

Vanessa jumped up then teetered a little, her arm catching herself on Susan's shoulder. "Matt and I are with you, love. Right, Matt?"

Matt's eyes widened in obvious excitement. "Hell yeah."

As the rest of the table stood up, Logan and I stayed sitting.

"Come on, what are you doing?" Susan asked, when we didn't move.

"Staying here." I remember being annoyed at Susan that night, something about her date being a jerk in the limo we'd shared. In the years she'd dated hetero, I'd never jived well with her guys. Logan had absolutely detested the guy.

Susan sent a dismissive glance at the dressed up people on the dance floor. "This shit is boring."

"It is kind of boring," Logan whispered.

"Then go," I snapped. "We can go party any time, this is the only time we can ever do prom."

"Except that we did it last year." Susan rolled her eyes, obviously annoyed at me too.

"Go." I gestured. "You can go too." I said to Logan. "I'm good here."

"Oh, Jay, I'll stay with you." Nessa fell back into her chair.

Her date sat too, leaning in to whisper something in her ear, making her mouth fall open, then she started giggling.

"That's cool, guys, you all go. I'm just going to go dance…"

"With who, yourself?" Susan challenged.

"Unlike some people here, I'm nice to people outside of our group of friends, so I have other friends." I challenged back.

"Fine Ms. Popular, be lame."

"I will. Go have a great time being drunk with your awesome date," I said, sarcasm dripping from my voice. I knew the real reason she wanted to go up to Brody's stupid suite.

"Whatever, Jay." Susan turned around, following the rest of our group who had already made their way toward the exit of the hotel's ballroom.

"You sure you're okay with us going?" Vanessa asked me, as she leaned into her date.

"Yeah," I said it perhaps a little too emphatically as I noticed that Matt's hand was most definitely up Nessa's skirt.

She jumped up. "Okay, we'll come back down in like an hour or something to hang out with you, promise." Grabbing her date's hand, Nessa rushed off through the crowd.

Logan's face was tense as he sat beside me.

I turned to him. "Want to go dance?"

Logan stared toward where Susan had walked off. "You think that dickhead is up at Brody's suite?"

"Yeah, that's how Susan knows him, through Brody."

"Maybe we should go check."

I closed my eyes. "Please don't go get in a fight tonight."

He squeezed my shoulder. "I won't, I promise. But, let's just go up there for a minute."

"You can go Logan, but I mean it, I'm not going."

He grinned over at me. "Are you going to make me pay for it if I go check on her?"

I punched him in the arm. "That depends."

"Depends on...?"

"Depends on if you come back in two hours wasted."

"You think I'm stupid?" he whispered in my ear before kissing me hard and deep.

"A little," I said as he moved away from me to stand.

He looked me up and down in my prom dress, grinning. "Well, I'm not that stupid."

"That remains to be seen," I called after him.

He shot me one more grin over his shoulder as he left.

"My friends are lame," I sung to myself as I stood to find another table to sit at.

Across the way, I crossed to the table that had most of the thespian crowd. "Hey y'all, mind if I join you?" I asked.

"Sure," several of the girls said.

Mike Diggs, who sat with his boyfriend, grabbed a chair from a neighboring table and dragged it across.

"Hey!" called a guy from that table.

I looked over. "Sorry, Josh, can I borrow this?"

"Oh, yeah of course, Jay. Where's Logan?"

"Upstairs." I tuned away quickly, not wanting to be pulled in with Logan's jock friends.

"Pippin," said one of the girls as I sat, continuing some conversation they must have been having.

Mike, unofficial leader of the thespians, shook his head. "No way, it's going to be West Side Story." He turned to me. "You and Nessa going to audition?"

"Maybe, when are auditions?"

"Not for another month," Theresa said, laughing. "But it's all we seem to be able to talk about."

"Are any of you thinking of heading to the dance floor?" I asked the table at large.

"Probably not," Theresa said.

My shoulders sunk a little. I sat with the group, talking about past musicals and theorizing about what this year's would be.

"Hey, wanna dance?"

Turning, I saw Cameron leaning down beside me, looking over.

"Yes!" I jumped up. "Thank god!"

He laughed. "Wow, you're excited."

"Yep!" I stepped over legs. "Later guys!"

"Later, Jay," a couple people called from behind me.

I grabbed Cameron's arm and pulled him toward the dance floor, making sure there was no way he could get out of the dance with me. "What happened to your date?"

"She's making out with Brody upstairs."

I turned to gape at him. "I'm sorry, Cameron!"

He shrugged. "She asked me. It's not like we're going out or anything. I didn't even want to go up there, if I knew you'd stayed, I would have come down a while back."

"That bad?"

"Just not really my scene. Logan and Susan are arguing on the balcony and everyone else is either getting messed up or hooking up."

"Yeah, I don't get it. We can do that any night for the rest of our lives but this night only comes once, ever. And we spent all this time getting ready and all this money..." I shook my head. "Whatever, forget them, let's go dance."

When we stepped on the dance floor, a fast song we both knew was on. Both Cameron and I sang along, jumping around each other. Cameron grabbed my hand and spun me around a couple times, dipping me dramatically and making me laugh.

A couple of our other friends came up after a few fast songs, surrounding us and we smiled in greeting, though I kept dancing with Cameron.

When a slow song came on, Miranda, a friend from the swim team, squeezed up close to me. "Yo Jay, wanna switch partners?" She grinned at me.

Glancing back, I saw my intended dance partner was Brian Foster, who was a cool guy and I was pretty sure Miranda's date.

"Sure." I shrugged.

"Sorry, Miranda." Cameron cut in. "I promised Logan that I'd dance with Jamie until he got back."

"Oh," she sounded pretty disappointed. "Well, later then."

"Yeah, sure, I'll find you guys." He put his arm around me and pulled me in for a slow dance.

I moved a little stiffly. "I didn't realize you're my babysitter."

Cameron pulled me closer to him and whispered, "I'm not, I just didn't want to dance with Miranda."

"Oh." I relaxed into the dance, laying my head against Cameron's shoulder. "Thanks for coming down and saving this night for me."

He hadn't responded for a while, and when he did, he said it so softly, I barely heard him. "Anytime."

We'd danced a couple more dances before Logan had come down and scooped me away from Cameron.

It was strange to think that that was the night Cameron had decided I was for him, especially since it was the night I'd lost my virginity to someone else. That memory with Cameron had always been overshadowed so much by what happened directly after. Back here, all these years later, laying with Cameron and looking at the scene through this lens, the memory sat badly.

I lay for a long while, running my fingers through Cameron's hair and not saying anything. After a little while, the thoughts that rattled around in my head grew so loud that I needed to speak them out loud. "Is that who you're in love with, Cameron?"

He looked up at me. "What?"

"The prom me, the Ultimate Sunshine Tour me, who I used to be?"

He exhaled and settled his head back down on my stomach. "No."

"Because you know... your gift and wanting to take me to that hotel... it just makes me think that maybe you're trying to revive something that never happened."

He groaned into my stomach.

"I'm sorry, I shouldn't do this to you now."

He gave me another amused look and croaked out, "No, Jamie, I'm not in love with you at seventeen. I might have been when I was seventeen, but now I'm in love with thirty-year-old Jamie."

"Okay." I looked away.

He squeezed me and when I looked down, his dark eyes were blazing into mine. "Hey, it's not about that, okay? I guess I'm—" he paused, "It was like you and Vanessa, Logan and Susan always had this shared history and it was a wall keeping the rest of us out."

"No, we're not like that."

"Not now, maybe, aside from with Susan. But, in high school and after, you guys were always together, and then there was the rest of us."

I shook my head. "No, it wasn't like that."

"It was." He stared at me. "I think I just want to remind you that we have a lot of history too, Jamie. Thirteen years of history."

"I know that."

"That's what you always had with Logan, so many memories no one could ever get close to that. You guys pretty much had your own language and it was annoying to hang out with you together or when Nessa and Susan were with you. And, I'm not trying to replace Logan, or say anything about it, I just want you to remember that I was there too because it was always you for me.”

I swallowed. “Until Nessa.”

“Ness was my best friend. We should never have gotten married. Yeah, we fell in love for a while, but it didn’t last long and then we were just friends again until everything ended badly. I wanted kids, she didn’t, I wanted to grow up, she didn’t—she still doesn’t. Oh—” He covered his mouth, climbed off me and rushed out of the room toward the bathroom.

Cringing, I called, “I’m so sorry, Cameron. I’m going to shut my fat mouth and let you be sick.”

“It’s fine!” I heard his hoarse voice through the hallway door.

After I heard the flush, I crossed to the hall to peer in the bathroom. Cameron was once again brushing his teeth.

“Would taking a shower make you feel better or worse?

“I’m not up for it yet. Can we just lay down on the bed and you keep massaging my head while I sneak my hands up your dress again?”

I laughed. “Yeah, come here.”

We did exactly what he said and I avoided the hard subjects, combing my fingers through his hair.

Day Eight

Unshackled

Day Eight: Four AM

I woke with someone kissing my neck. Blearily, I felt around me until I felt a warm, soft, damp body beside me.

"Did you shower?" I whispered, closing my eyes again.

"Yeah. I woke about an hour ago feeling a lot better," Cameron whispered. His hands lifted up my dress, which I must have fallen asleep in, lifting the material to over my hip.

"You woke up… better," I whispered as his mouth returned to my neck and hands pulled down the strap of my underwear.

"I woke up to you in that sexy dress covered in glitter," he whispered into my neck. "I'm taking this off you now." He pulled at my dress, and lifted it off my body when I shifted.

"Wow," he whispered as his hands came up to caress over my bra.

"I wore it for our date." I smiled at him.

"I thought we could have a reverse date now."

"A reverse date?" I reached my hands up to run my fingers through his hair.

His finger slipped under the bottom of my underwear, slipping up and down, and my breathing became heavy.

He deepened the pressure, whispering, "First we have sex, then we go watch the sunrise, then breakfast. A date, in reverse."

"I definitely like the sound of the first one," I breathed.

He grinned as his finger hooked around the bottom of my g-string. "I can tell."

Slowly, he pulled the material down my legs then used his hands to spread my legs apart.

"This is definitely our type of date," I said as he unhooked my bra.

"Sure is, baby." His mouth came down on mine and he kissed me with long, deep kisses as we caressed each other.

I was so ready for him that the moment he thrust inside of me, my eyes rolled back and I exploded around him.

An hour later, we stood in the shower, spent but also fully awake, and I was much more open to going out to watch the sunrise. Cameron and I stood, wrapped around each other, the hot water beating down on our shoulders.

"I'm glad you're feeling better," I said as I ran my hands up his back.

"Yeah, me too. I told you it was the burrito."

"Moral of the story is, don't cross women named Jamila."

He laughed before kissing my shoulder. "Lesson learned."

I pressed my body deeper into his. "How long until sunrise?"

"An hour."

"Good."

We barely made the sunrise, having to climb the east-facing embankment on his property rather than taking the drive Cameron had originally wanted us to take. Thankfully, as Cameron's property was nestled in the hills, the sunrise had waited for us. I folded myself under his arm, lying on one blanket and under another one.

"I can't remember the last time I watched a sunrise."

I arched my neck to look at him. "Me neither. Well, sunsets here are a little more spectacular with the ocean and all." I looked back to the sky, spreading with color and light. "But, I love it." Yawning, I laid my head on his chest and let my eyelids drift closed.

I woke with Cameron holding me and awkwardly trying to make his way down the embankment.

"I can walk," I said, but I nestled my head deeper into his chest. When he'd managed to maneuver me all the way into his house, I whispered, "I'll walk up the stairs."

"Nope." He just kept carrying me.

"You've been sick; you're going to kill yourself."

"I'm fine, Jamie." He continued up the stairs, setting me on the bed then curling up around me.

I woke again to a low rumbling sound. The same sound growled again, growing louder. Laughing, I asked, "Is that your stomach?"

"I'm hungry," his voice was muffled as his lips were pressed to my back.

"I can tell."

There was a loud gurgle as his stomach asserted itself once more. His lips tickled over my back as he spoke, "Let's go out for breakfast."

"I could make you something," I said into the pillow.

"The selection is getting pretty limited."

I groaned. "Does this mean we have to take another shower?"

"Not for the place I'm thinking of."

I mock glared over my shoulder at him. "You think I'm some sort of cheap date, do you?"

He leaned in, his mouth to my ear. "Baby, you are a sure thing."

I tried to punch him, but my movements were too awkward to make an impact. "Don't get used to it."

He leaned back, his hands going behind his head. "Nah, I'm going to up my game next date and not throw up all over."

"You're so sure you're going to get a second date?"

He leaned in to kiss my shoulder. "Yep, and a striptease."

My cheeks heated remembering that yes, I had promised to do a striptease for him when he'd been so cute and sick last night. Sitting up, I scooted off the bed. "I'm going to shower, but I'll be super quick."

We both ended up showering, though we threw on dirty jeans and sweatshirts and were out the door in less than twenty minutes.

"I'm so excited not to work tonight," I said as Cameron drove us down the hill.

"Yeah, I like the idea of you having Saturdays free."

"And you too, now your Saturdays are free of doing me favors."

He just smirked, flashing me a bright smile. "So when you introduce me around tonight, what are you going to call me?"

"Cameron." I blinked at him, my expression innocent.

"Uh-huh."

"What do you want me to call you?"

"Your boyfriend." He didn't even hesitate to say it.

"Cameron..."

He parked in a stall next to a small restaurant. "You told your dad I was."

I looked over, pursing my lips. "I kind of had to."

"You said you're not going to date anyone else."

"Yeah."

"You're living with me."

"For a little while.

"You're in love with me."

"Cameron..."

"And, we're now dating." He wiggled his eyebrows and gave me a small grin.

"Can we do this later?" I groaned.

"Fine." He reached for the door handle. "I just don't get what the difference is."

Outside the car, Cameron waited for me. "So I need to do a little catch up on work today. Do you mind if I leave you for a couple hours after we pick up Sarah?"

I stopped next to him. "Yeah, you never need to ask me that."

He shrugged. "Just checking in. I'll definitely be back in time for your benefit thing tonight."

I spun to the restaurant. It was a small building that seemed to sag on one side. A similar leaning sign had several of its letters absent. "Kiki's delicous fod," I read.

"It's better on the inside." Cameron put an arm around my back.

I leaned in and whispered, "Didn't you just get over food poisoning?"

The exterior off-white walls needed a fresh coat of paint, and they were the most appealing feature of the building. It didn't look promising.

"Trust me," Cameron said, grinning.

The bell on the door tinkled, alerting the big man behind the counter and about fifteen senior citizens of our arrival.

Seeing the crowd, I relaxed a bit. 'When in doubt, eat where the senior citizens were eating' was a good rule to live by.

"Sit anywhere," the guy behind the counter called as he turned away.

Cameron grabbed a couple menus from a bin and gestured for me to take the only open booth. More than one pair of eyes tracked us as we crossed over to take a seat.

"Morning," an elderly guy called as we passed.

"Good morning," Cameron and I called back.

Sitting on the red-vinyl seats, I whispered, "This place makes me want to have coffee so bad. Like, coffee, a cigarette and a real forlorn look on my face."

Cameron grinned, looking down at his menu. "What are you getting?"

I didn't even look at the menu. "Pancakes."

Two mugs slammed down on the table between us and without asking, the big gruff guy from behind the bar poured each of us a cup of coffee and walked away.

Touching the hot cup as little as possible, I pushed my coffee across the table. "They really don't skimp on atmosphere here. What do you think he'd do if I tried to order a tea?"

Cameron shook his head. "I wouldn't try it."

"What can I get you?" The guy said, popping up right next to us again. For such a huge guy, he sure was stealthy.

"Pancakes?" I looked up at him.

"Short stack or full order?"

"Short stack."

When Cameron ordered, he ordered four different meals.

As the guy walked away, I whispered across the table, "Should I have ordered more?"

Cameron shrugged, then slid out of his side of the booth to slide in next to me. "If you're still hungry, I'll share mine with you."

As much as I wished that I wasn't needy, I'd wanted him to sit next to me. I'd wanted his arm around me, his side against mine, my head on his shoulder. The outside world streamed around us, but in his arms, I could just be still. He was my safe harbor, had been for months, and maybe that was what terrified me so much. A safe harbor was a place of refuge, if you moved in, you lost it.

We said nothing. It was as if together, we could have a long exhale.

When the food came, all too soon, Cameron moved back to the other side of the booth.

I don't know what our waiter considered 'short', but there were probably eight pounds of pancakes set before me, already doused in syrup and butter. The waiter had to take three trips to get Cameron's plates, and we barely squeezed all of them on the table when he did.

After all our food was delivered, the guy just walked away, not asking if we wanted anything else, and I really didn't think it would be wise to call him back.

"Do you have an extra napkin?" I looked over at Cameron who was already shoving a big hunk of egg in his mouth.

"Sure." Leaning out of the booth, he grabbed a napkin from the nearest table.

"Ha." I covered my lap in the two tiny thin napkins and took my first bite of pancake. After the first bite, I knew why Cameron had chosen this restaurant. "Wow," I said, mouth full.

"Um, hm."

We were silent and content throughout the rest of our date, and by the time we returned to the car, we were both unbuttoning the top buttons of our jeans.

I glanced down at his unbuttoned pants. "Wanna drive to the lookout and make out before we have to pick up Sarah?"

He laughed.

"I'm so not kidding."

"No time to drive to the lookout, just come here." He reached for me.

As we were tucked away in an almost deserted parking lot, I thought, what the hell. I climbed across the center divider and straddled his lap. Leaning in, I kissed him deeply.

Cameron's arms came around me, moving down my back. He tasted like a mix of breakfast foods but it only made him more delicious, and I ran my fingers through his hair to pull him even closer to me.

A tap on the window made us both jump and look around.

An elderly man in a Bahamas-hat stood rapping his knuckles on our window again, he shook his head at us waving a finger. His elderly wife stood behind him, also shaking her head, but she grinned.

"Busted," Cameron said.

Then the man laughed and waved through the air before he gave us two thumbs up. He and his wife walked away, shooting us grins as they headed to their car.

Covering my face, I started laughing.

Cameron hugged me to him. "I love you, Jamie." Moving my hands away from my face with his, he snuck in one more kiss before reaching down and smacking my butt. "We should probably go get Sarah, so I can get to the shop."

I climbed off him. "I feel bad that you have to go in on a Saturday."

He gave me an exasperated look. "Jamie, you think I would have been working late yesterday if we didn't plan a date?"

"Good point. Guilt gone."

We took off toward the road. Today was one of those rare days in Coral Beach, where the sky was clear and the air warm. The roads were swamped with traffic, the cars all seemed to be heading to the beach.

"Too bad we no longer have a pool," I whispered.

"You have plans today?" Cameron glanced over.

"Not sure yet. Susan wanted to hang out, maybe."

"Just not you and Sarah hanging out alone, right?"

I rolled my eyes. "I hate this."

"Just be smart and stay safe."

I glared. "You know I am a card-carrying adult, right, Cameron? I'm pretty sure I have the brainpower to take care of me and my kid."

He gave me an exasperated look. "I'm not saying that. I just really need to get some work done and I have a meeting with a client, and I can't do either if I'm worrying about you."

I rolled my eyes. "Well, don't. You'll just have to trust that I can take care of myself, I'm not going to be babysat."

His hand came to rest on my leg. "I'm not trying to babysit you. There's just nothing stopping this guy from bothering you until Monday, and I have this really bad feeling that he's going to try to, especially if he finds you alone."

I stared out the window at my town, just seeming to wake up. "I'm going to be careful. But you know Cameron, so far he's just getting a kick out of freaking me out... but it's like he's so careful that he has to be afraid of getting caught or something."

"Sounds like pretty poor odds to bet your life on."

"That's a little dramatic. I feel like I'm giving him too much power over me, when really all I'm getting is some off comments and a couple creepy notes."

Cameron pulled up in front of my dad's house and turned to me. "You're scaring me here, Jamie. The guy broke onto our property to take pictures of us having sex which he delivered to your work. That's a little more than a creepy note."

My eyes widened and I paused. I'd definitely heard Cameron say '*our*' property instead of '*my*' property. Biting my lip, I looked away. "Yeah, you're right. And you don't need to worry; I'm going to be careful. I just have so many other things to worry about right now and I feel like he's just some creep that's getting way too much of my attention."

Cameron leaned in to give me a quick kiss. "He definitely is that."

Day Eight: Nine-fifteen

On the way up my father's porch steps with Cameron, I sent Susan a text.

Me: Is it okay if Sarah and I come over in a little while?

Susan: Whenever.

As I was about to put away my phone, I noticed that I had several text messages and a call from Amy that I must have missed when I checked my call log last night. Deciding that I'd check them in a minute, I stowed my phone and knocked on the front door of the house.

After a few seconds of waiting, the door swung open to my father's wide grin. "Good morning!"

"Morning, Dad." I stepped in to hug him, then squeezed past him.

"Cam." My dad clapped Cameron on the back. "Come on in, we still have some leftovers from breakfast."

"Oh, we ate like eighty pounds each, Dad."

"Good morning!" Sharon rushed over to hug us. She squeezed me and whispered, "Amy is upstairs."

When I pulled back, I saw red blotches ringing swollen eyes. Tilting my head, I gave her a questioning look.

"Sarah's in the living room." She leaned in. "Maybe you could go talk to Amy after you check on

Sarah. She probably doesn't want anyone else to know she's here though." She looked over at Cameron.

I nodded. "Everything okay?" I whispered really low.

Sharon's lips squeezed together and tears formed in her eyes.

"Sorry, I'll talk to her," I whispered in a very low voice.

When I turned, I found Cameron and my father had gone ahead into the living room.

"He's the best quarterback we've had in years!" my father was saying. "Have you seen that game?"

"The playoffs? I missed it."

"We're looking forward to quite a season this year." He held up two fingers. "It was close. Wasn't it Sarah?"

"Oh my god, Dad, you didn't have Sarah watching football reruns all night, did you?"

"Course I did, kiddo. Hey Sarah, ready?"

Sarah looked up from where she was watching cartoons on the massive couch. She threw up her hands along with my dad and they both yelled, "Touchdown!"

My dad turned a grin on me. "She loves it, just like you did. Too bad she's too young to take to the bar Thursday nights for the season."

"Dad!"

"Just saying." He took a seat beside Sarah, throwing an arm around her shoulders.

I took the seat on Sarah's other side, giving her a kiss on the forehead. "Hey baby."

She looked over. "Mom, can I stay at Grandpa's?"

"What kind of greeting is that?" I tickled her.

Giggling and squirming, Sarah called out. "All done tickles!" When I stopped tickling her, she looked up with a big grin. "More tickles!" As I reached to tickle her again, she screamed and giggled, "All done tickles."

"Okay, goofball, you can stay at Grandpa's for a couple more minutes, but then you're stuck with boring old mom." I kissed her on the forehead.

As Cameron had settled on my father's recliner and was again talking to my dad about football, I stood up and crossed over to him. Crouching down next to the recliner, I whispered, "Hey, I'm going to be a minute. I think my dad or Sharon can give me a ride if you need to split?"

Cameron shook his head. "I'll wait."

"You sure?"

When he nodded, I jumped up and hurried out of the room to the staircase. The old familiar staircase creaked its 'hello' at me as I ascended to the second story. A big bay window lit the hallway from one end, while the rest of the hall got progressively darker. On one side, my old room's door had been thrown open. As I passed, I saw the unmade bed and Sarah's open bag on the desk.

Across the hall, the door to Amy's old room was cracked open.

"Amy?"

A few seconds of silence went by, then Amy called, "Come in."

I pushed the door open, finding Amy sitting on her already-made bed with her computer open before her. She looked up as if startled from working. "Hey Jamie, you here to get Sarah?" Her voice was bright.

"Yep. What you working on?" I glanced at her screen, seeing only her bamboo-scene wallpaper and no open files.

Amy closed her laptop. "Just some work."

I nodded to the bed. "Can I sit?"

Amy stretched to set her computer on her desk. "Sure—of course, take a seat."

Instead of sitting where she gestured, I sat on her pillow directly next to her and threw an arm around her back.

"I'm fine Jamie." Her voice was filled with suppressed tears.

"Of course you are." I pulled her tighter to me. "Sharon just said something, so I wanted to make sure."

"Mom overreacts. It was just a stupid fight with Peter."

I pointedly ignored the tears she brushed off her face.

"What happened?"

"Nothing happened; I got a little tired so I took a taxi away from the party."

"And you came here?"

"It wasn't like that. I just... I needed to talk to someone and you didn't answer."

"Sorry."

"It's fine. I was tired and I didn't want to have to take another taxi. Peter agreed I should stay the night, he'll pick me up soon."

"Okay. What was the fight about?"

"Nothing." Her shoulders shook and she turned her face away.

"Amy... us against the world, remember? You can tell me."

"It's... it's stupid Jamie. Maybe I'm getting my period or something. He didn't do anything... and I just got really upset and left. But, he's not mad at me and... it's fine."

"That's just plain crazy, Amy. You never overreact. I'd know, I've known you since you were a fetus. Even in the uterus you were like 'birth, no prob, I have like ten contingency plans.'"

She breathed out a laugh. "That's not even funny."

"Then why are you laughing? Okay, you don't need to tell me what's going on but I want you to know that I know you're not overreacting to whatever it is."

She didn't say anything for almost a full minute while my gaze combed over her spotless room. Unlike the chaotic mess that my childhood bedroom still was, Amy's room had the exact same colorful, yet impeccably organized, scheme it always had. A series of color pencil still-life drawings were all framed in black along her wall. Each was exact in its shading and style.

"I was upset he didn't come with me to get my results from my pelvic exam." She inhaled, squeezing her eyes shut. "Something came up and he had to go."

"Why didn't you call me?"

A tear leaked out of her closed eyelids. "I did, but I already knew you were at work and even if you answered you couldn't get away last minute... same with Mom and no way was I calling Dad."

"Yeah, I'm sorry I didn't get your texts or see your missed call until just now."

"It's fine, Jamie."

"So, you went alone?"

She nodded. "It looks like I may have endometriosis."

"And that is?"

"Blocked fallopian tubes."

"Oh, so... they can fix that, right?" I squeezed her around her shoulders.

"They want to start me on hormone therapy, but that might take months and I would probably have to have surgery anyway."

"So what are you going to do?"

Her shoulders shook as almost silent sobs escaped her lips. "Peter says that maybe it was a blessing in disguise, that we might want to relocate in the next couple years and that we might want to put it off."

"I thought he was the one pushing the fertility testing?"

"He was... sort of. I think he changed his mind." Fat streams of tears coursed down her face, but she barely made a sound.

"Sweetheart." Turning, I hugged her and let her tears wet my shirt.

"I'm just a little extra emotional right now, I think." Her voice was barely audible trapped in my hug as she was.

"Hey, you're speaking to a freak-out specialist. This is nothing, okay?"

She sniffed, pulling away. Wiping the tears from her face with her manicured fingers, she said, "I'm fine."

"Of course you are, you're a badass bitch."

She breathed out a laugh while rolling her eyes. "So, enough about me, how was your date?"

"Awesome. Well, except for the part where Cameron got food poisoning and we fell asleep at eight o'clock."

"What?" Her eyes widened at me and she sounded a tad too amused at Cameron's pain.

I shrugged. "Bad fish for lunch, I guess. But, we had a nice morning. I guess it serves me right for trying to force my life into some set out schedule."

She glared, though it held little heat. "Was that about me?"

I held up my hands. "No, I promise, just about me and this silly soul detox thing." I glanced at the door, immediately having the fear that Cameron overheard me, which was completely ridiculous.

When I turned, Amy had relaxed just a little.

"I probably have to go. Do you want to come with me?"

She shook her head. "No, Peter's going to pick me up really soon. I'm free tomorrow if you and Sarah maybe want to catch a movie or something."

"I can't, tomorrow is the—"

"Ashes, sorry, I forgot." She glanced down at my wedding ring. Pointing, she said, "Wasn't that supposed to come off today?"

My gaze fastened on my ring. It was a small line of diamonds set in a gold band. The gold engagement ring had three diamonds that crisscrossed the wedding band.

Taking a deep breath, I pulled them up my finger. They had set so deeply in their groove, they resisted movement at first. There was a gliding pressure as the bands slid up to my first knuckle. When the bands refused to move any further, I stuck the whole finger in my mouth and pulled up gently with my teeth. The bands slipped over my knuckle with a sudden release of pressure. Moving my mouth away, I pulled the rings the rest of the way off with my fingers.

While setting them in my palm, I noticed the deep groove that remained on my ring finger. My eyes travelled back to my rings. "It feels weird."

"You want me to take them for you, for a little while? You know I'll keep them safe."

I laughed. "You think I'm going to relapse?"

"No, but it might make it easier."

I made a fist around the rings and reached forward, but paused. "Want me to wash them off for you first?"

She shook her head and held out a palm.

Taking a deep breath, I set the rings into her open hands.

A tear I didn't even realize I had shed fell onto my lower lip.

Amy nodded and tucked years of my life into her purse pocket, zipping it away.

I held up my hand to look at the divot in my finger. "It's like it's still there." Lowering my hand, I wiped away another tear. "I should get going before I try to take that back from you." Climbing off the bed, I turned back one more time. "Do you want to come tomorrow?"

She paused, her hand hovering from where she went to grab her computer back from her desk. "Do you want me there?"

"Only… only if you want to come."

"Of course I do. I'm sure Peter would love to come too, I'll just need to talk to him about it."

I nodded.

"I'll text you later after I talk to him about it. What time do you want us?"

"We were going to meet at nine at the Harrington's on Main."

"Okay, I'll get back to you as soon as possible about Peter."

"Thanks, Amy. I love you." Leaning forward, I gave another half hug before heading out of the room. "Oh, I owe Peter and his friend Carlos fruit baskets."

"I already sent Carlos your thank you card, I signed your name."

"Of course you did. Well, I plan to add mini-muffins or cookies or flowers."

"Not flowers."

"What's the matter with flowers?"

She laughed. "I love you, Jamie. I should get a little work done before Peter gets here."

And I was dismissed. On my way out, I stepped into my old room to grab Sarah's bag, but found that not only was the bag gone, the bed was made. I took one quick look around at the posters and photos haphazardly preserved in time, then headed back out. As I squeaked the old stairs with my descent, I wiped a couple more tears off my face before entering the living room.

Day Eight: Ten AM

My dad and Sharon walked us out to the car and gave us numerous goodbyes before we could leave.

"I'm sorry that took so long," I said as we backed out of the driveway.

"No problem, Jamie. I actually went upstairs to check on you and overheard you talking to Amy." He looked over with an apologetic expression. "I didn't listen, just grabbed Sarah's bag and headed back down."

I shrugged. "It's fine. I guess Peter and her got in a fight, but they seemed to have already made up. I just needed to check on her because Sharon seemed really worried—Sharon can get anxiety."

He shook his head. "Don't worry about it, babe, I have plenty of time to work in the shop. I'm not meeting Raphael until one, so I'm good."

I slowly turned to him. "Raphael... like, not the actor Raphael?"

Cameron nodded. "Yeah, him."

"He's your big client?"

"Yeah, he's a good guy, I like him."

I shook my head while rolling my head back and laughing all at once. "Cameron, I can't believe you didn't tell me about this. How are you not even the least bit excited?"

"I am." He shot me a grin. "You should see his cars."

"You are so crazy!" I threw an arm around the back of his seat and leaned in. "So, can I just happen by at your meeting with coffee, doughnuts and a thick autograph pad or something?"

Cameron chuckled. "I'll ask him for his autograph."

I bounced in my seat. "Thank you. But only if it's not weird, I don't want to jeopardize your work stuff."

"It's fine." He turned up his street. Reaching over, Cameron threaded his fingers through mine. He exhaled a 'huh' sound and lifted our joined hands up. His gaze fixed on my hand, then moved up to my eyes before he turned back to the road. "That's different."

I didn't respond.

After a second, Cameron dropped our joined hands back into my lap. He released me to shift, then grabbed my hand again. "Is Sarah still back there?"

When I looked over my shoulder, I found her passed out in her seat. "She's asleep."

"I could take your car." Cameron's finger worked back and forth over the divot in my ring finger as he talked.

"Would that be okay?"

"Doesn't matter to me." He shrugged. "I planned on getting a key made for you anyway, so I'll just take the spare to the hardware store so they can duplicate it then put it on your chain."

He pulled up to park next to my car, letting go of me.

"If you want to Cameron, but—just don't feel like you have to."

He gave me an exasperated look and leaned to set his forehead on mine. "You are commitment phobic. It's just a key Jamie, not a shackle."

"I'm not commitment phobic."

He gave me a quick kiss. "Baby, you are a classic case."

"Except for the fact I was with the same guy for twelve years."

"I'm not talking about that Jamie, I'm talking about you now." He kissed me again, quickly. "The same now-Jamie that I'm in love with."

I crossed my arms over my chest but couldn't make myself lean away. "Well, you snore sometimes, and you don't buy yourself groceries."

"Ha, you snore too."

"Liar! And you lie, because I don't snore."

Chuckling, he pulled away. "All right, now I really actually do have to go. Give me your keys."

After I did, he climbed out and I climbed over to take his place. I let him back out first, and then followed him down the hill. He shot me one last smirk as I pulled up next to him to turn inland.

Halfway there, Sarah announced, "I want juice."

"You're awake?" I looked into the rearview mirror where Sarah smiled out the window.

"We'll be at Aiden's in a second and I'm sure there's juice there, baby."

"But Mom, is there apple juice?"

"I don't know. We'll have to go see baby."

"Can I watch floor exercises at Aiden's house?"

"Nope, but you can play with Aiden and play on the trampoline."

Only Susan's new, but very dirty red car sat in the driveway as I pulled up. Sarah's seatbelt clicked just as I shifted into park. Her door swung open and blonde head shot past the window and up to Susan's house.

"Sarah!" I yelled as I threw open my door. "Sarah, you need to wait for me!"

She paid no mind, knocking on the door.

"Sarah, we don't just run off!" I rounded to her side of the car and crouched down by her open door. Switching up the child safety lock, I shut her door.

"Where's your mom, monkey?" I heard from behind me.

"Juice!" Spinning, I found Sarah pushing past Susan and into her house.

"I think she's after my juice." Susan gave me an amused look. "Good morning!"

I did an exaggerated face-palm. "Sorry, I forgot to put the child lock on Sarah's door."

"Is that Cameron's car?" She wiggled her eyebrows suggestively.

My eyes rolled as I walked up her driveway. "I'm living at his house, you dork."

"So, how was the date?"

"He got food poisoning."

Susan laughed loud and hard.

I poked her arm when I caught up to her. "You are so evil."

"What? That's classic, poor guy waits a decade to ask a girl out then barfs all over her on their first date."

"He didn't barf *on* me, and it was actually kind of nice in a weird way—for me at least, probably not for him."

As we stepped into her house, her mirth vanished, "So, I've been meaning to ask you…"

When she didn't continue, I turned to her, "Ask me what?"

Susan's fingers twined in the loose threads of the tapestry hanging on her wall. "I wrote something that I'd really like to say tomorrow."

"Of course, babe, you don't need to ask me."

"No, that's not it." She crossed her arms, and sighed. "My dad…"

I mirrored her, crossing my arms. "What about him?"

Susan ran a hand over her hair. "I know Jamie, but screw up that he is, he is Logan's dad. I think he should go with us."

I shook my head. "I planned on bringing Sarah."

Susan let out a heavy breath. "Jamie, he's changed a lot in the last couple months."

"I wanted this to be special, not some belligerent drunken scene."

"I swear he won't be drunk. If he is, I won't bring him, okay? I just—I eventually want him to be in Aiden and the baby's life. And, dad needs some closure. I don't see him getting healthy again without it. We all need closure, it never really happened."

Squeezing my eyes shut, I concentrated on breathing. "I don't want him to be in Sarah's life, not for a very long time."

"I know, Jamie, and that's up to you. But, I'm going to be brutally honest here, Logan wasn't just yours and his ashes aren't just yours. My dad needs this and I'll one hundred percent guarantee that he won't mess it up. You think I want him around Aiden when he's like that either?"

Closing my eyes, I whispered, "Shit, Susan."

Her big belly pressed into mine, her head coming to my shoulder.

"I didn't realize how much I wasn't ready to move on either when we made your stupid list. It hurts so bad, everything feels fresh. And I don't want my dad there, but I kind of need him there."

I swallowed, my arms going around her. "We should probably go check on our kids before they burn down your kitchen."

"I'm not going to push my luck and say who else needs to be there."

I let go of her, turning away. "I just don't want a scene. But, you're right, too, as much as I hate that you are. Logan's ashes don't really belong to me."

"So, I can invite them?"

"It doesn't mean that I'm going to talk to them, or play hostess or anything." I shook my head.

"That's fine, it won't be like that."

The refrigerator door hung open in the kitchen, exhaling cold mist lit by the fridge lights. I swung the door shut, turning to where I heard giggles. "Where's Beza?"

"She had to sub in for another wedding planner last minute."

We found the kids flipping on the trampoline, two juice-boxes at their feet skipping along the trampoline with its movement.

"Yo, baby, chuck those over to me!" Susan yelled.

"Hi Mom!" Aiden yelled.

"The juice boxes." She pointed.

Aiden grabbed one box and threw it out of the flap.

"The other one too."

"That one's Sarah's!" He shouted it with the type of indignation only an eight-year-old asked to pick up another kid's mess could muster.

"Sarah, throw out your box!"

Sarah did a perfect flip into the center of the trampoline, missing Aiden by inches.

"And watch out for each other. No collisions."

"Jesus." Susan lumbered halfway into the trampoline and grabbed the juice box. "Oh, gross, it's so sticky in there."

"We could just turn the hose on them," I suggested. "It's hot enough and I have Sarah's overnight bag here, she could wear yesterdays outfit while her stuff dries or something."

"I love the way you think." While Susan turned the hose on the kids, making them scream and run around trying to both catch and dodge the spray, Susan turned to me. "Oh, my god, I have something to tell you. So, yesterday when I crashed that PTA meeting, I walked in just as all these heinous women were ganging up on Beza because I guess she'd stood up for you when they were bad mouthing you, and then there was this moment of absolute beauty when they'd made the connection that I was both Beza's gay wife and another person from the video. The rest of the meeting was hilarious because they couldn't openly be rude to us. They're all so scared of not being politically correct."

"Tonight is going to be nuts. Oh, yeah, I forgot to tell you I'm coming."

"Yes! I wasn't going to go because Beza can't, but now there's no way I'm not going."

"Cameron is too, he wants to meet Patrick."

"Awkward. Why?"

"Jealousy, I think. He said something like, I want him to know who you're coming home to because you're such a flirt."

"That boy needs to cool his heels; you guys aren't even official yet."

"He wants to be."

"Well, duh." She rolled her eyes.

"He says I'm commitment phobic."

She gave me a skeptical look. "You kind of deserve to be. What does he think, that you're going to remarry the same year you were widowed by your lifelong best friend?"

The words hit me so hard, I had to take a step back. Tears started splashing down my cheeks again. Sitting down on a large garden pot, a flash of memory overtook my mind.

"I'm probably going to be the first groom ever to literally shit his pants after saying 'I do'!"

I could barely hear Logan's shout over the roar of the window whipping by the open airplane door. "And I definitely didn't imagine Bob here strapped to my back on our wedding day!"

"Just ignore me!" Bob yelled, doing his best to hide behind Logan's head.

"But, Jamie, I fucking love you! I've loved you for pretty much my whole life and I'm going to love you till the day I die!"

I glanced over at the officiator who crouched down holding onto a strap inside the airplane. He wore a yellow jump suit and a huge grin. "Your turn!"

I turned back to Logan. "I'd have to say I didn't expect to be strapped to a different guy on my wedding either!"

I felt Greg, the guy harnessed to my back laugh at that.

"And I still think we're crazy for doing this! But, I'm glad we're going to spend the rest of our lives being crazy together! I'll love you until the day I die, Logan, and then on until infinity."

The officiator yelled, "You may kiss the bride and jump out of the airplane!"

Leaning forward, we kissed.

"Brides first!" Logan shouted right after he pulled away, grinning like a maniac.

"You okay?" Susan asked, the hose sagging in her hand.

I wiped furiously at my face. "I don't know what's happening to me, Susan. It's like in the last couple of days memories are coming at me, sometimes they're so strong it feels like they're literally knocking me over."

She offered me a hand and I took it, but I didn't give her any of my weight as I stood.

"Hey Mom! Hey Mom! You can't get us!" Aiden shouted from the trampoline.

Susan turned the hose back on the kids. "I'm a firm believer that our brain protects us until we're ready to deal with stuff."

"Well, who decides that I'm ready? Because I'm pretty sure I'm really not."

Day Eight: Eleven forty-five

After playing the 'you can't get me' game and spraying the kids for a couple more minutes, Susan dropped the hose to her side. "I better turn this thing off or my neighbors are going to report me to the neighborhood committee or something."

"Really?"

"No, I'm just joking." She turned off the hose anyway, and went to sit on the bench. "Sorry you two, you can slide around up there or jump out."

They elected for the former, falling dramatically and giggling incessantly.

I took the seat beside Susan. "So, would you be happy or annoyed if I moved into the house across from you?"

"Are you kidding me?" She turned to me, shocked. "The place across the way?"

"I haven't even looked inside yet. It's just an idea."

"I have some money saved, not enough for a down payment, but maybe half."

I rested my head on her shoulder, laughing. "No way, you goof."

"I'm not even kidding at all, Jamie."

"I know... and I love you. But, I'm probably coming into a little money with selling the shop."

"Oh, yeah." Her arms crossed. "So you going to tell me about what's really going on with your place or what?"

Sitting up, I turned away.

"It's your neighbor, isn't it?"

I turned back to her sharply.

"I knew it! I just got this…" she gesticulated, "creepy, off feeling about him and then you reacted so strongly. And, then it's like you wouldn't go home."

I licked my lips. "I'm getting a restraining order."

"What? You let it get that bad without telling me?" She looked hurt.

Giving her a level look, I said in a low voice, "Come on, you know why I didn't tell you."

She threw up her hands. "You obviously told Cameron!"

"Only recently and when I absolutely had to. Cameron got, sort of involved…"

"He beat the crap out of the guy?"

"No, and he's not going to. I'm going to do this the police way, the law abiding way."

"That's got to be killing Cam."

"Maybe, but this guy is a total creep and he's really good at hiding it." It took me almost an hour to tell her the whole story from beginning to end. By the time I was finished, the kids looked like swamp monsters and Susan's eyes looked more flaming hot than the sun shining down from directly overhead.

"I'm going to kill that little creep." In her voice I heard that she was absolutely serious.

"Hence me not telling you." I rolled my eyes.

She got to her feet abruptly.

"Calm down, it's okay now; this can't be good for the baby."

"Shut up, Jamie." She walked into the house.

I let her go. Crossing to the trampoline, I peered through the net to where Aiden and Sarah looked to be making invisible snow angels.

"Are you guys playing in the snow?"

"No!" Aiden said like 'duh'. "We're in zero gravity, swimming through the Milky Way."

"Oops, my mistake."

"Come fly with us, Aunt Jamie!"

"Well, how could I refuse that?"

Doing a pull up on the trampoline, I climbed up and lay down between them. I laid my hands out to my sides over both of their heads.

"So where are we going?"

"Jupiter!" Aiden yelled.

"Purple planet!" Sarah yelled.

"To purple Jupiter we go!" I held up my hands like it was a steering wheel. "Ten, nine—"

"Aunt Jamie, we already did that. We're just floating through space now until we're caught in a tractor beam by the aliens and then we fight them."

I dropped my hands out. "Oops, my bad. I'm down with floating, but you'll have to teach me how to fight aliens."

"Don't worry, I will, it will be fine."

Tree branches swayed slowly above us, their leaves fluttering in hundreds of little dances. The sun angled just right to feed through a cluster of leaves, creating little moving shards of light. A few clouds reached into the sky, long, wispy shapes all in a hurry to be somewhere.

There was a big jostling movement and I looked over just in time to see Susan manage her way over the edge of the trampoline. "What are we doing?" She flopped down on Aiden's other side, her movements still a little jerky.

"Floating through space." Reaching over, I squeezed her shoulder.

She reached up, squeezed my hand once, then put her arm around Aiden. "We going to fight aliens?"

"Not yet, Mom. The aliens live on Jupiter."

"I think I see one." She reached up making a gun with her hand. "Pew, pew."

"Mom, they have supersized lasers, and turbo shields!"

"I brought us the new prototype mega shield, quick cover yourself up!" I motioned, throwing a sheet-type thing over our group and we all huddled under it while Aiden narrated the many projectiles that were coming at us.

It was a close thing, but in the end we prevailed over the alien horde. Susan, unfortunately had to be left behind in an alien prison on Neptune, but a rescue mission was in the works.

Lunch was eaten outside as the kids were a little wet and a lot dirty.

"We should probably clean them up before going tonight, what do you think?" Susan asked wryly.

"That is a good plan. I was actually hoping to change too, but I can't until Cameron gets home from work. Actually that should be around now. What time is it?"

"A little past two, but can't you just go there no matter what?"

"I could except for the... you know. Cameron made me promise I wouldn't be there without him."

"That's annoying."

"Yeah, tell me about it." I sighed. "I seriously need a better streak of luck right now."

She raised her eyebrows. "You need a piano dropped from a fifth floor window."

"And then boom! And then an anvil falls and there's a big lump on the duck's head like this high." Aiden held a hand about four inches from the top of his head.

"Oh, neat." I patted Aiden's shoulder then gave Susan a meaningful look. "Maybe we should talk about this some other time?" Stacking our empty plates, I hurried inside. After loading our plates in the dishwasher, I checked my phone since it was now permanently on silent.

Cameron had left both a voice message and a text message.

Cameron: I'm running a little late here, could I meet you at the benefit?

I texted back.

Me: Sure, no prob.

"Ugh." I stowed my phone in my purse and zipped it up with a bit too much force.

"What?"

I turned to see Susan dropping our cups in the sink.

"Cameron can't go back to the house. Looks like I'm showing up in sweats and Sarah's wearing yesterday's dirty clothes to the Principals and Principles benefit."

She held her hands out. "Or you could just wear anything I own and wash Sarah's clothes. We have three hours."

I looked at her, cringing. "I don't know."

"*Really*?" She popped out a hip. "I have way better clothes than you."

"Just not anything revealing, or anything with a swear word on it—or any leather."

"Do you have any idea how lame you sound? I wasn't going to dress you in club clothes."

"Or jeans I need to do anything special to get on or off."

She glared.

I gave in.

The rest of the afternoon was a slow progression of each of us showering after the other. When the kids were somewhat clean, Susan and I spent an unusual amount of time getting ready. We only checked on the kids periodically while they redecorated Aiden's room in drawings held up by numerous stickers.

Susan pulled the straightening iron through my hair as I applied make up.

"Darken your make up. Think tough," Susan said as she met my reflections gaze.

"It's pretty hard to look tough traveling with a pregnant lady."

"Sweetheart, I don't need to look tough, I am tough. You need to look scary so they back off before they even get the idea of making a scene or humiliating you."

I pulled the mascara stick from my eye. "I'm tough."

Her reflection almost rolled its eyes.

I turned a glare at her, jerking on my section of hair that was trapped in her straightening iron as I did. "I am tough. There's a big difference between being tough and being hard."

"Fine, I give you that one. I guess I mean you're not intimidating... whatsoever. People like Mindy and what's-her-face or like anyone ever don't even think twice about messing with you."

"Wow, that came off a lot like blaming the victim."

"Maybe you don't have to be the victim?"

"If I change who I am as a person? Thanks but I happen to like who I am."

"I didn't mean it like that, Jamie." She set the straightener down. "I happen to like you too, you're kind of like my best friend of twenty-something years, I'm just saying you should put on eye makeup. That's it, don't freak out on me."

"Fine." Just to appease her, I dusted a little on.

The jeans Susan picked out for me weren't obscenely tight, but came close to it, but she made up for it with a long loose draping shirt that almost, but not quite, covered my butt. At her insistence, I finished the outfit off with heels.

"Well, I'll at least be intimidating in my height." The moment I said it I overturned the thought. Whitney always, and I mean always, wore heels.

Susan looked at her phone. "You ready for this?"

Inhaling a shaky breath I said, "Not really... No, it'll be fine."

All too soon, the kids were in Susan's car and I was following her in Cameron's car to Coral Elementary.

When we had both parked next to each other in the lot, I remembered Cameron and checked my phone. There was only one message from him and it was recent.

Cameron: Almost done here, might be there near six. Probably going to head straight over from the shop.

Me: Cool, we just got here.

Climbing out of the car, I looked over its top to Susan. "Should I be pissed that Cameron is sort of flaking? Because I'm kind of relieved."

She shrugged. "Feel what you feel."

"I guess." Locking up his car, I walked around and grabbed Sarah's hand. As she held Aiden's and he Susan's, we looked pretty much like a human chain.

The Auditorium was transformed. The inside was made to resemble a fair, with small booths set up along the walls. Some booths were selling crafts or raffle tickets, while others gave out ice cream and other healthier snacks. Instead of vendor signs, above the booths the signs read things like 'respect', 'honesty', and 'diversity.' Strings of blue and red paper lanterns hung between them.

"Wow, this is amazing." I scanned the room. Between the booths, tables with red checkered table cloths and little bouquets led up to a small open dance floor. Several of the younger kids ran around the open area, loosely in line with a familiar pop song the DJ played from one side of the large stage at one end.

"I painted that sign with Bee yesterday." Susan pointed to a sign that read, 'Unity.' "Bee came up with a lot of the design stuff and painted most of the signs."

"I guess it really helps to have a wedding planner on the PTA."

"Yeah, she's not their leader or anything but everyone ran everything by her the whole meeting. It was pretty entertaining to watch."

"Too bad she got called away."

"Yeah, her boss loves doing that to her lately. Not very cool."

Sarah pulled at my hand. "I'm going to go dance now mom!"

"No gymnastics, baby, okay?"

"Can we have ice cream first? Aunt Jamie, can we go have ice cream first?"

"No ice cream!" Sarah pulled my hand, trying to escape to the dance floor.

"Aunt Jamie, please!"

"Aiden baby, that's something you'll have to convince Sarah of. I'll go get some ice cream with you if you want to go with me."

"No, I don't want to go with an adult!" He said 'adult' like he was saying, 'I don't want to go with a fart-machine'.

I shrugged. "Sorry, buddy." It wasn't like I would force my kid to go eat ice cream, especially since we hadn't had any dinner yet.

"Go dance, there will be plenty of ice cream." Susan nodded to the dance floor.

They walked off, Aiden obviously trying to convince Sarah, but I saw little hope in his cause. As much as Sarah liked ice-cream, convincing her to do anything she didn't want to do was something I rarely managed, even with eight years of on-floor experience.

"Ms. Scott?"

Both Susan and I turned, simultaneously saying "Yeah?"

"I'm sorry, we're both Ms. Scotts." I laughed, looking at the young, beautiful blonde with a high bun.

She stepped forward gracefully, her posture so straight it was as if a string attached her bun to the high ceiling. Her hand was sort of held out to both of us. "I meant both of you. I wanted to meet you both, I'm Charlize."

I took her hand, forcing a smile. "The dance teacher?"

Day Eight: Five-ten

It wasn't that big of a guess that Charlize was the now full-time dance teacher as she was wearing what looked like a leotard and a flowing dance skirt that wrapped around her tiny waist.

"Yes, that's me." She shook Susan's hand after mine. "I just came over to tell you that you both have very talented children."

"Thanks." Susan shot me a not so well disguised smirk.

Charlize didn't seem to notice and the aim of her smile bounced between us. "I've been meaning to talk to you, actually, just been so busy. We are working toward forming a competitive dance team for next year, and I believe that both Aiden and Sarah would really benefit from joining."

"Ah." I nodded while my gaze scanned the room. As I expected, the PTA mothers had all grouped together, and a couple of them were glancing our way.

Susan's voice pulled me back into the conversation, "Isn't that something that usually happens outside of a school?"

"Well, actually there are quite a few very good competitive dance teams within elementary schools across California. But sadly, yes, most teams are through private dance schools. This, in turn, limits the opportunity to those kids whose families can afford the high costs and time demands involved with having their child in a private dance program."

Nodding again, I said, "Thanks, but Sarah has gymnastics twice a week and she'll be competing in the Special Olympics next year."

"How nice for her. But, if it's all right for me to say, I think that dance would be a wonderful opportunity for Sarah. She's incredibly talented, but has very little interest in taking direction or following along with a team. Dance team could provide her lifelong team building and socialization skills."

As much as I hated it, she had a point.

Charlize turned to Susan. "Aiden also is very talented, but lacks self-confidence. He constantly second guesses himself and depends on humor to get him through uncomfortable social situations. He spends a lot of his time alone when he's not with Sarah or his friend Anthony. Dance team would give Aiden an opportunity to come out of his shell while at the same time strengthening his relationship with his peers. I believe his self-confidence would improve almost immediately."

"Hm." Susan nodded, seeming a little dumbstruck.

Charlize leaned forward, touching my arm. "Just keep it in mind. A couple of the dancers will be putting on a little performance later tonight and you can get an idea of what we do."

"Thanks," I said.

As Charlize walked away, Susan and I just gaped after her.

Susan blew out a loud breath and shook her head. "Holy shit, she almost convinced me. She. Is. Good."

"Sure is. But really, how many kids go to this school that couldn't afford private lessons?"

"Some, but who cares? You can't just screw over one group of kids to provide a special opportunity for another group."

"Yeah, I know."

"Looks like they're not going to just give up."

"I never really expected them too. Those ladies don't know how to not get their way."

"Hey Susie, Jamie!"

Susan visibly cringed as we turned around once more.

"Mindy, Whitney, how's it going?" They wore near-identical pant suits. Like usual, Whitney looked like she'd had her hair done up for prom, but unlike usual, Mindy matched her. Even though they looked almost nothing alike, there was a sameness to them.

Mindy smiled. "How funny, we all have names that end in an 'e' sound."

"Except for me," Susan said.

Whitney tilted her head, smiling beatifically at Susan. "Susan, we just wanted to come over and thank you for all the work you and Beza put into this event. You two are such contributors and givers to this school and this community."

"Yeah, that Unity sign does look really good." She smiled up at the Unity sign like, 'wow.'

A laugh bubbled up in my throat and I pushed the back of my palm onto my lips to force it back.

Whitney didn't miss a beat. "We'd love to thank Beza in person."

"Sorry ladies. Something came up at work; she's not going to make it."

Mindy shook her head. "That's too bad. She's the kind of person we love to see at these events."

Susan turned an almost combative look on Mindy. "What *kind of person* is that?"

Mindy took a small step back and straightened. "The involved kind."

"Ha, rude. Okay ladies, come out with it or move on." Closing my eyes, I turned my hand and literally covered my smile with it.

"I'm not sure what you mean." Whitney smiled. "But, like we said, it's wonderful to see you both here. Enjoy." She put an arm around Mindy and led her back to the other PTA parents.

"Oh, this is so much fun. We have to do this every weekend now you're not working Saturdays."

"It's definitely more fun with you." I laughed. "Mindy looked like she might pee her pants."

"It was way too fun screwing with her." She shrugged and gave me a wicked grin.

From the corner of my eye, I saw someone flip across the dance floor. "Shoot." I spun to see Sarah was indeed, lining up for another flip. Cupping my hands around my mouth, I shouted, "Sarah!" When she turned to look, I shook my head. "No flips."

Nervously, she started laughing and ran up to the nearest table, knocking a drink off of it. A group of people jumped away, one woman making a loud, 'ah!' sound.

"Crap," I mumbled, jogging over there. "Sorry! Sorry!" I picked Sarah up, who had begun to run off.

Wriggling in my arms and pushing at me, she laughed nervously.

"Sarah, stop."

She pushed at me harder, almost hitting.

"I got this Jamie." Susan called from behind me. When I turned, I found her laboriously getting down on the ground with a wad of napkins in her hand. "Aiden, go get me some napkins."

"Hi Jamie, you need any help?" I spun to find Patrick standing right next to me. In a quick look, I noticed that he wore a shirt that had #allkidscount on it.

Sarah smacked me again, not hard, and I managed to say. "I just need to take Sarah for a break, but Susan might need some help."

Turning, I fled the multipurpose room and walked out toward the front. As I walked, I notice that Patrick wasn't the only parent with that shirt. A couple parents wore the shirt, but more held one in their hand or under their arm.

Sarah's SDC teacher Ms. Ivy stepped up next to me. "Hey Jamie, do you want to take Sarah out to the play structure? I think it's fine if you guys go out, and it usually helps her reset."

"Thank you!"

She let me out the side door and followed along as we walked down the deserted hall toward the play structures in the field behind the school.

"I caught her doing something she wasn't supposed to do and sometimes that makes her freak out."

Ms. Ivy gave me a sympathetic smile. "Well, she's not alone in reacting that way, a lot of our kids do that."

"She really—" I cut off as Sarah pulled back in my arms and groaned into my face. "I'm sorry, baby." I sighed. "I know you don't like me talking about you to other people."

Ms. Ivy opened the back door of the hall, propping it open with a kick stand. "Be careful not to let this close until you come back in. But when you do come in, just be sure it is all the way closed."

"Sure, thank you so much." The moment I set Sarah down, she sprinted off toward the structure.

"And, Jamie?"

I looked back to see an apologetic smile on Ms. Ivy's face.

"Thank you so much for all you did with the video and speaking out. I know that couldn't have been easy at this school. You brought a lot of interest and awareness to what's going on here, a lot of parents came to talk to me and the other SDC staff expressing their support. And, in good news, it seems that the school is going to keep the second SDC classroom. So that's good." She paused, and I could feel the 'but' sentence coming. "However, unfortunately they're only opening it for a part-time position." She took a deep breath and blinked back the tears that were visibly forming in her eyes. "I wish I could survive on a part-time income..."

"I understand." I put a hand out to her arm but didn't quite touch her.

She nodded. "I wanted to tell you in person. I love these kids and if there was any way that I could manage it, I would." She wiped at her face. "But, there is success in that there will be two classrooms for at least part of the day, and at least for Sarah. She'll be in her regular day class in the afternoons anyway."

I nodded, biting my lip. "Thank you for telling me."

She sighed. "All right, I'll see you two inside soon."

Sitting down at a bench, I watched Sarah on the monkey-bars. She crossed once, then did the return journey skipping a bar. Repeat.

Maria's son Fernando ran past me, climbing straight up onto the playground.

Turning my head, I saw Maria walking up the hall.

Fernando went to the top of the slide, taking a seat but not going down.

"Sarah, your friend is here, do you want to go say hi?"

"Hi!" Sarah yelled, though she continued her monkey bar routine.

"Hey, Jamie." Maria came up and took a seat beside me. "Ms. Ivy said you were out here and I thought that Fernando could do with a break too. It's loud in there."

"Sure is." I turned to her.

She held up a t-shirt. "What do you think? I have a few set aside for you back in my car. I just set aside a range of sizes since you didn't tell me what you want. This one is for you, too"

"That's great." I took the shirt. Instead of black, this one was blue with the compound word perfectly centered on the chest.

I immediately pulled it on over my shirt. "How's the venture going?"

She barked a laugh. "We only have larges left. I should have brought more. It's my first time selling shirts and I just got the same amount of each size. They sold out so fast, didn't you see the line?"

"I saw a line. I didn't realize it was your booth."

"It happened right away. Even some of those awful ladies bought them, like it was trendy or something. I almost didn't want to sell it to them but I didn't want to make a scene." She shrugged.

I stared off at the two kids on the playground. "Did Ms. Ivy tell you about what's happening?"

"Yeah. Pisses me off."

"Kind of makes for a bittersweet victory, her still leaving." I sighed.

"Well, if we didn't do anything, they wouldn't have given this much, so I'm glad we did." She shrugged. "Felt good too."

"Yeah."

Standing, Maria said, "I should probably go check on my other kids. "Fernando!"

Little Fernando, who seemed to be either singing or talking to himself in the most adorable way while he still sat on top of the slide, didn't look over.

"Hi!" Kay ran past, running to join Sarah.

"Hi, Kay," I called though she was already on the monkey bars.

I paused before looking over my shoulder, knowing who approached.

Patrick gave a flat-handed wave and a closed-mouth smile. "Hi, Jamie, Maria."

"Hi, Patrick how are you?" She turned again to the play structure. "Fernando!"

"I'll be out here for another few minutes if you just want to run in and check, Maria."

"Oh, okay, thank you Jamie. I'll just be two minutes." She hurried off just in time for Patrick to take her seat on the bench beside me.

Day Eight: Six-fifteen

"Hey."

I grinned. "Hey there, rebel." I nodded to his shirt.

He looked adorable. The combed back blond hair and collar peeking out of the top of his t-shirt hinted that he had been dressed smartly before the t-shirt had very much altered his look.

"Hey there, rebel leader." He nodded back to mine, making me realize that I was probably as odd looking as he was. "So I hear congratulations are in order."

"Huh?"

"The judgment lien is being settled. You took the job and sold the shop?"

"Wow, yeah. I forgot for a second there, if you can believe it. So, I guess we're now kind of co-workers?"

"Definitely. Actually, it looks like I might even be placed at the Harrington's office on and off to do an internal audit. Which means, we'll probably work together directly for a month or so. I'm pretty sure I'm doing this evaluation for your benefit."

"Wow, an internal audit sounds intense."

"No, it's routine. Timepiece does it for all my father's companies about once a year. We just evaluate ways to optimize efficiency and improve organization. My father probably just wants to make sure you have all the tools you need for a smooth transition."

I grinned at him, though it was laced with suspicion. "Does Timepiece usually have their Senior Tax Manager do routine internal audits?"

Patrick's lips pinched before a smile crept up his cheeks. "Okay, you caught me."

I laughed. "So, what, you volunteered?"

"Traded for it. I thought you could use a friend at the company for a little while. I'm still full time at Timepiece, but I'll be in and out at all the Harrington's locations and as I said, I'll be able to help you transition."

I bumped into him with my shoulder. "Thank you. It makes me feel a lot better knowing you'll be around."

"Hey, I'm back!" Maria said, out of breath.

I turned to look at her. "Wow, that was fast." I gestured to Fernando. "He hasn't moved."

"Thanks for keeping an eye on him." She sat down on Patrick's other side.

I began to stand. "Well, I should probably head back into the festivities."

"You know, me too. I was just in and out but I should give those ladies a break from selling t-shirts."

Both Patrick and Maria stood just as Aiden ran past.

"Hi Aunt Jamie!" He didn't pause a second, just breezed past, heading to the monkey bars.

"Pretty soon the whole party is going to be out here." I turned, smiling, expecting to see Susan but instead found Cameron. "Oh, hey."

"Hey." A big, tired smile spread across his face. He didn't exactly stop beside me, more walked straight into me, his arm going around my shoulders. Kissing my forehead, he whispered, "Sorry I'm so late."

"No problem. Um, Patrick, Maria this is my—"

"Boyfriend," Cameron cut in, reaching a hand out to Patrick. "Cameron. Nice to meet you."

Patrick shook his hand. "Likewise." He took the slightest of steps back and I resisted the immediate urge to apologize to him with my eyes.

Cameron shook Maria's hand as well, saying, "Like the shirts."

"Thank you," Maria said.

"Yeah, Maria is the mastermind behind them. I guess she's almost sold out." I pulled mine forward so he could have a good look.

"Love it." To Maria, he said, "I'm guessing you only take cash."

"Yeah, but Jamie probably already got yours." She gestured to me.

I hadn't. When I'd been calculating who'd be getting the shirts I had been thinking of the people who'd been involved in the video. But I patted Cameron on the arm. "Yeah, I got you covered. We were about to head in, I wanted to check in with Susan."

"Sounds good to me." When the others had moved off, Cameron leaned in. "I actually need to talk to you about something."

"Well, it'll have to wait until after I clean all the pee off my shoes."

He looked down at my heels. "What pee?"

"From you pissing a circle around me." I raised my eyebrows.

He rolled his eyes but the slightest of smiles played on his lips. "That wasn't what I did."

I sighed, but I couldn't help a small smile in response. "Okay, I'm going to go get Sarah. Hopefully this will all go better with round two."

It took me a few minutes to coax Sarah and Aiden off the playground, and when I did the words 'ice cream' were definitely involved. Turning back, I was surprised to find Maria and Fernando had already left and Cameron was talking to Patrick. Nix that, Cameron was laughing with Patrick.

Patrick pointed into Cameron's face. "Freshman year Cantor Stadium. I knew you looked familiar. You guys killed us... not that I played that game."

"That was a good game, I remember your team mates invited us back to party at some frat house."

"Mine, actually, yeah I remember that too. Small world."

"Smaller town."

Patrick laughed. "Yeah, definitely is."

Kay pulled on Patrick's hand. "Dad... are we going or not?"

"Yeah, Kay bay, we'll go." He began to walk forward but turned to Cameron as he did and Cameron fell into step beside him. "So you still play ball? Weren't you kind of a big deal back then?"

I followed them, a few steps behind with Sarah and Aiden each holding a hand.

"Nah." He rubbed a hand over the back of his head. "Not any more. I own a custom body shop in town."

"Nice, actually I think Jamie mentioned that."

I hadn't. He was probably thinking of the time Whitney accused Cameron of being a mechanic in front of Patrick. It did make it sound like I was telling Patrick about Cameron though, which couldn't hurt.

Patrick leaned a little toward Cameron. "Do you work on older model Ferraris?"

"I definitely do."

"I'm talking pretty old."

"That's not a problem."

When we got back to the party, Aiden and Sarah immediately jerked away from me running toward the ice cream booth. "Walk, guys!" I called to little selectively-deaf ears.

I looked between where Cameron and Patrick had stopped, still locked in conversation to where the kids were narrowly missing people. I followed the kids.

When I caught up, they were already reaching for bowls of ice cream.

"You're welcome to take one too," the woman behind the counter said, giving me a smile and pointing to one of the bowls that had been set out.

"Thank you." Grabbing one, I followed the kids who had already found Susan sitting alone at a table in front of two empty bowls of ice cream.

"Hey," I said, lifting my spoon.

She waved, elevating her bare feet on an empty plastic chair. As the kids silently took the seats around her, she glanced up at me. "I hope it's cool I had Aiden lead Cam back, I needed to get off my feet or die." She lifted a swollen foot slightly.

"It's fine." I took the seat across from her. After checking over my shoulder that Cameron wasn't in hearing distance, I leaned forward. "He totally introduced himself to Patrick as my boyfriend."

Susan guffawed. "Subtle."

"Yeah, but now they're best friends. Look." I nodded back.

She leaned way too obviously to peer around me. "He's getting Cameron's number?"

"Something about cars."

"Figures." She gave me an apologetic look. "They're going to be best friends."

I rolled my eyes. "Of course they are. It's my lot in life."

"Could be worse, they could be crashing into the raffle booth, fists flying."

I stuffed a big bite of chocolate ice cream into my mouth and shrugged in agreement.

"How much longer are you going to be staying here? I'm pretty over this."

I looked back at the guys, then to Susan. "Hopefully not too much longer."

"Good evening, everyone!"

Susan and I turned to look at the stage.

Whitney smiled down, her hair and outfit still as impeccable as her makeup. "Hello. For those of you who don't know me, my name is Whitney Cooper. I am the president of the parent teacher alliance here at Coral Elementary. On behalf of the PTA, we'd like to thank you all for coming. Can we have a round of applause for everyone who contributed tonight?"

As everyone clapped, Sarah's hands flew over her ears.

I ran a hand over her arm and whispered, "It's okay, baby."

"Also, there's still a few minutes to buy raffle tickets everyone, the prizes were donated from local businesses—one of them being a gift certificate to Cordon Blue for a hundred dollars, so don't miss out." She smiled around at us. "All right, enough from me. I have the pleasure to introduce a group of students who have been working really hard along with our wonderful dance teacher, Ms. Charlize, who has been with us for a while now." She emphasized the last words clearly. Whitney held up her hands again, obviously signaling for us to clap.

I covered Sarah's ears as everyone around us clapped politely.

A group of perhaps ten girls and two boys ran on the stage. They wore normal street clothes, but they were all matching. I recognized Whitney's daughter in the crowd, beside her stood Kay.

"Ha, it's all the richest kids," Susan muttered.

A popular pop song came on and the group all struck a pose. Synchronized, they did a hip-hop/pop mash-up of dancing. Kay was good, at one point cart-wheeling along with another girl across the stage.

I put a hand on Sarah's shoulder, afraid that she'd try to join the group, but she just ate her vanilla ice cream placidly.

When the kids had struck their final pose, the whole room erupted in applause.

Grinning ear to ear, Charlize took the stage and crossed to the DJ booth to grab the microphone. I noticed that she'd changed her outfit somehow but not until she turned around did I notice she wore an 'all kids count' shirt over her leotard.

"That woman has some... testicles," Susan whispered from beside me.

"Hello," Charlize called, smiling around at the room. "It's so good to see these kids' hard work paying off. I've worked at this school for some time now and it's so wonderful to be at a place where all kids do count. We have a great group of kids, kids whose parents have already taught them the value of unity, diversity, honesty, kindness and understanding." She gestured to the different booths around the room as she spoke. "In this spirit, I would like to announce that Coral Elementary is forming a new open competitive team. We'll be holding informal practices for the rest of this year, but the team will start up in earnest at the start of next year. Anyone is welcome, no try outs are needed." She paused smiling, and after a polite applause, continued, "All right, thank you again and here is our principal."

As the principal took the stage, Susan leaned toward me. "That is such bullshit. She just totally tried to spin our message for her stupid dance team."

"Don't do anything Susan. The people who count, know."

"No, they don't."

"Please. Just don't, Susan."

She sat back, obviously unhappy about doing so.

The principal was already well into a speech about the school, its programs and what we were raising money for. At the end of her speech, she picked the raffle winners, most of which went to parents I didn't know. The principal held up a piece of paper. "Here we have a gift certificate to Cordon Blue for a hundred dollars, and it goes to..." She picked a name from the jar and read, "Susan Scott."

"Yes!" Susan managed off her chair, sticking her feet back into her shoes before she climbed up to the stage. "Thank you." She grinned wide as the woman handed her the certificate. "Yeah, wicked." When she'd managed back to the table, she held up the paper by her face.

Pulling out my phone I took a picture.

"Text that to Bee," she directed but I was already doing it. "All right Jamie, now that I got my winnings, we're out of here." To Aiden she said, "Hey baby, toss your bowl it's time to go home."

"No, mom, they haven't even started the dancing yet!"

"Tough."

I touched Sarah's head. "Us, too baby, we need to go get dinner."

Sarah didn't resist at all, just stood up and followed me.

We said our goodbyes to Aiden and Susan who planned to slip out, then Sarah and I made our way over to Cameron. He hadn't moved, still locked in conversation with Patrick. He had his hands up, gesticulating something. It was love, I could plainly see the bromance in their smiles.

"Hey guys," I said as we stepped up. When they both turned to me, startled from their conversation, I smiled. "So, I need to go get some dinner into Sarah and me, we're probably going to head out."

"Oh, yeah of course," Cameron took a step toward me.

"You don't have to go, Cameron, we could easily just go to a restaurant."

He shook his head and placed a hand at my back. "Nah, I'm going with you." Offering his hand, Cameron said, "Nice to meet you, man."

Patrick shook it. "Yeah, definitely. What are you guys doing tomorrow? You up for another Sunday barbeque?" This he asked me.

"Sunday barbeque?" Cameron asked, also looking at me.

"We—uh, Patrick had one last Sunday... with a lot of people. It was really fun." I cleared my throat, hoping to somehow dislodge the squirming feeling I had stuck in there. To Patrick, I said, "But, I can't tomorrow, sorry."

He gave me a small smile. "Maybe another Sunday, then."

I began to turn away. "Sounds like fun. See you later—"

"Hey, if you're free next weekend, we'd love to have you and your daughter over to our house for a barbeque." Cameron swung an arm over my shoulders. "Right, babe?"

I swallowed hard and faked a smile. "Sure."

"Sounds great," Patrick said, his gaze going between us.

Cameron smiled. "And, bring that car in anytime after Wednesday, man."

"I plan to." Patrick nodded. "See you at work Monday, Jamie."

"Yeah, see you." I turned in Cameron's arm and started for the door, my arm around Sarah.

On the way through the parking lot with Cameron and Sarah, I remembered to ask him, "Didn't you have something you wanted to tell me?"

"Yeah." Leaning over, he kissed me on the forehead and whispered, "You look beautiful."

"Thank you." I smiled.

Cameron paused by his car and pointed over his shoulders. "I parked your car a few cars back."

"Mind if we switch back? I kind of want to drive an automatic right now."

Cameron paused. "Sure. You want me to take Sarah?"

"Or we could switch her booster over, either way."

He shrugged. "I don't mind."

After we switched keys, I loaded Sarah up and headed to my car. I beeped the car unlocked and reached for the handle, but paused. For some reason, my car looked off. I moved to see it from different angles, but the more I looked, the more I decided I was imagining it.

Inside the car, Cameron had not only vacuumed and wiped down everything, he'd sprayed what smelled like a whole can of air freshener which

made me all kinds of paranoid about the car's
previous state.

Day Nine

Dust to Dust

Day Nine: Six-thirty

I woke with Sarah curled into me, her arm thrown over my head. Cameron's stronger arm wrapped around my waist. They're breathing was an even overlapping tempo, her high note then his low note.

Moving her arm from over my head, I tucked it into her side and pulled the blankets over her.

I rotated extremely slowly, hoping not to jostle either of them. There was almost no light in the room, meaning it was likely before sunrise. I was completely awake though, and no part of me wanted to be otherwise.

Today felt nothing like the day of Logan's actual funeral, but I couldn't help thinking about it. Strangely enough, my mother and Sharon had been the ones to arrange all the details of the funeral together. Neither I nor Susan had been in the mindset to arrange anything and my father was on twenty-four-seven Jamie and Sarah watch.

Sarah hadn't spoken in days, and all I could do as a mother was turn on the television, lie with her on the couch and once in a while grab her a yogurt. If my father hadn't made sure we both ate three square meals, I'm not sure we would have gotten through that first week. Both Sarah and I wore black dresses to the reception. Where they had come from was anyone's guess.

The house had been full of familiar faces, words had been exchanged, but as soon as they'd come out of lips, they'd been lost to my memory.

The moment that Logan's father had shown up the feeling in the reception had changed. He'd roamed around, drunkenly staggering through the house in a sort of trance.

I remember when I first met Logan's father, Mark, when he was in his early thirties, I'd thought he looked like a movie star with his golden hair and bright blue eyes. Logan had looked very similar to Mark around thirty. But, Mark had long since had any resemblance to his beautiful children.

As Mark entered the living room, I'd hugged Sarah tighter to me where we sat in the recliner.

I'd let go of Sarah very little in the last few days. She'd returned to nonverbal methods of communication and having bathroom accidents. Even though my mother had called it unhealthy, for these and other reasons, I didn't want Sarah to be away from me for a single minute.

Mark stood above me. I wasn't sure if he was swaying or my vision was messed up, but it was hard to focus on him.

I glared up, wishing that my gaze was a battering ram that could knock him over. He was a mess of worn down features. His hair stood out around his face, dripping wet.

"Go away. You're drunk," I said in greeting.

"I wanted to see... I want to see you and my granddaughter."

"Then you should have come sober." I looked away, rocking slightly in the recliner. Sarah blinked up, her gaze unwavering on his unsteady face.

As if the sadness crashed over him, Mark started sobbing beside us, a mess of tears in a room of stark dry grief. In that moment, I absolutely despised him. I hated him more than I'd ever hated anyone.

Sarah shocked me by uncurling from my arms. I thought about resisting as she climbed off my lap, but as she might have to go to the bathroom without having the words to tell me, I let her go.

Instead of walking toward the bathroom though, Sarah walked straight up to Mark and hugged him.

Climbing off the chair, I stood, then froze, staring at where Sarah held her sobbing grandfather. Others around the living room also watched on.

Mark lifted Sarah up, holding her as they hugged. Sarah patted his back. "It's going to be okay, it's going to be okay," she said the words I had been repeating incessantly to her. The first words I had heard her say in days.

Walking over, I reached up and took Sarah from his arms. "I don't want you to drop her."

He nodded, tears soaking his face. "I'll go."

"Thank you."

"Hey, Mark, I'll drive you." Beza had stepped up, her face stained with tears. She held out a hand and when he took it, they walked off together.

I rolled toward her on the bed, wrapping an arm around her.

For the millionth time, it occurred to me that maybe I shouldn't bring her today. We'd talked so little about what happened. I knew that she had in most ways processed the fact that Logan was gone, that he wasn't going to come back and that everyone was sad about it. Did she need to be drowning in everyone's grief again? Would it throw her into another non-verbal spell?

Sarah had gone to a therapist for six months, something my father had paid for as Sarah's insurance didn't fully cover it and there was no way that I could afford it.

I probably shouldn't have ended the appointments. But six months in, she'd seemed so much better day to day and had come from the sessions stressed out and prone to meltdowns over any small thing.

She might not be ready for this.

I wasn't ready.

For some reason, I'd decided to shed my tether of the coffee shop and the armor of my wedding ring and come to this day unstable and unprotected.

The room slowly lightened, the ceiling beams taking form above me. My bladder was full to the point of hurting, but I wasn't ready to move and chance waking the sleepers.

When I finally couldn't handle it anymore, I slowly maneuvered out of their limbs and scooted to the end of the bed. My feet ever so gently connected with the floor.

"Mom!" Sarah sat up abruptly, blonde hair sticking out in every direction. Seeing me, she said, "Mom, go to bed Mom."

I hushed her. "Cameron's sleeping baby. I have to go to the bathroom—"

"Go to bed, Mom."

I hushed her again.

"It's okay, I'm awake." Cameron said, his voice came out all jumbled and his eyes had not opened.

Sarah crawled across the bed and grabbed my arm. "Don't go to the bathroom."

I laughed a little out of exasperation as I said, "No, baby, I have to go pee." As she didn't seem to be letting go, I picked Sarah up and carried her to the bathroom, setting her down in front of the toilet. "You go first, and then you have to let me go."

Sarah took way too long. My bladder had nearly solidified in my abdomen when she'd finally come out. "Thank god." Rushing past her, I gently guided her out when she looked like she might stay.

When I came out of the bathroom, Sarah was jumping on Cameron's bed. And Cameron was still sleeping on it and bouncing.

"Sarah, no."

"Sarah, yes!" She smiled.

I rushed over, but when I got close, I heard the unmistakable sound of Cameron laughing. "How does she wake up with this much energy?" his voice was croaky.

"I'm pretty sure she bounced out of my womb." I lifted my hands out to her. "Come on goof ball, let's let poor Cameron sleep."

"Nah," he rolled and reached out to grab his phone from the side table. "We have to be there at nine right? I should probably get up."

"All right." I nodded.

Taking Sarah into her room—or, well, Cameron's guest room—I began searching through her stuff to see if I could find her black slacks. When I'd found an entirely black outfit, I held it out to her. "Hey, baby, how about you wear this today?"

"No, I'm going to get ready for gymnastics, Mom."

"Um, baby, we're going to do that special thing I told you about last night, before gymnastics. We're going to go talk about Daddy." I held out the black clothes.

She walked to her drawer with her gymnastics stuff in it. "No, I'm going to get ready for gymnastics then go talk about Daddy."

My hand dropped to my side. "Okay. Make sure you put sweats on over your leotard." Setting the black clothes on her bed, I walked out of the room, closing the door behind me.

When I entered Cameron's room, he was buttoning up his shirt. Taking a seat on the edge of the bed, I met his gaze. "I'm not sure I can do this."

He didn't respond, only kept my gaze. After our silence had lasted past all his buttons, he said, "You don't have to."

"Everyone is coming."

"They've waited a year, they can wait longer."

I nodded. "Sarah wants to wear her gymnastics clothes... and I don't really want to wear black."

"Then don't." He lifted my suitcase from where it still sat, propped against his wall. Setting it on the bed, he said, "Wear something you like. You know I cleared the top four drawers in my dresser for you."

"I know. I just haven't gotten a chance to unpack my stuff."

"Want me to do it?" He raised his brows.

"I'll do it later." Turning, I unzipped my bag and dug through the remaining clean contents. Each thing I pulled out didn't feel right until I pulled out a Licks Tour t-shirt. It was black, but had a big red mouth with its tongue sticking out. Even though it had been bought to fit my teenage self, I'd kept it all these years as a keepsake. After this past year of not taking very good care of myself, I thought that there was a possibility that it fit again.

Choosing my cleanest most respectable pair of shorts, I headed for the bathroom.

"You're really going to change in the bathroom?" Cameron chuckled.

"Really, really."

The shirt was tight in places it once hadn't been, but it still fit. Looking in the mirror I could almost picture waiting in line with Susan and Logan for the matching concert t-shirts. We'd barely had the money to buy them between us; the man at the souvenir counter had even spotted us a dime or a quarter or something.

Wearing it today felt silly and right at the same time.

The upstairs was empty when I exited the bathroom. The scent of eggs and cheese wafted up as I walked down the stairs. Sarah was already at the table, gymnastics uniform on and hair still sticking out in every direction. A bowl of cereal sat in front of her, a banana peel beside it, a change, for once.

"They think we're grabbing breakfast there but... thanks, this will be better anyhow."

"No problem. Like the shirt," Cameron said, grinning. He used a spatula to shovel eggs onto two plates. Thankfully, they were scrambled, another change.

"It's my armor, I guess we're going non-traditional." Crossing to the fridge, I pulled out a loaf of bread and opened the plastic to set two slices in the toaster.

Cameron came and stood close to me as I waited for the bread to toast, he lowered his voice and leaned in, "Logan would have hated to see you guys all done up in black anyway. He always told me that when he died he wanted us all to get wasted and talk about all the stupid things he did."

I breathed out a laugh. "We'd be there all day if we did that, not to mention the wasted part. Though, unfortunately, Mark might be."

Cameron shook his head. "Susan won't let that happen."

"We'll see."

After a quick breakfast, we only had time to load up in Cameron's car and head down to town to meet everyone. I sat in the passenger seat, holding Logan's heavy urn in my lap.

The feeling in the car was heavy and tense as we drove out of the driveway in silence.

"Do you mind?" I asked Cameron as I pushed in Sarah's kids CD which I had transferred over from my car.

"*Oh, Buffalo Gals will ye come out tonight, come out tonight, come out tonight.*

He looked over a little wryly.

"You better get used to the tunes if you want to ride with us," I teased.

"I guess it could be worse."

"What?" I asked, indignantly. "This is a classic, my mom used to sing this to me."

After a moment's pause, he said, "So would it be possible for me to drop you two off at Sarah's gymnastics then come back to pick you up at three?"

"Yeah, of course, but you know, you're welcome to hang with me while Sarah's in gymnastics."

"I would, but unfortunately I have to meet a client at one-thirty."

"Oh, yeah, sure. Someone new?"

"No, uh... Raphael." He stared determinedly at the road.

"Isn't he a bit of a demanding client, like Saturday and Sunday?" I watched his expression, because for some really weird reason, it felt like Cameron was hiding something.

"No, we actually had to cancel yesterday. Something came up." He paused. "Something work related." Glancing over, he gave me a quick, reassuring smile.

"Oh, okay." I hugged the urn and decided to let it drop. Who was I to begrudge Cameron his secrets? And, I trusted him above almost anyone. I didn't need to know every detail of his life to know that.

As we drove into the Harrington's parking lot, a crowd of over twenty familiar people gathered between cars. Chris was there with Shana and Melissa. Melissa and Shana were both petite next to Chris, I'd even say that Shana had diminished to smaller than petite in the months since I had seen her last.

Near Chris, my entire family stood. Even my mother stood in the crowd beside Susan. My father talked animatedly to Beza and Aiden. Very few people had actually elected to wear black, though Mark, who also stood beside Susan, did.

As we parked in a stall, another car pulled next to ours, also part of our group, Logan's buddy Mike and his pregnant wife. As Kimmy climbed out of the car beside us, her big pregnant belly came into view.

"Wow, she's so big," I whispered.

"You haven't seen them?" Cameron asked.

"No, not since the funeral. I actually haven't seen a lot of these people since the funeral."

Cameron made no move to get out, probably sensing my reluctance.

Behind us, Sarah's seatbelt clicked and I heard her pulling at the handle of her door. She huffed. "I need to go, Mom."

I took a steadying breath. "Okay, angel." Climbing out, I set the urn back in the seat, buckling it in before I let Sarah out.

When she made to run off, I blocked her path. "Wait for me and Cameron."

Cameron came to stand beside the car and I realized, though probably everyone already suspected that Cameron and I were together, we were coming in with a big sign on my forehead proclaiming it. So much for not being official, it seemed that train had departed whether I was on it or not.

Taking Sarah's hand in mine, we walked between the cars and into view of the group. No one really looked over at us until we stepped up beside them.

"Hey, kiddo!" My dad said, first to notice us and immediately taking me into his arms.

"I don't believe it!" Susan yelled way too loud from beside me.

When I pulled away from my dad to look at Susan, she wildly pointed between me and Beza. "She wore it for me because it doesn't fit right now."

When I looked, I saw that Beza wore a matching Licks Tour shirt. She reached out and gave me a hug, smiling and saying, "We're twins."

I couldn't help but grin. "We must have had some sort of brain connection this morning."

Everyone else insisted on hugging me, even Mark and my mother, which was way less weird than it should have been. I went to stand by Cameron again, who was just finished greeting everyone also.

"Can Sarah go in our car Aunt Jamie?" Aiden asked.

"We have her seat," Beza volunteered.

"Sure, okay."

"All right then." Susan looked around us. "Looks like we're all here. Everyone ready to go?"

A few people mentioned that they planned to go in to get coffee, but Amy yelled over them, "Everyone, coffee and pastries are on us." She gestured to Peter, my dad and Sharon. "We pre-ordered three to-go carafes of coffee and cups as well as pastries. We'll be bringing them all to the site. We also brought a couple tables for our belongings. If anyone wants to help carry it all from the car it will be appreciated."

Susan clapped and called out, "All right, we're going to caravan but just in case, anyone need directions?"

Everyone said they had it and drifted off to their respective cars.

I hung back to give Amy a hug. "Thank you, guys. I didn't expect you to go so above and beyond, but it helps to just be a passenger in all of this."

"Of course, it's no problem." Amy pulled back and sighed. "I completely don't agree with the fact that Susan invited Vanessa. I know that you guys talked about it, but you are completely within your rights to change your mind about her coming."

"What?" I looked around, I definitely hadn't seen Vanessa. "We talked about Mark coming, but nothing about Vanessa."

"Mom saw her in her car. She didn't get out of her car, but Susan said she might go to the site. Obviously, Susan completely overstepped."

"I noticed she also invited my mom." I gave Amy a meaningful look.

"That's different." The look she gave me said, 'and you know it.'

Exhaling heavily, I said, "I've already decided to just deal today—so that's what I'm going to do."

"Well, if you change your mind I have no problem asking her to leave for you."

I hugged her. "I guess we should go join this caravan, everyone is waiting on us."

They were, literally.

There were maybe fifteen cars in our caravan, Susan leading the group and my father, then us behind him. I glanced back a couple times to wave at Amy, who sat in the passenger seat as Peter drove.

"They seem better," Cameron commented as I turned back around.

I shrugged. "They always seem good when they're out in public."

"You don't like Peter?" Cameron asked.

"It's not that I don't like him..." I trailed off, because I was pretty much lying. "Amy really loves him. She's just got this idea in her head that somehow he's better than her when it's so the opposite."

He glanced into the rearview mirror. "I'd have to agree with you there."

Reaching over to touch his arm, I said, "I love you."

Giving me a smile, he took my hand and we took the turn down to the beach I'd only visited once before.

There wasn't really a parking lot at the state beach, though there were a few cars along the road. We all parked wherever we could find room. After Cameron parked, I sat in the car, clutching Cameron's hand and Logan's urn, watching as friends and family climbed out of their cars and greeted each other again.

Above us, the cloud layer stubbornly clung. I was grateful to those obstinate clouds because very few people were on this out-of the way beach. There were a few walkers, a few joggers, but no blankets were laid out, no tents pitched.

A few cars up, my father opened his back door and several people started unloading tables and cardboard coffee carafes, as well as large bakery boxes. There were also several clear boxes filled with flowers that my mother and Mike unloaded.

My gaze forward, I whispered, "You probably want to get out there..."

"The only people I'm here for are you, Sarah, and Logan."

Nodding, I stayed put.

When everyone was either on the beach or heading that way, I unbuckled my seatbelt.

Cameron squeezed my hand. "You ready?"

I shook my head and sighed. "No, but I'm going to do this any way."

Day Nine: Nine-twenty

Even though Cameron offered to carry the heavy urn, I knew it had to be me. As we approached, the group set up while chatting to each other a little ways up from the shore line. When I scanned the faces of the crowd, I didn't see Vanessa's among them. Most of the people there looked happy, or at least happy to see each other.

A few chairs had been set out, one that Shana was sitting in and another that Kimmy sat in beside her. Sarah sort of squeezed between them, her arms fastened around Shana who patted her hair with a blissful smile on her face. They'd also set up a couple tables, one for shoes, purses and those boxes of flowers, another for the food and coffee, and a third, empty table. Susan stood waiting by that third table.

When I stopped beside it, Susan said, "Mike used a level and made sure it was flat. It should be good."

"Okay," I mumbled. Careful not to jostle the table, I set the urn down. It took all my effort to step back, leaving it there alone.

As if she knew how hard it was for me to do, Susan swung an arm around me. "We're halfway there."

I nodded, not wanting to negate her statement but unable to respond with some other comforting cliché.

She didn't release me as she turned to the crowd. "Okay, guys." When she had everyone's attention, she called out, "I was thinking we'd form a sort of circle and talk for a little while."

The group spread out, forming a circle out from where Shana and Kimmy sat. Someone brought the free chair to Susan, who refused it, so the kids shared it beside Shana.

When we were all assembled, everyone stood in silence for almost a minute, waiting for someone to speak.

Susan, who'd been standing, eyes closed, opened her eyes. Her lashes were wet with tears that had already streamed down her face and off her nose. She didn't wipe them away, likely because she still held onto me on one side and Beza on the other. She cleared her throat.

"So, a few of you were here a year and a half ago when Logan and I walked into the ocean right here and spread my mother's ashes." She paused. "I'm going to be honest, if anyone told me that day that in a couple months I was going to lose Logan, or that a year and a half later I'd be here again, walking back into the ocean to spread his ashes, I would have punched them in the face."

She paused but no one made a sound.

Blowing out a breath, Susan continued, "A little over a week ago, when Jamie and I decided that it was finally time to do this, I was ready for it. I even pushed Jamie along, saying that it was time that she let go. But, I realize how stupid..." her voice broke, "How stupid I was being. Letting go of Logan is letting go of a part of my soul. My mom always told us she could feel us holding each other in her womb. I always

thought she was being sappy because we were
fraternal...obviously," she half laughed, half cried.
"But even after he was gone, even now, I felt him still
holding me." Letting go of me, she wiped her face, and
then replaced her hand around me.

"Mom!" Aiden climbed off the chair, running
across the circle he ran into Susan, hugging her across
her middle.

Susan ran a hand over his braids. "It's okay,
baby." She blew out a breath. "Okay, so, I'm going to
dry my tears and give you the eulogy that Logan and I
planned out and pinky-swore we'd give at each other's
funeral if one of us died first. I didn't have it in me to
say it the first time around but... I think I'm ready
now." Closing her eyes, she said, "Here lies Logan
Scott, defender of the weak, avenger of the wronged,
knight of the realm Scottotia. He fell while defeating
the mighty Yeti, Norgobogogo... or something like
that, as it ravaged the countryside and ate people. His
gruesome demise will be mourned by everyone in the
whole world—especially the girls." She blew out a
laugh, joining a few other people who were chuckling.
"So raise your glass..." she held up her hand, "Mine's
imaginary, and let's toast to the brave, honest, funny,
really, really good-looking guy who died at the hands
of his worthy foe."

Those who had coffees, raised them, the rest of
us just pretended.

"Skull!" Susan called out, and we all echoed
her.

After several people took a drink, and the circle
fell silent again, gazes all drifted to me. Some

expressions were concerned while others looked more apprehensive.

Sarah climbed off her chair, crossing over to me as Aiden had for Susan. She took a spot between Cameron and me, placing her hand on our joined hands.

I took a deep breath in, blowing it out slowly as I steadied myself. "I don't really have anything planned to say but, I think I might start by acknowledging the elephant that's here with us. Or, I guess, the elephant I feel is here with me, I don't know about you guys. Um, Logan passed in a way that really messed me up for a while."

Across the circle, Shana nodded in sympathy.

"I didn't say anything at his funeral, I didn't talk about it with anyone, really… but it was all that I could think about for a long time. When I thought of Logan, that's what I thought about, just that one moment and the couple of months that led up to that moment and that was it." I paused. "I wasn't getting over it, I didn't get over it at all. And when Susan and I decided last week that we were going to do this, I really didn't imagine how I could possibly go through with it. Because, for some reason, I needed his ashes, they got me through the day."

Cameron squeezed my hand while Sarah buried her face in my stomach.

"This whole year, I was so fixated on how Logan passed that I forgot I also lost my lifelong best friend. I forgot I lost the guy who I built the worst tree fort to ever get nailed to a tree with, and then spent every day in there with. I lost the guy who disrupted

697

eighth grade math to propose to our teacher so that he'd be thrown into Saturday detention with Mike, Susan and me."

"Which didn't work," Mike supplied, laughing.

"No, it didn't. I lost the worst football player to always somehow get played. My prom date. The traveler who was also the most turned around navigator the world has ever seen, who always got us so lost we'd be like in the wrong country or something, but it was amazing. The guy I jumped out of a plane with within moments after saying 'I do'. The man who cried while singing the first time he held our baby girl. I lost all of him, not just the bad bits. I couldn't move on before because... maybe I didn't want to, maybe I'd rather be angry than let go of the person I loved pretty much my whole life." I paused as tears soaked my face and crept down to my neck. Closing my eyes, I said, "I'm going to say this part to Logan, but I want you guys to hear it. Logan, the day I married you, I promised you that I'd love you until the day I die and then on until infinity, and I promise now again that that will always be true."

Susan squeezed me from one side and Sarah from the other. I kept my eyes closed for a while as the others began speaking.

Cameron was first, then around the circle. People shared mostly stories. Some of them I hadn't heard before, though many I'd been there for. A few people skipped, Kimmy and Peter among them.

When Mark was up, he didn't get very far into his story before he couldn't continue. The story was about when Logan was a boy and they had gone on a camping trip, but he didn't finish.

Susan broke ranks to cross over to him. I couldn't tell whether he was drunk or not. Actually, I found in that moment I didn't really care as much as I thought I would if he was drunk.

When we'd gone all the way around the circle, ending at Beza, Susan said, "We should probably get to it then."

"The kids want to speak," Shana said, pointing across the circle to Aiden and Sarah.

Leaning in, I looked at both of them. "You guys want to say something?"

"Um, yeah." Aiden stepped forward into the circle. "I loved my uncle Logan. He was really funny and he played with us a lot. I miss him and I wish he didn't die."

We all looked to Sarah.

"Baby, did you want to say something about your dad?" Shana asked.

"I don't want to miss my dad anymore." She buried her face in my stomach.

I let go of Cameron's hand and lifted her into my arms. Sarah curled into me, hiding her head.

Without any further cues, we all walked down to the shore. Cameron carried the urn as I was carrying Sarah and it was too heavy for Susan to be lifting. At the shoreline, Cameron helped unsnap the heavy lid to the urn and handed it to me.

My mother walked forward. "I'll take Sarah, Jay Jay."

Sarah's grip tightened around my neck. "No, stay with Mom!"

"You want to help me, baby? I'm going to walk in the ocean and pour out Daddy's urn."

She didn't respond, but didn't let up either. It was almost too heavy, having her clutched in one arm and the urn in the other.

With Susan and Mark beside me, we all walked forward as the foamy surf covered our ankles. The cold water rushed in before us, then out to splash up our legs.

I'd stood in the surf so many times, running through the wet sand with Sarah laughing, walking through it at night, thinking. Those many moments seemed to echo in the splash of the sea, as if I'd encoded my past into it.

And now, standing knee deep in the calm surf, I felt us encoding a new moment into the ocean, a goodbye that would always be waiting in the feel of salty water spray and the murmur of rushing water.

Sarah looked up and over at me.

I ducked in close to her, whispering, "Are you ready?"

"Are you ready?" she asked back. She might have been just repeating my words back at me, but somehow, I felt as if my little girl saw into my soul.

"Yeah, baby, I'm ready." Holding one side of the urn, I held it up to her. "Now we need to face away from the wind. You tell me when to go."

"Go," she said.

Tucking it most of the way into my body so I could get a good hold, I poured out the ashes into the water. They were a steady white flow, settling onto the shifting ocean surface.

When a good amount had poured out, I tipped the container back up and turned to Susan and Mark.

I held the half-filled urn out to them.

Susan reached out. "You ready, Dad?"

Mark murmured something I couldn't really hear, then reached up for the urn. Sarah and I stepped back as together they poured out the remainder of the ashes.

Something soft hit my leg and I looked down to see a flower float past me. It wasn't alone, on the beach, everyone tossed pink and white flowers into the frothing water.

My gaze came up and immediately met Cameron's. He'd rolled up his jeans and stood ankle deep, tossing flowers into the water.

'Hi,' he mouthed to me.

I nodded slightly as more flowers streamed past my legs.

Sarah tucked into me as we made our way back in to shore. I looked up as movement caught my eye. Far in the distance, near the parked cars, a woman watched us.

I knew it was her. I would know Vanessa anywhere.

Some part of me wanted to wave to her, to signal her to come, but I didn't.

When I'd made my way out of the ocean, I set Sarah down and turned away.

Day Nine: Eleven-ten

When the last flower had been thrown and the last words had been spoken, we watched the flowers travel the surf.

I sat beside Susan and Mark, though what I really wanted to do was curl up and nap. Sarah and Aiden had regained some of their energy, running up and down the sand with Beza and Cameron, picking up seaweed and rocks.

"We're going to clean up and head out, Jamie," Amy said as she came to stand in front of me.

I stood. "I'll help."

"No, no. We have it. Just relax, sit down, take a breath." She hugged me.

"Thank you for everything Amy, as always."

"I love you and I'm proud of you." She wiped away a tear as she pulled away.

"I guess I had it in me. Who knew?" I laughed.

"I did. Your mom is going to walk up with us, okay? So no awkwardness there."

"Thanks."

After saying goodbye to her and more family and friends, I sat again. Pretty soon it was just us seven, the flowers floating away and an empty urn.

I lifted the urn, looking at the wolf's visage, now somehow absent and lifeless.

"Why'd you pick that one?" Susan asked.

"I really have no idea." I laughed, looking at it.

"Could I hold onto it, just for a little while?" Mark looked up at me and in his gaze I could see how much rode on the answer and how much it cost him to ask.

"Not for forever," I said, not releasing it.

"No, I promise."

It took me a moment, but I forced myself to pass it to him.

He took it in his arms, clutching it to his chest. "Thank you, Jamie. I'll give it back to you."

"All right." I nodded.

Susan clapped her hands on her knees. "Okay, Dad, I'm going to need to take you back now, it's almost noon."

"Yeah, sweetheart, I should get back in time for lunch."

Susan turned to me. "We're going to head out."

"I gathered." Standing, I helped her up.

Susan smiled at me. "Hey, just think, with the assumption that Tuesday's task is going to be forgotten, after tomorrow's over it's all smooth sailing with your detox list."

"Yeah, hopefully. But, why am I getting the worst feeling that another storm is heading our way?"

"Don't talk like that. Think positive, it's all going to move past and you guys will be just fine."

I nodded. "You're right, it'll be fine."

She pointed at me. "Yoga tomorrow."

"No way." I laughed.

She lifted her hands. "Don't drop the ball. Exercise is not a one-time thing. Beza's cool with picking up the kids and you're going to need something to kill the time between when you and Cameron get off work."

"I have to go to the courthouse at four."

"I'll go with you. We'll leave yoga a couple minutes early it's only a block or two down."

"Oh, fine. But I better not be revealed as the fraud I am or I'm going to never live down the humiliation."

"It's fine, no one would care any way."

I pointed into her face. "Not funny, you better not tell anyone."

She rolled her eyes. "Like I would do something like that."

Cameron continued to play with Sarah down the beach after everyone else was left, building her a sand castle under her explicit directions.

Most of the flowers had ventured out to sea in their disjointed procession, though a few rode the waves. They rushed in up to shore where they lingered as the water sunk into the sand only to be scooped up by the next wave, repeating the cycle.

How quickly something so pivotal passes and yet it lingers for so long afterward.

Standing, I crossed to a flower that had been beached when the water came up unusually high. It was already soaked and leathery from its short time in the ocean. I tossed the flower back in, going for distance.

"You guys ready?" I asked.

Cameron looked up from where he sculpted a pretty good turret. "If you are."

Sarah stood up, grinned, then jumped onto Cameron's castle, spraying sand all over him.

"Sarah!" I laughed.

Cameron shook his head laughing, sand flying everywhere.

"It's all through your hair." I brushed my fingers through his hair, trying to get the sand out. "Maybe we should pick up something to-go and stop by the house so you can take a shower?"

He grinned up at me. "Nah, I'm good, I'd rather go out for lunch. I'll just get dirty at work anyway."

By the time we'd made it to the restaurant, the day had cleared enough that we elected to sit outside. We ordered burgers—humongous burgers.

"Look, I have a burger head." I held the burger up to my face.

Sarah burst into a fit of giggles.

Cameron held up his burger in front of his face. "How's it going? I'm Burgerman," he used a weirdly Germanic sounding accent.

I burst out laughing.

Sarah pointed at me. "You do it."

I held up my burger and tried to do an English accent, "I'm Burgerosa, queen of all burgers. Lettuce dance."

"Nice," Cameron said.

"I thought so." I took a big bite of the ridiculous burger.

Sarah giggled, then pointed to Cameron. "You do it."

None of us finished, though Sarah somehow got closest. We were a couple minutes late when Cameron dropped us off and Heidi was already waiting outside with the doors open.

"Sorry we're late," I called to her as I let Sarah out of the car.

"It's nothing. Come on in, I'm all ready for you."

I spent the entire session using my phone to read everything online that I could about what a general manager actually did. The Coffee Stop would be open tomorrow as per usual, but with the Jessicas and Chris again, as I was expected at the corporate office—with Cameron's new best friend, Patrick.

I shook my head, remembering that next weekend I had to eat dinner with just me, Patrick, Cameron and the kids.

"What are you thinking about that has you shaking your head?" Heidi asked, wryly from right in front of me.

I looked up to see Sarah and Heidi had snuck up on me without me noticing. "Oh, nothing, just silly stuff," I said as I stowed my phone.

"Well, Sarah did great." She turned to Sarah, "Keep up the good work, Hun." She smiled up at me. "You too seem really happy today, you have a good morning?"

I bit my lip. Now that I thought about it, I felt strangely happy, almost giddy. Sarah also kept smiling and laughing through lunch and the gymnastics practice. As I realized this, it suddenly felt wrong, like we shouldn't be feeling this way on this day of all days.

Misreading my hesitation, Heidi asked, "Not such a good morning?"

I hesitated. "It was great. Sarah did great, I mean. But the morning itself was intense."

"Something happened?"

"We, um, spread Logan's ashes this morning." Sudden tears pricked my eyes again, as if they'd never really left.

"I see." Heidi rubbed my shoulder. "Well, emotions go all over the place on days like that. Just remember to take care of yourself: eat, sleep and drink lots of water."

"Thanks, we will."

"Well, I need to go get the place ready for my next kids. I'll be seeing you Wednesday."

"Thanks, Heidi."

Cameron was waiting for us when we came outside, pulled up to the curb, his car running. He grinned wide as we climbed in.

"Meeting go well?"

"Excellent. I really think I'm going to be able to hire on a couple of guys soon." He held up a piece of paper for me to grab.

Taking it, I read:

Jamie,
Thanks for being a fan! Excited to meet you, you have to be a pretty awesome chick if you landed this fella.
Yours,
Raphael Rodriguez

I beamed at Cameron. "You *so* told him to write this."

He grinned back. "Nah, promise." Cameron was in such a good mood he sang along with Sarah's kid's CD all the way up to his house.

When we turned onto his road, I immediately saw the patrol car in his driveway beside my car.

Day Nine: Three-ten

A cop turned from the door of the house as Cameron parked behind my car.

She was petite, maybe five-foot nothing if she stretched, almost child-sized though her uniform bulked her out in some places. Her hair was combed up in a no-nonsense bun that stretched her beautiful features.

She waved at us with a flat hand moving up and down, her lips mouthed, "Roll down your window."

We both rolled down our windows simultaneously.

She stepped up to Cameron's, leaning down as if she'd just pulled us over on the highway for speeding.

She examined our faces. "Are you Cameron Robinson and Jamie Scott?"

Cameron nodded. "Yes, officer."

"Mr. Robinson, do you own a firearm?"

"Yes." He glanced over at me quickly, too fast to really gauge the expression.

"Are you armed at this time?"

"No, officer. The gun is in my gun safe."

"Ms. Scott, are you armed?"

"No, I don't own a gun." I shook my head for emphasis.

"I need to ask you a series of questions, Mr. Robinson. Would you prefer to speak here, inside, or at the station?"

"Inside."

She nodded slowly. "Could you please step out of the car, both of you?"

I leaned forward to get the officer's attention. "Um, officer, is it safe to bring my daughter out, too?"

She leaned back down, glancing into the back seat. "This is your daughter, Ms. Scott. Sarah Scott?"

"Yeah."

"What's your name?" Sarah smiled up and pointed into the officer's face.

"I'm Officer Evans."

"Who's your favorite gymnast?"

"I don't have one, sorry kid." A hint of a smile touched the officer's lips. To me, she said, "Yeah, that's fine, you can bring her out."

We exited the car slowly. Instead of letting Sarah out, I picked her up and held her to me as we walked to the door. The three of us walked up to the door first, the officer behind us.

"No one else is in the house?" The officer asked as Cameron made to open the front door.

"No."

The officer gestured to my car. "This is your car Ms. Scott?"

"Yeah," I said, pulling Sarah closer to me.

Cameron opened the front door to the sound of loud beeping. He disarmed the alarm, then gestured for us to come in.

Turning, I asked, "Can I go get Sarah settled somewhere with a movie?"

"I want to watch the beam finals."

The officer nodded. "That's fine."

I grabbed a box of crackers and a juice box, handing them to Sarah to carry, before grabbing my laptop. I carried it all and Sarah up to her room, setting everything on her bed. After setting up one of the gymnastics' playlists, I closed her door and descended into the big open room.

"What time did that happen?" I heard the officer asking as I rounded the staircase. She sat across from Cameron at his big slab of a dining room table.

"Maybe, ten-twenty, ten-thirty."

She wrote it down on a pad of paper in front of her.

"Is this about Clarke?" I took the seat beside Cameron.

The officer looked up at me, interested. "Clarke?" Something in her shrewd gaze reminded me so much of Gina. They both had that, 'I don't miss anything,' quality to their gaze.

"My next door neighbor." I looked at Cameron, then back. "He's been sexually harassing me. I just filed for a civil restraining order against him."

She wrote something down for a few seconds, and then looked back up. "Do you have an emergency protective order or a temporary restraining order in place now?"

"I talked to the chief, Rudy, he suggested the restraining order but didn't think an emergency protective order would work or something. I get the decision about the temporary one tomorrow at four."

She wrote it all down, then looked up toward Cameron. "What type of relationship do you have to Ms. Scott's neighbor, Clarke?"

Cameron sat up straight. "Until recently, I just talked to him in passing. He was always friendly, he had a good dog that I occasionally pet over the fence."

"And recently?"

"Recently he's been stalking my girlfriend and sneaking on my property to take pictures of us together to taunt her with."

She took a minute to write that down. "So, would you say that you are very angry at Clarke?"

Cameron and I looked at each other. I held a questioning look on my face while his looked more suspicious.

"Yes," Cameron finally said.

"Angry enough to threaten him?"

"No... not exactly."

She looked up and pinned Cameron with a disbelieving expression. "You say he's stalking your girlfriend and sneaking on your property and you're not angry?"

"I am. I'm definitely angry and extremely scared. He's delivered threatening messages to Jamie twice at her work, he's broken into her house and onto my property. His harassment of her only seems to be getting worse and more desperate. But, I also know how this sicko works."

"And how is that?"

"He only made inappropriate comments when she was alone, he went out of his way to make sure that she was isolated and that people wouldn't believe her. He only really accelerated his harassment when she began to push back and show signs she was trying to get help."

"How is that?"

"He cornered her in a laundry room and instead of following what he wanted her to do, which was stay with him, she lied to him to escape. After that, she refused to engage in conversation with him, she spoke to the management of their complex, then she moved out. Each thing has made him accelerate his harassment, while he's always very careful to not have anything lead back to him." Cameron paused as Officer Evans continued to write.

She looked up. "I'm still not following your logic here, sir. How is any of this discouraging you from threatening him?"

He inhaled deeply. "I think I know what you're here about. And, yes, I did talk to Clarke yesterday at his house. But I was really careful not to say anything whatsoever threatening."

I startled, looking at Cameron in absolute shock.

She examined him, not writing that part down. Her gaze stayed on him as she asked, "Ms. Scott, you didn't know about this confrontation?"

"It wasn't a confrontation," Cameron insisted.

"Ms. Scott, will you please answer the question?"

After staring at Cameron for a second, I shook my head. "I didn't."

That part she wrote down. "Mr. Robinson, could you please describe what happened yesterday?"

"I was working in my garage when my neighbor, Greg, who owns the auto glass shop one street over came in to say hello. He laughed, commenting that the car I was working on had the worst vandalism he'd ever seen. I'd not known what he was referring to so he took me outside to look at Jamie's car." Cameron paused to clear his throat. "The word 'whore' had been scratched into the driver's side door."

I inhaled sharply, making the officer look at me before turning back to Cameron.

He continued, "I'd only been there about an hour, so it must have been done then. Jamie and I swopped cars yesterday because Sarah was asleep in the backseat, and there was no sign of vandalism when I used it. Greg took some pictures. We called the police and they came by and made a report."

"Which officer was that?"

"I believe his name was Officer Martinez. He was going to send me a copy of the police report for Jamie, for evidence."

She nodded. "Please, continue."

"After the officer left, I buffed out the scratch and painted over it."

"You didn't tell Ms. Scott?" Her eyebrows went up in question though I thought she probably already knew from my reaction.

"She's going through a lot right now." Looking over at me, he said, "I'm sorry, baby."

I nodded just a little, not sure how to feel but I wanted to reassure him anyway.

"All right, you fixed her car, then what happened?"

"I cancelled my appointment with a client and while the paint dried I drove to Jamie's house."

"For what purpose?"

"I wanted to see if he vandalized anything else. I wanted to see if he'd broken into her apartment again. If he had, I didn't want her to discover it without me."

"Were you armed?"

"No." He shook his head.

"Did you stop at your house to pick up your firearm?"

"I did not. I just went straight there from the garage."

"Do you have anyone that can confirm this?"

After a second's pause, Cameron shook his head. "No."

"Please continue."

"I—uh, I got to Jamie's house and no one was outside. I used my key and checked her house, nothing had been disturbed. On my way out, Clarke was waiting for me."

"Waiting for you where?"

"He was on his side of the fence, leaning over it. I think he was expecting Jamie, when I walked out he seemed startled."

"Did you two speak?"

"Yeah, he tried to act casual, just asked me how I was doing. I gave him a look and told him that Jamie was my girlfriend and that I took threats against her safety very seriously. I began to walk away when he called out to me, saying that I should relax, take a load off. That he'd been watching some pretty great shows lately and maybe he could recommend some. I assumed he was talking about when he'd snuck on to my property and watched us together through my windows."

"I—" I paused to take a deep breath then said, "I have the photo he took of us that night in my car… if it helps." I wrapped my arms around my stomach, a little nauseated.

She looked at me. "That's not necessary right now. Please continue, Mr. Robinson."

"I turned back to him as he continued to talk. He said that it's been quiet with me and Jamie gone, that it's been nice. Though he didn't really mind the sounds Jamie makes. He said that he'd always found it so interesting that I came only on Thursdays and Saturdays, like we had a standing appointment. I said nothing as he talked, it didn't really make sense to me, why he'd break character when he had been so careful to not reveal himself to anyone but Jamie for so long." Cameron fell silent, staring off, his brow furrowed. "Then I figured he was taunting me, inferring that Jamie was a whore which meant he wanted me to react… probably violently."

"Did you do or say anything more to him?"

"Yeah, I said something. I told him that she was my girlfriend and that I loved her, that he should let it go and move on."

"You told him to move on… to harassing someone else?" She had a trace of cynical amusement in her voice.

"That's not what I meant."

"Um, hm." She turned to her pad and wrote for what felt like three minutes.

"I'm—going to check on Sarah, if that's okay?"

"Go ahead," she said, not looking up.

When I got back from checking on Sarah, she was still writing. As I sat, she looked over at Cameron and said, "I just have a couple more things I need. Have you had any long conversations with Clarke before yesterday?"

"Never."

"Have you ever discussed your personal history with him?"

"Not at all."

"So, you never told him that you have a misdemeanor assault charge on your record?"

"Never."

She turned to me. "Jamie, did you ever mention this to your neighbor?"

I shook my head. "Never."

"Thank you. What type of gun do you have Mr. Robinson."

"A model 110 shotgun."

She looked up and pinned him with her gaze. "That's the only gun you own?"

"Yes."

"Have you handled any other guns within this past week?"

He shook his head. "I have not."

"Not even a..." She flipped back a few pages on her pad and read, "Silver... maybe black hand gun, medium sized... normal-looking gun?"

"Definitely not."

I blinked at her. "That's the description he gave? Sounds like pretty much any gun but a rifle or shotgun."

She laughed under her breath, but didn't answer. "Would you be willing to open your gun safe for me, Mr. Robinson?"

He didn't hesitate. "Sure."

"Do you have any firearms that are loaded in there?"

"No, just the shotgun and it's unloaded."

"All right, Ms. Scott, if you could wait here, I have a couple questions I would like to ask you in private before I go."

"Okay. Can I go check on Sarah again while you guys go to the safe?"

She evaluated me for probably thirty seconds before she said, "Go ahead, we'll wait."

It only took me a minute and Sarah was totally fine, just watching the qualifying rounds and grinning. I took a seat at the table and waited for them to go off to Cameron's safe and return.

"All right, that's all I need from you Mr. Robinson. Ms. Scott, would you mind stepping outside with me for a minute?"

"Sure... yeah." I stood from the table.

She gestured for me to go first and I walked in front of her to the door, holding it open for her before making sure it was all the way closed.

"Walk with me." She gestured away from the house and toward the car.

Hesitantly, I walked beside her and stopped when she did. The height difference was much more obvious as I stood beside her.

"Ms. Scott, are you in an intimate relationship with your neighbor Clarke Allen?"

"No." I stuttered. "No, never."

"He said to me that you have had intimate encounters several times since he moved in a little over a month ago, do you feel that this is the truth?"

"No. Absolutely not."

"Have you ever asked or inferred to Mr. Allen that he owes you some type of monetary compensation?"

A sudden tear rolled down my cheek and I quickly wiped it away. "That's what he said?"

She didn't say anything, but her gaze was intense.

"No, I've never asked him for money. And, I've never, ever even touched Clarke in any way whatsoever."

Looking into her eyes, I tried to convey how truly scared I was when I said, "I really hope he never touches me, because any contact wouldn't be consensual, at least not from me. The only men I've been with my whole life were my late husband and Cameron. And, I've never once been paid for sex."

She examined my face and in her steadfast gaze, I could see that she believed me. "Thank you, Ms. Scott."

"Jamie." I paused, then asked, "Is Cameron going to be arrested?"

"I'm definitely not arresting him right now. I'm going to make a report, the report goes to a judge and he's the one who decides whether or not to issue a warrant."

"Thank you... for coming here and hearing our side too."

She nodded. "That's my job." Handing me her card, she said, "Keep this, call me if there's anything you would like to add to your statement."

I looked at her. "I quit my job, stopped working in the shop I usually do and moved out of my place. He doesn't have access to me anymore. Cameron stands in the way of that."

She nodded. "Thank you for your information, Ms. Scott, I have to leave now.

"Okay...bye. Thank you." Turning back, I walked into the house, locked the door and set the alarm. Cameron sat at the table, his head in his hands. Going behind him, I wrapped my arms around his body, kissing his neck and squeezing him to me.

He pivoted, and used his hands to guide me into his lap. "I'm sorry I didn't tell you."

Running my fingers through his hair, I said, "I get why you didn't, but don't do that again, okay? I need to know. I'm supposed to report everything to this officer. And just because I don't know about it doesn't make it go away." I leaned in and kissed him to soften the scolding.

"Are you going to call the other officer?"

"Yeah, in a second, I just wanted to check up with you first. You're being dragged pretty far down into this... I don't want you to—"

"Don't, Jamie."

"But I—"

"It's just wasted breath." He kissed me, slowly. "I'm not going anywhere."

Looking into his intent expression, I hoped so much that the justice system would let him keep that promise.

Day Ten

Digging up the Hatchet

Day Ten: Six-fifteen

I woke to the sound of Cameron's heartbeat, and the feel of fingers making slow circles on my shoulder.

"Is it time to wake up yet?" I asked into his shirt.

"Go back to sleep. You have forty-five minutes until your alarm goes off." He sounded wide awake.

"Is Sarah in here?"

"No," he whispered before kissing my hair.

"Is the door open, or closed?"

"Closed."

"Quickie?" I mumbled.

He laughed.

"I'm so not joking." I buried my face in his neck as my hands roved his body. "We can call it first-day-of-work stress relief. Or, maybe my-boyfriend-was-framed-by-my-stalker stress relief. Or it could just be called I-woke-up-feeling-like-a-quickie." I slipped my hand under his drawstring pants.

He gasped. His breathing was heavy as he asked, "Boyfriend?"

"So says you." I deepened my kiss on his neck as my hands roamed lower.

His hands pushed down at the elastic of my sleep shorts. "I guess . . . if it's for my girlfriend, I could help relieve some stress, but we have to be very quiet."

"Maybe we should lock the door?" I whispered.

"Yeah." He pulled away and rushed across the room, locked the door, then practically leaped back on the bed, making me laugh.

"Shh." He smiled and silenced me with a kiss. Our movements were almost frantic and desperate as our hands made quick work of undressing each other. Lying back on the pillows, I parted my legs so he could settle between my legs.

"We have thirty minutes," he breathed, before grabbing my hips and pushing into me.

"Forty," I moaned as my back lifted.

And I was right.

The alarm went off moments after he finished, while Cameron was still inside me.

Dazed, I reached for my phone and swiped to turn the alarm off. Cameron gave me one more kiss before rolling away and sprawling across the bed.

Wrapping myself in the sheet, I crossed the room to peek out of the bedroom door.

Sarah was still asleep in her room, her leg thrown over her blanket.

"I'm going to take the world's quickest shower." I glanced back to where Cameron still lay naked and sweaty.

"Uh-huh. Would you lock the door on your way out?"

After locking it, I snuck over to the bathroom. Leaving the door slightly ajar in case Sarah woke up and needed to come in, I took definitely-not-the-world's-quickest shower.

As I was about to turn the water off, Cameron startled the hell out of me by speaking from right outside the shower, "Leave the water on, I'm taking over."

Cameron's bed was freshly made with clean sheets, so I opened my suitcase and laid out every shirt I owned on the comforter. Ten minutes later, Cameron turned the water off and I was still in a towel, staring at my rather meager clothing choices.

"What do you think a general manager of a coffee shop chain wears?" I asked as Cameron entered the room, somehow already fully dressed.

"A suit?" Cameron suggested.

"Um, that's not going to happen."

"Wear this." He pulled up a sweater. "And some black pants. Done."

"Can we do another quickie? I'm getting stressed again."

He pulled me into him, his hands going around my towel. "Baby, you have to go in fifteen minutes if you want to get there in time."

"You're making it worse," I groaned.

"Just get dressed and you'll be fine." He kissed me. "You want me to wake Sarah?"

"No, if she's sleeping in, she probably needs it. I'll wake her to say goodbye if she's not up before I go."

"Sounds good, I'll see you downstairs."

I put on the outfit that Cameron suggested, really hoping that the day didn't get warm as all I could really wear that didn't show under the sweater was a tank-top.

Sarah threw open the door to Cameron's room and ran in, jumping on his bed. "Hey, goofball."

"Mom, come snuggle me."

Unable to resist, I climbed up and snuggled her in my arms. "I have to go to my job now, baby, but Cameron is going to take you to school."

"Mom, can I watch the cartoons from Grandpa's house?"

"If you do nice work at school, I'll see if I can find them for you as a reward, okay?"

"But, Mom, can I make bad choices at school?"

"You could, but then you won't get any TV at all." I sat up. "I'm going to go now, baby. Can you go get ready?"

She sat up, still a little bleary-eyed.

"Remember to brush your teeth, okay, baby? I love you." I kissed her forehead.

"I love you so much!"

Downstairs, I only managed to shovel a few bites of egg into my mouth and grab a banana before I had to run out the door. Cameron gave me one last kiss and reassured me that everything would be fine.

As much as I appreciated his effort, the fact that at least one judge, maybe two, were determining Cameron's—and my—fate today while I went to my first day at a job I was wholly unprepared for, felt very far from fine.

Halfway to the office building, I realized that all the buildings looked the exact same and I should have written down the number to the right building. I drove the rest of the way in a half-panic, until I got there and remembered which building it was.

After parking, I checked my phone to make sure a phone call hadn't come in saying that I should go somewhere else. A text from Patrick lit up as I checked it.

Patrick: You want to grab lunch today? I'll be in your building and neither of us will know anyone.

Me: I don't know. By that time, I'll probably be part of the 'in' crowd.

Patrick: Then I definitely want to eat with you.

Me: I guess.

Patrick: I'll take it. See you at noon at the café downstairs?

I texted that I'd be there and stowed my phone.
The building was just as I remembered it, bright and open. The atrium echoed a hundred sounds back at me. The voices must have originated from the people crossing the walkways overhead, or the large crowd squeezing into the café.
The security personnel at the desk was male today. He glanced between me and the ID picture a few times. "You lost some weight?"
"A little."
He handed the card back and turned to his monitor. "You're in the system, Ms. Scott. I just need to get a new photo of you, and then I'll issue a temporary pass. Your regular pass will be ready at the end of today."
"Thank you," I said.

"Just step in front of the camera here." He patted the desk.

Knowing the drill, I stepped in front of the camera and gave the camera an almost manic smile. The guard printed me a nametag that read, *Jamie Scott, Management,* then a bunch of numbers and letters.

I put the nametag on the breast of my sweater, but the fuzzy fibers rejected the not-so-sticky nametag. As I walked away from the desk to the elevators, I continued pressing on the nametag to try to get the thing to stick on.

The elevator dinged just as I got there, opening to reveal Nicole.

"Oh. Hi, Nicole."

She smiled, putting her hand to block the door of the elevator. "I was just checking to make sure you got through security." She glanced down and I realized I was pretty much grabbing my own boob.

I immediately dropped my hand and the name tag came with it, dropping to the ground. Cheeks heating, I reached for it. "The name tag won't seem to stick."

She grinned as I stood back up. "No problem, Jamie. I'll have them make you a pin."

She walked through the atrium toward the security desk and I stood awkwardly, not sure if I should follow her or just wait.

The elevator doors closed and a man rushed up hitting the button, making the doors reopen. I moved out of the way, wandering part way between the elevators and Nicole.

"I've got it," she called as she held up a nametag in plastic. She crossed the room fast for being in such high heels.

As we waited for the elevators to come back, Nicole turned to me. "I'm only here to take you up to the regional vice president. He'll be leading you through your orientation."

I looked up from where I was pinning the name tag to my sweater. "Douglass Maze?" I remembered his name from my paperwork.

"He goes by Doug."

I nodded and finished pinning.

As we stepped into the elevator, a horrible thought occurred to me. "What does Doug look like?"

Nicole looked at me, curiosity in her raised brow expression. "Well, he's about your age, tall . . ."

"Did he come visit The Coffee Stop?"

She nodded. "I believe he did, so maybe you guys don't really need to be introduced."

"Maybe not," I mumbled. The door dinged and the light on the five of the elevator's controls blinked out as the elevator opened.

"This way," Nicole said with an enthusiastic wave, probably sensing my reluctance. She led me into an almost identical reception hall, though the large floating photos were slightly different than I remembered. Nicole heaved open a heavy glass door and held it open so I could pass. The resemblance stopped there. We walked down a corridor with much larger offices on both sides. The receptionist didn't glance up as we passed.

We stopped at the very end in front of another middle-aged reception guy who didn't acknowledge us.

"Toby," Nicole sang in a teasing tone as we waited in front of his desk.

His head snapped up and he grinned widely as he saw us. "Sorry, Nicole." A blush crept up his cheeks. "So focused, you know." He had some sort of faint UK accent I couldn't place. His gaze hopped over to me and he seemed startled, as if I'd just popped into existence that very moment.

"Hi, I'm Jamie." I waved.

He smiled. "Are you also Ms. Scott?"

"Yeah," I said.

"Go on in, he's expecting you."

I nodded, my voice suddenly gone.

"All right, I'll see you later in the day, then," Nicole said.

Nodding again, I headed around the desk. My whole body tingled as I stepped up to the office. I wrapped my fingers around the large metal handle and pulled open the heavy door.

Inside, I noticed that the office wasn't as big as I'd expected it to be from the outside. The view was spectacular—nothing but ocean.

"Ms. Scott, nice to see you again."

Turning, I looked over to the large desk against one wall and the guy standing behind it. I'd already suspected that it would be him, but seeing him walking toward me, I knew that some evil deity out there had to be laughing his ass off right now. I really hated that fiend, whoever he was, because now I had to spend the next year with none other than the rude phone guy from my coffee shop as my direct boss.

Day Ten: Eight-fifteen

There was a faint, incessant clicking in the room, like a wall clock or one of those desk pendulums, but I saw neither.

Doug crossed the room to me. Something between a smile and a grimace touched his lips as he held out a hand for me to shake.

Shaking his hand, I said as brightly as I could, "Nice to see you again, Mr. Maze."

Smiling a little wider, Doug, the rude phone guy, gestured to his desk. "Why don't you take a seat, Jamie—is it all right if I call you Jamie? We like to keep things informal around here."

"Sure." When he pulled out his leather office chair for me, I took a seat and tried not to squeak on the leather as I crossed my legs.

"And feel free to call me Doug," he said as he lifted up his lapels and took the seat across the desk. He settled in to regard me, his face lit by the natural light. I wasn't quite sure why my first impression of him was that he was handsome. His face was too angular, and a frowned marred his face in resting position. Also, the smile he gave me didn't quite meet his eyes. He leaned back in his chair, regarding me.

Nothing sat on his desk, not a laptop or a speck of dirt.

He rocked a little in his chair. "So, this whole hiring process has been done in a bit of an unusual way, and I just wanted to talk a little bit, get to know each other. Usually, our HR department interviews people, and I make the decision." He paused as if I should respond. When I didn't—I had absolutely no idea what to say—he continued, "Usually this kind of position is filled internally. But Pat just told me he was hiring you, somewhat out of the blue, for a position that wasn't even available."

"Not available?"

"Sorry, I was just wondering, where did you go to college?"

I raised an eyebrow. "I didn't go to college."

The purse of his lips made me think he already knew this, which you'd think he would.

"But you've managed multiple shops at once?" he asked.

I shook my head slowly. My gaze flicked to the door, but returned to the dickwad. Honestly, if I hadn't signed that contract, I would so be walking out that door.

"How do you know Pat? Are you friends?"

No, Pat and I were not friends. I didn't like Pat much more than I liked Doug. Inhaling through my nose, I blew out a breath. I was stuck here for an entire year, minus three days. If I started this job, from the get go, letting this jerk speculate about me and how I got my job, this might be a really long year. "My first . . . encounter with Pat was when Timepiece sued me. Well, they sued my late husband's estate and he won. His company had a lien on my shop."

Again, he didn't look so surprised by the story. "The Coffee Stop?" he asked, like maybe I'd had a second shop hidden away somewhere.

"The same. I kept the shop, made a good profit. Pat visited often and eventually made an offer to buy it. Actually, he made two offers. I decided to sell, and then learned that the purchase of the shop was contingent on me taking this job. I'm here, and I have every intention of doing a good job . . . ." I gestured to him. "I only managed one shop, but I managed every part of it. I made a really high profit margin, and I know every aspect of the business."

He nodded, like this was what he wanted to hear. "That will probably be one of your biggest disadvantages here. You won't be able to micro-manage one shop; you'll have to manage several shops. It's easy enough to have one shop perform well, if it's all you're managing and it's in a prime location."

I gave half a shrug. "I guess that makes sense."

"It seems like we both agree that you should be moved to a less demanding position in the company."

I blinked slowly at him, my lips falling slightly apart. "No. I'm definitely up for taking a shot at the job."

His gaze, which had not wavered from mine, narrowed. "You're sure?"

"Yeah, really sure. So sure, I signed a contract saying it." I attempted to deliver this line with no sass.

He nodded like he was just being kind or something, and gave me an insincere smile. "Okay, but if you feel that it's too much of a load, please come talk to me and we'll find you a more fitting position."

I cranked a grin up on my face and said, "I'll be sure to do that, Doug." *When hell freezes over.* As of this moment, I was determined to rock the casbah out of this general manager job.

He hit the desk with both hands and gave me yet another wide, insincere smile. "Great, I'll show you to your desk. Let's get you started with training, then."

I gave him an even wider smile. "Thanks, sounds great."

When he rounded the desk, I stood, attempting to straighten my pants down my sides. As I went to grab my purse, my bag vibrated. Even though the phone was on silent, as it had been for days, the phone must have been next to my keys or something because a loud, jangling sound reverberated from my bag. "Sorry!" I said as a surge of embarrassment pushed up through me. My hand fished through the many and varied contents of my bag. As if the horrible first encounter with my new boss wasn't awkward enough, I had to come off as even more unprofessional. When I'd finally fished my phone out of my bag, I saw Pat Kelley Sr. flashing on the screen. "It's Pat," I mumbled as I answered it. "Hello?" I said into the phone.

"Jamie," Pat said over the phone. "How's your first morning going?"

"Great, I'm just meeting with Doug now," I glanced over at Doug.

His attention turned to a tablet, his hand swiping across the screen.

Pat continued, voice buzzing in my ear, "Good. I'm glad everything went smoothly so far. And you've met with my nephew."

"Nephew?" I asked, having no idea what he meant.

"Douglass, my sister's eldest son."

My gaze moved to Doug, who seemed not to have heard me, impossible as that was. I turned away, and walked toward the windows.

Pat continued, "Douglass is your supervisor, but I want to make sure that you know he does *not* have the power to fire you, demote you, or anything of that nature. I promoted him and gave him a lighter load. You'd think that would make him happy. Instead, he's taking it personally. If he takes it out on you, you call me right away and I'll talk to him. Okay?"

Grimacing at how supremely awkward this situation was, I muttered, "Yeah, of course." But I meant, 'Thank you for throwing me into a pile of dung, yet again.'

"I'll come by later in the week, and my son will be in and out to make sure everything goes smoothly. Keep in touch."

"Sure, I will," I said.

As I hung up, Doug peeled himself away from his desk. "You ready?"

"Yep," I said.

We said nothing as we walked back the way we came, past the reception desk and through the other identical doorway.

Color and hectic movement met us just on the other side. This side of the office building was way more my speed. A network of cubicles filled the entire space. Heads poked out of most of them. Colorful photos, posters, and decals, coated most of the available wall space.

"We're going to have to put you here with our design team until an office opens up," Doug said as he gestured to an open cubical.

"Looks great." I meant it.

A couple heads popped up or leaned over. Three cubicles down, a cute guy shot me a grin, before turning back to his desk.

I inhaled through my nose and turned back to Doug.

"All right, I've got a lot of reading material for you, and when you're finished, your computer has some videos in the orientation folder on your desktop. I'll come check on your progress at ten. If you've gotten through everything, we'll head out to the different store locations." He gave me yet another practiced smile, and then asked, "Do you have any questions for me?"

"Nope, I'm pretty sure I can figure it all out."

"Great. Well, if you do, I'll be in my office." With that, he turned and walked away.

It was a beautiful thing, him being gone. I wasn't sure what was worse news: that I was on the bad side of Pat's family drama, or that dickwad couldn't fire me and get me out of a year-long contract hanging out with him.

Grayish walls surrounded me on three sides as I took a seat at my new desk. My cubicle was in serious need of some concert posters. If I got a chance, I was going to steal a couple from The Coffee Stop.

A head of multi-colored hair popped over the far wall of my cubicle.

"Hello!" the woman called, giving me a wide smile. She had a deep voice, especially as she was probably close to ten years younger than me.

"Hi." I waved. "I'm Jamie Scott, I'm new today."

"Crystal James, nice to meet you." She reached over the cubical wall to shake my hand. "I've seen your video before, where you were singing."

"Cool," I said as I turned back to the folder that sat on my desk. I braced myself for the inevitable questions about Dream Big and the Rocketeers, and whether or not I could give some celebrity her number.

"So, does your whole life suck now that your video went viral, or is it cool? I've always been a little scared that one of mine will, even though I want them to."

I glanced up, and couldn't help smiling as that definitely wasn't the question I was expecting. "Well, people were blowing up my phone and showing up at my shop, but it cooled down over the weekend."

"Huh. Well, if you have any questions, feel free to ask me."

"Thanks," I said as she disappeared behind my wall.

The paperwork was basic and the videos even worse. Most of it was instructional on how to use the company phone-line, the email server, and connect to programs I'd been using for years.

On screen, a woman with a huge, frizzy perm walked into an office in a miniskirt while the words: *How to respectfully tell people that they're not dressing appropriately for work*, dissolved off the screen. As the poorly acted dialogue played, my mind wandered to the task I was supposed to complete today, and the nearly zero percent chance that I was actually going to do it. Susan had been right; this was the last challenging task that I had to do, especially since I obviously wasn't going to stop sleeping with Cameron tomorrow. But was I even capable of forgiving Vanessa? I didn't know.

I could almost speed-rewind our relationship in my mind.

"Don't you ever, ever call here again, Vanessa," Amy yelled into the phone, as I lay on my couch. I watched the tall stacks of boxes threaten to topple all over my soon-to-be former living room and decided that I'd never call Vanessa back.

I remembered back to the lines of mascara, dripping down Vanessa's face the day I'd held her through her tears. In front of my bedroom mirror, I wrapped my arms around her as she sobbed. By that night, she'd already betrayed me and soon she would play a large part in my husband's death. She'd been evading hanging out with me for weeks before that night, weeks where my marriage crumbled and her husband had helped me more and more along the way.

What was forgiveness anyway? Was it absolution? Did it mean I had to let her back into my life? Could I even do that? Did I want to? I had no answer for all these questions.

I forgave Logan. I'd decided that the amazing experiences that made up our life outweighed the bad choices he made in the end. But could I, or should I, do the same for Vanessa?

Another memory surfaced in my mind.

I pulled up to Vanessa and Cameron's house, hot tears dripping from my eyes as rain cascaded down my windshield. Both Cameron and Nessa's cars waited in the driveway, two matching sedans. I jumped out of my car door, immediately getting drenched as cold water washed down my bare arms.

"Crap," I whispered, before grabbing my jacket from the seat. It was too late. I was wet under the jacket. I circled the car, making sure Sarah's hood was up.

"Baby, I need to put my phone in my purse so it doesn't get wet," I told her.

"No," she said, her gaze still glued to the screen.

I paused, my hair and body drenched and only getting more drenched. But I couldn't think of the words to make her give me my phone. Hot tears leaked from my eyes, but cold water dripped down my cheeks. Reaching forward, I grabbed the phone. "Just turn it off."

"No," Sarah said.

"Baby, now!"

Wide eyes turned on me, and Sarah's hands fell away from the phone.

"Sorry. Sorry for yelling. Come on, sweetheart. Mommy is standing in the rain." I unbuckled her seatbelt and gently pulled her from her seat. I rarely carried Sarah when we walked

anymore now that she was seven, but I clutched her to me as we rushed through the rain to the house.

The door opened as we approached, Nessa framed in the doorway. "Jamie?" she asked, her melodic voice sounding surprised. Nessa, as always, looked beautiful and presentable even in yoga pants and an expensive jacket. Her blonde hair was heaped in a high bun at the top of her head.

"Hi, um, can we come in?" I asked as I rushed to the front door.

"Of course, come in right now." She jumped out of the way. "Jesus, you guys are soaked!"

I stepped into her front hallway, putting Sarah down. She squirmed to get away from me, and I pulled on her jacket sleeve, managing to take it off before she ran away from me. "I'm sorry, Ness, I just jumped in the car and drove. I ended up here—"

I looked down to the muddy puddle we'd made in her entranceway. "I'm making a mess—I'm just such a mess."

"Who cares about that?" She waved it away. "Take off your coat. Let me hang it up, Jay."

As I let her pull my coat off, the hot tears came again. "I'm just so mad at her, I can't even stand it."

"Your mom?" Nessa said as she hung mine, then Sarah's coat, on her coat rack.

"She has to have it her way . . . always. I told her that he couldn't handle it, I said just wait for me to tell him when it's the right time, but she just . . ." I punched through the air. "Ah, I could hit her I'm so mad."

Cameron came into view halfway down the stairs, his dark hair wet and swept back. A look of clear concern fell over his face. "Everything okay, Jamie?"

"Shit, sorry, Cameron. Hi! It's—everything's fine." I wiped back the wet hair sticking to my face.

"Love, let me get you a towel and a drink, okay?" Nessa wrapped her arm around my shoulders, even though they were wet.

"I'm sorry, guys," I said, trying to hold back tears, whether they were from sadness, anger or embarrassment, I wasn't sure. Today sucked in a big way.

"I'll go get the towel. And I'll keep an eye on Sarah so you guys can talk." Cameron turned.

"Thank you so much, Cameron," I called after him.

Vanessa squeezed my shoulders. "Let's go get you that drink. Wine or something harder?"

"Just a little wine, I have to drive Sarah home later."

"You don't if you don't want to; you guys are welcome to stay in our guest room." She smiled, and leaned in, her temple against mine as we walked.

"No, I—I want to be home when Logan gets back . . . if he even comes back."

At their wine cabinet, Vanessa selected a bottle. "Italian, yum." She poured half a glass for herself and a full glass for me. "In case you change your mind."

She handed it to me and I turned the crystal stem in my fingers before glancing up. "I think my little goblin is raiding your fridge," I said.

Vanessa glanced over her shoulder to where Sarah was taking the contents of her fridge out and placing it on the floor.

"Sarah—"

Vanessa rolled her eyes. "Oh my god, Jamie, I don't care. She's welcome to whatever. And she can make as big of a mess as she wants if it keeps her happy."

"Sarah," I called, "put the food back into the fridge, please."

Sarah didn't acknowledge me, but began setting things back in.

"Did something else happen since last night?" Nessa asked as her wine glass perched between her fingers.

I lowered my voice, as my emotion attempted to gush out of me. "Logan woke up drunk and just kept drinking all day. He was so mad, and just raving about her all day, one thing after the other. Sarah heard it all." My lungs pushed out a heavy exhale I couldn't stop. "Why did she have to—ugh." I gestured wildly, sloshing wine onto the floor. "Damn it! I'm sorry," I groaned.

She shook her head. "It's fine. Just drink. Take a sip before the rest is gone.

"I'm just so mad, and Susan is driving me crazy because she keeps calling me and she's completely on my mom's side. Like, seriously—" I shook my head.

"Jamie, drink your wine. I'm not kidding. You need it."

I set the wine glass down. "I should check on Sarah."

But when I looked, Cameron and Sarah sat on the floor in front of the fridge, eating strawberries. A big fluffy towel sat folded on the couch right next to us. The sight made me start to cry again.

"See." She handed me my glass. "Now partake in my vino-therapy, that's an order. And you know what? Forget about Susan. She needs to butt out. Just ignore her for a couple days, okay? This is between you, Logan, and your mom."

"I don't think I can ever forgive her," I said before taking a sip. A cool, acidic yet mild, taste washed over my tongue.

"Now that's crazy," Vanessa responded before taking a sip of her drink. "Your mom shouldn't have gone around you and told Logan, but she did it because she loves Sarah . . . and you. I'm one hundred percent on your side here—but, as your best friend for life, there's no way I'll let you never forgive her either."

My phone buzzed near my leg, waking me from my memories.

Day Ten: Ten-forty

Extracting the phone from where it sat on top of my purse, I checked the screen.

Cameron: How's your first day going?

Glancing around and finding no one looking my way, I typed a response.

Me: It's already boring me to death. Hopefully soon, I'll be able to do something other than read stuff I already know and watch info videos from the 80s. Did Sarah get to school okay?

Cameron: She's good. Seemed happy. I'll leave early today so we can go to the courthouse.

Me: You don't have to. Susan is going with me after we go to prenatal yoga.

Cameron: Something you want to tell me?

Oops, looks like I forgot to tell Cameron about that one. I couldn't help but crack a little smile as I typed my response.

Me: No, sorry! Nothing to worry about there.

Cameron: Who said I was worried?

"You are so busted."

I glanced up, startled to see Patrick's face as he leaned into my cubical desk. "Holy shit," I whispered, as my cheeks heated.

"Are you already slacking on the job?" he asked, grinning.

I leaned in. "Actually, I'm ahead. Your cousin hates me," I whispered the last part.

"Doug?" he asked, an eyebrow rising.

"Uh huh."

"Oh, I doubt that." He set his elbow on his cubical. "So, I wanted to ask if you'd like to go for a celebratory drink after your first day of work . . . and by drink, I mean milkshake with our kids?"

"Today?"

"Yep," he grinned again. "I've thought of some semi-inappropriate jokes to tell you, but obviously can't do it here."

"That sounds awesome, but I have plans today after work. What about tomorrow?"

"Tomorrow sounds good," he said. "You ready to go check out all the locations you'll be supervising?"

I sat up straight in my desk chair. "I get to go with you?"

"Until lunch time, my ten o'clock meeting cancelled. After lunch, unfortunately, I'll have to go back to the mother ship and Dougy is taking over," he said.

"Ha. There are so many things I want to comment on in that statement, I just don't know where to start." Grabbing my purse from the floor, I practically jumped from my chair.

He patted the cubical wall. "I'm not supposed to be training you, just so you know. I'm just going along with you while I'm doing my audit, simultaneously."

I shrugged. Stepping up beside him, I said, "Sounds good. Do you know if I have to check in with Doug, or can I just go?"

"I think you're good. I volunteered to take you around, so he already knows."

"Okay, good," I said under my breath.

We fell in beside each other as we walked through the halls.

"Being here always feels like stepping into an alternate universe." He held the large swinging door open for me. "It's the exact same as the building I go to every day, but the people and decorations are different."

"Ha, I can imagine that'd be weird. Are all the buildings the same?" I asked.

"Yeah, my dad probably got a discount on it or something." He shot me a wry smile.

Pressing the button outside the elevator, I leaned against the felt wall and looked back to Patrick's grinning face. "So, does your whole family work for your father's various companies?"

He looked a little embarrassed as he rubbed the back of his neck. "Basically. It's a little complicated. My father is very into *grooming* people for his needs, if that makes any sense to you."

I glanced around; making sure no one was in earshot. The reception area was empty, the receptionist busily worked on her computer, white ear-buds in her ears.

"Just his family, or outside people too?"

Patrick avoided eye contact when I tried to catch his gaze. "Mostly with family. I'm pretty sure he's already trying to groom Kay, though. It started with me in middle school, about the time I decided I wanted to be a professional football player."

The door to the elevator dinged open.

Stepping inside, I teased, "Professional football player, you say?"

He finally met my gaze with a smirk. He hit the button for the first floor. "I was thirteen. I was never even close to good enough, not like Cameron." He raised his eyebrows, still smirking.

"Cameron was good," I said, because there was an expectant silence after his words.

"He seems like a good guy."

I nodded. "Definitely a good guy."

"So, I noticed he introduced himself as your boyfriend . . ."

I forced down a nervous grin. "That he did."

He leaned in a little. "So you guys are officially together?"

"Yeah." It came out a lot less certain than I intended.

"Exclusively?"

The elevator slowed, stopped, and the doors opened to a group of young people.

"Going down?" a girl asked, as she glanced at the arrow at the side of the door.

"Yep," I said, stepping in closer to Patrick to make room as five people stepped onto the elevator.

We took the rest of the ride in silence while I attempted to come up with an answer for him. The answer should be "yes." I was pretty sure the answer was yes, Cameron and I were together. Did I want to be with Patrick too? I . . . didn't think so. Did I want things to change between me and Patrick? Not really. I liked this innocent flirtation we shared.

I wasn't sure if I could keep the flirtation and the exclusive boyfriend status.

Damn it. I knew I couldn't string him along, even if I really liked the smiles and smirks and dreamy, flirty eyes Patrick shot my way. Maybe I was a huge flirt. But if Cameron knew and accepted that about me, did I have to stop being a flirt? I hoped not.

As the doors slid open and the crowd emptied out of the elevator, I turned to Patrick. "Yeah, I'm pretty sure we are."

He gave me a mirthless grin. "Too bad."

We followed the crowd into the large, echoing atrium. Turning, I grimaced a little as I said, "I really like you and I want to be friends, in a real way."

He nodded. "Good, I do too. And I do like Cameron. I hope we can all be friends."

"Well, we are going to have a friendly dinner this weekend . . . which will be fun." Maybe I couldn't hide all the awkwardness I felt, because Patrick laughed.

I shot an amused glance toward him. "Yeah, uh-huh."

"All right, I have time to take you around to two of the locations before lunch. You want to take one car or two?"

"I'm all for saving gas."

We took his car since it was the nicer of our two cars. It had all-white leather interior, and that sort of smell that made you think a kid probably never barfed in his back seat. The area around Kay's seat, however, had a very different feel. The leather wrinkled all around the black booster, and there was definitely some familiar pink ink-type stains on the fold-down arm rest.

As we drove out of the parking lot, Patrick turned to me. "Hey, I was meaning to offer, if you ever need a day, Kay would love to have Sarah over after school."

I cringed a little as I responded, "Um, that's really nice, but you have really nice stuff in your house, and sometimes Sarah just spontaneously starts flipping around. It's usually better if I'm on hand for social stuff."

He blew out a laugh. "I really don't care about my furniture. It all came with the house, remember?"

"That's what everyone says. And then something irreplaceable gets damaged—I really should be there."

"Yeah, no problem." We lapsed into silence as Patrick took the onramp to the freeway.

Thankfully, traffic was light until was got closer to downtown Coral Beach.

Patrick turned to me. "So, why do you think Dougy hates you?"

"Dougy?" I laughed, relaxing into the leather seat.

"He's my little cousin. We used to call him baby Doug, but we're not allowed to do that anymore."

"Ha."

He smirked. "So?"

"I guess your dad carved my job out of Dougy's responsibilities, and Doug is taking it personally. He tried to demote me in the first five minutes of me being there, something I guess he's not supposed to be able to do."

"He'll get over it. Doug is—he's the baby of the family. He definitely has something to prove, but he's a great guy." Patrick flicked down his blinker, and merged between two cars into the right lane.

"I just hoped your dad would give me the guilt job and be done with it. But now I'm neck deep in some family politics thing, too?" I mumbled the last part, not knowing if it was going too far.

To my surprise, Patrick laughed, "Trust me, with my dad, he gave you a guilt job, is using you in some family politics play, and has some other agenda."

"*Great.*"

"But he also wants you to stay for a couple years and sees something special in you. If I know anything about him, it's that he'll first throw you in the deep end to test what you're made of, and then he'll try to find a way to keep you very invested in his aspirations."

"How does he have so much energy with so many employees?"

"He doesn't. I'm just talking about the way he acts with family . . . and he's kind of been treating you that way. But he might act differently with you."

"Why does being treated like family sound like a bad thing?"

Patrick turned into the parking lot of a Harrington's I'd never been to before. After he pulled into a stall and shifted into park, he said, "It is, and it isn't. My father takes nepotism to a whole new level. He's unapologetic about it, too." He turned to me. "At the same time, he likes to play all of us against each other. For example, remember my brother, Derek?"

"Yeah."

"Well, my father put Derek and my older sister in direct competition to take over as Timepiece's CEO when my uncle retired. They did everything short of seriously injuring each other to prove themselves to him. When my sister was promoted, it got so bad, my father needed to move Derek to a different company. Still, I think he brought me on at Timepiece to make my sister insecure in her position. But unlike everyone else in the family, I refuse to play his games. My sister and I get along just fine. You ready to go?"

"Oh, yeah," I said, breathing out a laugh.

As we walked toward the building, he said, "Hey, I don't want to freak you out. My father is usually great to his employees. And if he starts enticing you to compete with Doug, or trying to get you to come to family events, just refuse to play his games."

"You say you don't want to freak me out, and then you say something so freaky." I shook my head.

He opened the door for me. "I'm sorry. I'm sure it's not going to be like that with you. I already told you I have problems with my father."

Day Ten: Eleven-fifteen

As we stepped into Harrington's, the smell of vanilla hit my nose. It wasn't the sickly sweet smell of vanilla syrup; it was the cloying scent of vanilla air freshener. Modern pop music played low in the shop, I wasn't quite sure what was playing it was so low.

Several patrons waited in line, while three girls and a middle-aged guy worked through the line. I craned my neck, looking to the back. "Is this one a drive-thru?"

"Nope." He gave me a confused look. "Didn't Doug give you the floor plans?"

"Yeah, of seven shops." I rolled my eyes.

"You want to go back and meet everyone?"

"Let's go through the line. I don't want to freak anyone out, and I'd rather just get a good feel for the shop—the *shops*."

Also, I wanted some sort of tea latte. It was about that time. The line moved relatively quickly, quickly enough that neither Patrick nor I felt the need to make conversation.

"Hello, welcome to Harrington's. What can I get for you?" the man asked with a slight southern twang.

I glanced behind me to make sure that we were the last in line, which thankfully we still were. I turned back to the guy and waved. "I'm going to order in a second. I just started working for Harrington's today and I want to introduce myself first." I waved. "Hi, I'm Jamie."

A huge, unexpected smile broke across his bristly face. "You are so nice. Are you going to be working here?"

I grinned back. "Sort of. I'll be in and out. I might cover a few shifts if needed. Mostly, I'll be stocking and fixing things if they need to be fixed."

"That's great. I'm Bob. It's really nice to meet you. I'll introduce you around. Hey, Jenna!"

"What?" The girl next to him called over a low whining sound. Her attention was still fixed on the pitcher of milk she was heating at the espresso machine. Heavy makeup lined her eyes, and her lips were painted vermillion.

"Jamie, this is Jenna. She's our store manager. Over there is Camilla and Lucy."

The girls waved, though they busily worked on other tasks.

"Jamie just started work here," Bob said.

"I'll mostly be in the corporate office, but I'll be coming in and out of here, as well." I pulled out a piece of paper and pen, and wrote my number very clearly across it. "I'm going to leave you guys my number. Anything you need, any suggestions you have, whatever, call or text me."

Jenna glanced over at me, brow furrowed. "I usually talk to Doug."

"Cool, think of me as, like, Doug's personal assistant that has the power to change things."

Patrick peered down at me, a decidedly amused expression on his face. He looked back to Jenna. "And I'm Patrick, Doug said you have papers for me here?"

"Oh, yeah." She looked around. "Camilla, would you finish this for me?" When she returned with a stack of papers to hand over to Patrick, Jenna asked me, "So, I call you now?"

Obviously Doug told her about Patrick, but didn't think to mention me. My best guess: Dougy thought he would just demote me in the morning and be done with it. *Lovely*.

I shrugged. "I think some sort of memo will go out later this week with instructions. If you feel comfortable with switching over to call me, that's fine. If not, you're welcome to wait." I pushed my number further across the counter. "Just save my number and pass it around. I'm happy to come and help with anything."

"Okay. Nice to meet you. We'll all be sure to save your number," Jenna said, turning back to her machine.

"Can I get you two anything to drink, since you're here?" Bob asked.

"Oh, please," I said.

When both Patrick and I had drinks in our hand, we headed for the door when I saw the culprit for my growing headache. Walking over, I pulled a plug-in vanilla scented air freshener from the wall.

I held it up, turning to the crowd working behind the counter. "Hey, any of you object to me tossing this?"

They all looked over.

Jenna stepped toward me. "I don't think you should do that. Doug put those in himself." She bit her lip and released it, making a small crescent dent in her thick lipstick.

"Oh no, Doug said I can fix whatever. I just want to make sure it's cool with you guys," I called.

They looked at each other.

"Sure," Jenna said.

"I hate those things." Bob grinned.

"There's another one back here. You want that one too?" Lucy said, raising thick black eyebrows above the rims of her glasses.

I took it from her. After I walked out with Patrick, I tossed both into the outside trash can. "Nasty."

"That was . . . interesting," Patrick said, before taking a sip of his drink.

I turned to him as we may our way through the parking lot. "How was that interesting?"

"You didn't tell them you're the general manager."

I stopped outside my car door. "I did."

"No, you said you were 'Doug's personal assistant who has the power to change things.'" The idea obviously amused him because a huge smirk played across his lips.

Climbing in the seat, I waited for him to start the car before I responded. "I'm not into throwing my weight around."

He didn't respond, just backed out of the space and merged back onto the road.

"What?" I asked, because I felt an unspoken criticism in the silence between us.

His gaze stayed glued to the road. After a short pause, he said, "You're going to have to throw your weight around at some point," he shrugged, "and if no one respects your authority . . ." The words hung in the air. When I didn't respond, he said, "But I'm not supposed to be training you, so don't worry about anything I say."

Rolling back my shoulders, I decided, "I'm just going to go with what feels natural for me. If I suck as a boss because of it . . . I'll cross that bridge when I get to it."

He nodded. "Well, obviously my father thinks you're doing something right. So hey, that's probably a good plan—even if it's unconventional."

I glanced over. "Do you agree with me, or are you just being nice?"

He grinned.

"I'll think about it. And, please, keep it coming with the advice. I'm just sort of winging it."

He blew out a laugh. "Well, if I were you, I wouldn't go through the line. I'd just tell them you're taking the air fresheners away, not ask permission. If you ask permission, they might say no out of loyalty to tradition, even if they want them gone. Also, I wouldn't throw them away. Just put them somewhere no one can find—in case it becomes an issue."

"Hmm, thank you." I filed all the info in my head as we moved to the next location.

As much as I appreciated the advice, I played it the same in the next two locations. Walking out with my third drink, this time a vanilla steamer I couldn't finish, I turned to Patrick as he popped his trunk.

"Your trunk is going to smell like a cupcake for the rest of your life, my friend," I said as I set three more vanilla air fresheners in.

"Just as long as none of them spill in there." He cringed a little.

I cringed back. "Those things have to be the nastiest inventions humans have ever made."

He chuckled before asking, "Where do you want to grab lunch before I hand you over to Dougy?"

"Seriously, you've got to cut that out or I'm going to call him that by mistake, which would make him hate me even more. And as for lunch—would you mind dropping in on The Coffee Stop? I want to pick up some of the stuff in my office to decorate my cubical."

"Sure. I've never been there," he said.

"Really?" I asked as I climbed back in the car.

He buckled his seatbelt, and said, somewhat sheepishly, "Yeah, I knew you worked there, and since I also went to your bar once in a while, I didn't want to seem like I was following you, or something."

The smile dropped off my face as a wash of unease filled me—not from him, but from the lingering creepiness of my own personal stalker, Clarke. I peered around the parking lot at the palm trees shifting shadows over the long stretch of concrete.

"Everything okay?" Patrick asked.

I startled. "Oh, yeah, I'm sorry. Wow, here I am, acting like a crazy person. What you said just reminded me of something that I've been sort of trying to repress."

"Is it the guy who's bothering you? Because the moment after I said that, I remembered you're going through something. I'm sorry."

"No." I shook my head. "It's fine. But, yeah, I'm getting a restraining order. Or, well, I find out if the judge is going to order a temporary one today at four."

He turned to me sharply. "Really, it's that bad?"

"Unfortunately."

A silence settled over us the rest of the way to The Coffee Stop. A pool of dread formed in my stomach, expanding at a slow rate. I needed to put it from my mind. If I was going to rock this job, I needed to be sharp. And then there was the Vanessa thing.

I decided I was taking my pass. Vanessa would be my tomorrow task. I wasn't ready, and there was way too much other shit going on in my day today to let all my issues with her mix in.

The moment I decided, it was as if a cape weighted with lead was lifted off my shoulders. I would forgive Vanessa tomorrow.

Instead of parking in my usual spot by the mural, Patrick pulled directly up to my shop—my former shop. New green leaf buds emerged all over the tree that reached up in front of The Coffee Stop.

The day felt warm, the shop even warmer. The moment I stepped into the shop, the smell of warm coffee and butter overwhelmed my senses. It smelled like home.

"I can see why you didn't like the vanilla things," Patrick said as he stepped in after me. "This smells like one of those French shops that sell bread. So much better.”

“Right?” I said. The line reached all the way to the door, and I had to press my back to the wall to scoot around the crowd.

When Patrick followed me, by being a lot smarter and asking people to move out of his way, he gazed around with a smile. “Nice.”

“You like it?”

He grinned. “Very . . . you.”

“I’ll take that as a compliment.”

“Do. Want to head into your office?” He glanced over his shoulder to where Chris and the two Jessicas worked behind the coffee bar.

I smiled and waved at Chris, who gave me an exaggerated wave and smile in return before turning back to his customer.

“Hey, Jamie.”

I jumped as someone stepped out of line, and then looked up to Cameron’s smirk. Laughing, I shook my head. “Oh my god, Cameron, you’re always sneaking up on me.”

Leaning in, he asked, “You didn’t get my text?”

Being this close, I couldn’t help but notice he smelled a lot like my body wash. I grinned. “No, you texted me?” For some reason, a spark of mischief lit in his dark gaze.

“Yeah, I definitely did.” He looked over my shoulder, and his eyelids widened. “Oh hey, man. Nice to see you again.”

“Oh . . .” I stepped out from between them.

“Yeah, you too.” Patrick offered his hand.

Cameron looked between us. "So you two are working together? That's good."

"Yeah," I said, just as Patrick said, "A little."

Cameron smiled, a little absently. "Well . . . I'm going to jump back in line. I have to meet a client in fifteen minutes."

"Want me to just grab you something? I'm going back there," I said, throwing a thumb back over my shoulder.

"No, I'll wait in the line."

"I have to be heading on back there." Patrick offered Cameron his hand again. "See you soon, yeah?"

"Yeah, buddy, sounds good."

After they shook, Patrick headed off and Cameron immediately pulled me in for a hug.

"If you pinch my ass or something, I'm going to punch you in the face, Cameron. I shouldn't even be hugging you, I'm working," I whispered into his ear.

He laughed, loud and hard and squeezed me once before letting me go. "I'm glad you're here. I just came out of habit and then remembered that you wouldn't be here. I did text." He raised his eyebrows.

"Now I really have to check this text. You keep giving me this little look when you say that." I poked his side.

"Excuse me, are you in line?" A woman in line asked.

"Oh," he looked back, "yeah, sorry." He turned back to me, another small smile playing on his lips. "See you at five-fifteen at the house?"

"Yeah, that works fine."

"You sure you don't want me to leave early?"

"No, really. Susan and I have it handled." I touched his arm. "I'll see you soon, yeah?"

"Yeah." He shot me one more grin before stepping back into line.

After dodging through customers, I paused just beyond the coffee bar. Pulling my phone from my purse, I ran my finger over the smooth screen, checking to see Cameron's text and if I missed anything else important.

When I saw that there were no missed calls from Sarah's school, I checked my text messages.

Cameron: Found myself in your coffee shop. Are you here? Need any stress release on your lunch break?

Glancing over my shoulder, I met Cameron's dark, heated gaze.

My cheeks grew tight as I fought a smile. "I wish," I mouthed at him.

He shot me a quick wink before looking away to step forward in line.

Turning, I entered the all-too familiar behind the counter frenzy.

"Hey there, foxy," Chris called as I stepped around the counter.

I pointed at him. "Hey, that's foxy boss to you."

He raised his hands in placation. "Sorry, sorry, I'll remember next time."

"Aren't you supposed to be off?"

"Just staying through the rush." He turned to the next person in line. "Hey Mike, you want your usual?"

I patted his big shoulder as I squeezed past.

"Hey Jessicas, how's it going?"

The Jessica on the machine smile widely. "Good, Jamie. How's your first day going?"

"Really good, but I'm missing this place like crazy." I grabbed up a rag and began wiping down a spill near the espresso machine. "I'm kind of thinking my first project here should be getting you guys another person, huh?"

The Jessica at the bagel counter spun. "That'd be awesome. I mean—not that we can't handle it, because we can. But usually we have three people and nothing close to these kinds of crowds."

I nodded before pulling out the trash, which was completely full, as was the recycling. "I'm on it. My first project." Pulling the string to the trash bag, I tied it off. "I'll just take these back. Anything you guys need restocked?"

"Sixteen ounce cups would be good," Chris called.

Yanking the heavy trash out, I set a new liner in before heading to the back. "I'm on it!" It took me a couple minutes to set my poor crew up and meet Patrick in my office.

I found him staring at his phone, thumbs moving fast across his screen.

"Whatcha playing?" I asked, leaning in.

"Oh." He looked up, looking a little busted himself. "Ah, just one of Kay's games. Nothing." He turned the phone to face me, showing a bunch of little cartoon birds.

"Cool. So, I'm thinking maybe we should just pick up what we need here and get something at a drive-thru on the way to the office to give these guys a break."

He shrugged, stowing his phone in his pocket. "I'm down." Slowly, he turned. "Did you actually go to all of these concerts?"

"No, I wish. Maybe two-thirds of them. Some are from when my mom was a teenager. My dad contributed a couple, but it's really much more my mom's thing. Also, some pretty amazing celebrities have visited my dad's bar," I pointed to a signature on one of the posters, "And even after they divorced, he got signatures for her."

Patrick leaned in. "Wow."

"I know, right? Yeah, but since I have limited room, I'm only taking the ones that I've actually been to." Lifting a poster off the hook, I set it on my desk before reaching up to grab another poster.

"Uh, you want some help?" When I looked over at Patrick, I noticed he was sort of leaning, obviously trying to get out of my way in the very small space.

"I'm sorry. My office is so small," I said.

His eyebrows rose. "Do you want me to leave?"

"No, I—let's just get what you need, then I'll grab my stuff and we can go."

He smiled. "I'm just here for you. Here, uh, I'll step out."

I pressed myself against the wall so he could step out.

I grabbed three more posters, as that was probably all that would fit on my cubical wall and I felt bad having Patrick doing all this stuff for me. Especially since, obviously, even this morning he thought maybe we still had a chance. The heavy poster frames dug into my arms as I maneuvered back out of my office.

"Hey, let me take that for you," Patrick said, and then he just did.

"Uh—um, okay, are you sure?" I asked.

He laughed. "Lead the way."

We snuck out the back and walked down the alley to Patrick's car. The air felt completely still, the warm day whispering that summer was close.

"Oh, here, I'll take that, I don't want to put it in with the poison." I fake coughed, "Sorry, I mean air fresheners."

After I climbed in my seat, he handed over the stack of frames, setting them in my lap. He leaned into my door with a smirk. "You really don't like those things."

"They're actually really bad for you, and they smell like ass."

"All right."

When he was next to me and we were on our way to drive-thru Mexican, I peered over at him. "Do I really have to wait for milkshakes or do I get to hear your semi-inappropriate jokes now?"

"Milkshakes."

"You're no fun."

My phone vibrated again in my bag, and I had to maneuver my purse over the frames. Extracting out my phone, I saw Pat's name again on the screen.

"Shit, it's your dad."

"Ignore it." Patrick pulled into the Mexican drive through parking lot.

"I can't ignore it."

He looked over. "Trust me, ignore it."

Gritting my teeth, I groaned before answering, "You've reached Jamie."

"Hello, Jamie, it's Pat. I only have a minute to talk. My wife, Caroline, knew a little about your case when I told her you joined the team. She's planning you a dinner this Friday evening, I couldn't stop it. It's just going to be my family there, very casual; I hope you can make it."

I turned wide eyes on Patrick. "Oh my god," I mouthed.

"Say no," he mouthed back. Instead of pulling into the drive-thru, he pulled into a parking spot and shut off his engine.

"Hello, did you go somewhere?" Pat said over the phone.

"Um, Pat, that is so kind of your wife, but I have plans—um, with your son, actually, and my boyfriend, and Kay and Sarah, and—"

Patrick waved his hands. 'No, just say that you can't, nothing else,' he mouthed.

But it was way too late for that. "Bring them along. Patrick Jr. will be coming too; I'll force him if I have to. Does six work for you?"

"Pat, I—"

"Too early?"

"No, uh, it's just that—"

"Okay, great, I'll tell Caroline to expect three of you guys. How was your first day? Is Doug giving you any trouble?"

"Nope, that's fine, but I—"

"I'm sorry Jamie; I really have to head in to a meeting."

Patrick shook his head.

"I can't go this Friday," I said into a dead phone.

Day Ten: Twelve forty-five

I looked at Patrick. I looked at the phone. "Holy shit. Is that what it's always like?"

Patrick started up the car. "Pretty much." He pulled into the drive-thru.

"How am I going to get out of it?"

"Unfortunately, you probably can't. If you try to call him back, he won't answer or respond for at least twenty-four hours. When you do get through to him, my mother will have 'already bought all the supplies' and you can cancel, but she'll be very disappointed."

"Shit."

"The best way to get out of it is just tell him an absolute 'no' when he first asks, no explanation." He rolled down his window to order our food.

We didn't have time to sit and eat together; by the time we pulled into Harrington's corporate office, there was a call on my cell phone from an unknown number that turned out to be Doug.

"Are you back here or still visiting sites?" he asked in greeting.

"We're pulling in now."

"Great, I'll be down in just a second, we can just go from there," he said.

"I—uh, have stuff to bring up. Can I meet you up there?"

There was a way too lengthy pause, before he answered, "Sure, that's fine. Just meet me in my office."

I hung up and turned to Patrick. "Tell me how to fix this. This is just my first day and Doug is like giving me weird awkward silences for extremely reasonable requests."

"I'm not sure I have a good answer for you there," Patrick said as he began to walk toward the building. "I just always reassure everyone that I've got as much as I can handle, and I'm not looking for any more responsibility."

"Okay . . ."

We were not alone in the parking lot; perhaps forty or more other people threaded through the parking lot and parked cars, heading in toward the shiny, curved building.

"Want to switch?" Patrick asked, looking between the food in his hands and the stack of frames in mine.

"Nah, I'm good. So, is this just today or do I get to work with you more?" I asked.

The question made him happy, a twitch of a smile playing on his cheek. "I'll come by tomorrow, definitely. I have some actual work to do so I probably can't ride around with you tomorrow. But I'll definitely be available for lunch."

"Sounds good."

My arms started to complain by the time we were in the elevator, frames digging into my inner elbows. The smell of the Mexican food tortured my empty stomach. Patrick took me to my cubical and pulled out my burrito, giving me a quick hug before rushing away.

I unwrapped the top of my burrito and turned to find Doug standing only a few feet.

"Oh," I said, mouth full of fish and salsa. Quickly, I chewed and swallowed.

"Hey, Doug. I was just heading to you."

"Good, we're running pretty late. Could you maybe stay just until we get through visiting all of the shops?"

"I—can't, I have to pick up my daughter at two forty-five."

He glanced at his watch. "That means we only have forty-five minutes to visit four more locations, Jamie."

"I'm ready." I held up my burrito. "I can eat and walk."

He turned away. "Yeah, let's go."

I stayed several feet behind, trying to eat my burrito as quietly as humanly possible.

"So, Jenna called in and said you don't like my air fresheners . . . that you tossed them in the trash." Doug didn't turn as he talked.

Jenna was officially my least favorite of all the people I'd met today, not counting Doug—as I'd technically met him a few days before. I chewed the food in my mouth, tasting sour cream and guacamole. After swallowing, I admitted, "Yeah, sorry. I didn't throw away the ones from the other shop, though. They're in Patrick's trunk, I can grab them tomorrow."

"You took all of them out?"

Crap, I could already tell this was going to be a thing.

"I did. I'm probably going to take them out of the other stores too. Am I overstepping, or can I do that?" Another good question, that I'm not going to ask, was if every change I made would be overstepping, because I had a feeling it might be.

He didn't answer right away, so I focused back on my burrito as we stepped back out into the parking lot.

"You can make that decision, that's fine. But, I'd like them returned. I bought them myself and if they're not going to be used, I'll take them home."

I cringed. "Oh, sorry. Yeah, I'll bring them in and I'll replace the ones I tossed. I shouldn't have done that."

"It's fine. I'm thinking we should take separate cars. We probably won't get through all the locations and you'll likely want to leave from wherever we are in time to go pick up your kid."

"Yeah, thanks." As we walked toward our cars, I tried to hold out an olive branch. "Do you have any kids?"

"Nope." He didn't even turn around.

"How about pets?" I asked as I crinkled my burrito wrapper into a ball.

"I have a dog. My car's right here." He pointed. "I'll see you at the location on main."

"Great—okay, see you there." I waved before turning again toward where I thought my car should be, but wasn't.

Scanning the lot, I realized I was in the entirely wrong row. Doug pulled out of his space and I waved to him, a little awkwardly. I waited until he had pulled away to cut between cars and rush over to where the car sat.

We only had time to visit two locations. Doug introduced me to the nervous young baristas as their new general manager, Jamie. And, yes, I would be sending out more information later in the week. Obviously, that was a task that he didn't mind handing over to me. He took the air fresheners out himself, stowing them in his trunk.

"This was fun, we should do it again," I said as we stepped back out in the parking lot.

Stone-faced, he responded, "Sure, let's try for eight o'clock at the Hoover street location. We can finish this quickly in the morning, and hopefully get back on track."

I grinned. "Sounds good. Thank you for everything, Doug. I'll see you tomorrow bright and early."

"Thank you also, Jamie. See you in the morning." He turned, climbing back into his car.

"Oh, you hate me so much," I whispered as I climbed into my car. Usually, I couldn't give a rat's ass, but I really, really didn't want my boss to hate me.

And I was right, he totally hated me. Resentment stiffened his back and shortened his tone. It was in the manner of how he informed me that he checked on The Coffee Stops' social media sites, and noticed they didn't reflect recent changes.

Yes, I hadn't logged onto the shop's social media sites since the change, but I'd had a hell of a weekend. Okay, that was a lie. I'd been avoiding the sites since Amy posted the video. The very idea of feeding through the online drama made my skin itch. I chose to abstain and avoid.

I pulled into Sarah's school as groups of children spilled out of the doors along the school's outer wall. My car crawled along as chatting women crossed to their cars, kids trailing behind them. My usual stopping point stood open, so I pulled into it and shifted into park.

"Jamie!" I heard Beza's voice as I stepped out of my car.

Spinning, I saw Beza stepping out of one of one of the doorways. Aiden looked around at the other kids distractedly behind her.

"Jamie, what are you doing here?" Beza asked.

"Oh crud, Beza, I totally forgot!"

She grimaced. "Do you have your clothes for yoga?"

"Oh my god, no. I remembered I was going, but I forgot all my stuff this morning and forgot again on the way back from school. Oh, she's going to kill me." My hands went to my forehead.

"I'm going to call her; she's probably on her way in." Beza pulled her phone from her bag as I pulled mine from my purse. As I pressed the button to turn my phone on, text messages flashed across my screen.

Susan: Where are you?

Susan: You better not be standing me up

Susan: You are fired

I quickly typed in a response.

Me: I completely forgot. I'm at the school right now. I am so sorry!

Susan: Come here now!

Me: I forgot my stuff, too.

Susan: Ugh! Fired. Fine, I'll go to this crap alone.

Me: I am so sorry!

She didn't respond.

"Mom!" Sarah plowed into me as I stowed my phone.

"Hey baby," I said as my hands went around her. I peered up to Ms. Brown, whose pretty, patterned dress matched a new pair of glasses.

"Hey Jamie," she said as she waved and backed away. "I have to go to a meeting, but Sarah had a great day!"

"Awesome."

"See you ladies tomorrow!" she said, as she spun and rushed off, her dress swishing around her legs.

Squeezing Sarah to me, I turned back. "I am so sorry, Beza."

She sighed. "It's fine, Jamie, it'll work out fine."

"Do you want my list of excuses?"

She reached up and patted my arm. "Honey, it's fine. Do you want me to take Sarah, anyway?"

"No, I—it'll just run smoother if I take her now. I even forgot to tell her she was going to your house after school, I'm such a mess." I shook my head.

"First day at a new job and everything else, it's perfectly understandable. Aiden and I have some errands to run anyway. And Susan will get over it by tomorrow." She rubbed my arm one more time, and then turned to Aiden. "You ready to go, baby?"

He looked up as if Beza just woke him. "What?"

"Ready to go?"

"Isn't Sarah coming?" he lisped through his words.

"Not today."

He waved. "Hi, Aunt Jamie!"

"Hey, cutie. You guys have a good night," I said, steering Sarah toward the car.

Minutes later when we were both in the car and Sarah was singing along to her kids' CD, I realized I had time to kill and absolutely nowhere to go. Also, I was going to have to take Sarah with me to the courthouse at four.

I drove away from the curb only to park again in a stall.

Running through my options, nothing really shone out as a good choice. Everyone I knew besides Susan and Beza were at work. As there was an hour and fifteen minutes to kill, most activities either took more than that or less. We could go bowling, maybe, but that place was even over-stimulating for me.

I looked into my rearview mirror. "Do you want to go hang out at the playground, Sarah?"

"No, I want to go home," she said, smiling.

"Well, we can't do that. How about a restaurant?"

"Can we watch floor exercises?" she asked, kicking the seat in front of her.

We had no place to go. We had no home. God, I hated Clarke so much. If he was standing in front of me, I'd freaking hit him with my car.

As if my thought sparked him into existence, a shiny blue four-door sedan just like Clarke's rolled down the street.

"Shit." My stomach plummeted all the way to my toes and I ducked down behind my steering wheel.

"Shit!" Sarah yelled from the backseat.

Most of the car was obscured by a short hedge so I couldn't read the license plate, but it looked just like his car.

The car stopped at the crosswalk to let three older kids cross.

My hand fished wildly through my purse, trying to pull out my cell phone. The hard surface hit my fingers and I yanked it out. When I looked back, the kids stepped up on the far sidewalk, and the car began driving away. I unlocked my phone, opened the camera app and snapped a photo just as the car turned onto another street.

I looked down at my camera screen. A blue blurred out bumper turned just so its license-plate was at an angle where no letters showed. "Damn it," I whispered.

"Mom, I want to watch floor exercises."

I turned to Sarah, smiling in the back seat. "Yeah, yeah sure honey. I'm . . . let's go to Cameron's garage and you can sit in his office and watch floor exercises," I mumbled as I turned the keys in the ignition.

As I backed up, I called Cameron with my phone on my lap. As I pressed the button for speaker, the ringtone buzzed through my phone's speaker.

The phone rang several times before Cameron's voice came on the speaker, "Hello, you've reached Cameron at Custom Auto, please leave a message after the tone." I hung up just at the beep and dialed again, only to get the voicemail.

"Crap. Crap," I whispered under my breath.

"Mom, can I play with your phone?" Sarah asked from the backseat.

"Uh, not right now, baby," I called back as I took another turn, a little too fast, onto the street Cameron's body shop sat on.

Cameron's shop sat neatly on one corner, giving little sign that it was a body shop at all. No pileup of cars in desperate need of repairs waited outside, just a long tan building with a small red sign that read Custom Auto. I parked along the street, not wanting to take the only open space in his four stall lot, and I went around to grab Sarah out.

I grabbed the handle of Cameron's swinging glass door, held it open for Sarah, and then followed her in.

Oil, paint and a car air freshener scent sat heavy in the room. Sarah ran immediately to an empty desk and scooted up into Cameron's swiveling chair. She spun around. "Mom, can I watch floor exercises?"

"In a second, baby." Louder, I called, "Hello?"

"Oh, sorry. I'm coming," a familiar female voice called.

Surprise washed through me and the blood rushed out of my face.

"I'm coming!" Her voice got closer as my feet rooted to the spot.

The universe obviously already decided for me and it wasn't going to let me have a skip day, it seemed. The universe was a total bitch.

"Hey, how can I—" Vanessa stepped through the door, and stopped dead.

Day Ten: Three O'clock

I can't remember the day that Vanessa and I became best friends, not like I could with Logan and Susan. I know it was before Logan and Susan, probably over some game of house in Kindergarten. Vanessa had been my other half. I was silly and happy, she was silly and sad. As Logan and Susan had each other, Vanessa was that to me—my Halloween costume partner every year, the friend that came over every day after school. In seventh grade she pretty much moved into my mom's house because her mother had a new boyfriend that didn't want kids. Thankfully, that relationship ended in her mother deciding that she'd never date again.

Framed in the doorway, I couldn't help but notice that she'd lost weight, maybe ten pounds. Her beautiful features tucked in closely to her face, especially sunken in around the eyes. She wore low-riding jeans and a flowy top, her blonde hair piled high on her head.

Sarah dove out of Cameron's chair and sprinted to collide with Vanessa's legs.

"Holy shit," she said, before looking down to Sarah who was gripping Vanessa's diminished waistline. "Oh my goodness, Sarah. You're so big," she whispered, before glancing up to me. "I'm sorry, Jamie, I—this is probably not okay with you—I just stopped in to pick something up and Cameron asked me to watch the shop for a minute while he ran out. I—I'm sorry."

I wiped away a tear that ran down my face, completely without any words to speak.

"I–Sarah, you have to let go now, baby," Vanessa said.

"No. She can hug you, if you want," I said roughly as another tear caught in the crease under my nose.

"Okay," she whispered as her hands rubbed down Sarah's head. "Wow, you're big, monkey."

The door opened behind me and I practically jumped as I turned around to see Cameron entering backwards with his hands full of boxes. "Hey, is Jamie here?" he asked, before he even turned.

When he did turn, he stopped to look between us. "Oh, hey."

I swallowed. "Hey."

He crossed the room, setting the boxes down on his desk quickly before walking back to me. His hand went to the small of my back. "Hey, everything okay? I thought you were heading to yoga. Did something happen?"

"I–I completely spaced after work and just drove to Sarah's school."

"Oh, okay." He turned back to Vanessa. "Thank you so much for watching the shop for me, Ness."

"Yeah, it was no problem." I could hear the emotion she was holding back in her voice. She looked back down. "Sarah, love, now I really need to go." She stepped just slightly away and Sarah let her go.

Sarah smiled. "I love you so much."

Vanessa sniffed and blinked rapidly. "I love you . . . uh–um, I love you so much, too. I'm going to go now. I'll see you later." She waved as she passed us, heading determinedly out the door.

The door closed behind her with a whooshing sound.

"You okay, baby?" Cameron asked.

"Um . . . I—" I turned to the door. Blowing out a breath, I whispered, "I'm going to be right back, is that okay?"

"If . . . you want to," he said, unsure.

"I don't know," I mumbled as I followed out of the door.

Vanessa stood feet away, sobbing with her hand on the handle of her car. She glanced over her shoulder, seeing me, eyes already red. "Oh, I . . . I'm sorry, Jamie. I swear, I'm leaving. I—"

"I was planning on calling you today."

After a long pause, she asked, "Really?"

I scrubbed a tear away with the palm of my hand. "Yeah. I couldn't do it, but I was planning on it."

Another silence stretched between us, before she said, "Okay."

"Maybe I'll try again tomorrow. I can't promise anything, though."

"You don't have to," she said. "I know it—I know it means nothing. But, I just wanted to tell you that I'm happy that you and Cam are together now. You don't . . . I—"

"Thank you."

She nodded.

"I don't want to carry it around with me anymore. It's just—it's hard."

She nodded, again.

"I'm going to go back in." I gestured over my shoulder.

She wiped at her nose, which was running. "Okay."

Turning, I pulled open the door to Cameron's shop and stepped inside.

Cameron glanced up from where he was leaning in toward his desk.

"That one!" Sarah poked Cameron's computer screen, scooting it back a little.

"Oh yeah," Cameron said. He turned back to the computer and clicked his mouse, making some instrumental music blare out of his speakers. After turning the knob on his little detached speaker, Cameron stepped away and toward me. "Hey, baby."

"Hey," I breathed.

He wrapped his arms around me, pulling me against him. "I'm sorry about Vanessa being here. She was picking up some papers, and I needed to step out because some parts came—"

"You don't need to apologize, Cameron."

He kissed my forehead. "Okay. I just need to do one more thing before I can close up, do you mind waiting?"

"You don't need to close up early."

He squeezed me even tighter. "I want to. I'm interviewing a lady tomorrow, seems like a good fit. If things work out, I'm going to be free after two-thirty every day."

"That'd be really nice," I said.

Cameron locked the front door before going back into his shop.

I sat down in one of his waiting room chairs, staring off while Sarah's Olympics announcers analyzed a move. There were so many things I needed to do, I knew that, but I couldn't quite think of what they were. My face felt heavy, like a metal mask weighed down my features.

Absently, I pulled out my wallet and extracted my worn detox list from its fold. On day ten now, there were so many tasks above me, and almost nothing after. Five inches above, and only half an inch below.

I'd worked through all the hard steps, especially as I'd already decided that I wasn't going to stop sleeping with Cameron, I was going to do the opposite. How had Susan put it? Something like: quit him or make him for real. I chose the latter. But if I was through all the hard parts, why did it feel like the worst was yet to come? Why did it feel like my huge challenge, the one that was really going to knock me on my ass, was just around the corner?

I looked to the space under the list. Underneath number thirteen, where Susan had written, 'be happy,' was the faint remains of task fourteen. It was my vetoed task, the one we'd erased from the list. If I leaned in really close though, I could just barely see: number fourteen, talk to my mother.

I closed my eyes.

It was the task that everyone thought I should have done a long time ago. I knew that. If I forgave Logan and Vanessa, I should be able to forgive my mother, I knew that, too. She didn't do anything wrong. She didn't deserve my anger. All these things I knew. I really, really did.

Yet, I also knew when Susan added it to the list, I wasn't going to be able to do it.

"Are you guys hungry?" Cameron's voice called, though he was muffled by distance.

Opening my eyes, I quickly grabbed the list from where it sat on my lap and shoved it in my purse.

Just as I straightened up, Cameron stepped through the open door. "I was thinking of ordering some pizza after the courthouse, what do you think?"

"Yeah, sounds good."

"Cool, I'm good to go. Too bad we have two cars."

"Or if you would be okay driving Sarah, I could just pop in and then head to your house."

Cameron stood up straighter, but he didn't respond for a second. "Do you feel safe doing that?"

"Yeah, it's a courthouse. Besides I've been alone all day. I think I just need to avoid being at my usual haunts alone." The moment I said it, I remembered I hadn't told Cameron about thinking that I saw Clarke's car outside of Sarah's school. Although, I didn't think this was exactly the right moment to tell him.

"What if we take one car to the courthouse and Sarah and I wait in the car?"

Standing, I grabbed my purse. "If you're okay with that. I just don't really want to make Sarah go through the security and have to be there for all this stuff. If you're okay waiting outside, I'd really appreciate it."

"Yeah, no problem."

We took my car because Sarah's booster was already in there and I was parked in a two-hour zone, anyway. Sarah's game music blared out of my phone in the backseat as we parked. "Maybe I should just leave her with my phone," I mumbled, looking in the backseat. Looking back to Cameron, I said, "I'll just be in and out."

The day beat down so hot that I pulled off my sweater. Upon seeing that my entire tank-top was a carpet of sweater fuzz, I put it directly back on. The courthouse cast a long shadow over the stairs that led up to it. Passing into the shadow felt like a relief from the heat, but for some reason, I had the thought: turn around.

I glanced over my shoulder, looking to where I could still see Cameron and Sarah's figures in my car.

Slowly, I turned. This whole situation was making me nervous and incredibly paranoid.

A small line formed outside the security check point, and I took my place behind a pair of older men in suits. Different security guards manned the station this time, and they didn't pay any attention to me as I put my purse through the scanner and stepped through.

Several people took the elevator up with me; two younger guys in baggy clothes with earrings shot me looks over their shoulder, but got off at the second floor with the rest. The county clerks' office door again stood open, several people waiting inside. I didn't know if I should wait in the ten person line or just off where a group of six other people waited. I stepped into the line, my gaze combing over the room.

"You can't be fucking serious," came a whisper at my ear.

Gasping, I spun to find Clarke standing directly behind me.

My mouth fell open as my eyes met his livid gaze. In my mind I had stretched him, made him taller, bigger, fanged, but he looked so small, so familiar. He was probably only a couple inches taller than me and his face looked entirely normal, like he could have stepped out of any shop downtown, just strolling around. He looked pissed off, though, like he might hit me.

A scream dried up in my throat, right along with all of my words.

He leaned in so close that I could feel the space between the bristles on his jaw and my cheek. "You really think I'm going to let a prostitute get me arrested?"

I dodged, and rammed into the person behind me in line.

The person cried out, and I jumped away.

I looked over my shoulder to see the elderly woman I stood behind in line had fallen onto the younger man who stood beside him.

"Watch out!" the young guy yelled.

"I'm so sorry—I . . ."

"That guy pushed her," someone else said from behind me.

I spun back to see a tall woman with a shaved head behind me in line, pointing toward the clerk's door. Clarke had vanished.

"I saw it, he pushed her," the woman said as she stepped up.

"No—uh, he didn't push me, but he scared me so bad that I fell back. I'm so sorry, are you okay?" I put an arm out to the elderly woman, who turned to me.

"I'm fine, just a little shocked, is all." She patted my hand.

"He didn't push you?" the tall buzzed-hair woman asked, looking almost like she didn't believe me.

"He leaned in and called me a whore, but he didn't actually push me. I'm actually here to get a restraining order against that guy." I pointed back. "That guy is my neighbor and I have an ongoing police report going for him. Do you think that maybe you could be a witness for me?"

She nodded. "Yeah, of course I can."

"You saw his face, right?" I asked her, looking up into her piercing blue gaze.

She shook her head. "I wasn't really paying attention to him. I think he went up over there . . ." she pointed across to the other side of the office. "And he got a packet. Then I saw him . . . well, what looked like push you, but I guess not." When I asked, she gave me her number and said that she'd definitely talk to the cops. Unfortunately, the people in front of me in line hadn't seen Clarke's face either.

When I looked around the room, no one else faced my way or would make eye contact. The clerk behind the desk looked over a couple times, but turned back to help the man in front of her.

Even in a crowded room, I barely had a single witness.

I wanted to rush out of there. I wanted to scream. Instead, I waited in line until it moved up to the front.

When I stepped up to the clerk, the same clerk I had talked to on Friday evening, she asked, "Everything okay back there?"

"The . . . the guy I filed to get a restraining order against was here, he leaned in and whispered something really nasty to me. You didn't see what happened, did you?"

"I didn't." The clerk's lips pressed together. "Well, I'm sorry you had to deal with that here." She shook her head.

"Thanks." Inhaling deeply, I said, "You told me that the judgment on whether I could get a temporary restraining order would be here today at four."

"Name?" she asked.

"Jamie Scott."

"Yeah, we have it. Go on ahead down to that side of the counter and an associate clerk will grab it for you." She pointed down the counter. She pointed to the place that Francine had said Clarke had gone to get papers.

"Oh," I whispered, voice hoarse. "Tha—thank you." Numb, I walked down the counter to another woman.

She looked up through thin-rimmed glasses. "Name?"

"Jamie Scott."

She searched through a group of sealed manila folders.

She grabbed one from the stack, and then asked, "Can I see your ID please?"

After I handed it to her, she handed me the packet with my name on a white label in the right-most corner.

"Thanks," I mumbled as I turned away.

My steps echoed loudly on the hallway floor as I walked from the clerk's office. I stood outside the elevator for a couple minutes, my hand reaching for the button.

I didn't want to ride the elevator alone. The thought embarrassed me so much, but it was true. God, Clarke had turned me into such a chicken-shit. He cowed me. I should have hit him or yelled out; instead I fell back onto an elderly woman.

Pressing the button, I stepped back from the elevator. When another group exited the clerk's office and waited with me for the elevator, I was more relieved than I'd admit out loud.

Day Ten: Four-twenty

My expression had to say a thousand words, because as I walked toward the car, Cameron jumped out.

"What happened?" he asked, leaving his car door open to cross over to me.

I cleared my throat. "Clarke was in the office, and they didn't issue the temporary restraining order." My voice broke as I said the words. I held up the open manila folder.

"What the fuck?" Cameron asked, taking the folder, but keeping his gaze on me.

"They gave me a court date, but they didn't give me the temporary restraining order."

"Did he follow you in there?"

"No, he was there before I even got in there."

His gaze skirted all over the lot. "What the hell?" he said the words almost to himself. "Did he do anything to you?"

"He said that he's not going to let a prostitute get him arrested." I shook my head.

His expression darkened, jaw clenching. "I'm getting really fed up with letting this guy call you a prostitute."

"He's said it so much I'm almost wondering, does he actually think I'm a prostitute or something?"

His gaze narrowed. "No, he's just a real sicko."

I looked away. "God. Why wouldn't they just— now he knows I'm trying to get a restraining order against him, and I don't even have it. And I have to have someone give him a notice to appear." I made a loud annoyed voice and shook my head. "Why does this have to be so hard?"

Cameron's arm came around me. "Let's just get home and really go through the papers. I'll order some pizza on the way."

"Thank you. That sounds awesome."

Cameron drove on the way back to his garage, and followed me closely up to his house in his car. Sarah ran up to the house, probably so ready to be out of the car.

Inside the house, thankfully, Sarah immediately ran upstairs to play with her doll. Cameron and I sat down at the table, spreading out the paperwork between us. No new revelations popped out of it. I was granted a court date, but nope, not the temporary restraining order.

"I should call the police to report what happened today," I said it all on a sigh, because everything I was doing didn't seem to be making a difference.

"I'll head upstairs, check on Sarah and if it's okay with you, I'd really like to shower. My sinuses are feeling a little irritated from this stuff I sprayed on a car today. It's not toxic, but it feels uncomfortable."

"Yeah, of course, Cameron," my voice threaded with laughter, even though laughing was the last thing I felt like doing.

The officer that had been assigned to my case, Kelly Oliver listened quietly while I explained every detail of my last encounter with Clarke. After she took down Francine's number she asked, "How do you think he knew you were going to be in there?"

"It doesn't make any sense to me, actually. Oh, I forgot to mention that I thought I saw his car outside of Sarah's school right after the school got out. If it was him, maybe he followed me all day, but that wouldn't make any sense either because he was there before me, picking up a packet."

"I'll look into it," she said, before pausing. "So, that's pretty scary—the possibility of him being outside of Sarah's school. Why don't you describe that to me?"

A knock came at the door.

"Shoot, sorry, there's someone at the door."

"I'll stay on the line if you want to answer it."

I wasn't sure if I should, but I heard the pipes from the shower running upstairs. Slowly, I crossed the room, leaning in to peer through the peep-hole.

"Oh, it's just the pizza guy," I said over the phone, though it was more for my own sake. I covered the receiver. "One second!"

Running back to the table, I grabbed my purse and returned to the door. With the phone balanced against my ear, I opened the door to a teenage-looking guy holding up a big red bag.

"Pizza delivery," he said with a big smile.

I fished through my purse for my wallet, grabbed out the money and handed it over. "Keep the change," I said as I stuffed my wallet back into my purse and grabbed the pizza from him.

After setting my purse and the pizzas on the table, I told the officer every detail of seeing what might have been Clarke's car. She had me email the picture, even though I warned her how bad it was.

Both Sarah and Cameron came down as I was finishing with the email, or more floated down, chasing the smell of the pizza.

I pushed send just as Sarah took the seat beside me.

"My fourteen-day soul detox?" Cameron asked in a voice like he was reading the words.

I spun to see Cameron, freshly washed and in new clothing, standing by the door, a wrinkled piece of paper held up in his hand.

"Oh, uh—" I reached toward him, but it was too late. "Cameron?"

He looked up at me. "I found this lying by the door." He glanced to the floor, like maybe there was some sort of mistake. "This is yours?" he said it as a question, but at the same time, it didn't sound like a question. He looked back to the paper.

"I'm . . ." But I didn't know what I was. I was a freaking idiot. I was having a hell of a day. I was somehow stupid enough to drop that piece of paper out of my purse.

"This doesn't look like your handwriting," he said.

"Susan wrote it."

He looked back to me, dark gaze questioning. "Did she write this, tell you to do this?"

God, I almost wanted to throw Susan under the bus and say 'yep, it was all Susan.' As if I hadn't been a bad enough friend to her today.

"It was my idea to change my life, and her idea to do a list. We wrote the list together, she contributed some, I supplied others." I sucked my lower lip into my mouth and chewed on it, waiting for him to respond.

His eyelids narrowed, posture going defensive. "So is number eleven here your wording or hers?"

Number eleven. I had it memorized, the task I wasn't going to do: stop sleeping with her ex-husband. I swallowed. "It was . . . my wording."

He nodded, looking back to the paper. "Well, looks like you've done everything else on this list. I wondered why you quit coffee . . ."

I looked down again, not able to hold his eyes.

Crossing the room, he set the paper before me.

"I obviously changed my mind," I said as he begun to back away from me.

He ran a hand through his hair. "Ah, Jamie," he said under his breath before turning back to the stairs and heading up them.

My eyelids heated as I turned back to the table.

Sarah had opened the pizza box and was eating directly out of it, her face and shirt covered in tomato sauce.

"Hey baby, uh, we're going to go . . ."

She stopped chewing. "No, stay home," she said.

"Baby, let's go to Grandpa's house, yeah? Let's stay with Grandpa and Grandma tonight?"

"No! Stay home!" She threw down her pizza.

My head fell into my hands.

Fuck fixing my life. Fuck the universe. After working my ass off for almost two weeks to improve my life, the only lesson I learned was that I should never try to better my situation.

If you tell the universe that you really want to change, they'll send a freight train to crash through your life.

Standing up, I went in search of Cameron's liquor cabinet. Vanessa must have taken their entire wine cabinet in the divorce, but there had to be a secondary source. Yeah, he didn't have any food, but he was a guy so I figured there was a high probability that he had liquor.

All I found was one completely full bottle of whisky. It was dusty and tucked high in a cupboard. I cracked the cap off and poured myself a tall glass. I lifted the glass, but as the astringent smell hit my nose, I pulled it away.

Logan's image surfaced in my mind, gray-faced and trudging to the coffee maker.

He grabbed the bottle of whisky out of the fridge and opened the lid.

"Jesus, Logan," I hissed as I stepped in close to him.

Bleary eyes turned to me. "Oh, hey, baby." He went to pour the whisky into his coffee.

"Logan, stop. Seriously, it's seven in the morning."

He smirked, his hand going to my hip. "Sweetie, don't act like my mom. I'm a grown man."

Emotion filled my voice, but I kept my voice low, "I'm not acting like your mom, I'm acting like her mom." I pointed to Sarah who watched us over her cereal, sitting at our kitchen table. I continued,

"And, she's watching her daddy drink while she eats breakfast."

"You're right." He gave me a quick kiss before grabbing the mug and the bottle, and walking into our bedroom. The door closed.

Damn it. I hated whisky.

Sighing, I poured my entire glass into the sink before I shoved the bottle back into its cupboard.

Crossing back to the table, I took the seat beside Sarah, who had managed to eat half the pizza.

Cameron didn't come out of the room, nor did I go in. I helped Sarah with her homework, then into a shower before getting ready for bed. I lay with her in her bed as she began to fall asleep.

"I love you so much, Mommy," she said as she smiled over at me.

I brushed her hair from her forehead. "Girlie, it's all about you for me. You're my number one, you know that, right?"

She didn't answer, and soon she closed her eyes and sunk into her pillow. Eventually, I stood. Crossing to the other side of the hallway, I hesitated before knocking on Cameron's door.

"Come in," he called.

I considered doorbell ditching him, or door knock as it were, just spinning on my heel and dashing back down the stairs. God, I was such a chicken shit. Instead, I turned the knob and entered the room.

Cameron lay on the bed, his attention on a television playing on the far wall. He didn't look over as I entered.

"What are you doing?" I asked.

"Watching sports," he said.

"You don't like watching sports."

His jaw clenched.

"Do you want food?" I asked.

"I'll go grab some pizza later."

"Do you want us to leave?"

He finally looked over. "Of course not."

I took a step forward. "Are we going to talk about this? Because, I can tell you what it all was—"

"Can we do it tomorrow, Jamie? It's just, you've been through a lot today and I don't think I can talk about this without getting angry. I really don't want to fight with you while all the Clarke stuff is so fresh."

"Okay." I gestured over my shoulder. "I'll go sleep with Sarah."

He rolled his eyes. "No, you'll sleep here." His hand patted the bed beside him.

"No, I won't, because if I'm next to you and you're super pissed off at me, I'll obsess and I won't go to sleep. I'll just lay there hating the tension between us."

He grabbed the remote, turned off the TV and held out an arm. "Come here."

Like a little kid, I almost wanted to refuse, but I walked over to him. I paused a few feet from the bed. "Get in here," he said.

"Fine." I crawled in beside him.

He scooted down beside me and lowered his voice, "Jamie, what you wrote there, it fucking pissed me off, and I think you can tell that."

I sucked on a tooth. "Yeah."

"Yeah, it did. But I don't want you to leave. I'm not breaking up with you. And I definitely still want you in my bed."

"Yeah."

"But I'm still mad. I don't want to be, I know you are unsure about us—"

"Was unsure about us."

He raised his brow, and continued, "And, even if you wrote down that you wanted to stop 'sleeping with Vanessa's ex-husband' a little over a week ago—"

I held up a hand. "I—"

"Please, Jamie, I really, really don't want to fight about it yet."

My hand dropped to the bed. "Okay."

"I'm just saying that I'm angry about it, about the wording, and I'm going to be tonight, maybe tomorrow. If you can handle that, I'd like to talk about it tomorrow."

Even though I was pretty sure that it would kill me not to explain myself, I said, "I can handle that."

"Thanks, baby," he said before he rolled over and turned back to the television. He reached up with the remote and turned the television back on. It was some sports' channel and they were talking about basketball.

Not quite feeling better about my day, I climbed off the bed and walked to the bathroom to shower.

Day Eleven

The Long Run

Day Eleven: Seven O'clock

I woke in Cameron's arms. He had moved in his sleep, rolling practically on top of me. We'd melded to each other in our sleep.

Moving as little as possible, I reached forward and pressed snooze on the screen of my phone. I held my breath as I repositioned myself in Cameron's embrace, settling in.

For a couple hours yesterday, I was sure he would leave me. Like, seriously, who wouldn't? I'd kept him at arm's reach for a year, sleeping with him regularly, having him help me out a couple nights a week. All the while, I knew he was in love with me and I had no intention of being with him long term. Then, I try to break up with him, tell him I'm going to date around, but keep him on the hook. After all that, he gets tangled in the fucked up shit that's blasting through my life, and he finds out I had a big plan to dump his ass today. Actually, I referred to him as 'her ex-husband.'

God, I was such a fucked up mess. And Cameron has done nothing but love me, nothing but wait me out. He's stuck with me through my rejecting him, the spasmodic way I treated our relationship, Patrick, and being falsely accused of assault. He waited patiently, giving me love, support, and a lot of hot sex along the way.

I'd been so sure that I needed to leave him by today. The idea now turned my stomach. It was like considering removing one of my organs, my liver or small intestine. I knew I was in love with him. I knew that he'd been my safe harbor. What I didn't realize was that Cameron had become Sarah and my home, our family.

Sarah already realized it, she had moved right in. Cameron was her family, no questions asked, so much, she told me flat out that she wasn't going anywhere.

Even though I'd fought it so hard along the way, I couldn't even understand why now.

Yes, Cameron had known about Logan and Vanessa's affair. And, yes, I had a really, really hard time getting over that. But if I looked deeply inside of me, to the person I had been while Logan was falling apart all around me, I wasn't sure what I would have done had our situations been reversed.

How had Susan put it? We'd all look pretty bad on paper, but life was too messy for that. And, Cameron and I had been messy, we might always be messy. Everything in my life had always been chaotic, like standing in the path of the blossoms as the twirled and whirled down the street. A beautiful chaos.

The alarm on my phone rang out again, and Cameron's arm moved as he rolled away from me.

Slowly, I sat up in bed and climbed away from him. I grabbed up the clothes I laid out for myself last night and headed to the bathroom.

After my quick shower and dressing for work, a knock rattled the bathroom door.

"Sorry, one sec," I called before I opened the door to Sarah. Her eyelids were wide and legs moving in the international pee-pee dance.

"Oops, sorry, angel," I said as I skirted around her.

Reentering the bedroom, I found Cameron's bed empty and made. For some stupid reason, I had to blink tears back.

Fighting with Cameron fucking sucked. I didn't like it. I waved my hands and made all my stupidity vanish.

I walked slowly downstairs to find Cameron breakfasting on leftover pizza.

"Pizza?" I tried to tease.

He looked up, giving me a slight smile. "Yeah, this is actually much closer to my usual breakfast. There's plenty more if you want some."

"My first stop is a coffee shop today, so I'll just grab something there. Thanks for . . . taking Sarah to school again."

He rolled up his eyes and shook his head. "You don't need to thank me every day, baby. I'm just going to keep doing it, it's easy and she seems to like me taking her."

"I'm not going to stop appreciating it, though." I swallowed. "I love you, Cameron."

He set his chin in his hand, looking up at where I stood over him. "I know that."

"Good."

"I love you, baby. We'll talk later today, okay?"

I nodded. "I'm going to go say goodbye to Sarah, then take off, yeah?"

"Okay. Want to hang out at the shop again until I can get off work? I'll probably be able to finish up a little early."

"Yeah, but I . . . I told Patrick that Sarah and I would go with him and Kay to ice cream right after school. So, after that, I'll come right over."

He nodded, looking back to his pizza. "Patrick," he said before taking another bite of pizza.

"Is becoming my friend, just my friend." I nodded.

He took another bite, and then nodded. "I'll see you after, then."

"Yeah." I backed away, before turning back to head up the stairs.

Sarah sat on her bed, pulling up purple socks.

"I'm going to go, baby. Cameron will drive you to school again, you okay with that?"

She grinned up at me. "I love you so much, Mom."

"I love you too, monkey."

"Mom, what's your favorite color?"

"You know, I don't really have one . . . maybe green?"

"Your favorite color is green. Ask me what my favorite color is."

"What's your favorite color?"

She grinned even wider. "Purple."

I laughed. "Thank god, because if it was suddenly yellow we would have to buy you all new stuff, huh?" I kissed her on the top of her head. "Are you going to make good choices today?"

"No."

I tickled her. "What?"

"Good choices!"

"Okay, that's what I wanted to hear. And after you make good choices, we're going to go get ice cream with Kay. Does that sound nice?"

She nodded so enthusiastically she almost tumbled forward off the bed.

"Careful there, cutie," I said with a laugh.

I stepped away, but I didn't want to leave her. I wanted to stay, to blow off work and have her play hooky, so that we could both just hang out. It was a stupid thought as it was only my second day and my boss already hated me.

I turned, heading for the door.

"I love you so much, Mom."

Turning back, I said, "You too, cutie. Have a good day at school."

Cameron waited for me at the bottom of the stairs. When I stood before him, he reached up, hand going around the back of my neck. "You have a good day at work, baby."

"You too."

Leaning in, he kissed me lightly before stepping away.

I arrived at the Harrington's location ten minutes early, but Doug's car already waited outside. When I stepped in, I immediately found him sitting at a table, busily working on a tablet. As the line wasn't too bad, I decided to wait in it before I walked to greet him, prolonging the inevitable on purpose.

After grabbing some food and drinks, I crossed the small dining area and plopped into the wobbly seat across from him. "Morning," I sang.

He glanced up from his tablet. "Just one second, please."

"No prob," I said before taking a big bite of muffin. It was good, not great, but edible.

I was halfway through before Doug looked up. "Sorry, important email. Good morning."

I held up a bag. "Want a muffin?"

He looked at the muffin bag, brow furrowing. "You know we're allowed to take them for free, right?"

I shrugged. "Well, I bought this one for you, if you want it."

"Um . . . sure." He took the bag, but didn't take the muffin out.

Thinking that maybe he just felt uncomfortable, I started on the second half of my muffin. "So, what's on the docket for today?" I asked once my mouth was clear of crumbs.

He pulled a section of muffin out of the bag. "This location and another, before you do some more training at the office."

"Jamie," I heard the barista call.

"Oh, that'll be our drinks." I stood.

He paused with the piece of muffin halfway to his face. "Jamie, you didn't have to order my drink."

"It's my second day; you have to allow me to suck up a little bit." Cocking a cheeky eyebrow, I walked over to the coffee counter and grabbed our drinks.

"Americano," I said, setting the drink before him.

He took the cup, scooting it closer. "Well, just remember that you don't have to pay in the future."

"Sure."

He glanced at his watch. "Looks like we're on the clock now. How about I show you around the shop, introduce you to the crew, and then we'll head off?

We did just that and only did a quick breeze through the second location as well. My car clock only read eight forty-five when I started it up to head into the corporate office.

I purposefully lost Doug on the way, even though he told me to "follow him." I knew he was only a couple car lengths away, but I appreciated the distance. I might be determined to charm the hell out of him, but it felt really nice to be away from his *energy*, as Susan would put it. In that line of thought, I parked in a row several down from where I saw him parking and headed in. We met at the door.

Doug talked on his phone, acknowledging me with a smile that looked more like a grimace before we walked to the elevator.

"Yes, that's definitely possible," he said into the phone. "Oh." He glanced at me. "Yeah, she's with me now." He was silent for a minute before he held the phone out to me. "It's Pat."

Great.

"Heya, Pat," I said into the smartphone.

"Hello, Jamie. I've arranged for you to be able to tour our roasting facility today, but unfortunately neither Doug nor Patrick are available to go with you. Do you feel comfortable heading off there alone, or would you like me to go with you?"

Oh my god, no. I cleared my throat. "I'm sure I can handle it."

"Good, that's what I like to hear. Caroline wanted me to make sure that Sarah didn't have any allergies or a special diet."

"About Friday, Pat."

"What about Friday?" he asked, sternly.

I paused. "Oh, fine. No, she isn't on any special diet, but she's super picky, so please don't be offended if she doesn't eat anything. Also, Sarah spontaneously does gymnastics. She knows she's not supposed to, but does it anyway. Often things get broken, so we rarely go to people's houses if they're not family or close friends."

The elevator spread open to our floor.

"That's not a problem; all of our important possessions are insured."

"If you say so," I mumbled as I followed Doug to his office. If he strong-armed me into a dinner, I wasn't going to feel bad about the consequences.

"All right, please pass me back to Doug. Remember to call me if you have any questions or if Doug is acting like an ass."

Jesus.

"Cool, thanks," I said, dryly before handing the phone back to Doug, who was attempting to look inconspicuous in his own office. "I'll be at my cubical?" I whispered it to Doug, like a question.

Taking the phone, he nodded.

I tried not to run out of there, even though I had the very essential job of decorating my cubical. The concert photos and posters waited patiently for me, just where I had left them yesterday. Unfortunately, the tacks I brought from Cameron's just fell out when I hung my frames on them. When I tried two tacks, the frames still refused to hang. I stood up. "Psst, Crystal."

Her multi-colored head of hair shot up from her side. "Hey, Jamie. What can I do for ya?"

"How do you hang the pictures on your cubical wall?"

She held a finger up to her purple lipstick, then ducked back behind her wall. A moment later, she handed over a roll of adhesive strip.

"It's my secret, use as much as you want."

"Thank you!" I whispered emphatically as she ducked back into her cubical.

Doug appeared as I was sticking the last poster in. "You must really like music," he said.

"Um, sort of . . . yeah. I love music, but my mom is really, really into it. She was a backup singer for some pretty big names before she had me. Growing up, she took me to concerts all the time. Then I continued to go with my husband, so most of these are memories." He didn't respond, so I said, "Sorry, that's probably way more explanation than you needed. I can be a bit of an over-sharer." My cheeks heated.

"It's fine. Here is our list of distributors and information on how we make orders and such. It probably won't take you more than a couple hours. After lunch, you're scheduled to visit our local roaster, and have a tour. I tried to reschedule my meeting, but

it looks like that's impossible, so you'll have to visit
alone."

"No problem," I said as I took the folder.

Day Eleven: Nine-twenty

The information was only a little less boring than yesterday's. Harrington's only worked with one distributor, a company that I was pretty sure was also owned by Pat from its associated address. The ordering system was ridiculously simplistic compared to the system we had in The Coffee Stop, as we worked with several micro-distributors. I got the orders from each store manager, analyzed the needs, and input them into a program installed in the computer that would automatically order it from the website. It was efficient, I'd give them that. But where was the randomness of having a special, or having a barista invent some drink that could be incorporated into the menu if it was amazing? Maybe there was more than I could read from a program, but it all just seemed kind of like a creativity deadener.

When I got to the waste reports, I had to recheck the numbers. Each shop produced three to five times the amount of waste that The Coffee Stop produced. It didn't make any sense to me.

Standing, I walked over to Doug's office and knocked on the door.

"Come in," he called from the other side.

I poked my head in. "I just have a question. Do you have a minute?"

His smile didn't quite reach his eyes, but he smiled. "Come on in, I have a minute. What are you confused about?"

Walking in just a little, I asked, "Do you guys have a separate disposal program for your coffee grounds?"

He blinked at me. "I'm a little confused about what you mean."

"Like, a separate trash can with an opening just for the portafilter."

He stared at me blankly, his forehead furrowing.

"Um, the hopper the grounds go in to make the espresso." I gestured with my hands as I talked.

Realization lit his gaze. "No, we don't have that."

"Oh, uh—" I walked to the chair across from him and took a seat. "So wet grounds are incredibly heavy and take a lot of room with the amount you go through. So, at The Coffee Stop, we had a landscaping company drop by early each morning before opening to grab out grounds. They're really good fertilizer, I guess."

"At what expense?" he asked.

"Free. We donated it. They were a pretty small company but there are some much larger ones that I'm sure would be interested. Also, the mushroom farm south of the city might be interested; I was told that it's good for mushroom growing. It would cut waste costs by a lot."

"Great, I'll look into it," he said, turning back to his tablet.

"Or I could," I suggested.

He didn't look up at me as he continued, "I really want you to concentrate on training this week.

We can talk about waste management when you're through your basic training."

"Okay, but just so you know I'm talking about cutting your waste charges in half or more. You might even find a way to get a tax cut for it."

He exhaled out of his nose. "Sounds great, I'll definitely look into it. How is your training going?"

"Good, I have about two more pages."

"Great, I'll come out with what I had planned for tomorrow since you're so ahead."

"Thanks." Turning, I walked out of the office. Plan for the future: just make the changes, talk to Doug after. Officially, I was almost positive that I could do it without getting in trouble. Now, I'd just shot myself in the foot because it looked like Doug was married to his broken system. Maybe I read him wrong and he'd actually look into it, but I seriously doubted it. Dumb-ass.

Back at my desk, I finished the training in a couple minutes and sat, not wanting to go back into Doug's office to ask for something to do.

Crystal jumped up from behind her cubical. "Coffee run! What can I get everyone?" She went around the room, ending at me. "Coffee?"

"How about a tea?" I handed her a five.

"What are you, English?"

Grimacing, I admitted, "Nope, I'm in recovery."

Her purple lips made a perfect 'o'. "You don't drink coffee?"

"My friends had an intervention on me recently."

"Please never, ever, introduce me to your friends." She took my money. "What kind of tea?"

After I told her, she scampered off.

Doug's assistant, I think his name was Terry—no, Toby—came through with another folder of stuff, taking the first. "Here you go, love," he said with his adorable accent as he touched my shoulder.

"Thanks, Toby."

When he grinned, a little dimple turned up in his cheek. "You ever need anything, just call over. I'll be your assistant as well, when you're finished with training."

"Nice, that's the best news I've had all day." I grinned back.

Crystal returned with my tea, so I slowly sipped it as I worked through the new folder.

Unfortunately, this training was on incidents and when to involve human resources. Also, the info covered how I should handle injuries, disciplining employees and firing with due cause. While some of it was interesting, the more I read, the less enthusiastic I felt about being the general manager. Obviously, this was a huge part of my job, handling all the big, negative issues at the locations. This, I was without a doubt, unqualified for.

I'd never disciplined Chris once, not once in six years. For some reason, I hadn't even considered it. I finished with the training just as Patrick stopped by my cubical.

"I like it," he said, looking around at my posters.

"Thank you." It did look pretty great.

"It looks like your office, not an inch of wall space." His voice had a distinctly teasing edge.

"Well, there's limited wall space." And, there was, the frames even had to touch at some places to fit.

Standing, I grabbed my purse.

"Want to eat out or in?" he asked.

"Definitely in. The food is that much closer." Holding up the folder, I said, "I just have to drop this with Toby on the way out. Oh, we're still doing ice cream after school today, yeah?"

"Sure."

"Good, because I told Cameron we were."

His eyebrows rose. "How'd that go?"

Opening the door into the reception area, I held it open for Patrick, making him smirk. "Fine," I said. "He thinks I'm an incurable flirt, but I think he'll get over it." Shrugging, I wondered if I shouldn't have said that and I cringed a little.

The downstairs deli was packed, every table filled with groups eating off of trays.

"I'm surprised we don't have a Harington's down here," I said as I grabbed a tray.

They do have a little coffee station over there," he pointed into the deli, "but all of these are run by yet another of my father's companies that have locations in office buildings all over here and in LA."

"Wow, talk about having your fingers in a lot of pies," I said.

Lunch went by too quickly and before I knew it, I had said goodbye to Patrick and was on my way to the roaster. Unfortunately, my phone's navigation system told me to go the wrong way on a one way and I had to go completely around a circuitous route to find the roaster.

The warehouse building smelled like coffee beans from a block away. This was my favorite smell on Earth, even with my unfortunate coffee-sobriety status. Nose in the air and grinning manically, I walked into the main office ten minutes late.

"Hello, can I help you?" a woman asked as she looked up from the desk.

"Oh, I have it," a middle-aged man said as he stood from where he leaned against the wall. He stowed his phone. "Jamie?"

I reached out a hand. "And, you must be José."

He shook my hand with a strong grip. "Yep, nice to meet you. I'm going to show you around. Just so you know, Harington's roasters don't require people to speak English to get a job here so, I can help if you need any help with interpreting."

"Thank you. I grew up in a bilingual family, Spanish and English, but I don't speak any other languages."

"Where is your family from?" he asked me in Spanish.

"My stepmom is from Cuba," I responded.

"Your Spanish does have a little bit of a Cuban accent. Where is she from? My father is from Santiago."

"She's from Santa Clara, but I've never been there. My sister has, though; she's trying to get dual citizenship, actually." Or, Amy had been before her husband put a nix on her plans.

Touring the facilities was one of the highlights of the job thus far. First, it smelled amazing and second, I got to speak in Spanish the whole time with José, something I almost never did. The head roaster had prepared a coffee tasting from me, and for the first time in eleven days I broke my coffee-sobriety. I only took a small sip of each roast, breaking the layer of grounds, inhaling the scent then using a spoon to pull the grounds away. By the time I left the facility, I knew that if I didn't haul-ass, I'd be late for Sarah.

A sense of urgency over took me, and I pressed on my gas pedal, getting back to the freeway as quickly as I could.

Day Eleven: Two-thirty

Low, gray cloud-cover clung to Coral Beach, a discus of gray in an otherwise clear sky. An unusual amount of traffic clogged up the streets leading to Sarah's school, and I had to resist laying on the horn more than once. When two trucks stopped to talk to each other, I considered moving the one in front of me with my front bumper. They passed something between them and the truck in front of me roared off. I took the street to Sarah's school going a little too fast and caught my breath as I felt an out of control momentum for a second.

I forced myself to slow down a few blocks up from Sarah's school as kids crossed the street with no thought to traffic. When I finally made it to my spot, I parked and jumped out. Sarah wasn't there yet, but really, that didn't *mean* anything. That type of thing happened all the time. I scolded my heart to stop racing, but it didn't listen.

My gaze combed the lot, not seeing her or Ms. Brown anywhere.

"Okay, okay," I mumbled as I headed into a door while a teacher held it open. The hall had almost emptied of children, even though I was only, maybe, five minutes late. Down the way, I saw another kid from Sarah's class with his aide. The boy screamed, the high-pitched sound echoing through the halls. His aide—I think his name was Mr. Hale—held the little boys hands at his sides, in more of a protective hold than a restraining one, likely stopping him from injuring himself.

The boy screamed again, trying to kick Mr. Hale. The aide took the blow and continued to murmur words to the boy.

For a moment, I considered offering to help. When I found Sarah, if they still needed help after I picked up Sarah, I'd offer.

Spinning around, I gazed down the length of each hall until I was at Sarah's special day classroom. Even though she didn't end her day here, I remembered that the last time I was in a panic she'd been here with Ms. Brown. When I pulled at the handle, the door didn't open. Craning my neck, I looked around the announcement papers taped to the window and into the classroom, the room sat dark.

Turning, I jogged to room twelve, finding an open door. When I stepped in, Ms. Nelson glanced up from where she was sweeping a pile of detritus into a large black dustpan-bucket. She grinned, blonde eyebrows rising up her young face. "Hey, there. How are you doing?"

Waving, I said, "Kind of freaking out, honestly. Have you seen Sarah?"

Her lips pressed together as she shook her head. "No, but I'll keep an eye out."

"Thanks," I said as I ducked back out of the classroom.

"Hey, Jamie," I heard from behind me.

I turned, almost losing my balance.

Patrick grinned, his hand holding a grinning Kay, whose hair was plated messily in two French braids.

My gaze darted between them. "Have you seen Sarah?"

Patrick glanced around him. "Uh, no."

Kay shook her head and sent more strands to fall loose. "She didn't go to class today."

I blinked at her. "What?" Scrambling for my purse, I grabbed out my phone. After quickly unlocking the screen, I called Cameron.

"Hey, baby," he answered on the second ring.

"Hey . . . uh, you took Sarah to school today, right?"

"Yeah, of course." His voice turned serious, "Everything okay?"

"It's probably fine. I'll call you back when I find her, okay? Love you." I hung up, stowing my phone in my back pocket.

"Here, we'll search this way." Patrick gestured over his shoulder.

"Okay, thanks. Could you check the school garden? She likes it there. I'm going to the office," I said.

A familiar tall, thin woman rounded the corner. I'd met her before, remembered her pretty, tired features but couldn't quite think of her name. "Oh," she said in a relieved voice. "Sarah's mom. So, you've already picked up Sarah?"

My mouth dried, tongue suddenly sand paper in my mouth. I tried to swallow. "No, I'm looking for her."

Her eyelids widened. "You didn't get her?" she asked, like maybe I was confused and I actually did pick her up.

"No!" Taking a deep breath, I said, "Sorry, no. I'm looking for her. Where's Ms. Brown?"

"She has the stomach flu. We had Sarah in resource after lunch period because we were short-staffed. She did great, but . . . uh, she was supposed to be with Mr. Hale. There was an incident with another student—here, come with me to the office." She walked backward toward the office as she spoke.

I looked back over my shoulder to where I had seen Mr. Hale, torn between following her and running back.

As the woman already turned into the office, I rushed after her to see the principal on a two-way radio.

She turned to me, dark curls bouncing from a loose bun. Her mouth set into a grave line. "You don't have Sarah?"

"Obviously," I snapped.

She nodded. "We're going to have all the available staff search for her, Ms. Scott. Mr. Hale just noticed that she's gone, so she's probably not far."

"Unless someone took her," I muttered. "I'm going to go look." I didn't even finish my statement before I was sprinting out of the office. When my phone rang, I answered it while running, "Cameron?"

"Did you find her?"

"No, not yet," I breathed heavily while sprinting. "I have this horrible, horrible feeling. I think I saw Clarke drive by her school this time yesterday . . ." I paused to look out the open front doors of the school, but only a few lingering parents and kids stood talking around the bike racks.

"I'm getting in my car right now; I'll be there in five minutes."

Breaking into a sprint again, I breathed, "Can you drive around the streets around the school first?"

"Yeah," he said.

Mr. Hale rushed up to meet me and I paused, though my body tipped from side to side. "I just took my eyes off her for one second; Michael was having a meltdown, injuring himself . . ."

"Where were you standing?" I tried not to yell, but my words rasped out harshly.

"Back here," he said, pointing toward the door I had originally come in through.

We both rushed to the entrance, and I saw Patrick and Kay jogging back from up the parking lot. When Patrick saw me, he slowed and shook his head. Pointing behind him up the street, he called out, "She's not in the surrounding areas over there. We didn't see her in the garden either. You want us to drive around?"

"Please, could you take the areas on that side of the school? I pointed the other way," I said.

He nodded. "Right away. Come on, Kay bay." He grabbed Kay's hand; she looked up, her hair now sticking out in all directions around a bloodless face. Eyes wide, she followed behind Patrick as he led her, but her gaze stayed on me.

I dialed the number on my phone for my contact at the police, Officer Oliver. The number rang until a voicemail picked up, saying that I'd reached Officer Oliver and if this was an emergency to dial nine-one-one. "Kelly, it's Jamie. I'm here to pick

Sarah up from school and she's not here. I'm absolutely terrified that Clarke took her. The whole school is looking. Please, please call me back as soon as you get this—"

The phone beeped, and then a mechanical voice said, "If you are satisfied with your message, please press one—"

I pressed one, disconnected and then called Beza.

"Hey, lovely lady," she sang as she answered.

"Beza, are you still at the school? Sarah is missing."

"I am heading right back," she said.

"Okay, I'm going to go now, call me if you find anything."

"Does Sarah elope?" Mr. Hale asked.

"Yes!" I shouted. "It's in her IEP! You guys should know this!" Waving my hand, I cried, "Shit, I'm sorry. Sorry." I ran off, back into the school. Poles shot by me, windows flashed their glare into my eyes before I burst out the back door. Remembering myself, I grabbed the door before it could close and trap me back here. The heavy door hit my palm, sending pain shooting up my arm

No one played on the playground. Absolutely no one remained on the large stretching field behind the school. Ducking back into the hall, I called nine-one-one, but the dispatcher said that the police were already on their way.

And to confirm this, as I rushed back to the front, sirens blared closer.

Red lights flashed through the parking lot as I reentered it. An officer stood outside of his car, talking to the principal. He towered a full head taller than her, and his close-cut afro made him even taller.

The principal held out a shaky hand toward me. "That's Sarah's mother."

"I'm Sarah's mom, has anyone found her?" I panted out the question as I stopped beside the officer.

"Not yet." The principal glanced around, her curls bouncing wildly around her head.

I looked around, too, seeing teachers run past through the window. "Were the bathrooms checked? All of the classrooms?"

"Yes, but the teachers and staff are double checking everywhere. Also, the parents who are still here are calling other parents to see if they saw anything. The school secretary and guidance counselor are on it too . . ." Her voice trailed off. "We're looking. This has never, ever happened before."

"No one reported seeing Sarah after Mr. Hale, at all?" I asked.

"Not yet," she said on a breath.

The officer leaned down so that we were eye to eye. Even his head was big; he was the kind of guy you'd expect never to see outside of an action movie. "Is it possible that someone else picked her up?" he asked.

"No, my boyfriend is driving around the neighborhood looking for her, so are my friends. My other family would never pick her up without telling me."

"Her father?"

"Died."

He nodded. "Do you have a photo of her on hand?"

"In my phone." I fiddled it out of my pocket. Glancing at the text messages from Patrick, Cameron and Beza, all of which were still looking further out, I pulled up a recent photo of Sarah. Her gymnastics uniform showed from the torso up, but the close-up was on her face as she grinned widely with hands flung out in an 'I just rocked that routine' way. I held out my phone to the officer.

He nodded. "How old is she?"

"Eight."

"Can you send that photo to an email address via your phone?"

I sent the picture, following his instructions. After I sent the picture, I answered about thirty questions about her diagnosis, behaviors, and sensitivities. After it all, I broke off to tell him, "But there's someone, a person who's been bothering me and I'm really scared he's involved. My former neighbor, his name is Clarke . . . Clarke *Allen*. I have an ongoing report going with Officer Kelly Oliver."

The officer's weight shifted toward me. "He's been threatening you?"

"Threatening, harassing, and stalking, but I can't prove any of it yet. I tried to get a restraining order, but only got a court date a week off."

The officer nodded and held up a finger, while stepping back. He spoke into a two-way receiver much larger than the principals, "The mother says there is a possible kidnapping suspect." He held the radio near his ear as an indecipherable voice crackled through the speaker. He pressed the button at the side of the radio. "Clarke Allen, a neighbor, lives at . . ." he looked up to me. When I gave him the address, he recited it into the radio. "Do you know where he works?" he asked me.

"A car lot. I think it starts with a 'b', something 'Auto' . . . I don't know." I shook my head.

As the officer relayed my words, I tried to remember. He told me once. It was almost two months ago when he'd been there a couple weeks and I'd still been dismissing the creepy comments as my imagination.

Clarke stepped out of his door just as Sarah and I approached. His dog, Buster, was an explosion of hair, bounding out of his apartment.

"Buster!" Sarah cried, reaching up to where Buster was jumping onto the fence that divided where he had a fenced front yard. Sarah pushed her hair into Buster's hair, her arms going around him.

"This is okay?" I asked Clarke as I gestured to Sarah snuggling Buster with wonton abandon.

He waved his hand in the air. "Buster loves it. So, Jamie, I've been meaning to mention, I noticed your car's pretty beat up, ever think of trading it in for a newer model?"

I put the top of Busters head. "Not really in my budget right now."

"The lot I work at—Best Deal Auto over on Main—we have your same car, last year's, I could get you a hell of a deal." His eyebrows rose and voice turned suggestive, "What do you say, Jamie, don't you want a new ride?"

I woke from the memory as the officer asked, "Could it be Best Deal Auto?"

I nodded. "That's it."

"Okay, an officer knows it." He paused for a minute and we all waited for a prolonged silence before another crackle came over the radio.

"I wish you had told the school," the principal said, her gaze hard on mine.

"God, me too," I mumbled. "I thought you guys were required to get substitutes for the aides."

She shuffled her weight away, obviously uncomfortable. "No one could cover."

The officer said into his radio, "Yes, sounds good." The voice responded, again, indecipherable, before the officer stowed the radio. He looked back to me. "They have a Clarke Allen on their staff. We've got an officer heading there now. I'd suggest you double check with any family member that might have picked her up, however unlikely. Nine times out of ten, it's a mix up—"

My hands gestured wildly. "This isn't a mix up!"

"Ma'am, I need you to stay calm and rational." He held out a hand to me. "I'm a father too, and I can imagine how hard a request like that can be, but for Sarah's sake, you need to stay rational."

"Sorry, I—" I scrubbed my sweaty, tear-covered face, breathing heavily into my hands. I hadn't even noticed that I was crying or sweating. Inside my body was going insane but outside, my skin, face, everything numbed. "I'll text them, but I know no one else was supposed to pick her up."

"When she's run away before, where did she go?" the officer said, his low-timbre voice breaking through the fog encroaching on my mind.

"She's never actually run away. She's run off, but someone always caught up." Swallowing down a sour taste, I whispered, "I have a hard time believing that an eight-year-old was running through the streets and no one noticed her while there were hundreds of parents walking around. And I thought I saw Clarke's car around near the school yesterday as I was picking Sarah up."

"We're looking into it." He stepped off, talking to another officer while we waited. I sent out a group text to all of my local contacts, including my mom and Vanessa.

Me: Sarah was missing when I went to pick her up from school. The teacher watching her got distracted as they waited for me. Sarah vanished. She's still missing. Beza, Cameron and Patrick are driving around the school, looking for her. Police are here. Spread this message, post about it, do whatever.

The officer returned, looking like he was going to say something but halted as a crackling sound came over his radio. He leaned his head, listening. His gaze met mine. "We found your neighbor, he's at work. His boss and others can attest to him being there since this morning."

Day Eleven: Three-thirty

I looked away and around at the lingering parents. Most were looking back at us, concern radiating from their expressions. The gray sky sunk down upon us, defying the usual patterns of the weather here. The charged air hovered, buzzing through the spaces between bodies.

Blinking rapidly, I turned back to the officer. "Clarke has used other people before to deliver threats. He's very careful."

The officer nodded, I still didn't know his name but I had already memorized every detail of his kind face, every scar, every wrinkle in these last minutes. He said, "We'll continue to look into it. But for now, I want you to focus on contacting friends and family and thinking of any other detail that might be relevant. Where might she go? Has she ever walked home before, or to a friend's house, and—"

"Ice cream." I looked up, feeling a surge of realization. "I told her we were going out for ice cream after school . . . maybe, maybe she's on the path to go get it. We've walked it before. Coral Beach Ice Cream Shoppe, it's right over there, like half a mile that way on the other side of the beach park." I spun toward the path, then back to the officer who talked into his radio. "I'm going to run it."

He held out his hands. "Ms. Scott, I suggest you stay here."

I shook my head. "Sorry, sir, there's no fucking way I'm staying here. I just feel it, she's there." My feet took me away from the parking lot and toward the path to the ice cream shop before my mind caught up.

Adrenaline spiked in me as I bent in and sprinted forward. My eyes saw everything and I didn't break stride at the road. Palm trees streaked across my vision as I curved through the beach park, looking back and forth with my every footfall.

In the distance, a police cruiser streaked by, its siren blaring and lights flashing.

Sarah always froze up when she heard the sirens, covered her ears, and occasionally even began screaming. As much as I didn't want my little girl in distress, I hoped so badly she heard those sirens, froze up and stood somewhere holding her ears.

The hope that surged through me leaked out each time my dress flats hit the cement. Each time I turned the corner and scanned what I could see, finding her not there, my certainty dripped away. When I made it to the end of the beach park, I almost didn't want to cross the street, as if that one little distance would shatter the thin layer of hope I coated myself in.

A police cruiser waited in the lot, its light circling and driver-door open. The red light passed me, then again, as I panted at the street corner. An officer left the shop alone, descending quickly down the steps.

A tear splashed my face as I trudged the short distance that might as well been a hundred foot plunge off a cliff. It wasn't my hope that was shattering, it was me; I was shattering.

"She's not in there?" I shouted, hoarsely to the officer talking into her radio. Dimly, I registered that I knew her: Officer Evans. She'd only been over to Cameron's house two nights ago, but it felt like a lifetime away.

"I'm sorry, Ms. Scott, no, but another officer is going around the building. Would you like a ride back to the school?"

My hands pinched into the cramps at my sides as I swayed. "I'm—I'm going to check the bathrooms and under the tables. Not that you didn't, but—"

"I understand. Go ahead." She gestured toward the decorative little shop.

I grabbed the wooden handrail and teetered up the step. The painted wood slicked against my sweaty palms. Yanking open the door, I almost jumped at the soft jingle of bells.

The older man behind the counter glanced up, wrinkles creasing around his eyes.

"Sorry." I held out my hands. "I'm Sarah's mom; I just know she might be scared. I need to check the shop, please."

"Of course. I'm sorry you're going through this, if I see anything, I'll call the police. I'll be sure to ask anyone who come in here," he said, gruffly.

Sniffing back emotion, I said, "Thank you."

She wasn't in the shop. I'd known it before I stepped in, that she wasn't there; but hope was such a cruel captor, lingering past the point all the evidence screamed that optimism was misplaced. I ducked under the tables, searched the bathroom and even looked into the back, with the kind ice cream man's permission. The shop closed in around me. She was not there.

Two officers waited outside as I trudged back down the steps.

"How about we take you back to the school, Ms. Scott?" Officer Evans said, her lip tucking up into a jagged line.

"Thanks," I murmured before climbing into the backseat of the patrol car.

Plastic crinkled under me as a disinfectant smell stung my nose. The mesh separating the front and back seats distorted their figures as they climbed into the front seats. I had no idea what the second cop looked like, or even if they were male or female. Blinking, I turned to the window as they pulled out of the small lot.

The sky sunk even further, crouching in on the unsuspecting ground. My gaze combed through figures as we drove the short distance back to the school, a young woman jogging with her poodle, a man blowing lawn clippings off the path, not Sarah, not Sarah.

Three more cruisers sat in the lot, three turning red lights out of sync.

Beza stood next to the officer who had interviewed me before, cheeks stained with tears.

When the car stopped, I wrenched at the handle of the door, but it didn't open. I tapped on the mesh. "Please let me out."

Officer Evans turned her head, profile disjointed in the spaces between the mesh. "Of course, Ms. Scott, just one moment."

When she finally opened the door, I practically dove out of the door. "Did something happen? Did you find her?" I yelled.

Beza looked up, startled. "No, Jamie. Uh—" she wiped her face. "I'm sorry, I'm just upset. No, they haven't found her yet."

Squeezing my eyes shut, I silently sobbed as tears splashed down my face, tears of relief, and tears of terror.

"Honey, I—" Her arms went around me.

I fell into her hug. My sweat slimed onto her but I needed a hug so much that I was too selfish not to grasp tighter. "Where's Aiden?" I whispered when I could let her go.

"Patrick took him and Kay to get something to eat and so they could calm down. Cameron is driving around, a little further out now. Also, Susan, your dad, mom, Sharon, Chris, and Amy are all on their way or already driving around, they're visiting the places she likes too. Vanessa is too. Have you checked your phone?"

"Not for a couple minutes, but I felt the texts buzzing." I sobbed out the words, "I thought I knew where she was."

"I know, I know." She patted my back.

"Ms. Scott?"

I looked up to see the officer I'd talked to earlier standing inches away.

"Ms. Scott, we've called in the child abduction response team, even though we're still not sure about the nature of the disappearance. Now, I'm going to ask you to do something for me, okay?"

Because he seemed to be waiting for a response, I nodded.

"I'm going to ask you to go wherever Sarah considers home, or her favorite place, her safe place, okay?" When I opened my mouth he raised a hand. "Please, I need you to listen. Go to her safe place, the first place that comes to mind when I say those words, and I need you to have two phones. You will use your personal phone only to receive messages and calls, and a secondary phone for any outgoing calls. I want you to keep your phone open, if someone isn't calling specifically to tell you that they have Sarah or know where she is, you call them back immediately on the secondary phone."

Beza held out her smartphone to me.

Taking it and pressing my fingers into its red leather case, I whispered, "Thank you."

The officer continued, "No matter how much you're tempted, do not leave Sarah's safe place unless someone tells you that they have her. Do you understand?"

I didn't answer for a second, my breaths coming heavily in the space between us. "I want to look for her."

"Other people can and will be looking for her, a lot of other people, officers and civilians. But, Sarah only has one mommy to find, so you need to be in a place that she can easily find you."

Wiping at my cheeks, I whispered, "Okay . . ." I nodded. "Okay," I said stronger.

"Good. Are you safe to drive?" He looked at me sternly, like he was asking if I'd drunk a forty on my mad dash to find Sarah.

"I'm safe to drive."

The moment the officer stepped away, Beza turned to me, "How about I come with you to help if you need another person? Should I meet you at your apartment . . . oh, sorry, I forgot you moved out."

"No, uh, Cameron's house," I said, before clearing my throat. "We've fully moved in there, so she probably considers that home now. I'll meet you there." I looked away, not able to meet her gaze as I said the words.

Her hand came up and fingers squeezed my arm. "She's going to be found."

"Yeah, I know." *I am going to find her*, but I didn't say that.

"We should probably get going," I murmured, before jogging to where my car still waited.

While the officers re-parked, clearing a path for me, I scanned my text messages. Most were in the group thread I created, begging for updates, saying where they were, and where they were heading. I typed in a new message.

Me: If you have information, please text my phone or Beza's phone outside of this group text. Do not call my phone unless you know where Sarah is. If you need to reach me, call Beza's phone.

I added Beza's phone number and pressed send before turning my ringer on.

The cops pulled haphazardly out of my way and I pulled out before driving slowly through their parked cars. My whole drive, I rolled along, ignoring the honks. I gazed out more from the side windows than my front window. Sarah did not stand outside of the convenience store, or play in the yards I passed. I looked for streaks of blonde streaming behind a small girl dressed in all purple, but she wasn't there.

Something in me had told me not to leave her today as she giggled on her bed, something had said, 'stay home, stay with her.' But my head got in the way. I couldn't mess up my stupid new job with my horrible new boss. That moment, that moment of turning from her, that was the biggest mistake of my life.

I pulled into the all too familiar lot outside of my duplex complex and circled the lot. When I saw Clarke's little blue car in his space, I kept driving. Sarah wasn't anywhere around the complex, but I didn't really expect her there.

I felt so frazzled, for a second I forgot which spot was mine—forty-two or forty-three—before I remembered and pulled in. The air turned to a thick viscous gas that resisted my movements as I stepped from my car and took the familiar pathway that led to the secluded area where only Clarke and units were. I didn't try to be quiet as I unlocked my door, rattling my keys in the lock before turning it and stepping inside.

The deadbolt clucked as I turned it. A ding sounded on my phone, but it had been dinging constantly since I turned it off silent. Leaning back against my door, I read through my most recent messages. No one had texted outside of the group message, except for Cameron.

Cameron: Where are you?

Wiping away a hot tear, I stowed the phone in my back pocket. Going to my television set, I pressed the power button on the remote, and then switched the channel to the news station. A commercial played for a local DUI lawyer group. *Don't serve time, call Stewart and associates.* A creepy little jingle played while their phone number displayed on the screen.

Walking slowly, I searched through the apartment. My bedroom gaped back, empty, as did Sarah's room. They were more than empty, they felt foreign, just a vacuous space with unclaimed furniture.

The only window in my bedroom looked down to one of my better paying neighbor's back yard. It was one in a long line of fenced yards that stacked between the units. The top of Clarke's fence reached just between our window ledges.

Crossing to the window, I pulled up the tabs on the window screen and on an exhale of breath, popped it out of the tracks. The top of the screen resisted, deciding it wouldn't cooperate. Taking slow measured breaths, I pressed down a constant pressure, pulling at the screen. With a soft snick sound, it released its track.

Ever so slowly, I set the screen on the wall further in the bedroom. Leaning into the window, my face pressed against the cold glass. When I couldn't see what I was looking for, I took another step back and pressed my face harder against the pane.

I saw it. Just barely, the lip of Clarke's window stuck out. A line of metal stripe peeking into my view, meaning the window was cracked open. I stepped back from my window, my face peeling from the glass.

Pausing, I closed my eyes and blew out a breath. I could do this. My legs threatened not to support me and a hot, sticky anxiety clotted in my throat, but I would fight it, and do this anyway.

Tip-toeing back to my bathroom, I opened the cupboard slowly and reached up to pull down a big jar of petroleum jelly.

My fingers scooped into the pot as I returned to the window. I slathered the goopy jelly on the hinges and tracks, then wiped the excess off on my pant leg.

Stepping back, I examined my work. If this didn't work, I was out of ideas.

Crossing back to the bathroom, I stepped in, closed the door and turned on the faucet. My hands shook as I again pressed on the contact for Officer Kelly Oliver.

"Please answer, please answer," I chanted as the dial tone rang into my ear.

"You've reached Officer Oliver. Jamie, is that you?"

"It is," I said.

"Jamie, I got your message, I'm sorry I didn't get back to you. I am busy working to retrieve Sarah along with a good percentage of the force. You hold tight at your house, okay? I will update you as soon as we have something."

"I'm almost sure it's Clarke," I whispered.

"Jamie, he has several witnesses placing him at his job during the time of her disappearance. We're following other leads right now."

"That's what Clarke does; he makes it impossible for me to blame him. Why would he be driving around outside of her school, Kelly? He planned this."

"Jamie, we've continued to patrol his work and residence area and we see no sign of your daughter."

I grabbed the spout of the sink and held onto the warm metal like it was the only thing stopping me from floating off to sea. Closing my eyes, I said, "I need you to stay on the line. If you can, please, record the call."

Her voice grew suddenly stern, "Jamie, that's really not what I want to hear right now. Are you in a safe location?"

I lowered my voice, "Please, will you do that for me? Will you record this call? All I'm asking is that if he admits that he took her, you come in and arrest him."

"Jamie, think about what you're doing. Just because we think it unlikely that he's responsible for Sarah's disappearance today doesn't make Clarke Allen any less dangerous for you. He's threatened you; he's invaded your home. You're panicking. This is not a rational decision."

"Please, please come," I whispered into the phone.

I pressed the speaker button. "Jamie, I strongly advise . . ." her voice trailed off as I lowered the speaker volume all the way down.

"You might hear some silence, Kelly. I can't hear you anymore."

Tipping my head up, I whispered, "Dear God, or Universe, or whoever is making all this happen. Come on, cut me a break. Please. Just, get her back to me. Or, just make sure she's safe. That's all I want in this world." I wiped another tear, and then opened the door to my bathroom.

Day Eleven: Four forty-five

As I pressed my fingers into the crank of my bedroom window, the strangest, most horrible memory surface in my mind. The memory was another absolute low point in my life and it had very little to do with the horror that Sarah was in right now, the horror I was about to face.

My mother stood before me, dark circles ringing her beautiful crystal blue eyes. I reached in to grab Sarah's backpack from the back seat but turned when my mother snapped, "Jamie, you cannot keep doing this. This is so wrong; I won't be part of it."

I had glanced back to the open doorway of my house. "Mom, shh . . ."

She paced up the length of the car, shaking her head. "No, no way, Jay Jay."

"First, you're making a really huge deal out of this. Second, it's not your business, Mom. This is between my family. Okay? Butt out."

She halted and her blonde eyebrows rose high over glaring eyes. Her mouth set in an expression that sent an immediate jolt of guilt through my stomach.

"I'm sorry I said butt out, but not the rest. You're always trying to run my life for me but I'm an adult . . ." I pointed to my chest, "I can make decisions, as an adult, that are mine to make. Okay?"

She shook her head. "Not okay, Jamie. He's her father, he needs to know. You can't keep Sarah's diagnosis from him. You can't move her into the special day program without his consent. It's not right and I'm not even sure that it's legal." She pointed into the house. "You owe it to him, and you owe it to her."

I pointed into the house, too. "Mom, he lost his mother a month ago, okay. Four fucking weeks ago."

Her head rocked back. "Don't swear at me."

"He's not himself . . . okay, he's drinking every night. He doesn't talk to me; he won't call Susan. I'm going to tell him, when he can handle it. Sarah is fine. I'm not even sure she needs to be in Special Day." I mumbled.

Her hands came up to my arms. "Honey, Sarah needs to be in Special Day class. She needs to be in speech and occupational therapy, she needs these things. And Logan needs to know." The look she gave me brooked no argument. She was a warrior— a short, blonde, middle-aged warrior, defending a small child.

"Mom, you need to let me do this."

Blinking, my mind returned to my fingers as they slowly, ever so slowly, turned the window crank. With a wet suction sound, the metal of the window separated from its frame. The muscles of my back and neck clenched, as I waited for the window's usual loud creek.

I rotated the crank once, centimeter by centimeter. The window shifted open one inch and then two. I paused, grasping the crank. If you see me through this one little crank, I swear to god I'll never make you work again.

Breathing in through my nose, I turned the crank again. I had three inches. On the fourth inch a high-pitched hissed warned of a creek coming, I pulled my hand away. It had to be enough.

Grasping my phone, I rotated it in my hand just so it could slip through my window. The rough siding outside scraped against my knuckles as I squeezed my hand through. Petroleum jelly slicked onto the back of my hand and up my arm, along with a grimy, black substance. My elbow didn't want to squeeze through the crack so I turned my arm out and pushed it through, ignoring the sting as it scraped along the siding. My arm refused to push out past my upper bicep, the sill squeezing my arm so tight that my fingers tingled.

Peeking one eye through the crack and closing the other, I could just see the lip of the sill and the open window. My hand couldn't quite maneuver close enough to set the phone on.

I glanced down to the drop into Clarke's yard that my phone could very easily fall into. Inching my fingers down the length of the phone, I moved it until only two fingers pinched the end.

My thumb immediately complained, but I ignored it. I connected the end of the phone with the sill, feeling the solid support. If the sill was like mine, it was only about six inches thick and flat, hopefully wide enough. I pushed the phone onto the ledge scooting it in.

My hands could barely touch it now and I could just barely see it tip. I wrenched my hand forward, ignoring the squeezing pain in my arm and shove the phone onto the ledge. It stayed.

As I slipped my arm back through the grimy, jelly coated window, I watched the tiny shiny metal spot that I could see of my phone. It was secure, it wasn't falling off.

Black stains coated my entire arm, and splotched across my chin and cheek. As quickly as I could I scrubbed the substance off and shrugged on an old sweater that sat crumpled in the back of my closet, thankfully overlooked in Cameron's packing.

Catching my reflection in the bathroom mirror, I pivoted to peer into desperate, bloodshot eyes. Around those eyes skin puffed out, red and irritated. My reflection looked like a woman driven mad, not at all like the reflection I remembered. I backed away, and then stomped through the apartment. Slinging my purse over my shoulder, the weight hit my tender shoulder.

My fingers threw open the deadbolt and shook the handle before I turned it. I exited my apartment slowly, stepping out a few feet before I turned back.

A cold, calm feeling settled low in my belly, into my wrists and numbed my fingers as I lifted my keys back to my lock.

Before my key had completely turned in my lock, Clarke's door opened. A fuzzy mass of hair rushed out, jumping up on the fence beside me, black nose peeking out, and tongue lulling from his panting mouth.

"Buster," I whispered, as a realization came to me. If Sarah had seen Buster, she would have followed him anywhere. If someone else helped Clarke, if he drove the car and actually did the kidnapping, Sarah might have climbed right in for Buster.

Clarke stepped out a moment later. Gone was the pretty boy, gone was the affable mask. His mouth snarled while his dark eyes shot loathing into mine. "You sent cops to my work, you stupid bitch," his worded came out a dark, angry snarl.

"Where's Sarah?" I snarled back.

The snarl dropped from his face, slowly morphing into a grin. He chuckled, his gaze combing over me, taking me in.

I took a step closer, though my ankle threatened to roll when I did. My gaze drove into his. "Where is she?"

He flung an arm out to his open door. "Why don't you come inside, Jamie the whore?"

"Is she in there?" I asked.

He only smirked.

When I made my way slowly down the length of his fence, he kept pace with me like a predator. As if he was being some kind of gentleman, he opened the gate and stepped back to let me pass.

Even though I knew the gate was small and still open, as I stepped through it felt as if a metal gate shot down behind me.

Clarke offered me his hand, like we were heading into a restaurant for a date, not heading into his apartment after he kidnapped my daughter. I ignored it, hoping that if he thought I didn't see it, he wouldn't force it on me.

"Stay, Buster," he called out.

The door loomed before me, a wormhole, a black hole, ready to suck me in and tear me apart. As my foot passed over the lip of the door from cement to tile, I sucked in a breath. The tangy, almost overwhelming scent of freshly spray air-freshener hit my senses, so thick it clotted in my throat. The apartment spread mirror shape and proportion to mine, though looked almost completely opposite. Where my furniture was cheap, worn in, and heavily used, his could have been used in a magazine spread for male furniture set ups. His wide screen spanned the entire wall, mounted high over a glass entertainment center. His couches gleamed back at me, pleather—or probably leather. A beer sat on a coaster on his glass coffee table.

A door slammed behind me, making me jump. Why was I just standing here? A low metallic sound clanked as Clarke locked the front door.

"Sarah?" I yelled as I charged into the apartment. The strap of my purse wrenched me back. Spinning, I found Clarke's hand firmly wrapped around my purse strap.

"Let me take that for you," he said as he yanked it from my arms.

"Give it back." My voice came out much more calm and stern than I thought I could ever manage.

He unzipped my purse quickly just as my phone rang inside it. "You don't mind if I—" He held up the phone which displayed the name 'Cameron.' "Looks like you have a client call." He waved the phone in my face. "You want to get it?"

"Sure," I said, reaching for the phone.

Clarke tossed the phone, sending it flying through his open kitchen and clattering into the sink. "Oh, sorry, that slipped right out of my hand." He raised an eyebrow. "I'll go get that for you." Walking over to the sink, he turned the faucet on. "Crap, did it again." He held up the phone, whose screen flashed solid white to solid black. "Here you go, he must have hung up." Walking back, he stowed the phone back in my purse soaking wet before he zipped the purse up and handed it back to me.

I let the purse hang from his hand and rushed through his apartment. His space was almost the exact same dimensions as mine; though where my room was in my apartment, Clarke had a large sprawling office that looked to have never been used. She wasn't in there, or in the closet. When I turned back, Clarke stood filling the doorway.

Holding my chin up, I avoided his gaze and walked straight up to him. "Let me check your bedroom, please?"

He flung his hand out like, 'go ahead', but didn't move from the doorway.

As I knew it was the only way past, I squeezed into the space between the doorframe and his body.

Clarke pressed in, his body flush against mine while the corner of the doorframe dug into my back. "You smell like you want to get fucked," he whispered as his pelvis pressed into mine, his erection digging into me.

"No! Stop!" I shouted. My hands pushed hard against his chest, beating against his heavy weight.

He pressed harder against me, forcing out all my air. The he stepped back, chuckling. "I thought you wanted to go into my bedroom?"

I teetered, gasping in air as I grabbed onto the door frame to stay vertical. Without saying another word, I ducked my head down and peeked only quickly into the spotless bathroom that reeked like male body spray, before walking into Clarke's bedroom.

I forced myself not to look at his window, not to check if the phone was still there. Clarke's gaze sat heavily on my back. A loud clunk sounded behind me, followed by a click. Again, I forced myself not to look.

A fleece blanket with a giant football spanned his large bed. Sport memorabilia hung framed all around the room. A football jersey stretched in a tall frame. The colors were the same as the local university had, the university that Cameron played for a long time ago. A signed football sat in a glass box on his dresser.

Immediately, I knew Sarah wasn't in here. Still, I pushed his clothes aside in his closet, finding only an expense array of brand new sneakers. Going down to my hands and knees directly, I searched under his bed, finding only a clean stretch of floor.

I looked up at him; he'd crossed the room to stand only inches from me. Grabbing onto his bed, I got to my feet.

"Don't get up, I like you down there," he said as he smirked.

"Where is Sarah?" I asked.

He stepped closer, one dark brow rising. "Not here."

"I see that. You don't have her?" I asked, articulating carefully.

His hand came up, fingers rising to just barely brush against my hair. "I didn't say that." His gaze came to mine and he smiled, lips parting over perfect white teeth.

"Where is she?"

"I'll tell you . . . if you ask me really nicely. Why don't you go ahead and get back on your knees? I liked seeing you down there."

I shook my head. "Clarke—"

"Beg me, whore."

I swallowed, hard. "I'm not a whore. Do you really, actually think I'm a whore? Is that what this is about?"

"Get down on your knees," he articulated each word slowly.

"Okay, I'll beg you. But just so you know, I absolutely do not consent to anything whatsoever sexual. All I want is my daughter back." I climbed down to my knees, scooting just a little bit back on his clean tile floor. I forced my gaze up the length of his body, and into his smirking face. "Please, tell me where my daughter is, I beg you."

"Not yet," he said.

Day Eleven: Five-fifteen

Clarke's grin shouted his glee and his gaze whispered of victory. His expression almost looked awestruck, like he'd just got handed exactly what he wanted out of the blue, perverted lottery winner.

His hand reached forward, threading through my hair.

"Don't touch me," I snapped.

What were the cops waiting for? Clarke admitted he had Sarah. Did they have to get a warrant to break in through his door? Had my phone disconnected? I was as close as I possibly could be to the window, but maybe it wasn't close enough. Maybe Officer Oliver hadn't heard Clarke's confession.

His hands dug deeper into my hair, and when I grabbed his wrist, his open palm clenched into a fist, grabbing a handful of my hair and pulling a couple strands out with it.

"You have no idea how much it turns me on to have Cam's whore on her knees before me, ready to eat my dick."

"You get your dick near me and I will bite it off. Where is my kid?" I shouted.

He yanked so hard on my hair, I grunted through clenched teeth as pain shot through my skull. "Stay very still," he said, almost calmly. He reached to his waistline with one hand, pulling open his button.

Tears fell from my eyes as I met his gaze. "Don't you fucking dare."

Clarke's lips parted as his eyes glazed with lust. The hand not in my hair grabbed my wrist, squeezing hard until I released his arm. He blew out a laugh. "Shit. I wish he was here, I wish he could watch as I fuck every single part of you until you moan out my name."

"Who are you talking about?" My gaze darted around the room as my mouth fell open. "Cameron?"

"Too bad if he comes anywhere near me, he'll immediately be arrested, the fucker." He sucked on his teeth as if he was savoring the moment.

"You *want* Cameron?" I asked, putting a shitload of sexual innuendo into the words.

His hand clenched harder in my hair. "No, you stupid bitch. I want Cam to get fucking hit by a bus. I want him to take a gun to his own head and blow out his brains all over my wall. I'd happily clean up that mess."

"Sounds like you two have a history."

Clarke pulled me closer, gripping even tighter when I resisted. "You know what I really want?" His eyebrows rose, over eyes sparking with excitement. "I want him to break in here to find me bending you over, taking it. Then, he'll be arrested because he broke the restraining order I have against him. I want him to take a swing at me, just to ensure that he'll go away for a while." Clarke yanked me to him again as I pushed back, and I knew that if I didn't do it, no one else was going to stop him from raping me.

Maybe all the cops needed was time to get a team together, or to obtain a warrant. I had to believe that someone would break down that door and force Clarke to give up Sarah's location.

Arching my head back as far as his grip would allow, I asked Clarke, "So, what? Did you have a hard on for Cameron and he rejected you? He's not gay."

Immediately, the lust doused from his eyes, replaced by rage. "Shut the fuck up." He twisted my wrist, wrenching it so hard I would have fallen if his hand wasn't clutching my hair. "Cam is a fucking psychopath. He's a psycho living among us. He deserves to be in prison, but he gets to walk around banging sluts against walls."

Breathing hard, and knowing what was coming, I said, "Let me guess, you were on his team in college and no one noticed you."

He laughed through his words, "No, you dumb bitch. You really think he's some great guy, don't you? That everyone liked him? Cam sucker-punched me and broke my cheekbone. My eyeball fell into my face, I had to get surgery."

"No, he didn't."

"Yeah, he did," he drew out the words like he thought I was stupid.

"Then why didn't he get arrested? Why would you have to make a fake police report now?"

"He's a psychopath, there were ten witnesses and all of them lied to the police. I had to pay for my surgery with a year-long repayment plan, thousands of dollars. And you know what? Cam introduced himself to me like he didn't even know me two days after I moved in here. He talked to me every time he came for a poke, shot the shit with me, no fucking clue that he sucker-punched me and ruined my whole fucking life. I got kicked off the team, I got blamed.

Then he goes and gets charged with assault again a few months after. Because he's a psycho and everyone is always on his side. But not anymore."

My mouth fell open just a little. I knew that story, or at least the part where Cameron beat up a guy and everyone lied to the police for him. "You raped a girl," I said, glaring up into his dark, enraged gaze.

"Says one bitch." He leaned down until his face was level with mine. "If I raped her, why didn't she ever report it, tell me that? She got drunk, had sex, was scared her parents would find out and lied to her friends. A bitch lies, and then I get sucker-punched, my face gets broken, and everyone takes the psycho's side." He spat the words into my face.

"I'm a little confused here, Clarke," I snapped, my breaths coming fast. "If you're innocent and Cameron's a psycho, and all of this is just getting your just desserts at Cameron, then why are you tormenting me, why did you kidnap my kid? It's just a little confusing, don't you think?"

He released a breath and straightened out, his hand releasing its grip in my hair a little. Letting out a forced-sounding chuckle, he said, "That was just for fun, Jamie. I like watching a whore squirm. Anyway, with a girl like you, I figured you'd give me a piece sooner or later. Maybe I could send Cameron a video or a nice picture of you taking it."

I didn't believe that for one second. And when I thought over all the things he did in the past two weeks, it all made a sick sort of sense. Cameron had thought the catalyst for why Clarke started harassing me more aggressively was when I started fighting back, but that wasn't it. The catalyst was when Cameron started to really act like my boyfriend.

Clarke corned me in the laundry room while Cameron was having fun playing with the kids in the pool. He took my underwear out while I was wrestling around with Cameron. Clarke was humiliating me, punishing me. When he took a picture of me having sex, it was on Cameron's property, something he took the time and effort to find. When he scratched 'whore' in my door, it was while my car was at Cameron's shop. Clarke kept shaming and humiliating me, but most of it centered on Cameron.

It was so clear and so simple, but I never made the connection, "You're scared of Cameron. You're afraid of him, so you punished me instead of him. You humiliated and tormented me, because I was the easier target—"

Clarke backhanded me. Even though I saw him reach back for the blow, when the back of his hand connected with my cheek, the shock and pain deadened all my senses. My hands flew to my cheek as I cried out. Blinking, I shook my head, seeing white spots.

"I'm not scared of him. He sucker-punched me. If he tried to take me in a fair fight, he'd be dead." He shook out his hand, looking at it then back at me. His gaze fixed on my cheek, forehead furrowing as his other hand loosened on my hair. "That never happened. None of this ever happened, yeah? You hear me?"

I nodded, causing a new bout of pain in my head.

"You want Sarah to come home safe, none of this ever happened."

A loud banging came from the front of the house.

Clarke released my hair, head popping up. When the banging came again, a small grin played at the corner of his mouth. He turned back, his voice almost taking a teasing edge, "You think that's Cameron?"

The moment his grip let go of my hair I crawled away from him, using the bedside to pull myself from the floor. My knees and legs ached so much that I half-sat, half-crumpled onto the bed. My head swam, the room tipping from side to side.

Clarke crossed over to his dresser and opened his top drawer. Reaching in, he grabbed a phone and shut the drawer.

My voice rasped as I yelled, "Clarke! Where is Sarah?"

He glanced down, almost disinterested. "Jamie, if you ever want to see Sarah again, take off your clothes and lie in my bed. You were just fucked and you loved every second of it."

He focused back on his cell phone, pressing the screen three times. He held the phone to his ear, nervous excitement buzzing off him like a child when the lights go down and he knows his cake is coming. Clearing his throat, he said into the phone, "Um, yes, this is Clarke Allen. I recently obtained a restraining order against Cameron Robinson, and I believe that he's at my door. He may be armed."

Closing my eyes, I begged the Universe that even though it seemed to be turning a deaf ear to me so far, just let that not be Cameron. Let it be the police.

"Yeah, I'll wait," I heard Clarke say, though I squeezed my eyelids even tighter together.

Whoever was listening, if there was some force listening, I asked that it would make sure that Sarah was safe and Cameron was far, far away.

The pounding came again.

"Oh," Clarke sounded surprised, "That's the police at my door."

I clasped my hands together. *Thank you, thank you.*

"Can I ask what this is about?" His voice had taken a different tone; the charmer was gone, now he sounded more affronted, like the wronged party.

"Oh, okay. Yeah, I'll let them right in." He turned to me, tapping his phone against his leg. "So, your boyfriend was spotted in the area, they want to *check in with me.* Can't really get out of that, so how about you stay in here and don't make a sound? If you're really, really quiet, I'll take you to your daughter, afterward." He patted my shoulder. "Yeah? You can wait on taking off your clothes." He crossed the room and shut the door, closing me in.

I waited until I heard muffled voices in the distance. Though my legs screamed their protest, I stood and crossed the room to Clarke's window. Tears pricked my eyes as I saw that not only was my phone still there, I had somehow managed to get the phone just a little bit past the open window.

Grabbing the crank, I turned it as quickly as I could until the window opened all the way past my little black smartphone. I grabbed it from the sill and slid my finger across the screen to unlock it. The phone app opened, showing that a phone call was still open and on speaker phone.

A message popped up on the screen: 'Five percent of your battery remaining.' Pressing the speaker phone off, I turned up the volume and brought the phone to my ear.

"Hello, are you still there?" I whispered.

"Jamie," Officer Oliver's voice came over the phone harshly, "Are you okay? Are you seriously injured?"

I blinked back tears. "I'm fine, but I couldn't get him to tell me where Sarah is."

"Jamie, Clarke doesn't have Sarah, he never did. She's been found, she safe and uninjured."

"Are you . . ." My words came out no more than a breath. Clearing my throat, I asked louder, "Are you sure?"

"Yes, she's at Mr. Robinson's house with him and several other people."

Sobs broke through my throat. "Oh my god. She's safe? You're completely sure that she's safe?"

"One hundred percent."

My hands grabbed onto the window sill for support, clean metal rasping against my skin. "What happened?" I sobbed.

I didn't care if Clarke heard me; I didn't care if he came back in. I couldn't be quiet, the sobs took over.

"Sarah ran all the way down to her gymnastics gym. Her teacher Heidi phoned the police."

"What?" I shook my head. "That's like . . . six miles. She would have crossed some *major* intersections."

"A man actually walked a good portion of it with her. His name is Mitchell Frost."

"Who?"

"He says he knows you and Sarah from your coffee shop, that he's known Sarah since she was really little. Mitchell was sleeping on the street near the warehouse district area and recognized Sarah as she ran past. He escorted her all the way to the studio to make sure that she arrived safely and waited for the police with her teacher. After he made a report, he took off."

"Mitch? Did he call himself Mitch? I know a Mitch. He comes into the shop, but . . . oh my god. He . . . he probably saved her life."

"Probably did."

A knock rattled Clarke's door.

I lowered my voice, "Someone is knocking on Clarke's bedroom door. I'm inside."

"That should be the police. They should have already made the arrest."

Day Eleven: Six O'clock

Officer Evans waited at the door, her lips scrunched up like she was physically holding in words. When I peered down at her, she asked, "Do you need an ambulance, Ms. Scott?"

Slowly, I rotated my injured wrist. It was definitely sore, maybe even sprained, but not broken. "I think I'm okay," I said, my voice going hoarse.

She nodded. "Your daughter was found, she's safe."

"Thanks." I held up my phone. "Officer Oliver already told me. Is Clarke still here?" I looked over her head, really only able to see the hallway and a sliver of living room.

"No, he's being taken to the station for processing. I know you probably want to get back to your daughter, but I'm going to ask you to stay and make a statement while all the details are fresh in your mind. Can you do this for me?"

"Can I call her first? I just . . . I need some proof."

She nodded. "Yes, of course. Do you want to stay here?"

"Not at all." I shook my head, but my cheek screamed in protest. I raised my hand and brushed my fingers across already puffy skin.

Officer Evans stepped out of the doorway, backing up until she turned into the living room.

Another police officer stood, a clunky-looking camera raised and pointing at my purse on the ground. A large wet spot leaked through on one side where probably Beza's phone sat. Looks like I owed Beza a big apology and a new phone.

"The neighboring apartment is yours?" Officer Evans asked as her hands went to her hips in what looked like a practiced stance to put me at ease. When I nodded, she said, "Why don't you make your call from there. After you're finished with your call, I'll conduct my interview with you in there. If you feel comfortable, I'd also like you to walk me through today's events in here before we conclude our interview. Do you need anything from your purse?" She pointed down to my bag.

"My keys."

"Do I have your permission to open your bag?" she asked.

"Yeah." I nodded.

Grabbing a latex glove from her back pocket, she pulled the blue rubber over one hand. "Anything dangerous or hazardous in your purse?" She asked as she crouched down.

"No."

Her hands went to the zipper. "No weapons, hypodermic needles or drug paraphernalia?"

My eyes widened. "Definitely not."

She opened the purse slowly, folding out the sides so the contents were laid bare. With her gloved hand, she lifted out my keys. "Are these the keys you need?"

"Yeah."

Nodding, she stood and handed them to me.

"Thank you. Um, did you guys record the conversation I had with Clarke?"

"We did." She nodded. "Ms. Scott, I would advise you to never try anything like that in the future without the explicit direction of the police. Privacy and eavesdropping laws are very strict in California, and if it hadn't been an officer at the other end of the phone, *and* if you hadn't been in there to gather evidence about a possible kidnapping, you could be facing some very serious consequences right now. An officer of the law is one of the only parties exempt from eavesdropping laws, if it had been anyone else I'd have to be arresting you right now."

I blinked rapidly. "I thought I was supposed to be recording Clarke to get evidence for the restraining order?"

"You might be protected under that statute, as well, I'll have to look into it. But, in the future, I'd advise you to always follow the direction of an officer of the law. Officer Oliver specifically told you not to approach Mr. Allen, that she believed you to be in imminent danger, and you ignored her orders."

"He actually approached me," I said.

She only gave me a level look like I wasn't fooling anyone. Gesturing toward the open door, she said, "This way, Ms. Scott."

I followed, feeling well and truly cowed as well as sore, beaten and humiliated. I hadn't looked into the legality of my actions, nor really considered it. It was kind of shocking to even consider that Clarke could have been viewed as the wronged party in all of this if I hadn't accidentally slipped by the law.

I followed through the house, and straight past Buster who had been leashed to a tether in the front yard. He tried to run to me as I passed, but reached the end of his tether and sat, panting. Several other officers stood on the sidewalk just outside his yard, either talking to each other or into radios. I didn't recognize any of them and none of them looked over as I passed.

I let myself into my apartment, turning on the light.

Officer Evans grabbed my doorknob. "I'll return in about ten minutes. If you finish before, just step out and ask for me, okay?"

"Yeah." I grasped my phone, turning the screen on and off absently.

"I'm glad you're all right, Ms. Scott," she said, before closing the door behind her.

Immediately, I unlocked my phone and dialed Cameron.

"Jamie," his voice barked out after the first ring.

"It's me."

"Holy fuck," he said on a breath. "They told me if I try to get to you, they'll be forced to arrest me before I get to the building. I'm still thinking about heading back there."

"Don't come, I just need to make a police report and then I'm heading home." Walking to my old kitchen table, I took a seat and rested my elbows on the table. "Can I talk to her? I just need to hear her voice."

"Yeah, she's in the living room with your mom and dad, just one second." There was a mechanical type sound and a few seconds of silence before I heard Cameron say, "You're on speaker phone with Sarah."

"Baby?" I asked.

She didn't respond.

"Here, she's watching cartoons, I'll pause it." Some of the background sound stopped.

"Can you turn it on?" I heard Sarah's voice say.

Sobs rippled through my chest and my voice broke as I said, "Angel, it's mom on the phone."

"Mom, can I watch cartoons with Grandma?"

"Yeah, baby, of course. I just wanted to talk to you for a second, okay? Did you go to gymnastics today?"

"Yes," she said.

"Baby, we don't go until Wednesday, and only, only ever with mom. Okay?"

She didn't respond at first, and then asked, "Mom, is today Wednesday?"

"No, baby, it's Tuesday. If you go to gymnastics without mom, you could get very hurt. You could get so hurt, you could never do gymnastics again. Please, only go with mom."

She didn't say anything and I waited for her through the silence. I needed her to understand. Finally, she asked, "Can I watch cartoons with Grandma?"

Exhaling heavily, I said, "Yeah, for a little while."

The background music turned on again and Cameron said, "You're just talking to me now."

"Hey."

"She wore through her shoes, if you can believe it." The cartoon sounds lessened as he talked, as if he walked away from it.

"Clarke was arrested," I said.

"Just get home."

A knock rapped against my door.

"Okay, I will as quickly as possible. I love you."

He paused, before his voice grew gruff, "I love you, too."

When I opened the door, Officer Evans nodded inside. "Mind if I come in?"

When I stepped out of her way, she entered, walked across the room and took a seat at my table. "You don't mind, do you?" she asked.

"No, please. Do you want anything to drink?" I blew out a laugh. "I mean, do you want some water? I already moved out of here."

"No, I'm fine. But you might want to grab a glass of water, it's important to stay hydrated after traumatic events."

When I opened my cupboard, it didn't feel real. Like the cups and furniture and room itself were all a set. Even after I poured myself a glass of water from the sink and took a big sip, it still felt removed, like I was in a house made of paper walls.

Sitting on the chair, I set my glass before me.

Officer Evans glanced up from where she was writing something on a pad. "I want to inform you that I am recording this conversation, do you object to this?"

"No," I said.

"All right, Ms. Scott, I want you to go over the events of today. Add in as many details as you possibly can with always remaining truthful and as exact as possible. You have the right to not answer any question I ask you, do you understand?"

"Yeah."

"Okay, please start at when you left the school today, unless you feel there is other information that you need to add from before that."

Before she'd told me how close I had been to breaking some really serious laws, I'd just assumed I was completely in the right. I wasn't sure how exactly I should proceed or if I should leave anything out. I started off slowly, choosing my words with care. But, when she asked me if I went home with the intention of recording a conversation with Clarke, I knew I had a choice: be honest and maybe be charged with something, or lie and risk being found out.

"I did," I articulated.

She wrote it down. "Why did you suspect him of kidnapping despite the fact the police had told you that it was very unlikely?"

"He . . . he's been harassing me for a while, almost since he moved in. I talked to my landlord asking to be moved to another apartment, stating that I felt unsafe. Instead of moving me and Sarah, the manager of the building told Clarke and offered that he could move apartments. That same day, or that next day, Clarke hired some guy to come into my work to tell me that Clarke wasn't moving and neither was I. So, knowing that he's hired people in the past and that he was particularly careful in hiding his harassing me, I decided to confront him."

"It seems like a pretty big leap from sexual harassment to kidnapping."

"He also broke into my house, took pictures of me sleeping with my boyfriend . . . I reported all this stuff."

She nodded. "Please continue."

"I was almost sure that I saw his car outside Sarah's school at her pick up time the day before. I took a picture and reported it to Officer Oliver."

As she continued to ask me questions she already must know the answers to, I just played along. I had to believe that she was helping, not trapping me. I explained to her exactly how I'd set up my phone and 'delivered' it onto Clarke's property. I showed her the window and the petroleum jelly I'd used to stop the hinges from creaking. Even though I wasn't sure it was in my best interest, I reenacted putting the phone onto Clarke's window ledge with a stationary pad.

We sat back down and Officer Evans regarded me seriously. "Do you think that you can go over the details of your encounter with Clarke now?"

"Yes."

"Okay, I want you to recite the words as closely as you can remember them. Sometimes closing your eyes helps. If it becomes too much for you, we can take a break or finish the interview tomorrow. Do you agree to this?"

I nodded. "I can do it."

"Now when you exited your apartment, how was the interaction initiated, did you knock on his door?"

"No."

"Please proceed."

Closing my eyes, I brought my mind back to exiting my apartment, to that strange calm and clarity that had settled in me. "I left noisily, I knew he'd come out to gloat or threaten me. I took my time locking my door. His dog came out first, jumping on the fence. Then Clarke followed. He said, 'You sent the police to my work, you bitch.'" Opening my eyes, I found the officer's gaze on my face.

"Keep going."

My eyes closed, again as my hand gripped onto the edge of the table. "I asked where Sarah was. He told me to come into his house. I asked if she was in there and he only grinned at me."

"He didn't tell you he had her?"

I opened my eyes. "Not specifically, not yet. But it was very much implied. He didn't deny it. He told me to come into his house." I continued the story, explaining about how he'd grabbed my purse and poured water on Beza's phone. How he'd pinned me against the wall while I was looking for Sarah. The words he whispered, '*You smell like you want to be fucked.*' When I got to the part about him telling me to get down on my knees and beg for Sarah's location, my voice came out in a jumbled mess.

"Let's take a little break here, Jamie."

My eyes opened, again.

"I suggest you drink a little water and take some deep breaths before you continue."

Nodding, I took another sip of water. When I was calm enough to continue, I told her about when things began to be violent.

"So there was physical restraint?"

I lifted my arm. "My wrist, my hair. He undid his button . . ." I flinched as the memory slammed through my mind.

"Just the button?"

"I figured the police were on their way so I started saying things to piss him off, to get him talking. He made it perfectly clear he planned to rape me, he was holding me down on my knees, he was undoing his pants. I decided that I'd rather be hit than raped, so I . . . I tried to make him mad."

The horrible statement lingered in the air as I took another gulp of water.

"Did you indicate to him that you were an unwilling partner?"

"Yeah, I told him that I would bite off his dick if he tried."

A smile twitched at the side of her mouth, but vanished almost instantly. "Did you feel that at any time you could safely leave?"

"No, he told me that I needed to do these things to get my kid back. I was scared to even fight him off because I thought that maybe it would mess up my chances of getting Sarah back." I gestured with my hands. "I was just hoping that if I got him talking long enough, you guys would show up and be able to get Sarah's location from him."

She nodded. "So you felt that there was a threat of violence if you tried to escape the whole time?"

"To Sarah, yes."

"And he physically restrained you against your will, posing an implied threat of rape on you."

"A little more than implied, he said that I was, 'ready to eat his dick,' and then unbuttoned his pants."

"I want you to go over in detail every time he touched you, violently or not. If you can pair the actions with the words he said when he did them, that would be ideal."

After a minute of describing the different things he said and did, I couldn't keep my eyes closed anymore. I didn't want to be back there, even if I sacrificed details in my telling.

When I paused again, she leaned in. "I'm sorry for making you relive this, Ms. Scott. Unfortunately, you will probably have to retell your experiences a number of times in the near future if you want to press charges against Mr. Allen."

"Did he even break the law?" my voice came out weaker than I wished, disheartened. I'd voluntarily gone into his apartment, hadn't I? He hadn't kidnapped Sarah, he didn't even outright say he did when I thought about it, just weaseled around the admission.

"It looks like he did break a couple laws. Do you wish to press charges?"

"I do."

"Do you wish to be issued an emergency protective order against Clarke Allen until your upcoming court date?"

I squeezed my eyes closed. "Please."

"Good. Due to the new evidence, I'm fairly confident that a judge will reevaluate this case with urgency."

"Thank you."

"All right, Ms. Scott, if you feel you are able, I am going to ask you to walk me through the events from when you entered Clarke's apartment to when you left it."

Walking Officer Evans through my encounter with Clarke was its own level of Hell. By the time I was finished, every inch of my body ached. The camera man snapped pictures of my bruises, which they said were already beginning to purple.

"If you could come into the station sometime in the next two days, I'd like to get a second set of photos on your injuries," Officer Evans said when the photographer finished.

"I will." I rubbed my eyes. "Can I go home? Is that okay?"

"Yes, Ms. Scott. I'll be in touch the moment we get the decision on the emergency protective order." She reached up to touch my arm but seemed to think better of it and nodded. "Do you feel all right to drive?"

"I do, thank you."

The knowledge that Clarke was right now in jail, gave me the freedom to feel safe to do anything.

Day Eleven: Seven-forty

Lit streetlights passed over the windshield in a slow, even pattern as I made my way out of Coral Beach and up the hill that Cameron's house waited on. My rearview mirror shone in reds and oranges from the sunset I was leaving.

As I pressed on the gas pedal, my calf cramped like a clamp on my bone. It wasn't alone; parts of my body ached that weren't even whatsoever injured. It was especially true in my lower back, which seemed to be in an all-out brawl with my spine.

Cars clotted up Cameron's driveway, all familiar. Like a couple others, I just pulled to the side of his road. As I stepped out of my car and trudged up the pavement, I considered that I probably should have called Cameron to tell him I was heading back. Oh well, too late now.

His porch light shone bright in the waning daylight, a light at the end of my horrible day. When I made it to the door, I decided to just turn the knob rather than knock. It turned.

The smell of pizza tempted me toward where I heard raised voices yelling out. Well, to be fair, my father didn't need to elevate his voice, ever, to be at a raised level. Amy also shouted, something about my dad not needing to be informed of everything. Deciding that the pizza could wait, I avoided the dining area and the voices. Across the large open area on the other side if the staircase to the upstairs, a couple heads poked out of Cameron's couch. Cartoon characters moved across the screen before them, two pigs danced around, the third laid bricks.

Walking slowly, I crossed the space until I looked down at Sarah and my mother. On another couch, Aiden slept, his head on Beza's lap while her fingers played through his braids.

I almost didn't want to break their moment with my beaten, dirty self, knowing that their little moment of peace would evaporate. But I was selfish, and I needed to be with my baby girl.

Walking slowly around the couch, I took the seat beside her, careful to keep the bruised side of my face pointed away.

My mother's head came up sharply, her red ringed eyes fixing on me. "Jay Jay?" she asked like she wasn't quite sure if it was me.

"Hey, Mom," I whispered.

Sarah glanced up at me, grinned, and then snuggled into me as my arm went around her.

I looked back to my mother, as silent tears dripped down her face. Holding out my palm, I offered her my hand.

Hesitantly, she reached over Sarah's lap and clasped hands with me.

"I thought about you a lot today, Mom," I said.

"Well, I have to say same here, honey." With her other hand, she wiped the tears from under her eyes.

Across the way, I saw Beza and the tracks of tears that ran down from her eyes. "Beza, I owe you a new phone. I'm really sorry."

Her lip pushed out. "I'm just glad you don't owe me a new friend, Jamie, and Aiden a new aunt and Sarah a new mom," her words came out harshly, angrily, especially for Beza.

Running my teeth over my lips, I said, "Yeah." Because there was not much I could say.

"She's already fucking here," I heard Susan's voice cry out from deeper in the house.

Glancing back, I saw a very angry pregnant woman charging at me. She was like a small blonde bull, plowing into the living room, a crowd of angry familiar faces following behind her.

I felt glued to the couch, especially as I held both Sarah's shoulder and my mother's hand.

They surrounded us, Susan first, then my father, Sharon, Chris, Peter and Amy.

"What the hell, Jamie?" Susan shouted from directly in front of me, blocking out the television screen singlehandedly.

Sarah grumbled, and then broke away from me to leave me alone with the angry mob. My mother, thankfully stayed, strangely being my biggest comfort.

Amy's hands went up to cover her mouth as everyone's gaze combed over my full face.

"Jamie?" my dad's voice boomed out.

"Oh my god," Susan said as angry tears sprayed from her eyes. "You could have died, you stupid bitch."

"That's what he called me," I mumbled. "Guys, not right now, okay?"

A hand went to my shoulder, and Cameron's voice came from behind me. "I'm going to have to second that. Anyone who feels they can't hold it in, needs to take off and come back later. We've all had a bad day, but I'm pretty sure Jamie's day was a whole lot worse."

My dad regarded Cameron seriously. "You're going to kick her family out?"

"Only if I have to," Cameron responded.

My dad's lower lip tucked up, and he regarded me very seriously. "All right, I don't think I can hold it in. Out of respect for you and your home, I'm going to have to leave." He nodded, then turned to Sharon. "Mind taking me home, honey?"

"Of course, you go to the car and I'll meet you there," she said.

His feet pounded away, echoing through the now hushed house.

I cleared my throat and looked between the angry faces of the people I love, finding a desperation and distraught marring their faces. I'd put them through the ringer, that was obvious. They wanted something from me—that was obvious from their expressions as well—but I had nothing to give them.

Clearing my throat, I said, "I feel bad about this, but I can't offer you any apologies for doing what I did." I closed my eyes. "Obviously, in retrospect, it was the wrong decision. But, in the moment, I was sure Clarke had Sarah. When he found me outside my house, he told me he had her. I didn't see any other choice."

I opened my eyes to see a couple heads shaking and Susan storming away. She grabbed her jacket from the chair, almost sending it toppling to the ground as she stormed out after my father.

"Beza, you want some help carrying Aiden to the car?" Chris asked on a sniff.

"Yeah," she said, her voice still raw and harsh.

Amy was the next to storm off, Peter quickly following behind. She did knock over her chair as she yanked her purse from it and left Peter to right it. He gave me an apologetic smile and wave as he followed. They left with a bang of the door slamming closed.

Sharon walked up to me, her hand going to grasp my free hand so that my arms were crossed and holding hands with the two women who raised me. Skin puffed out around her dark eyes and new deep wrinkles had carved between her brows. A tear still clung to her cheek. She squeezed my hand. "Te amo," she said, fiercely.

"I love you, too."

"Te amo," she repeated, squeezing my hand harder.

"I know you do," I whispered, looking down.

Nodding, she released me. She crossed the room and grabbed her purse from where it sat on the table before following my father out.

My mother stayed for a few minutes longer, until I told her that I had to get Sarah to bed. She reached to hug me but pulled back when I hissed with pain.

I cringed. "I'm sorry, Mom, it so isn't you or your hug. I just hurt my arm trying to . . . do something and I'm sore all over." I gestured to my body with my hand with a messed up wrist as opposed to messed up full arm.

"Of course, honey." She touched my hair.

I cringed again, I couldn't help it. My scalp was one of the most sensitive parts about me.

Lifting up hands in surrender, she said, "I'll just say that I love you, and this was one of the scariest days of my life. I really hope you saying that you thought about me while you were in danger means that you're ready to let me back in."

"Can we do this later, Mom?" I looked away.

"Honey, it's a sign." She took a deep breath. "I won't say anything more. I'm going to go. I'll be waiting by the phone for your call."

I almost laughed out of exasperation, realizing that I even missed this part of her. She was still my guilt-trip mom. "I love you, Mom. I love you. And I miss you. I'm trying to work my stuff out, okay?" I sniffed. "It's just taking some time."

"Okay, honey." She reached for me, but drew back her hand. Walking over to Sarah, who still stood before the television, she pulled her in a tight embrace. "Never, ever walk away by yourself again, baby. You need to wait for Mom. Yeah?"

"Yeah," Sarah said as her head rested on her grandma's shoulder.

"Never, ever, again. You scared your grandma so much." She held her for one more moment before giving Cameron a hug, too, and walking to the door.

My mother opened the door to Susan, who had her hand up to knock.

We all paused at the door, until Susan walked in and grabbed me to her. I bent forward over her belly, getting a face-full of messy blonde hair. "I'm so mad at you," she sobbed, before releasing me and turning to hobble back down the steps. My mom walked with her, stopping by her car that waited, door open, engine running.

I closed the door before crossing the house to take a seat beside Sarah on the couch. Swinging an arm around her, I pulled her in close to me. "It's time for bed, baby."

Cameron turned off the TV. "How about I get Sarah to bed so you can shower and eat?" He didn't quite meet my gaze as he said it.

I looked to Sarah, torn between letting her out of my sight and satisfying the empty feeling inside me that was beginning to feel like nausea. The idea of washing any lingering trace of Clarke's touch off of me was the kicker. I said, "All right, thank you."

I gave Sarah an extra-long bedtime hug and kiss, before heading off to the mostly devoured pizza box.

As I took my first bite of pepperoni pizza, my phone vibrated in my purse. I pulled it out to find an unknown local number flashing across the screen. My hand shook a little as I answered and the thought that Clarke was already out buzzed through my mind. But he wasn't out. That was crazy. "Hello?" I answered.

"Jamie, this is Officer Kelly Oliver."

"Hey," I said.

"Hey, I'm calling to inform you that a judge approved your emergency protective order and I have the paperwork waiting here for you at the station."

I needed to concentrate on my breathing for a few seconds because the relief was so great. "Thank you so much."

I could hear a smile in her voice as she said, "Of course. Call me if you think of anything else, or if anything comes up, okay? I'll give you what updates I'm allowed to by law."

"Thank you, Kelly—Officer Oliver. You do not know how relieved I am.

"I don't suppose that I do, but there are a couple of us at the station that are feeling some relief as well . . . one of them being the chief. He had some pretty strong words to say about your decision to go in there against my advice."

"He and my dad can rag on me together over a beer at the bar. My guess is they already are."

She breathed a laugh before her voice turned serious, "I really, really hope you'll never consider doing anything like that again."

"I swear I never will. Thank you for everything. You really saved me today."

She sighed. "Not as quickly as I would have liked. Well, I need to go. I will be in touch soon. Will you be coming into the station tomorrow?"

"I'll try, I work tomorrow."

"I suggest you take a day off, Jamie. You might not even be aware of all of your injuries yet."

Looking around the large open room, I knew she was right. I couldn't go to work tomorrow, no way in hell. And I definitely wasn't about to send Sarah to that school. "You're right. Thank you."

"You have a good night, or well, a better one."

"Thanks. Thank you."

After I hung up, my gaze grazed over the familiar large open space of Cameron's A-frame.

Unlike the emptiness that now consumed my old apartment, this space felt worn in and warm, like my favorite Aerosmith On Tour long-sleeved t-shirt.

Right now, right in this second, I felt safe, I felt home. I finished my slice of lukewarm pizza before looking back to my phone. Unlocking the screen, I looked at the time: eight thirty-two. It was probably not too late to call Doug. Two days in and I was already fumbling my new job.

Honestly, after the day I had, they could keep the fucking job, I'd give them the money back. Or I'd just tell them never to send it, since my account hadn't received anything yet.

The phone rang twice, and then Doug's now familiar voice said, "You've reached Douglass Maze."

"Hey, Doug, it's Jamie." I took a moment to come up with the right phrasing.

"Good, you got my message."

My head came up. "No—I must have missed that."

"Yeah, well, Patrick told me about what you went through today and thought you might need a day off."

For one humiliating instant, I thought he was talking about what happened with Clarke. "Yeah, my daughter ran off. It was terrifying."

"I imagine you wouldn't want her out of your sight for the next twenty-four hours."

Nodding, even though he couldn't hear me, I said, "That would be really nice."

"Well, since you already got through most of what I had planned for you tomorrow, I can just send you some links and email some reading material so you can finish up from home. If that works for you, of course."

My head fell into my hand, but I was careful not to touch the huge bruise forming above my cheekbone. "That works amazingly. Thank you so much, Doug."

"I'll see you Thursday. Expect an email from me around eight, eight-thirty tomorrow."

"Okay, thank you again."

"No problem, sleep well." He disconnected.

As I set my phone back down, Cameron's voice came behind me, "Are you going to take a shower?"

Slowly, I crawled out of my seat and turned around.

He stood a few feet away, his face worn and his eyes exhausted. His dark hair stuck out wildly around his beautiful face. He was still wearing his work clothes. A large black stain smeared across his stomach.

My hands dug into the sides of my filthy dress pants. "I am definitely going to take a shower."

He offered me his hand, and I had to blink away the memory of Clarke, strangely, offering me his hand outside of his apartment. I blinked, again, furiously. "Sorry, I—" Walking forward, I took his hand and noticed the cuff of red, raw skin around my wrist. Reaching forward, I pulled my sweater sleeve down.

Cameron looked at me, dark gaze pinning me. "Jamie, that's nothing to your face. You can't hide this from me."

Even though all I wanted was to hide this from him, I lied and said, "I'm not trying to."

Day Eleven: Eight Forty-five

After I checked on Sarah, Cameron helped me undress in his room, pulling my sweater sleeves so I could carefully maneuver my arms out of them. Cameron leaned in, peering at the sleeve of the button-up I'd worn for work. "What's all that black stuff?"

When I brushed my fingers over the black striped marks on my sleeve, my shoulder complained at even that much contact. Sighing, I said, "You know my window in my bedroom?"

"Yeah."

"Well, it creaks really loud every time I open it, usually. So I spread petroleum jelly all over it, I've seen my mom do it with hinges. Anyway, the window opened a couple inches before it started to creek. All this . . ." I gestured up and down my arm, "it's from me squeezing my arm out of the window to put my phone on Clarke's windowsill."

Little puckers formed around Cameron's brows and his eyes bounced through the room like he was trying to picture it.

"My whole idea was kind of crazy . . . and could have gone very wrong, I know that."

His dark gaze came back to mine and he gave me a look that was half disbelieving and half furious.

"You're mad at me," I stated the obvious.

He didn't respond, just continued to regard me.

"I thought when you defended me downstairs maybe I got out of it." I tried to make it sound teasing, but it came out flat and defensive.

"Baby." His hand came up to carefully cup the uninjured side of my face. "I will always defend you. But that doesn't mean that when it's just you and me I'm not going to call you on your bullshit."

A tear fell onto my cheek. My voice came out raw and angry, "You have no idea—"

"Yeah, I do." His fingers tapped his chest and he leaned in closer to me. "If someone has a gun to our heads, I take the bullet. Me." He tapped his chest harder.

I looked away to my suitcase still propped against one wall. The image that Clarke forced on me drove into my mind—Cameron, dead, his brain-matter splattered across Clarke's pristine wall. Clarke stands with a bottle of bleach, grinning. I shook my head furiously, ignoring the screaming pain the movement shot into me.

"Yes, Jamie. Yes. Thirty minutes. For thirty minutes I thought you were being raped—or worse. The police wouldn't let me anywhere near you. I tried, I drove up and they told me that if I didn't turn back right then, they'd be forced to arrest me for contempt of court. They told me that they wouldn't let you be injured or raped, *but nothing else*." His eyes closed.

"Clarke didn't rape me," I whispered.

"No. But he hurt you. He's a sick fuck, completely obsessed with you—"

"He's not obsessed with me."

His hand rose to my face again and his expression melted from anger to concern. "Jamie, of course he's obsessed with you. He might be arrested, but he's still going to come after you, probably even more now that you gave him what he wanted."

I was too weary to fight him and too exhausted to keep standing. Blowing out a breath, I backed up and slumped onto his bed. "Cameron, I wish I hadn't talked to him, or I wish I could just erase all of today. But weirdly, I get Clarke now, I get what he was doing and why he was doing it, and it had nothing to do with me. Who Clarke is really obsessed with is himself, it was all about himself. He really, honestly, thinks he's the victim in this situation." I held up a hand, "And I'm not saying that he's not completely insane, but that is what he thinks."

"How could he possibly be the victim?"

I looked up into Cameron's beautiful, concerned face. One of my all-time favorite faces attached to one of the people I loved most in this world. I couldn't tell him. Inhaling deeply, I said, "He's crazy, but in his mind, you and I are the bad guys who deserve to be punished. He didn't really want to rape me, he wanted to punish us. He did everything to humiliate and debase me because he was trying to hurt you and hurt me."

"From what I saw, he seemed to only be focused on you," he said, shaking his head just slightly.

"He's scared of you, but he was trying to punish you, too. He got a restraining order against you—"

"I know."

"He wanted to arrange it so you would get arrested."

Cameron nodded and looked off. "Maybe he just didn't want to see you happy with another guy after you rejected him so many times."

"Maybe," I said. I would have to leave it at that. It was a reasonable answer, a rational one. It wasn't the real answer, but as answers went, it fit. The truth I wish I could shield Cameron from forever was that Clarke started to punish me because he didn't want to see Cameron happy.

Cameron straightened and pointed at me. "Jamie, that doesn't make him any less dangerous. If he has a victimhood complex, he's going to see himself as the victim of this arrest."

"True. But now at least I have an emergency protective order until the trial."

"Good," he said the word on a breath of relief.

"Also . . ." I rubbed the soreness out of my neck as I continued, "I feel like I was making him way more powerful in my mind than he really was. In my mind he was this super-spy serial killer. But in real life, he's kind of pathetic. A young guy obsessed with himself and the past. In his mind, nothing was his fault— kind of like a creepy little goblin."

His eyebrows rose. "Creepy little goblin?"

I laughed, but then closed my eyes and felt the mirth dissipate like mist. "Stuck, like he was stuck and felt that if the people he thought were responsible suffered, it would make his life better." I shook my head. "Maybe, I'm reading too much into it. Maybe I'm just reflecting my problems onto his situation, but I felt like I understood him."

Cameron just regarded me with concentration, like he didn't know how to respond.

I tried to explain, "I'm not saying that anything he did was whatsoever justified, or that you or me deserved any of it—"

"Jamie, I get what you're saying." He reached out, brushing his fingers along my jaw-line. "You pity Clarke. You have sympathy for the devil."

"Sort of. Thanks for the Stones reference . . . that's a great song." I gave him a half smile. "And if I don't get into the shower pretty soon, I'm going to have to sleep like this."

Cameron crouched down on the floor before me, and made eye contact as he pulled off my shoes. "Let me take care of you."

The sight of Cameron kneeling down before me was such a stark contrast from how Clarke held me to crouch before him. They were two such opposite men, caught in parallel lives. The difference between them felt like the difference between love and hate.

Cameron's fingers deftly unhooked my pants, and I lifted my butt so he could gently pull both my pants and underwear down my legs. When my pants peeled over my knees, he paused, his gaze going between my knees and my eyes.

"Are they bruised?"

"Yeah."

I didn't even want to look at them. Instead, I watched Cameron as he slowly maneuvered my pant legs over my feet. Kneeling between my legs, he unbuttoned my shirt then carefully pulled the material over my uninjured shoulder. My wrist throbbed when I had to bend it to pull through my sleeve, but it managed through. After Cameron unhooked my bra and helped me slip the straps over my injuries, he asked, "Would you let me help you in the shower?"

"Please," I whispered, looking down at him. "I love you, Cameron."

"Baby, you're it for me, I think you know that."

Day Twelve

Remembering How to Love

Day Twelve: Seven thirty-five

I woke up crying, and I wasn't even sad. My eyelids pushed open through the soppy, junky wetness. My arm tightened around Sarah's still sleeping form. I had carried her in last night, scooped her up and brought her to sleep in the big bed. I held her, and Cameron held me.

As my eyes met the dim, early morning light, I tried to recall the dream before all the details slipped from my mind.

Sarah and I sat on a boat as a burbling river carried us downstream. Raw wood planks, splintered from age, stretched under us. Sarah faced forward and I toward the back. A steep canyon with trees poking out rose around us. The shadows found us and released us just as quickly.

Sarah reached over the side of the boat.

"Careful, baby," I told her.

Her fingers trailed through the passing water, paths of luminescence streaming behind each finger. "Sarah, is the river time?" she asked in a way that I knew she was telling me to ask her the question.

"Angel, is the river time?"

"Yes." She smiled at me. A big, happy smile.

I looked over her head, expecting to see more of the river, but instead an ocean waited behind her. Another boat sailed out over the lapping sea, heading to the horizon. As the sailboat disappeared from view, tears fell from my eyes. Then, in the way of dreams, the boat I sat on turned, and both Sarah and

Tears forged a path over the bridge of my nose, pooling on the pillow under me. The echo of the boat's movement under me took a moment to dissipate after I'd woken, as if I'd actually traveled in my sleep.

My cheek throbbed, pressure building around the bone. Perhaps I should have gone to the emergency room for an X-ray; I was sure my fancy new insurance had already started.

My body protested movement. I also had the very real risk of waking Sarah and Cameron, but both the throbbing in my cheek and the parallel pain at the back of my head demanded that I get up. I maneuvered Cameron's arm off me and unpeeled myself from the bed. I hissed at the pain in my knees, but I managed to get up and off the bed.

When I turned back, Sarah mumbled something before rolling away.

Cameron opened his eyes blearily, shut them, then mumbled, "Do you need . . ." but trailed off.

I caught sight of my reflection in the mirror. I looked terrible. A purple triangle spread across my cheek. Reddish tendrils spread up to the outside of my eye. I'd gone to bed with wet hair, which had dried in a manner that would make Medusa cringe.

Unfortunately, if I even brought my fingers near where Clarke had grabbed me, a stabbing pain reverberated through my skull. I satisfied myself with brushing out everywhere else and making peace with the big poof coming out of the side of my head.

Downstairs, I learned about the joys of having cold pizza for breakfast, while holding a towel-covered ice pack to my cheek.

Virtually every person I loved was furious with me, besides Sarah. I was beat up all to hell. I'd been through one of the worst twenty-four hour periods of my life. Yet, strangely, I felt happy. So happy, in fact, that if my bruised cheek didn't strictly forbid it, I would have been smiling right now.

Perhaps my happiness stemmed from the dream, or from the fact that Clarke was in jail, or that by some miracle, Mitch had seen Sarah running past him yesterday.

A little body plopped into the seat beside me. I turned to see Sarah blinking around the room. Medusa would probably have been envious of Sarah's hairdo; some sections of her hair even managed to defy gravity and stick out in a vertical position.

"Hey, baby," I said as I attempted to smooth down her hair with my better arm. Catching sight of the dark cuff around my wrist, I hid my arm from her.

Peering up at me with one eye closed, one open, she raised a hand toward my face.

Gently, I intercepted her hand. "Baby, don't touch Mommy's face right now, okay? Are you hungry? Do you want a yogurt?"

"I want pizza," she said.

"You want me to heat it up for you?"

"No." She giggled.

As I was eating it straight from the box, I couldn't really object, so I scooted it between us and we ate in silence.

I finished my pizza, suffering for every delicious bite with echoing throbs in my cheek. I looked down at Sarah. "I had an amazing dream with you in it, baby. We were floating down a beautiful river in a little boat."

"Was there gymnastics in it?"

"Nope."

"What did you dream about?"

"A beautiful boat. What did you dream about baby?" I asked. I could tell that's what she wanted.

"Gymnastics."

"That must have been a good dream. Do you feel happy?"

"I feel happy and excited. Do you feel happy and excited, Mom?" It was probably just a kid question, but like so many times before, I felt like she could look into my soul.

"I do, baby." I nodded.

"First school, then gymnastics." She took another slice of pizza and tried to shove half of it in her mouth.

"Small bites, baby." When I was sure she wasn't choking, I said, "Today, we're going to do it a little different. We're not going to go to school today. First, we're going to go to the police to thank them for looking for you. After that, we're going to find our friend Mitch and say thank you to him, too. Then, gymnastics. And after gymnastics, we need to go get you some new shoes."

She peered up at me. "Are the other kids in school?"

Instead of answering, I looked away. Honestly, I wasn't sure how to answer. I really didn't want her to feel rewarded for running off, but at the same time, I wasn't ready to let her go back to school. Not yet.

Turning back, I asked, "Sarah, why did you run to gymnastics?"

She looked at me but didn't answer. It was an answer only she could give and an answer I would probably never receive. I considered punishing her by taking gymnastics away for a couple of weeks, but I wasn't sure that would help anything. Sarah only paid attention to consequences when she was calm and rational, and I'd only ever seen her elope in a panic. She eloped when a car backfired, or a person shouted at her, or something popped out at her unexpectedly. It didn't seem like punishment would fix that.

I placed my elbow on the table and my forehead in my hand. I whispered, "Maybe we need more help."

When I peeked over at Sarah, she took another bite of pizza.

Setting down my icepack on the table, I asked her, "Do you remember Dr. Artie? You liked his waiting room with all the toys."

"Yes," she said.

"Do you want to go back and see him, to talk about your day and stuff?"

Sarah nodded. "Dr. Artie talks about Daddy."

"Do you want to talk about Daddy?" I asked her.

"Yes."

Sniffing, I said, "Okay, I'm going to call him, see if I can make an appointment."

"Dr. Artie loves gymnastics," she said with a smile.

"Does he love gymnastics?"

She nodded with enthusiasm. "His favorite gymnast is Peter Vidmar. Peter Vidmar did not compete in the London Olympics."

"Oh." I cleared my throat. "Baby, you can talk to me about Daddy, too, if you want." When she didn't respond, I added, "You don't have to. But if you ever want to . . . you can talk to me about anything."

She turned away.

I dropped the subject so she could finish the rest of her pizza. Touching her shoulder, I said, "I'm just going to be right back, okay?"

"Okay, Mommy." She gave me a view of a grin full of pizza.

"Gross." I tickled her side as I stood to head upstairs.

I found Cameron in his room. He was buttoning a work shirt over a white undershirt and his hair was still wet.

I leaned my good shoulder against his wall.

"You're awake?"

"Yep. I went downstairs but it seemed like you two needed a moment." He grinned over as his hands dropped to his sides. "What's the plan for today?"

"Don't you have to go in to work?" I asked.

"I can stay out until about eleven," he said.

"I need to buy Sarah some new shoes, go to the police station so they can photograph my injuries, and I need to find Mitch."

"Find Mitch?" he asked.

"Yeah. He's a regular at The Coffee Stop. I think he's homeless. I'm pretty sure he saved Sarah's life yesterday."

He nodded. "The Mitchell who walked her all the way to the gym."

"Yeah." I bit my lip and looked away. "Maybe there's something I can do for him. I don't know. He never lets me just give stuff to him. He always wants to help me, to earn it. I think he might be an alcoholic or drug addict or something. He's come into the shop pretty messed up before. But he did something that I can never, ever repay, and then just left."

Cameron nodded. "I'll help you find him."

"I think he works at a gas station. Maybe if Chris stops being mad at me, he'll tell me the next time Mitch comes into the shop." I sighed.

"We'll find him," Cameron said, before walking over to me. "And your friends and family will forgive you."

"Maybe. Everyone but Susan." I laughed mirthlessly.

"I bet you ten dollars Susan will show up today to have it out—your dad and Amy, too." He pressed a soft kiss on my lips. "I'll bet you ten dollars each."

"So if they show, I'll have to be yelled at by three loud, crazy people, and be out thirty dollars? I'm not sure I want to take that bet."

"Maybe we should make the bet more enticing." He quirked his eyebrows.

I gestured from my face down my body. "You really want all this?"

He grinned, not taking his gaze from my eyes. "Always. But this time it would have to be very, very carefully."

"Fine, I'll take your bet, you tempter. But instead of a bet, let's call it my reward for surviving my nearest and dearest."

Day Twelve: Eight-twenty

After Cameron headed downstairs, I dressed quickly in my *I love Cash, Johnny Cash* t-shirt, knowing that I needed an extra boost today and hoped that Johnny could see me through. When I pulled up my jeans and buttoned them, I pulled at the waistband, surprised that I didn't need a belt. Maybe Susan was onto something with her 'women since the beginning of the holiday season would argue you can gain twenty pounds in two weeks' speech.

After pulling on my shoes, I crossed the bathroom and found Sarah passing on the way to her bedroom.

"I'm getting ready for gymnastics, Mom," she said, grinning. She reached up and wiggled her front tooth.

"Wow, baby. Is it loose?"

She jumped back. "Don't touch it!"

"Sorry, sorry." I held up my hands. "Gymnastics isn't until later. Dress normally and we'll take your gymnastic clothes with us like every other Wednesday."

As I stepped in front of the mirror, my bruised cheek greeted me. It looked worse than it had when I'd woken up. Maybe it was just the light, but my cheek looked almost purple. I hadn't realized Clarke's strike had been so powerful. I wouldn't consider my life up until this point as gentle, but the abuse and torment I'd undergone in the last twenty-four hours was worse than anything I'd really experienced in my life. Losing Logan and discovering how deep his

illness ran was nothing to the feeling of losing my
baby and thinking she was in the hands of a
psychopath. Truth or not, the torture of yesterday
would eclipse all else.

So why did I feel so much better?

As I stepped out of the bathroom, a blank space
of wall stretched before me. The photo that used to
occupy that space had been there for as long as
Cameron and Vanessa had the house, but I hadn't
really looked at it in years. Perhaps Cameron had
moved it, but I could have sworn that I saw it there a
few days ago. It was conspicuous in its absence.

A slight feeling of suspicion rose within me. I
knocked gently on Sarah's door. "Sarah?"

She opened the door, wearing her gymnastics
outfit.

"Baby, did you take the photo from the wall?"

"Yes," she said, nodding.

"Where is it?"

She pointed to her wall. The wood-framed
photo hung at a slant, half covering Sarah's Olympics
poster.

I crawled over the bed to grab it, but paused as
my gaze passed over the faces on the photo. It was a
group shot of the day Vanessa graduated from college.
Cameron, Logan, me, Susan, Beza and Amy crowded
around a grinning Nessa in her red cap and gown. We
were all huddled around her in a too-small diner
booth. Nessa's mother sat to one side with Susan and
Logan's parents, Mark and Colleen, beside her. Mark
looked like an entirely different person back then,
clean and handsome.

A small smile touched my lips when I saw the sliver of my mother's face in the corner of the photo.

After all this time, the scene was still so clear in my mind.

"Wait, wait, I can do it this time!" My mother laughed as she set the timer on her huge hunk of a camera. As she'd done every other time she didn't make it in time to us, she walked to the other side of the restaurant booth wall, tucked her blonde hair behind her ears and leaned down to check the picture.

"Two pregnant ladies here, Mom!" I yelled. I was sweating from being sandwiched so close to all of my best friends.

My mom smiled, though her eyes were on the picture. "This one is going to be good!" She gestured. "Get closer, Colleen!"

"Get a move on, lady!" Susan yelled as she crowded me on my other side.

"Okay, what are we going to yell this time?" Logan asked, looking over Nessa to me.

"Nessa's most embarrassing moment," I suggested.

"No!" Nessa objected with a laugh. Her cheeks had already ripened to a brighter shade of red than her cap and gown.

"Too late. Embarrassing moment! Go!" Susan yelled.

"When a bird pooped on Nessa's head in front of Josh Davies!" I yelled as everyone else yelled out

other exclamations. People turned to us, though our words jumbled into a mess and I was sure no one else could really hear what we'd said.

Amy started laughing so hard she was snorting, and the rest of us were laughing just as loud. The camera stopped ticking, and my mother dove for us, but once more didn't make it into the picture.

Laughter lit up each of our faces. Two pregnant bellies peeked over the booth. It was a moment of potential, a moment of the purest happiness with no death, cheating, depression, or hatred.

My fingers touched the glass over our elated faces. I didn't blame myself for destroying this; it was Logan and Vanessa's fault—along with circumstances beyond any of our control. But I didn't want it destroyed forever, either. Somehow, someway, the universe gave me the power here. It gave me the power to bring this back, to forgive the people here, to move on, and to give this to Sarah. I'd already decided to pull myself out of the anger and resentment, to move on and forgive, my head was just taking time to catch up.

Sarah crawled onto the bed beside me, looking up at the picture I was still touching. I pointed to my stomach. "That's you in there." I pointed to Beza's belly. "And that's Aiden in there."

"Don't take it, Mom," she said, pushing my hands away from the picture as if I might break it with my touch.

"Well, it's Cameron's picture. I'm sure it's important to him. You should ask him if you could borrow it for a while. But first, you need to put something over your gymnastics outfit, baby."

Of course, Cameron said yes, and from his small smile, I suspected he'd already noticed that Sarah had moved the photo into her room. After searching through Sarah's cupboard, the only shoes I could find for her to wear were her sparkly, purple rain boots. I packed a spare outfit in her backpack, and remembered to slip in her homework for the week.

Clouds skipped across the blue sky as we exited out into the almost, but-not-quite summer warmth. Sarah rushed to my car, climbing in as soon as I clicked the button to unlock it. Since my wrist was sore and I wasn't in the mood to drive, Cameron volunteered.

"Kids' CD!" Sarah demanded as soon as we were settled in the car.

"Kids' CD, what?" I prompted, looking back at her.

"Kids' CD, Mom."

I smiled, and then grimaced because the action hurt my cheek. "I'm thinking of a polite word."

"Please!"

"All right." I turned the CD on and put the volume on low.

"You have any idea where to start looking for this Mitch guy?" Cameron asked as he turned the car around.

"Would it be okay to do the police station first, just to get it over with?"

His hand came over the center divider and his fingers laced through mine. "Yeah. I'm ready for all this to be behind us." He said nothing for a minute, and then glanced over. "I had a thought."

"Just one?" I asked.

He cracked a smile. "What if we moved?"

"Moved? Like to a new house?"

"Yep."

An unexpected flood of warmth surged through my chest and excitement fluttered in my stomach. Amazingly, not only did I want to do just that, I absolutely loved the idea.

But no.

"Cameron, what about your house?"

He took a deep breath in, as if he was steadying himself. "I've been thinking of selling it. It's about to be summer and the market is good. We could get a place in town. It would be more convenient for both of us.

"But you built that house yourself. I don't want you to do that." It was a bald-faced lie, because a million images ran through my mind. The picture of Cameron, Sarah, and I smiling through house searching, carrying boxes, and moving around furniture thrummed through my mind. I shook my head.

Cameron squeezed my hand. "I built it for a different life, Jamie. I'd already been thinking about it for a while. And honestly, after what happened, I think we both need a fresh start without bad memories."

I wasn't exactly sure what bad memory he meant—his marriage, the accident, Clarke—there was too much to pick from. Was it even possible to make a fresh start with someone you had over a decade of history with? Because he seemed to be waiting for an answer, I said, "A lot to think about, but it sounds really nice."

Cars packed the police station parking lot, and after circling twice we ended up parking in a metered street-side spot three blocks away. Sarah insisted on holding both Cameron and my hands all the way to the entrance of the police station.

"Maybe I should have called ahead," I said after we stepped inside. I glanced around. Unlike the last time I came here, the station was full and a long line stretched from the desk partitions all the way to the entrance. Soft chatter and a low buzzing resonated through the office.

Sarah looked up. "Mom! Can we go now?" She brought up our hands to cover her ears.

"Shoot," I mumbled.

"You could just step outside and call them now," Cameron suggested, nodding to the swinging door we'd just entered through.

I pointed at him with my free hand. "Cutting the line, I like the way you think."

"I'll wait here in case they don't let you cut."

Sarah joined me outside, hopping up and down the steps as I pulled up Officer Oliver's phone number on my phone. Three minutes later when we'd reentered the station, a female officer exited the heavy door into the waiting area. As the woman I was pretty sure was Officer Oliver examined the space until her gaze caught on mine, I realized I didn't know what Officer Oliver looked like. She'd been my lifeline when I'd walked into Clarke's apartment yesterday, the sound of safety and security for the past week, but I'd never actually met her.

The officer walked straight over to us. She was around forty, tall, and her shoulders were wide for a woman. Her prominent nose and direct stare gave her an almost hawkish look as she crossed the space. She stopped and nodded. "Officer Oliver. You're Ms. Scott?"

"Yeah, I'm Jamie, and this is Cameron and Sarah."

She nodded to Cameron, but her expression softened as she turned a smile to Sarah. Thick lines creased across her forehead. "I've heard a lot about you, Miss Sarah. Are you doing okay?"

"Thank you!" Sarah yelled.

Her smile widened. "You're welcome. Let's all head back to see the chief."

As Officer Oliver led us back, she looked between Cameron and I. "I'm glad you both came in so early."

"Both?" I asked, not knowing if she meant Sarah, who skipped beside me, or Cameron.

"Yeah." She looked to Cameron, her smile falling away. "Have you thought about getting an emergency protective order as well?"

His brow furrowed. "From Clarke?"

"Yeah."

"What? Is he out?" I asked.

She nodded and spoke in a low voice, "Yes, he was released on bail this morning. I could help you get an emergency protective order, Mr. Robinson. I believe the judge would pass it based on the evidence."

"Thank you, but I don't really think I need one," Cameron said.

Officer Oliver halted before the heavy metal door to regard Cameron. "I'd have to disagree with you, sir. I'd suggest you talk to the chief about it or, like I said, I can take care of it for you."

Cameron's brow furrowed. "Thanks, I'll think about it." From his tone of voice, I could tell that he'd already made up his mind against it.

There was a loud buzzing followed immediately by a clunking sound, and then Officer Oliver opened the door for us.

"Clarke still has a restraining order against Cameron, right?" I asked as I passed her.

"I don't think that's something you can rely on here." She walked the short remaining distance and leaned her shoulder against the chief's door. "I'll just peek in here and see if he's busy. You three hold tight."

The moment she stepped inside, Sarah looked up. "Mom, can I have your phone? Mom!"

"Uh, yeah." I pulled it out of my purse and handed it over before turning back to Cameron. "Maybe she's right, Cameron." Going to my tiptoes, I whispered, "Clarke is nuts, he's as likely to go after you as he is me."

It was even more likely now that I knew the truth of Cameron and Clarke's history, but I couldn't tell Cameron that. If he knew Clarke was obsessed with him and not me, he'd blame himself for everything that had happened; I was certain of that. The way I saw it, there was only one person to blame, and that was Clarke.

Cameron leaned in even closer, so close his lips brushed my ear, "I dare Clarke to come after me."

He said it with such stone-cold anger, I immediately moved away. "Don't say that," I whispered back, though no sound left my lips.

As the door opened and Officer Oliver ushered us in, I begged the universe not to take Cameron up on his dare.

Day Twelve: Nine O'clock

In a quiet and calm voice, Chief Greer handed me my ass.

He sat back, leaning his bulk against the backrest of his leather chair, looking deceptively relaxed. I didn't know if my dad put him up to it or he just took the task on himself, but the chief managed to pack a butt-load of scorn in every question he asked me about what happened with Clarke.

When he told me, "Thankfully, for your sake, stupidity isn't illegal; but it does have a high mortality rate," Cameron must have had enough because he leaned into the desk and said, "With all due respect, Chief, you need to stop talking to Jamie that way."

I put a hand on Cameron's back.

Chief Greer looked like he was going to respond to that, so I quickly said, "It's okay, Cameron. He's my dad's friend. Rudy, please watch what you say in front of my kid."

We all glanced over to Sarah who slouched in the chief's big office chair, captivated by the game she was playing on my phone.

Chief Greer's lips pursed and his big, bushy eyebrows came together. He was silent for a moment. Finally, he looked up and met my gaze. "Mike's been a good friend of mine for a long time. Things could have easily gone very differently."

When he paused again, I nodded. "Yeah, I know."

"But I'll admit, maybe I'm taking this too personally." He blew out a breath and stood. "All right, let's get you photographed so you can get out of here."

Officer Oliver returned with a camera, and we stayed in the chief's office for the light. Photographing and cataloguing my injuries took another twenty minutes of me standing around the office, pivoting this way and that. Chief Greer must have warmed up to me in that time, because when I asked if Sarah could thank the Officer who was in charge of looking for her, he pulled a man who looked like an action hero into his office. The chief introduced him as Officer James.

Even crouched down in front of Sarah, he was still a few inches taller than her. "Hey, Sarah. Are you listening to your mom and staying safe?" he asked.

She just stood there, eyes wide, staring at him.

"Baby, he asked you a question," I prompted, touching her shoulder.

"Thank you!" Sarah shouted.

He grinned. "You're welcome. Now, I want you to make sure that you stay near the adults who are taking care of you, okay?"

Jumping up and down, her blonde hair whipped in all directions. She made a loud, agitated sound and spun on her heel. She ran toward the chief's desk, reaching toward the papers sitting on there.

"Whoa." I intercepted her, grabbing her up and holding her to me, seeing exactly where that was going. "Baby, wait, no," I said as I struggled to hold her before she calmed. "Sarah, you're not in trouble."

Officer James stood, towering over all of us.

"She has a hard time when she thinks she's in trouble," I explained.

He nodded. "I can understand that. Most people do. I have to head back out there. You guys take care of yourselves."

"Thank you so much for everything you did yesterday," I said.

"I'm just glad everything turned out all right." He nodded and left the office.

We didn't have anything else to do at the police station, so with a final goodbye and thank you to the chief and Officer Oliver, we headed back out.

My default ringtone blared out of my purse as we walked through the waiting area of the police station. When I managed to extract it, I saw Amy's face flashing across my screen.

When I looked up, Cameron held the station door open for me.

"Amy," I said as I squeezed past him.

A smile flitted across his lips. "See, I'm winning already."

"I guess you are," I mumbled as a hot tingle flooded my belly. If he followed through with our bet, though, I was pretty sure I would be the winner.

"We'll hang out here if you want to take that," he said, nodding over to Sarah who was again hopping up and down the stairs.

I took a steadying breath. "Yeah, okay."

Taking a few steps away from him, I answered the call. After a second's pause, I answered, "Amy?"

"You never apologize," she said.

"Um . . ." I didn't really know how to respond to that, so I took a seat on the steps and didn't say anything.

"I'm pretty sure that's what upsets me the most, Jamie. Our whole lives, you've never apologized for anything, and you still don't." She wasn't yelling, her words were crisp—Amy's version of holding back tears. "Say something." She paused for so long, I knew she was waiting me out.

I cleared my throat. "I know I've felt sorry for things, I've certainly screwed up a lot of times."

"See, that's just it, you say stuff like that." Her voice changed to a low tone, "'I'm a fuck up, Amy,' 'Maybe I'm just stupid, Amy.'" Her voice went back to usual, "But you never just come out and apologize."

"Amy, I'm sorry about a lot of things, but I'm not sorry about yesterday."

The phone went dead.

"And she hangs up on me," I mumbled. Pulling the phone from my face, I waited.

Above, the sun broke through the fog layer, revealing a long stretch of blue.

The phone rang again and I answered without looking. "Hey, Amy."

She was silent for a moment before saying, "Sometimes I think you just don't get how much you mean to me."

"Yeah, I do, because you mean the same to me." A tear fell onto my cheek and I wiped it away.

There was a thumping sound on the other end of the call. "I have to go, I'm standing against the women's restroom door at work and someone is trying to get in." The thumping came again, and the phone disconnected.

Leave it to Amy to punch me straight through my heart then go back for a second strike. Staring off, I tried to remember the last time I'd apologized to someone. I was sure I'd apologized to Cameron sometime recently. The idea that I never apologized was pretty crazy, and I was almost positive that she was wrong.

"You ready to go?" Cameron asked before he stepped out of the way as a bickering couple walked out of the station and between us. Behind him, Sarah was still jumping up and down the stairs. I stood, brushing off my behind. "Yeah, I'm sorry."

See, apology.

Not a second after Amy accused me of never apologizing, I did just that. I had a feeling that wasn't the type of apology she meant, though.

Walking toward Cameron, I said, "Amy says I never apologize about anything. That's not true, right? Just Amy being Amy." I tried to sound offhanded.

His lips pursed like he was trying to stop something from coming out. The silence dragged on.

"I do too apologize," I said.

He looked like he was fighting a smirk. "I didn't say anything."

"Yeah, exactly, you didn't say anything." I gestured to him.

Now he was definitely smirking.

"Now that I think about it, I don't remember you ever apologizing either."

"Apologizing for what?" The smirk had morphed into a full-blown smile.

"Um . . ." I looked away, not able to think of anything substantial off the top of my head. Looking back, I accused, "How about when you didn't tell me about the car?"

"I apologized that night."

"Says you."

"You came back inside from talking to the officer and gave me a hug. I pulled you into my lap and apologized."

Damn it, he was right.

"I apologize all the time," I said.

"Yeah," he said, but it didn't hold much weight as he'd paused way too long when I'd first asked him. I glared, but I wasn't angry.

"I do apologize. That's just one of those things you can accuse someone of because it's so broad that they can't defend themselves."

He stepped in and gave me a quick kiss.

I let him kiss me, even though he didn't deserve a kiss.

"Next time you apologize for something big, just point it out to me."

"Oh, you'll know. I'll tattoo it on your chest in your sleep. 'I'm sorry,' in big, fat letters."

He smiled again and stole another kiss. "You don't want to know what retaliatory tattoo I'll put on you."

"What?"

"How about: 'I'm not sorry' right on your ass."

I laughed. Peeking around Cameron, I saw Sarah was far enough away that she couldn't hear us.

Cameron glanced back, too. "We should probably get off their steps, huh? I'm going to need to take off pretty soon and I want to help you find Mitch."

"Yeah, I'm *very* ready to get out of here."

When we were all loaded up in the car and halfway to the gas station I thought Mitch was talking about when he'd told me about his interview, Cameron turned to me. From the look on his face, I knew I wasn't going to like what he was going to say.

"What?" I asked.

"I want you and Sarah to stay at the shop while I work." When I opened my mouth to say something, he continued, "Just until we have a better idea of what's going on with Clarke."

"I—"

"Jamie, I know you don't want me to tell you what to do—"

"Jesus, Cameron stop interrupting me." I laughed, exasperated. "I was going to say 'yeah'. I'd rather stick close to you—at least until I need to take Sarah to gymnastics."

"Good. How about I take you guys over there and pick you up, too?"

I looked over. "Look at you pressing your luck the moment I give in. Fine," I said on an exhale.

"I was actually thinking of calling around, maybe hiring private security."

"What? I thought stuff like that costs tens of thousands of dollars."

He looked back to the road. "Don't worry about that, baby, I'll figure it out. No matter what it costs, it'll be worth it to me. Just until he goes to court and is safely in jail."

"I could probably pay for some of it," I mumbled. "It hasn't come in as of yesterday, but I'm supposed to have money coming in. Maybe I should check; I have an app for that." Peering over my shoulder, I found Sarah very busy with my phone. I decided that it could wait.

"Jamie, I'll take care of it."

Perhaps this was one of those male-ego moments where he was going to set in his heels no matter how women's lib I got on his ass. Or, maybe this was something he had to do for his own sanity—I could understand that, but I couldn't completely let it go either. "If we're planning on living together, you're going to have to get used to me paying for stuff."

"We could just get a joint account and share everything," he said.

That sounded like a big step. Even with my pay raise and advance, I was sure Cameron made twice as much as me and had more savings than I did. That wasn't even touching on the fact that he was talking about selling a property that was probably worth close to a million dollars.

He glanced over, like I was supposed to answer his suggestion.

I grimaced. "I'm sorry, Cameron, it's just too much to think about right now."

"We'll talk about it later." His hand covered mine a bit awkwardly as he was trying to avoid my wrist. "This it?" He nodded toward a gas station on our side of the three-lane road. A large red and white sign read, 'Discount Gas, Full Service Station.'

"I think so."

The car's blinker ticked and Cameron drove into the gas station. He pulled up next to a set of old pump stations likely last updated before I was born.

A teenager with outgrown black hair and a red zit in the middle of his nose rushed up to Cameron's side of the car. He knocked on Cameron's window with a bent finger.

As soon as Cameron rolled down his window, the guy said, "Excuse me, sir, your gas tank is on the other side of your car." He sounded a little stressed about it.

I leaned down over the center divider so the boy could see my face. "Sorry, does a guy named Mitch work here?"

The kid blinked at me, looking a little shocked. For a second, I'd forgotten I was sporting a bruised cheek and a fluff of hair coming out of the side of my head. Cameron hadn't stared and none of the cops had gawked—but I was sure they were trained to be tactful.

This guy was definitely gawking, but he didn't say anything. He didn't answer my question either, so I asked again, "I'm looking for a guy named Mitch. Does he work here?"

The guy scratched the top of his greasy hair, his gaze still on the side of my face, then flicking away. "Uh . . . um, no. He might have worked here before. I only started a couple days ago."

"Oh. Sorry, this must be the wrong gas station. Do you know if there are any other full service stations around here?"

He scratched his head again. "Uh, nope."

I looked away. Annoyance surged through me and all directed at this kid. I knew it was completely unwarranted. He was just some guy who'd been hired for a job he'd applied for. But it looked like Mitch didn't get the job he'd been so excited about. Clearing my throat, I said, "Thanks, I must have gotten it wrong."

"That's all good. Do you guys want some gas?"

Cameron pulled around and the teenager filled up my tank. Sarah's electronic game music blared in the otherwise silent car as the guy stood outside my door, pumping the gas. I pulled down the vanity mirror and glanced at my face, then turned up the mirror. I'd avoided putting on makeup when we left the house so my bruises could be photographed, but it was just damn stupid of me that I hadn't brought any concealer with me.

"Anywhere else you can think of to look for Mitch?" Cameron asked as we drove out of the station.

"I think I should probably just buck up and text Chris," I mumbled. I glanced into the backseat at Sarah. "He won't be out of work until we have to be heading to the shop anyway."

"We could just go to the store."

I pointed to my face. "I'm their boss, remember, how am I going to explain this? Let's just drive up and down the streets near downtown."

"Chris will be the first one to forgive you. He probably already has."

I shrugged. "I'll call him later, when he can answer. No point in trying to contact him now."

"Or you could just apologize for scaring him, and he'd be completely over it."

"I'm not going to apologize . . . and it's not because I don't apologize; it's because in this specific situation, I don't think I should."

Cameron grinned. "Chicken."

"Shut up," I said, rolling my eyes, but the motion hurt my cheek so I stopped.

"What are you going to do if you find Mitch?" Cameron asked.

I shrugged. "I'm not really sure. I was thinking of offering him money, but he'll never accept money from me. I don't know. I guess I'll figure it out in the moment."

"I have an idea, if you'd like to hear it."

I smiled over. "Sure, let's hear it.

"I was thinking that if he's still looking for a job, I could hire him to clean the cars. If he's good at it, I could even extend the job to detailing."

"I–I bet he'd really appreciate that. But Cameron, can you afford to do that? Aren't you planning on hiring someone else?"

He looked over at me. "Yeah, an admin. She starts next week. If he'd be willing to work for minimum, I could afford it. I'd have to charge a detailing fee to my customers, but I'd make it work. Jamie . . . I couldn't pay him enough for what he did yesterday."

I knew he meant it, and I nodded because I couldn't agree more.

"Can I ask you something?" Cameron asked when we'd passed halfway through the backstreets of the downtown area.

"You just did," I said, putting my knees up against the dashboard.

"All right, then I'll just ask. What's the fourteenth thing on your list?"

"Huh?" I looked over, a little surprised.

"Well, today is 'feel loved' right?"

"Remember what love feels like," I mumbled.

"Do you?" He smiled.

I touched my lips, and through my fingers, I said, "Yeah, even though everyone I love hates me right now."

Now it was his turn to roll his eyes. "They don't. Everyone you love loves you, same as they did yesterday, same as they did before you wrote your detox. So, are you going to tell me or not?"

"Tell you what?" I asked.

"The fourteenth task."

"Oh." I looked back out the window as we turned down a street that bordered a park. I didn't see any of the usual homeless crowd hanging out on the benches. "To call my mom," I muttered.

"Oh," he said. He didn't say anything more as we continued to weave through the streets.

Day Twelve: Eleven-fifty

After driving around every downtown street and not finding any sign of Mitch, we headed straight back to Cameron's shop so he wouldn't be late to meet his first client.

As Cameron dove into work, Sarah and I sat in Cameron's office in a somewhat-dazed silence, listening to the wall clock tick away. Two large, frosted windows lit the small office space with a natural white glow. The glass door gave a narrow view of the street beyond and a blur of cars passing, but most was impossible to see. The privacy felt nice and disconcerting at the same time, especially now that Clarke was on the loose again.

Sarah sat in Cameron's desk chair, swiveling back and forth. The high-pitched tones of her game blared out of my phone in her lap. I knew she'd already played with my phone way more than I should have allowed today, but I needed her distracted right now for my own sanity. Ever since Cameron asked me about the fourteenth task, all I could think about was my mother and the day our relationship went to shit.

I didn't know what had prompted her to call Logan that day—I didn't even remember that much about the phone call she and I had where she told me what she did. Maybe I'd repressed the details of that phone call. I did remember that she said that lying to Sarah's father in such a fundamental way was immoral, unethical, and beneath me.

That I remembered.

But as I stared forward at a luminescent chart of two-tone colors on Cameron's wall, the memory of the night after my mother told Logan flooded my mind.

My phone dinged as the door to our house slammed. As Logan stumbled loudly down our hall toward me, I glanced at the text lighting up my screen.

Mom: Sweetheart, please call me back. We need to talk more. I love you and I only want what's best for you and Sarah, always.

I swiped over the message and deleted it just as Logan lurched into the kitchen. I tensed, waiting for the argument I knew was coming.

"I hate your mother," he muttered as he swayed in the doorway. "Our family is none of her damn business."

My lips parted in surprise. I'd been sure he'd direct all his hatred at me. I stared across our taxes spread over the kitchen table to where he was staring my way, but not quite looking at me. "Logan, please don't say anything bad about her. I'm mad at her for getting into our business, too, but I still don't want to hear it," I told him.

"You would say that," he grumbled. Going into the kitchen cupboard, he pulled down a plastic bottle of whisky. "Always taking everyone's side but mine."

I was relieved to see him grab a glass, and then disappointed to see he didn't even add ice, just poured it full of liquor.

As he lifted the glass to his lips, I studied him. He looked like shit. Dark circles ringed his eyes and light stubble poked out around his jaw. His skin had lost its youthful glow and now had a grayish undertone. A large brown stain spread across the side of his jeans, and the rest of his clothing was just as dirty, like he'd been wearing that outfit for a few days.

Seeing me stare at him, he said, "I'm sorry, baby. You're mad at me, huh? You are. I can tell you are."

Knowing that this was the end of me getting anything productive done, I gathered up the papers on the table. Sighing, I said, "No, I'm not mad at you, Logan. I told you, I'm pissed off at my mom."

"She's a bitch," he said.

I dropped the papers. "Damn it, Logan. I know you're drunk and mad but I told you not to say shit like that about her."

He gestured wildly with his arms. "Our family isn't her business. She needs to get a life." His glass slipped from his fingers, hitting the counter and rolling across the floor. "Damn it. Damn it. I'll clean it up." He lost his balance and crashed into the counter.

I rubbed my fingers over my eyes. "I'll get it." Standing from the table, I crossed over to the kitchen sink and pulled out some paper towels.

"You hate me," Logan muttered as he stumbled away.

"That's insane." Getting to my knees, I started mopping the liquor off the side of the cupboards.

"You and your mom fucking hate me. There is nothing wrong with my daughter."

I looked up to find him pointing at me.

"No one said there was anything wrong with her," I said.

"She's got a learning disability, or maybe ADHD, or whatever." He was still pointing at me, accusing me of something.

"Logan, there's nothing wrong with Sarah. There's nothing wrong with autism."

"She's not going into Special Ed class and getting bullied by half her school. You're not doing that to my daughter." He pointed his finger to his chest. "I'm her father. I get to decide, too."

I grabbed the fallen glass and stood, setting it on the counter with a soft clunk. "Logan, her special day class isn't like that. Kids aren't such assholes as they were when we were her age. Everyone's been really great. You'll see—"

He threw up his hands. "You just decided and that's it? You just decided that she has this thing and she's going to be in Special Ed, and I don't get a fucking say in it?"

"Damn it, Logan! We knew! I told you three years ago I wanted to get her checked out but you didn't want me to. I'm relieved. I'm not even upset! I thought I would be, but I'm not. I'm so relieved because now when I take her to school she's not miserable! There are people there that can make sure she's not hurting herself or running off or anything. She used to just scream and cry, and she hasn't been doing that in her new class. She loves her teacher and her aide. They have her in speech and occupational therapy, they say they can help her with all this shit that I've been scared about for so long. She hasn't changed at all. She's the exact same as she's always been."

He swayed toward me, then back. "So you've just decided, and that's it? You don't even tell me. You don't even fucking tell me! And they're okay with that? I don't remember signing anything. Last time I remembered, I was still her dad and that meant something."

I took a breath to steady myself, my hands clenching into fists. My nails dug into my palms. "I lied to the school and I forged your signature. I'm not sure I needed to, but I did do it."

"That's—" He shook his head, "Damn it, Jamie. Why didn't you just talk to me? I have a right to know this stuff."

I threw the soaked paper towel into the sink, shaking my head. "When was I supposed to talk to you about this? You're never here, and when you are here, you're wasted. I bet you won't even remember this conversation tomorrow."

"Yeah, I will. This is one conversation I promise you I'll remember. It's the moment that I realize that my wife doesn't fucking love me." He took the glass I'd just picked up from the ground and poured it full of the brown liquor.

My phone rang, breaking me from the memory. I blinked around at Cameron's office and across his desk to where Sarah sat curled in Cameron's office chair. Her finger moved. The ringtone cut off abruptly and her game music started up again.

"Sarah," I said, reaching across the desk.

"Nope, it's my turn on the phone," she said, like she had a say in it.

"Sarah, give me my phone, baby. I hope you're not doing that every time someone calls me."

She continued to ignore me.

"Five, four, three, two—"

She passed over the phone right as it dinged with a text. Then she smiled and asked, "Mom, can I play with the phone?"

"Nope."

"Can I watch floor exercises?"

"Baby, you've had enough screen time. Why don't you start on your homework?"

"Nope. Homework is boring."

"Too bad. Homework is your job." I pressed the button to light up the screen, finding a text from Patrick there.

Patrick: Hey, just wanted to check in and make sure you and Sarah were doing okay with everything that happened yesterday.

I chewed on my thumb nail for a second, wondering if he knew about *everything* that happened. Deciding that there was only one way to find out, I typed in my response.

Me: Thanks, Patrick. We're okay. Sarah and I are playing hooky today, recovering a little bit from the stress. Did Beza tell you what happened?

Patrick: Susan did. She picked Aiden up right after the police found Sarah. I'm glad everything turned out okay.

I blew out a breath. I wasn't sure what I was going to tell my new coworkers when they saw my face tomorrow when I wasn't quite ready to tell Patrick.

The door to the outside swung open, making me jump in my seat and spin around.

A huge man took a step inside and looked around the office with a sweeping glance. His gaze seemed to stop on me, but I couldn't be sure if he was looking at me because his dark sunglasses and hat obscured most of his face. "Is Cameron here?" he asked in a strangely familiar voice.

"Yeah, in the shop. You can go on back or I can call him." I pointed toward the door-less entry to the shop.

"I'll head back," he said. The man's face didn't turn from me and he stared for so long, alarm bubbled in me.

"Can I help you?" I whispered.

He must have heard the alarm in my voice, because he said, "Oh, I'm sorry." He pulled his hat and glasses off, and then I was the one staring.

"Whoa," I whispered. "You're Raphael Rodriguez, aren't you?"

Holy. Shit.

He didn't look exactly the same as he did on screen, especially as he had hat hair. He towered over me, big and muscular, but he wasn't quite the wall of muscle I'd always imagined. His face was handsome in a chiseled way, but still had human details like some missed hairs on the tip of his chin and a wrinkle outlining the side of his left eye.

"Are you okay?" he asked, his voice tinged with concern.

I met his light-brown gaze and realized he was studying me as well, but his stare was fixed on my cheek. Raising my hand, I stopped short of touching my swollen bruise. "Yeah, I'm okay."

His eyes flitted over to Sarah, who had somehow managed to steal my phone in the minute I set it down on the desk. Looking back to me, he asked in a low voice, "Did someone hit you?"

If he hadn't sounded so concerned, I'd have been a bit offended at the personal question. I nodded, slowly. "Yeah, but the guy's in jail . . . or, he was in jail and likely going back. He's not someone who I'm close to, just crazy and mean."

"Oh, okay." He nodded. Holding out a hand to me, he asked, "You're Jamie? I recognize you from that video of you singing."

I shook his hand. "Yeah, and you're Raphael. I recognize you because you're extremely famous."

He grinned, but it dropped fast. "Anything I can do to help?"

I shook my head. "No, but—wait!" A smile formed on my face. I quickly forced it down as a sharp pain shot through my cheek. "Actually there is something that you could do. You don't have to, though."

His brow furrowed and two distinct lines formed between his eyebrows. "I wouldn't have offered if I didn't mean it. What can I help you with?"

"Could I take a video of you where you say hi to my friends for me? They're big fans—I mean huge fans."

"Yeah, no problem." He nodded.

I reached back across the desk toward Sarah. "Sorry for being so typical, you probably get this all the time, but this really is doing me a huge favor."

It took us a minute to film the video, and he smiled as he headed back into the shop. Before he'd completely disappeared, I called out, "I apologize in advance, but there's a high probability that they'll show up to meet you."

He turned and waved. "It's fine. Actually, I'd like to meet them, too. I've definitely heard of them both."

Returning to sit, I pulled up the video in the app and watched Raphael Rodriguez's extremely recognizable smile light up my phone screen. "I'm Raphael Rodriguez and I want to say hello to Susan and Beza Scott, and their son Aiden." He gave another dazzling smile and the recording ended.

I uploaded the video to the texting app, and group texted Susan and Beza, before realizing that Beza no longer had a phone.

Not thirty seconds later, my phone dinged.

Susan: Holy fuck.

Susan: Where the hell are you? Did you just run into him somewhere? Where are you?!

Susan: Like for real, where the hell are you? I'm driving to where you are right now.

Me: Cameron's shop. Can you send this on to Beza?

Susan: She hasn't picked up a new phone yet. Damn it, I just remembered I'm mad at you.

Me: He says he's heard of you guys and he'd like to meet you.

I gave her a second. The phone beeped.

Susan: You tricky bitch. Damn it, I'm heading there anyway. Did you like touch his arms, or what?

Me: Creepy.

Susan: I'm getting in my car now; I'll be there in five.

Four minutes later, Susan pushed the front door open. Her hair and eyes were wild and her face gleamed with excitement.

She pointed at me. "Don't think you're off the hook. Where the ef-word is he?"

In my mind, I grinned. I was so off the hook. Nodding through the door to the shop, I said, "Back with Cameron."

She stalked toward the door, but stopped short. "How do I look?"

"Your hair is kind of nuts."

She looked at me like she really didn't want to say something, but she needed to. "Okay, fine, fix it. And, holy cow look at your face."

"It looks worse than it feels." I stood, and went to smooth down her blonde hair.

"You guys going to sit this one out?"

"Yep."

"Hey cutie, like the boots. Are you doing okay?" Susan asked down to Sarah, patting her on the head.

Sarah didn't respond.

"Sarah? Earth to Sarah?" Susan said louder, as I finished her hair, but Sarah still ignored her.

When I peeked around Susan, I found that Sarah had snuck my phone onto her lap. "Sarah, you rascal. I told you to do your homework."

"No use now, her brain has downloaded. Is she doing okay?" Susan asked.

"Fine. I think she's fine," I said.

Susan spun around to face me and took a deep breath before whispering, "Okay, I guess I'm going in there."

I tried not to sigh in relief because I was expecting her to say something about how much I sucked at life.

She shook out her hands at her sides. Susan and Beza knew all kinds of famous people, but I'd never seen her like this about any of them. As if she read my thought she said, "Holy . . . ef-word, I'm nervous. All right, wish me luck."

"Good luck."

After she headed into the shop, I focused on helping Sarah do her homework.

When we were just finishing with her math worksheet, laughter rang out from the garage. I walked over and tried to peek through the doorway but the front bumper of a truck blocked my view of where the group was standing.

As I turned back, I found Sarah bent over her assignment, giggling.

"Uh oh," I said as I returned to her.

I sat beside her and looked down at her latest assignment.

"Say, 'you rascal.'" Sarah giggled and pointed at me.

Her assignment was to connect the right words with their pictures, but Sarah took a circuitous route all the way around the pictures until the lines were in an indecipherable tangle.

"You rascal," I said, even though I knew I shouldn't encourage her.

She fell into another bout of hysterics.

I suppressed a laugh and took the seat across from her. "Okay, baby. We're going to have to do this again with Cameron's highlighter." I held up his highlighter and after her laughter finally subsided, she took it.

Her nose scrunched up in mischief, and she began another circuitous route with the highlighter.

My hand slapped over her assignment and got highlighter on my thumb for my trouble. "Uh, uh, uh, Sarah. Do it right this time or no more phone."

She didn't say anything but when I lifted my hand, she began doing the assignment the right way.

Minutes later, Susan emerged back through the door, her face flushed and her eyes glowing.

Sarah jumped up from the desk and rushed over to her.

"Hey cutie. I didn't even get a nod on the way in and now you're all full of love for me?"

"Let's play together on my mom's phone," Sarah said.

"Uh, uh," I said, just as Susan said, "I wish I could baby, but I have to get back to work. I'm already a little bit late." Susan looked back to me. "So, you want to hang out later?"

I tried to look completely neutral as I said, "Sure, but Sarah has gymnastics at three. We're free after."

"I'll just meet you at Sarah's studio and we can chill, if that's cool with you?"

I narrowed my eyes on her. "Are you using this as an excuse to tear me a new you-know-what?"

"I don't know, maybe. I haven't quite made my mind up on that one yet." She shrugged.

"Fine, but do you think maybe you could give us a ride there? We only have one car."

She rolled her eyes. "You're going to get me fired."

"They won't fire you, and not because you don't deserve it either, but because you're pregnant. I love you. Get your prego-butt to work."

"Love you both. See you at two thirty-ish."

Day Twelve: Two Forty-five

"Hey, Cameron," I called out, poking my head into the back.

The low timbre of conversation across the shop halted and Cameron stepped into view. "Hey," he said, a small smile playing on his lips like he was surprised and happy to see me, even though I'd been here for hours.

"Sarah and I are heading over to gymnastics." I threw a thumb behind me.

He jogged over. "You want me to give you a ride?"

"No, I arranged it with Susan. She's taking us. She just texted she's leaving work."

He leaned in a little and his fingers brushed over my hip. "I love you, baby."

"Why?" I asked, leaning against the doorframe. "*Why?*"

"Uh-huh, rain compliments on me, I feel like crap."

"Because from the moment I met you, I woke up each morning hoping I'd get to spend a little time with you. And even when I spend every day with you, it's never enough." Leaning in, he gave me a quick kiss and then smiled. "Good enough?"

I grinned. "That'll do."

His hand brushed up and down my side. "I like that you're not scared anymore."

"Scared of what?"

"Us being in love."

I blew out a laugh and admitted, "Oh, I'm still terrified, I'm just not going anywhere."

"That'll do," he said my words back at me, and then nodded into the workshop. "I'll just finish up here with Raphael and head over to the gym to pick you up. We can grab a bite to eat or something before we head home. That work?"

"Sure. That'll be great."

He took a step backwards, but then stopped. "Your sister and Susan reached out, now all you need is your dad."

"A little awkward for me to want to have a showdown with my dad for that reason," I said, fighting a smile.

He shrugged. "Whatever gets you through it." He took another step and though I wanted to grab him and pull him to me, I didn't.

With one more smile, he walked back into the shop.

My phone rang once behind me before Sarah's game music took over.

Turning, I shook my head. "Monkey, don't do that. It could be important." When I took the phone from her, it beeped with a text.

Susan: Here.

We found Susan waiting in the car in the small lot. As I buckled up beside her, she regarded me with a look somewhere between annoyance and amusement.

"So, inviting me to meet my all-time favorite actor doesn't erase the fact that you almost broke my heart yesterday. You know that, right?"

I gave her a hopeful smile, because her tone was more sardonic than biting. "But it helps. He's a pretty cool celebrity, right?"

She pointed at me. "Not the point." Starting up the car, she drove out of the lot, turning onto the main road. "You don't even want to know what I was thinking . . . and considering, while you were in there. I honestly considered putting my unborn baby at risk for you . . ."

I didn't respond, because if I did, I'd have to point out the hypocrisy in what she said. Susan, my dad and Amy were the ones most likely to do exactly as I did the day before; they also were the ones who were the angriest at me for doing it. But, I bit my tongue because saying something would be like fanning the dying embers of her anger.

"It was dumb—to the extreme." She looked at me. "Say something."

"Nope."

"Fine," she said, turning back to the road. When we were almost to the studio, Susan turned back. "I know why you did it, I just . . ." She shook her head. "All right, Jamie, we can call a truce but I want something in return."

"Of course you do," I said.

"Every—" she glanced back toward Sarah, "ef-ing detail."

I sighed. "Honestly, I'm not sure I want to relive every detail, Susan."

She looked back to the road. "I don't need the details of that stuff. I just need to know why you did it, what's going on with this creep, if you're going to do it again and what's going to happen to him. I don't know enough, you've been keeping me out of the loop—on purpose—and I need to be in the loop again or I'll lose it, Jamie."

"Yeah, we'll talk—when Sarah's doing her thing, we'll talk."

"Cool."

Halfway through Sarah's gymnastic session I started talking about what had gone through my head before I walked into Clarke's apartment yesterday. As Sarah flipped up and down the beam, Susan and I huddled together on the seats against the wall. She stared at Sarah as I told the story, but from her expression, I knew she was listening to me. I stopped at the point where I had set the phone outside Clarke's window.

"You are insane," she whispered.

"Maybe," I said.

"I would have just gone over and beat the crap out of him," she said, folding her arms over her chest.

"Yeah, I know."

"Still kind of want to. He should be glad I'm this pregnant," she grumbled. "You think he's done being obsessed with you, or is this just going to get worse?"

"It's not about me."

She regarded me, seriously. "You are insane and delusional."

My head fell into my hands. "I'm not. Clarke is obsessed with Cameron. I was just his means of tormenting Cameron—an easy target."

She shifted in her chair so she could fully face me. "What are you talking about?"

"This has to stay between us."

"I'm not promising anything until you tell me what the hell you're talking about. What do you mean he's obsessed with Cameron? Like in a sexual way?"

I hushed her, looking around to see if Heidi and Sarah could hear us. Heidi was clapping her hands rhythmically as Sarah practiced spinning in place on the mat. Both were completely unaware of our conversation. "No. At least I don't think so. They have a history, I guess. Cameron punched him in the face in college and messed up his face. Everyone took Cameron's side and Clarke was kicked off his team."

"Not—not . . ." Susan stared wide eyed at me. She stood.

"Susan?"

Her eyes darted quickly around me, but more like she was thinking than looking at anything.

"His name was Allen," she whispered. Tears splashed down her face.

"You knew him? That's his last name, Clarke Allen. He—I thought he raped someone, one of Vanessa's friends. Logan and I were gone then."

She looked off, her jaw clenching.

"Susan?" I asked, again. When she didn't answer, I stood and came around to stand in front of her.

Her gaze met mine. "That guy was so damn lucky that Cameron got there first, so damn lucky," she whispered. "I can't believe that fucker is still around, hurting the people I love."

"Who did he hurt, Susan?" When she didn't answer, I grabbed her shoulders and tried to pull her back to the present, but it didn't work.

My phone rang from my purse, blaring out my default ringtone. I let it go to voicemail.

"Fucker," she whispered again. "He stalked you for weeks. Fucker!"

"What is going on?" I hissed.

My phone started blaring from inside my handbag again. I glanced between where my bag slouched on the floor and Susan's distant eyes. "Susan, talk to me."

"He . . . what he did to Nessa, that guy deserves to die."

My hands dropped. "Nessa?"

My phone stopped ringing, then immediately started up again. I ignored it, but when it rang the fourth time, I broke away from Susan.

My shaky fingers extracted my phone from my purse. Shock smacked me in the face as Vanessa's picture flashed across my screen.

"Oh my god, it's Vanessa," I whispered. I closed my eyes for a second, thinking maybe I was seeing things, but when I opened my eyes, her face was still smiling from my screen.

I hit the button on the phone and slowly lifted the phone to my ear. "Hello?" I whispered.

"Jamie?" Nessa sobbed.

"Yeah, Vanessa, you okay?"

"Jamie—oh my god, Jamie—Cameron has been hit by a car."

I sat down, missed the chair, and fell hard onto the ground. My hip screamed out in pain.

"Jamie?" Vanessa called out.

I blinked around as my vision narrowed. Memories closed in.

"Cameron, what are you doing here? Is everything okay?"

Nothing.

"Do you want to come in? Talk to me! You're scaring me. What happened?"

"Vanessa just called me from the hospital, but I didn't go to the hospital. I came here."

"Jamie? Jamie are you there?" Vanessa yelled into my ear.

"Uh . . . what?" I shook my head.

"A car hit him—I dropped off some papers—I was driving away when I heard the crash. He's being loaded into the ambulance, going to the hospital; they won't let me ride with him. He's alive—I think he's alive—"

"Mr. Scott was pronounced dead on the scene, Ms. Scott. We believe that the crash killed him instantly . . . He didn't suffer."

"Thank you. But you have to say that, don't you?"

"That was what I was told by the medical examiner, ma'am."

Susan crouched down in front of me, and somehow Heidi and Sarah were right beside her.

"Honey, what's going on? Let me help you up, did you fall?" Heidi reached out her hands.

Susan began speaking, but the high-pitched buzzing in my mind drowned out her voice.

"Oh, Mike, you're home, honey. Did you get a chance to stop by the morgue?"

"I did. Is Jamie around?"

"No. I'm pretty sure she's upstairs napping with Sarah."

"Good—I really think we should encourage her to have Logan cremated. She never needs to see that. If only I could un-see it."

"Jamie!" Susan grabbed the phone from my hand.

Sarah climbed onto my lap, her knees hitting me in my stomach. She pressed her face to mine, her small fingers gripping onto my hair. I winced from the pain ringing through my scalp, but didn't pull her away.

"Give your mom some space, honey," Heidi said, though Sarah didn't move. "Jamie, can you talk? Are you injured?"

Behind her, Susan yelled into the phone, "You need to calm down, Ness. Which hospital are they taking him to? Nessa, take a breath. Calm down and talk to me. I need to get Jamie there."

Heidi's hand rubbed my shoulder, but we were all silent as we listened to Susan.

"General . . . are you sure?" Susan paused. "We're going to see you there."

"Did you want to write a eulogy for him, honey?"

"What would I say, Dad? Here lies the man who ripped up my heart and destroyed my entire life?"

"How about: Here lies your lifelong best friend, your husband of nine years and the father of your child?"

"Just leave me alone! Everyone just needs to leave me the hell alone!"

"Okay, honey, okay."

Susan hung up the phone and turned to me. "Jamie, Sarah, get up. I'm taking you to the hospital."

Slowly, I blinked up at her. "What?"

"Jamie, Nessa's freaking out. From what I can tell, Cameron is alive and on his way to the hospital. Pull it together. We need to go meet him there."

"Susan, I think she needs a moment—" Heidi protested.

"No, she needs to pull it together and go. I'd pick you up myself, Jamie, but I'm too pregnant for that."

"Jamie, one day, you're going to move on and meet someone who treats you better than Logan did, which probably won't be that hard to find, honestly."

"Should I look for someone who treats me like Peter treats you?"

"Maybe you should. Seriously, I don't even know why I try to talk to you."

"Amy—I'm just not very good company lately. And getting into another relationship sounds like the stupidest decision I could ever make. I'd rather spend the rest of my life alone in this crappy apartment."

"That sounds horrible. I hope you change your mind on that, and soon."

"Jamie!" Susan yelled.

"What?" I whispered.

"We need to go to the hospital. Please, pull yourself out of this."

Sarah squeezed me even harder.

Clearing my throat, I said, "Baby. Baby. Sarah, you need to get up." That's what I said, but I didn't let go of her, and she didn't let go of me. I was only faintly aware that her face was smashed against mine.

When we didn't move, Susan put her hand on the seat of the chair, and lowered herself to sit beside Sarah and me on the floor. Her hand ran over Sarah's hair. "This isn't the same, guys. We need to get up and see what's going on. Don't check out."

Pulling my head back and my face away from Sarah's, I forced myself to look into her concerned eyes. "He was our safe harbor."

"Cameron is alive. This isn't what happened to Logan. This is a new, different situation. Get up, Jamie."

It took Sarah and me another five minutes to untangle and trudge out to the car. Tense silence hung in the spaces between us as Susan whipped around street corners. The beautiful day zoomed by. Like the universe, the blue sky felt like a liar and a thief.

As Susan merged onto the highway, another horrible memory crashed into my mind.

I lay on my couch, staring off at nothing in my new apartment. My body curled around Sarah who napped in my arms. The few possessions Timepiece allowed us to keep piled high around us, tucked in hastily packed boxes. Amy had wanted to stay and unpack them the day before, but I'd needed her gone. I'd needed everyone gone.

A knock came at my door, a familiar titter. I knew who it was.

"It's open," I called out in a hoarse voice. When the knock came again, I unpeeled myself from Sarah and the cushions. As I trudged to the front door, my steps fell heavy and hard.

I inched the door open, poking my head out. My mother stood a few paces from the door, a hesitant smile on her face. Her hair combed back into a neat twist. The pink sweater she wore looked closer to a work outfit than her usual weekend bohemian-type outfits. Was today a weekday? I had no idea. Outside, the lighting hinted at it being afternoon, though I didn't remember eating lunch.

"What are you doing here, Mom?" I croaked.

"Hey, Jay Jay." She reached out to me, but when I didn't move any closer, her hands dropped. "I wanted to come help you and Sarah set up your new place. I called about a hundred times, but it never goes through and your voicemail box is full."

"That's because I don't want you calling me," I said.

She took a slight step back, her brow furrowing.

"Ever again," I told her.

She shook her head. "Jay Jay . . . Honey."

"I want you out of my life, Mom. Forever." An unwanted tear rolled down my face, and I wiped it away.

My mother didn't cry. She more looked like she didn't know what was going on. Her purse dropped off her arm, but she didn't seem to notice.

"I told you . . . I told you to stay out of it, Mom. I told you it was none of your business. Now he's dead. Now my husband's dead and Sarah is never going to have a father again. You couldn't just stay out of it." I stepped back through my door, ready to close it.

"Honey," she whispered, blinking at me. "He is . . . was her father. He needed to know. My talking to him about it had nothing to do with why he died."

"Yeah, it did. He didn't need to know because he wasn't right in the head, Mom. I was going to talk to him when he wasn't so fucked up about his mother. That's what you just can't get. He didn't understand what was going on with Sarah. He thought it was *something that it wasn't—he didn't get that there was nothing wrong with her because he was always, from that point forward, drunk. All he knew was that I lied to him and hid things from him, and then he cut me out. He cut me out and cheated on me with my best friend and now he's dead. You did this to me. You ruined my life, Mom."*

She shook her head. Her lips parted but no words came out.

"I do not want you in my life anymore, Mother, never again," I annunciated every word.

"Jay Jay, I—"

I closed the door. I didn't slam it, just closed it with a quiet snick that punctuated my decision to cut my mother out of my life forever. Leaning into the wall, I slipped down the side, my chest heaving with sobs.

Day Twelve: Four o'clock

As we pulled into the General Hospital's underground parking garage, the astringent, sour smell of urine filled the car.

"Sarah?" I whispered, spinning around to look frantically into the backseat. "Oh my god, baby, are you okay?"

She rocked back and forth in her chair, humming in agitation. Wetness discolored her lap.

Unbuckling my seatbelt, I scurried over the center divider to fall into the seat beside her. "Baby, it's okay," I said as tears began pouring down my cheeks. "Baby!"

She rocked harder, covering her ears. It was as if I wasn't even there.

I ran my hands over her head. "Baby. Angel, it's going to be okay. Angel, look at me, we're going to be okay."

Susan pulled into a parking spot, and turned around to me. "Jamie, do you have any spare clothes?" she asked.

I nodded, breathing hard. "In her backpack. She won't even look at me."

"Okay, I'm going to take her to my house right now. It's only a minute away from here and she can have a shower, and then we'll head straight back or stay there, whatever's better for Sarah at the time."

"I can't leave her like this. I—" I leaned in closer, close enough that I finally caught Sarah's attention. "Sarah?"

"All done car!" she shouted, still rocking back and forth.

"Sarah! Sarah! Do you want to go shower at Aunt Susan's or change in the hospital with me?"

She screamed and thrashed wildly in her seat, her hand hitting me straight on my bruised cheek.

Agony exploded through my face and I rocked back, blinking wildly. I couldn't stop the cry of pain that ripped from my mouth.

"Jamie! Jamie, let me take Sarah to my house." Susan grabbed my shoulder as I blinked back into full awareness. "I can handle this. Sarah needs a shower and a safe place to calm down. The best thing for Sarah now is to be around people who are calm, and you are not calm."

"I can't just leave her like this!" I sobbed, my hands covering my face.

"Let me take care of her for a little while. I know what to do."

"Oh god, Susan," I cried.

"Damn it, Jamie, you're making it worse. You need to go into the hospital, get your head on straight and see what's actually going on. You're stuck in the past, both of you are. As far as we know, Cameron is alive and okay. The best thing you could do for Sarah right now is to bring him home safe."

Even though Susan's words had the ring of truth, I waited for Sarah's meltdown to subside. By the time she stopped thrashing, the pain in my cheek had subsided as well. I combed my fingers through Sarah's hair. "Baby, you need to get cleaned up. Are you okay going with Aunt Susan while mommy stays here?”

She pushed my hand away. “Go away, Mom!” she shouted.

My eyes closed and I blew out of my nose. “Okay, will you call me when she’s in the shower?” I asked Susan.

Her hand squeezed my shoulder. “Yes, love. Now you need to go. I’ve got this, okay? You need to figure out what’s going on. Don’t just assume the worst.”

Turning back to Sarah, I tried to hold in my sobs. “I love you so much, baby.”

“Jamie,” Susan said in a firm, quiet voice. “Please go before this starts all over again.”

“Okay, okay.” I climbed out of the car, wiping furiously at my face as I did.

A yellow halogen light popped above me as I hurried away from Susan’s running car. I jogged for the long strip of natural light interrupting the artificially lit cement structure. A truck whizzed by. Stumbling, my breath caught, but I kept going. At the edge of the garage, cement stairs ascended back into the daylight.

A family passed me as I emerged onto the sidewalk. The mother smiled up at her son who sat on his father’s shoulders, “I’m so proud of you,” she said in Spanish.

Tears clouded my vision so much that I couldn’t see my way anymore. So I stopped.

“Are you okay?” someone asked me.

When I wiped my eyes, I found the family had stopped a few feet from me, looking over with concern clear in their expressions.

"Fine, I'm sorry," I sobbed.

The mother's hand touched my back. "Do you need help?"

"No, no. I'm sorry. Thank you so much, but I'll be okay." I waved, and rushed further along the sidewalk toward the front entrance of the hospital emergency room.

A big, red-and-white cross towered over me as I lined up behind the group funneling into the front doors. Two women in scrubs laughed beside me, and the smell of cigarette smoke stung my nose. I hung back as the group pressed closer.

As the crowd scattered into the building, I blinked around the long wide hall that the entrance led into. People walked in both directions as signs shouted out their different destinations in blue and white letters.

"Out of the way!" someone called as an empty stretcher rolled from one side of the hall to the other. Several people lined up to squeeze through a wide door that read, 'Emergency Room Intake'. Another group headed for the door across the hall with a sign that read, 'Waiting Room'.

"Out of the way please," someone bellowed behind me.

I pressed my back against the wall as a woman in scrubs wheeled a man in a wheelchair past. The man winced; his arms wrapped around his stomach while he hyperventilated into a facemask.

My fingers pressed hard into the wall I stood against as people streamed past me. Looking back to the waiting room, I tried to force myself to walk toward it. A long, empty chasm opened between the room and me, and the chasm kept growing. Spinning on my heel, I dodged people and sprinted out of the hospital doors. My feet slapped against the pavement down the sidewalk and back the way I came. When I found the stairs, I flung myself down them. At the bottom, I had nowhere else to go so I just kept running, my squeaking footsteps echoing around me.

The garage ended three levels below where only a few cars ventured to park. A bank of elevators and a metal door that led to the emergency stairs met me at the furthest reaches of the space.

I let myself into the stairwell, and slumped down onto the bottom step. "What the fuck, universe?" I whispered. I turned up my face and yelled, "What the fuck do you want? What is wrong with you?" My breath escaped in halting gasps.

The universe returned nothing but the low rumble of cars driving around the parking garage outside the stairwell.

My phone beeped.

I pulled my phone from my purse, dropped it, and then lifted it up again, clicking on the screen. By some miracle the phone not only hadn't cracked in the fall, it had one bar of service. A text lit up on my screen.

Susan: Sarah's in the shower and calm now. If it's cool with you, we'd like to keep her here, make sure she eats, and maybe put on a movie.

My fingers shook as I typed in two words.

Me: Sounds good.

Susan: Any news?

I started to type out, 'I couldn't go in,' but I deleted the message.

Me: I'll call you when I have some.

Swiping through my contacts, I pressed on a name I hadn't called in months.

She answered on the second ring. "Jay Jay?"

"Mom," I sobbed.

"Honey, what's the matter?"

"I—I need you, Mom. I don't think I can do this again, I don't think I can do it again . . ."

"Baby, talk to me. What's going on? Where are you?" I could hear tears in her voice.

"I'm in the stairwell at the bottom of the parking garage of the General Hospital. Cameron was hit by a—a car," I cried.

"Oh, Jay Jay, I'm on my way, baby."

I don't know how long it took, but my mother found me. I gripped onto the metal railing, the metal warm under my fingers.

The heavy door opened, and I braced to see some random doctor or nurse trying to get by, but my mother stepped in. She looked just the same as she always did—beautiful and hip, with her long blonde hair and bright blue sweater. People always said that I was an exact copy of her, only younger. Well, they said that before I'd lost fifteen pounds and a year of my life.

She didn't shy away from me or ask my permission, she took a seat on the metal stair beside me and pulled me into her arms.

"I'm so sorry," I sobbed. "I'm sorry, Mom."

She squeezed me, making hushing sounds.

"It wasn't your fault. I don't know why I said that to you that day at my apartment. I don't even know why I was so mad at you. You didn't do anything wrong. I should have told Logan. It was his fault for reacting that way and for being an alcoholic—he'd already been acting that way, I just didn't want to admit it to myself."

"Baby, it's okay. It's fine. I'm not mad at you. I was never mad at you." She rocked me into her, like I was a little kid again.

"I'm a horrible person. You should be mad at me. I'm so sorry."

"You're not horrible at all. Are you mad at Sarah when she hits you because she's having a hard time? I just missed you—that's all, I just missed you."

"I couldn't go up there. I couldn't go in there. I don't think I could take it, Mom. I'm not strong enough for this shit."

"We're going to do this together, baby."

"I'm sorry I said 'shit'," I whispered.

She blew out a breath. "You say whatever you have to say."

My phone rang and I reached for it but my hand fumbled and it slipped off the step again. "Shit. Sorry. That's probably Susan."

It wasn't Susan. It was Vanessa.

I looked up into my mother's eyes, two blue circles surrounded in red and white. "Could you answer it, Mom? I just—I can't. I held up the still ringing phone.

"Yeah." She took it gingerly, like the phone was delicate. Biting her lip, she answered the call then pressed the phone to her ear. "Vanessa?" She paused. "Yeah, it's me—but Jamie's here." She paused for a minute, obviously listening intently. Her hand squeezed my knee and she nodded, her gaze on mine. "He woke up . . . has a concussion. He had surgery on his leg, there was a cut all the way into his bone, but it looks like it will heal. . . Oh, oh." She made a face. "We can't go see him yet, but they say soon." She paused again, and then looked at me. "Vanessa has to go do a couple things, but she's offering to head over to Cameron's to pick up a change of clothes for you and him and bring it by, and anything you need from the store."

I nodded, but I said, "I don't have my keys."

My mother relayed the message. "She knows where Cameron keeps the spare . . . unless he moved it, do you know?"

"I think he said it was in a shed?"

My mother nodded. "She knows where it is. Should she grab anything else?"

"Would she mind grabbing some clothes for Sarah? I'll take it to Susan's later."

My mother relayed the message. "She says sure," she said to me. After saying goodbye, she handed over my phone. Her brow furrowed. "Are you two talking again?"

"No." I shook my head. "But I kind of want to again . . . I don't know."

We stood together, brushing off the dust from our pants. There was a definite dark streak on the back of her light-blue jeans. "Stairs or elevator?" My mom asked, looking up to the long channel above us.

"Elevator." I wiped at my face, avoiding all the tender parts. "Now I actually do want to get up there, even if they're not going to let us in." When I blinked, my eyeballs felt tender. In contrast, a bubbly warmth rose in my chest, and I almost felt like laughing.

"So on our way up why don't you tell me about your soul detox—only if you're up to it?"

I stopped with my hand wrapped around the scratchy handle of the metal door. "Oh my god, that busybody. Every single time. How much did Susan tell you?"

My mother smiled. "Probably most of it, but I haven't been updated in a couple days. I'm proud of you for taking charge of your life that way."

I opened the door, pushing my weight against it to hold it open for her. "I still don't really feel in charge."

"Tell me about it."

So, I did. As we took the elevator up to the street level and meandered through the chaos of the emergency room, I told my mother all the details of the past two weeks. In the Emergency Room, we were told that Cameron had been moved to the main hospital, so I continued my story as we hiked across the complex and waited in a crowded, well-lit waiting area. My mom listened as she always did, with total and complete concentration.

To my amazement, it felt as if the past year had not driven us apart. She didn't hesitate to smile or to cry, she didn't hesitate to take my hand and squeeze it. The whole thing made me a little sad, because I realized that I'd missed her. I hadn't just missed her in the past year, I'd been trying to function without my whole heart intact. Maybe Susan was right, maybe I had been punishing myself. Perhaps I was shoving all the people and things that would let me heal away. And, in my self-loathing, I'd pushed away the people who could help heal Sarah's wounds as well.

The image of the boats and the river from my dream surfaced in my mind again, and in the distance, the sailboat disappearing from view.

Day Twelve: Six-fifteen

When my lower back ached from sitting and exhaustion was setting in, I looked over to the waiting room reception desk. The stern receptionist sitting there in her scrubs had already given us the brush off twice—once right after we entered and once about fifteen minutes ago. But I considered bugging her one more time.

"What do you think they're making us wait for?" I asked my mom.

My mother's gaze broke away from where she watched a pair of toddlers play with a play-kitchen on one side of the waiting room. "I could go ask again," she volunteered.

"Yeah," I said, but I immediately changed my mind. "No, I don't want them to get mad and then not let us back there or something." They'd already had two nurses come out to tell us that the doctor said Cameron was stable, that he was doing well and we could see him soon.

My phone rang from under my leg, buzzing against my jeans. "Hopefully that's Susan," I muttered. But again I was surprised as 'Officer Oliver' lit across my screen. "Mom, I'm going to get this, will you text or call me if there's an update?"

When she agreed, I rushed out to the hall. "Officer Oliver?" I answered.

"Hello, Ms. Scott." She sounded exhausted. "How are you? Are you at the hospital?"

"I'm okay. Do you know about Cameron?" I headed down the hall and out a glass sliding door, into a small courtyard area. Somehow, in the past few hours since I reentered the hospital, the clouds rolled in.

"I do." She sighed. "I know you guys are going through a lot right now, but I was wondering if I could come and take your statement. I could come to the hospital if you don't want to leave."

I sat on a cement bench, rubbing my arm against the first touch of the afternoon chill. "I'm sorry, Officer Oliver, but I wasn't there. Sarah and I were at her gymnastics studio."

"We know that. We were able to take a statement from Mr. Rodriguez who witnessed the incident. But while Mr. Allen is still living, we need to treat this as a criminal investigation."

I stood up. "Mr. Allen—you mean Clarke?"

"Yes, while he is still living we need to move forward with this investigation."

"I'm really confused, here." I paced to one side of the garden. "What does Clarke have to do with this?" As I paced back, I kicked the bud of a dandelion, sending the fluff raining down.

"I can't really tell you too many details, Ms. Scott. I can tell you that Mr. Allen appears to have been the driver of the car that hit Mr. Robinson."

I stopped. "What?"

"Given the prior self-confessed history, we are pursuing a criminal investigation against Mr. Allen, even in his present state."

"His present state?" I whispered.

My phone beeped against my ear. When I pulled it away, I saw my mother's picture on the screen.

"We can't make that public knowledge," Officer Oliver was saying when I pressed the phone back to my ear.

"I think I need to go. I think they're going to let us in to see Cameron. I'll give you a statement if you come by the hospital, though I don't know much."

"Okay, I'll call before I head there, should be in about an hour."

The phone beeped again.

"Okay, thank you. I'm going to disconnect now." I clicked over the call. "Mom?"

"They're calling us in," she said in greeting.

"Okay, I'll be in there in two seconds." I hung up and stowed the phone in my back pocket. Small drops of water splattered onto my face and ears and I glanced up, seeing delicate lines of water and feeling the gentle, cold touch of the drizzle.

For a moment, just an instant, there was only me and the rain. Thoughts of seeing Cameron broke me from my momentary trance, and I rushed back into the hospital.

A nurse led my mother and me through the heavy swinging doors. "Right this way," she said, gesturing down a wide, overly bright hallway. As we walked, she tapped her pink painted nails on her clipboard, making a light, continuous titter. We passed room after room, most with blue paisley curtains drawn. Disjointed television conversations and music blared out from the rooms. She paused to open a door and held it open for us. "He's in here. You guys can go ahead in. I'll be back soon to check on him."

Cameron sat propped up on an adjustable hospital bed. His eyelids were half-closed over his beautiful deep-set eyes, one of which was entirely red around the pupil. Cuts crisscrossed his forehead and arms, a few bandages scattered among them. Blood matted his hair, making it look as if he had big, red strands interspersed with his dark hair. Thick white casts encased both his legs.

"Baby," he whispered, smiling through the word.

Tears filled my eyes and poured down my cheeks, tracing my nose and dripping down my neck. I fell to my knees next to his bed, leaned forward and kissed his fingers. His fingers rubbed up my uninjured cheek. "Come here," he said.

"I thought that you died for a little while today, Cameron. I'm really happy right now," I sobbed.

"You sound happy," he mumbled. "Why don't you get off the floor and sit with me, huh? I can't go down there with you."

I pressed my face into his mattress, inhaling the starchy fabric scent. I felt out of control, like I had when I ran from the hospital. As embarrassing as it was to be breaking down on his floor, this was where I was.

Something squeaked behind me, and then a hand touched my shoulder. "Here, honey, I brought you a chair. Let me help you up."

It took me a second, but I climbed into the rolling chair and was able to see Cameron again. My mother rolled me forward until I was directly beside his bed.

His fingers moved across my knuckles. "I've been thinking about you."

"Ditto," I said, sniffing.

"I've been thinking about our house—our new house. I want to build it," he slurred.

Glancing up, I looked for the morphine drip, and saw it hanging. "Okay," I said, nodding.

"Let's just sell everything—everything, and start fresh."

"Sure, sounds good."

Cameron went on describing our house, and somehow, I was both crying and smiling as I listened to him. Likely it had everything to do with the fact that he was loopy as hell and I couldn't even remember the last time I saw Cameron tipsy.

"Hey, sweetheart." My mother ran her hand over my hair. "I was thinking about running to Susan's and checking up on Sarah. Would that be okay?" she asked.

I looked up at her. "Yeah, that would be great. Thanks, Mom."

"Do you want her to stay with me tonight? I could take the day off work tomorrow, if you think she needs an extra day," she said.

"You'd do that? You don't mind?" I whispered.

"It would be my joy, Jay Jay. I can bring her by here too, so she can see Cameron, unless you think that's a bad idea?"

Emotion I couldn't hold back filled my voice, "I think that's a great idea. Thank you so much, Mom."

"I told you, it's my joy." She ran her fingers through my hair again. "Hey honey, mind stepping out with me a minute? I had a thought I wanted to share with you about what we were talking about earlier."

"Okay, Mom." I squeezed Cameron's hand before standing.

Just outside the door, my mom smiled, standing exactly eye to eye with me. "I just wanted to share something with you, about you feeling like you're not in control of your life."

When she paused, I nodded for her to go ahead.

Her gaze veered a little ways away from mine. "I don't know if this is true or not, but I've always thought that no matter what else is going on, whether times are good or bad, the only way you'll ever be happy is if you're honest with yourself. Sometimes being honest with yourself also means accepting things that you don't want to be true."

I blew out a laugh. "Maybe I should have just talked to you and not done this whole stupid detox, which basically upended my entire life."

She smiled. "Maybe that's what you needed."

Tears welled in my eyes again. "Thanks for— just forgiving me."

"Always, angel." After pulling me in for a hug, my mom headed off down the hallway and away from me.

"Hey," Cameron said as I reentered his room. "Wanna join me on here?" His smirk was just a little bit lazy.

"Is there a way I could do it without hurting you?" I took a seat beside him because I already knew the answer to my question. Reaching up, I touched one of the few places on Cameron's cheek that wasn't cut up. Bristles brushed over my fingertips. "I need to tell you something—to confess something."

"Now?" One of his eyelids drooped.

"I'm afraid that if I don't do it now, I won't ever tell you. I know you probably don't want to hear this stuff right now, but—"

"Just tell me, Jamie," he slurred.

I closed my eyes. "This was all kind of my fault, what happened today."

A knock came at the door and the nurse from before stuck her head in, light reflecting off her glossy black hair. "All right if I come in?"

I was going to object when Cameron's eyes slipped closed. I was being selfish. "Yeah, come on in," I said to the nurse.

"I just want to check up here. Vanessa is here to see you, Mr. Robinson, if you want me to send her in? And there's a police officer asking to speak to you, Ms. Scott." she said as she passed me on the way to the tubes that crisscrossed out of Cameron's arm.

"Yeah, I'm expecting her." I stood. "I guess we'll talk about it later," I said, running my thumb over his fingers.

"Are you going to take off?" he asked, fighting his eyes back open.

"Do you want me to?"

"Never," he said with a goofy smile. "But I understand if you have to."

"I don't. I'm just going to step out to talk to Officer Oliver." I was also stepping out to give Cameron a moment with Vanessa, but I wasn't going to say that one out loud.

The nurse left me to find my own way out, heading to the next door over. As all the hallways looked the same, I got turned around twice before noticing a red exit sign with an arrow.

The moment I stepped past the swinging doors, Officer Oliver's hawkish gaze found me. With amazement, I realized that it was only this morning that I met her for the first time in person ever. I felt like I knew her for a long time. The directness of her stare and her energy was so similar to Gina's. Gina, I probably should call and update her.

"Ms. Scott," she said, giving me a slight nod as I approached.

"Hey, thanks for coming into the hospital." I looked toward the windows. "If it's stopped raining, I know a pretty private place to talk. It might be a little wet."

She nodded again. "I'm not going to need you to give a statement, unless you feel like you want to, but at this point, we're not pursuing any charges. I just got a call that Clarke Allen passed away from his injuries as I was entering the hospital."

I grabbed onto the smooth surface of the nurse's desk. "You did?"

"I was already here and thought you might prefer to hear the news in person."

"I do, thank you," I whispered. My gaze drifted over the crowd around us. "Is there anything you can tell me about what happened?"

She inhaled deeply, her shoulders seeming to widen even more. "Clarke Allen seems to have borrowed a car from the wife of a coworker earlier today with her permission, though she does claim she was unaware of the purpose. He then drove to Custom Auto and, we believe, parked in the alley behind the shop and waited for Cameron to walk out to his, or your, vehicle."

"He would have been blocked in. It's a dead end."

"When the car hit Mr. Robinson, his body went over rather than under the car. We believe that Mr. Allen lost control of the unfamiliar vehicle before he collided into the side of the shop. This started a fire. Raphael Rodriguez—" she cleared her throat, "I mean, Mr. Rodriguez witnessed most of this incident from the mouth of the alley, as he had also been en route to his car. He was able to pull Cameron away from the fire and call nine-one-one."

"Oh, god." I rubbed my face. "Clarke was a terrible person, worse than I even knew yesterday," I whispered. He was a rapist and an attempted murderer, but weirdly, I didn't feel happy or even relieved.

Officer Oliver nodded, solemnly. It didn't seem like she was nodding because she agreed with me, but rather as a signal that the conversation was over. "I will ask Mr. Robinson to come in and give a statement once he's recovered, but as I said, we are not at this time pursuing a criminal investigation against anyone involved, so it can be at his convenience.

"Thanks, I'll tell him." I lightly tapped the nurses' desk beside me.

After another moment of silence, Officer Oliver stepped away, but looked back, "I hope it's okay that I inquire, but is everything okay with your daughter?"

"Yeah, she's doing all right. I–I think I'm going to start her back in therapy. She had a great special needs therapist when my husband first died. She'll be okay—we'll be fine."

After Officer Oliver left, my mind drifted as my feet returned me to the courtyard. Lights shone from different areas of the garden, brightening as the sky purpled. The enclosed space smelled of fresh plants and rain. Though the bench was wet, I sat down anyway. The wet concrete had a grainy feel on my hands as I buried them under my knees.

As much as I didn't want it to happen, all my moments with Clarke fed slowly through my head. His college football jersey and ball, framed, even though he'd been kicked off the team, flicked through my head. With that image came more, him standing outside the laundry room, him just standing casually outside the house while Cameron was inside, taunting me.

I rubbed my forehead, wanting the images gone, but they continued. He was a bad man, a horrible man. He'd stalked and hit me, raped Vanessa, tried to kill Cameron—and nearly succeeded. I shouldn't have any sympathy for him. But I'd seen a connection between us, and I couldn't break or dismiss it. In some dark part of me, I was stuck and angry and reveling in the misery. I knew I wasn't like him, not at all, but I wanted my heart to march a parade at the news of his passing, and it simply wasn't.

Day Twelve: Eight O'clock

The hospital door swished open, making a popping sound as I left the garden and the cooling evening. I waited, half in and half out for a couple to pass. A man smiled down as a woman smiled up from a wheelchair as they slowly moved through the hall. Stepping in behind them, I took a slow pace back the direction I'd come from.

I turned at the waiting area, stepping through the doorway to find myself face to face with Vanessa.

We both halted, our eyes locking together like magnets.

Neither of us said a word.

Her usually perfectly made-up face looked like it had been freshly scrubbed—I said usually, but I supposed I didn't really know what was usual for her these days. Her blonde hair was a mess around her face, curls frizzing out at odd angles. She was still beautiful, always beautiful.

"Hey, Jamie," she said, under her breath.

"Hey," I said.

"Excuse me," someone said.

Turning, I found another couple waiting behind me. "Oh, sorry," I said as I took a step into the waiting room and out of their way. I looked back to Vanessa, standing just that little bit closer. "So, Cameron seems like he's okay. Loopy, but okay," I said.

"Yeah. That was terrifying."

I glanced around the waiting room. Only a few people occupied the room now, the crowd from earlier almost completely gone.

Vanessa hefted her purse higher on her shoulder, grabbing my attention. She cleared her throat before saying, "I'm sorry I called you like that. I heard the crash and saw the fire . . . I wasn't thinking straight. You, of all people, didn't need a phone call like that. I always mess everything up, even when I'm trying to do the right thing."

I shook my head. "It's fine, Nessa—everything turned out fine."

We devolved into silence, a heavy cloying silence that I didn't know how to break.

Vanessa pivoted and hefted up her purse again. "I should probably go. There are some clothes for you and Sarah there. I brought her a dress and some stretch pants, I hope that works."

"That's perfect." Nodding, I stepped out of her way. "I'll see you later?"

"That would be wonderful," she whispered.

She walked forward to pass me, but paused and turned back. "I noticed your car at Cameron's shop when I was there. You have a car here, right?"

"I—no, I guess I don't have a car here." I looked away. That was pretty damn stupid of me, and I hadn't even realized that I didn't have a car with me this whole time. What if there was an emergency with Sarah? I'd totally blanked on that one.

Nessa shrugged, paused, and then asked, "Do you want a ride to your car? It didn't look damaged from what I saw."

Without meaning to, I took a step back.

"Or maybe I could have Joseph help me bring it to the hospital and drop it off—if you want me to?" she said in a rush. "That would be better. I'm sorry, Jamie—I don't want to be . . . I'm sorry, I—"

"No, Nessa, a ride to my car would be great." I rocked back and forth on my heels. "Thank you, I'd love a ride. I just need to get my stuff and get my keys from Cameron."

Cameron was half-asleep when I reentered his room, and when I mentioned my keys, he peered down to his hospital gown. "I'm pretty sure they're in my pants." It took me several minutes to track down a nurse who could show me where Cameron's personal effects had been stored.

With a promise to be right back, I left Cameron and returned to Vanessa, who hadn't moved an inch from where I'd left her. We said nothing more as we made our way out of the hospital complex and toward the parking garage I'd originally come from.

No stars shone above us, only a dark gray expanse. Lines of mist buzzed around the streetlights that lit our path down to the underground garage. Nessa and my steps echoed loud in the quiet between us.

She pointed to the black sedan I'd seen her in at Cameron's garage a couple days ago—the day I had designated to forgive her.

"When'd you get the new car?" I asked.

It took her a moment to respond, likely because of the reason behind her losing her old car. "About a month after the accident."

Her car smelled so familiar when I climbed in, like hibiscus and coconut oil—like her. The interior lit up with a multitude of blue lines as her engine purred. She didn't stick a key in, but pressed a button.

Her hands gripped the steering wheel as if she was steadying herself, before she looked over her shoulder and backed out of the space. The same tense silence locked us in for the entire drive to Cameron's shop—an expectant, almost fearful silence. When we pulled up, her headlights showed no damage to the front of Cameron's shop. The only noticeable difference was the banner of police tape that blocked the alley.

Even after Vanessa parked, she continued staring out of the windshield, her back ramrod straight. "Can I—can I say something?" she whispered, but then she shook her head. "Actually, no."

"What?" I asked.

"It probably won't make you feel any better."

"Just tell me, Nessa."

"I'm not trying to make you think any better of me by saying this. I—I've just thought of telling you this a lot since what happened. I thought that maybe it would make you feel a little better, but it might make you feel worse."

"Nessa . . ." I sighed. "If you don't tell me, I will go insane from wondering. Just do it."

"Okay." She closed her eyes. "I don't remember much of it . . . the times we were actually together, Logan and I. It happened. I'm not saying that it didn't. But we were both so fucked up that it was always gross and dirty and horrible. Afterwards we'd always vomit and cry, Logan would throw stuff, and it was horrible for both of us—it wasn't love, not even close."

Sobs ripped through my chest and I felt tears drip down my face. I wrapped my arms around my chest, leaned forward and cried. It was a hideous picture, a horrendous image in my mind, and it brought me no happiness and no relief. It was all just ugly.

When I could rein my emotions in, I wiped the tears off my face the best I could without touching my bruises. I looked to Vanessa, tears stained her cheeks. Sniffing hard to try to stop more tears from falling, I took a deep breath. "I've got to go. My mom is going to bring Sarah by the hospital soon."

"Okay," she said through sobs.

Even after everything, part of me wanted to comfort her. But I just couldn't. I couldn't.

"I'm going to go." I opened my car door and stumbled back out into the night. The cool dew brushed over my hot cheeks.

Vanessa opened her car door. "Wait, wait—Jamie. I'll go back there with you. It's dark," she managed. "I shouldn't have said anything. I knew better, and I still—I'm such a fuck up. I'm sorry for even bringing it up." She hesitated halfway out of her car, watching me expectantly.

"Yeah," I said.

Her brow furrowed.

"Sorry. I meant 'yeah, walk back with me'—if you want to. I'd appreciate it," I said.

Nessa took a second to untangle herself from her car door, her breaths coming heavy as she did. "Okay," she whispered, "Okay." We walked toward the alley together.

I fished my phone out of my bag, turning on the flashlight app. Beside me, Nessa did the same.

We stopped at the alley's mouth, our beams shining on the yellow tape stretched across it.

"Um . . . so, I don't think we should touch anything but your car back there. The police said they're doing a criminal investigation," Nessa said.

"They've closed the investigation. The guy who did this to Cameron died from his injuries." I looked over at her. With my beam pointed away, I could barely see her face, though small traces of light touched her messy hair. The idea of telling her who Clarke really was flashed through my mind, telling her that Clarke was Allen and that Allen was dead. But I stopped myself. I knew if I told her the truth, she would fall apart. And, selfish though it might be, I didn't have it in me to comfort her right now. I'd ask Cameron to tell her, or he'd just do it without me asking.

Nessa's phone dropped from her fingers, skittering further in the alley, sending light flashing in all directions. "Oh shit," she whispered, ducking under the police tape and scrambling to get it. She took a moment to right herself, and then turned to me; shadows obscured her expression. "I need to go, Jamie."

"Okay." Shining my light further into the alley, I said, "No one's here, I'll be fine."

"No—I'll wait. I'll just wait right here, shine my light in from here." She moved quickly over to the wall. "I'll take down the police tape so you can get out."

"Thanks, Nessa." I nodded once before heading into the alley and away from my once best friend.

Day Thirteen

Wading into Happiness

Day Thirteen: Seven O'clock

My phone buzzed beside my arm, waking me. My back protested as I straightened from the chair I sat on. After swiping off my phone alarm, I rolled up, stretching.

Across the semi-dark room, Cameron still slept in his hospital bed; his face looked even more bruised up this morning. A low beeping came from the white rectangular machine pulled up to his left.

Grabbing the bag Vanessa had left for me in the time I was gone from the room, I peeked up and down wide halls of the hospital, finding that several staff already walked around. Crossing over to the bathroom, I did the best I could to get ready for work before returning to Cameron.

He still slept, and as I didn't want to disturb him. I scavenged for a pen and an old receipt out of the bottom of my purse and wrote him a quick note. After I finished, I tucked the note into his hand and leaned in. "I love you, Cameron. I'll be back after work," I whispered.

"Okay, baby," he muttered through barely moving lips, though his eyes didn't open. Not wanting to disturb him more, I let myself out of the room and headed down the hallway. My shoes squeaked on the tile, reminding me that I still hadn't bought Sarah new shoes, which meant she still only had her rain boots to wear. I headed out of the hospital and into the garage, where I had parked my car last night.

Sarah had come right before her bedtime, stopping in to see Cameron. "Say: hey, sport!" she had yelled at him when she'd arrived, and seemed mollified when he'd managed it and a smile. She hadn't wanted to stay, though. It had been good. At least, I'd hoped it had been good.

The elevator opened into the garage to reveal my car. A matte, grayish tint discolored the side of the sedan that had faced the fire, dissipating into the car's red glossy color. Too bad Cameron no longer owned an auto body shop, but rather an office attached to a burnt pile of timber and machinery with a ripped-open car sticking out of it all. I hadn't lingered long to examine the scene when I picked my car up the night before, but from what I saw in the beam of my phone's flashlight, the damage was extensive.

Climbing into my car, I drove out of the hospital complex, paying the ungodly fee at the toll booth before merging onto the highway. The fog from yesterday had yet to dissipate, and it cast a shadow over Sea Breeze Way and the many cars attempting to park at the long line of buildings.

I clicked the button on my remote to lock the car before heading in, even though I doubted any thief would pick it among its neighbors at this point. As I crossed the parking lot, I shot off a quick text to my mother.

Me: How's everything going?

Mom: Great! Sarah's still asleep, I figured she needed it. I talked to the school, they understand.

Of course they did, they were probably delighted that Sarah was taking a couple family days. My guess was that they were worrying right now that I'd sue them for not having a substitute aid the day Sarah eloped.

Most of the crowd headed for the café, the line so long that it overflowed into the atrium. I walked with several other people to the elevator bank, squeezing in beside them. Suit shoulders lined up before me and I tried not to touch anyone as we ascended.

"This is me," I said when the elevator stopped, squeezing out between shoulders.

Standing in the entrance area, I looked to the coffee-themed wall hangings. The designs screamed corporate; clean, crisp lines webbed out around doctored photos of coffee beans and lattes. The coffee drinker couple featured on one hanging looked like super models who'd been dressed down to look funky and normal. Looking at those oddly dressed models, reality hit me: I was never going to be able to give the Harington's locations the feel of The Coffee Spot. You didn't buy that feeling, or make clever advertisements that shouted it or policy that feeling into being. The feeling Pat wanted for his chain had to grow from its incarnation, it was in every interaction that had ever occurred in the shop, every pastry and coffee ever consumed. And it never came with a high turnover rate or a corporate line of products.

I saw my future here spread out before me— chasing another man's impossible dream while caught in a power struggle with his insecure nephew.

Nodding to the receptionist, I let myself into Doug's side of the office and made my way to Toby's desk. He looked up at me, freezing with the Danish halfway in and halfway out of his mouth. His cheeks ripened to a deep red color.

"It's cool, Toby. Finish your pastry. I'm just looking for Doug."

"Hmm." He nodded to the office. Holding up a finger, he pressed a button on his phone and picked the receiver up. He chewed fast and swallowed heavy, and then said in his slightly accented voice, "Jamie Scott is here, hoping to see you." He paused before hanging up the phone. Giving me a wide smile with icing and phyllo pastry clinging to his lower lip, he said, "Go on in."

I pushed open the door.

Doug sat at his desk in his spacious, empty office, his attention fixed on his tablet. He didn't look up or acknowledge me as I took the seat across from him.

As he continued to ignore my presence, I tapped my foot, looking over my shoulder to the view of the crashing waves in the distance. A gray sky spread out over a gray sea, and my mood was gray as well.

"Did you get a chance to review the material I emailed?" Doug asked, still not looking up.

"I didn't," I said.

He didn't respond for a second, before he leaned back in the chair and aimed an insincere smile my way. "It's fine, I'm sure you can catch up this morning. Did you have a nice day with your daughter?" His gaze skipped over to my cheek.

"My boyfriend got hit by a car," I said, "So, not that good, really. But thank you for giving me the day off."

He blinked at me, slowly. "Is he okay?"

I nodded. "Sort of, he's in the hospital recovering."

"I hate to have to ask you this, but is your life usually so filled with crises?"

My fingers gripped the seat of my chair. "It has been lately, but I expect it to stop being filled with crises."

"You have a lot of responsibility for someone who's already showing to be unreliable."

I stared forward at a face that grew more and more ugly to me.

"You should be able to pull up the work assigned to you yesterday in your email—"

"Doug, I don't want this job," I said, interrupting him.

He paused, before asking, "You don't want your job?"

"I don't."

Slowly, he sat up straight. "I completely understand. I do have some ideas for a position better suited to your skill set. Here, let me have Toby print you up a proposal—I will come up with one for you, it won't take long." Leaning forward, he grabbed his phone.

"No, you misunderstood me, I don't want the job—any job here." I shook my head and stood. "I'm sorry; I know I've just been wasting your time."

He leaned a little over his desk, his brow furrowing. "You signed a year-long contract."

"I know, I'm sorry, but I'm breaking it."

"The sale of your shop was contingent on you taking the job for a year—you can't just walk away. We can find a better job for you within the company."

"Nope, I'm going to walk away. If that means I lose all the money from the sale of the shop . . ." I shrugged, "That is what it is."

"Per the terms of your contract, we have the right to sue you for damages if you break this contract."

I froze. Crap. That was right.

Likely seeing my hesitation, Doug leaned in over his desk and said, "Jamie, you're wanted at this company. I'm not proposing that we lower your salary or change your job title. You can't really leave this position—"

"I *can't* leave?" My brow furrowed. "That doesn't sound exactly legal."

He held out his hands. "You didn't let me finish my sentence. What I was saying is that you have a legal responsibility to stay in this job position, as per the agreements you signed."

"I know, and I regret that." I looked back to the gray sea. "I guess I'll just have to deal with it if Harringtons sues me. I know how it works, and this time I have almost no assets to take." They couldn't take my car as I needed it to work, and I was pretty sure there was a 'head of household' exemption from wage garnishment. No matter what, I'd figure it out. Turning back, I asked, "Do you have a box? I already moved my stuff into the office."

"I think we need to call Pat and have a sit down." He reached for his phone. "I'd really recommend against this move."

"Thanks, but I'm going to do it anyway." I nodded. "Yep, that is what I'm going to do." Not really expecting to get my box, I turned for the door. I walked through the office, through one set of swinging doors and into the other. Not wanting to be escorted out by security or something like that, I rushed to take down the framed posters I'd hung only a few days ago, scraping off the adhesive tape from the back and stacking them up quickly.

My phone rang before I stacked all of them, and Pat's number flashed across my screen. I set the frame down on the pile and blew out a heavy breath.

"Hello, Pat," I answered.

"Do not leave, Jamie, I'm on my way to speak to you," he said. The phone went dead.

I looked to my concert posters; they begged me not to chance leaving them. With one last glance around the rows of cubicles, I took down the final poster, grabbed up the stack and headed for the elevator.

"Hey, Jamie," Crystal said as I passed. She smiled wide, holding up two coffee cups in her hands.

"Hey," I said, but I didn't stop.

No one else said a word to me as I descended to the first floor and cut across the atrium. Just as I closed my trunk with the posters inside, my phone rang again.

"Where are you?" Pat asked in greeting.

"At my car," I said.

"Please come back in here so we can discuss this situation."

I spun on my heel, looking back to the long line of glass waves.

"I've gone to a lot of trouble on your behalf, Ms. Scott; the least you could do is come up here and have a conversation with me."

I cleared my throat. "Yeah, all right. I'll head up."

"Meet me in the conference room you had your original meeting in," he said, and then disconnected. Obviously he wasn't big on words of farewell.

Taking a steadying breath, I walked back between the parked cars, returning to the geometrical glass wave.

As I reentered the building, I already felt like an outsider. I'd never truly felt part of this corporate scene, but yet, I felt distinctly different. Few people walked around. A lady rushed toward the elevators, her coffee spouting from the hole in her cup like a tiny blow-hole. I didn't rush to join her, rather slowed down and let the elevator doors close. The moment the elevator doors reopened, my phone dinged with a text. Stepping inside, I fished through my purse and pulled my phone out.

Patrick: Are you back at work? Do you want to grab lunch today?

Not sure what to answer, I stowed the phone just as the doors to the elevator slid open. A young, pretty receptionist I vaguely recognized from the original meeting with Nicole stared at her screen as I approached. She startled, seeming to wake from her typing.

"I have a meeting with Mr. Kelly," I told her.

"No worries. You don't need to check in with me anymore." She nodded to my nametag.

Pat waited for me in a chair facing away from the door. I knew that he heard me enter the room, but he didn't look over until I rounded the table and took the seat across from him.

I really didn't know how I could have missed the similarities between him and his son, especially as they shared a name. The only big difference between them was their hair. Patrick was blond and his father gray. Pat's nose sat more prominently on his face, and wrinkles crisscrossed his brow. But truly, they were very similar.

"Hi, Pat," I said.

His blue eyes pinned me to the spot. "Here we are again, Jamie. And only a week later." His hands folded together on the table.

I leaned in. "Trust me, it's been one hell of a week."

His gaze darted to my cheek, then back up to my eyes. "You've just come out of a long-term litigation situation. Do you really want to enter into one again?"

Taking a deep breath in, I decided, "If that's how it's got to be. I'd be okay with us going back on the deal, if that's possible. I don't want the shop back. I just want to be done. None of the money has gone through to my account yet, so if you're okay with me just signing over the shop to Timepiece in repayment of the debt, I'd be fine with that."

His expression, if possible, grew stonier. "It's a little late for negotiations of that kind, Jamie. Do you not remember the stack of papers we had you sign, not to mention the time, effort, and money we'd invested to promote your success in this position?"

"Pat . . ." I held my hands out to my sides, "I'm sorry, but I realized something this morning. I realized that I don't want to spend another day feeling stuck, feeling trapped. I took this job for the wrong reasons. My neighbor was sexually harassing and stalking me, I was in incredible debt, and my daughter and I were nearly homeless." I held up a hand. "I'm not saying this to sway you, it's just the truth. I made a mistake deciding to stay stuck in the trouble that Logan landed me in for another year. And, that's what this job is for me, it's being stuck paying back someone else's debt for another year of my life. I've paid enough. I'm done."

"You're saying you took this job under duress?"

I gave him a look. "You knew I took this job under duress, Pat. You just didn't know that I took it because we were in serious danger."

He gave me a questioning look that bordered on challenging. "And you're not in danger now? You don't need a steady income now?"

"I'm not in danger. I do plan to provide a steady income . . . just not with this job." I shook my head. "It's not right for me."

"May I ask where you're planning to find employment?" he asked this question with challenge also.

Feeling a touch of concern, I folded my arms and met his gaze. "You're not threatening to sabotage me, are you?"

His eyes rolled to the ceiling. "Of course not, Jamie. I just asked. You can decide whether or not you want to answer."

"I don't know. Chris offered me a job helping him start his business." The moment I said it, I remembered that said business was now going to be funded by Pat.

He obviously remembered too, because he blew out a breath that suspiciously sounded like a laugh.

"Or something else."

"You expect that to be different?" One of his brows rose.

"Yeah, I do." And I did. Suddenly, I realized that I didn't need to be here. Pat was either going to sue me or not, and I'd already decided to leave regardless. I set my hands on the table, looking directly into his piercing blue eyes. "Pat, I'm really sorry for wasting your time. I didn't plan to do this. But at the same time, I'm going to move on now from all of this," I gestured around me, "no matter what that brings." Standing, I scooted out from the chair.

He stood, too. "If Chris does as well as I expect him to with that shop, I will be more than justly rewarded in my investment."

"I expect you will," I said, readjusting my sweater down my sides. "I don't want to mess up Chris' deal with you. I suggested that before I remembered that you were his investor. I'll look for work elsewhere." Leaning forward, I offered him my hand over the table. "Thank you for all of your time, Pat."

He left me hanging and said, "I do expect to see, at the very least, return on my investment within five years."

My hand dropped. "Chris is amazing, I'm sure he'll do a fantastic job."

"I expect you both will. Unfortunately, Jamie, I have to run to a meeting. Perhaps we can discuss this in more detail tomorrow at the dinner? I'll call Chris and have him come."

"Uh—" my mouth hung open, "Um, Pat, I was thinking the dinner would be off."

"No, that's ridiculous. Caroline's already bought all the ingredients and has everything planned." He shook his head. "You guys will love the meal. She was a professional chef for years before I *convinced* her to take over one of my businesses. She's expecting you at six, and as your schedule will be wide open, I don't expect that will be a problem for you."

"Cameron can't come, he has two broken legs," I said.

"That's why humans invented wheelchairs. Trust me, he'll want to come."

I couldn't help it, I laughed.

Pat didn't laugh, but the corner of his lips twitched before he nodded and turned to the doors.

"Chris hasn't hired me yet," I called after him.

"Chris is a very smart young man," Pat said back, though he didn't turn around and simply walked out of the conference room.

Day Thirteen: Eight-forty

As I stepped outside the office building, the fog layer began to break and small canals of blue fissured into the gray sky. A sparrow skipped among the clouds, swinging up and around.

Turning back to the parking lot, I realized I had to go tell Chris—who was pissed off at me—that his investor kind of, sort of, decided that he needed to hire me. True, Chris had already offered to hire me, but I really wanted it to be his choice and not because some crazy rich guy liked to play god with my life.

Sitting in my car, I tried to call Chris, but it rang five times and went to voicemail. Deciding not to leave a voice message, I opted for a text instead.

Me: Hi. I have lots of news. Mind if I drop by the shop to talk to you?

I waited for a response, shooting off a quick text to my mother and getting the response that everything was great over there. I also responded to Patrick.

Me: I actually quit.

Patrick: Are you serious?

Me: One hundred percent serious.

Patrick: Okay.

He then sent nothing more. When Chris didn't respond after a few minutes, I tossed the phone onto the passenger seat and turned the keys in the ignition.

It took ten minutes to return to town, and as I expected, a crowd lined up to the door of The Coffee Stop when I drove by. Someone stole my usual parking spot by the library, and I had to park several blocks down. When I made it to the shop, I had to squeeze past the line just to get through the door.

Customers filled the tables, most playing with their smartphones or typing on laptops. Small changes scattered about the shop as well. A display case with brand-logo mugs stood to one wall. Little Harrington's products, mints and gift card holders, peppered the counter.

The biggest change was the display case filled with Harrington's typical pastries and none of Chris' usual delights. I walked over to the case, getting a sideways look from an elderly woman in line.

Doug had made all of these changes while I was the general manager without saying a word to me. It just affirmed that getting the hell out of working for that jerk was very much the right decision for my life.

Chris stood at the counter, grinning and taking a man's order, writing it on a cup. "Double mocha, no whip. Gotcha. Can I get your name?" As he looked to the man, his gaze skipped to me. He gave me a wide smile, but it was as if a shadow passed over his expression as he nodded and returned to his customer.

Obviously Chris was still a little upset, or at least I thought that was what his change in expression meant. Like Susan, it was as if he remembered to be upset with me. As I wandered through, one of the Jessicas peeked up from the espresso machine. Her eyes widened under her thick-rimmed glasses and she gave an excited wave. "Are you coming to check out our site?" she asked me. Her hands went to her milk pitcher. "Do you want me to make you anything?"

"Uh, no. I'm just here hoping to get a word with Chris. It seems like this might not be the best time." I wasn't quite sure what I'd been thinking in the first place, nine o'clock at the shop had always been busy, just not this busy.

"I can switch places with him?" she suggested.

"Uh," I looked around, "I'm not actually your boss anymore—I'm doing something else now. So, asking you to do that feels a little unethical . . ." I said, extremely awkwardly.

"Oh," she said, and then she looked away. After a second, she met my gaze again and waved through the air. "You know what, it's fine for a minute. Sorry to hear about the reassignment though, I was really looking forward to you being our manager." She leaned forward. "Don't tell Doug that, though," she mock-whispered.

"Of course not," I said. I didn't correct her assumption that I'd been reassigned. When I thought about it, it was an easy assumption to make from the odd way I'd worded my statement earlier.

Jessica held up a hand and headed over to Chris. He smiled and nodded, passing the cup he'd been writing on over to her.

"Hey there, Jamie," he said, not looking at me but instead at the line of cups near the espresso machine.

"I'm sorry to bug you, Chris," I said.

"That's fine. How are you feeling?" The smile crossing his face seemed pretty genuine, if a shade less warm than usual.

"So, Clarke is dead," I said.

His eyelids went wide and gaze focused on me. "What?"

"Well, I'll give you the abbreviated version, and then maybe you can call me after work? So, Clarke hit Cameron with a car and died from his injuries. Cameron is in the hospital alive but banged up. He's healing—I probably should have led with that."

"Wait . . ." Chris shook his head as if to clear it. "Can you back up here for a second? What happened to Cameron?"

"Clarke hit him with a car. He has two broken legs. I'm pretty sure he's going to be okay."

Chris leaned into the bar. "Holy s—word, Jamie."

I held up a finger. "And, one more thing."

His brows shot up. "You're serious?"

"Well, it's not of the same caliber as the other news, but it's why I'm here."

"Chris?" Jessica called.

He looked back to where Jessica held up a cup. Behind her the crowd had only grown.

"Sorry, I'll leave you to work. I have to talk to you—well, I'm hoping to talk to you before Pat does, specifically. I dropped by because I wanted to make sure you'd pick up my call later."

He grinned at me. "Don't be crazy, Jamie, I'd always pick up your calls. Even if you did scare the—you know what—out of me yesterday. So, just tell me."

"After work—I shouldn't take any more of your time."

He mock glared. "That's just cruel."

I shrugged. "I need to ask you, well, it's kind of a favor but not exactly. Call me when you're free—before you talk to Pat."

He shook his head, a smile on his lips. "I'm off at eleven and don't have class until one. You want to talk then?"

"Yeah, I really do."

His smile fell. "Cameron's really going to be okay?"

"Yeah, I think so."

"Can't say I'm unhappy that guy won't be bothering you guys anymore." He didn't look at me as he said it. Pulling off the portafilter, he banged it over the trashcan and dumped out the grounds before he filled it with espresso and timed the shot. "I don't want to say I'm happy someone died, but I'm definitely relieved."

"Yeah." I tapped the counter. "I'll let you get back to work. If Pat reaches you before I do, just remember that the decision is one hundred percent up to you, okay?"

"Now you're just being unforgivably confusing. What are you talking about, Jamie?"

I grinned. "There's just no way we could cover all of it now. It wouldn't be fair to you. I'll tell you after work. Love you, Chris."

He shook his big, bristly head slowly. "Fine, fine, be that way. I'll talk to you soon. Want a green tea latte?"

"I'm good, thanks." I backed away from the counter. "Oh, and could you call me if Mitch comes by? I'm trying to find him."

"Sure, but I haven't seen him all week."

"Oh, okay. Well, thank you." I waved before turning and squeezing between bodies until I could leave the shop.

Stepping out into the day, I looked up into the leaves of the tree that grew directly outside The Coffee Stop. It looked back, arching down over me. I crossed over and ran my hand over its coarse trunk.

"You started all of this," I told the tree, but the tree didn't respond. It probably already knew that when it dropped its blossoms on me, it set a snowball effect in motion on my life. "I'm not sure whether I'm grateful, yet," I whispered. It was a lie, I was grateful.

The wind rattled its leaves, and one flittered down beside me. When I'd written 'be happy' for today, I'd imagined something very different, but I guess the universe doesn't let you choose how it delivers you happiness.

"All right, then." I patted the tree once more before turning back to the sidewalk.

A block away, I called my mother.

"Hey, sweetheart," she answered on the second ring.

"Hey, Mom. I kind of quit my general manager job."

"You did?"

I stopped to let a car pass on the street. "I am now jobless and possibly going to be sued."

"Sued?"

"Well, from the way we left things it didn't really sound like Harringtons was going to sue me. However, I never really know what Pat, the guy who owns Harrington's, is going to do. So yeah, the point is I quit my job."

"Well, how do you feel about it?" she asked.

I paused and halted my steps. "Oh my god. I feel so relieved, Mom. I feel like doing a freaking happy dance up the street."

"Good, then it's good. And no matter what this guy Pat decides, we'll figure everything else out."

"Thanks, mom. How's Sarah?" I asked as I continued toward my car.

"Sarah is great. We're making some breakfast—our second breakfast—then we're going to get cracking on this week's workload. Her teacher emailed it all over to me, so she'll be caught up for tomorrow."

"Thanks, Mom. You're so much better at that stuff than I am. I was thinking that I'd go see Cameron for a minute then head over to you—" I paused, again, as I saw a figure sitting huddled deep in the alley behind the library. With their body turned from me this way, I couldn't see their face.

"Take your time, honey," my mother said.

"Mom, I have to go."

"All right, see you later, Jay Jay."

I hung up. Narrowing my eyelids, I tried to peer into the alley. "Hello? Is that you, Mitch?"

The figure shifted.

I stepped toward the alley, but hesitated, not quite ready to commit to walking in. "Mitch? Excuse me?"

The figure shifted again, and then glanced back. It wasn't Mitch. I was pretty sure it wasn't even a man.

"Fuck off," the person called.

"Yeah, okay," I mumbled before continuing on to my discolored car.

I drove around the downtown streets on my way out, but I didn't find Mitch. Several other homeless people lingered about this morning, a group near the Grocery Mart, another group lying around the park, but Mitch wasn't among them. I had no idea what I could offer him now, anyway. I couldn't offer him a job, or a substantial amount of money. I had almost nothing.

I gave up after about twenty minutes and headed for the hospital.

Day Thirteen: Nine forty-five

A nurse with a lopsided gait and a big smile led me into Cameron's room when I arrived to at his hospital wing.

"How are you doing this morning, Mr. Robinson? I brought someone to see you," she said as we entered.

Cameron's bruised, tired eyes shifted from her to me. "I'm doing better now." His lips formed into something that I could almost call a smile.

"Good, that's good. Everything here looks good," she said while checking over his tubes and machinery. "All right. You two have a nice morning. I'll be back to check on you in about an hour."

"Hey, baby," Cameron whispered as the nurse closed us in.

Rolling the chair up to his bed again, I sat beside him. "Hey there."

"I think I might need some stress release," he whispered.

I laughed. "We might have to wait a day or two on that one." Carefully, I brushed his dark hair away from his forehead. It was a little damp, the crusted blood completely gone from his dark locks. His bandages looked clean and fresh.

"If you say so." He grinned, dazedly. "Did you sleep here last night?"

I nodded.

"You didn't have to do that, I bet you're in pain now."

"I'm fine, but . . . can I tell you about my crazy morning?" I asked him.

"Please."

I told him everything. When I was done telling him about the job and everything that Pat said, I told him about what Officer Oliver had told me the night before, and everything I had yet to tell him about Clarke.

When I told the part where Susan admitted that it was Vanessa who was raped, Cameron whispered, "Vanessa told me that Clarke was really the Allen I beat up, Jamie. She made the connection yesterday when she talked to the police after the accident."

"She knew?"

"Yeah. She was pulling away from the shop while the accident happened and heard the crash. She'd been there when the ambulance took me, and talked to the police while the firemen pulled Clarke from his car."

"Oh. Last night, when she took me to my car, I—I thought she didn't know. I guess that means she knows he's dead now." I leaned onto the handrail of his bed and trailed my fingers over a stretch of his arm that was free of any injuries. "Vanessa never told me about it. I had no idea that happened to her."

Cameron moved his other hand, and webbed his fingers through mine. "She never told anyone, not even me. Yesterday was the first time I'd ever heard her say that he raped her."

I sat up a little straighter. "But you punched him. How did you know about it if she never told you?"

He looked away, staring up at the ceiling. And from his expression, he was staring into the past as well. "She called me in the middle of the night one night when we were both living in the dorms. I was in my room sleeping, but I ran out to find her. She couldn't really describe where she was, so it took me a while to find her. I knew she went out to a party with a date that night. She refused to tell me beforehand who he was because she already knew I didn't like the guy and she didn't want me to act stupid." He looked back, misery clear in his face. "I found her in an alley. She was so confused. Her skirt was on backwards, her shirt was—she looked bad. There was piss on her, on her shirt and in her hair. It reeked."

My hands flew up to cover my mouth.

He continued. "I knew she was on something, not just booze, but something else. I called the police and when the ambulance came, they wouldn't let me go with her. I convinced a friend to give me a ride to the hospital, but they wouldn't let me in to see her."

"Oh my god."

"Allen was on my team. He was a senior, and a real asshole. He despised me for some reason. He was popular with the Greek crowd, but the entire football team hated him. The coach hated him more than anyone. He was a good player, but a real dick on and off the field. He was probably eighty pounds heavier back then, and I swear his face was different."

"He said he had to get surgery after you hit him."

"Maybe that was it." He sighed. "That next day he was telling everyone that Vanessa had gotten really drunk when he took her out and wet his bed. It was like he was bragging about it or something. She'd come into school a pretty big deal, as she was somewhat famous from the pop group. He was calling her 'the bed-wetter'. A bunch of other guys also started calling her that. She hadn't come back that day and I was out of my mind worried, and I lost it. I hit him and I did it in front of most of the team and the coach."

"And they told the cops that he swung first."

"Yeah, but they did it more because they hated him than out of any loyalty to me. The coach had wanted him off the team for a while, and he used the fight as a third strike against Allen. Vanessa returned about a week later and never said anything to me about it."

"I think she told Susan. She knew," I said.

"Maybe she did. Ness wasn't the same after she came back, though. First, it was the drinking, and then she was constantly going home with dickheads at the bar. Susan and I tried to help, but Vanessa didn't want our help. When I caught my old-ass, married boss with her bent up over his desk, that's when I lost my shit again. She was eighteen and he was in his sixties and a real slimy pervert too."

I squeezed his hand. "I would have punched him, too."

"After I got out of jail, I thought she was . . . I don't know, better, maybe. I started working at the body shop and we started being a little more than best friends. Maybe I thought I could fix her, as stupid as that was."

His dark hair again fell over his forehead, and I brushed it back. "You were nineteen."

"Yep, and pretty dumb. Also, you and Logan decided to get married at twenty. I'm not proud to admit it, but I was pretty determined to move on with my life. I really thought she was better."

"Maybe she was."

"No, just better at hiding it. I didn't realize that she was still sleeping around in *that way* until a few years into our marriage. Most of our marriage was just me trying to get her help. It hadn't been romantic for a long time. Then it happened with Logan—that was the first time she admitted it. She said that neither of them knew if it actually happened the first time."

I swallowed and pulled my hand from his, gripping the bar. "I feel like I should have known about it, if it had been going on so long. Am I really that oblivious to what's happening with my friends?"

He reached up and grabbed my hand again.

"I knew she got stupid when she drank," I continued as a hot tear dropped onto my cheek. "I knew she was really depressed . . . She never told me about any of this."

"I think she didn't want you to know—you more than anyone, Jamie." Reaching up with some effort, he wiped my tear away.

"Am I super judgmental or something?"

"No. You were maybe just a little sheltered back then—idealistic. You thought she was smart and beautiful and had her shit together—you always told her that she was. I think she tried really hard to be the person you thought she was. She's talked to me a little about it recently."

"That's good that she has you to talk to," I mumbled, though I meant it. "Is she—is she doing better now?"

"Not for a while there, but recently she seems a little better. She tried to kill herself about six months ago."

"She did?"I whispered as tears filled my eyes.

"Yeah. She stayed in a hospital for a little over a month because of it. I think that helped her. We put the divorce off for a while, though we've been legally separated since right after the crash."

"Oh. I just assumed you guys were divorced."

"We are now . . . we have been in all but the legal system since the crash."

"You never told me."

His brows rose and there was a distinct look of challenge in his bruised and battered face. "I tried to bring it up a couple times. You shut me out every time I tried to talk about us."

I blinked, realizing that he was right. I'd never even asked Cameron if he and Vanessa were divorced. He'd called her his ex-wife. I'd just assumed, or maybe I just hadn't cared. "I guess that says a lot for what kind of person I've been to you in the last year."

"Hey, I told you. One day you were going to be ready to move on, and I was there, patiently waiting for that day."

I gave him a look. "Patiently? I'd say you made your move pretty fast."

"You're probably right." He grinned. "Maybe I did."

We didn't talk much after that, just held each other's hands and tumbled into our own thoughts. I didn't know if learning about what Vanessa went through made me feel worse or better about what happened with Logan—the whole thing just made me sad and sickened.

And, underneath it all, I really missed my best friend. Mess, adulterer and home-wrecker that she was, I really missed her in my heart.

I looked back to Cameron, and when his gaze came back to mine, I said, "I think love is permanent. Maybe that's what screws us up so much, that even after people break your heart, you still love them just as much as you ever did." I was thinking of Logan and Vanessa, but also of the way I treated my mother and the way she'd forgiven me so easily.

My phone rang from my purse, and I broke from Cameron to go check it. Chris' big smile greeted me from my phone screen.

"It's Chris." I gave Cameron a nervous smile. "Fingers crossed."

"Yeah," he said.

"Of course I'd hire you, Jamie," Chris said in greeting.

Damn it. I winced. "Pat got to you first?"

"Yeah, I didn't feel right letting it go to voicemail. But you should have just flat out told me in the shop today, there's no way I'd ever say no."

"Are you sure? I don't want to have Pat put pressure on you or anything."

"How stupid do you think I am, Jamie? If you think I'd ever pass up an opportunity to hire you, then you're taking crazy pills."

"You big jerk, you're making me cry." I wiped the tears away.

"I'm sorry, Jamie, can't have that. Well, I have officially given my two weeks' notice to Harringtons, and Pat says he already has some ideas on a space for us."

"Of course he does. I have a feeling that we're going to have to be very careful on how involved we let him be. He's like a somewhat nefarious fairy godfather."

"Pat's all right," Chris said, making me worry even more. "We'll figure it out tomorrow at dinner, I guess. He says you and Cameron are coming?"

I looked over to Cameron. "I have a feeling that Cameron might want to sit this one out, but I'll ask him."

"Will you also ask him if it's cool if I stop by to visit him later after class today? I just want to see that he's okay."

Cameron obviously overheard because he smiled and said, "Yeah, tell him I'd love it if he came by whenever."

A few seconds after I hung up with Chris, a knock came at the door and the nurse popped her head in. "Mind if I come in to do a couple assessments before lunchtime?"

"Come on in," Cameron said.

"I should probably go check on Sarah," I told Cameron. "I'll be back tonight."

"Don't sleep here, baby. I'd rather you be comfortable."

I shrugged. "I'll come by no matter what. If Sarah needs me to stay with her tonight, I probably will. I'll bring her by, if you want?"

He looked like he wanted to roll his eyes, and said, "Of course I want you to bring her by."

The nurse turned around to give us a moment of privacy. I leaned down and gave Cameron a quick kiss. "I love you," I whispered, before standing straight.

Day Thirteen: Eleven-fifteen

As I drove away from the hospital, my stomach grumbled. And I realized I'd forgotten to eat breakfast. Obviously even after two weeks, I hadn't been miraculously cured of my forgetfulness. I pulled off into a side of Coral Beach I rarely visited. It wasn't that far from my apartment, but in the opposite direction of Sarah's school.

A long line of little shops abutted a neighborhood area. A small full service gas station sat at the end of the street.

"Full service," I mumbled as I continued to the end of the street and pulled up to a pump.

Inside the booth, a man moved around, but I couldn't quite see him. Muffled by my closed windows, I heard the man call out. "Coming! I'm coming! I'll just be there in one second!"

I rolled down my passenger window. "Mitch?"

Mitch appeared at the doorway. His attendant uniform transformed him, though his worn work pants had two distinctly dirty patches in the knees. His hair looked relatively clean, combed back with a few strands falling forward. A huge smile broke across his face, revealing his gapped-teeth. "Jamie? Are you here for gas?" he asked, sounding extremely excited about the idea.

"No, I'm here to see you. Here, I'll get out." I turned to climb out of the car.

"Oh no, Jamie. No, you're not supposed to get out really. I'm supposed to come around. Here, you stay there. Stay there and I'll get your gas." He rushed around the car, standing by my door so that if I did open it, I might accidentally hit him.

When I rolled down my window, he smiled again. "What type of gas does your car take?"

I grabbed the edge of my window and leaned out so that I could fully see his face. "Oh—um, you see Mitch, I just picked up gas yesterday, so it's almost full. But, I've been looking for you to thank you. You—you might have saved my daughter's life when you walked her all the way across town to the gymnastics studio."

"Ah, nah, Jamie. You don't need to thank me. It wasn't that long of a walk. It wasn't a really big deal."

"Mitch believe me—it was the biggest deal of my whole life, okay? I'm going to be thankful to you every day for forever."

"Ah, well, thanks Jamie. Thank you for saying that." He nodded. "How about I get your gas? How about I do that for you?"

Because he seemed like he really wanted to, I said, "Uh, okay, it'll only be like a quarter of a tank."

"That's fine, that's good. What does your car take? We have really good gas here."

"You know, let's do premium. I don't usually do it, but let's do premium today."

He grinned wide. "That's—that's coming right up, right now."

I popped my gas tank cover and watched out the window as Mitch rushed to the other side of my car to fill up my gas. It took less than a minute, and when he was done he grinned again. "That will be seven dollars and twenty-three cents."

I handed him a twenty. "The rest is a tip."

His eyes widened. "Uh, no, Jamie. That's too big of a tip. It's usually a dollar or two, sometimes nothing."

I held up a hand. "Just this first time, let me give you a big tip. As . . . like, a congratulations on getting the job tip."

"Well, okay then. Just this once I think it's okay. I'll go get your receipt." He rushed off toward the booth and disappeared from view. A few seconds later he reemerged, holding up the receipt like it was something awesome he'd found.

"You know, Jamie, it just made my day that you came here to see me. It really did, it just made my day." He nodded for emphasis.

"What days do you work?" I asked.

"Tuesday through Saturday, four-thirty a.m. to eleven-thirty a.m., every week." He punctuated every word with a nod.

"Okay, I'll be sure to come get gas from here while you're working as much as possible."

Another huge grin broke across his face. "That would be so nice of you. I would really like that. And, maybe Chris too. Do you think that Chris might want to come by, too?"

"Well, I can't speak for him, but I'll definitely tell him you'd like him to." I scratched my forehead. "Mitch, is there anything else I can do for you? I could bring you lunches, or—"

"Oh no, Jamie, they give me lunch here."

"Is there anything else . . . money?"

He shook his head, furiously. "No, no—I have a job and I'm making money and I'm doing really well for myself."

"Sure looks that way from here. I like your uniform."

He stepped back so that I could clearly see the blue shirt with its wide yellow collar.

"They already made me a nametag," he pointed to his yellow nametag.

"Very nice."

A car turned into the station, pulling up to the next pump.

"Oh," he said, jumping a little. "Well, I really need to go, Jamie, but I will see you soon."

"It was great to see you, Mitch. Thank you again, with all of my heart."

"Oh. No seriously, Jamie, it was not a big deal," he called, but he was already rushing away to the other car.

I sat for a moment, wanting to get out and do something more for Mitch, but not really knowing how to go about it.

A car pulled up and parked by the booth before an elderly man in the same uniform Mitch wore stepped out. The man gave a smile and wave to Mitch, who didn't notice, before heading to the booth. Mitch rushed over to the booth, then back to the car with a receipt, never once glancing my way. On his return to the booth, he did notice me, pausing to smile again.

I leaned out of my window. "You get off your shift now, right? Can I give you a ride somewhere?"

"Oh, no. I'm fine, Jamie. I like the bus."

"You sure? Because it's no problem at all. I'd like to give you a ride to say thank you for walking Sarah—but you don't have to, of course," I rushed to say in case he felt uncomfortable with the idea.

"Well, if it's a thank you. Okay, that would be nice. I have to check out. It might be five minutes, could you wait five minutes?" he asked, looking back and forth between the booth and me.

"Take your time, I have nothing to do."

After Mitch rushed forward, I pulled off to park next to the elderly man's car. It only took a couple minutes before he knocked on my window.

"It's open," I said, nodding and pointing.

Mitch sat down in my passenger seat slowly, scooting in more than sitting down. Carefully, he buckled himself in, and then turned to smile at me.

"Where to?" I asked.

"Um . . . I'm living at the Palms, do you know where that is?" he asked.

"The hotel?"

"Yeah, yeah the hotel. It's a really nice place. I really like it."

"That's great. Yeah, I know where that is." I backed out of my space, turning onto the street and heading toward the highway. "So . . . you have a place to live, that's good," I said, cautiously.

He shrugged. "It's okay, I like it. I miss some of my friends at camp, they're good people. Maybe I'll go back there, I don't know."

"Are you thinking of maybe getting an apartment—sorry if that's invasive. I'm just asking because if you need any help, I'd be happy to help you."

"Thank you, Jamie. Thank you. But I'm no good at that stuff, paying the bills and having a place and all that. I like where I live, it's an easy place to live."

"Well, okay. But if you ever change your mind I'd be happy to help."

"I'm going to head to the coffee shop soon, Jamie. I've been so busy, been really busy."

I winced. "Uh . . . Mitch, I need to tell you something. I quit the coffee shop, and Chris just gave his two weeks."

Mitch's smile fell.

"Oh, I'm sorry. Chris and I are starting a cupcake shop, actually—it probably won't be open for a while." I gripped the steering wheel harder. "Do you like cupcakes?"

"Well—no, but . . ." he looked at me, looking like he was thinking hard about something, "How old does a kid have to be to eat cupcakes?"

"Um, like one or a little older maybe," I said. "How come?"

"Well, I don't know if she likes cupcakes, but if she does, I'll bring her to your shop."

"Sorry Mitch, who?"

"Well, if her mother lets me, I will. You said that your shop won't be open for a while, so by that time, maybe she'll let me."

I nodded slowly. "Do you have a niece?" I asked.

"She's my daughter. Hannah, my daughter. I don't really see her. Her mom is a very nice woman—I shouldn't have left her. She lives with her mom now and I don't really see Hannah," he said.

Seeing a familiar sign with a neon palm tree that read 'The Palms Hotel' approach near the highway entrance, I flicked up my blinker. "Oh. That's wonderful, Mitch, you have a daughter? Is that why you got the job? So you can see her?"

"I don't know if she'll let me see Hannah, Jamie. But—if I'm clean and I have some money coming in, I think she'll let me see her. And, if Hannah likes cupcakes I will definitely take her to your shop."

I pulled into a space in the crowded parking lot. A man pushing a grocery cart full of trash glared over, mumbling from a few spaces down as he wheeled his cart by. A guy smoking a cigarette out of the hotel office window yelled at the homeless man, and the man kept wheeling his cart along.

"Maybe . . . could I get you a room at another hotel, Mitch?"

"Oh, no, Jamie. I like it here—I have friends here." He opened his car door.

"Mitch," I called.

He turned back.

"We'll always have a cupcake for Hannah. If you ever need anything, I'll do my best to help you."

He grinned. "Well, I don't know if she likes cupcakes, but that's really nice, Jamie. Thank you for the ride." With another grin, he stepped up to the car and headed toward the line of rooms.

Hearing the smoking office guy really start to shout at the homeless man, I backed out of the space and drove away.

After calling my mom quickly, I picked up food for all of us. I drove down the side streets all the way through town, and turned onto the street that ran along the state beach. Even though it was midday on a Thursday, the beach was filling up with blankets and tents. I pulled over along the road a few spaces up from where my mother was just climbing out of her car.

"Mom," I called as I stepped from my car.

She looked over her shoulder. "There you are."

"I brought burritos." I held up the bag as I crossed over to the car. Sarah let herself out of her side of the car, jetting off toward the beach.

"Sarah, yo! Wait, baby!" I called.

She did, stopping to cartwheel back and forth.

"Oh thank god, I thought she might run again," I grumbled.

"Oh honey, I did want to tell you some pretty good news. I received an email the principal is going to have a safety meeting for all school staff, implementing new safety procedures. She didn't say anything specifically about the special needs kiddos, but it did say 'due to recent breaches in safety'."

"Well, maybe that's good. I have a hard time believing that the school will step up."

"I asked Sarah about why she ran. I hope that's okay."

"Did you get anything?"

My mother shook her head. "I'll keep trying, though." She grabbed a blanket from her trunk. When I turned back to the beach, she leaned in and said, "I love the idea of having a picnic here, honey."

I looked around at Logan's beach. "Let's make this our thing, like every Sunday or something, with Susan and Beza too, if they want."

Walking over, she put an arm around me and rubbed my back. "That sounds very nice. So, I was wondering. Are you and Cameron thinking about having more kids?"

I rolled my eyes. "Oh my god, Mom, I can't even . . ." Shaking my head, I laughed and we all headed down Logan's beach for our picnic.

Day One Hundred and Fourteen

Floating On

Day One Hundred and Fourteen: Seven-thirty

My eyes opened to early morning light and the certainty that Cameron and I were about to be married. It was clear as day in my head, the wedding cake we'd picked out, Sarah's purple flower-girl dress, the dance routine our friends had not so subtly planned to surprise us with. But as the bed became more and more real around me, I realized that Cameron and I weren't actually engaged. Today was a day for a party, but a very different sort of party.

Also, Cameron and I weren't even close to thinking of marriage. We'd only been officially together for less than four months. Sure, we'd been in some weird in-between stage for over a year, but that didn't really count.

Cameron shifted behind me, pressing closer against my back.

Sighing, I snuggled deeper into his arm. His hand rubbed up and down over my hip.

"You waking up, baby?" he asked in a low growly voice that sent shivers all through me.

"Mm-hmm. I probably should already be downstairs making cupcakes," I mumbled into my pillow. My eyes closed again.

The hand that had been rubbing over my hip slipped onto my belly and slid lower. "I was thinking that the cupcakes could wait a little while," he whispered.

"Mm—do you?" I managed, nuzzling my body even closer to him.

"In fact, I'm positive they can wait." His hand slipped down past the lining on my underwear.

"You're going to get me in trouble, big trouble. Amy is going to kill me if I don't bake those cupcakes," I said, biting my lip.

"Amy is supposed to be here in an hour and a half right? Meaning we probably have another hour before she shows up."

"An hour of assigned baking," I whispered, but at the same time I really didn't want him to remove his hand.

"Well, the way I figure it, Amy is going to be here three hours before your mother brings Sarah home and five hours before the party actually starts. Plenty of time to make . . ." he leaned in closer and whispered, "Cupcakes."

"Amy definitely told me they had to be done before she got here . . . but, maybe I could do them in, like, half an hour."

"Uh huh." His hand slipped into my underwear.

"Maybe we have forty-five minutes." I drew a sudden breath in as he began to rub me in the most delicious way.

"Or an hour," he whispered. As his hand continued to work me, his other hand went under and around me. His fingers ventured up my shirt to cup my breast. My pleasure built and I couldn't help but grind back against him, feeling him grow hard against my backside.

His fingers sped up their pace and soon I was whimpering. I tensed. "Wait, Cameron. Slow down, baby, slow down. I'm going to. . ."

"I want you to," he growled into my ear.

The orgasm ripped through me, I couldn't stop it. As the pleasure rippled through me, Cameron yanked down my panties, pulled my legs apart and entered me from behind.

I pulsated hard around him as he began even strokes.

"Oh god, baby, you feel so good," he moaned, deep inside of me.

"I—I love you," I whispered as my next orgasm kept building.

After Cameron had me from behind, he rolled me on top of him, and I rode him with long slow movements.

Just as my pleasure was building close to yet another orgasm, my phone rang from the nightstand.

"Damn it, that's probably Amy," I breathed.

"Not yet," he said, gripping my hips and rolling us over once more so he was on top. "Let's—turn off your phone."

I reached up and pulled him to me. "Then she'll only show up early," I whispered onto his lips as he continued to drive deep inside of me.

We ignored three more phone calls before Cameron collapsed on top of me, waves of pleasure still rippling through me.

The phone beeped.

"Damn it," I whispered as I blindly reached to the nightstand.

When my screen lit up, there was a text from Amy on it.

Amy: I swear to god, Jamie, if you're not done with those cupcakes, I'm heading over there right now and doing them myself.

I texted a quick response.

Me: They're done.

"She's going to kill me when she gets here," I whispered.

Cameron didn't move off me, lying boneless over me like a big, sweaty, muscled blanket. "There's more than enough time to make the cupcakes. I told you not to let her plan this."

"I didn't ask her to, she just started planning things."

As we rushed through a quick shower, I peeked up into his beautiful face and couldn't help but smile.

"What?" he asked, as he rubbed shampoo in his hair.

"I had a dream that we were planning on getting married," I said.

He raised a brow at me. "Did you try to run away to a different country?"

"Actually, I was really excited about the wedding in the dream."

He looked a little surprised. "You were?"

"I was."

His hands came down and went to my hips. "Here, switch places with me so I can rinse off my hair."

We switched places and as he put his head up under the flow, I ran my fingers through his wet hair to help wash out the suds.

His gaze met mine through the curtain of water. "You're not asking me to marry you, are you?"

"Don't be crazy," I said.

He grinned a sexy little grin. "Because I'd at the very least want a ring."

"Ha, ha," I said.

"Your turn." He turned me into the spray, lathering soap into my hair.

"That feels really, really nice." I said, closing my eyes and reveling in the massage. After all the soap had washed out and I stepped out of the spray, I met his gaze again. "I mean, what would be the point?"

"The point of what?"

"Getting married," I said.

He made a face like he was really considering it. "Taxes . . . health insurance . . . I could introduce you to people as my wife—especially men."

"Nice."

He leaned down. "I could come home to fuck my wife."

"I kind of like the sound of that."

"I thought you would." His arms came around me, pulling our wet bodies together. "We could have a wedding, invite all our friends."

"Yeah, but we see too much of them anyway."

"And, if I'm being real about it, I could adopt Sarah, if you both wanted me to," he said.

"You'd want to do that?"

"That surprises you?" he asked.

It didn't. I just had never thought of it before. My head rested against his shoulder. "Are you asking me to marry you?"

"Nope." Leaning down, he kissed my shoulder. "One day, you'll be ready to marry me, I don't mind waiting for that day."

My head rose and I met his intent gaze. "Always so sure of yourself." Leaning in, my lips met his. His lips glided slowly over mine as the water cascaded down onto us. My back met the tile and his body pressed mine into the wall. His tongue slipped past my lips just as I felt him grow ready again pressed against my center.

In the distance, the doorbell rang.

I broke away. "Crap, that's got to be Amy."

Cameron chuckled as he moved back away from me. "I'd say let her wait, but we probably should make those cupcakes."

When I managed to get dry, dressed and downstairs to open the front door, Amy greeted me with an expectant expression. "That took a while."

"I was in the shower. You're early."

She clutched two big bags overflowing with what looked like purple crepe paper.

I reached for her bag but she didn't hand it over.

"Are the cupcakes cooling?" she asked.

"I didn't make the cupcakes. I lied about the cupcakes."

"Jamie!" Her eyes widened. "*Seriously?*"

"Amy, we have eight hours, and my mom is taking Sarah to do all these awesome things, so you have me as your slave all day. It will be fine," I said, and even the sour expression she gave me couldn't break the happiness that lingered on from this morning.

"Fine. Just take this." She shoved a bag at me.

I took the bag, which was way heavier than I expected it to be. "Holy shit, Amy, what do you have in here, textbooks?"

"Party decorations, utensils and plates, a couple platters, that's likely what's heavy." She brushed past me, bee-lining for the kitchen.

The moment she set down the bag, she turned the dial on the stove to preheat. Glancing around quickly at Cameron's A-frame, she said, "I can't believe that you guys are moving out of this house to move into a tiny little house in town."

"*Amy,*" I groaned the word.

"Fine, fine. So, who's coming to help us set up?"

"Susan is," I said.

Amy stood straight, clutching my cupcake pan. "With a two-month old?"

"I think she just wanted to hang out."

Amy's eyes widened, but she didn't say anything as she turned to my cupboard. "Please tell me that you at the very least bought the ingredients?"

"Everything on the list Chris gave me, I swear. And the instructions are in that drawer."

As she began pulling supplies from the cupboards and fridge, I took a seat at the big slab table.

"Patrick is going to come a little early with Kay and bring some stuff for the grill," Cameron said as he descended into the living room.

"Well, that's good," Amy said.

I pointed at Cameron. "You are such a friend stealer. There was a time when Patrick texted me, and now you've gone and completely stolen him from me."

"He's still your friend." Cameron leaned down. "And I'm trying to forget about the time when Patrick used to text you all the time."

"First of all, it wasn't all of the time. Second, we were only ever friends. And, third, he could still text me, there's no rule saying he can't."

Cameron made a face. "Yeah, there pretty much is."

"You told him he can't text me?"

"No, I didn't say a word to him. But there's an unspoken guy code, you don't flirt over text messages with your buddy's girlfriend. It's kind of obvious."

I propped my head up on my hand, because I knew he had a point. Though, I still wasn't one-hundred percent down with him basically usurping my friendship with Patrick. He and Patrick took Sarah and Kay to do stuff and while I thought it was incredibly sweet, I had been excited to have a new friend. Now, I was just the best friend's girlfriend.

"Well, at least this place is clean," Amy called from the kitchen. "You guys want to start by putting up some decorations?"

"We will in a second," Cameron said, and then he leaned in toward me. "First, breakfast. You hungry?"

"Starving," I whispered.

"I'm not even getting anywhere near that stove, so do you want your pizza warm or cold?"

"Cold works," I whispered. Louder, to Amy I said, "We'll start doing decorations right after we eat. You hungry?"

"No, I ate before I came." It sounded more like a scolding than an answer, but I let it go. We'd spent a lot of time together since her and Peter's split and I'd learned to let most things go.

Over in the kitchen, Amy beat at a bowlful of batter like it was her cheating, soon-to-be-ex-husband's head. As if to confirm she was indeed imagining what I thought she was imagining, Amy said, "Peter wants to sell the house and pretty much everything we own before the divorce is final."

"Weird. Is that a bad idea?" I asked, not really sure how to proceed with the conversation. "Thanks," I whispered as Cameron set a plate of cold pizza beside me and plopped down in the seat next to me.

"I'm having my lawyer look into it," she said. "But it definitely means he's moving away."

Good riddance. I didn't say it, even though I was thinking it. Instead, I focused on my cold pizza.

Amy clanged the mixing bowl onto the counter. "When you're done eating, can you put the paper cups into the muffin tin? No—you know, I'll do it."

"I'll do it in two seconds, Amy," I said, mid chew.

"No," she sighed the word, "It's no problem, Jamie."

By the time I finished my pizza, Amy had the cupcakes in the oven so I turned my attention to decorating.

As I combed through the decorations Amy brought over, she turned to Cameron and asked, "Are you planning to sell or rent this place when your new place closes?"

Cameron set his and my plates into the sink. "I'm open. Is this place somewhere you'd like to live?"

She turned away. "Oh, I'm not talking about for me. I was just curious." She walked over to the bags I was fishing through and upended one. Purple paper plates and cups skittered down the length of the counter. "I won't even have furniture," she said as she gathered the supplies.

I raised my eyebrows, "I have an entire storage container full of furniture just sitting there. All I took out was the furniture dad made for Sarah. Everything else is still in there. There's pretty much an entire house full of stuff I can't use but don't have the heart to sell."

She shook her head. "No guys, I really wasn't talking about me."

"Okay . . ." I drew out the word.

"Here, Jamie, go hang up the crepe paper." She shoved the purple rolls of paper at me.

Day One Hundred and Fourteen: Nine O'clock

Taking the hint that Amy wanted some space in the kitchen, I grabbed Cameron's hand and tugged him into the conjoined living room.

He leaned into me. "If she's determined to do all this work, we could just head back upstairs."

"Ha, ha," I whispered, "As tempting as that sounds, I would really prefer to keep all my limbs.

"I'm with you there. I'm a pretty big fan of your limbs."

Cameron and I decked the living room in crepe paper. Or, more, I stood on a chair taping up the streamers while Cameron 'spotted' me. Translation: he grabbed my ass every time Amy wasn't looking. When all the paper was out and the house looked like a purple fairy had tee-peed the entire space, Cameron and I hesitantly reentered the kitchen.

"All right, the mini-quiches are cooking, the cupcakes are cooling and the veggies are chopped. I have everything set out so you guys can start on the potato salad." She pointed over to where she had indeed set out a potato salad station. "I'm just focusing on everything that needs to be cooled down by the party. I still think we should have had this catered."

"Uh huh," I muttered as I cut hard boiled eggs in half and scooped the yolks into a separate bowl, "And I still think we should have ordered pizza, so I guess this is halfway in-between and a lot more work."

Amy turned. "And, Cameron, I hope it's okay, the bounce house people are going to be here in a couple minutes. Could you show them where to set up?"

I glanced over. "Bounce house?"

"Oh yeah, I forgot. Dad paid for it, it's part of his present."

Cameron, who'd been leaning next to me, looked almost relieved to have an excuse to leave. "Yeah, no problem."

The knock came minutes later, and Cameron accompanied several guys into the yard with a giant, deflated blue and white bounce house. I watched out the window as the men set up. A chill passed through me, as it did every time I looked into the backyard. It was one of the main reasons that Cameron and I wanted to move before we could find the right property to build our dream house. It was the reason we usually kept the windows to the backyard closed.

Clarke's malice still lingered in the place he'd watched us from.

A few weeks ago, Vanessa and I had gone out to Clarke's grave. Even though I knew he was dead, we'd both needed to put him behind us.

We drove separately, Cameron driving with me and a young, good-looking guy with her. Vanessa and I hesitated beside each of our cars, likely as all the communication we'd had up to that point had been over text.

The guy with Nessa stepped into the space between cars. "I'm Joseph," the guy said, offering me his hand. Except for having dark hair, Joseph looked nothing like Cameron. He stood barely an inch taller than Nessa, and he had a lean frame. His bristly beard did nothing to hide how youthful his features were.

After I shook his hand, he offered to shake Cameron's with a smile.

"Nice to meet you, man," Cameron said. After the handshake, Cameron crossed over to give Nessa a quick hug before returning to me.

"Hey, Nessa," I said, waving across the distance.

She gave me a small smile before tucking her hair behind her ears. Like me, she wore comfortable clothes—yoga pants, a long sweater and running shoes.

"We're twins," I said, a little awkwardly, pointing between us.

"Oh god, never again." She raised a hand to her face.

"I know, right?" I said.

She shook her head. "Oh, so embarrassing, we were so dumb. And neither of us brought spare clothes so they made us wear our stinky PE clothes all day." To Joseph, she explained, "Jamie and I tried to be conjoined twins one Halloween—I know, really bad taste, but we were eleven and my mom made the costume for us—her idea, we didn't even know what being conjoined meant. Jamie spent the night and we went to school like that."

"We just thought that they would have to let us sit in on each other's classes. But, the teachers were not fans. We got sent to the principal's office and it was pretty serious," I said.

"God, my mom. She thought she was funny but it was so not." She looked back to me. "That's so embarrassing. We were so weird and awkward back then."

I smiled. "Like hair day?"

She laughed. "Oh god, no."

I noticed the guys listening to us, their gazes darting back and forth.

"So, uh, I guess it's over here," I pointed deeper into the graveyard, "If you guys are ready to head in."

Vanessa nodded, but she didn't step away from her car. "I might hang back just a little."

"Yeah, whatever works for you," I said.

Cameron, Joseph and I walked a little way ahead, counting gravestones and looking for fresh grass. Above us the June gloom lingered, a thin grey layer sitting high above. No one else wandered the space, likely because it was a Monday morning.

"Eighty-two down," I said pointing up a few rows.

We headed toward the standard grey stone, seated on top of a thicker base.

Cameron took my hand as we made our way around to the face of the gravestone. Even though I knew what we were going to find at the end of this walk, my stomach still flipped seeing his name inscribed in crisp letters in the stone.

'Clarke Allen, Beloved Son,' it said.

A small bouquet of white daisies adorned the grave.

Cameron squeezed my hand once, and I squeezed his back. A bird flew overhead, flapping furiously before gliding past. I looked back down, and I felt nothing—no anger, relief, joy, sadness. I felt nothing. For a second, I imagined that I could look down past the deep layers of dirt and into the buried coffin.

I didn't know what shape Clarke's body was in when he died from his injuries, but I imagined his face intact. I imagined his body, never rotting, chemically preserved, stuck forever in his last act of hatred. And still, I felt nothing.

"I'm done here," I said, looking up at Cameron.

"Yeah, me too. Done with this guy forever."

"Me too. Fucker," Joseph said, and then he spit on the grave.

Surprised, I jumped a little.

Cameron turned to Joseph and clapped him on the back. "I think we'll give you guys your space."

Nessa nodded when we passed her. I glanced over once, seeing Joseph hanging back while Nessa stood before Clarke's gravestone. Quickly, I turned away, and Cameron and I wandered out to wait by our car.

In the time that had passed, Vanessa and I had texted more and more. However, today would be the first time we'd see each other in person again.

Pulling the provided plastic wrap over the top of the potato salad, I carried it over to the fridge. Half the contents had to come out for the bowl to fit in, and I had to get on my knees to shove condiments into every tiny space left.

"Yo!" I heard Susan's voice from the direction of the front door as I put my weight into shoving a ketchup bottle between two plastic food storage containers.

"Yo yourself," I called just before the ketchup popped back out at me. Standing, I held the container up. "Ketchup doesn't need to be refrigerated, right?"

Susan smiled. "Never is in the restaurants." From a little front baby-pack, a pair of big brown eyes blinked at me.

"Oh, baby Miles," I gushed. As I went to put down the ketchup, my sister swooped in and beat me to the baby.

Amy didn't run over, but her stride was fast and determined. "Hey Susan, hey, baby Miles," she said, but she was talking only to the baby. "Wow, he drools quite a bit. Is he already teething?"

He did have drool all over his chubby face.

"Oh, I've got a towel for that," Susan said, reaching into her big bag.

Amy touched little Miles' sock-covered foot. "Oh, could I do it? Could I maybe hold him for a minute?"

"Uh—yeah, sure Amy," Susan said, seeming a little surprised. "Here." She did a complicated move with the pack and passed over her little chubby baby.

"Jesus, what are you feeding him?" I asked.

"He loves to eat. It's kind of his thing, along with gurgling, smiling, and messing his pants.

Amy held Miles like he might explode if she moved too much, her arms stiff and eyes wide. Miles immediately reached up and yanked a lock of Amy's dark hair.

"Oops . . . Here, how about you go sit on the couch and I'll put him in your arms? Let's put up your hair." Susan reached to take her son back, and untangled his hand from Amy's hair.

Amy reached up to her hair. "How should I put it up? Should I put on a hat?"

Susan managed to situate Miles in Amy's lap. After, she half hugged half fell on me in the kitchen. "I'm pretty sure I've fucking lost my mind—I'm so tired," she said in a quiet voice. "And I can't have coffee, because then Miles will be wired, too."

I glanced around. "Where's Aiden?"

"Already in that huge castle outside," she said.

When I glanced outside, there was a huge blue and white castle taking up most of the yard and a little boy bouncing in it.

"Hey, go pass out in Sarah's room for a bit. I've got the kids and Amy will set up the party. Actually, Amy may not even realize you're gone and I'll set up the party."

Susan looked at me with eyes so shadowed they looked almost bruised. "I'm just going to do it and pray you don't change your mind."

"I won't." I gave her a quick hug, the carrier scrunching up between us.

Ten minutes later, nasal snores sounded from up the stairs. As I predicted, Amy didn't move an inch from the couch. Her party stress obviously forgotten, she made weird faces and weirder sounds at the baby while I prepared the burger patties for the barbeque.

"Cool if I come in?" someone called from the door.

I looked up to see Patrick, standing framed in the doorway.

"Yeah, come on in," I called, waving nasty meat covered hands at him.

"Yum, burgers," he said with a wide smile.

I wiped back my hair with my bicep. "Yeah, looks like you brought something too?"

"Steaks. A lot of them," he said, holding up a wrapped package with two hands. "Kay also brought a present for Sarah, but I think she abandoned it near the bounce castle, I'll go get it." He set down the big wrapped butcher package.

Miles began to cry. It started as a low whimpering cry, but turned into a full blown wail.

"Oh no!" Amy said, looking around frantically. "Where's Susan—I, oh god, Jamie come here."

"Mind if I help—?" Patrick asked, crossing over to Amy.

"Um, it's not my baby. I can't really give you permission."

"It's cool, Susan and Patrick are friends. She won't care. I'd do it, but. . ." I held up my meat-covered hands.

Miles continued to wail and Patrick scooped him up, holding him to his shoulder. "I'm going to take this little guy with me and walk around a bit, that cool?" Patrick asked.

"Susan would love that, she's trying to nap," I said.

Miles' cry was already beginning to abate as Patrick lightly bounced him.

Patrick grinned. "I'll take him to go watch his brother and send Kay in with the present."

Amy joined me in the kitchen, and immediately began unwrapping packages, but her gaze kept sneaking to the window where Patrick stood with Miles outside the bounce castle.

After twenty more minutes of enduring her longing looks, I told Amy, "Go, I've got this. Go be with that baby."

"I'm fine," she said. "I've forgotten how to be with babies."

"You did awesome. Babies cry, Amy. Go be with the baby," I shooed her away, gesturing with my meat-covered hands.

"Fine. If you're sure you've got this."

"One hundred percent positive," I said.

A minute later, Amy stood next to Patrick, her hand tickling a now smiling little Miles' foot.

Day One Hundred and Fourteen: Five Forty-five

"We're late! It's my fault! Where's the birthday girl!" my dad bellowed as he hugged me, his bristly mustache tickling my arm.

"Out in the bounce castle you ordered. We haven't seen any of the kids yet," I said as I moved on to hug Sharon.

"Those things are like black holes. I doubt we'll see them until we tell them there's cake," Sharon said as she hugged me.

"You're probably right," I said.

"Well, you have a full house," my dad said, looking around. My father and Sharon knew most of the people, but I introduced them around to the parents' of Sarah's schoolmates.

Both Sharon and my father gave Vanessa a long hug when they saw her.

"You know Chris and Melisa," I said, stopping by the couple. "And this is Pat; he's the investor for CJ's Cupcakes." I wanted to add that Pat was also a huge pain in my ass who invited himself to my daughter's birthday party, but I didn't. Actually, to be perfectly honest, Pat was kind of growing on me. I was pretty sure that angel investors weren't supposed to be as involved as he insisted on being, but as Chris was ultimately in charge and so easygoing that he let Pat be involved, there wasn't much I could do about it.

My father offered Pat his hand. "I believe I know your son and granddaughter."

"They're around here somewhere," Pat replied, shaking my father's hand.

"Here, I'll show you," I said, half to escape Pat and half because I thought that Patrick might be out with Cameron. After getting them each a drink and leaving Sharon to coo over baby Miles along with half of the party, I led my father outside.

As we passed the bounce house that rocked back and forth, my father called out, "Birthday girl, oh, birthday girl! Come give your grandfather a hug!"

A second later, Sarah peeked out of the flap, then immediately bounced out and scurried over to my father. She ran into his waist, her arms fastening around him. "I have presents for Sarah!" she shouted.

"You do?" he asked, lifting her up.

"Say, I have presents for you!" she threw her arms around his neck.

"What, you wanted presents?" he teased.

"Yes!"

"Well, maybe Grandma Sharon brought some, you'll just have to go see her and ask."

When he set her down, she made to run off again but I blocked her path to tickle her. "Hey, give me some of those hugs! I haven't seen you all party, monkey!"

She giggled. "No tickles!"

"Okay, okay." I grabbed her to me, giving her a quick kiss and hug.

As Sarah ran into the house with her blonde static- ridden hair streaming around her, my father turned to me. "Sharon and I are still happy to pay for her therapy sessions, honey, keep that in mind."

"Thanks, Dad. Cameron and I are managing, just managing, but we got it. His new shop is up and running, so the income is becoming steady. Plus, CJ's is scheduled to open in two months so . . . fingers crossed, things are looking up."

My father's arm came around me, and he squeezed me to him. "I'm proud of you, honey."

I smiled up. "For what?"

He nodded to the window.

I turned slightly, looking at the view inside. Almost everyone I loved sat in the living room, all of them laughing. My mother sat next to Vanessa, and they huddled close together, deep in conversation. Beside both of them, a still sleepy Susan sat hand in hand with her father. Sarah bounced around the group, probably wanting them to tell her she had presents.

"Mark's five months sober, I guess. Thought that was pretty cool," I said.

"He looks a lot better."

"Where's Amy?" I asked.

Both my father and I craned our necks, scanning the crowd, until we heard a snort of laughter from deeper in the yard. We glanced at each other before wandering further in. On the other side of the bounce house, Amy covered her nose, cheeks heating but still laughing. Across from her and also laughing, stood Patrick.

"She's drinking beer," I whispered, pointing at the bottle of beer clutched in her hand.

"Never liked Peter," my dad said, too loudly.

I hushed him, pulling him toward where Cameron stood over the barbeque, talking to Nessa's boyfriend of all people. They were both smiling, at least.

"Hey," I said, waving and coming closer.

"Good to see you, Cam!" my father called.

"Oh my god, that smells so good," I said, standing over the sizzling steaks. They smelled *so* good that I immediately felt saliva pooling in my mouth.

"I was just going to carry these in," Joseph said before nodding to us and carrying a tray of steaks off.

"And I'll take the next set, let you two have a moment of peace," my dad said, as always really loudly, before following after Joseph with another tray of steaks.

I stepped into Cameron, my arms going around him. "This turned out very nice," I said.

His hand threaded through the back of my hair. "This turned out perfect."

"Shh . . . Don't jinx it," I whispered into his shoulder.

As I held onto Cameron, a thousand moments floated through my mind. A flower bumped against my leg then drifted into the ocean. Tears formed tracks down Chris' cheeks as he smiled down at his future. Mitch stepped back to show me his uniform. Maria held up a #allkidscount t-shirt like a warrior's standard. Cameron wrapped his arms around me to watch the sunrise. Sarah sat beside me, hair sticking in all directions, pulling the pizza box toward her. Thousands of moments passed under us and all around us, like petals in the wind, and we continued on our way, always.

Looking up into Cameron's dark eyes, I grinned.

"Why are you so happy?" he asked.

I kissed him, and whispered, "I just am."

And, I was. I just was.

Leaning back a little ways, I said, "So . . . I was thinking . . ." When I paused, he raised a brow at me, so I continued, "I was thinking about my dream last night."

"The one where we were getting married?" he asked, squeezing me a little tighter to him.

"Yeah, that one."

When I didn't continue, he leaned down so that we were eye to eye. "What were you thinking about your dream from last night?"

"Definitely not something that I'd want Amy to plan."

His mouth looked distinctly like it was fighting a grin. "Definitely not."

"And, my dad would kill me if I didn't let him give me away this time. So, we'd have to do it on the ground."

He chuckled. "Yes, definitely on the ground."

"Pretty much everyone that I'd want to invite would demand to be in the wedding party, so maybe I won't have bridesmaids—Susan and Amy might fight to the death over maid of honor if I tried."

"They'd be pretty evenly matched," he said, not even trying to fight his smile now.

"We don't have much money," I said, making a face. "So we'd have to like, have a pot luck wedding."

He leaned down and whispered over my lips, "I love pasta salad."

"How can you make pasta salad sound so sexy?" I asked.

He grinned. "Are you asking me to marry you, Jamie?"

"I think I am." I kissed him, but pulled away quickly. "I don't have a ring for you, though."

"That's okay, I have one for you."

I pulled back further. "You do?"

"Of course I do, I was just waiting for you to ask me first."

A huge grin spread across my face. "Wow."

"Wow, baby," he said back.

A summer breeze blew by, smelling salty and a little briny. Over our heads, a leaf drifted down, sliding over the barbeque and falling onto my foot. Someone in the distance squealed. And I looked up into Cameron's beautiful face, and saw forever in his eyes.

I laughed, and he laughed too.

My hand went to his face, brushing his hair away from his forehead. "I think everything is going to be okay."

Leaning down, he kissed me once, softly. "Yeah, baby, everything is going to be just fine."

THE END.

If you enjoyed this book, please consider reviewing on Amazon.

Acknowledgements

I want to give a special thanks to my sisters Abra and Anna, for their amazing support and ideas. I'm sending a whole truckload of thank yous to my mother for always helping me.

I also want to send a huge thanks to my beta readers Gretel and Anne. Both of them have helped me with a couple books now, and I couldn't be more grateful for how much time and thought they have gifted me with. I'd like to say a big thank you to Elizabeth from the Chick Lit Chikadees Blog for beta reading Volume One and for her awesome suggestions.

Also, I'm sending a huge thanks to my editor Monique Fischer, who never ceases to amaze me. It's always a pleasure to work with her.

www.ingramcontent.com/pod-product-compliance
Lightning Source LLC
Chambersburg PA
CBHW070726120726
47910CB00001B/3